of love & life

Three novels selected and condensed
by Reader's Digest

The Reader's Digest Association Limited, London, Montreal

# of love & life

ISBN 978-0-276-44446-3

www.readersdigest.co.uk

The Reader's Digest Association Limited, 11 Westferry Circus, Canary Wharf, London E14 4HE

and in Canada
www.rd.ca

The Reader's Digest Association (Canada) ULC, 1100 René-Lévesque Blvd. West, Montréal, Québec, H3B 5H5 Canada

CONTENTS

Twenties Girl

Sophie Kinsella

Hello!

My new book, Twenties Girl, is about twenty-something Lara Lington, who gets an unlikely visit from none other than the ghost of her great Aunt Sadie! Sadie is a feisty, 1920s girl with firm ideas on fashion, love and the right way to dance . . . and she has a mission for Lara: track down her missing necklace. Lara and Sadie make a hilarious, sparring duo and at first it seems as though they have nothing in common. But as the mission turns to intrigue and then romance, perhaps they can learn some surprising lessons from one another.

It's a fun, sparkly book, with two great heroines, and I really hope that you enjoy it.

Best wishes and happy reading!

Sophie Kinsella

One

THE THING ABOUT LYING to your parents is, you have to do it to *protect* them. It's for their own good. I mean, take my parents. If they knew the truth about my finances/love life/plumbing/council tax, they'd have heart attacks and the doctor would say, 'Did anyone give them a terrible shock?' and it would all be my fault. Therefore they have been in my flat for ten minutes and already I have told them the following lies:

1. L&N Executive Recruitment will start making profits soon.
2. Natalie is a fantastic business partner and it was a brilliant idea to chuck in my job to become a head-hunter with her.
3. Of course I don't just exist on pizza, cherry yoghurts and vodka.
4. Yes, I did know about interest on parking tickets.
5. Yes, I did watch that Charles Dickens DVD they gave me for Christmas, it was great, especially that lady in the bonnet. Yes, Peggotty. That's who I meant.
6. I was actually *intending* to buy a smoke alarm at the weekend, what a coincidence they should mention it.
7. Yes, it'll be nice to see all the family again.

Seven lies. Not including all the ones about Mum's outfit. And we haven't even mentioned The Subject.

As I come out of my bedroom in a black dress, I see Mum looking at my overdue phone bill on the mantelpiece.

'Don't worry,' I say quickly. 'I'm going to sort that out.'

'Only, if you don't,' says Mum, 'they'll cut off your line, and it'll take ages for you to get it installed again, and the mobile signal is so patchy here. What if there was an emergency?' Her brow is creased with anxiety.

'Er . . . I hadn't thought about it. Mum, I'll pay the bill. Honest.'

Mum's always been a worrier. She gets this tense smile with distant, frightened eyes, and you just know she's playing out some apocalyptic scenario in her head. She looked like that throughout my last speech day at school, and afterwards confessed she'd suddenly noticed a chandelier hanging from the ceiling on a rickety chain and became obsessed by what would happen if it fell down on the girls' heads.

Now she tugs at her black suit, which has shoulder pads and weird metal buttons and is swamping her. Dad's wearing a suit made out of a dull black fabric which flattens all his features. He's actually quite handsome, my dad, in a kind of fine-boned, understated way. His hair is brown and wispy, whereas Mum's is fair and wispy like mine. They both look really great when they're relaxed and on their own territory—like, say, when they are playing in their local amateur orchestra, which is where they first met. But today, nobody's relaxed.

Mum glances at my stockinged feet. 'Where are your shoes, darling?'

I slump down on the sofa. 'Do I *have* to go?'

'Lara!' says Mum. 'She was your great-aunt. She was 105, you know.'

'So what? I didn't know her. None of us knew her. This is so stupid. Why are we schlepping to Potters Bar for someone we didn't even ever meet?' I hunch my shoulders up, feeling more like a sulky three-year-old than a mature twenty-seven-year-old with her own business.

'Uncle Bill and the others are going,' says Dad. 'And if they can make the effort . . .'

'It's a family occasion!' puts in Mum brightly.

My shoulders hunch even harder. I'm allergic to family occasions.

'It won't take long,' Mum says coaxingly.

'It will. And everyone will ask me about . . . things.'

'No, they won't!' says Mum at once, glancing at Dad for back-up. There's silence. The Subject is hovering in the air. Dad plunges in.

'So! Speaking of . . . things.' He hesitates. 'Are you generally . . . OK?'

'Oh, you know,' I say after a pause. 'I'm fine. I mean, you can't expect me just to snap back into—'

'No, of course not!' Dad backs off. 'But you're . . . in good spirits?'

I nod assent.

'Good!' says Mum, relieved. 'I knew you'd get over . . . things.'

My parents don't say 'Josh' out loud any more, because of the way

I used to dissolve into heaving sobs whenever I heard his name.

'And you haven't . . . been in touch with him?' Another euphemism. What Dad means is, 'Have you sent him any more obsessive texts?'

'No,' I say, flushing. 'I haven't, OK?'

It's so unfair of him to bring that up. In fact, the whole thing was totally blown out of proportion. I only sent Josh a few texts. Three a day, if that. Hardly any. And they weren't obsessive. They were just me being honest and open, which you're *supposed* to be in a relationship.

I mean, you can't just switch off your feelings because the other person did, can you? So you write your true feelings down in a text, simply because you want to share them, and the next minute your ex-boyfriend changes his number and tells your parents. He's such a sneak.

'Lara, I know you were very hurt, and this has been a painful time for you.' Dad clears his throat. 'But it's been nearly two months now. You've got to move on. See other young men . . . go out and enjoy yourself . . .'

I can't face another of Dad's lectures about how plenty of men are going to fall at the feet of a beauty like me. I mean, for a start, there aren't any men in the world, everyone knows that. And a five-foot-three girl with a snubby nose isn't exactly a beauty. OK, I know I look all right sometimes. I have a heart-shaped face, wide-set green eyes and a few freckles over my nose. But take it from me, I'm no supermodel.

'So, is that what you did when you and Mum broke up that time in Polzeath? Go out and see other people?'

Dad sighs and exchanges glances with Mum.

'We should never have told her about that,' she murmurs.

'Because if you'd done that,' I continue, 'you would never have got back together again, would you? Dad would never have said that he was the bow to your violin and you would never have got married.'

This line about the bow and the violin has made it into family lore. Dad arrived at Mum's house, all sweaty because he'd been riding on his bike, and she'd been crying but she pretended she had a cold, and they made up their fight and Granny gave them tea and shortbread.

'Lara, darling.' Mum sighs. 'That was very different, we'd been together three years, we were engaged—'

'I know!' I say defensively. 'I know it was different. I'm just saying, people do sometimes get back together. It does *happen.*'

There's silence.

'Lara, when you break up with someone,' Dad says, 'it's easy to look back and think life would be perfect if you got together again. But—'

He's going to tell me how life is an escalator. I have to head him off.

'Dad. Listen. Please.' Somehow I muster my calmest tones. 'You've got it all wrong. I don't want to get back together with Josh. That's not why I texted him. I just wanted *closure*. I mean, he broke things off with no warning, no discussion. I never got any answers. It's like . . . unfinished business.'

There. *Now* they'll understand.

'Well,' says Dad at length. 'I can understand your frustrations . . .'

'That's all I ever wanted,' I say as convincingly as I can. 'To understand what Josh was thinking. To talk things over.'

And to get back together with him, my mind adds, like a silent, truthful arrow. *Because I know Josh still loves me, even if no one else thinks so.*

'Anyway, you mustn't worry about me,' I say, 'because I've accepted that Josh doesn't want to talk. I've realised that it just wasn't meant to be. I've learned a lot about myself, and . . . I'm in a good place. Really.'

Dad and Mum exchange looks. I have no idea whether they believe me, but at least I've given us all a way out of this sticky conversation.

'I'm so glad you've come through this.' Mum kisses the top of my head. 'Now, we'd better get going. Find yourself some shoes, chop chop!'

As we pull up in the drab little car park of the Potters Bar Funeral Centre, I notice a small crowd of people outside a side door. Then I see the glint of a TV camera and a microphone bobbing above people's heads.

'What's going on? Something to do with Uncle Bill?'

'I think someone's doing a documentary about him,' Mum puts in. 'Trudy mentioned it. Because of his book.'

This is what happens when one of your relations is a celebrity. You get used to TV cameras being around. And people saying, when you introduce yourself, 'Lington? Any relation to Lingtons Coffee, ha ha?' and being gobsmacked when you say, 'Yes.'

My Uncle Bill is *the* Bill Lington, who started Lingtons Coffee from nothing at the age of twenty-six, and built it up into a worldwide empire of coffee shops. His face is printed on every single coffee cup, which makes him more famous than the Beatles or something. His autobiography, *Two Little Coins*, came out last month and is a best seller.

Of course, I've read it from cover to cover. It's all about how he was down to his last twenty pence and bought a coffee and it tasted so terrible it gave him the idea to run coffee shops. So he opened one, and started a chain, and now he pretty much owns the world. His nickname is 'The Alchemist' and, according to some article last year, the entire business world would like to know the secrets of his success.

That's why he started his 'Two Little Coins' seminars. I secretly went to one a few months ago. Just in case I could get some tips on running a new business. There were 200 people there, all lapping up every word, and at the end we had to hold two coins up in the air and say, 'This is my beginning.' It was totally cheesy and embarrassing, but everyone round me seemed really inspired. Personally speaking, I was listening hard all the way through and I *still* don't know how he did it.

'Maybe you and Natalie will write a book about your business one day!' says Mum, as though she can read my mind.

'Global domination is just round the corner,' chimes in Dad.

'Look, a squirrel!' I point hastily out of the window. My parents have been so supportive of my business, I *can't* tell them the truth.

To be strictly accurate, you could say Mum wasn't *instantly* supportive. In fact, when I first announced I was giving up my marketing job and taking out all my savings to start a head-hunting company, having never been a head-hunter, she went into total meltdown.

But she calmed down when I explained that I was going into partnership with my best friend, Natalie. And that Natalie was a top executive head-hunter and would be fronting the business at first while I did the admin and marketing and learned the skills of head-hunting myself. And that we already had several contracts lined up.

It all sounded such a brilliant plan. It *was* a brilliant plan. Until a month ago, when Natalie went on holiday, fell in love with a Goan beach bum, and texted me a week later to say she didn't know exactly when she'd be coming back, but the details of everything were in the computer and I'd be fine and the surf was fabulous out here, I should really visit, big kisses Natalie xxxxx.

I am never going into business with Natalie again. Ever.

As we approach the funeral centre, I hear Uncle Bill's distinctive drawl carrying on the air, and sure enough, there he is, with his leather jacket and perma-tan.

'Family's the most important thing,' he's saying to an interviewer. 'Family is the rock we all stand on. If I have to interrupt my schedule for a funeral, then so be it.' I can see the admiration pass through the crowd. One girl, who's holding a Lingtons takeaway cup, is clearly beside herself and keeps whispering to her friend, 'It's really him!'

'If we could leave it there for now . . .' One of Uncle Bill's assistants approaches the cameraman. 'Bill has to go into the funeral home. Thanks, guys. Just a few autographs . . .' he adds to the crowd.

We wait patiently at the side until everyone has got Uncle Bill to scribble on their coffee cups and funeral programmes, while the camera films them. Then, at last, they melt away and Uncle Bill heads our way.

'Hi, Michael. Good to see you.' He shakes Dad's hand, then immediately turns back to an assistant. 'Have you got Steve on the line yet?'

'Here.' The assistant hastily hands Uncle Bill a phone.

'Hello, Bill!' Dad is unfailingly polite to Uncle Bill. 'It's been a while. How are you doing? Congratulations on your book.'

'Thank you for the signed copy!' puts in Mum brightly.

Bill nods briefly at all of us, then says straight into the phone, 'Steve, I got your email.' Mum and Dad exchange glances. Obviously that's the end of our big family catch-up.

'Let's find out where we're supposed to be going,' murmurs Mum to Dad. 'Lara, are you coming?'

'I'll stay out here for a moment,' I say on impulse. 'See you inside!'

I wait until my parents have disappeared, then edge closer to Uncle Bill. I've suddenly hatched a demon plan. At his seminar, he said the key to success for any entrepreneur was grabbing every opportunity. Well, I'm an entrepreneur, aren't I? And this is an opportunity, isn't it?

I wait until he seems to have finished his conversation, then say hesitantly, 'Hi, Uncle Bill. Could I talk to you for a moment?'

'Wait.' He lifts a hand, and puts his BlackBerry to his ear. 'Hi, Paulo. What's up?' He beckons to me, which I guess is my cue to speak.

'Did you know I'm a head-hunter now?' I give a nervous smile. 'I've gone into partnership with a friend. We're called L&N Executive Recruitment. Could I tell you about our business?'

Uncle Bill frowns at me for a moment, then says, 'Hold on, Paulo.'

Oh, wow! He's put his phone call on hold! For me!

'We specialise in finding highly qualified, motivated individuals for senior executive positions,' I say. 'I wondered if maybe I could talk with someone in your HR department, maybe put a pitch together . . .'

'Lara.' Uncle Bill lifts a hand to stop me. 'What would you say if I put you in touch with my Head of Recruitment and told her, "This is my niece, give her a chance."?'

I feel an explosion of delight. My gamble paid off!

'I'd say thank you very much, Uncle Bill!' I manage, trying to stay calm. 'I'd do the best job I could, I'd be so grateful—'

'No,' he interrupts. 'You wouldn't. You wouldn't respect yourself.'

'Wh-what?' I stop in confusion.

'I'm saying no.' He shoots me a dazzling white smile. 'I'm doing you a favour, Lara. If you make it on your own, you'll feel you've *earned* it.'

'Right.' I swallow, my face burning with humiliation. 'I mean, I *do* want to earn it. I *do* want to work hard. I just thought maybe . . .'

'If I can come from two little coins, Lara, so can you.' He holds my gaze for a moment. 'Believe in yourself. Believe in your dream. Here.'

Oh, no. Please no. He's holding out two ten-pence pieces to me.

'These are your two little coins.' He gives me a deep, earnest look, the same way he does on the TV ad. 'Lara, close your eyes. Feel it. Believe it. Say, "This is my beginning."'

'This is my beginning,' I mumble, cringing all over. 'Thanks.'

He nods, then turns back to the phone. 'Paulo. Sorry about that.'

Hot with embarrassment, I edge away. So much for grabbing opportunities. I just want to get through this stupid funeral and go home.

I head round the building and through the front glass doors of the funeral centre to find myself in a foyer with upholstered chairs and posters of doves. There's no one about, not even at the reception desk.

Suddenly I hear singing coming from behind a pale wood door. Shit. It's started. I'm missing it. I hurriedly push the door open—and sure enough, there are rows of benches filled with people. I edge in and find myself a space as unobtrusively as possible.

As I look round, trying to spot Mum and Dad, I'm overwhelmed by the sheer number of people here. And the gorgeous cream and white flower arrangements. A woman at the front is singing 'Pie Jesu', while near me, a couple of people are sniffing. I feel a bit chastened. All these people, here for my great-aunt, and I never even knew her.

The atmosphere is so emotional that suddenly I can't help it, I feel my eyes pricking too. Next to me is an old lady in a black velvet hat.

'Do you have a handkerchief, dear?' she whispers.

'No,' I admit, and she immediately snaps open her large, old-fashioned patent bag. She offers me a packet of tissues.

'Thanks,' I gulp. 'That's really kind. I'm the great-niece, by the way.'

She clasps my hand. 'It's an honour to meet any relative of Bert's.'

'Thank you—' I begin automatically, then halt. Bert?

I'm sure my aunt wasn't called Bert. She was called Sadie.

'You know, you look a lot like him.' The woman's surveying my face.

Shit. I'm in the wrong funeral.

'Actually,' I say wildly, 'I've just got to . . . er . . . Thanks so much for the tissue . . .' I hastily start making my way back towards the door.

'It's Bert's great-niece.' I can hear the old lady's voice following me. 'She's very upset, poor thing.'

I practically throw myself at the pale wooden door, and find myself in the foyer again, almost landing on Mum and Dad. They're standing with a woman in a dark suit with woolly grey hair.

'Lara! Where were you?' Mum looks in puzzlement at the door. 'What were you doing in there?'

'Were you in Mr Cox's funeral?' The woman looks taken aback.

'I got lost!' I say defensively. 'I didn't know where to go! You should put signs on the doors!'

Silently, the woman points at a plastic-lettered sign above the door: BERTRAM COX—1.30 P.M. Damn. Why didn't I notice that?

'Anyway.' I try to regain my dignity. 'Let's go. We need to bag a seat.'

Bag a seat. What a joke. I've never been at anything as depressing as this, my whole entire life. OK, I know it's a funeral. It's not supposed to be a riot. But at least Bert's funeral had lots of people and flowers and music and atmosphere. At least that other room *felt* like something.

This room has nothing. It's bare and chilly, with just a closed coffin at the front and 'Sadie Lancaster' in crappy plastic letters on a notice board. No flowers, no singing, just some muzak piped out of speakers. And the place is practically empty. Just Mum, Dad and me on one side; Uncle Bill, Aunt Trudy and my cousin Diamanté on the other.

I surreptitiously run my gaze over the other side of the family. Uncle Bill is sprawled on his chair, typing on his BlackBerry. Aunt Trudy is flicking through *Hello!*, probably reading about all her friends. She's wearing a tight black dress and her blonde hair is swept artfully around her face. Aunt Trudy married Uncle Bill twenty years ago, and I swear she looks younger today than she does in her wedding pictures.

Diamanté's platinum-blonde hair sweeps down to her bum and she's wearing a minidress covered with a skull print. Really tasteful for a funeral. She has her iPod plugged in and is texting on her mobile. Diamanté is seventeen, and has two cars and her own fashion label called 'Tutus and Pearls' that Uncle Bill set up for her. (I looked at it online once. The dresses all cost £400 and everyone who buys one gets their name on a special 'Diamanté's Best Friends' list and half of them are celebs' kids. It's like Facebook, but with dresses.)

'Hey, Mum,' I say. 'How come there aren't any flowers?'

'Oh.' Mum immediately looks anxious. 'Trudy said she would do it. Trudy?' she calls over. 'What happened about the flowers?'

'Well!' Trudy closes *Hello!* and swivels around. 'I know we discussed it. But do you know the price of all this?' She gestures around. 'And we're sitting here for, what, twenty minutes? Flowers would be a waste.'

'I suppose so,' Mum says hesitantly.

'I mean, I don't begrudge the old lady a funeral.' Aunt Trudy leans towards us, lowering her voice. 'But you have to ask yourself, "What did she ever do for us?" I mean, I didn't know her. Did you?'

'Well, it was difficult.' Mum looks pained. 'She'd had the stroke, she was bewildered a lot of the time . . .'

'Exactly!' Trudy nods. 'She didn't understand anything. It's only because of Bill that we're here.' Trudy glances at Uncle Bill fondly. 'He's too soft-hearted for his own good. I often say to people—'

'Crap!' Diamanté rips her iPod speakers out of her ears. 'We're only here for Dad's show. He wasn't planning to come till the producer said a funeral would "massively up his sympathy quotient". I heard them talking.'

'Diamanté!' exclaims Aunt Trudy crossly.

'It's true! He's the biggest hypocrite on earth, and so are you. And I'm supposed to be at Hannah's party, right now,' Diamanté says resentfully.

'Hello?'

We all look up to see a woman in a dog collar heading towards us.

'Many apologies,' she says, spreading her hands. 'I hope you haven't been waiting too long.' She has cropped pepper-and-salt hair, dark-rimmed glasses and a deep, almost masculine voice. 'My condolences on your loss.' She glances at the bare coffin. 'I don't know if you were informed, but it's normal to put up photographs of your loved one . . .'

We exchange awkward looks. Then Aunt Trudy gives a sudden click of the tongue. 'I've got a photo. The nursing home sent it on.'

She rummages in her bag and produces a battered Polaroid. It shows a tiny, wrinkled old lady, hunched over in a chair, wearing a shapeless, pale mauve cardigan. Her white hair is a translucent puff of candy floss. So that was my great-aunt Sadie. And I never even met her.

The vicar looks at the print dubiously, then pins it onto a big notice board, where it looks totally sad and embarrassing, all on its own.

'Would any of you like to speak about the deceased?'

Mutely, we all shake our heads.

'I understand. It can often be too painful for close family. I'll be glad to speak on your behalf. If you could perhaps just give me some details. Tell me everything about Sadie that we should be celebrating.'

'We didn't really know her,' Dad says apologetically. 'She was very old.'

'Was she ever married?' the vicar prompts.

'Er . . .' Dad's brow is wrinkled. 'Was there a husband, Bill?'

'Yeah, I think there was. Don't know what he was called, though.' Uncle Bill hasn't looked up from his BlackBerry. 'Can we get on with this?'

'Of course.' The vicar's smile has frozen. 'Well, perhaps just some small anecdote from the last time you visited her . . . some hobby . . .'

There's another guilty silence.

'She's wearing a cardigan in the picture,' ventures Mum at last. 'Maybe she knitted it . . . Maybe she liked knitting.'

'What about from earlier in her life?' The vicar sounds slightly outraged. 'No achievements? Stories from her youth?'

'Jeez, you don't give up, do you?' Diamanté looks at her mother scornfully. 'Can't you tell we're only here because we have to be? She didn't do anything special. She didn't achieve anything. She was nobody! Just some million-year-old nobody.'

'Diamanté!' says Aunt Trudy in mild reproof. 'That's not very nice.'

'It's true, though, isn't it? I mean, look!' She gestures round the empty room. 'If only six people came to my funeral I'd *shoot* myself.'

'Young lady.' The vicar takes a few steps forwards, her face flushing with anger. 'No human on God's earth is a *nobody*.'

'Yeah, whatever,' says Diamanté rudely.

'Diamanté.' Uncle Bill lifts his head. 'Enough. Obviously I regret not visiting Sadie, who I'm sure was a very special person, and I'm sure I speak for all of us.' He's so charming, I can see the vicar's ruffled feathers being smoothed. 'But what we'd like to do now is send her off with dignity. I expect you have a tight schedule, as do we.' He taps his watch.

'Indeed,' says the vicar after a pause. 'I'll just prepare.' With a last disapproving look around us all, she heads out again.

Aunt Trudy immediately turns in her seat. 'What a nerve, giving us a guilt trip! We don't *have* to be here, you know.'

The door opens and we all look up—it's my sister. Tonya. This day just got about 100 per cent worse.

'Have I missed it?' Her pneumatic drill of a voice fills the room as she strides down the aisle. 'I just managed to scoot away from Toddler Gym before the twins had a meltdown.'

She's wearing black trousers and a black cardigan trimmed with leopardprint, her thick, highlighted hair pulled back in a ponytail.

'How are the boys?' asks Mum, but Tonya doesn't notice. She's totally focused on Uncle Bill.

'Uncle Bill, I read your book! It was amazing! It changed my life. I've told *everyone* about it. It's so inspiring! Isn't it a fantastic book?'

She's such a suck-up, I want to hurl. Mum and Dad obviously feel the same way, as neither of them answers. Uncle Bill isn't paying her any attention either, so reluctantly she swivels round on her heel.

'How are you, Lara? I've hardly seen you lately! You've been hiding!' Her eyes start focusing in on me with intent as she comes nearer and I shrink away. Uh-oh. I know that look.

My sister Tonya basically has three facial expressions: 1. Totally blank and bovine; 2. Loud, showy-offy laughter; and 3. Gloating delight masked as sympathy as she picks away at someone else's misery. She's addicted to the Real Life channel and books with tragic, scruffy kids on the cover, called things like *Please, Grammy, Don't Hit Me with the Mangle*.

'I haven't seen you since you split up with Josh. What a shame. You two seemed so perfect together!' Tonya tilts her head sorrowfully.

'Well, it didn't work out.' I force a smile. 'I've moved on. I'm happy.'

'Tonya, sit down,' Mum says tactfully. 'How did the school visit go?'

Blinking hard, I get out my phone and before I can stop it, my finger scrolls down to Photos. Don't look, I tell myself firmly. Do *not* look. But it's an overwhelming compulsion. I have to have one quick look . . . My fingers are scrabbling as I summon up my favourite picture. Josh and me. Standing on a mountain slope, arms round each other, both with ski tans. Josh is smiling at me with that perfect dimple in his cheek.

We first met at a Guy Fawkes party in Clapham. Josh was handing round sparklers to everyone. He lit one for me and asked me what my name was and wrote 'Lara' in the darkness with his sparkler, and I laughed and asked his name. We wrote each other's names in the air till the sparklers went dead, then edged closer to the fire and reminisced about the fireworks parties of our childhoods. Everything we said chimed. We laughed at the same things. I'd never met anyone so easy-going. I can't imagine him being with anyone else. I just can't . . .

'All right, Lara?' Dad is glancing over at me.

'Yes!' I say brightly and jab off the phone before he can see the screen. As organ muzak begins I sink back in my chair, consumed with misery. I should never have come today. I hate funerals and—

'Where's my necklace?' A girl's distant voice interrupts my thoughts. I glance round to see who it is, but there's no one behind me.

'Where's my *necklace*?' the voice comes again. It's high and imperious and posh-sounding. Is it coming from my phone? Didn't I turn it off properly? I pull it out of my bag—but the screen is dead. Weird.

'Where's my *necklace*?' Now the voice sounds as though it's right in my ear. I flinch, and look all around in bewilderment.

What's even weirder is, no one else seems to have noticed.

'Mum.' I lean over. 'Did you hear something just now? Like a . . . voice?'

'A voice?' Mum looks puzzled. 'No, darling. What kind of voice?'

'It was a girl's voice, just a moment ago . . .' I stop as I see a familiar look of anxiety coming over Mum's face. I can almost see her thoughts, in a bubble: *Dear God, my daughter's hearing voices in her head.*

'I must have misheard,' I say hastily, just as the vicar reappears.

'Please rise,' she intones, 'and let us all bow our heads. Dear Lord, we commend to you the soul of our sister, Sadie . . .'

This vicar has the most monotonous voice. My eyelids are just about to close when I hear the voice again, right in my ear.

'*Where's my necklace?*'

That made me jump. I swivel my head round from side to side—but again, there's nothing. What's wrong with me?

'Lara!' Mum whispers in alarm. 'Are you OK?'

'I've just got a bit of a headache,' I hiss back. 'I might go and sit by the window . . . get some air.'

Gesturing apologetically, I get up and head to a chair near the back of the room. The vicar barely notices: she's too engrossed in her speech.

'Where's my *necklace*? I *need* it.'

I turn my head sharply, hoping to catch the speaker this time. And then suddenly I see it. A hand. A slim, manicured hand, resting on the chairback in front of me.

I move my eyes along, incredulously. The hand belongs to a long, pale, sinuous arm. Which belongs to a girl about my age. Who's lounging on a chair in front of me, her fingers drumming impatiently. She has dark, bobbed hair, and a silky, sleeveless, pale green dress.

I'm too astonished to do anything except gape. Who the hell is that?

As I watch, she swings herself off her chair as though she can't bear to sit still, and starts to pace up and down. Her dress falls straight to the knee, with little pleats at the bottom which swish about as she walks.

'I need it,' she's muttering in agitation. 'Where is it? Where *is* it?'

Her voice has a clipped, pinched accent, just like in old-fashioned black and white films. I glance wildly over at the rest of my family—but no one else has noticed her.

Suddenly, as though she senses my gaze on her, the girl wheels round and fixes her eyes on mine. They're so dark and glittering, I can't tell what colour they are, but they widen incredulously as I stare back.

OK. I'm starting to panic here. I'm having a hallucination. A full-on, walking, talking hallucination. And it's coming towards me.

'You can see me.' She points a white finger at me. 'You can see me!'

I shake my head quickly. 'I can't.'

'And you can hear me!'

'No, I can't.'

I'm aware of Mum turning round to frown at me. Quickly I cough, and gesture at my chest. When I turn back, the girl has gone. Vanished.

Thank God for that. I thought I was going crazy. I mean, I know I've been stressed out recently, but to have an actual *vision*—

'Who are you?' I nearly jump out of my skin as the girl's voice punctuates my thoughts again. She's striding down the aisle towards me. 'Who are you?' she demands. 'Where is this? Who are these people?'

Do *not* reply to the hallucination, I tell myself firmly. It'll only encourage it. I swivel my head away, and try to pay attention to the vicar.

'Who are you?' The girl has suddenly appeared right in front of me. 'Are you real?' She raises a hand as though to prod my shoulder and I cringe away, but her hand swishes straight through me.

I gasp in shock. The girl stares in bewilderment at her hand, then at me. 'What are you?' she demands. 'Are you a dream?'

'*Me?*' I can't help retorting in an indignant undertone. 'Of course I'm not a dream! You're the dream!'

'I'm not a dream!' She sounds equally indignant.

'Who are you, then?' I can't help shooting back.

Immediately I regret it, as Mum and Dad both glance back at me.

The girl juts her chin out. 'I'm Sadie. Sadie Lancaster.'

Sadie . . .? No. No *way*. My eyes are flicking madly from the girl in front of me to the wizened old woman in the Polaroid, and then back again to the girl. I'm hallucinating my dead, 105-year-old great-aunt?

The hallucination girl looks fairly freaked out, too. She starts looking round the room as though taking it in for the first time. For a dizzying few seconds she appears and reappears all over the room, examining every corner, every window, like an insect buzzing round a glass tank.

She's hovering at the coffin, staring down at it. I can see her reading the name 'Sadie Lancaster' on the plastic notice board. I can see her face jolt in shock. After a few moments she turns towards the vicar, who is still droning on in her monotone: 'She was a woman who lived to a great age. I look at her picture and I see a woman who led a beautiful life. Who found solace in small things. Knitting, for example.'

'*Knitting?*' the girl echoes incredulously.

'So.' The vicar has obviously finished her speech. 'Let us all bow our heads for a final moment of silence before we say farewell.' She steps down from the podium, and the organ muzak begins again.

'What happens now?' The girl looks round, suddenly alert. A moment later she's by my side. 'What happens now? Tell me! Tell me!'

'Well, the coffin goes behind that curtain,' I murmur quietly. 'And then . . . er . . .' I trail off. How do I put it tactfully? 'We're at a crematorium, you see. So that would mean . . .'

The girl's face blanches with shock, and I watch as she starts fading to a weird, pale, translucent state. It almost seems as if she's fainting—but even more so. For a moment I can almost see right through her. Then, as though making some inner resolution, she comes back.

'No.' She shakes her head. 'That can't happen. I need my necklace. You have to stop the funeral.' She looks up, her eyes dark and glittering.

'*What?*' I stare at her. 'I can't!'

'You can! Tell them to stop!' As I turn away, trying to tune her out, she appears at my other side. 'Stand up! Say something!' Her voice is as insistent and piercing as a toddler's. 'Stop the funeral! *Stop it!* I must have my necklace!' She's an inch away from my face. 'Stop it! Stop-it-stop-it-stop-it!' The girl's voice rises to the most penetrating shriek. I'm going schizophrenic. There's no way I can ignore her. She's like a banshee. I can't stand this any longer. I'm clutching my head, trying to block her out, but it's no good.

'OK! OK! Just shut up!' In desperation, I get to my feet. 'Wait!' I shout. 'Stop! You have to stop the funeral! STOP THE FUNERAL!'

To my relief, the girl stops shrieking.

On the downside, my entire family has turned to gape at me as if I'm a lunatic. The vicar presses a button in a wooden panel set in the wall, and the organ muzak abruptly stops.

'Stop the *funeral*?' says Mum at last. 'But why?'

'I . . . um . . . I don't think it's the right time. For her to go.'

'Lara.' Dad sighs. 'I know you're under strain at the moment, but really . . .' He turns to the vicar. 'I do apologise. My daughter hasn't been quite herself lately. *Boyfriend trouble*,' he mouths.

'This is nothing to do with that!' I protest indignantly.

'Ah. I understand.' The vicar nods sympathetically. 'Lara, we'll finish the funeral now,' she says, as though I'm a three-year-old. 'And then perhaps you and I will have a little talk. How about that?'

She presses the button again and the organ muzak resumes. A moment later, the coffin starts moving creakily away on its plinth, disappearing behind the curtain. Behind me I hear a sharp gasp, then—

'Noooo!' comes a howl of anguish. 'Nooo! Stop! You have to stop!'

To my horror, the girl runs up onto the plinth and starts trying to push the coffin back. But her arms keep sinking through.

'Please!' She looks up and addresses me desperately. 'Don't let them!'

I'm starting to feel genuine panic here. I don't know why I'm hallucinating this, or what it means. But it feels real. Her torment looks real. I can't just sit back and witness this.

'No!' I shout. 'Stop!'

'Lara—' Mum begins.

'I mean it! There's a just cause and impediment why this coffin cannot be . . . fried. You have to stop!'

The vicar presses the button again, and the coffin comes to a standstill.

'Lara.' The vicar turns to me. 'Do you have a reason for wanting to stop your great-aunt's funeral?'

Oh God. What am I supposed to say? 'It's because . . . er . . .'

'Say I was murdered!' I look up in shock, to see the girl right in front of me. 'Say it! Then they'll have to put off the funeral. Say it!' She's beside me, shouting in my ear again. 'Say it! Say-it-say-it-say-it—'

'I think my aunt was murdered!' I blurt out in desperation.

I have seen my family looking at me, gobsmacked, on a number of occasions in my time. But nothing has ever provoked a reaction like this. They're all turned in their seats, their jaws hanging in incomprehension like some kind of still-life painting. I almost want to laugh.

'*Murdered?*' says the vicar at last.

'Yes,' I say forthrightly. 'I have reason to believe there was foul play. So we need to keep the body for evidence.'

Slowly, the vicar walks towards me, narrowing her eyes.

'Murdered . . . how?' she says.

'I'd rather discuss that with the authorities,' I shoot back as though I'm in an episode of *CSI: Funeral Home*.

'You want me to call the police?' She looks genuinely shocked now. Oh *God*. Of course I don't want her to call the bloody police.

'Yes,' I say after a pause. 'Yes, I think that would be best.'

'You can't be taking her seriously!' Tonya explodes. 'It's obvious she's just trying to cause a sensation!'

'My dear,' the vicar says curtly to Tonya, 'that decision does not rest with you. Any accusation like this has to be followed up. And your sister is quite right. The body would have to be preserved for forensics.'

I think the vicar's getting into this. She probably watches TV murder mysteries every Sunday evening. Sure enough, she says in a low voice, 'Who do you think murdered your great-aunt?'

'I'd rather not comment at this time,' I say darkly. 'It's complicated.'

'Are we finishing this or not?' Uncle Bill says. 'Because either way, my car's here and we've given this old lady enough time already.'

'More than enough!' chimes in Aunt Trudy. 'Come on, Diamanté, this is a farce!' She begins to gather up her celebrity magazines.

'Lara, I don't know what the hell you're playing at.' Uncle Bill scowls at Dad as he passes. 'She needs help, your daughter. Bloody lunatic.'

'Lara, darling.' Mum gets out of her seat and comes over, her brow crinkled in worry. 'You didn't even know your great-aunt Sadie.'

'Maybe I didn't, maybe I did.' I fold my arms. 'There's a lot I don't tell you.' I'm almost starting to believe in this murder.

The vicar is looking flustered. 'I think I'd better call the police. Lara, if you wait here . . . I think everyone else should probably leave.'

'Lara.' Dad comes over and takes my arm. 'Darling.'

'Dad . . . just go.' I muster a noble, misunderstood air. 'I have to do what I have to do. I'll be fine.'

I'm left alone in the silent room. And it's as if the spell has suddenly broken. *What the bloody hell did I just do?* Am I going mad?

I sink into a chair and exhale. At the front of the room, the girl is staring at the photo of the little, hunched old woman.

'So, *were* you murdered?' I can't help saying.

'Oh, I shouldn't think so.' She's barely acknowledged me, let alone said thank you. Trust me to have a vision with no manners.

'Well, you're welcome,' I say moodily. 'You know. Any time.'

The girl doesn't even seem to hear. She's peering round the room as if she doesn't understand something.

'Where are all the flowers? If this is my funeral, where are the flowers?'

'Oh!' I feel a squeeze of guilt. 'The flowers were . . . put somewhere else by mistake. There were lots, honestly. Really gorgeous.'

'And where were all the people?' She sounds perplexed.

'Some of them couldn't come.' I cross my fingers behind my back, hoping I sound convincing. 'Loads wanted to, though—'

'Where's my *necklace*?'

'I don't know where your bloody necklace is!' I exclaim. 'Stop bugging me! You realise I'll never live this down? And you haven't even said thank you!'

There's silence and she tilts her face away, like a caught-out child.

'Thank you,' she says at last.

''S OK.'

I find myself eyeing her more closely. Her hair is dark and shiny and the tips frame her face as she tilts her head forward. She has a long, white neck and now I can see that her huge, luminous eyes are green. Her cream leather shoes are tiny—size four, maybe—with little buttons and Cuban heels. I'd say she's about my age. Maybe younger.

'Uncle Bill,' she says at last. 'William. One of Virginia's boys.'

'Yes. Virginia was my grandmother. My dad is Michael. Which makes you my great-aunt—' I break off. 'This is crazy. How do I even know what you *look* like? How can I be hallucinating you?'

'You're not hallucinating me!' She looks offended. 'I'm real!'

'You can't be real,' I say impatiently, 'you're dead! So what are you, then, a *ghost*?'

'I don't believe in ghosts,' the girl says disparagingly.

'Nor do I.' I match her tone. 'No way.'

The door opens and I start in shock.

'Lara.' The vicar comes in. 'I've spoken to the police. They'd like you to come down to the station.'

Two

IT TURNS OUT they take murder quite seriously at police stations. Which I suppose I should have guessed. They've put me in a little room with a table and plastic chairs, and posters about locking your car. They've given me a cup of tea and a form to fill in, and a policewoman told me a detective would be along in a moment to talk to me.

'What am I going to say to a detective?' I exclaim, as soon as the door has closed. 'I don't know anything about you! How am I going to say you were murdered? With the candlestick in the drawing room?'

Sadie doesn't even seem to have heard me. She's sitting on the window ledge, swinging her legs. She's all in my mind, I tell myself firmly just as the door opens and a detective, wearing plain clothes, walks in. Oh God. I am in such trouble.

'Lara.' The detective holds out his hand. He's tall and broad, with dark hair and a brisk manner. 'DI James.'

'Hi.' My voice is squeaky with nerves. 'Nice to meet you.'

'So.' He sits down in a businesslike way and takes out a pen. 'I understand you stopped your great-aunt's funeral.'

'That's right.' I nod with as much conviction as I can muster. 'I just think there was something suspicious about her death.'

DI James makes a note, then looks up. 'Why?'

I stare blankly back at him, my heart pounding. I have no answer. I should have made something up, very quickly. I'm an *idiot*.

'Well . . . don't *you* think it suspicious?' I improvise at last. 'Her just *dying* like that? I mean, people don't just die, out of the blue!'

'I believe she was 105 years old.'

'So what?' I retort, gaining confidence. 'Can't people of 105 be murdered, too? I didn't think the police were so *ageist*.'

DI James's face flickers, whether with amusement or annoyance I can't tell. 'Who do you think murdered your great-aunt?' he says.

'It was . . .' I rub my nose, playing for time. 'It's . . . rather . . . complicated . . .' I glance helplessly up at Sadie.

'You're useless!' she cries. 'You need a story or they won't believe you! Say it was the staff at the nursing home! Say you heard them plotting.'

'No!' I exclaim in shock before I can help myself.

DI James gives me an odd look. 'Lara, do you have a genuine reason for believing something was amiss with your great-aunt's death?'

'Say it was the staff at the nursing home!' Sadie's voice is in my ear like a screeching brake. 'Say it! *Say it!* SAY IT!'

'It was the staff at the nursing home,' I blurt out. 'I think.'

'What grounds do you have for saying this?'

'I . . . er . . . I overheard them whispering in the pub. Something about poison and insurance. I thought nothing of it at the time.' I swallow feebly. 'But the next moment, my great-aunt's dead.'

DI James gives me a penetrating look. 'You would testify to this?'

Oh God. 'Testify' is one of those scary words, like 'tax inspector' and 'lumbar puncture'. I cross my fingers under the table and gulp, 'Ye-es.'

'What's the name of the nursing home? What area is it in?'

I stare back at him steadily. I have no idea. I glance at Sadie.

'Fairside,' she says slowly. 'In Potters Bar.'

'Fairside, Potters Bar,' I repeat.

There's a short silence. DI James stands up. 'I'm just going to consult with a colleague.' He stands up. 'I'll be back in a minute.'

The moment he's left the room, Sadie gives me a contemptuous look. 'Is that the best you could do? Your story was utterly hopeless.'

'You try making something up on the spot!' I reply defensively. 'And that's not the point! The point is—'

'The point is, we need to delay my funeral.' Her eyes are intense and pleading. 'It can't happen. You can't let it. Not yet.'

'But—' I blink in surprise as she disappears right before my eyes. God, this is annoying. I feel like Alice in Wonderland. Any minute she'll reappear with a flamingo under her arm, shouting 'Off with her head!'

Leaning back in my chair I try to process everything. But it's too surreal.

'They're going to pursue it!' Sadie appears again. 'They think you're *probably* deluded, but they're going to follow it up anyway, just in case.'

'Really?' I say incredulously.

'That policeman's been talking to another policeman,' she explains. 'He showed him your notes and said, "Got a right one here."'

'A "right one"?' I can't help echoing indignantly.

Sadie ignores me. 'But then they started talking about some other nursing home where there *was* a murder. Sounds *too* ghastly. And one policeman said maybe they should put in a phone call just in case, and the other agreed. So we're all right.'

'You may be all right, but I'm not!'

As the door swings open, Sadie adds quickly, 'Ask the policeman what's going to be done about the funeral. Ask him. Ask him!'

'That's not *my* problem—' I begin, then hastily stop as DI James's head appears round the door.

'Lara. I'm going to ask a detective constable to take a statement from you. Then we'll decide how to progress.'

'Oh. Er . . . thanks.' I'm aware of Sadie glaring at me. 'And what will happen to . . .' I hesitate. 'How does it work with the . . . body?'

'The body will be kept at the mortuary for now. If we decide to proceed with an investigation it will remain there until we file a report to the coroner, who will demand an inquest, should the evidence be sufficiently credible and consistent.'

He nods, and whisks off. As the door closes I subside. I'm suddenly feeling shaky all over.

'You realise I've just committed perjury?' I say to Sadie. 'You realise they might *arrest* me?'

'"They might arrest me,"' Sadie echoes mockingly, perched on the window ledge. 'Have you never been arrested before?'

'Of course I haven't!' I goggle at her. 'Have you?'

'Several times!' she says airily. 'The first time was for dancing in the village fountain one night. It was *too* funny.' She starts to giggle. 'We had some mock handcuffs, you know, as part of a fancy-dress costume, and while the policeman was hauling me out of the pond, my friend Bunty locked her handcuffs round him as a lark. He was livid!'

She's in paroxysms of laughter by now. God, she's annoying.

'I'm sure it was hilarious.' I shoot her a baleful look. 'But personally, I'd rather not go to jail, *thank you.*'

'Well, you wouldn't have to if you had a better story.' Her laughter stops. 'At this rate they won't even proceed with the investigation. We won't have any time to find my necklace.'

'Look,' I say. 'Why do you need this necklace so badly? Why this one particular necklace? Was it a present or something?'

For a moment she's silent, her eyes distant.

'It was a present from my parents for my twenty-first birthday,' she says at last. 'I was happy when I wore it.'

'Well, that's nice,' I say. 'But—'

'I had it all my life. I wore it all my life.' She sounds suddenly agitated. 'No matter what else I lost, I kept that. It's the most important thing I ever had. I *need* it.'

She's so thin and pale, she looks like a drooping flower. I feel a pang of sympathy for her, and am about to say, 'Of course I'll find your necklace,' when she yawns elaborately, stretching her skinny arms above her head, and says, 'This is *too* dull. I wish we could go to a nightclub.'

I glare at her, all my sympathy gone. Is this the gratitude I get?

'If you're bored,' I say, 'we can go and finish your funeral if you like.'

Sadie claps a hand over her mouth and gasps. 'You *wouldn't.*'

'I might.'

A knock at the door interrupts us, and a jolly-looking woman in a dark shirt and trousers puts her head round it. 'Lara Lington?'

An hour later, I've finished giving my so-called 'statement'. I've never had such a traumatic experience in my life. What a shambles.

First I got my timings all wrong, and had to convince the police-woman it had taken me only five minutes to walk half a mile. I ended up saying I was training to be a professional speedwalker. There's no *way* she believed me. I mean, do I *look* like a professional speedwalker?

Then I said I'd been to my friend Linda's before visiting the pub. I don't even *have* a friend called Linda, I just didn't want to mention any of my real friends. She wanted Linda's surname, and I blurted out 'Davies' before I could stop myself.

Of course, I'd read it off the top of the form. She was DC Davies.

To her credit, the policewoman didn't flicker. She just thanked me politely and found me the number of a cab firm.

I'll probably go to jail now. Great. I glower at Sadie, who's lying on the desk, staring up at the ceiling.

'Right, well.' I pick up my bag. 'I'm off.'

Sadie sits up. 'You won't forget my necklace, will you?'

'I doubt I will, my entire life.' I roll my eyes. 'However hard I try.'

Suddenly she's in front of me, blocking my way to the door. 'No one can see me except you. No one else can help me. Please.'

'Look, you can't just say, "Find my necklace"!' I exclaim in exaspera-tion. 'I don't know anything about it. I don't know what it looks like—'

'It's made of glass beads with rhinestones,' she says eagerly. 'It falls to here.' She gestures at her waist. 'The clasp is inlaid mother-of-pearl—'

I cut her off. 'Well, I haven't seen it. If it turns up, I'll let you know.'

I swing past her, push the door open into the police-station foyer and take out my phone. I get out the minicab firm number DC Davies gave me, and start keying it into my phone.

'Hey!' A voice interrupts me and I pause. 'Lara? Is that you?'

A guy with sandy hair in a polo neck and jeans is waving at me. 'It's me! Mark Phillipson? Sixth-form college?'

'Mark!' I exclaim, suddenly recognising him. 'How are you doing?'

'I'm fine! Great.' He comes across with a concerned expression. 'What are you doing at the police station? Is everything OK?'

'Oh! Yes, I'm fine. I'm just here for a . . .' I wave it off. 'Murder thing.'

'*Murder?*' He looks staggered.

'Yeah. But it's no big deal. I mean, obviously it *is* a big deal . . .' I correct myself hastily at his expression. 'I'd better not say too much about it . . . Anyway, how are you doing?'

'Great! Married to Anna—remember her?' He flashes a silver wedding ring. 'Trying to make it as a painter. I do this stuff on the side.'

'You're a policeman?' I say disbelievingly, and he laughs.

'Police artist. People describe the villains, I draw them; it pays the rent . . . So how about you, Lara? Are you married? With somebody?'

'I was with this guy for a while,' I say. 'But it didn't work out. But I'm fine about it now. I'm in a really good place, actually.'

Mark looks a bit disconcerted. 'Well . . . see you, Lara.' He lifts a hand.

'Don't let him go!' Sadie's voice makes me jump. 'He can help!'

'Shut up and leave me alone,' I mutter out of the corner of my mouth, shooting a bright smile at Mark. 'Bye, Mark. Give my love to Anna.'

'He can draw the necklace! Then you'll know what you're looking for!' She's suddenly right in front of me. 'Ask him! Quickly!'

'No!'

'Ask him!' Her banshee voice is coming back, piercing my eardrum.

'Mark!' I call. 'I've got a tiny favour to ask you, if you've a moment . . .'

'Sure.' Mark shrugs.

We go into a side room, with cups of tea from the machine. We pull up chairs to a table and Mark gets out his paper and artist's pencils.

'So.' He raises his eyebrows. 'A necklace. That's a new one.'

'I saw it once at an antique fair,' I improvise. 'And I'd love to commission one like it, but I'm so bad at drawing things, and it suddenly occurred to me, maybe you could help . . .'

'No problem. Fire away.' Mark takes a sip of tea, his pencil poised over the paper, and I glance up at Sadie.

'It was made of beads,' she says, holding up her hands as though she can almost feel it. 'Two rows of glass beads, almost translucent.'

'It's two rows of beads,' I say. 'Almost translucent.'

'Uh-huh.' He nods, already sketching circular beads. 'Like this?'

'More oval,' says Sadie, peering over his shoulder. 'Longer. And there were rhinestones in between.'

'The beads were more oval,' I say. 'With rhinestones in between.'

'No problem . . .' Mark is already rubbing out and sketching longer beads. 'Like this?'

For another five minutes, Mark sketches, rubs out, and sketches again, as I relay Sadie's comments. Slowly, gradually, the necklace comes alive on the page.

'That's it,' says Sadie at last. 'That's my necklace!'

'Perfect,' I say to Mark. 'You've got it.'

For a moment we all survey it in silence.

'Nice,' says Mark at last, jerking his head at it. 'Unusual. Reminds me of something.' He frowns at the sketch for a moment, then shakes his head. 'No. Lost it.' He glances at his watch. 'I'm afraid I have to dash . . .'

'That's fine,' I say quickly. 'Thanks so much.'

When he's gone I pick up the paper and look at the necklace. It's very pretty, I have to admit. Long rows of glassy beads, sparkling rhinestones and a big, ornamental pendant in the shape of a dragonfly, studded with even more rhinestones. 'So this is what we're looking for.'

'Yes!' Sadie's face is full of animation. 'Exactly! Where shall we start?'

'You have to be joking!' I stand up. 'I'm not looking for anything now. I'm going home and having a nice glass of wine. And then I'm having a chicken korma with naan. Newfangled modern food,' I explain, noticing her bemused expression. 'And then I'm going to bed.'

The next day the sketch of the necklace is all I have left. Sadie has disappeared and the whole episode feels like a dream. At ten to nine I'm sitting at my desk, sipping coffee and staring down at the picture. What on earth got into me yesterday? The entire thing must have been a figment of my imagination.

'Hi!' There's a crash as Kate, our assistant, swings the door open, knocking over a bunch of files, which I'd put on the floor while I got the milk out of the fridge. We don't have the biggest office in the world.

'So, how was the funeral?'

'Not great. In fact, I ended up at the police station. I had this weird mental flipout.'

'God!' Kate looks horrified. 'Are you OK?'

'Yeah,' I say. 'I'm fine now. Were there any messages?'

'Yes.' Kate reaches for her notebook with a super-efficient manner. 'Shireen kept calling all yesterday. She's going to call you today.'

'Great!'

Shireen is our one piece of good news at L&N Executive Recruitment. We recently placed her as operations director at a software company, Macrosant. In fact, she's about to start next week.

'Anything else?' I say, just as the phone rings. Kate checks the caller ID and her eyes widen.

'Oh, yes, another thing,' she says hurriedly. 'Janet from Leonidas Sports called. She said she was going to ring at nine a.m. This'll be her.'

My stomach is bubbling with nerves. Leonidas Sports is our biggest client. They're a massive sports-equipment company with shops all over the UK and we've promised to find them a marketing director.

Rephrase that. *Natalie* promised to find them a marketing director.

'I'll just put you through,' Kate is saying, and a moment later the phone on my desk rings. I glance desperately at Kate, then pick it up.

'Janet!' I exclaim in my most confident tone. 'Good to hear from you. I was just about to call.'

'Hi, Lara,' comes Janet Grady's familiar hoarse voice. 'Just phoning for an update. I was hoping to speak to Natalie.'

'Oh, right! Well, unfortunately Natalie's still . . . er . . . poorly.'

This is the story I've been spinning, ever since Natalie didn't make it back from Goa.

'But we're making great headway,' I continue. 'We're working through the long list and there's a file of very strong candidates here on my desk.'

'Can you give me any names?'

'Not right now!' My voice jumps in panic. 'I'll fill you in nearer the time. But you'll be very impressed!'

'OK. Well, as long as you're on top of it. Best to Natalie. Goodbye.'

I replace the receiver and meet Kate's eyes, my heart thumping. 'Remind me, who do we have as possibles for Leonidas Sports?'

'The guy with the three-year gap in his CV,' says Kate. 'And the weirdo with the dandruff. And . . . the kleptomaniac woman.'

I wait for her to continue. She gives a tiny, apologetic shrug.

'That's *all*?'

'Paul Richards pulled out yesterday,' she says anxiously. 'He's been offered a position at some American company. Here's the list.' She hands me a sheet of paper and I stare at the three names in despair.

God, head-hunting is hard. Before we started up the company, Natalie always made it seem so exciting. She was always full of such amazing stories about her work, I couldn't help feeling envious. Writing promotional website copy for a car manufacturer seemed really dull in comparison. So when Natalie suggested a start-up, I jumped at the chance.

The truth is, I've always been a bit in awe of Natalie. She's always been so glossy and confident. And when we first started the company, it all worked brilliantly. She brought in some big bits of business for us at once and was constantly out, networking. I was writing our website and supposedly learning all the tricks from her. It was all going in the right direction. Until she disappeared and I realised I hadn't actually learned any tricks at all.

Natalie's really into business mantras, and they're all on Post-its around her desk. I keep sidling over and studying them, trying to divine what I'm meant to do. For example, 'The best talent is already in the market' is stuck up above her computer. That one I do know: it means you're not supposed to go through the CVs of all the bankers who were fired from an investment bank last week, and try to make them sound like marketing directors. You're supposed to go after *existing* marketing directors. But how? And what if they won't even speak to you?

'We have three weeks to find a marketing director for Leonidas Sports.' I'm trying desperately to stay positive. 'OK.' I slap my hand on the desk. 'I'm going to make some calls.'

'I'll make you a fresh coffee.' Kate springs into action. 'We'll stay here all night if we have to.'

I love Kate. She acts like she's in a film about some really thrusting multinational company, instead of working for two people in a ten-foot-square office with mouldy carpet.

'Salary, salary, salary,' she says.

Kate's got into reading Natalie's mantras, too. Now we can't stop quoting them at each other. The trouble is, they don't actually tell you how to do the job. What I need is a mantra telling you how to get past the question, 'May I ask what it is in connection with?'

I swing my chair over to Natalie's desk to get out all the Leonidas Sports paperwork, just as the phone starts ringing.

Kate picks up the phone and says, 'L&N Executive Recruitment . . . Oh, Shireen! Great to hear from you! I'll put you through to Lara.'

'Hi, Shireen!' I say cheerfully. 'All set for the new job? I just know it's going to be a great position for you—'

'Lara.' Shireen interrupts tensely. 'There's a problem.'

'Problem?' I force myself to sound relaxed. 'What kind of problem?'

'It's my dog.'

'Your *dog*?'

'I'm intending to take Flash into work every day. But I just phoned Human Resources about setting up a basket for him, and they said it was impossible. They said it wasn't their policy to allow animals in the offices. Can you believe it?'

She clearly expects me to be as outraged as her. I stare at the phone in bewilderment. How has a dog suddenly entered the picture?

'Shireen, listen to me. I'm sure you're really fond of Flash. But it's not usual to take dogs into the workplace—'

'Yes, it is!' she interrupts. 'There's another dog in the building. I've heard it every time I've been in. That's why I assumed it would be fine! I never would have taken this job otherwise! They're discriminating against me.'

'I'm sure they're not discriminating,' I say hurriedly. 'I'll call them straight away.' I put down the phone, then quickly dial the HR department at Macrosant. 'Hi, Jean? It's Lara Lington here, from L&N Executive Recruitment. I just wanted to clarify a small point. Is Shireen Moore permitted to bring her dog to work?'

'The whole building has a no-dog policy,' says Jean pleasantly. 'I'm sorry, Lara, it's an insurance thing.'

'Of course. Absolutely. I understand.' I pause. 'The thing is, Shireen believes she's heard another dog in the building. Several times.'

'She's mistaken,' Jean says after a tiny beat. 'There are no dogs here.'

'None at all? Not even one little puppy?' My suspicions have been aroused by that pause.

'Not even one little puppy.' Jean has regained her smoothness. 'As I say, there's a no-dog policy in the building.'

'And you couldn't make an exception for Shireen?'

'I'm afraid not.' She's polite, but firm.

'Well, thanks for your time.'

I put the phone down and tap my pencil on my notepad for a few seconds. Something's up. I bet there is a dog there. But what can I do about it? I can't exactly phone Jean back and say, 'I don't believe you.'

With a sigh, I redial Shireen's number.

'Lara, is that you?' She picks up straight away.

'Yes, it's me. I called Jean and she says no one else in the building has a dog. She says it's an insurance thing.'

'They're lying,' Shireen says. 'There is a dog in there.'

'Shireen . . .' I feel like banging my head against the desk. 'Couldn't you have mentioned the dog before? At one of the interviews, maybe?'

'I assumed it would be OK!' she says defensively. 'I heard the other dog barking! You can tell when there's a dog in a place. Well, I'm not working without Flash. I'm sorry, Lara, I'll have to pull out of the job.'

'Nooo!' I cry out in dismay. 'I mean . . . please don't do anything rash, Shireen! I'll sort this out, I promise. I'll call you soon.' Breathing heavily, I put the phone down and bury my head in my hands. 'Crap!'

'What are you going to do?' ventures Kate anxiously.

'I don't know,' I admit. 'What would Natalie do?'

Both of us instinctively glance towards Natalie's desk.

'She might tell Shireen she *had* to take the job and threaten to sue her if she didn't,' says Kate at last.

'She'd definitely tell Shireen to get over herself.' I nod in agreement.

The truth is that now I've got to know the way Natalie does business, I don't really relate to a lot of it. What appealed to me about this job was working with people; changing lives. I thought it must be so much more satisfying to help people's careers than to sell cars. But that aspect doesn't seem to feature highly on our agenda. I mean, I know I'm a novice but your job is one of the most important things in your life, surely. It should be *right* for you. Salary isn't everything.

There again, that'll be why Natalie's the successful head-hunter and I'm not. And right now, we need commission.

Trying to look as though this is a decisive piece of action instead of a cop-out, I push the phone aside and start leafing through the post. A bill for office paper. An offer to send all my staff on a team-building trip to Aspen. And at the bottom of the pile, *Business People*, which is like the celebrity magazine of business. I open it and start flipping through the pages, trying to find the perfect marketing director for Leonidas Sports.

'Yes . . . yes . . .' Suddenly I become aware of Kate making semaphore signals across the room. 'I'm sure Lara would be able to make space for you in her diary, if you could just hold on a moment . . .'

She presses HOLD and squeaks, 'It's Clive Hoxton! . . . The one who said he wasn't interested in Leonidas Sports?' she adds at my blank look. 'The rugby guy? Well, he wants to have lunch and talk about it!'

'Oh my God! Him!' My spirits shoot back up. Clive Hoxton is marketing director at Arberry Stores and used to play rugby for Doncaster. He couldn't be more perfect for the Leonidas Sports job.

'Play it cool,' I whisper urgently.

Kate nods vigorously. 'Let me just see . . .' she says down the phone. 'Lara's schedule is very packed today, but I'll see what I can do . . . Ah! Now, what a stroke of luck. She has an unexpected vacancy. Would you like to name a restaurant?'

She grins broadly at me. Clive Hoxton is an A-list name.

'All fixed up.' Kate puts the phone down. 'You're having lunch today at one o'clock.'

'Excellent. Where?'

'Well, that's the only thing.' Kate hesitates. 'I asked him to name a restaurant. And he named . . .' She winces. 'Lyle Place.'

My insides shrivel. 'You have to be kidding.'

Lyle Place opened about two years ago and was instantly christened 'the most expensive restaurant in Europe'. It has a massive lobster tank and a fountain and loads of celebrities go there. We should never, never, *never* have let him name the restaurant.

Oh my God, I think I'm going to faint. Except I can't, because Clive Hoxton has just asked me to run through the spec of the job again.

I'm sitting on a transparent chair at a white-clothed table. If I look to my right I can see the famous giant lobster tank. Over to the left is a cage of exotic birds, whose cheeping is mingling with the background whooshing sound from the fountain in the middle of the room.

'Well.' My voice is quite faint. 'As you know, Leonidas Sports has just taken over a Dutch chain . . .'

I'm talking on autopilot. My eyes keep darting down to the menu. Every time I spot a price, I feel a fresh swoop of horror.

Ceviche of salmon, origami style £34. That's a starter. A *starter.*

Half a dozen oysters £46.

'Obviously the board want a new marketing director who can oversee this expansion . . .' I have no idea what I'm blabbering about. I'm psyching myself up to peek at the main courses.

Fillet of duck with three-way orange mash £59.

My stomach lurches again.

'Some mineral water?' The waiter appears at the table and proffers a blue-tinted Plexiglas square to each of us. 'This is our water menu. If you like a sparkling water, the Chetwyn Glen is rather fun,' he adds.

'Ah.' I force myself to nod intelligently and the waiter meets my eyes without a flicker. Surely they all get back into the kitchen and start snorting with laughter. 'She paid fifteen quid! For water!'

'I'd prefer Pellegrino.' Clive shrugs. He's a guy in his forties with greying hair, froggy eyes and a moustache, who hasn't smiled once since we sat down.

'A bottle of each, then?' says the waiter.

Nooo! Not *two* bottles of overpriced water.

'So, what would you like to eat, Clive?' I smile. 'If you're in a hurry we could go straight to main courses . . .'

'I'm not in any hurry.' Clive gives me a suspicious look. 'Are you?'

'Of course not!' I backtrack quickly. 'No hurry at all!'

Not the oysters. Please, please, please, not the oysters . . .

'The oysters to begin with,' he says thoughtfully. 'Then I'm torn between the lobster and the porcini risotto.'

The lobster is £90; the risotto only £45.

'If you can't decide,' the waiter puts in helpfully, 'I could bring you both the lobster *and* a reduced-size risotto.'

He could *what*? Who asked him to interfere, anyway?

'Great idea!' My voice is shrill. 'Two main courses! Why not?'

I feel the waiter's sardonic eye on me and instantly know he can read my thoughts. He knows I'm skint.

'And for madam?'

'Right. The truth is . . . I went for a big power breakfast this morning. So I'll just have a Caesar salad. No starter.'

'One Caesar salad, no starter.' The waiter nods impassively.

'And would you like to stick to water, Clive?' I desperately try to keep any hint of hope out of my voice. 'Or wine . . .'

'Let's see the list.' Clive's eyes light up.

'And a glass of vintage champagne to start, perhaps?' suggests the waiter with a bland smile. He is a total sadist.

'I could be persuaded!' Clive gives a lugubrious chuckle.

At last the waiter departs, having poured us each a zillion-pound glass of vintage champagne. I feel giddy. I'm going to be paying off this lunch for the rest of my life. But it'll be worth it. I have to believe that.

'So!' I say brightly, raising my glass. 'To the job! I'm *so* glad you've changed your mind, Clive.'

'I haven't,' he says, swigging half his champagne down in one gulp.

I stare at him, unnerved. 'But I thought—'

'It's a possibility.' He starts to break up a bread roll. 'I'm not happy with my job at the moment and I'm considering a move. But there are drawbacks to this Leonidas Sports gig too. Sell it to me.'

For a moment I'm too choked with dismay to answer. I'm spending the price of a small car on this man and he might not even be interested in the job? I take a sip of water, then look up, forcing my most professional smile. I can be Natalie. I can sell this to him.

'Clive. You're not happy in your current post. For a man with your gifts, this is criminal. You should be in a place which will *appreciate* you.'

I pause, my heart thumping hard. He's listening attentively.

'In my opinion, the job at Leonidas Sports would be the perfect move for you. You're a former sportsman—it's a sporting goods company. You love to play golf—Leonidas Sports has a whole golfwear line!'

Clive raises his eyebrows. 'You've done your research, at any rate.'

'I'm interested in people,' I say honestly. 'And knowing your profile, it seems to me that Leonidas Sports is exactly what you need at this stage. This is a fantastic, unique opportunity to—'

'Is that man your lover?' A familiar, clipped voice interrupts me and I jump. That sounded just like—? No. Don't be ridiculous.

I take a deep breath and resume. 'As I was saying, this is a fantastic opportunity to take your career to the next level.'

'I said, "Is that man your lover?"' The voice is more insistent and, before I can stop myself, I swivel my head.

No. This can't be happening. She's back. It's Sadie, perched on a cheese trolley. Ignore her. It's a hallucination. It's all in your head.

'Lara? Are you OK?'

'Sorry, Clive!' I hastily turn back to him. 'Just got a bit distracted there.' I take a deep,calming breath. 'Clive, this is a unique chance to work with a great brand, to—'

To my horror, Sadie has materialised right in front of me. 'Have you found my necklace yet?' she demands accusingly.

It's taking every ounce of will-power to ignore Sadie. 'In my opinion, this job is a great strategic move, and furthermore—'

'Stop ignoring me! Stop talking! Stop—'

'Just shut up and leave me alone!'

Shit. Did that just come out of my mouth?

From the shell-shocked way Clive's bulbous eyes have widened, I'm guessing the answer is yes. The buzz of clashing cutlery and conversation seems to have died away all around.

'Clive!' I give a strangled laugh. 'Obviously I wasn't talking to *you* . . .'

'Lara.' Clive fixes me with a hostile gaze. 'Please do me the courtesy of telling me the truth. This isn't the first time this has happened to me.'

'It isn't?' I peer at him, bemused.

'I've had to put up with it in board meetings, in directors' lunches . . . It's the same everywhere. These hands-free sets are a bloody menace.'

Hands-free—does he mean . . . He thinks I was on the phone!

'I wasn't—' I begin automatically, then stop myself. Being on the phone is the most sane option available to me. I should go with it.

'But this really is the pits.' He glowers at me. 'Taking a call during a one-to-one lunch. Hoping I might not notice. It's disrespectful.'

'I'm sorry,' I say humbly. 'I'll . . . I'll switch it off now.' With a fumbling hand I reach up to my ear and pretend to switch off an earpiece.

'Where is it, anyway?' He frowns at me. 'I can't see it.'

'It's tiny,' I say hastily. 'It's actually . . . um . . . embedded in my earring.' I hope I sound convincing. 'New technology. Clive, I'm really sorry I was distracted. But I am very sincere about wanting to place you with Leonidas Sports. So if I could maybe just recap—'

'You have to be joking. You think I'm going to do business with you now? You're as unprofessional as your partner.' To my horror, he gets to his feet. 'I was going to give you a chance, but forget it.'

'No, wait! Please!' I say in panic, but he's already striding away, between the tables of gawping diners.

With a shaky hand I reach for my champagne and take three deep gulps. So that's that. My best hope is gone.

And what did he mean, I'm as unprofessional as my partner? Has he heard about Natalie disappearing off to Goa? Does everyone *know*?

'Will the gentleman be returning?' My trance is interrupted by the waiter approaching the table. He's holding a wooden platter bearing a dish with a silver dome on it.

'I don't think so.' I stare at the table, my face burning with humiliation.

'Shall I return his food to the kitchen?'

'Do I still have to pay for it?'

'Unfortunately, madam, yes.' He gives me a patronising smile.

'Then I'll have it.'

'*All* of it?' He seems taken aback.

'Why not? I'm paying for it, I might as well eat it.'

'Very good.' The waiter deposits the platter in front of me and removes the silver dome. 'Half a dozen fresh oysters on crushed ice.'

I've never eaten oysters before. I've always thought they looked gross. Close up, they look even grosser. But I'm not admitting that.

The waiter retreats and I stare fixedly at the six oysters in front of me.

'Oysters! I *adore* oysters.' To my disbelief, Sadie appears in front of me again. She sinks into Clive's vacated chair with a languid movement, looks around and says, 'This place is rather fun. Is there a cabaret?'

'I can't hear you,' I mutter savagely. 'I can't see you. You don't exist.'

'Where's your lover gone?'

'He wasn't my lover,' I snap in low tones. 'I was trying to do business with him and it's all spoiled because of you. You've ruined everything.'

'Oh. I don't see how I could do that if I don't exist.'

'Well, you did. And now I'm stuck with these stupid oysters that I don't want and can't afford, and I don't even know how to eat them . . .'

'It's easy to eat an oyster!'

'No, it isn't.'

Sadie shakes her head disapprovingly. 'Pick up your fork. The shell-fish fork. Go on!' Casting her a suspicious look, I do as she says. 'Ease it around, make sure it's detached from the shell . . . now give it a squeeze of lemon and pick it up. Like this.' She mimes picking up an oyster and I copy. 'Head back and swallow the whole thing. Bottoms up!'

It's like swallowing a piece of jellified sea. Somehow I manage to slurp down the whole thing, and take a swig of champagne.

'You see?' Sadie is watching me greedily. 'Isn't that too delicious?'

''S OK,' I say reluctantly. I survey her silently for a moment. She's all in my head, I tell myself. My subconscious has invented her. Except, my subconscious doesn't know how to eat an oyster. Does it? My brain is edging very slowly to the only possible conclusion.

'You're a ghost, aren't you?' I say at last. 'You're not a hallucination. You're a proper, real-live ghost. So, what, am I *psychic*?'

My head is prickling all over as this revelation hits me. I can talk to the dead. Maybe I'll start talking to more ghosts. I could be famous! With a surge of excitement, I lean across the table.

'Do you know any other dead people you could introduce me to?'

'No.' Sadie folds her arms crossly. 'I don't.'

'Have you met Marilyn Monroe? Or Elvis? Or . . . or Princess Diana? What's she like? Or Mozart!' I feel almost dizzy as possibilities pile into my head. 'This is mindblowing. You have to describe it! You have to tell me what it's like . . . *there*.'

'Where?' Sadie tosses her chin.

'*There*. You know . . .'

'I haven't been anywhere.' She glares at me. 'I haven't met anybody. I wake up and it's as though I'm in a dream. A very bad dream. Because all I want is my necklace, but the only person who can understand me refuses to help me!' She looks so accusing I feel a surge of indignation.

'Well, maybe if you didn't come along and ruin everything, that person might *want* to help you. Did you think of that?'

'I didn't ruin everything!'

'Yes, you did! My candidate walked out!'

For a moment, Sadie looks cornered—then her chin juts out. 'I didn't know he was your candidate. I thought he was your lover.'

'Well, my business is probably sunk now. And I can't afford any of this stupid food. It's all a disaster and it's *all your fault*.'

'I'm sorry,' Sadie says. 'I apologise for causing you so much trouble. If I could communicate with anyone else, I would do so.'

Now, of course, I feel bad.

'Look,' I begin. 'It's not that I don't *want* to help—'

'It's my final wish.' Sadie's eyes are dark and velvety and her mouth is in a sad little 'o' shape. 'It's my only wish. I don't want anything else. Just my necklace. I can't rest without it. I can't . . .' She breaks off, and looks away as though she can't finish the sentence.

I can tell this is a sensitive area. But I'm too intrigued to let it go.

'When you say you "can't rest" without your necklace,' I venture delicately, 'do you mean "rest" as in sit down and feel relaxed? Or do you mean "rest" as in pass on to . . . *there*?' I catch her stony gaze and amend hastily, 'I mean, the Other . . . I mean, the Better . . . I mean the *After*—'

God, this is a minefield. How am I supposed to put it? What's the politically correct phrase, anyway?

'So . . . how does it work, exactly?' I try a different tack.

'I don't *know* how it works! I haven't been issued with an instruction pamphlet, you know.' Her tone is scathing, but I can see an insecure flash in her eye. 'I don't *want* to be here. I've just found myself here. And all I know is, I need my necklace. And for that, I need your help.'

'Sadie.' I exhale sharply. 'If I find you your necklace, will you go away and leave me in peace?'

'Yes.'

I fold my arms sternly. 'If I look for your necklace as hard as I can, but can't find it, will you still go away?'

For a few moments, Sadie glowers at me. 'Very well,' she says at last.

'OK. It's a deal.' I reach into my bag, pull out the necklace sketch and unfold it. 'All right. Think back. Where did you last have it?'

Three

FAIRSIDE NURSING HOME is in a leafy residential road: a red-brick, double-fronted building with net curtains in every single window. I survey it from the other side of the road, then turn to look at Sadie, who has been following me in silence ever since Potters Bar Station.

'So, that's where you used to live,' I say with awkward brightness. 'It's really nice! Lovely . . . garden.' I gesture at a couple of mangy shrubs.

Sadie doesn't answer. I look up and see a line of tension in her pale jaw. This must be strange for her, coming back here.

'Hey, how old are you, anyway?' I say curiously. 'I mean, I know you're 105 really. But now. As you are . . . here.' I gesture at her.

Sadie looks taken aback by the question. She examines her arms, peers at her dress and thoughtfully rubs the fabric between her fingers.

'Twenty-three,' she says at last. 'Yes, I think I'm twenty-three.'

I'm doing calculations in my head. She was 105 when she died. Which would mean . . . 'You were twenty-three in the year 1927.'

'That's right!' Her face suddenly comes alive. 'We had a pyjama party for my birthday. We drank gin fizzes all evening and danced till the birds started singing . . . Oh, I miss pyjama parties.' She hugs herself. 'Do you have many pyjama parties?'

Does a one-night stand count as a pyjama party?

'I'm not sure they're *quite* the same . . .' I break off as a woman's face peers out of a top-floor window at me. 'Come on. Let's go.'

I head briskly across the road and up the path to the wide front door, and press the security buzzer.

'Hello?' I call into the grille. 'I don't have an appointment, I'm afraid.'

There's the sound of a key in a lock, and the front door opens. A woman in a blue nurse's uniform beams at me. She looks in her early thirties, with her hair tied back in a knot and a plump pale face.

'Can I help you?'

'Yes. My name's Lara and I'm here about a . . . a former resident. Sadie Lancaster.' I glance at Sadie. She's gone. She's left me in the lurch.

'Sadie!' Her face softens. 'Come in! I'm Ginny, senior staff nurse.'

I follow her into a lino-floored hall smelling of beeswax and disinfectant. Through a door I glimpse a couple of old ladies sitting in chairs with crocheted blankets over their knees.

'Are you a relation?' Ginny asks, showing me into a reception room.

'I'm Sadie's great-niece.'

'Lovely!' says the nurse. 'We've been expecting someone to call, actually. Nobody picked up her stuff.'

'That's what I'm here about.' I hesitate, gearing myself up. 'I'm looking for a necklace which I believe once belonged to Sadie. A glass bead necklace, with a dragonfly set with rhinestones.' I smile apologetically. 'I know it's a long shot, and I'm sure you don't even—'

'I know the one.' She nods.

'You know the one?' I stare at her stupidly. 'You mean . . . it exists?'

'She had a few lovely bits.' Ginny smiles. 'But that was her favourite.'

'Right!' I swallow, trying to keep calm. 'Could I possibly see it?'

'It'll be in her box. If I can get you to fill in a form first . . . do you have any ID?'

'Of course.' I scrabble in my bag. I can't believe it. This was so easy!

As I fill in the form, I keep looking round for Sadie, but she's nowhere to be seen. Where's she gone? She's missing the great moment!

'Here you are.' I thrust the form at Ginny. 'So, can I take it away? I'm nearly next of kin . . .'

'The lawyers said the next of kin weren't interested in having her personal effects,' says Ginny. 'Her nephews, was it? We never saw them.'

'Oh.' I colour. 'My dad. And my uncle.'

'We've been holding onto them in case they changed their minds . . .' Ginny pushes through a swing door. 'But I don't see why you can't take them.' She shrugs. 'It's nothing much, to be honest. Apart from the jewellery . . .' She stops in front of a pinboard and gestures fondly at a photo. 'Here she is! Here's our Sadie.'

It's the same wrinkled old lady from the other photo. She's wrapped in a pink lacy shawl, and there's a ribbon in her white candy-floss hair. I feel a slight lump in my throat as I gaze at the picture. I just can't relate this tiny, ancient, folded-up face to Sadie's proud, elegant profile.

'Her 105th birthday, that was.' Ginny points to another photo. 'You know, she's our oldest-ever resident! She had telegrams from the Queen!'

A birthday cake is in front of Sadie in this photo, and nurses are crowding into the picture with cups of tea and wide smiles and party hats. I feel a crawling shame. How come we weren't there?

'I wish I'd been there.' I bite my lip. 'I mean . . . I didn't realise.'

'It's difficult.' Ginny smiles at me without reproach. 'Don't worry. She was happy enough. And I'm sure you gave her a wonderful send-off.'

I think back to Sadie's miserable, empty funeral and feel even worse.

'Er . . . kind of. Hey!' My attention is suddenly drawn by something in the photograph. 'Wait! Is that *it*?'

'That's the dragonfly necklace.' Ginny nods easily. 'You can have that photo, if you like.'

I take down the photo. There it is. Just visible, poking out of the folds of Great-Aunt Sadie's shawl. Just as she described it. It's real!

'I'm so sorry none of us could make the funeral.' Ginny sighs as we resume walking down the corridor. 'We've had such staff problems this week. But we toasted her at supper . . . Here we are! Sadie's things.'

We've arrived at a small storeroom lined with dusty shelves, and she hands me a shoebox. There's an old hairbrush inside, and a couple of old paperbacks. I can see the gleam of beads coiled up at the bottom.

'Is this *all*?' I'm taken aback, in spite of myself.

'We didn't keep her clothes.' Ginny makes an apologetic gesture.

'But what about stuff from earlier in her life? What about . . . furniture? Or mementos?'

Ginny shrugs. 'Sorry. I've only been here five years and Sadie was a resident for a long while. I suppose things get broken and lost.'

'Right.' Trying to hide my shock, I start unpacking the meagre things. Someone lives for 105 years and this is all that's left? A shoebox?

As I reach the jumble of necklaces and brooches at the bottom, I feel my excitement rising. I untangle all the strings of beads, searching for yellowy glass; for a flash of rhinestones, for the dragonfly . . . It's not there.

'Ginny, I can't find the dragonfly necklace.'

'Oh dear!' Ginny peers over my shoulder in concern. 'This is strange. Let's check with Harriet. She did the clearout.' I follow her back down the corridor, and through a door marked 'Staff'. Inside is a small, cosy room, in which three nurses are sitting, drinking cups of tea.

'Harriet!' says Ginny to a pink-cheeked girl in glasses. 'This is Sadie's great-niece, Lara. She wants that lovely dragonfly necklace that Sadie used to wear. Have you seen it?'

'I don't want it for me,' I say hastily. 'I want it for . . . a good cause.'

'It isn't in Sadie's box,' Ginny says. 'Do you know where it could be?'

'Is it not?' Harriet looks taken aback. 'Well, maybe it wasn't in the room. Now you mention it, I don't remember seeing it. I'm sorry, I know I should have taken an inventory. But we cleared that room in a bit of a rush.' She looks at me defensively. 'We've been so stretched . . .'

'Do you have any idea where it could have gone?'

'The jumble sale!' pipes up a thin, dark-haired nurse sitting in the corner. 'It wasn't sold by mistake at the jumble sale, was it?'

'What jumble sale?' I swivel round to face her.

'It was a fundraiser, two weekends ago. All the residents and their families donated stuff. There was a stall with lots of jewellery.'

'No.' I shake my head. 'Sadie would never have donated this necklace. It was really special to her.'

'Like I say.' The nurse shrugs. 'There were boxes of stuff everywhere. Maybe it was collected by mistake.'

I try to organise my thoughts. 'So can we track it down? Do you know who was at this jumble sale?' Doubtful looks are exchanged round the room and I sigh.

'We do!' The dark-haired nurse suddenly puts down her cup of tea. 'Have we still got the raffle list?'

'The raffle list!' says Ginny, brightening. 'Of course! Everyone who came to the sale bought a raffle ticket,' she explains to me. 'They all left their names and addresses in case they won.'

Five minutes later I'm clutching a four-page photocopied list of names and addresses. There are sixty-seven in all.

'Well, thanks.' I smile, trying not to feel too daunted. 'I'll investigate this lot. And if you *do* come across it . . .'

'Of course! We'll all keep an eye out, won't we?' Ginny appeals round the room, and there are three nods.

I follow Ginny back through the hall, and as we approach the front door she hesitates. 'We have a visitors' book, Lara. I don't know if you'd like to sign it?'

'Oh.' I hesitate awkwardly. 'Er . . . yes. Why not?'

Ginny takes down a big, red-bound book and leafs through it. 'All the residents have their own page. But Sadie never had very many signatures. So now you're here I thought it would be nice if you signed, even though she's gone . . .' Ginny flushes. 'Is that silly of me?'

'It's sweet of you.' I feel renewed guilt. 'We should have visited more.'

'Here we are . . .' Ginny's flipping through the cream pages. 'Oh, look! She did have one visitor this year! A few weeks ago. I was on holiday, so I missed it.'

'Charles Reece,' I read, as I scrawl 'Lara Lington'. 'Who's he?'

'Who knows?' She shrugs.

Charles Reece. I stare at the name. Maybe he was Sadie's dearest friend from childhood. Or her lover. And now he doesn't even know she's dead and he wasn't invited to the funeral. We really are a crap family.

'Did he leave any contact details, this Charles Reece?' I look up.

'I don't know. I can ask around, though . . .' She takes the book from me and her face lights up as she reads my name. 'Lington! Any relation to the coffee Lington?'

Oh God. I really cannot face it today.

'No.' I smile weakly. 'Just a coincidence.'

'Well, it's been a real pleasure to meet Sadie's great-niece.' As we reach the front door, she gives me a friendly hug. 'You know, Lara,

I think you have a little of her in you. You both have the same spirit.'

The nicer this nurse is to me, the crappier I feel. I'm not kind. I mean, *look* at me. I never even visited my great-aunt.

'Ginny.' A red-haired nurse beckons her. 'Can I have a quick word?' She draws her to one side and murmurs under her breath. I just catch the odd word. '. . . strange . . . police.'

'*Police?*' Ginny's eyes have widened in surprise.

'. . . don't know . . . number . . .'

Ginny takes the slip of paper, then turns to smile at me again. I manage a rictus grin, totally paralysed with horror.

The police. I'd forgotten about the police. I told them Sadie was murdered by the staff at the home. Why did I say that? What was I *thinking*?

'Lara?' Ginny peers at me in alarm. 'Are you all right?'

She's going to be accused of homicide, and she has no idea. And it's all my fault. I'm going to ruin everyone's career and the home will be shut and boarded up and all the old people will have nowhere to go . . .

'Lara?'

'I'm fine,' I manage at last. 'Fine. But I have to go.' I start backing out of the front door on wobbly legs. 'Thanks so much. Bye.'

I wait until I'm safely down the path and back on the pavement, then whip out my phone and speed-dial DI James's number, almost hyperventilating in panic.

'DI James's office.' A woman's crisp voice interrupts my thoughts.

'Oh, hello.' I try to sound calm. 'This is Lara Lington speaking. Could I speak to DI James or DC Davies?'

'I'm afraid they're both out. Can I take a message? If it's urgent—'

'Yes, it's very, very urgent. It's to do with a murder case. Could you please tell DI James I've had a . . . a . . . a realisation.'

'A realisation,' she echoes, obviously writing it down.

'Yes. About my statement. Quite a crucial one.'

'I think perhaps you should talk to DI James personally—'

'No! This can't wait! You have to tell him it wasn't the nurses who murdered my great-aunt. They didn't do a thing. They're wonderful, and it was all a terrible mistake, and . . . well . . . the thing is . . .'

My mind is doing double backflips trying to work out a solution that involves both being honest and buying time for Sadie.

'It was someone else,' I blurt out. 'A man. It was *him* I overheard in the pub. I got confused before. He had a plaited goatee beard,' I add randomly. 'And a scar on his cheek. I remember it really clearly now.'

They'll never find a man with a plaited goatee and a scar on his cheek.

'A man with a plaited beard and a scar . . .' The woman sounds as if she's trying to keep up. 'And what is this man supposed to have done?'

'Murdered my great-aunt! I gave a statement but it was wrong. So if you could just cancel it out . . .'

There's a pause, then the woman says, 'Dear, we don't just cancel out statements. I think DI James will probably want to talk to you himself.'

Oh God. The thing is, I really, *really* don't want to talk to DI James.

'Fine.' I try to sound cheery. 'No problem. As long as he knows the nurses definitely didn't do it. If you could write that message on a Post-it or something? "The nurses didn't do it."'

'"The nurses didn't do it,"' she repeats dubiously.

'Exactly. In big capitals. And put it on his desk.'

I ring off and head down the road, my legs weak. I think I just about got away with it. But honestly, I'm a nervous wreck.

Two hours later, I'm not just a nervous wreck. I'm exhausted. In fact, I'm taking a whole new jaded view of the British populace. It might seem like an easy project, phoning a few people on a list and asking if they've bought a necklace. It might seem simple and straightforward, until you've actually tried it yourself.

I rub my ear, which is glowing from being pressed against the phone, and count the scribbled-out names on my list. Twenty-three. Forty-four to go. This was a crap idea. I'm never going to find the necklace. I fold up the list and put it in my bag. I'll do the rest tomorrow. Maybe.

I head into the kitchen, pour myself a glass of wine, and am putting a lasagne in the oven when Sadie's voice says, 'Did you find my necklace?' I start, crashing my forehead against the oven door, and look up. Sadie's sitting on the sill of the open window.

'Give me some *warning* when you're going to appear!' I exclaim. 'And anyway, where were you? Why did you suddenly abandon me?'

'That place is deathly. Full of old people. I had to get away.'

'*You* were old,' I remind her. 'Look, that's you!' I reach in my jacket pocket and produce the picture of her, all wrinkled and white-haired.

'That's not me.'

'It is! A nurse at the home said it was you on your 105th birthday!'

'I mean, it's not *me*. I never felt like that. No one feels like that inside. This is how I felt.' She stretches out her arms. 'Like this. A girl in my twenties. All my life. The outside is just . . . cladding.'

'Well, anyway, you could have warned me you were leaving.'

'So did you get the necklace? Do you have it?'

'Sorry. They had a box of your stuff, but the dragonfly necklace wasn't in there. Nobody knows where it's gone. I'm really sorry, Sadie.'

I brace myself for the tantrum . . . but it doesn't come. She just flickers slightly, as though someone turned the voltage down.

'But I'm on the case,' I add. 'I'm calling everyone who came to a jumble sale they had at the home recently, in case they bought it. I've been on the phone all afternoon. It's been quite hard work, actually,' I add. 'Quite exhausting.'

I'm expecting some gratitude from Sadie at this point. But she just sighs impatiently and wanders off through the wall.

'You're welcome,' I mouth after her.

I head into the sitting room and am just flicking through the TV channels when she appears again. She seems to have cheered up.

'You live with some very peculiar people! There's a man upstairs lying on a machine, grunting.'

'What?' I stare at her. 'Sadie, you can't spy on my neighbours!'

'What does "shake your booty" mean?' she says, ignoring me. 'The girl on the wireless was singing it. It sounds like nonsense.'

'It means . . . dance. Let it all out.'

'But why your booty? Does it mean wave your shoe?'

'Of course not! Your booty is your . . .' I get up and pat my bum. 'You dance like this.' I do a few 'street' dance moves, then look up to see Sadie in fits of giggles.

'You look as though you've got convulsions! That's not dancing!'

'It's modern dancing.' I glare at her and sit down. I'm a bit sensitive about my dancing. I take a gulp of wine and look critically at her.

'Look, Sadie . . . what *are* you?' I say on impulse.

'What do you mean, what am I?' She sounds affronted. 'I'm a girl. Just like you.'

'A dead girl,' I point out. 'So, not *exactly* like me.'

'You don't have to remind me,' she says frostily.

I watch as she arranges herself on the edge of the sofa, obviously trying to look natural despite having zero gravity.

'Do you have any special superhero powers?' I try another tack. 'Can you make fire? Or stretch yourself really thin?'

'No.' She seems offended. 'Anyway, I *am* thin.'

'Do you have an enemy to vanquish? Like Buffy?'

'Who's Buffy?'

'The Vampire Slayer,' I explain. 'She's on TV. She fights vampires—'

'Don't be ridiculous,' she cuts me off tartly. 'Vampires don't exist.'

'Well, nor do ghosts!' I retort. 'And it's not ridiculous! Don't you know anything? Most ghosts come back to fight the dark forces of evil or something. They do something *positive*.'

Sadie shrugs, as though to say, 'What do I care?'

Maybe she's going to shed light on mankind's plight or the meaning of life or something like that. Maybe I'm supposed to learn from her.

'So, you've lived through the whole twentieth century,' I venture. 'That's pretty amazing. What was it like living through World War Two?' To my surprise, Sadie looks quite blank. 'Don't you *remember* it?' I say incredulously.

'Of course I remember it.' She regains her composure. 'It was dreary and one's friends got killed, and I'd rather not think about it.'

She stands in front of the mantelpiece and peers at a photo of me. It's from Madame Tussauds and shows me grinning next to the waxwork of Brad Pitt.

'Is *this* your lover?' She turns round.

'I wish,' I say sardonically.

'Don't you have any lovers?' She sounds so pitying, I feel piqued.

'I had a boyfriend called Josh until a few weeks ago. But it's over. So I'm single at the moment.'

Sadie looks at me expectantly. 'Why don't you take another lover?'

'Because I don't want to just take another lover!' I say, nettled. 'I'm not ready!'

'Why not?' She seems perplexed.

'Because I loved him! And it's been really traumatic! He was my soul mate, we completely chimed . . .'

'Why did he break it off then?'

'I don't know. I just don't know! At least, I have this theory . . .' I trail off, torn. It's still painful talking about Josh. But on the other hand, it's quite a relief to have someone fresh to download to. 'OK. Tell me what *you* think.' I kick off my shoes and sit crosslegged on the sofa. 'We were in this relationship and it was all going great—'

'Is he handsome?' she interrupts.

'Of course he's handsome!' I pull out my phone, find the most flattering picture of him and tilt it towards her. 'Here he is.'

'Mmm.' She makes a so-so gesture with her head.

Mmm? Is that the best she can do? I mean, Josh is absolutely, definitively good-looking, and that's not just me being biased.

'I honestly thought he was The One. But then . . . Well, there was this time when I . . . I did the wrong thing. We were walking past a jeweller's shop and I said, "That's the ring you can buy me." I mean, I was *joking*. But I think it freaked him out. Then, a couple of weeks later, one of his mates broke up from a long-term relationship. It was like shockwaves went through the group. The commitment thing hit them and none of them could cope, so they all ran. All of a sudden Josh was just . . . backing off. Then he broke up with me, and he wouldn't even talk about it.'

I close my eyes as painful memories start resurfacing. It was such a shock. He dumped me by email. By *email*.

'The thing is, I *know* he still cares about me.' I bite my lip. 'I mean, the very fact he won't talk proves it! He's scared, or he's running away, or there's some other reason I don't know about . . . But I feel so powerless.' I feel the tears brimming in my eyes. 'How can I make things better if I don't know what he's thinking?'

There's silence. I look up to see Sadie sitting with her eyes closed.

'Sadie? *Sadie?*'

'Oh!' She blinks at me. 'Sorry, I do tend to go into a trance when people are droning on.'

'I wasn't droning on! I was telling you about my relationship!'

'You're terribly *serious*, aren't you?' Sadie says.

'No I'm not,' I say at once, defensively. 'What does that mean?'

'When I was your age, if a boy behaved badly, one simply scored his name out from one's dance card.'

'Yes, well.' I try not to sound too patronising. 'This is all a bit more serious than dance cards. We do a bit more than dance.'

'My best friend Bunty was treated terribly badly by a boy named Christopher one New Year. In a taxi, you know.' Sadie widens her eyes. 'But she had a little weep, powdered her nose again, and tallyho! She was engaged before Easter!'

'Tallyho?' I can't keep the scorn out of my voice. 'That's your attitude towards men? *Tallyho?*'

'What's wrong with that?'

'What about proper relationships? What about commitment?'

Sadie looks baffled. 'Why do you keep talking about commitment? Do you mean being committed to a mental asylum?'

'No!' I try to keep my patience. 'I mean . . . were you ever married?'

Sadie shrugs. 'I was married for a spell. We had too many arguments. So I left him. I went abroad, to the Orient. That was in 1933. He divorced me during the War. Cited me for adultery,' she adds gaily. 'But everyone was too distracted to think about the scandal by then.'

In the kitchen the oven pings to tell me my lasagne's ready. I wander through, my head buzzing with all this new information.

'D'you mean Asia?' I hoick out my lasagne and tip some salad onto my plate. 'Because that's what we call the Orient these days.'

I sit down and look at my lasagne, but I'm not hungry any more. I feel all churned up and frustrated over Josh.

'If I could just talk to him. But he won't accept my calls or meet up.'

'*More* talking?' Sadie looks appalled. 'How are you going to forget him if you keep talking about him? Darling, when things go wrong in life, this is what you do.' She adopts a knowledgeable tone. 'You lift your chin, put on a ravishing smile, mix yourself a little cocktail . . . and out you go.'

'It's not as simple as that,' I say resentfully. 'And I don't *want* to forget about him. Some of us don't give up on true love. Some of us—'

I suddenly notice that Sadie's eyes have closed again.

Trust me to get haunted by the flakiest ghost in the world. One minute shrieking in my ear, the next making outrageous comments, the next spying on my neighbours . . . I take a mouthful of lasagne and chew it crossly. Maybe I could get her to spy on that guy upstairs when he's making a racket, see what he's actually doing . . .

Wait. Oh my God. I nearly choke on my food. With no warning, an idea has flashed into my mind. A fully formed, totally brilliant plan.

Sadie could spy on Josh.

She could get into his flat. She could listen to his conversations. She could find out what he thinks about everything and tell me, and some-how I could work out what the problem is between us and solve it . . .

This is the answer. This is it. *This* is why she was sent to me.

'Sadie!' I leap to my feet. 'I've worked it out! I know why you're here! It's to get me and Josh back together!'

'No, it's not,' Sadie objects at once. 'It's to get my necklace.'

'You can't be here just for some crummy old necklace. Maybe the real reason is you're supposed to help me! *That's* why you were sent! I bet you're my guardian angel.' I'm getting carried away here. 'I bet you've been sent back to earth to show me that actually my life is wonderful, like in that movie.'

Sadie looks at me silently for a moment, then surveys the kitchen.

'I don't think your life's wonderful,' she says. 'I think it's rather drab. And your haircut's atrocious.'

I glare at her furiously. 'You're a crap guardian angel!'

'I'm *not* your guardian angel!' she shoots back.

'How do you know?' I clutch at my chest determinedly. 'I'm getting a very strong psychic feeling that you're here to help me get back together with Josh. The spirits are telling me.'

'Well, I'm getting a very strong psychic feeling that I'm *not* supposed to get you back together with Josh,' she retorts.

'Well, I'm alive, so I'm boss,' I snap. 'And I say you're supposed to help me. Otherwise, maybe I won't have time to look for your necklace.'

'Very well,' she says at last, with a huge, put-upon sigh. 'It's a terrible idea, but I suppose I have no choice. What do you want me to do?'

I haven't felt as zippy as this for weeks. It's early the next morning, and I feel like a brand-new person. I'm standing outside Josh's building, feeling bubbly with excitement. Everything's going to plan. I've located his window and explained the layout of the flat. Now it's up to Sadie.

'Go on!' I say. 'Walk through the wall! This is so cool!'

'I don't *need* to walk through the wall.' She shoots me a disparaging look. 'I'll simply imagine myself inside his flat.'

'OK. Well, good luck. Try to find out as much as you can.'

Sadie disappears, and I crane my neck to survey Josh's window, but I can't see anything. I feel almost sick with anticipation. This is the nearest I've been to Josh in weeks. He's in there, right now. And Sadie's watching him. And any minute she'll come out and—

'He's not there.' Sadie appears in front of me.

'Not there?' I stare at her, affronted. 'Well, where is he? He doesn't usually leave for work till nine.'

'I've no idea.' She doesn't sound remotely interested.

'What did the place look like? Is it a real mess? Like he's been letting himself go? Like he doesn't really care about life any more?'

'No, it's very tidy. Lots of fruit in the kitchen,' Sadie adds.

'Oh. Well, he's obviously taking care of himself then . . .' I hunch my shoulders, a bit discouraged. It's not that I *want* Josh to be an emotional wreck on the brink of meltdown, exactly, but . . . well. You know. It would be quite flattering.

'Let's go.' Sadie yawns. 'I've had enough of this.'

'I'm not just leaving! Go in again! Look around for clues! Search on his desk. Maybe he's in the middle of writing a letter to me or something. Go on!' Without thinking, I try to push her towards the building, but my hands sink straight into her body.

'Urgh!' I recoil, feeling squeamish.

'Don't do that!' she exclaims.

'Did it . . . hurt?'

'Not exactly,' she says grudgingly. 'But it's not pleasant to have someone's hands poking through my stomach.'

She whisks off again. I close my eyes and try to wait patiently. But this is totally unbearable, being stuck outside. If it were me searching, I'd find something, I know I would. Like a diary full of Josh's thoughts. Or a half-written email, unsent. Or . . . or *poetry*. Imagine that.

'Wake up! *Lara?*' I open my eyes to see Sadie in front of me again.

'Did you find something?' I gasp.

'Yes. As a matter of fact, I did!' Sadie looks triumphant. 'He's having lunch with another girl on Saturday.'

'What do you mean, he's having lunch with another girl?'

'There was a note pinned up in the kitchen. "12.30–lunch with Marie."'

'Who's Marie?' I can't contain my agitation. 'Who's Marie?'

Sadie shrugs. 'His new girlfriend?'

'Don't say that!' I cry in horror. 'He hasn't got a new girlfriend! He wouldn't have! He said there wasn't anyone else! He said . . .'

I trail off, my heart thumping. It never even occurred to me that Josh might be seeing another girl already. It never even crossed my mind.

'Did it say where they're having lunch?'

Sadie nods. 'Bistro Martin.'

'Bistro Martin?' I think I'm going to hyperventilate. 'That's where we had our first date! We always used to go there! Go in again.' I wave my hands agitatedly at the building. 'Search around! Find out more!'

'I'm not going in again!' objects Sadie. 'You've found out all you need to know.'

'You're right.' Abruptly I turn and start walking away from the flat. 'Yes, you're right. I know which restaurant they're going to be at, and what time. I'll just go along and see for myself—'

'No! That's not what I meant! You *can't* be intending to spy on them.'

'I have to.' I look at her, perplexed. 'How else am I going to find out if Marie's his new girlfriend or not?'

'You *don't* find out. You say "Good riddance", buy a new dress and take another lover. Or several.'

'I don't want several lovers,' I say mulishly. 'I want Josh.'

'The worst thing a girl can do is trail after a boy when a love affair is dead,' Sadie says disdainfully.

'But what if it's true love?'

'True love!' echoes Sadie with a derisive laugh. 'You're so old-fashioned!'

'*Old-fashioned?*' I echo incredulously.

'You're just like my grandmother, with your sighing. You even have a little miniature of your beloved in your handbag, don't you? Don't deny it! I've seen you looking at it.'

It takes me a moment to work out what she's talking about.

'It isn't a miniature, actually. It's called a mobile phone.'

'Whatever it's called. You still look at it and make goo-goo eyes, and then you take your smelling salts out of that little bottle—'

'That's Rescue Remedy!' I say furiously. God, she's starting to wind me up. 'So you don't believe in love, is that what you're saying?'

A postman shoots me a curious look and I hastily put a hand to my ear as though adjusting an earpiece. I must start wearing one as camouflage.

Sadie hasn't answered me, and as we reach the tube station I stop dead to survey her, genuinely curious. 'You were really never in love?'

There's the briefest pause, then Sadie says, 'I had fun. That's what I believe in. Fun, flings, the sizzle . . .'

'What sizzle?'

'That's what we called it, my friend Bunty and I.' Her mouth curves in a reminiscent smile. 'It starts as a shiver, when you see a man for the first time. And then he meets your eye and the shiver runs down your back and becomes a sizzle in your stomach and you think, *I want to dance with that man.*'

'And then what happens?'

'You dance, you have a cocktail or two, you flirt . . .'

'Do you . . .?' I want to ask, 'Do you shag him?' but I'm not sure it's the kind of question you ask your 105-year-old great-aunt. Then I remember the visitor to the nursing home. 'Hey.' I raise my eyebrows. 'I know there was someone special in your life.'

'What do you mean?' She stares at me, suddenly tense.

'A certain gentleman by the name of . . . Charles Reece?'

She looks blank. 'I've never heard of him.'

'He came to visit you in the nursing home. A few weeks ago.'

Sadie shakes her head. 'I don't remember.' The light in her eyes fades as she adds, 'I don't remember much about that place at all.'

'I suppose you wouldn't . . .' I pause awkwardly. 'You had a stroke, years ago.'

'I *know*.' She glares at me.

Suddenly I realise my phone is vibrating. I pull it out of my pocket and see that it's Kate.

'Hi, Kate!'

'Lara? Hi! Um, I was just wondering . . . are you coming into work today? Or not?' she adds quickly, as though she might have offended me by asking. 'I mean, either way is great, everything's fine . . .'

Shit. I've been so absorbed in Josh, I'd almost forgotten about work.

'I'm just on my way in,' I say hastily. 'Is anything up?'

'It's Shireen. She wants to know what you've done about her dog. She sounded quite upset. She was talking about pulling out of the job again.'

Oh God. I haven't even *thought* about Shireen and her dog.

'Could you phone her back and say I'm on the case and I'll call her really soon? Thanks, Kate.'

I put my phone away and massage my temples briefly. This is bad.

'We have to go.' I start hurrying towards the tube. 'I've got a problem.'

'Another man problem?' asks Sadie.

'No, it's my client.' I march down the tube steps. 'She wants to take her dog to work, and they're saying it's not allowed, but she's convinced there's another dog in the building because she heard barking. But I mean, what am I supposed to do about it? I'm stuck. Human Resources are denying there's any other dog, and there's no way to prove they're lying. I can't exactly get into the building and search every office—'

I stop in surprise as Sadie appears right in front of me.

'Maybe not.' Her eyes sparkle. 'But I can.'

Four

MACROSANT IS HOUSED in a massive block on Kingsway, with big steps and a steel globe sculpture and plate-glass windows. From the Costa Coffee across the road, I have a pretty good view of it.

'Anything dog-like,' I'm instructing Sadie, behind an open copy of the *Evening Standard*. 'The sound of barking, baskets under desks, dog toys . . .' I take a sip of cappuccino. 'I'll stay here. And thanks!'

I flick through my paper and have just ordered a second cappuccino when Sadie materialises in front of me. Her cheeks are flushed. I pull out my mobile, smile at the girl at the next table, and pretend to dial.

'So?' I say into the phone. 'Did you find a dog?'

'Oh, that,' Sadie says, as though she'd forgotten all about it. 'Yes, there's a dog, but guess what—'

'Where?' I cut her off in my excitement. 'Where's the dog?'

'Up there. Floor fourteen, room one-four-one-six. In a basket under a desk. It's the *dearest* little Pekinese—'

'Did you get a name?'

'Jane Frenshew.' She hugs herself. 'I've just met the most *delicious* man.'

'What do you mean, you've met a man?' I'm scribbling it all quickly on a piece of paper. 'You can't meet a man. You're dead. Unless—' I look up. 'Ooh. Have you met another ghost?'

'He's not a ghost.' She shakes her head impatiently. 'But he's divine. He was in one of the rooms I walked through. Just like Rudolph Valentino.'

'Who?' I say blankly.

'The film star, of course! Tall and dark and dashing. Instant sizzle.'

'Sounds lovely,' I say absently.

'And he's just the right height,' Sadie continues, swinging her legs on a barstool. 'I measured myself against him. My head would rest on his shoulder perfectly if we went dancing together.'

'Great.' I finish writing, grab my bag and stand up. 'OK, I need to get back to the office and sort this out.'

I head out of the door and start hurrying towards the tube, but to my surprise Sadie blocks my way.

'I want him.'

'I'm sorry?' I peer at her.

'The man I just met. I felt it, right here. The sizzle.' She presses her concave stomach. 'I want to dance with him.'

Is she joking?

'Well, that would be nice,' I say. 'But I've got to get to the office . . .'

As I move forward, Sadie thrusts a bare arm across my path.

'Do you know how long it is since I've danced?' she says with sudden passion. 'Do you know how long it is since I've . . . shaken my booty? All those years, trapped in an old woman's body. In a place with no music, with no life . . .'

'OK,' I say quickly. 'Fair enough. So, let's dance at home. We'll put on some music, dim the lights, have a little party . . .'

'I don't want to dance at home to the wireless!' she says scornfully. 'I want to go out with a man and enjoy myself!'

'You want to go on a *date*?' I say disbelievingly, and her eyes light up.

'Yes! Exactly! A date with him.' She points at the building.

What exactly is it about being a ghost that she doesn't understand?

'Sadie, you're *dead*.'

'I know!' she says irritably. 'You don't have to keep reminding me!'

'So you can't go on a date. Sorry. That's the way it is.' I shrug, and start walking again.

'Ask him for me.'

'What?'

'I can't do it on my own.' Her voice is fast and determined. 'I need a go-between. If you go out with him on a date, I can go out with him on a date. If you dance with him, I can dance with him too.'

She's serious. I almost want to burst out laughing.

'You want me to go on a date for you,' I say, to clarify. 'With some random guy I don't know. Just so you can have a dance.'

'I just want one last little burst of fun with a handsome man while I still have the chance.' Sadie's head falls forwards and her mouth pouts into a sad little 'o' shape again. 'One more whirl round a dancefloor. That's all I ask for before I disappear from this world.' Her voice descends to a low, pitiful whisper. 'It's my last desire. My final wish.'

'It's not your final wish!' I say, a bit indignantly. 'You've already had your final wish! It was searching for your necklace, remember?'

For an instant Sadie looks caught out.

'This is my other final wish,' she says at last.

'Look, Sadie.' I try to sound reasonable. 'I can't just ask a stranger on a date. You'll have to do without this one. Sorry.'

'You're really saying no,' Sadie says, her voice cracking with emotion. 'I was in that nursing home for years. Never any visitors. Never any laughter. Never any life. Just oldness . . . and loneliness . . . and misery.'

'It wasn't my fault,' I say feebly, but Sadie ignores me.

'And now I see the chance of a sliver of happiness. A morsel of pleasure. Yet my own callous, selfish great-niece—'

'OK!' I stop in my tracks. 'OK! Whatever! Fine! I'll do it.'

'You're an angel!' Sadie's mood has instantly flipped to giddy excitement. 'I'll show you where he is! Come on!'

I follow her towards the massive steps and push my way into the huge, double-height foyer.

'So where is he?' I look around the echoing marble chamber.

'Upstairs! Come on!' She's like a puppy straining at the leash.

'I can't just walk into an office building!' I hiss back, gesturing at the security barriers. 'I need a plan. I need an excuse. I need . . . *aha*.'

In the corner is a stand signed GLOBAL STRATEGY SEMINAR. A pair of bored-looking girls are sitting behind a table of name badges.

'Hi.' I approach briskly. 'Sorry I'm late.'

'No problem. They've only just started.' One of the girls reaches for her list, while the other stares resolutely at the ceiling. 'And you are?'

'Sarah Connoy,' I say, grabbing a name badge at random. 'Thanks. I'd better get going . . .'

I hurry to the security barriers, flash my name badge at the guard and hurry through into a wide corridor. I have no idea where I am. The building holds about twenty different companies.

'Where's this guy, then?' I murmur out of the side of my mouth.

'Twentieth floor.'

I head for the lifts, nodding in a businesslike way at all the other passengers. At floor twenty I get out of the lift and find myself in another massive reception area with a granite desk manned by a scary-looking woman in a suit. A plaque on the wall says TURNER MURRAY CONSULTING.

Wow. Turner Murray are the really brainy ones who get asked to sort out big businesses. This guy must be pretty high-powered, whoever he is.

'Come on!' Sadie is dancing ahead towards a door with a security panel. Two men stride past and one of them gives me a curious look. I follow the men and as we reach the door, one of them punches in a code.

'Thanks.' I nod in my most businesslike way, and follow them in. 'Gavin, the European figures don't make sense,' I say into my phone.

The taller man hesitates as though he's going to challenge me. Shit. I hastily increase my speed and walk straight past them.

'I have a meeting in two minutes, Gavin,' I say hastily. 'I want those updated figures on my BlackBerry . . .' I leave them behind as I turn a corner in the corridor.

'So where is he?' I turn to Sadie.

'Hmm.' She's peering around. 'One of these doors along here . . .' She heads along an empty corridor and I cautiously follow. This is surreal.

'Yes!' Sadie appears by my side, glowing. 'He's in there!' She points to a solid wooden door labelled ROOM 2012.

'OK, let's get it over with.' I rap sharply, twist the door handle and take a step inside the room.

Twenty suited people seated round a conference table all turn to look at me. A man at the far end pauses in his PowerPoint presentation.

I stare back, frozen. It's not an office. It's a conference room. I'm standing in a company I don't belong to, in a great big meeting I don't belong to, and everyone's waiting for me to speak.

'Sorry,' I stammer at last. 'I don't want to interrupt. Carry on.'

Out of the corner of my eye I've noticed a couple of empty seats. I pull a chair out and sit down. The woman next door to me eyes me uncertainly for a moment, then pushes along a pad of paper and a pen.

'Thanks,' I murmur back.

I don't quite believe this. No one's told me to leave. Don't they realise I don't belong here? The guy at the front has resumed his speech and a few people are scribbling notes. Surreptitiously I look round the table. There are about fifteen men in this room. Sadie's guy could be any of them. There's a sandy-haired guy across the table who looks quite cute. The man giving the presentation is quite good-looking too. He has wavy dark hair and pale blue eyes. He's gesturing at a graph, and talking with an animated voice.

'. . . and client satisfaction ratings have increased, year-on-year . . .'

'Stop right there.' A man standing at the window, whom I hadn't noticed before, turns round. He has an American accent, a dark suit and chestnut-coloured hair brushed straight back.

'Client satisfaction ratings aren't what we're about,' the American says. 'I don't want to perform work that a client rates as an A. I want to perform work that *I* rate as an A . . .'

I tune out as I notice Sadie sliding into the chair next to me. I push my pad across and scribble, '*Which man?*'

'The one who looks like Rudolph Valentino,' she says.

For God's sake. '*How would I know what bloody Rudolph Valentino looks like?*' I scribble. '*Which one?*'

'Him, of course!' Sadie appears in front of the American man with the frown, and gazes at him longingly. 'Isn't he a dove?'

'Him?' Oops. I spoke out loud. Everyone turns to look at me, and I hastily try to sound as though I'm clearing my throat: 'Hrrrm hrrrm.'

I survey the American guy dubiously. I suppose he is quite good-looking in that classic preppy way. His hair springs up from a broad, square brow, and his eyes *are* penetrating. But honestly. He's so totally not my sort. Too intense. Too frowny.

The American guy suddenly consults his watch. 'I have to go.

Apologies for hijacking the meeting, Simon, carry on.'

'Quick!' Sadie's voice resounds in my ear, making me jump. 'Ask him on a date! He's leaving! You promised! Do it! Do-it-do-it-do-it—'

'*OK!!!!!!*' I scrawl, flinching. '*Just give me a second.*'

Mr American Frown is pushing some papers into his briefcase.

I *can't* do this. It's ludicrous.

'Go on! *Go on!*' Sadie is trying to push me. '*Ask!*'

Blood is pulsating round my head. My legs are trembling under the table. Somehow I force myself to raise a hand.

'Excuse me?' I say in an embarrassed squeak.

Mr American Frown turns and surveys me, looking puzzled. 'I'm sorry, I don't think we've been introduced. You'll have to excuse me, I'm in a hurry—'

'I have a question.'

Everyone round the table has turned to look at me. I can see a man whispering, 'Who's that?' to his neighbour.

'OK.' He sighs. 'What is it?'

'I . . . um . . . It's just . . . I wanted to ask . . .' My voice is jumpy and I clear my throat. 'Would you like to go out with me?'

There's a staggered silence, apart from someone spluttering on their coffee. My face is boiling hot, but I hold steady.

'Excuse me?' says the American man, looking bewildered.

'Like . . . on a date?' I risk a little smile.

Suddenly I'm aware of Sadie beside him. 'Say *yes!*' she shrieks into his ear, so loudly that I want to flinch on his behalf. '*Say yes! Say yes!*'

To my astonishment, I can see the American man cocking his head as though he can hear some distant radio signal. Can he *hear* her?

'*Say yes! Say yes!*' Sadie's yelling increases to an unbearable level.

This is unreal. The American man can definitely hear something. He shakes his head and takes a couple of steps away, but Sadie follows him, still yelling. His eyes are glazed and he looks like he's in a trance.

No one else in the room is moving or speaking. They all seem pinioned by shock; one woman has her hand clapped across her face as though she's watching a train wreck.

'*Say yes!*' Sadie screams. '*Right now! Say it! SAY YES!*'

'Yes.' The American man nods desperately.

There's a gasp all round the table, and a hastily stifled giggle. Everyone turns to gape at me, but I'm too dumbfounded to reply. He said yes. Does this mean . . . I actually have to go on a date with him?

'Great!' I try to gather my wits. 'So . . . I'll email you, shall I? My name's Lara Lington, by the way. Here's my card . . .'

'I'm Ed.' The man still looks dazed. 'Ed Harrison.' He reaches in his inside pocket and produces his own business card.

'So . . . um . . . bye then, Ed!' I pick up my bag and hurriedly beat a retreat. I can hear someone saying, 'Who the bloody hell was that?' and a woman saying in an urgent undertone, 'You see? You just have to have the *guts*. You have to be *direct* with men. Stop the games. Lay it out there. If I'd known at her age what that girl knows . . .'

I'm still in a state of shock as Sadie catches up with me, halfway across the ground-floor reception lobby. My mind keeps rerunning the scene in total disbelief. Sadie communicated with a man. He actually *heard* her. I'm not sure how much he heard—but obviously enough.

'Isn't he a peach?' she says dreamily. 'I knew he'd say yes.'

'What went on there?' I mutter incredulously. 'What's with the shouting? I thought you couldn't talk to anyone except me!'

'Talking's no good,' she agrees. 'But I've noticed that when I really let off a socking great scream right in someone's ear, most people seem to hear something faint. It's terribly hard work, though.'

'I thought I was the only person you were haunting,' I can't help saying childishly. 'I thought I was special.'

'You're the only person I can be with instantly,' says Sadie after pondering a moment. 'I just have to think of you, and I'm with you.'

'Oh.' Secretly, I feel quite pleased to hear this.

'So, where do you think he'll take us?' Sadie looks up, her eyes sparkling. 'The Savoy? I *adore* the Savoy.'

She seriously envisages all three of us going on a date together? A weird, freaky, threesome-with-a-ghost date? OK, Lara. Stay sane. He won't really claim a date. He'll tear up my card and blame the incident on his hangover/drug habit/stress levels and I'll never see him again.

Feeling more confident, I stride towards the exit.

As soon as I get back to the office I put a call through to Jean, sit back in my swivel chair and prepare to relish the moment.

'Hi, Jean,' I say pleasantly. 'It's Lara here. I'm just calling about your no-dog policy again, which I totally understand. But I was just wondering why this rule doesn't extend to Jane Frenshew in room 1416?'

Ha! I've never heard Jean so squirmy. At first she denies it. Then she tries to say it's due to special circumstances and it doesn't set any precedent. But it only takes one mention of lawyers for her to cave in. Shireen can bring Flash to work! It's going to be put in her contract tomorrow and they're throwing in a dog basket! I put down the phone and dial Shireen's number. She's going to be so happy! Finally, this job is *fun*.

And it's even more fun when Shireen gasps incredulously down the phone. 'I couldn't imagine anyone at Sturgis Curtis taking the same trouble,' she keeps saying.

I put the phone down, glowing, and look up to see Kate gazing at me with avid curiosity.

'How did you find out about the other dog?' she says.

'Instincts.' I shrug.

'I'll go on a coffee run to celebrate!' Kate says brightly. The minute she's closed the door behind her, Sadie comes over to my desk.

'So.' She regards me expectantly. 'Are you going to ring him?'

'Who?'

'Him!' She leans right over my computer. '*Him!*'

'You mean Ed Whatsit? You want me to *ring* him?' I shoot her a pitying glance. 'Do you have no idea how things work? If he wants to ring, he can ring.' *Which he won't, in a million years*, I silently add.

I delete a few emails, and type a reply, then look up again. Sadie is sitting on top of a filing cabinet, staring fixedly at the phone. As she sees me looking, she jumps, and quickly looks away. She swishes over to the window, then back to the phone. Then she heaves a heavy sigh.

There's no way I can sit here all afternoon with her swishing and sighing. I'm going to have to be brutally honest.

'Look, Sadie,' I say. 'About Ed. He won't call.'

'What do you mean, he won't call?' Sadie retorts. 'Of course he will.'

'He won't.' I shake my head. 'There's no way on earth he's going to call some loony girl who blagged her way into his meeting. He's going to throw my card away and forget all about it. Sorry.'

Sadie is staring at me with reproach. 'He's going to call,' she says.

'Fine. Whatever you think.' I turn to my computer and start typing. When I glance up she's gone. Finally, some space. Some silence!

I'm in the middle of typing a confirmation email to Jean about Flash, when the phone rings. I pick it up absently. 'Hello, Lara speaking.'

'Hi there. This is Ed Harrison.'

'Um . . . hi!' I look wildly around for Sadie, but she's nowhere.

'So, I guess we're going on a date,' says Ed stiffly.

'I . . . guess we are.'

'There's a bar in St Christopher's Place,' he says. 'The Crowe Bar. You want to have a drink there?'

He's suggesting a drink because that's about the quickest date you can have. He really doesn't want to do this. So why did he call?

'Good idea,' I say brightly.

'Saturday night, seven thirty?'

'See you there.'

As I put the phone down, I feel surreal. I'm actually going on a date with Mr American Frown. And Sadie has no idea.

'Sadie.' I look around. 'Sa-die! Can you hear me? He called!'

'I know,' comes Sadie's voice from behind me, and I swivel round to see her sitting on the windowsill, looking totally unruffled.

'Your guy called! We're going on a—' I break off as it hits me. 'Oh my God. *You* did this, didn't you? You went and shouted at him.'

'Of course I did!' she says proudly. 'It was simply *too* dreary waiting for him to call, so I decided to give him a little nudge.' Her eyebrows lower disapprovingly. 'You were right, by the way. He *had* thrown the card away. It was in his bin. He wasn't planning to call you at all!'

She looks so outraged, I have to bite back a laugh.

'Welcome to modern dating. How did you change his mind?'

'It was terribly hard work!' Sadie looks affronted. 'First I just told him to call you, but he absolutely ignored me. He kept turning away from me and typing more quickly. So then I looked at his typewriter—'

'Computer?' I interject.

'Whatever it is,' she says impatiently. 'I told him it would break down and he would lose his job unless he called you. He moved quite quickly after that.' Sadie tosses her hair back triumphantly. 'And so he telephoned you. Aren't you impressed?'

I gaze back at her, speechless. She's blackmailed this guy into going on a date with me. She's messed with his mind. She's forced him into a romance that he had no intention of pursuing.

She is the only woman I've ever known who could make a man call. Ever.

OK, it took supernatural powers, but she did it.

'Great-Aunt Sadie,' I say slowly. 'You're brilliant.'

It's twelve thirty on Saturday and I've been sitting in Bistro Martin for twenty minutes. I'm in the corner, tucked out of sight, wearing a baseball cap just to be on the safe side.

Josh is booked at one of the tables in the window—I peeked at the reservations list. I have a pretty good view of it from my corner seat, so I'll be able to study this so-called Marie pretty carefully. Even better, I'll be able to listen to their conversation, because I've bugged the table.

This isn't a joke, I've genuinely bugged it. Three days ago I went online and bought a tiny remote microphone in a pack called 'My First Spy Kit'. When it arrived I realised it was designed for ten-year-old boys rather than adult ex-girlfriends, as it also came with a plastic 'Spy's Logbook' and 'Cool Code Cracker'. But so what? I've tested it out and it works! It only has a range of twenty feet, but that's all I need. Ten minutes ago I casually sauntered past the table, pretended to drop something, and slapped the tiny sticky pad of the microphone on the underside of the table. The earpiece is hidden under my baseball cap. I just have to switch it on when I'm ready.

And OK, I know you shouldn't spy on people. But the point is, when it comes to love there's a different set of morals. All's fair in love or war.

'I think he's coming now!' Sadie says beside me. I had talked her into being my assistant, although all she's done so far is wander about the restaurant saying disparaging things about people's outfits.

I risk a glance towards the door. Oh God—it's him. And her. They're together. I take a deep gulp of wine, then raise my eyes again.

She's blonde. Quite skinny, in orange pedalpushers and one of those crisp white sleeveless tops that women wear in ads for low-fat yoghurt or toothpaste. Her arms are tanned and there are streaks in her hair as though she's been on holiday.

As I shift my gaze to Josh, I feel my stomach go all slithery. He's just . . . Josh. Same fair floppy hair, same goofy lopsided grin as he greets the maître d', same faded jeans, same canvas sneakers, same shirt—

Hang on. I stare at him in disbelieving shock. That's the shirt I gave him for his birthday. How can he be doing this? Does he have no heart? He's wearing *my* shirt in *our* place. And he's smiling at this girl as though no one exists but her.

'They look very well suited,' says Sadie brightly in my ear.

The maître d' is showing them to the window table. Keeping my head down, I reach into my pocket and switch on the microphone. The sound is faint and buzzy, but I can just about hear his voice.

He's ordering a bottle of wine. Great. Now I have to watch them get all merry. I take a few olives and munch disconsolately. Sadie has slid into the seat opposite and is watching me with pity.

'I warned you, never be a trailer.'

'I'm not being a trailer! I'm just . . . trying to understand him.'

I glance over at Josh, who is smiling at Marie while the waiter uncorks a bottle. I could be watching our own first date. It was just the same, all smiles and amusing little stories and wine. Where did it go wrong? How did I end up sitting in a corner bugging him?

And then the solution hits me, with total clarity. I lean over towards Sadie with sudden urgency. 'Go and ask him.'

'Ask him what?' She makes a face.

'Where it went wrong! Get inside his head! Make him talk! This is the only way I can get to him—' I break off as a waitress approaches the table, her notepad out. 'Oh, hi. I'd love some . . . um . . . soup. Thanks.'

As the waitress moves off I gaze entreatingly at Sadie. 'Please. I've come all this way. I've made all this effort.'

There's a moment's silence—then Sadie rolls her eyes. 'Very well.'

She disappears, then a moment later reappears right by Josh's table. I push my earpiece more firmly into my ear and listen to Marie's rippling laugh as she tells some story about horse riding.

'Your childhood sounds amazing,' Josh is saying. 'You have to tell me more.'

'What do you want to know?' She laughs.

'Everything.' He smiles. I'm watching in horror. They've got that whole eyes-meeting frissony thing going on.

'*Why did you break up with Lara?*' Sadie's voice is so piercing through my earpiece I nearly jump out of my chair.

Josh has heard her, I can tell. His hand has stopped, halfway through pouring out fizzy water.

'My two brothers tormented me, all through my childhood.' Marie is speaking, obviously unaware of anything. 'They were so evil . . .'

'*Why did you break up with Lara? Talk to Marie about it! Talk, Josh!*'

'. . . found frogs in my bed, in my satchel . . . once even in my cereal bowl!' Marie laughs, and looks up at Josh, clearly expecting him to respond. But he's frozen like a statue as Sadie yells, '*Say it, say it, say it!*'

'Josh?' Marie says. 'Did you hear a word I said?'

'Sorry!' He shakes his head. 'Sorry! It's weird. I was just thinking about my ex, Lara.'

'Oh. What about her?'

'I don't know.' Josh screws up his face, looking perplexed. 'I was just thinking what it was about her and me that went wrong.'

'Relationships end,' Marie says easily. 'Who knows why?'

'Yes.' Josh still has a faraway look in his eyes, which isn't suprising as Sadie is yelling like a siren in his ear, '*Say why it went wrong! Say it out loud!*'

'I suppose she was a bit intense,' Josh blurts out. 'She used to read me out "relationship issues" from some magazine and want to talk about how similar we were to some other random couple. That annoyed me. Why did she have to analyse everything? Why did she have to unpick every single row and conversation?'

'That does sound annoying.' Marie nods sympathetically.

'*What else?*' Sadie is shrieking at Josh. '*What else?*'

'She used to litter the bathroom with her creams and crap.' Josh frowns distantly at the memory. 'Every time I tried to shave I had to fight through this thicket of pots. It drove me mad.'

'What a pain!' says Marie, over-brightly. 'Anyway—'

'And it was the little things. Like the way she used to sing in the shower. I mean, I don't mind singing, but the same song every bloody *day*? And she didn't want to open her mind. She's not interested in travelling, not interested in the same things as me . . . Like, I once bought her this book of William Eggleston photography—I thought we could talk about it but she just flipped through with zero interest . . .'

Josh suddenly seems to notice Marie. 'I'm sorry! I don't know why Lara keeps popping into my head. Let's talk about something else.'

'Yes, let's do that.' Marie smiles stiffly.

'Soup? Excuse me, Miss, didn't you order the soup? Excuse me?'

Suddenly I realise a waiter is standing by my table with a tray of soup and bread. I have no idea how long he's been trying to get my attention.

'Oh, right,' I say, quickly turning to him. 'Yes, thanks.'

The waiter deposits my food and I pick up a spoon, but I can't eat. I'm too flabbergasted by everything Josh just said. How could he have felt all this and never mentioned it?

'Well!' Sadie bounces up to me and slides into the seat opposite. '*That* was interesting. Now you know where it all went wrong. I agree about the singing,' she adds. 'You are rather tuneless.'

'Well, thanks.' I keep my voice low and gaze morosely into my soup. 'You know the worst thing? He never said any of this stuff to my face. None of it! I could have fixed it! If he'd just given me a chance . . .'

'Shall we go now?' She sounds bored.

'No!' I take a deep breath. 'Go and ask him what he liked about me.'

'What he liked about you? Are you sure there was anything?'

'Yes!' I hiss indignantly. 'Of course there was! Go on!'

Sadie shrugs and heads back across the restaurant. Josh is sipping his wine and skewering olives with a metal pick while Marie talks. He has a bemused look on his face and keeps trying to edge his head away from Sadie, who's yelling, '*What did you love about Lara? Say it!*'

'I loved the way she had so much energy,' he says in a desperate rush. 'And she was quirky. She always had some cute necklace on, or a pencil stuffed into her hair or something . . . And she really *appreciated* things.'

'Are we talking about your ex-girlfriend again, by any chance?' There's a steely edge to Marie's voice. Josh seems to come to.

'Shit! Marie, I don't know what's got into me. I don't know why I'm thinking about her.' He looks so freaked out I almost feel sorry for him.

'If you ask me, you're still obsessed,' Marie says tightly.

'I'm not obsessed! I'm not even interested in her any more!'

'So why are you telling me how great she was?' I watch as Marie pushes back her chair and stands up. 'Call me when you've got over her.'

'I have got over her!' Josh exclaims angrily. 'This is ridiculous. I hadn't *thought* about her until today.' He pushes back his chair, trying to get Marie's attention. 'Listen to me, Marie. Lara and I had a relationship. It was fine, but it wasn't great. And then it finished. End of.'

Marie is just shaking her head. 'Which is why you bring her up in conversation every five minutes.'

'I *don't*!' Josh almost yells in frustration, and a few people at nearby tables look up. 'Not normally! I haven't talked about her or thought about her for weeks!'

'You need to sort yourself out,' Marie says, not unkindly. She picks up her bag. 'See you, Josh.'

As she moves swiftly between the tables and out of the restaurant, Josh sinks back into his seat, looking shell-shocked. Somehow I suppress an urge to run over and fling my arms around him.

'Are you satisfied now?' Sadie returns to my side. 'You've ruined the path of true love. I thought that was against your creed.'

'That wasn't true love.' I scowl at her.

'How do you know?'

'Because I know. Shut up.'

We both watch in silence as Josh pays his bill, reaches for his jacket and gets up to leave. His jaw is tight and his easy saunter has gone, and I feel a flash of guilt. But I know I'm doing the right thing. Not just for me, but for Josh. I can make it work between us, I *know* I can.

All the way home, I'm deep in thought. Josh is vulnerable. He's confused. It's the perfect time for me to rekindle our love. But I have to *use* what I've learned. I have to change myself.

I keep obsessively tracking back over everything he said, trying to remember every detail. And every time I reach one particular phrase, I squirm and wince. *It was fine, but it wasn't great.*

It's all blindingly clear now. Our relationship wasn't great because he wasn't honest with me. He didn't tell me any of his little niggles. And they all built up in his head and that's why he chucked me. But it doesn't matter—because now I know what the problems are, I can solve them! All of them! I've put together an action plan and I'm going to start by tidying up my bathroom. As soon as we get back to my flat I stride in, full of optimism, to find Sadie heading me off.

'What are you going to wear tonight?' she demands. 'Show me.'

'Later.' I try to get past her.

'Not later! Now! Remember, this is my date. You're representing me. You need to look divine.'

'All right!' I head into my bedroom. 'What about . . . this?' I pull a maxi skirt and my new corset top from Topshop out of the wardrobe.

'*Stays*? And a long skirt?'

'It's the maxi look, OK? It's really fashionable, actually. And these aren't stays, it's a corset top.'

Sadie touches my corset top with a shudder. 'My mother tried to make me wear stays to my aunt's wedding,' she says. 'I threw them on the fire, so she shut me in my room.'

'Really?' I feel a spark of interest. 'So you missed the wedding?'

'I climbed out of the window, took the motor, drove to London and had my hair shingled,' she says proudly. 'When my mother saw it, she went to bed for two days.'

'Wow.' I put the clothes down on the bed and look at Sadie properly. 'You were a real rebel. Were you always doing things like that?'

'I did rather torture my parents. But they were so stifling. So *Victorian*. The whole house was like a museum.' She shudders. 'My father disapproved of the phonograph, the Charleston, cocktails . . . *everything*. He thought girls should spend their time arranging flowers and doing needlework. Like my sister, Virginia.'

'You mean . . . Granny?' Suddenly I'm fascinated to hear more. I only have hazy memories of Granny. 'What was she like?'

'Horribly virtuous.' Sadie makes a face. '*She* wore stays. Even after the whole world had stopped wearing them. She was the dullest girl in Archbury. And then she married the dullest man in Archbury.'

This is ringing bells in my mind. *Archbury*. I know I've heard it . . .

'Hang on!' I say suddenly. 'Archbury House. The house that got burned down in the 1960s. Was that your house?'

It's all coming back to me now. Years ago, Dad told me about the old family home, Archbury House. He said that he and Uncle Bill had spent summers there when they were little boys, and then moved in when their grandparents died. After the fire, the land was sold off and a close of new houses was built in its place.

'Yes. Virginia was living there with her family by then. In fact, she caused the fire. She left a candle alight.' There's a moment's silence before Sadie adds with an acidic edge, 'Not so perfect, after all. I lost all my things,' she says distantly. 'All the things I was keeping there while I was abroad. All destroyed.'

'That's awful,' I say, feeling inadequate.

'What does it matter?' She suddenly seems to come to, and gives me a brittle smile. 'Who cares?' She whirls away towards the wardrobe and points imperiously. 'Get out your clothes. I need to see them all.'

'Whatever.' I grab an armful of hangers and dump them on the bed. 'So, tell me about your husband. What was he like?'

Sadie considers for a moment. 'He wore a scarlet waistcoat at our wedding. Other than that, I remember very little about him.'

'How could you marry someone you didn't love?'

'Because it was my only way to escape,' says Sadie. 'I'd had the most terrible row with my parents. My father had stopped my allowance, the vicar called every second day, I was locked in my room every night . . .'

'What had you done?' I say. 'Had you been arrested again?'

'It . . . doesn't matter,' says Sadie, after a slight pause. 'I had to leave. Marriage seemed as good a way as any. My parents had already found a suitable young man. And believe me, they were hardly lining up in their droves in those days.'

'Oh, well, I know about that,' I say, rolling my eyes in sympathy. 'There are *no* single men in London. None. It's a well-known fact.'

I look up to see Sadie gazing at me with a kind of blank incomprehension. 'We lost all ours in the War,' she says.

'Oh. Of course.' I swallow. 'The War.'

World War One. I hadn't quite put that together.

'The ones who survived weren't the same boys they'd been. They were wounded. Broken to bits. Or full of guilt because they'd survived.'

The room is quiet, save for the tinny sound of the TV upstairs.

'But even if there weren't many men around,' I venture, 'did you have to settle? What about waiting for the right guy? What about love?'

'What about love! Goodness, you play a monotonous tune.' She surveys the mound of clothes on the bed. 'Lay them out so I can see properly. I'll choose your dress for this evening.'

'OK.' I start spreading my clothes out on the bed. 'You choose.'

'And I'm in charge of your hairstyle and make-up,' Sadie adds firmly. 'I'm in charge of everything.'

'Fine,' I say patiently.

I walk back to the bathroom and look at my pots of creams and cosmetics, all balanced on the counter round the basin. Hmm. Perhaps Josh had a point. Maybe I don't need apricot scrub and oatmeal scrub *and* sea-salt scrub. I mean, how scrubbed should skin be, anyway?

Half an hour later I've got everything organised into rows and have assembled a whole carrier bag of ancient, half-empty pots to chuck out. If Josh saw this bathroom he'd be so impressed!

Feeling delighted with myself, I make a cup of tea. Next on my list is to find that photography book he was talking about. It must still be round here somewhere. Maybe under the sofa . . .

'I've found it!' Sadie's excited voice springing out of nowhere nearly makes me knock my head on the coffee table.

'I've found you a frock,' she announces. 'Come and see! We have to go out! It's in a shop!'

'A shop?' I stop and stare at her. 'What do you mean, in a shop?'

'I was forced to go out.' She lifts her chin defiantly. 'There was nothing in your wardrobe. So I went out, and I found an *angel* of a dress! You simply have to buy it! Come on! Get your purse!'

'Well, OK,' I say at last. 'As long as it doesn't cost a zillion pounds.' I reach for my bag. 'Come on, then. Show me.'

I'm expecting Sadie to lead me to the tube station and drag me to Oxford Circus or somewhere. But instead she veers round the corner and into a grid of backstreets I've never explored.

We pass rows of houses and a little park and a college. I'm about to tell Sadie that she must have got her bearings wrong when she turns a corner and makes a triumphant flourish.

'There!'

We're in front of a tiny parade of shops. There's a newsagent and a dry-cleaner and, right at the end, a tiny shop with a wood-painted sign reading VINTAGE FASHION EMPORIUM. There's a mannequin in the window wearing a long satin dress and gloves up to the elbow.

'This is by *far* the best shop you have in your area,' says Sadie emphatically. 'I've found everything we need. Come on!'

Before I can say anything she's disappeared into the shop. I have no choice but to follow her. The door gives a little 'ting' as I enter and a middle-aged woman smiles at me from behind a tiny counter. She has straggly dyed hair in a vivid shade of yellow, and is wearing what looks like an original seventies kaftan in a wild green circular print.

'Hello!' She smiles pleasantly. 'I'm Norah. Have you been here before?'

'Hi.' I nod back. 'This is my first time.'

'Were you interested in a particular garment or era?'

'I'll . . . just have a browse.' I smile back. 'Thanks.'

I can't see Sadie, so I start wandering around. I've never been into vintage clothes, but I can tell there's some pretty amazing stuff here.

'Where are you?' Sadie's voice pierces my eardrum. 'Come here!'

She's beckoning from a rack towards the back. I head towards her.

'Look!' She gestures in triumph. 'Perfect.'

Sadie is pointing at a 1920s flapper's dress. A bronze silk flapper dress with a dropped waist, little beaded capped sleeves and a matching cape. The store tag reads 'Original 1920s dress, made in Paris.'

'Sadie!' I find my voice. 'I can't wear that on a date! Don't be stupid!'

'Of course you can! Try it on! I've found you some matching shoes, too.' She points at some bronze-coloured dancing slippers. 'And some proper make-up.' She whirls over to a glass counter and gestures at a Bakelite case next to a sign reading, 'Original 1920s make-up set.'

'I had a set just like this.' She's gazing at it fondly. 'This is the best lipstick that was ever made. I'll teach you how to do yours properly.'

'I know how to do my lipstick properly, thanks—'

'You have no idea,' she cuts me off crisply. 'But I'll teach you. And we'll marcel your hair. There are some irons for sale.' She points at a cardboard box inside which I can see a weird-looking, metal contraption. 'You'll look *so* much better if you make an effort.'

'Sadie, just stop it!' I hiss. 'I'm not getting any of this stuff—'

'Go and try the bronze dress on!' Sadie shoos me forward. 'Go on!'

'Stop it!' I hiss. 'I don't want to try it on!' My frustration bubbles over. 'Get real! This is the twenty-first century! I'm not wearing a flapper's dress on a date! It's just not happening!'

For a few moments, Sadie seems too taken aback to reply.

'But you promised. You promised I could choose your dress.'

'I thought you meant normal clothes!' I say in exasperation. 'Not this.' I pick up the dress and brandish it at her. 'It's fancy dress!'

'But if you don't wear the dress I choose, then it might as well not be my date at all. It might as well be your date!' Sadie's voice starts rising; I can tell she's cranking up into a scream. 'I might as well stay at home!'

I sigh. 'Look, Sadie—'

'He's *my* man! It's *my* date!' she cries passionately. 'Mine! With my rules! This is my last chance to have some fun with a man and you want to spoil it by wearing some frightful, dreary outfit—'

'I don't want to *spoil* it—'

'You promised to do things my way! *You promised!*'

'Is everything all right?' Norah appears and eyes me suspiciously.

'Yes!' I try to compose myself. 'I was just . . . er . . . on the phone.'

'Ah.' Her face clears. She nods towards the bronze silk flapper dress, still in my arms. 'You want to try that on? Wonderful piece.'

'I . . . um . . .'

'You promised!' Sadie's about three inches from me, her chin set, her eyes fiery. 'You promised! It's my date! Mine! *Mine!*'

She's like a relentless fire-engine siren. I jerk my head away, trying to think straight. There's no way I can cope with a whole evening of Sadie yelling at me. My head will explode. And let's face it, Ed Harrison thinks I'm a nutter anyway. What difference does it make if I turn up in a flapper dress? Sadie's right. It's her evening. I might as well do it her way. 'All right!' I say at last, cutting across Sadie's insistent voice. 'You've talked me round. I'll try on the dress.'

Five

IF ANYONE I KNOW SEES ME, I will die. I will *die*.

As I get out of the taxi I look up and down the street. No one in sight, thank God. I have never looked so ludicrous in my life. This is what happens when you let a dead great-aunt take control of your looks.

I'm wearing the flapper dress from the shop, which I only just managed to zip up. My feet are squished into the dancing slippers. Six long bead necklaces are jangling round my neck. Circling my head is a black headband, beaded with jet, and sticking out of that is a feather.

My hair has been tortured into a series of waves and curls, which took about two hours to do with the marcel irons. When it was done, Sadie insisted I smother it in some weird pomade stuff which she also found in the vintage shop, and now it feels rock solid to the touch.

And as for my make-up. Did they honestly think this was a good look in the 1920s? My face is covered in pale powder, with a spot of rouge on each cheek. My eyes are heavily outlined in black kohl. My lids are smeared with a lurid green paste which came out of the old Bakelite case. I still don't know exactly what's on my eyelashes: some weird black goo which Sadie called 'Cosmétique'. She made me boil it up in a frying pan and then smear it all over my lashes.

'Let me see.' Sadie appears beside me. She's in a gold dress, with gloves up to her elbows. 'You need to touch up your lipstick.'

With a sigh I reach in my bag for the pot of red gunk and pat yet more colour onto my exaggerated Cupid's bow.

'You look divine!' Sadie hugs herself with excitement. 'Come on, then!'

I begin to follow her up the street towards the Crowe Bar sign, barely able to walk in my vintage shoes. As I reach the door, I realise she's disappeared. Where's she gone?

'Sadie?' I turn round and scan the street.

'He's in there already!' She suddenly appears, looking even more hyper than before. 'He's absolutely swoonsome. How do I look?' Sadie's smoothing her hair down and I feel a sudden pang of compassion for her. It can't be much fun, going on a date and being invisible.

'You look great. If he could see you he'd think you were really hot.'

'Hot?' She looks confused.

'Sexy. Pretty. You're a hottie. It's what we say.'

'Oh, good! Now, before we go in, remember this is my date.'

'I know it's your date,' I say patiently.

'What I mean is . . . be me.' She fixes me with an urgent look. 'Say whatever I tell you to say. Do whatever I tell you to do. Then I'll feel as though it's really me talking to him. Do you understand?'

'Don't worry! You feed me the lines and I'll say them. I promise.'

'Go on then!' She gestures at the entrance.

I push through the heavy frosted-glass doors and find myself in a chic lobby with low-level lighting. There's another set of double doors ahead, beyond which I can see the bar. As I pass through, I catch a glimpse of myself in a tinted mirror and feel a clench of dismay. I look like a twenties-o-gram. And I'm standing in a minimalist bar full of cool people in understated Helmut Lang.

As I'm edging forward, all prickly with self-consciousness, I spot Ed. He's sitting at a table about ten yards away, in a conventional trousers-and-jacket combo, drinking what looks like a conventional gin and tonic. He looks up, glances my way, then does a double take.

'You see?' says Sadie. 'He's transfixed by the sight of you!'

He's transfixed, all right. His jaw has fallen and his face has turned a pale green colour. Very slowly he gets to his feet and approaches me. I can see the bar staff nudging each other as I walk through the bar, and from a nearby table comes a sudden gasp of hilarity.

'Smile at him!' Sadie is insisting loudly in my ear. 'Walk towards him with a shimmy and say, "Hello, Daddy-O!"'

It's not my date, I remind myself. It's Sadie's. I'm only acting a part.

'Hello, Daddy-O!' I say brightly as he draws near.

'Hi,' he says faintly. 'You look . . .' He moves his hands helplessly.

All around, the buzz of conversation has died to a halt. The whole bar is watching us. Great.

'Say some more!' Sadie is hopping around in excitement. 'Say, "You look pretty dapper yourself, you old thing." And twirl your necklace.'

'You look pretty dapper yourself, you old thing!' I fix him with a sickly smile, swinging my beads around so hard that one of the necklaces catches me in the eye. Ow. That hurt.

'Right.' Ed seems barely able to talk for embarrassment. 'Well. Can I . . . get you a drink? A glass of champagne?'

'Ask for a swizzle stick!' instructs Sadie. 'And smile! You haven't laughed once!'

'Could I have a swizzle stick?'

'A swizzle stick?' Ed frowns. 'Why?'

'Say, "To stir the bubbles out, darling!"' she hisses.

'To stir the bubbles out, darling!' I giggle brightly and twirl my necklaces for good measure.

Ed looks like he wants to sink into the floor. I don't blame him.

'Why don't you take a seat?' he says. 'I'll bring over the drinks.'

I head over to the table where he was sitting, and pull up a chair.

'Sit like this,' commands Sadie, adopting an affected pose with her hands on her knee, and I copy as best I can. 'Open your eyes wider!' She looks restlessly around at all the clusters of people sitting in groups and standing at the bar. The hum of chatter has resumed and there's a low throbbing of lounge-style music. 'When will the dancing start?'

'There *isn't* any dancing,' I mutter. 'It's not that kind of place.'

'No dancing?' she says fretfully. 'But there has to be dancing! Dancing is the whole point! Don't they have any snappier music?'

'I don't know,' I say sarcastically. 'Ask him.' I jerk my head towards the barman, just as Ed appears before me with a glass of champagne and what looks like another gin and tonic. I should think it's a treble. He sits down opposite, puts down the drinks, then lifts his glass.

'Cheers.'

'Chin-chin!' I say with a dazzling smile, give my champagne a brisk stir with a plastic swizzle stick and take a glug. I look up for Sadie's approval—but she's disappeared. I surreptitiously look around and spot her behind the bar, yelling something in the barman's ear.

'So . . . did you have far to come?'

My attention is wrenched away. Ed's talking to me. And there's no Sadie to feed me any lines. Great. I'm actually going to have to make conversation.

'Er . . . not too far. Kilburn.'

'Ah. Kilburn.' He nods as though I've said something profound.

While I'm trying to think of something to say, I run my eyes over him. He's taller than I remember, with a broader, firmer frame and the same 'V' of frown lines that he had in the office.

'So, Ed!' I make a heroic effort and smile at him. 'From your accent I'm guessing you're American?'

'That's right.' He nods, but doesn't volunteer any more.

'How long have you been over?'

'Five months.'

'How do you like London?'

'Haven't seen much of it.'

'Oh, you must! You should go to the London Eye, and Covent Garden, and then you should take a boat to Greenwich . . .'

'Maybe.' He gives me a tight smile. 'I'm pretty busy at work.'

That is the lamest thing I ever heard. How can you move to a city and not bother to get to know it? I *knew* I didn't like this guy.

I glance up to see Sadie by my side, her arms folded sulkily.

'That barman is very stubborn,' she says. 'Go and tell him to change the music.'

Is she nuts? Shooting her a discreet glare, I turn back to Ed.

'So, Lara,' Ed says. 'What do you do?'

'I'm a head-hunter.'

Immediately Ed looks wary. 'You're not with Sturgis Curtis, are you?'

'No, I have my own company, L&N Executive Recruitment.'

'Good. I wouldn't have liked to offend you.'

'What's wrong with Sturgis Curtis?' I can't resist asking.

'They're vultures from hell. They pester me every day. Do I want this job? Am I interested in that job? They use tricks to get past my secretary . . . I mean, they're *good*.' He shudders. 'They even asked me to sit at their table at the *Business People* dinner.'

'Oh, wow.' I'm impressed. I've never been to the *Business People* dinner, but I've seen it written up in the magazine. It's always held at a big hotel in London and it's pretty glam. 'So, are you going?'

'I'm speaking at it.'

He's *speaking*? Oh my God, he must be really important. I had no idea. I look up to raise my eyebrows at Sadie, but she's vanished.

'Are you going?' he asks politely.

'Er . . . not this year.' I try to imply this is just a temporary blip. 'My firm wasn't quite able to make up a table.'

Bearing in mind tables hold twelve people and cost £5,000 and L&N Executive Recruitment has precisely two people and about minus £5,000.

'Ah.' He inclines his head.

As I swizzle my drink again I realise the music has stopped. I turn to look at the barman, and he's standing by the CD player behind the bar, obviously experiencing a momentous struggle between his own will and the sound of Sadie shrieking in his ear. What is she up to?

At last, with a visible capitulation, the barman takes a CD from its box and slides it into the machine. The next minute, some scratchy, old-fashioned, Cole Porter-type band music starts filling the air. Sadie sweeps up behind Ed's chair, a beam of satisfaction on her face.

'At last! I knew that man would have something suitable in his drawer. Now ask Lara to dance!' she instructs Ed. '*Ask her to dance!*'

Oh God. No way. *Resist her*, I silently message Ed. *Don't listen.* I'm sending him my strongest telepathic signals. But it's no good.

'Lara.' He clears his throat. 'Would you like to . . . dance?'

'OK.' Hardly able to believe what I'm doing, I stand up. I follow Ed to a tiny patch of spare floor next to the barstools, and he turns to face me. For a moment we both just stare at each other, paralysed by the enormity of the situation. This is a 100 per cent non-dancing scenario. We're not on a dance floor. This isn't a club, it's a bar. No one else is dancing. The jazz band is still playing its scratchy music through the speakers and some bloke is singing about his fancy shoes. There's no beat, there's no nothing. There's no way we can dance.

'Dance!' Sadie is flitting between us like quicksilver. '*Dance!*'

With a look of desperation in his eyes, Ed starts moving awkwardly from side to side. He looks so miserable, I start copying him, just to make him feel better. I've never seen less convincing dancing in my life.

Out of the corner of my eye I can see everyone turning to watch us. Ed's eyes are focused far ahead, as though he's having an out-of-body experience. This is the most excruciating experience of my life.

'Dance properly!' I turn my head to see Sadie regarding me in horror. 'That's not dancing! *This* is how to dance.'

She starts some twenties Charleston-type dance, all flying legs and elbows and knees. Her face is beatific, and I can hear her humming along to the music. At least *someone's* having fun.

As I watch, she shimmies right up to Ed and places a slender hand on each of his shoulders. Now she's running a hand adoringly down his cheek. 'Isn't he blissful?' She runs both her hands down his chest, circling his waist and skimming down his back.

'Sadie!' I hiss as her hands travel even further down his body.

'I'm sorry, what did you say?' With an obvious effort, Ed focuses on me. He's still dancing, totally oblivious to the fact that he has a twenty-three-year-old flapper running her hands voraciously all over his body.

'I said . . . let's stop.' I avert my eyes from Sadie, who's trying to nibble his ear.

'No!' protests Sadie furiously. 'More!'

'Great idea,' says Ed at once and starts back towards our chairs.

'Ed? Ed Harrison?' A blonde woman steps into his path. She's wearing beige trousers and a white shirt and an expression of incredulous glee. At the table behind her, I can see several other business types watching avidly. 'I thought that was you! Were you just . . . *dancing?*'

As Ed surveys all the faces at the table, it's obvious his nightmare has just got about fifty times worse. I almost feel sorry for him.

'That's . . . that's right,' he says at last, as though he can't quite believe it himself. 'We were dancing.' He seems to come to. 'Lara, do you know Genevieve Bailey from DFT? Genevieve, Lara. Hello, Bill, Mike, Sarah . . .' He's nodding at all the people sitting round the table.

'Your dress is adorable.' Genevieve flicks a condescending glance over my outfit. 'Going for the twenties look, obviously.'

'It's original.' I nod.

'I have no doubt!'

I smile back as best I can. 'I'll just touch up my make-up,' I say. 'I'll be back in a minute.'

In the Ladies', I get out a tissue, wet it and scrub at my face.

'Where did you learn to dance?' Sadie asks.

'I didn't. You don't learn to dance. You just pick it up.'

'Well, it shows. You're terrible.'

'Well, you're totally OTT,' I retort, stung. 'You looked like you wanted to jump his bones right there!'

'Jump his bones?' Sadie frowns. 'What do you mean?'

'It means . . . you know.' I stop awkwardly. 'It's like a pyjama party. Except you take off your pyjamas.'

'Oh, that.' Her face clicks with recognition. 'What an odd phrase. We used to call it sex.'

'Oh,' I say, discomfited. 'Well, we do too—'

'Or barney-mugging,' she adds.

Barney-mugging? And she calls 'jump his bones' an odd phrase?

'Well, whatever you call it. You looked like you wanted to do it with him right there in the bar.'

'Do you think he'd like me? If he could see me.'

'Yes,' I say as convincingly as I can. 'I think he'd love you.'

'I think so too.' She looks satisfied. 'Your headdress is crooked, did you realise?'

I tug at it and survey my reflection grumpily. 'I look so *ridiculous*.'

'You look divine. You're the prettiest girl in the place. Apart from me,' she adds airily.

As we head back to the bar, I see that Ed is still chatting to Genevieve.

'Lara!' Genevieve greets me with a fake smile. 'I'm so sorry. I don't want to disrupt your evening *à deux* with Ed!'

'No worries.' I give her an equally fake smile.

'So how did you two meet?'

I can't help a surreptitious glance at Ed who looks uneasy.

'It was in the office, wasn't it?' I say, to help him out.

'In the office. Yes.' Ed nods in relief.

'Well!' Genevieve laughs—a bright, trilling laugh. 'Ed, you *are* a dark horse! I had no idea you had a girlfriend!'

For a split second, Ed's and my eyes meet. I can see he's about as keen on that idea as I am.

'She's not my girlfriend,' he says at once. 'I mean, that's not . . .'

'I'm not his girlfriend,' I chime in. 'We're just . . . it's kind of a one-off.'

'We're just having a drink,' Ed supplies.

'We'll probably never see each other again.'

'Probably not,' Ed affirms. 'Definitely not.'

We're both nodding in total agreement. In fact, I think we've bonded for the first time.

'I see.' Genevieve looks totally confused.

'Let me get you another drink, Lara.' Ed gives me the warmest smile he has all evening.

'No, I'll get them!' I beam back at him. There's nothing like knowing you only have to spend ten more minutes with someone to make you feel suddenly generous towards them.

'What do you mean?' A voice is shrieking behind me, and as I turn I see Sadie heading towards me. 'It's not a one-off! You made a promise!'

'I kept my promise!' I hiss out of the side of my mouth as I approach the bar. 'I've done my side of the deal.'

'No, you haven't!' She glares at me in outrage. 'You haven't even danced properly with him! You've just shuffled round dismally.'

'Too bad.' I get out my phone and pretend to be speaking into it. 'You said you wanted a date. I've given you one. The end. A glass of champagne and a G&T, please,' I add to the barman.

Sadie's silent. I swivel round and see her back beside Ed. She's yelling in his ear. Oh God, what's she doing?

I pay for the drinks as quickly as I can and hurry back across the bar. Ed is staring into the middle distance, that glazed, transfixed look on his face again. Genevieve is in the middle of an anecdote about Antigua and doesn't even seem to have noticed Ed's faraway expression.

'And then I saw my bikini top!' She trills with laughter. 'In the sea! I never lived that one down.'

'Here you are, Ed,' I say, and hand him his G&T.

'Oh. Thanks.' He seems to come to.

'*Do it now!*' Sadie suddenly shrieks in his ear. '*Ask her NOW!*'

'Lara.' Ed focuses on me with what looks like some difficulty. 'Would you like to be my guest at the *Business People* dinner?'

I do not *believe* it. In shock, I swivel my eyes to Sadie's—and she's looking at me with an expression of triumph.

'Don't say yes on my account,' she says carelessly. 'It's up to you.'

Ooh. She's *good*. I didn't even realise she was paying attention to the conversation. There's no way I can turn down an invitation to the *Business People* dinner. I'll be able to network . . . make contacts . . . It's a massive opportunity. I can't say no. I just can't. *Damn* her.

'Yes,' I say at last, stiffly. 'Thank you, Ed, I'd love to come.'

'Good. That's great. I'll send you the details.'

We both sound as though we're reading lines from cards. Genevieve is looking back and forth between our faces, bewildered.

'So, you *are* a couple,' she says.

'No!' we both reply in unison.

'No way,' I add for emphasis. 'Not at all. I mean . . . never. Not in a million years.' I take a sip of champagne and glance over at Ed. Is it my imagination, or does he look just the tiniest bit offended?

I last about another twenty minutes, listening to Genevieve show off about practically every single holiday she's ever been on. Then Ed glances at me, and my empty glass, and says, 'Don't let me keep you.'

Don't let me keep you. If that isn't code for 'I can't stand a moment more in your company', I don't know what is.

'I'm sure you have dinner plans,' he adds politely.

'Yes!' I say brightly. 'I do, as it happens. Absolutely. Dinner plans.' I do a pantomime sweep of my watch in front of my eyes. 'Goodness, is that the time? I must run. My dinner companions will be waiting.' I resist the temptation to add 'At Lyle Place, with champagne.'

'Well, I have plans too.' He nods. 'So maybe we should . . .'

He made dinner plans. Of course he did. He probably has a whole other, superior date lined up.

'Yes, let's. It's been . . . fun.'

We both stand up, make general parting gestures at the business people, and head out of the bar onto the pavement.

'So.' Ed hesitates. 'Thanks for . . .' He makes as though to lean in for a peck on the cheek, then clearly decides against it and holds out his hand instead. 'That was great. I'll let you know about the dinner.'

His face is so easy to read it's almost pitiful. He's already wondering how the hell he got himself into this one—but having invited me in front of a crowd, he can hardly back out now.

'So . . . I'm going this way,' he adds.

'I'm going the other way,' I respond at once. 'Thanks again. Bye!' I turn on my heel and start striding down the street. What a fiasco.

Things are on the up. I feel it in my bones. Even this second date with Ed is a positive thing. Going to the *Business People* dinner will be a great chance for me to meet loads of senior professionals.

'Kate!' I say on Monday morning. 'I need all my business cards, and I need to buy one of those little holders, and I need all the back issues of *Business People*—' I break off in surprise. She's clutching the phone with one hand and circling the air wildly with the other. 'What's wrong?'

'It's the police! They want to come and see you.'

'Oh, right.'

A chunk of ice seems to descend nastily into my stomach. The police. I was hoping the police might just forget all about me.

'Shall I put them through?' Kate is totally agog.

'Yes, why not?' I try to sound confident. 'Hello. Lara Lington speaking.'

'Lara, it's DC Davies here.' She's pleasant but brisk. 'I'm in the area and was wondering if I could pop by for a chat. Are you free now?'

'Yes, I'm free.' My voice has risen to a petrified squeak. 'See you then!'

I put the receiver down, hot in the face. Why is she following this up? Aren't the police always supposed to be chasing car fines and ignoring murders? Why couldn't they ignore *this* murder?

I look up to see Kate staring at me. 'What do the police want?'

'Nothing to worry about. It's just about my great-aunt's murder.'

'*Murder?*' Kate claps a hand over her mouth.

I keep forgetting how 'murder' sounds when you just drop it into a sentence.

'The one whose funeral you went to?'

'Mm-hmm.' I nod.

'No wonder you were so upset! That's awful. How was she killed?'

Oh God. I really don't want to go into the details.

'Poison,' I mumble at last.

'By who?'

'Well.' I clear my throat. 'They don't know.'

'They don't *know?*' Kate sounds totally outraged. 'God, the police are useless! They spend their whole time giving you parking tickets and then someone's actually murdered and they don't even care—'

'I think they're doing the best they can,' I say hastily. 'They're probably giving me an update. In fact, they've probably found the culprit.'

Even as I'm speaking, the most horrific thought is hitting me. What if that's true? What if DC Davies is coming here to tell me they've found the man with the scar and the plaited beard? What do I do then?

The buzzer goes, and Kate leaps up to answer it.

It'll all be fine, I tell myself fervently. It's no big deal. But as soon as I see DC Davies walking through the door, I can feel my calmness disintegrating into childlike panic.

'Have you found the murderer?' I blurt out anxiously.

'No,' DC Davies says, giving me a strange look.

'Thank God.' I subside in relief, then realise how that might sound. 'I mean . . . why not? What are you doing all day?'

'I'll give you some privacy,' says Kate, backing out, while simultaneously mouthing 'Useless!' behind DC Davies's back.

'Have a seat.' I gesture to a chair. 'So, how are things progressing?'

'Lara.' DC Davies gives me a long, hard look. 'We have found no evidence to suggest that your great-aunt was murdered. According to the doctor's report, she died of natural causes. Essentially, old age.'

'Old *age*?' I adopt a shocked expression. 'Well, that's just ludicrous.'

'Unless we can find any evidence to suggest otherwise, the case will be closed. Do you have any evidence?'

'Um . . .' I pause. 'Not what you'd call *evidence*. Not as such.'

'What about this phone message you left?' She pulls out a piece of paper. '"The nurses didn't do it."'

'Oh, that. Yes.' I nod several times, playing for time. 'I realised I'd got a tiny detail wrong in my statement. I just wanted to clarify things.'

'And this "man with a plaited beard"? A man who didn't even appear in your original statement?' The sarcasm in her voice is unmistakable.

'Absolutely.' I cough. 'Well, it suddenly came back to me. I remembered seeing him in the pub at the time and thinking he looked suspicious . . .' I trail off, my face hot. DC Davies is looking at me like a teacher who's caught you cheating in the geography exam.

'Lara, I'm not sure you're aware of this,' she says in calm, even tones. 'But wasting police time is a criminal offence which can carry a penalty of imprisonment. If you have made a malicious accusation—'

'I wasn't being malicious!' I say in horror. 'I was just . . .'

'What, exactly?' Her eyes are fixed on mine. Suddenly I'm scared.

'Look, I'm sorry,' I say in total panic. 'I didn't mean to waste your time. I just had this very strong instinct that my great-aunt was murdered. But maybe . . . thinking about it in the cold light of day . . . I got it wrong. Maybe she did die of old age. Please don't prosecute me.'

'We're not going to charge you this time.' DC Davies lifts her eyebrows. 'But consider this a warning.'

'All right,' I gulp. 'Thank you.'

'The case is closed. I'd like you to sign this form, confirming that we've had this talk.'

'OK.' I nod humbly, and scribble my signature. 'So what will happen now with the . . . the . . .' I can hardly bring myself to say it. 'What happens to my great-aunt?'

'The body will be handed back to the responsibility of the next of kin in due course,' says DC Davies in a businesslike way. 'Presumably they'll then arrange another funeral.'

'And how soon will that be?'

'Maybe two weeks, maybe a little longer.'

Two *weeks*? What if I can't find the necklace by then?

After DC Davies has left, I yank open my desk drawer. I have to find Sadie's necklace. I pull out the list of names and rip off the second sheet.

'Kate,' I say as she comes back into the office. 'New job. We're trying to find a necklace. Long, glass beads with a dragonfly pendant. Any of these people might have bought it at a jumble sale at the Fairside Nursing Home. Can you ring this lot?'

There's a tiny flicker of surprise in her eyes, then she takes the list and nods, like some loyal army lieutenant. 'Absolutely!'

I run my finger down past all the scribbled-out names and dial the next number. After a few rings a woman picks up.

'Hello?'

'Hi there! My name's Lara Lington, you don't know me . . .'

It's two hours before I finally put the phone down and look up wearily at Kate. 'Any luck?'

'No.' She sighs. 'Sorry. How about you?'

'Nothing.'

I slump back in my chair. We've ruled out every single number. I don't have anywhere else to turn. What am I going to do now?

'Shall I go on a sandwich run?' says Kate tentatively.

'Oh. Yeah.' I muster a smile. 'Chicken and avocado, please. Thanks.'

'No problem!' She bites her lip anxiously. 'I hope you find it.'

I'll just have to go back to the nursing home. There *has* to be an answer. A thought suddenly strikes me. That visitor she had, Charles Reece. I never followed him up. I might as well tick every box. Fishing for my mobile, I find the number for the nursing home and dial.

'Hello, Fairside Nursing Home,' answers a female voice.

'Hi! This is Lara Lington, Sadie Lancaster's great-niece.'

'Oh yes?'

'I was just wondering . . . can anyone tell me anything more about a visitor she had just before she died? A Charles Reece?'

'Just a moment.'

As I'm waiting, I get out the sketch of the necklace and study it as though for clues. Maybe I should secretly have a copy made. I could get it distressed, tell Sadie it's the original, she might just fall for it . . .

'Hello?' A cheerful voice rouses me from my thoughts. 'Lara? It's Sharon here, one of the nurses. I was with Sadie when Charles Reece visited, in fact I signed him in. What do you want to know about him?'

'Well . . . what exactly happened during his visit?'

'He sat with her in her room for a bit, then he left. That's it.'

'Right. So . . . could he have taken a necklace from her?'

'Well, it's possible.' She sounds doubtful.

'Can you tell me what he was like? How old was he?'

'In his fifties or so, I'd say. Nice-looking chap.'

'And there's nothing else you can tell me about him?' I add.

'Well.' She laughs. 'It's just funny, you being called Lington.'

'How come?' I stare at the phone, puzzled.

'Ginny says you're not related to that Bill Lington off the coffee cups?'

'Er, why do you ask?' I'm suddenly alert.

'Because that's exactly who he looked like! I said it at the time, to the girls. Even though he had dark glasses on and a scarf, you could see it. He was the spitting image of Bill Lington.'

Six

IT MAKES NO SENSE. None. It's crazy, whichever way you look at it.

Was it really Uncle Bill? But why would he visit Sadie using a fake name? And why wouldn't he mention it? And as for the idea that he might have had anything to do with her necklace disappearing . . . I mean, he's a multimillionaire. Why would he need some old necklace?

I feel like banging my head against the window to make all the pieces fall into place. But since at this very minute I'm sitting in a plushy chauffeur-driven limo provided by Uncle Bill, I probably won't. Just to get this far has been a total hassle. I don't want to jeopardise things.

I've never phoned Uncle Bill in my life, so at first I wasn't sure how to get in touch with him. (Obviously I couldn't ask Mum and Dad or they'd want to know why I needed to see Uncle Bill.) So I rang Lingtons' head office, eventually got through to one of the assistants, and asked if I could make an appointment to see Uncle Bill.

It was as if I'd asked to see the President. Within the hour, about six assistants started sending me emails, coordinating a time, changing the time, organising a car, asking me to bring ID, asking what Lingtons beverage I'd prefer in the car . . . All for a ten-minute meeting.

The car pulls off the road and approaches a pair of enormous gates. As the car stops by the gatehouse and a security man approaches, Sadie suddenly pipes up from the seat opposite. 'Goodness. That's a rather large house. How on earth did he become so rich?'

'I told you,' I say under my breath as I give my passport to the driver. He hands it to the security guard and they confer as though I'm some sort of terrorist.

'You said he ran coffee shops.' Sadie wrinkles her nose.

'Yes. Thousands of them. All round the world. He's really famous.'

There's a pause, then Sadie says, 'I should have liked to be famous.' There's a trace of wistfulness in her voice and I open my mouth to say automatically, 'Maybe you will be one day!' Then, as the truth hits me, I close it again, feeling a bit sad.

By now the car is purring up the drive, and I can't help gazing out of the window like a child. I've only been to Uncle Bill's mansion a few times in my life and I always forget how impressive and intimidating it is. It's a Georgian house with about fifteen bedrooms and a basement with two swimming pools in it. *Two*.

I'm not going to get nervous, I tell myself firmly. It's just a house. He's just a person. But, oh *God*. Everything's so grand. As we approach the entrance, a tall guy in a black suit and shades with a discreet earpiece is coming down the spotless white steps to greet me.

'Lara.' He clasps my hand as though we're old friends. 'I'm Damian. I work for Bill. He's looking forward to seeing you. I'll take you round to the office wing.'

It's a vast, light room with a vaulted ceiling and a glass sculpture on a podium and a sunken seating area. Six men in suits are getting up from chairs, as though finishing a meeting. And there, behind his massive desk, is Uncle Bill, looking lithe in a grey polo neck and jeans. He's more tanned than he was at the funeral, and he's cradling a Lingtons coffee mug in one hand.

'Thanks very much for your time, Bill,' one of the men is saying fervently. 'We appreciate it.'

Uncle Bill doesn't even reply, just lifts a hand like the Pope. As the men file out, Damian ushers me forward to a chair.

'Lara, have a seat,' Uncle Bill says.

As I sit down I'm aware of Damian moving away and the soft swoosh of the door closing behind me.

There's silence apart from Uncle Bill tapping something into his BlackBerry. I look at the wall of pictures of Uncle Bill with famous people. Madonna. Nelson Mandela. The England football team.

'So, Lara.' At last he looks up. 'What can I do for you?'

'I . . . um . . .' I clear my throat. 'I was . . .'

I had all sorts of punchy openers prepared. But now I'm actually here, in the inner sanctum, they're all drying up on my lips.

'Lara?' He frowns questioningly.

'I went to Aunt Sadie's nursing home last week,' I say in a rush. 'And apparently she had this visitor a few weeks ago who looked just like you, called Charles Reece, and it didn't make any sense to me, so I thought I'd come and ask you . . .' I trail off.

'Jesus Christ,' he mutters. 'Lara, are you still claiming Sadie was murdered? Is that what this is about? Because I *really* don't have time . . .'

'No, that's not it!' My face is boiling, but I force myself to persevere. 'I don't really think she was murdered. I went there because . . . because I felt bad that no one had ever shown any interest in her. When she was alive, I mean. And there was another name in the visitors' book, and they said the guy looked exactly like you and I was just . . . wondering.'

There's silence. For a few moments Uncle Bill looks as though he's weighing up exactly what to say.

'Well, it looks as though both of us had the same instincts,' he says at last, leaning back in his chair. 'You're right. I did go and see Sadie.'

My jaw drops in astonishment.

'But why did you use the name Charles Reece?'

'Lara.' Uncle Bill gives a patient sigh. 'I have a lot of fans out there. I'm a celebrity. There are a lot of things I do that I don't trumpet. Charity work, hospital visits . . .' He spreads his hands. 'Charles Reece is the name I take when I want to stay anonymous.' He meets my eyes with a friendly twinkle, and for a moment I can't help smiling back.

It kind of makes sense. Uncle Bill is such a rock star. Taking a pseudonym is the sort of thing he'd do.

'But at the service, you said you'd never visited Aunt Sadie.'

'I know.' Uncle Bill nods. 'And I had my reasons for that. I didn't want to make the rest of the family feel in any way guilty about not having visited themselves. Especially your father. He can be . . . prickly.'

Prickly? Dad's not prickly.

'Dad's fine,' I say tightly.

'Oh, he's great,' Bill says immediately. 'An absolutely fantastic guy. But it can't be easy being Bill Lington's big brother. I feel for him.'

Indignation surges through me. He's right. It's not easy being Bill Lington's big brother because Bill Lington is such an arrogant *tosser*.

'You don't need to feel sorry for Dad,' I say as politely as I can. 'He doesn't feel sorry for himself. He's done really well in life.'

'You know, I've started using your dad as an example in my seminars.' Uncle Bill adopts a musing tone. 'Two boys. Same upbringing. Same education. The only difference between them was, one of them *wanted* it. One of them had the *dream*.' He sounds like he's rehearsing a speech for some promotional DVD. God, he's up himself.

'So, Lara.' He focuses back on me. 'It was a pleasure to see you. Damian will show you out . . .'

'There's something else,' I say hastily. 'I just wondered, when you visited Aunt Sadie . . .' Oh God. How am I going to put this? 'Did you see . . . or possibly take, by accident . . . a necklace? A long necklace with glass beads and a dragonfly pendant?'

I'm expecting another patronising sigh and a dismissive comment. I'm not expecting his eyes to become suddenly sharp and wary.

As I stare back, I feel almost breathless with shock. He knows what I'm talking about. He *knows*. The very next moment the wariness has disappeared out of his eyes and he's back to empty politeness.

'A necklace? Do you mean something of Sadie's?'

What's going on? I saw the recognition in his eyes, I know I did. Why is he pretending he doesn't know about it?

'Yes, it's just an old piece I'm trying to track down.' Some instinct tells me to act cool and unconcerned. 'The nurses at the home said it had disappeared, so . . .' I watch Uncle Bill sharply for a reaction, but his bland mask is perfectly in place.

'Interesting. Why do you want it?' he asks lightly.

'Oh, no particular reason. I just saw a photo of Sadie wearing it at her 105th birthday and I thought it would be nice to find it.'

'Fascinating.' He pauses. 'Can I see the photo?'

'I haven't got it on me, I'm afraid.'

'Well, I'm afraid I don't know what you're talking about. And I'm pressed for time, so we'll have to leave it there.'

He pushes back his chair, but I don't move. He knows something about it. I'm sure he does. But what do I do? What options do I have?

'Lara?' He's standing by my chair, waiting. Reluctantly I get to my feet. As we approach the door, it opens and we're greeted by Damian and a woman dressed in an immaculate black suit.

'All done?' Damian says.

'All done.' Uncle Bill nods firmly. 'Give my best to your dad, won't you, Lara? Goodbye.'

Damian hurries past me and the two men head to the other side of the room. The door is already closing. I stare after them, almost exploding with frustration. What's going on? What *is* it with this necklace?

'Hi, Lara, I'm Sarah,' the woman in the black suit says. 'Your car is waiting for you at the front. I'll take you there now.'

Damn. If she escorts me out, there's no way I can sidle off or poke around any drawers or anything.

'Well, it's been so great to see you, Lara!' she says as we reach the door. Her fake gushiness makes me wince. 'Come back soon!'

The limo driver opens the car door and I'm about to step in when Sadie appears right in front of me, blocking the way.

'I've found it!' she says dramatically. 'It's in the house! I saw it in a bedroom upstairs, on a dressing table! It's here! My necklace is here!'

'You're absolutely sure it's yours?'

'Of course I'm sure!' Her voice rises shrilly and she starts gesturing at the house. 'I could have picked it up! I *tried* to pick it up! Of course, I couldn't . . .' She clicks her tongue in frustration.

'Lara, is there a problem?' Sarah is hurrying down the steps again. 'Would you like a different car, Lara? Or to go to a different location?'

'This car's fine, thanks,' I say brightly. 'Get in the car,' I mutter to Sadie out of the side of my mouth. 'Can't talk here.'

I quickly slide inside. The car door clunks and we glide away towards the gates. I check the glass partition is closed, then flop back and look at Sadie.

'This is unbelievable! How did you find it?'

'I just went looking.' She shrugs. 'I walked past a dressing table and there it was.'

I can't believe it. I'm popping with anger. Uncle Bill just sat in front of me and said he didn't know anything about any dragonfly necklace. Without a single flicker. He's a lying . . . *liar*.

'Something's going on,' I say. 'There has to be a reason he took it and a reason he's lying. But what? Why is it so important to him? Does it have some kind of history or collector's value?'

'Is this all you're going to do?' Sadie explodes. 'Talk, talk, drone, drone? You need to walk through the door and *get* it! At once! It'll be easy,' she adds confidently. 'You can take off your shoes.'

'Right.' I'm nodding. But I don't feel *absolutely* prepared for this.

'Well, come on then! Stop the car!'

I open the glass partition between us and the driver. 'Excuse me. I'm feeling carsick, so could you let me out, please? I'll go home by tube.'

The car pulls over and the driver looks round dubiously. 'I'm supposed to take you home to your door.'

'Don't worry!' I say. 'Honestly, I just need some fresh air, thanks . . .'

I'm already on the pavement. I bang the door shut and give the driver a little wave. He shoots me one last suspicious glance, then turns and heads back towards Uncle Bill's house. As soon as he's out of sight, I start retracing my path, keeping unobtrusively to the side of the road. I round a corner, see Uncle Bill's gates ahead and pause.

The gates are closed and they're massive. The security guard is there in his glass box. CCTV cameras are everywhere. I take a deep breath and approach the gates, looking as innocent as possible.

'Hi! It's me again, Lara Lington,' I say into the intercom. 'I left my umbrella behind. Silly me!' After a moment, the guard opens the pedestrian gate for me and leans out of his window.

'I've spoken to Sarah. She doesn't know anything about an umbrella, but she's coming down.'

'I'll meet her, save her the trouble!' I say brightly and hurry past before he can protest. OK, I'm past one hurdle.

'Tell me the minute he looks away,' I mutter to Sadie out of the side of my mouth. 'Say "Now".'

'Now!' she says suddenly, and I dodge to the side of the path. I take a few steps across the grass, then drop down, roll behind a hedge and come to a stop like someone in an action film. Through the hedge I can see Sarah crunching down the drive.

'Where is she?' I hear her voice drifting up from the front gates.

'. . . saw her a moment ago.' The guard sounds baffled.

Ha! Actually, not ha. They might start looking for me with Rottweilers in a minute.

'Where is it?' I whisper to Sadie. 'Guide me. And keep a lookout!'

We start making our way over the lawn towards the house, dodging from hedge to water feature to prize-winning sculpture.

'There!' We turn the corner and Sadie nods at a set of French doors on the first floor. They're ajar and open onto a terrace with steps up to it from the garden.

'Keep guard!' I mutter to Sadie. I slip off my wedges, creep towards the steps and run up them silently. Cautiously I approach the French doors and catch my breath. There it is.

It's lying on a dressing table, just inside the room. A long, double row of beads in shimmering yellow glass, with the most exquisite carved dragonfly, inlaid with mother-of-pearl and studded with rhinestones. It's Sadie's necklace. Iridescent and magical, just as she described it.

As I gaze at it, I feel overcome by emotion. After all this time . . . here it is. Just a few feet away from me.

'It's stunning.' I turn back to Sadie, my voice a little choked.

'Get it! Stop talking! *Get it!*'

'OK, OK!'

I swing the French doors open, take a step inside and am just reaching towards the necklace when suddenly I hear footsteps approaching the room and the door is thrown open. Shit. Someone's coming in.

In panic, I reverse onto the balcony and duck to one side.

'What are you doing?' demands Sadie from below. 'Get the necklace!'

'Someone's in there! I'll wait till they've gone!'

In an instant Sadie is up on the terrace and poking her head through the glass into the room.

'It's a maid.' She glares at me. 'You should have grabbed it!'

'I'll get it in a minute when she's gone! Just keep a lookout!'

Suddenly my heart jumps as the French doors start moving—but they're not opening. They close with a firm clunk. The next thing I hear is the click of a key being turned. Oh no.

'She's locked you out!' Sadie darts into the room, then out again. 'Now she's gone! You're stuck! You're stuck!'

I rattle the French doors, but they're firmly locked.

'You idiot!' Sadie is beside herself with fury. 'Why didn't you grab it!'

'I was about to!' I retort defensively. 'You should have gone to check if anyone was coming!'

'Well, what are we going to do?'

'I don't know! I don't *know*!'

There's silence as we face each other, panting slightly. 'I need to put my shoes on,' I say at last. I head down the steps, and slip on my wedges. For a few moments neither of us meets the other's eye.

'I'm sorry I wasn't quicker at grabbing it,' I mumble at last.

'Well,' says Sadie, clearly making a supreme effort. 'I suppose it wasn't *completely* your fault.'

'Let's go round the house. We may be able to slip in somewhere. Go inside and see if the coast is clear.'

As Sadie disappears, I creep cautiously over the grass and start moving along the wall of the house. I'm making slow progress because every time I pass a window I duck down and crawl on my stomach.

'There you are!' Sadie pops out of the wall beside me. 'Guess what?'

'Jeepers!' I clasp my chest. 'What?'

'It's your uncle! I've been watching him! He's just been to the safe in his bedroom. He looked in it, but he couldn't find what he wanted. Then he banged it shut and started shouting for Diamanté.'

'My cousin.' I nod. 'Another of your great-nieces.'

'She was in the kitchen. He said he needed a private word and sent all the staff away. Then he said an old necklace was missing from his safe and did she know anything about it?'

'Oh my God.' I stare back at her. 'Oh my God! What did she say?'

'She said no, but he didn't believe her.'

'Maybe she's lying.' My mind is working overtime. 'Maybe that's her bedroom, where the necklace was.'

'Exactly! So we have to get it now, before he realises where it is and locks it away again. There's no one around. All the staff have got out of the way. We can go through the house.'

My heart pumping, I follow Sadie to a side door and in through a laundry room. She beckons me through a pair of swing doors, down a passage, then holds up a hand as we reach the hall, her eyes widening warily. I can hear Uncle Bill shouting, his voice increasing in volume.

'. . . private safe . . . how *dare* you . . . code was for emergencies only . . .'

'. . . not bloody fair! You never let me have *anything*!'

It's Diamanté's voice, and it's getting closer. Instinctively I dart behind a chair and sink down. The next moment she strides into the hall.

'I'll *buy* you a necklace.' Uncle Bill comes striding in after her. 'That's no problem. Tell me what you need.'

'You always say that!' she shrieks at him. 'You never listen! That necklace is perfect! I need it for my next Tutus and Pearls show! My whole new collection is based on butterflies and insects and stuff! I'm *creative*, in case you hadn't realised—'

'If you're so creative, my love,' says Uncle Bill with a sarcastic edge, 'why have I hired three designers to work on your dresses?'

'They're . . . *assistants*!' she screams back. 'It's *my* vision! And I need that necklace—'

'You're not using it, Diamanté.' Uncle Bill's voice is ominous. 'And you're going to give it back to me right now!'

'No, I'm not!' She runs up the stairs, closely followed by Sadie.

Uncle Bill looks furious. 'Diamanté!' he shouts. 'Come back here!'

'Fuck off!' comes a distant cry.

'Diamanté!' Uncle Bill starts to stride up the stairs himself. 'That's it—'

'She's got it!' Sadie's voice is suddenly in my ear. 'She's taken it. We need to catch her! You go round the back. I'll guard the front stairs.'

I get to my feet, run back down the passage, through the laundry room and out onto the lawn. I sprint breathlessly round the house, not caring if anyone sees me—and stop dead in dismay. *Shit.*

Diamanté is in a black, open-top Porsche, heading down the gravel at speed towards the front gates, which are hastily being opened by the security guard. 'Noooo!' I wail before I can stop myself.

As Diamanté pauses to exit she flicks a V sign back at the house, and the next minute is out on the road. In her other hand I can just see Sadie's necklace, wrapped around her fingers, glinting in the sunshine.

There's only one possibility. They're not rhinestones, they're diamonds. The necklace is studded with rare antique diamonds and worth millions of pounds. It's *got* to be that. There's no other reason I can think of why Uncle Bill would be so interested in it.

I have a plan, and it's a pretty good one. First of all, I found out all about Diamanté's next Tutus and Pearls catwalk show. It's this Thursday at the Sanderstead Hotel, 6.30 p.m., private guest list. Then I emailed Uncle Bill's flunky, Sarah, and said I'd really like to support Diamanté in her fashion venture and could I come and talk to Uncle Bill about it? Maybe I would just drop round to the house, I suggested. Maybe tomorrow! And I added a few smiley faces for good measure.

Sarah immediately emailed back that Bill was busy right now and I *shouldn't* come tomorrow, but she could talk to Diamanté's personal assistant. And the next thing I knew, two tickets were biked to my door.

The only downer is that the second and crucial part of my plan—to persuade Diamanté to give me the necklace after the show—has failed so far. Her assistant won't give me her mobile-phone number. She did allegedly pass on a message, but obviously I haven't heard anything.

There's only one thing for it. I'm going to have to go along to the show, wait till it's over, then grab Diamanté and somehow talk her into giving the necklace to me. Or, you know. Pinch it.

With a sigh I swivel round to survey Sadie. Today she's wearing a silver dress. It's backless except for two thin silver straps over her shoulders, and a rosette at the small of her back. Of all the ghost dresses she's worn, this is my favourite.

'The necklace would look amazing with that dress,' I say impulsively.

Sadie nods, but doesn't say anything. There's a low-slung, dispirited cast to her shoulders. We were so near to it. And then we lost it.

'Tell me again . . . *why* is the necklace so special to you?'

'I told you,' she says. 'When I wore it, I felt beautiful. Like a goddess. Radiant.' She leans against the window frame. 'You must have something in your wardrobe that makes you feel like that.'

'Er . . .' I hesitate. I can't honestly say I've ever felt like a goddess. Or particularly radiant, come to that.

Kate has left the office early to go to the orthodontist, and all the phones are quiet. Maybe I'll leave too. It's nearly time, anyway. I glance at my watch and feel a shot of anticipation.

I adjust the pencil stuffed into my hair, stand up and check over my outfit. Quirky printed T-shirt from Urban Outfitters. Cute little pendant of a frog. Jeans and ballet pumps. Not too much make-up. Perfect.

'So . . . I thought we could go for a walk, maybe,' I say super-casually to Sadie. 'It's such a nice day.'

'A walk?' She peers at me. 'What kind of walk?'

'Just a walk!' Before she can say any more, I close down my computer, set the office answering machine and grab my bag. Now my plan is about to come to fruition, I'm quite excited.

It only takes twenty minutes to get to Farringdon, and as I hurry up the tube steps I glance at my watch. Five forty-five. Perfect. I head to the corner of the main road, and pause.

'What are you waiting for?'

'No one,' I say defensively. 'I'm just . . . hanging out. Watching the world go by.' I lean casually against a pillar box to prove my point, then hastily move away as a woman approaches to post a letter.

Sadie appears in front of me and scans my face, then suddenly inhales as she sees the book in my hand. 'I know what you're doing! You're trailing! You're waiting for Josh! *Aren't* you?'

'I'm taking control of my life.' I avoid her eye. 'I'm showing him I've changed. When he sees me, he'll realise his mistake. You wait.'

'This is a very bad idea. A very, very bad idea.'

'It's not. Shut up.' I'm not going to listen to a word Sadie says. I'm totally psyched and ready to go.

Ever since that lunch, I've totally transformed myself. I've kept the bathroom tidy. I've stopped singing in the shower. I've made a resolution never to mention anyone else's relationship, ever. I've even looked at that William Eggleston photography book, but I think it would seem a bit of a coincidence to be actually holding it. Which is why I'm clutching a book called *Los Alamos*, which is another collection by him. Josh is going to see me so differently. He's going to be amazed! Now I just have to bump into him accidentally-on-purpose as he leaves his office. Which is about 200 yards away.

'Listen.' I turn to Sadie. 'You might have to help me out a bit.'

'What do you mean, help you?' she says haughtily.

'Prompt Josh a bit. Tell him he likes me. Just to make sure.'

'Why will he need telling?' she retorts. 'You said he was going to realise his mistake when he saw you.'

'He will,' I say impatiently. 'But he might not realise it *straight away*. He might need . . . a nudge.' I catch my breath. Oh my God. There he is.

He's sauntering along, his iPod in his ears, carrying a new, cool-looking laptop bag. My legs are suddenly trembling but there's no time to lose. I take a step out from my hiding place, and then another and another, until I'm right in his path.

'Oh!' I try to adopt a tone of surprise. 'Er . . . hi, Josh!'

'Lara.' He rips out his earphones and gazes at me warily.

'I'd forgotten you work round here! What a coincidence!'

'Yee-esss,' he says slowly.

Honestly. He needn't look quite so suspicious.

His eyes alight on the book in my hand and I can see the jolt of surprise. 'Is that . . . *Los Alamos*?'

'Oh, yes,' I say carelessly. 'I was looking through this fantastic book called *Democratic Camera* the other day. The pictures were so amazing, I just *had* to go and buy this.' I pat it fondly, then look up. 'Hey, didn't you quite like William Eggleston, too? Or was that someone else?'

'I love William Eggleston,' says Josh slowly. 'It was me who gave you *Democratic Camera*.'

'Oh, *that's* right.' I slap my head. 'I'd forgotten.'

I can see bewilderment in his face. He's on the back foot. Time to press home my advantage.

'Josh, I've been meaning to say . . .' I give him a rueful smile. 'I'm sorry for all those texts I sent you. I don't know what got into me.'

'Well . . .' Josh coughs awkwardly.

'Will you let me buy you a drink? Just to make it up? No hard feelings?'

There's silence. I can almost see his thought processes. *It's a reasonable suggestion. It's a free drink. She looks sane enough.*

'OK.' He puts his iPod away. 'Why not?'

I shoot a triumphant look at Sadie, who is shaking her head. Well, I don't care what she thinks. I march Josh into a nearby pub, order a white wine for me and a beer for him and find a table in the corner. We raise our glasses and sip, and I open some crisps.

'So.' He clears his throat, clearly feeling awkward. 'How are things?'

'Josh.' I lean my elbows on the table and look at him seriously. 'You know what? Let's not *analyse* everything. God, I'm sick of people who analyse everything to death. I'm sick of unpicking conversations. Just live. Enjoy life. Don't think about it!'

Josh stares at me over his beer, looking totally confused. 'But you used to love analysing. You used to read that magazine, *Analyse*.'

'I've changed.' I shrug casually. 'I buy less make-up. My bathroom is totally empty. I was thinking I might like to travel. To Nepal, maybe.'

I'm sure I remember him mentioning Nepal, one of those times.

'You want to go travelling?' He seems taken aback. 'You never said.'

'It came to me recently,' I say earnestly. 'Why am I so unadventurous? There's so much out there to see. Mountains . . . cities . . . Kathmandu.'

'I'd love to see Kathmandu,' he says, looking animated. 'You know, I was thinking about going there next year.'

'No!' I beam at him. 'That's amazing!'

For the next ten minutes we talk about Nepal. We look like a happy couple. I know, because I keep checking our reflection in the mirror over the bar.

'I'd better shoot,' Josh suddenly says, looking at his watch. 'I've got squash practice. It's been good to see you, Lara.'

'Oh, right,' I say, taken aback. 'Great to see you, too.'

'Thanks for the drink.' I watch in slight panic as he picks up his laptop case. This isn't how it's supposed to go.

'This was a good idea, Lara.' He smiles. 'Let's stay in touch.'

'Have another drink!' I try not to sound desperate. 'Just a quick one!'

Josh looks at his watch again. 'OK, a quick one. Same again?' He heads towards the bar. The minute he's out of earshot I hiss, 'Sadie!' and beckon her over from the barstool where she's been sitting throughout.

'Tell him he loves me!'

'But he doesn't love you,' says Sadie.

'He does! He does really! He's just scared to admit it, even to himself. But you saw us. We were getting on amazingly. If he just had a little nudge in the right direction. Please . . . *Please* . . .'

Sadie gives an exasperated sigh. 'All *right*.'

A microsecond later she's at Josh's side, bellowing in his ear, '*You still love Lara! You made a mistake! You still love Lara!*'

I can see him stiffen and shake his head, trying to rid himself of the noise. He looks so dazed that if I weren't feeling so anxious I'd laugh.

'*You still love Lara! You still love Lara!*'

As Josh carries the drinks over and sits down next to me, he seems transfixed. I shoot Sadie a grateful smile and sip my wine, waiting for Josh to declare himself. But he just sits rigid, his eyes distant.

'Is there something on your mind, Josh?' I prompt in a soft voice.

'Lara . . .' He stops.

I look desperately at Sadie for more help. He's *so* nearly there . . .

'*You love Lara! Don't fight it, Josh! You love her!*'

'Lara. I think maybe I made a mistake. I think I still love you.'

Even though I knew he was going to say it, there's a huge, romantic swell in my heart, and tears start pricking my eyes.

'Well, I still love you, Josh,' I say, my voice trembling. 'I always did.'

I'm not sure if he kisses me or if I kiss him, but suddenly our arms are wrapped round each other, and we're devouring each other. (OK, I think I kissed him.) As we draw apart eventually, Josh looks even more dazed than before.

'Well,' he says after a bit.

'Well.' I lovingly mesh my fingers with his. 'Here's a turnup.'

'Lara, I have this squash thing.' He glances at his watch. 'I need to . . .'

'Don't worry,' I say generously. 'Go. We can talk later.'

'OK.' He nods. 'I'll text you my new number.'

'Great.' I smile.

I won't bring up the fact that I think it was a total over-reaction to change his mobile number just because of a few texts I sent him. We can talk about that another time. No hurry.

As he flips open his phone, I glance over his shoulder—and feel a jolt of sheer amazement. He's still got a photo of us on his screen. Him and me. Standing on a mountain in our skiwear at sunset. We're in silhouette, but I remember the moment vividly. We'd been skiing all day and the sunset was spectacular. We asked this German guy to take a picture. And Josh kept the photo! All this time!

'Nice picture,' I say in a deadpan, casual way, nodding at it.

'Yeah. Makes me feel good whenever I look at it.'

I knew it. I *knew* it. He does love me. He just needed a nudge.

My phone burbles with a text and Josh's number pops up on my screen. I've got him back again. He's mine!

We head out of the pub, hands clasped, and pause at the corner.

'I'll get a cab,' says Josh. 'Do you want to—'

I'm about to say, 'Great! I'll share it with you!' But then the new Lara stops me. *Don't be too eager. Give him space.*

I shake my head. 'No, thanks. I'm going the other way. Love you.'

'Love you.' He nods. A cab stops and Josh bends to kiss me again before getting in.

'Bye!' I wave as it pulls off, then turn away, hugging myself, zinging all over with triumph. We're back together! I'm back with Josh!

Seven

I CAN NEVER RESIST telling people good news. So by the following morning I've texted all my friends that Josh and I are back together. And some of his friends, just because I happened to have their numbers programmed in my phone. And the guy at Dial-a-Pizza. (That was a mistake. He was pleased for me, though.)

'Oh my God, Lara!' Kate's voice bursts through the office door at the same time as she does. 'You made up with Josh?'

'Oh, you got my text?' I say nonchalantly. 'Yeah, it's cool, isn't it?'

'It's amazing! I mean . . . it's incredible!'

She doesn't need to sound *quite* so surprised. But it's nice to have someone pleased for me. Sadie's got such a downer on the whole thing. She hasn't said she's happy for me once. But I don't care, because I've got my most important phone call of all to make, and I am *so* looking forward to it. I dial the number, lean back and wait.

'Michael Lington.'

'Oh hi, Dad, it's Lara,' I say in a casual tone. 'I just thought I'd let you know that Josh and I are back together again.'

'What?' says Dad after a pause.

'Yes, we bumped into each other yesterday,' I say airily. 'And he said he still loved me and he'd made a huge mistake.'

There's another silence at the other end of the phone. Ha. This is such a sweet moment!

'So it looks like I was right, doesn't it?' I can't resist adding, 'I *said* we were meant to be together.' I shoot Sadie a gloating look.

'Lara . . .' Dad doesn't sound as happy as I thought he would. In fact, he sounds pretty stressed. 'Are you absolutely *sure* that you and Josh . . .' He hesitates. 'Are you *sure* that's what he meant?'

'You can call him if you like! You can ask him! We bumped into each other, and we had a drink and we talked about stuff and he said he still loved me. And now we're back together. Just like you and Mum.'

'Well. That's quite . . . incredible. Wonderful news.'

'I know. It just goes to show. Relationships are complicated things, and other people shouldn't barge in and think they know all about it.'

'Indeed,' he says faintly.

'Hey.' I cast around for something to cheer him up. 'Dad, I was thinking about our family history the other day. And I was wondering, have you got any pictures of Great-Aunt Sadie's house?'

'Sorry, darling?' Dad sounds like he's having trouble keeping up.

'The old family house that burned down. In Archbury. You showed me a photograph of it once. Have you still got it?'

'I think so.' Dad's voice is wary.

'That photo's the only thing we've got left of the house, isn't it?'

'Not quite the only thing,' says Dad. 'You know, the oak desk in the hall came from that house.'

'In our hall? I thought everything was lost in the fire.'

'A very few things were salvaged.' I can tell Dad's relaxed a little.

'They were put in a storage unit and left there for years. It was Bill who sorted it all out, after your grandfather died. He was at a loose end. I was doing my accountancy exams. Strange to imagine, but Bill was the idler in those days.' Dad laughs. 'That was the year your mother and I got married. That oak desk was our first piece of furniture. It's a wonderful piece of original Art Nouveau.'

'Wow.'

I'm riveted by this story. Maybe it was Sadie's own desk! Maybe it has all her secret papers in it! As I put the phone down, Kate is industriously working. I can't send her on yet another coffee run. But I'm desperate to tell Sadie what I just heard.

'Hey, Sadie!' I type in a new document. 'Not everything was lost in the fire! There were some things in a storage unit! Guess what? We have a desk from your old house!' I gesticulate at her and point at my screen.

'I know that desk was saved,' says Sadie, after reading my message. 'I was sent a list of things at the time in case I wanted to claim anything. Hideous crockery. Dreadful furniture. None of it interested me.'

'It's not dreadful,' I type. 'It's a wonderful piece of Art Nouveau.'

'It's minging,' Sadie says, and I can't help giggling.

'Where did you learn that word?' I type.

'Picked it up.' Sadie gives an insouciant shrug.

Across the room, the phone rings and a moment later, Kate says, 'I'll just put you on hold.' She looks up anxiously. 'Lara, it's Janet from Leonidas Sports. Shall I put her through?'

'Yes. Just give me thirty seconds.' I psyche myself up, then lift the phone in my breeziest, top-recruitment-consultant manner. 'Hi, Janet! How are you? Did you get the short list?'

Kate emailed the short list to Janet last night.

'I hope you're as excited by it as I am!' I add brightly.

'No, I'm not,' Janet says in her usual hoarse, peremptory tones. 'Lara, I don't understand. Why's Clive Hoxton on the list?'

I know my lunch with Clive didn't end brilliantly. But the truth is, he'd be perfect for the job. And I might be able to talk him round.

'Clive's a really bright executive, Janet.' I launch into my spiel. 'He's experienced in marketing, very dynamic, ripe for a move—'

'I know all that.' Janet cuts me off. 'But I bumped into him at a reception last night and he was shocked to learn he was on the short list.'

'Really?' I summon a tone of astonishment. 'How strange. As far as I was aware, we had a great meeting, he was enthusiastic—'

'He told me you were on the phone to another client throughout and he never wanted to do business with you again.'

My face flushes. Clive Hoxton is a mean sneak.

'Well.' I clear my throat. 'Janet, I'm baffled. All I can say is we must have had mixed messages . . .'

'What about this Nigel Rivers?' Janet has clearly moved on. 'Is he the man with the dandruff? Applied to us once before?'

'It's a lot better these days,' I say. 'I think he's using Head & Shoulders.'

'And what about this Gavin Mynard?'

'Very, very talented,' I lie at once. 'A very creative guy who has been overlooked. His CV doesn't reflect his . . . wealth of experience . . .'

Janet sighs. 'Lara.'

I stiffen with apprehension. Her tone is unmistakable. She's going to fire me, right now. I can't let it happen, I can't, we'll be finished . . .

'And of course, I have another candidate!' I hear myself saying.

'Another candidate? You mean, not on the list?'

'Yes. Much better than any of the others! In fact, I'd say this candidate is definitely your person.'

'Who is it?' says Janet suspiciously. 'Why don't I have the details?'

'Because . . . I just need to firm things up first.' I'm crossing my fingers so hard they hurt. 'It's all very confidential. This is a high-profile person we're talking about, Janet. Believe me, I'm excited.'

'I need a name!' she barks angrily. 'I need a CV! Lara, our in-house meeting is on Thursday. Can I speak to Natalie, please?'

'No!' I say in panic. 'I mean . . . Thursday. Absolutely! You'll have all the information on Thursday. I promise. And all I can say is, you'll be bowled over by the calibre of this particular candidate. Janet, I must dash, great to talk . . .' I put the phone down, my heart thumping.

Shit. *Shit.* What am I going to do now?

'Wow!' Kate looks up, eyes shining. 'Lara, you're such a star. I knew you'd do it! Who's this amazing high-profile candidate?'

'There isn't one!' I say desperately. 'We have to find one!'

By seven o'clock my neck is aching and my eyes are red-rimmed. I've made a new, emergency long list of candidates, using old issues of *Business People*, the internet and a copy of *Marketing Week*. But none of them will even take my call. Let alone talk about a job. I have forty-eight hours. I'm going to have to invent a top marketing director.

On the plus side, they had a half-price offer on Pinot Grigio at

Oddbins. The minute I get in, I turn on the TV and start glugging the wine down at speed. By the time *EastEnders* starts I've got through half a bottle and my work troubles are receding nicely.

I've been texting Josh all day, just to keep my spirits up. And he's sent two texts back! Quite short ones, but even so. He's at some dreary conference in Milton Keynes and he said he can't wait to be back home. Which obviously means he can't wait to see me!

I'm just debating whether to send him another light, friendly text asking him what he's doing, when I glance up and notice Sadie sitting on the fireplace in a pale grey chiffony dress.

'Oh, hi,' I say. 'Where did you get to?'

'The cinema. I watched two films.' She shoots me an accusing look. 'You know, it gets very lonely during the day. You're so preoccupied with your work.'

'Well, I'm sorry I have to earn a living,' I reply, a little sarcastically.

'Have you got the necklace yet?' she says.

'No, Sadie,' I say tetchily. 'I haven't. I've had a few other problems today.' I wait for her to ask what those problems are, but she just shrugs.

'Josh has been texting me, isn't that great?' I add, to annoy her. She stops humming and gives me a baleful look.

'It's not great. The whole thing is absolutely false.'

'It's *not* false. It's real. You saw him kiss me, you heard what he said.'

'He's a puppet,' says Sadie dismissively. 'He said whatever I told him to say. I've never known anyone so weak-willed!'

'That's rubbish,' I say coldly. 'OK, I know you nudged him a bit. But he would never say he loved me unless there was a basis of truth. He was obviously expressing what he really feels, deep down.'

Sadie gives a sarcastic laugh. '"What he really feels, deep down." Darling, you're too amusing. He doesn't *have* any feelings for you.'

'He does!' I spit. 'Of course he does! He had my picture on his phone, didn't he? He'd been carrying it round all this time! That's love.'

'It's not love. Don't be ridiculous.'

'Well, you've never even *been* in love! So what would you know about it? I really believe Josh has deep feelings for me—'

'*It's not enough to believe!*' Sadie's voice is suddenly passionate. 'Don't you see that, you stupid girl? You could spend your whole life hoping and believing! If a love affair is one-sided, then it's only ever a question, never an answer. You can't live your life waiting for an answer.'

She flushes and turns away.

Bloody hell. What was that outburst all about? I thought Sadie didn't care about love. But just then, she sounded as if . . .

'Is that what happened to you, Sadie?' I say tentatively to her back. 'Did you spend your whole life waiting for an answer?'

Instantly, she disappears. No warning. She just vanishes. There's got to be a story here. I switch off the TV and call loudly into thin air.

'Sadie! Tell me! It's good to talk about things!' The room is silent, but somehow I'm sure she's still there.

'Whatever.' I shrug. 'Thought you had more guts than that.'

'I do have guts.' Sadie appears in front of me, looking furious.

'So tell me.' I fold my arms.

'There's nothing to tell,' she says, her voice low. 'It's simply that I *do* know what it's like to think you're in love. I know what it's like to squander all your hours and all your tears and all your heart on something which turns out to be nothing. Don't waste your life. That's all.'

'What happened? Did you have a love affair? Sadie, tell me!'

She sighs. 'It was a long time ago. Before I went abroad. Before I was married. There was . . . a man.'

'The big row with your parents!' I suddenly put two and two together. 'Was that because of him?'

Sadie tilts her head forward in assent.

'Did your parents catch you together? Were you . . . barney-mugging?'

'No!' She bursts into laughter.

'So what happened? Tell me! Please!'

'They found sketches.' Her laughter dies away and she hugs her chest. 'He was a painter. He liked to paint me. My parents were scandalised.'

'What's wrong with him painting you?' I say, puzzled. 'They should have been pleased! I mean, it's a compliment, an artist wanting to—'

'Naked.'

'*Naked?*'

'I had a drape over me. But my parents . . .' Sadie presses her lips together. 'That was a dramatic day, the day they found the sketches.'

'So they saw you . . . your . . .'

'They became absolutely hysterical.' She gives a tiny snort, almost a laugh. 'It was funny, but it was dreadful, too. His parents were as angry as mine. He was supposed to be going into law.' She shakes her head. 'He would never have made a lawyer. He was a great big shambles of a man. He painted all night, and drank wine, and smoked gaspers back to back . . . We both did. I used to spend all night with him at his studio. In his parents' shed. I used to call him Vincent, after Van Gogh. He called me Mabel.' She gives another tiny snort.

'*Mabel?*' I wrinkle my nose.

'There was a maid at his house called Mabel. I told him I thought it was the ugliest name I'd ever heard and they should make her change it. So he instantly started calling *me* Mabel. Cruel beast that he was.'

Her tone is half-jokey but there's a strange flickering in her eyes.

'I used to creep out of the house when everyone was asleep, climb down the ivy . . .' Suddenly she looks really sad. 'When we were discovered, everything changed. He was sent to France, to some uncle, to "get it all out of his system". As if anyone could ever stop him painting.'

'What was his name?'

'His name was Stephen Nettleton.' Sadie breathes out heavily. 'I haven't said that name aloud for . . . seventy years. At least.'

'So what happened? After that?'

'We were never in touch with each other, ever again,' she says.

'Why not?' I say in horror. 'Didn't you write to him?'

'Oh, I wrote.' She gives a brittle smile that makes me wince. 'I sent letter after letter to France. But I never heard from him. My parents said I was a naive little simpleton. They said he'd used me for what he could get. I wouldn't believe them at first, hated them for saying it. But then . . .' She looks up, her chin set, as though defying me to pity her. 'I was like you. "He does love me, he really does!"' She puts on a mocking, high-pitched voice. '"He'll write! He'll come back for me. He *loves* me!" Do you know how it felt when I finally came to my senses?'

There's a taut silence.

'So what did you do?' I hardly dare speak.

'Got married, of course. Stephen's father conducted the service. He was our vicar. Stephen must have known, but he didn't even send a card.'

She lapses into silence and I sit there, my thoughts teeming. She got married to Waistcoat Guy out of revenge. No wonder it didn't last.

'Didn't you ever think about following Stephen to France?'

'I had my pride.' She gives me a pointed look and I feel like retorting, 'Well at least I got my guy back!'

'Did you keep any of the sketches?'

'I hid them.' She nods. 'There was a big painting, too. He smuggled it to me, just before he left for France, and I hid it in the cellar. My parents had no idea. But then of course the house was burnt and I lost it.'

'Oh God.' I sag in disappointment. 'What a shame.'

'Not really. I didn't care. Why should I care?'

'Maybe he never got your letters,' I say hopefully.

'Oh, I'm sure he did.' There's an edge to her voice. 'I smuggled them out of the house and into the postbox myself.'

'Is he still alive now?' I'm gripped by irrational hope. 'We could track him down! We could Google him, I bet we'd find him—'

'He died young.' Sadie cuts me off. 'Twelve years after he left England. They had the funeral in the village. I was living abroad by then. I wasn't invited, anyway. And I wouldn't have gone.'

I'm so horrified, I can't reply. Not only did he leave her, he *died*.

Sadie's face is drawn as she gazes out of the window. I feel sudden tears spring to my eyes. She loved this artist. It's obvious. Underneath all the bravado, she really loved him. All her life, probably. How could he not have loved her back? Bastard.

'It's so sad.' I rub my nose. 'It's just so sad.'

'It's not sad,' she retorts at once, her old flippant air returning. 'It's the way things are. But that's why I know.' She suddenly rounds on me. 'I *know* that you'll never work things out with your chap. Your Josh.'

'Why?' I glare back at her defensively. Trust her to bring Josh into it.

'Because you can want and want and want.' She turns away again, hugging her knees. 'But if he doesn't want you back, you might as well wish the sky were red.'

I'm not panicking. Even though it's Wednesday and I still don't have a solution and Janet Grady is on the warpath. I'm beyond panic. I'm in an altered state. Like a yogi. I've been dodging calls from Janet all day.

I'm doomed. All in all, you'd think now would not be the best time to be glammed up and going to a party.

Nevertheless, here I am in a taxi, glammed up and going to a party.

'We're here!' Sadie peers out of the window. 'Pay the driver! Let's go!'

Bright flashes from cameras are filling our taxi and I can hear the hubbub of people greeting each other. I see a group of about ten people in evening dress arriving on the red carpet leading up to the Spencer Hotel, where the *Business People* dinner is taking place. According to the *Financial Times*, 400 of the top business talents in London are going to be gathered here tonight. And some of them have got to be top-level marketing executives. And some of them have got to want a new job. Surely.

So this is my last-ditch plan. I'm going to find a candidate for Leonidas Sports tonight, at the dinner.

I glance at my reflection in the window. Needless to say, Sadie took charge of my outfit again. I'm in a black, sequinned vintage dress with fringed sleeves and beaded Egyptian-style medallions at the shoulders. Over this I'm wearing a cloak. My eyes are heavily kohled, I have a long gold snake bracelet, and on my head is a close-fitting diamanté mesh cap that Sadie found at some antique market.

Tonight I feel a lot more confident, though. For a start, everyone else will be dressed up too. And even though I protested about the cap, I secretly think I look quite cool. I look kind of glam and retro.

Sadie's dolled up too, in a fringed dress, all turquoise and green, with a peacock feather shawl and the most ludicrous headdress with a diamanté waterfall cascading past her ear.

'Let's go!' Her legs are twitching. 'I can't wait to start dancing!'

For God's sake. She's obsessed. And if she thinks I'm dancing with Ed in the middle of the bar for a second time, she needs to think again.

'Sadie, listen,' I say firmly. 'It's a business dinner. There won't be any dancing. I'm here to work.'

'We'll find some,' she says confidently. 'You can always find dancing.'

As I get out, people in evening dress are everywhere, shaking hands confidently and laughing and posing for the cameras. Just for a moment I feel all twingey with nerves. But then I glance at Sadie and raise my chin, just like she does.

'Hi, Lara.' Ed's voice greets me from behind and I turn. There he is, looking as square-cut and handsome as I might have expected. His dinner jacket fits him perfectly, his dark hair is brushed back perfectly.

'Hi.' I take Ed's hand before he gets any idea of kissing me. He's looking my outfit up and down with a quizzical expression.

'You look very . . . twenties.'

Well spotted, Einstein. 'Yes, well.' I shrug. 'I like twenties clothes.'

'No kidding,' he says, deadpan.

'You look delicious!' says Sadie joyfully to Ed. She flings herself at him, wraps both arms round his chest and nuzzles his neck.

Urgh. Is she going to do that all night?

We're approaching a small group of photographers and, at a signal from a lady with an earpiece, Ed stops with a slight roll of his eyes. 'Sorry, I have to do this, I'm afraid.'

'Shit!' I say in panic as the camera flashes blind me. 'What do I do?'

'Stand a little side-on,' he murmurs reassuringly. 'Chin up and smile. Don't worry, it's natural to freak out. I did media training for this stuff.'

As we head into the hotel I'm looking round, trying to see if there's anyone I could approach about the Leonidas Sports job.

Meanwhile, Sadie has been glued to Ed's side, stroking his hair and rubbing her face against his. As we come to a halt in front of a reception table she suddenly dips down and pokes her head into his dinner-jacket pocket. I'm so disconcerted, I jump.

'Sadie!' I mutter furiously behind Ed's back. 'What are you doing?'

'Having a look at his things!' she says, standing up. 'There wasn't anything very interesting, just some papers and a pack of cards.'

'Mr Harrison!' A woman in a chic navy cocktail dress has swooped down on Ed. 'I'm Sonia Taylor, head of PR at Dewhurst Publishing. We're so looking forward to your speech.'

'Pleased to be here.' Ed nods. 'May I introduce Lara Lington, my . . .' He looks at me dubiously, as though searching for the word. 'Date.'

'Hello, Lara.' Sonia turns to me with a smile. 'What line are you in?'

Oh, wow. The head of PR at Dewhurst Publishing.

'Hi, Sonia.' I shake her hand. 'I'm in recruitment; do let me give you my card . . . *No!*' An involuntary cry leaves my lips.

Sadie has bent down and plunged her face into Ed's trouser pocket.

'Are you all right?' Sonia Taylor looks concerned.

'I'm fine! Really, really fine . . .'

'That's good.' Sonia gives me a slightly odd look. 'I'll just find your name badges.'

'Lara, is something wrong?' Ed turns to me with a puzzled frown.

'Um . . . no!' I manage. 'It's all good, all good . . .'

'Goodness!' Sadie's head reappears. 'I got a good view there.'

I clap a hand over my mouth. Ed eyes me suspiciously.

'Sorry,' I manage. 'Just coughing.'

'Here we are!' Sonia turns back from a table and hands us each a badge. 'Ed, can I steal you for a moment to run through the order of events?' She smiles stiffly, then leads Ed away.

I pull out my phone as camouflage, then wheel round to Sadie.

'Don't do that again! You put me off! I didn't know where to look!'

She raises her eyebrows wickedly. 'Just wanted to satisfy my curiosity.'

'Well, don't! That woman Sonia thinks I'm a complete flake now.'

Sadie gives a shrug. 'Who cares what she thinks?'

It's as if a switch flips inside me. Doesn't she realise how desperate I am?

'*I* care!' I round on her furiously and she shrinks back. 'Sadie, why d'you think I'm here? I'm trying to build up my business! I'm trying to meet important people! I've got to find a candidate for Leonidas Sports by tomorrow! If I don't do something soon, we'll go bust. I've been totally stressed out and you don't even care.' My voice is suddenly shaking a bit. 'Anyway. Do what you like. Just stay away from me.'

'Lara—' Sadie starts to speak, but I stride away from her towards the main banqueting room. Around me, tables are filling up with dynamic-looking men and women. I can see Ed walking towards me.

'How's it going? Sorry to abandon you.'

'No worries.'

'We're on Table One.' He leads me towards the stage and I feel a flicker of pride. Table One at the *Business People* dinner!

'Lara, I have a question,' says Ed as we walk. 'Please don't take this the wrong way.'

'I'm sure I won't,' I say. 'Fire away.'

'I just want to get something straight. You don't want to be my girl-friend. Is that right?'

'That's right,' I nod. 'And you don't want to be my boyfriend.'

'No,' he says, emphatically shaking his head. We've arrived at the table by now. 'So what are we doing here together?'

I'm not sure how to answer. The truth is, there is no sane reason.

'Friends?' I suggest at last.

'Friends,' he echoes doubtfully. 'I guess we could be friends.'

He pulls out my chair and I sit down. By every place is a programme with *Guest Speaker: Ed Harrison* written across the bottom.

I flick to the back of the programme and feel a little kick when I find my own name in the list. Lara Lington, L&N Executive Recruitment.

'You don't strike me as a typical head-hunter,' says Ed.

'Really?' I'm not quite sure how to react. Is that good or bad?

'You don't seem obsessed with money, for a start.'

'I'd like to make more money,' I say honestly. 'Lots more. But I sup-pose that isn't the main point for me. I've always seen head-hunting as a bit like . . .' I break off, embarrassed, and take a sip of champagne.

'What?'

'Like matchmaking. Matching the perfect person with the perfect job.'

Ed looks amused. 'That's a different way of looking at it. I'm not sure most people around here would consider they were having a love affair with their jobs.' He gestures round the crowded room.

'Maybe they would if it was the right job, though,' I say eagerly. 'If you could just match people up with exactly what they want . . .'

'And you'd be Cupid.'

'You're laughing at me.'

'I'm not. I like it as a theory. How does it work in practice?'

I sigh. There's something about Ed that makes me lower my guard.

'Not great. In fact, right now, pretty shit.'

'That bad, huh?'

'Even worse.'

Ed is watching me quizzically. 'You're in a partnership, right?'

'Yes.'

'So, how d'you decide who to go into partnership with?' he says lightly. 'How did that all happen?'

'Natalie?' I shrug. 'Because she's my best friend and I've known her for ever and she's a very talented, top head-hunter. She used to work for Price Bedford Associates, you know. They're huge.'

'Out of interest, who told you she was a very talented, top head-hunter?'

I stare at him, feeling slightly wrong-footed. 'No one had to *tell* me. She just *is*. I mean . . .' I meet his sceptical gaze. 'What?'

'It's none of my business. But when you and I first . . . met, I did a little asking around. Nobody had even heard of you.'

'Great.' I take a slug of champagne. 'There you go.'

'But I have a contact at Price Bedford and he told me a little about Natalie. Interesting.'

I feel a sudden foreboding. 'Tell me.' I put my glass down. 'Please, Ed. What did he say?'

'Well, the story goes that she lured a number of high-profile people onto a list for some anonymous "blue-chip job" that didn't exist. Then she tried to offer them up to some less-than-blue-chip client and claim this was the job she'd meant all along. The shit hit the fan, big-time. The senior partner at her firm had to step in, calm things down. That's why she was fired.' Ed hesitates. 'But you knew this, right?'

I stare at him, speechless. Natalie was fired? She was *fired*?

She told me she'd decided to quit Price Bedford because she was undervalued and she could make far more money working for herself.

'Is she here tonight?' He's looking round the room. 'Will I meet her?'

'No.' I manage to find my voice. 'She's not around at the moment.'

I can't tell him she's left me in the lurch to run the company all by myself. I can't admit that it's even worse than he thinks. She never told me she'd been fired. She told me everyone in the industry was dying to set up with her but she wanted to link up with someone she really trusted. An old friend. I was bowled over. I quit my job the next week and took out all my savings. I'm such a gullible *idiot*. I feel tears trembling on the brink of my lashes.

'Lara?' Sadie's shrill voice comes in my ear. 'Lara, come quick! I need to talk to you.'

I really don't feel like talking to Sadie. But nor can I keep sitting here with Ed looking at me with so much concern. I think he's guessed this is all a total shock to me.

'I'll be back in a second!' I say over-brightly and push my chair back. I head across the room, trying to ignore Sadie jabbering in my ear.

'I'm very sorry,' she's saying. 'I thought about it and you're right, I was selfish and thoughtless. So I decided to help you, and I have! I've found you a candidate! A wonderful, perfect candidate!'

'What?' I turn. 'What did you say?'

'You may think I'm not interested in your work, but I am,' she announces. 'You need a trophy and I've found you one. Aren't I clever?'

'What are you talking about?'

'I've been listening in on everyone's conversations!' she says proudly. 'I was starting to think it was hopeless, but then I heard a woman called Clare whispering to her friend in a corner. She's not happy. Things are getting so bad at her place, she's thinking of quitting.'

'Right. So the point is—'

'She's a head of marketing!' Sadie says triumphantly. 'It was on her badge. She won an award last month, you know. But her new chief exec didn't even congratulate her. He's a total pig,' she adds confidingly.

I swallow, trying to stay calm. An award-winning marketing head who wants to move jobs. Oh God. I would die and go to heaven.

'She's over there!' Sadie gestures at the other side of the room.

'Is she into sports? Exercise?'

'Brawny calves,' says Sadie triumphantly. 'I noticed them at once.'

I hurry to a nearby board and look through the list of guests. Clare . . .

'Clare Fortescue, Marketing Director of Shepherd Homes?' I feel a jab of excitement. 'I wanted to talk to her, but I couldn't get through!'

'Well, she's here! Come on, I'll show her to you!'

My heart is thumping as I cross the crowded room.

'There!' Sadie is pointing at a woman with glasses in a royal-blue dress. She has dark hair, a mole on her nose and is on the short side.

'Hi!' I walk up to her and take a deep breath. 'Clare Fortescue?'

'Yes?' she says briskly.

'May I have a quick word?'

'Well . . . OK.' Looking a bit puzzled, Clare Fortescue allows me to draw her away from the group she's in.

'Hi.' I give her a nervous smile. 'My name's Lara Lington and I'm a recruitment consultant. I've been meaning to make contact with you. Your reputation has spread, you know.'

'Really?' She looks suspicious.

'Of course! In fact I must congratulate you on your recent award!'

'Oh.' A pink tinge comes to her ears. 'Thanks very much.'

'I'm recruiting for a marketing-director position right now,' I say, lowering my voice discreetly, 'and I just wanted to mention it. It's a really exciting sportswear company with massive potential and I think you'd be perfect. You'd be my number-one pick.' I pause, then add lightly, 'But of course, you may be very happy where you are right now . . .'

There's silence. I can't tell what's going on behind Clare Fortescue's glasses. My whole body is so tense I can't even breathe.

'Actually, I have been thinking about a move,' she says at last, quietly. 'I might very well be interested. But it would have to be the right situation.' She gives me a bullet-like look. 'I'm not compromising myself.'

Somehow I manage not to whoop. She's interested *and* she's tough!

'Great!' I smile. 'Maybe I can call you in the morning. Or if you had a few minutes to spare right now, we could have a chat? Just quickly?'

Ten minutes later I walk back to the table, giddy with joy. She's going to send me her CV tomorrow. She used to play right wing in hockey! She's a perfect match!

Sadie seems even more thrilled than me.

'I knew it!' she keeps saying. 'I knew she'd be right!'

'You're a star,' I say joyfully. 'We're a team. High-five!'

'High what?' Sadie looks perplexed.

'High-five! Don't you know what a high-five is? Hold up your hand.'

OK. It turns out high-fiving a ghost is a mistake. That woman in red thought I was trying to hit her. Hastily I resume walking. I arrive at the table and beam at Ed. 'I'm back!'

'So you are.' He gives me a quizzical look. 'How's it going?'

'Brilliantly, since you ask.'

'Brilliantly!' echoes Sadie, and jumps into his lap. I reach for my champagne glass. Suddenly I'm in the mood for a party.

Eight

TONIGHT IS TURNING OUT to be one of the best evenings of my life. The dinner is delicious. Ed's speech goes down fantastically. Afterwards, people keep coming over to congratulate him, and he introduces me to everyone. I've given out all my business cards and set up two meetings for next week, and Clare Fortescue's friend has just come over to ask discreetly if there's anything I can do for *her*.

The only slight pain is Sadie, who's got bored by business talk and has started on about dancing again. She's been out exploring, and according to her there's some tiny nightclub down the street which is perfect and we *have* to go there immediately.

'No!' I mutter, as she pesters me yet again. 'Ssh! The magician's doing another trick!'

As we all sip our coffee, a magician is doing the rounds of the tables. He's asking Ed to choose a shape on a card and saying he'll mind-read it.

'OK,' says Ed, choosing a card. I glance over his shoulder, and it shows a squiggle shape.

'Focus on the shape and nothing else.' The magician, who is wearing a jewelled jacket, fake tan and eyeliner, fixes his gaze on Ed. 'Let The Great Firenzo use his mysterious Eastern powers and read your mind.'

There's a hush round the table. The Great Firenzo takes both hands up to his head as though in a trance.

'I am communing with your mind,' he says, his voice low and mysterious. 'The message is coming in. You have chosen . . . this shape!' With a flourish, he produces a card that exactly matches Ed's.

'Correct.' Ed nods, and shows his card to the table.

'Amazing!' gasps a blonde woman opposite.

'Pretty impressive.' Ed is turning his own card over, examining it. 'There's no way he could have seen what I picked.'

'It's the power of the mind,' intones the magician, swiftly collecting the card from Ed. 'It's the power of . . . The Great Firenzo!'

'Do it to me!' begs the blonde woman excitedly. 'Read my mind!'

'Very well.' The Great Firenzo turns to face her. 'But beware. When you open your mind to me, I can read all your secrets. Every deepest, darkest one.' His eyes flash and she giggles.

'I find ladies' minds are often easier to . . . *penetrate.*' The Great Firenzo raises an eyebrow suggestively. 'They are weaker, softer . . . but more delightful within.' He grins toothily at the blonde woman.

We all watch as the blonde woman picks a card, studies it for a moment, then says decidedly, 'I've chosen.'

'It's the triangle,' says Sadie. She's behind the back of the blonde woman, looking down at the card.

'Relax. Do not resist, sweet lady. Let Firenzo probe your thoughts. I promise . . .' He gives the toothy smile again. 'I'll be gentle.'

Euuw. He thinks he's so hot, but he's a total sleazeball. *And* sexist.

'Only The Great Firenzo has such powers,' he says dramatically, looking around the table at us all. 'Only The Great Firenzo can—'

'Actually, I can too,' I say. I'll show *him* who's got a weaker mind.

'What?' The Great Firenzo shoots me a look of dislike.

'I can commune with the mind too. I know what card she chose.'

'Please, young lady. Do not interrupt the work of The Great Firenzo.'

'I'm just saying.' I shrug. 'I know what it is.'

'No, you don't,' says the blonde woman, a little aggressively.

'I *do* know!' I say indignantly. 'I'll draw it. Does anyone have a pen?' A nearby man holds one out and I start drawing on my napkin.

'Lara,' says Ed in a low voice, 'what exactly are you doing?'

'Magic,' I say confidently. I finish my triangle and thrust the napkin at the blonde woman. 'Is that right?'

The blonde woman's jaw drops. 'She's right.' She turns her card over and there's a gasp round the table. 'How did you do that?'

'I told you, I can do magic. I too have mysterious powers. They call me "The Great Lara".' I catch Sadie's eye and she smirks.

'Are you a member of the Magic Circle?' The Great Firenzo looks livid. 'Because our protocol states—'

'I'm not in any circle,' I say in a pleasant tone. 'But my mind's pretty strong, I think you'll find. For a lady.'

The Great Firenzo looks totally put out.

I glance over at Ed. 'Very impressive. How d'you do that?'

'Magic.' I shrug innocently. 'I told you. I have mysterious Eastern mind-reading powers.'

'The Great Lara, huh?'

'That's what my disciples call me. But you can call me Greatie for short.'

'Greatie.' His mouth is twitching and suddenly I see a smile pop out at one corner. A real, genuine smile.

'Oh my God! You smiled! Mr American Frown actually smiled!'

Oops. Maybe I *have* had too much to drink. I didn't mean to call him Mr American Frown out loud. For an instant Ed looks a bit taken aback—then he shrugs, as deadpan as ever.

'Must have been a mistake. Won't happen again. Shall we go?'

On the street the air is clear and there's a warmish breeze. The hotel doorman is surrounded by people waiting for taxis, so Ed and I walk down onto the pavement.

'If we walk this way . . .' I say, squinting at a street sign, 'we should be able to pick up a taxi.'

'I'm in your hands,' says Ed. 'I don't know this area.'

'Is there any area you *do* know?'

'I know my route to work.' Ed shrugs. 'I know the park opposite my building. I know the way to Whole Foods.'

'Don't you think if you come and live in a city you should respect it enough to get to know it? London is one of the most fascinating, historic, amazing cities in the world!' My voice rises. 'I mean, why did you take a job here if you weren't interested in the place? What were you planning to do?'

'I was planning to explore it with my fiancée,' Ed says calmly.

His answer slightly takes the wind out of my sails. What fiancée?

'Until she broke it off with me, a week before we were due to come,' Ed continues conversationally. 'She asked her company to transfer her London placement to someone else. So you see, I had a dilemma. Come to England, stay focused and do the best I could, or stay in Boston, knowing I'd see her almost every day. She worked in the same building as me.' He pauses a second, before adding, 'And her lover.'

'Oh.' I stare at him in dismay. 'I'm sorry. I . . . didn't realise.'

'No problem.'

His face is so still, it almost seems like he doesn't care—but I'm getting to understand his impassive style. He does care, of course he does. Suddenly his frown is making more sense. And that closed-up expression. God, what a bitch his fiancée must be. I can see her now. Big white American teeth and swingy hair and killer heels.

I feel so sorry for him, I think I should probably stop giving him a hard time. But some stronger instinct in me makes me push on.

'So you just take your route to work and back again every day,' I say. 'You go to Whole Foods and the park and back again and that's it.'

'Works for me.'

'How long have you been over here again?'

'Five months.'

'Five months?' I echo in horror. 'No. You can't exist like that. You have to open your eyes and look around. You have to move on.'

'*Move on*,' he echoes in mock-amazed tones. 'Wow. Right. Not a phrase anyone's said to me much.'

OK, so I'm obviously not the only one who's given him a pep talk.

'I'll be gone in two more months,' he adds curtly. 'It hardly matters whether I get to know London or not.'

'So, what, you're just treading water, just existing, waiting until you feel better? Well, you never will! Not unless you *do* something about it! People break up,' I say. 'It's just the way things are. And you can't dwell on what might have been. You have to look at what is.'

As I'm saying the words, I have a weird flash of déjà vu. I think Dad said something like this to me once about Josh. But that was different.

'Life is like an escalator,' I add wisely.

When Dad says that to me I get all annoyed because he just doesn't understand. But somehow it's different when *I'm* giving advice.

'An escalator?' echoes Ed. 'Thought it was a box of chocolates.'

'No, definitely an escalator. You see, it carries you on regardless.' I mime an escalator. 'And you might as well enjoy the view and seize every opportunity while you're passing. Otherwise it'll be too late. That's what my dad told me when I broke up with this . . . this guy.'

Ed walks on a few paces. 'And did you take his advice?'

'Er . . . well . . .' I brush my hair back, avoiding his eye. 'Kind of.'

I'm not sure I want to get into this conversation actually. Maybe now is the moment to find a cab.

'Taxi!' I wave my hand at a passing cab but it sails past, even though its light is on. I *hate* it when they do that.

I turn back to see Ed standing stock-still on the pavement.

'Lara,' he says. His face is confused and his eyes a little glassy. 'I think we should go dancing.' He nods. 'It would be a perfect way to round off the evening. It just came to me out of the blue.'

I don't believe it. *Sadie*. I whirl round on the pavement, searching the darkness, and suddenly spot her, floating by a lamppost.

'You!' I exclaim furiously, but Ed doesn't even seem to notice.

'There's a nightclub near here,' he's saying. 'Come on. Let's have a quick dance. It's a great idea. I should have thought of it before.'

'How do you know there's a nightclub here? You don't know London!'

'Yeah, right.' He nods, looking a bit flummoxed himself. 'But I'm pretty sure there's a nightclub down that street.' He gestures. 'Down there, third left. We should go check it out.'

'I'd love to,' I say sweetly. 'But I must just make a call. There's a conversation I need to have.' I direct the words meaningfully at Sadie. 'If I don't have this conversation then I *won't be able to dance*.'

Sulkily, Sadie descends to the pavement and I pretend to punch a number into my phone. I'm so angry with her, I almost don't know where to start. 'What's all this?' I say, gesturing at Ed.

'I want to dance!' she says. 'I had to take extreme measures. And don't look at me like that!' She suddenly rounds on me. 'I wouldn't need to if you weren't so selfish. I know your career's important, but I want to go dancing! That's why we're here. It's supposed to be my evening. But you take over and I don't get a look in. It's not fair!'

She sounds almost tearful. And suddenly I feel bad.

'OK. You're right. Come on, let's go dancing.'

'Wonderful! We'll have such a good time. This way . . .' Her spirits restored, Sadie directs us through some tiny Mayfair streets I've never been down before. 'Nearly there . . . Here!'

It's a tiny place called The Flashlight Dance Club. Two bouncers are standing outside, looking half asleep, and they let us in, no question.

We descend a set of dim wooden steps, and find ourselves in a large room carpeted in red, with chandeliers, a dance floor, a bar, and two guys in leather trousers sitting morosely at the bar. A DJ on a tiny stage is playing some J-Lo track. No one's dancing.

'Listen, Sadie,' I mutter as Ed goes up to the bar. 'There are better clubs than this. We should go somewhere there's a bit more happening.'

'Hello?' A voice interrupts me. I turn to see a slim, high-cheeked woman in her fifties, wearing a black top and gauze skirt over leggings. 'Are you here for the Charleston lesson?'

Charleston lesson?

'I'm so sorry,' the woman continues. 'I suddenly remembered we had an arrangement.' She stifles a yawn. 'Lara, isn't it? You're certainly wearing the right clothes!'

'Excuse me.' I smile, hauling out my phone, and turn to Sadie. 'What have you done?' I mutter. 'Who's this?'

'You need lessons,' Sadie says unrepentantly. 'This is the teacher. She lives in a little room upstairs. Normally the lessons are during the day.'

I stare at Sadie incredulously. 'Did you wake her up?'

'I must have forgotten to put the appointment in my diary,' the woman is saying as I turn back. 'It's not like me . . . thank goodness I remembered! Out of the blue, it came to me that you would be here.'

'Here's your drink.' Ed arrives by my side. 'Who's this?'

'I'm your dance instructor, Gaynor.' She holds out her hand and, looking a bit bewildered, Ed takes it. 'Have you always been interested in the Charleston?'

'The Charleston?' Ed looks mystified.

I feel a bit hysterical. The truth is, Sadie always gets her way. She wants us to dance the Charleston. We're going to dance the Charleston. I owe it to her. And it might as well be here and now.

'So!' I smile winningly at Ed. 'Ready?'

The thing about the Charleston is it's more energetic than you realise. And it's really complicated. And you have to be really coordinated. After an hour, my arms and legs are aching. It's relentless.

'And forwards and back . . .' the dance instructor is chanting. 'And swivel those feet . . .'

'Charleston, Charleston . . .' The music is tripping along, filling the club with its peppy beat.

Ed is grimly crossing his hands back and forth over his knees. He shoots me a quick grin as I look at him, but I can tell he's concentrating too hard to talk. He's quite deft with his feet, actually. I'm impressed.

I glance over at Sadie, who's dancing in bliss. She's amazing. *So* much better than the teacher. Her legs are twinkling back and forth, she knows a zillion different steps and she never seems to get out of breath.

Sadie catches my eye, grins and throws back her head in rapture. I guess it's a long time since she got to sparkle on the dance floor. I should have done this before. I feel really mean now.

The only trouble is, now I've got a stitch. I head to the side of the dance floor and an empty table. What I need to do is to get Ed to dance with Sadie. The two of them alone. Somehow. Then I really will have made her evening.

'OK?' Ed has followed me off.

'Yes. Fine.' I mop my brow with a napkin. 'It's hard work!'

'You've done very well!' Gaynor comes over to us. 'You're very promising, the pair of you! Shall I see you again next week?'

'Er . . . maybe.' I don't quite dare look at Ed. 'I'll call you, shall I?'

'I'll leave the music on,' she says enthusiastically. 'You can practise!'

As she goes, hurrying across the floor, I nudge Ed. 'Hey, I want to watch you. Go and dance on your own for a bit.'

'Are you crazy?'

'Go on! Please! You can do that one-two thing with your arms. I want to see how you do it. Pleease . . .'

Rolling his eyes good-humouredly, Ed heads out onto the floor.

'Sadie!' I hiss and gesture at Ed. 'Quick! Your partner's waiting!'

Her eyes widen as she realises what I mean. In half a second she's out there, facing him, her eyes lit up joyfully.

'Yes, I'd love to dance,' I hear her saying. 'Thank you so much!'

As Ed starts swinging his legs back and forth, she synchronises with him perfectly. She looks so happy. She looks so right. Her hands are on his shoulders, her headdress is bobbing, the music is fizzing along, it's like watching an old film . . .

'That's enough,' says Ed suddenly with a laugh. 'I need a partner.' And to my dismay he barges right through Sadie, towards me.

I can see the shock on Sadie's face. As she watches him leave the floor she looks devastated. I wince, wishing so hard he could see her . . .

'I'm really sorry,' I mouth at Sadie as Ed drags me onto the floor.

We dance a while longer, then head back to the table.

'I've had a good time.' Ed drains his glass and smiles at me. A full-on, proper smile. Crinkled eyes, uncreased brow, everything! I almost want to shout, 'Geronimo! We got there!'

'So have I.'

'I didn't expect to end the evening like this. But it's great!'

'Different.' I nod.

He rips open a bag of peanuts and offers it to me and I watch him as he crunches them hungrily. Even though he's looking relaxed, the frown lines are still faintly etched on his brow.

'Ed,' I say on impulse. 'Let me take you sightseeing. You should see London. I'll show you around. At the weekend sometime?'

'I'd like that.' He seems genuinely touched. 'Thanks.'

'No problem! Let's email.' We smile at each other and I drain my Sidecar with a slight shudder. (Sadie made me order it. Totally revolting.)

Ed glances at his watch. 'So, are you ready to go?'

I glance over at the dance floor. Sadie's still going strong, flinging her arms and legs around with no sign of flagging. No wonder all the girls in the twenties were so skinny.

'Let's go.' I nod. Sadie can catch up with us when she's ready.

We head out into the Mayfair night. The street lanterns are on, mist is rising from the pavements and nobody's about. We head to the corner and after a couple of minutes, flag down a couple of cabs. Ed ushers me into the first taxi, then pauses, holding the door open.

'Thanks, Lara,' he says in that formal, preppy way he has. I'm actually starting to find it quite endearing. 'I had a good time. It was . . . quite a night.'

'Wasn't it!' I adjust my diamanté cap, which has fallen lopsided with all the dancing, and Ed's mouth twitches with amusement.

'So, should I wear my spats for sightseeing?'

'Definitely.' I nod. 'And a top hat.'

Ed laughs. I think it's the first time I've ever heard him laugh. 'Good night, twenties girl.'

'Good night.' I close the door and the taxi roars off.

Next morning I feel a bit dazed. Charleston music is ringing in my ears and I keep having flashbacks to The Great Lara. The whole thing feels like a dream. Except it's not a dream, because Clare Fortescue's CV is already in my inbox when I arrive at work. Result!

Kate's eyes are like saucers as I print out the email.

'Who on earth's this?' she says, poring over the CV. 'Look, she's got an MBA! She's won a prize!'

'I know,' I say nonchalantly. 'She's a top, award-winning marketing director. We networked last night. She's going on the Leonidas short list.'

By ten o'clock the new list has been sent off to Janet Grady. I flop back in my chair and grin at Kate, who's staring at her computer screen.

'I've found a picture of you!' she says. 'From last night. "Lara Lington and Ed Harrison arrive at the *Business People* dinner."' She hesitates, looking puzzled. 'Who's he? I thought you were back with Josh.'

'Oh, I am,' I say at once. 'Ed is just . . . a business contact.'

'Oh, right. He's quite good-looking, isn't he? I mean, Josh is too,' she amends hastily. 'In a different way.'

Honestly, she has no taste. Josh is a million times better-looking than Ed. Which reminds me, I haven't heard from him for a while.

I wait till Kate has gone to the bathroom and then dial his office.

'Josh Barrett.'

'It's me,' I say lovingly. 'How was the trip?'

'Oh, hi. It was great.'

'Missed you!'

There's a pause. I'm pretty sure Josh says something in response, but I can't quite hear.

'I was wondering if your phone was going wrong?' I add. 'Because I haven't received any texts from you since yesterday morning. Are mine getting through OK?'

There's another indistinct mumble. What's wrong with this line?

'Josh?' I tap the receiver.

'Hi.' His voice suddenly breaks through more clearly. 'I'll look into it.'

'So, how about lunch tomorrow? And we can take it from there.'

'Sure,' he says after a pause. 'Great.'

'Love you,' I say tenderly. 'Can't wait to see you.'

There's silence.

'Josh?'

'Er . . . yeah. Me too. Bye, Lara.'

I put down the phone. I feel a bit dissatisfied, but I don't know why. Everything's fine. So why does it feel like there's something missing?

Briskly, I turn back to my computer and find an email waiting in my inbox from Ed. Wow, that was quick off the mark.

Hi, twenties girl. Great evening last night. Re your corporate travel insurance. Might want to look at this link. I've heard they're good. Ed

I click on it and find a site offering reduced insurance rates for small companies. That's so typical of him: I mention a problem once, and he instantly finds a solution. Feeling touched, I reply:

Thanks, twenties guy. I appreciate it. Hope you're dusting off your London guide.
PS Have you demonstrated the Charleston to your staff yet?
Immediately an answer pops back.

Is this your idea of blackmail?

I giggle, and start browsing online to find a picture of a dancing couple to send him.

'What's funny?' says Sadie.

'Nothing.' I close down the window. I won't tell Sadie I'm emailing Ed. She's so possessive, she might take it the wrong way.

She starts reading the *Grazia* which is lying open on my desk, and after a few moments orders me, 'Turn.' This is her new habit. It's quite annoying, actually. I've become her page-turning slave.

'Lara!' Kate rushes back into the office. 'You've got a special delivery!'

She hands me a bright-pink envelope printed with butterflies and ladybirds, with 'Tutus and Pearls' emblazoned across the top. I rip it open to find a note from Diamanté's assistant: *Diamanté thought you might like this. We look forward to seeing you later!*

It's a printed sheet with details about the fashion show, together with a laminated card on a chain, reading 'VIP Backstage Pass'. Wow. I've never been a VIP before. I've never even been an IP.

I turn the card over in my fingers, thinking ahead to this evening. Finally we'll get the necklace! After all this time. And then—

My thoughts stop abruptly. Then . . . what? Sadie said she couldn't rest until she got her necklace. That's why she's haunting me. That's why she's here. So when she gets it, what will happen? She can't . . .

I mean, she won't just . . . She wouldn't just . . . *go?*

I stare at her, suddenly feeling a bit weird. This whole time, I've only been focused on getting the necklace. I've lost sight of what might happen *beyond* the necklace. 'Turn,' says Sadie impatiently, her eyes avidly fixed on an article about Katie Holmes. 'Turn!'

In any case, I'm resolved. I'm not letting Sadie down this time. The minute I see this bloody necklace I'm grabbing it.

'**K**eep your eyes peeled,' I mutter to Sadie as we walk through the bare white lobby of the Sanderstead Hotel. Ahead of us, two skinny girls in miniskirts are heading towards a pair of double doors decorated with swags of pink silk and butterfly helium balloons. That must be it.

Nearing the room, I see a gaggle of well-dressed girls milling around, knocking back glasses of champagne. There's a catwalk running through the centre of the room, and rows of silk-swagged chairs.

I wait patiently as the girls ahead of me are ticked off, then step forward to a blonde girl in a pink prom dress. She's holding a clipboard and gives me a chilly smile. 'Can I help you?'

'Yes.' I nod. 'I'm here for the fashion show.'

'Are you on the list?'

'Yes.' I reach for my invitation. 'I'm Diamanté's cousin. I've got this, by the way.' I brandish my VIP backstage pass at her. 'I could just go hunting. But if you could locate her, it would help . . .'

'OK,' the girl says after a pause. She reaches for her teeny jewel-encrusted phone and dials a number. 'Some cousin wants to see Diamanté.' She adds in a barely concealed murmer, 'No, never seen her before. Well, if you say so . . .' She puts her phone away. 'Diamanté says she'll meet you backstage.' She points down the corridor to another door.

'Go ahead!' I instruct Sadie in a whisper. 'See if you can find the necklace backstage! It must be easy to spot!' I follow a guy with a crate of Moët down the carpeted corridor, and am flashing my VIP pass at a bouncer when Sadie reappears. 'Easy to spot?' she says, her voice trembling. 'You must be joking! We're never going to find it! *Never!*'

'What do you mean?' I say anxiously as I walk in. 'What are you—'

Oh, no. Oh, bloody hell. I'm standing in a large area filled with mirrors and chairs and about thirty models. They're all tall and skinny and are wearing skimpy, diaphanous dresses. And they're all wearing at least twenty necklaces piled round their necks. Chains, pearls, pendants. Everywhere I look there are necklaces. It's a necklace haystack.

'Lara! You came!'

I wheel round to see Diamanté teetering towards me. She's wearing a tiny skirt covered in love hearts, a skinny vest, a studded silver belt and patent stiletto shoe boots. She's holding two glasses of champagne and she offers one to me.

'Hi, Diamanté. Thanks so much for inviting me! This is amazing!' I gesture around the room, then take a deep breath. The important thing is not to seem too desperate or needy. 'So anyway.' I aim for a light, casual tone. 'I have this huge favour to ask you. You know that dragonfly necklace that your father was after? The old one with the glass beads?'

Diamanté blinks at me in surprise. 'How d'you know about that?'

'Er . . . long story. Anyway, it was originally Great-Aunt Sadie's, and my mum always loved it and I wanted to surprise her with it.' My fingers are crossed tightly behind my back. 'So, maybe after the show I could . . . er . . . have it? Possibly? If you didn't need it any more?'

Diamanté stares back at me for a few moments, her eyes glazed.

'My dad's a fuckhead,' she says at last, with emphasis.

I stare at her uncertainly until the penny finally drops. Oh, great. She's pissed. She's probably been drinking champagne all day.

'Yes,' I say quickly. 'He is. And that's why you need to give the necklace to me. *To me*,' I repeat, very loudly and clearly.

Diamanté's swaying and I grab her arm to steady her.

'The dragonfly necklace,' I say. 'Do-you-know-where-it-is?'

Diamanté turns her face to survey me for a minute.

'You know, my dad found out you were coming today. He called me up. He was like, What's she doing on the list? Take her off. I was like, Fuck you! This is my first cousin or whatever.'

'Your dad . . . didn't want me here? Did he say why?'

'I said to him, Who cares if she's a bit of a psycho?' Diamanté talks right through me. 'Be more *tolerant*. Then, you know, *he* was on about that necklace. He offered me all these substitutes. I was like, don't patronise me with *Tiffany*. I'm a designer, OK? I have a *vision*.'

The blood is beating hard in my ears. Uncle Bill is still after Sadie's necklace. I don't understand why. All I know is, I need to get hold of it.

'Diamanté.' I grab her shoulders. 'Please listen. This necklace is really, really important to me. To my mum. I totally appreciate your vision as a designer and everything . . . but after the show, can I have it?'

Diamanté looks blank. Then she puts an arm round my neck and squeezes hard. 'Course you can, babe. Soon as the show's over, 's yours.'

'Great.' I try not to give away how relieved I am. 'Great! That's great! So where is it right now? Could I see it?'

'Sure! Lyds?' Diamanté calls to a girl in a stripy top. 'D'you know where that dragonfly necklace is?'

Lyds is shrugging indifferently. 'Don't remember. It'll be on one of the girls somewhere.'

It'll be in the haystack somewhere. I look round the room hopelessly. Models are everywhere. Necklaces are everywhere.

'I'll look for it myself,' I say. 'If you don't mind—'

'No! The show's about to start!' Diamanté starts pushing me towards the door. 'Lyds, take her in. Put her in the front row. That'll show Dad.'

'But—'

It's too late. I've been ushered out. As the doors swing shut, I'm hopping with frustration. It's in there. Somewhere in that room, Sadie's necklace is hanging round a model's neck. But which bloody one?

'I can't find it anywhere.' Sadie suddenly appears beside me. To my horror, she seems almost in tears. 'I've looked at every single girl. I've looked at all the necklaces. It's nowhere.'

'Sadie, listen. I'm sure it's on one of the models. We'll look really carefully at each one as they go past and we'll find it. I promise.'

Thank God I'm in the front row. As the show starts, the crowd is six deep and everyone's so tall and skinny there's no way I would have got a view from further back. Pink spotlights start flashing onto the catwalk and a Scissor Sisters track thumps through the speakers.

Opposite me on the other side of the catwalk, taking his seat in the front row, is Uncle Bill. As I stare in horror, he looks up and catches my eye. My stomach lurches. I feel frozen.

After a minute he smiles calmly in greeting. Numbly, I do the same. Then suddenly the first model is on the catwalk, wearing a white slip dress printed with spiders' webs and doing that sashay-model walk. I stare desperately at the necklaces jangling round her neck, but she whizzes past so quickly, it's almost impossible to get a good view.

I glance over at Uncle Bill and feel a prickle of horror. He's scanning the necklaces too.

'This is useless!' Sadie appears from nowhere, and leaps up onto the catwalk. She goes right up to the model and peers intently at the jumble of chains and beads and charms round her neck. 'I can't see it! I told you, it's not there!'

The next model appears and in a flash she's examining that girl's necklaces, too. 'Not here either.'

'Super collection,' a girl next to me exclaims. 'Don't you think?'

'Er, yes,' I say distractedly. 'Great.' I can't look at anything except the necklaces. I'm feeling a growing foreboding, a sense of failure—

Oh my God! There it is! Right in front of me. Wound around a model's ankle. My heart is hammering as I stare breathlessly at the pale yellowy beads, casually twined into an anklet. An *anklet*.

Sadie suddenly follows my gaze and gasps. 'My necklace!' She zooms up to the oblivious model and yells, 'That's mine! It's mine!'

The moment that model is off the catwalk I'm going after her and I'm getting it. I don't care what it takes. I glance at Uncle Bill—and to my horror, his eyes are glued on Sadie's necklace too.

The model is sashaying back now. She'll be off the catwalk in a minute. As I glance across, I see Uncle Bill getting to his feet.

I leap to my feet too, and start making my way out, muttering apologies as I tread on people's feet. At least I have an advantage: I'm on the side of the catwalk nearer the doors. Not daring to look back, I fling myself through the double doors, and sprint up the corridor to the backstage area, flashing my pass at the bouncer guy on the door.

The backstage area is mayhem. Girls are ripping clothes off, having clothes put on, having their hair dried, having their lips touched up . . .

I look around in panic. I've already lost sight of my model. I start moving between all the hair stations, dodging rails of clothes, trying to catch a glimpse of her, when I become aware of a row at the door.

'This is Bill Lington, OK?' It's Uncle Bill's assistant, Damian, and he's obviously losing his rag. '*Bill Lington*. Just because he doesn't have a backstage pass—'

'No backstage pass, no entry,' I can hear the bouncer saying in a flat monotone. 'Rules of the boss.'

'He *is* the boss,' snaps Damian. 'He paid for all this, you moron.'

'What did you call me?' The bouncer sounds ominous and I can't help smiling—but my smile dies as Sadie materialises, her eyes desperate.

'She's gone!' she gulps. 'That model girl has taken my necklace. She was hailing a taxi and I dashed back to get you, but I knew you'd be too slow. And when I returned to the street . . . she'd gone!'

'A *taxi*?' I stare at her in horror. 'But . . . but . . .'

'We've lost it again.' Sadie seems beside herself. 'We've lost it!'

'But Diamanté promised I could have it!'

I'm hollow with dismay. I can't believe I've let it slip away again.

Massive cheers and whoops are coming from the main hall. The show must have finished. A moment later, models stream into the backstage area, followed by a pink-faced Diamanté.

'Fucking fantastic!' she yells at everyone. 'You all rock! I love you all! Now let's party!'

I struggle through the melee towards her. 'Diamanté!' I call over the hubbub. 'The necklace! The girl wearing it has gone!'

Diamanté looks vague. 'Which girl?'

'She's called Flora,' Sadie says urgently in my ear.

'Flora! I need Flora, but apparently she's gone!'

'Oh, Flora.' Diamanté's brow clears. 'Yeah, she's gone to Paris for a ball. On her dad's PJ. Private jet,' she explains at my blank look. 'I said she could wear her dress.'

'But she's taken the necklace too!' I'm trying really hard not to scream. 'Diamanté, please. Call her. Call her now. Tell her I'll meet her. I'll go to Paris, whatever it takes. I *need* to get hold of this necklace.'

Diamanté gapes at me for a moment, then raises her eyes to heaven. 'My dad's right about you,' she says. 'You're nuts. But I quite like that.' She gets out her phone and speed-dials a number.

'Hey, Flora! Babe, you were awesome! So are you on the plane yet? OK, listen. Remember that dragonfly necklace you had on?'

'Anklet,' I interject urgently. 'She was wearing it as an anklet.'

'The anklet thing?' says Diamanté. 'Yeah, that one. My crazy cousin really wants it. She's gonna come to Paris to get it. Where's the ball? Can she meet you?' She listens for a while. 'Oh, right. Yeah. Totally . . . Of course . . .' At last she says to me, 'Flora doesn't know where the ball is. It's like, some friend of her mum's holding it? She says she wants to wear the necklace 'cause it suits her dress, but then she'll FedEx it to you.'

'Tomorrow morning? First thing?'

'No, after the ball, yeah?' says Diamanté. 'I dunno what day exactly, but as soon as she's done with it she'll send it. She promised. Isn't that perfect?' She beams and lifts her hand to give me a high-five.

I stare back at her in disbelief. *Perfect?* The necklace is on its way to Paris and I don't know when I'll get it back. How can this in any way be perfect? I feel like having a total meltdown. But I don't dare. There's only the thinnest, most fragile chain linking me to the necklace now, and the strongest link in it is Diamanté. If I piss her off, I'll lose it for ever.

'Perfect!' I force myself to smile back and high-five Diamanté. I take the phone and dictate my address to Flora. Now all I can do is cross all my fingers. And my toes. And wait.

Nine

WE'LL GET THE NECKLACE BACK. I have to believe it. I *do* believe it. But still, both Sadie and I have been on edge since last night. The truth is, I feel like I've failed her. The necklace has been within my reach, twice. And each time, I've let it get away.

Neither of us is chatting much this morning. In fact, Sadie has been silent for a while. As I finish typing my emails at work I watch her sitting, staring out of the window.

Sighing, I shut down my computer. The necklace will come back. I have to believe it. Meanwhile, I have a life to lead. I have a boyfriend to meet for lunch. I push back my chair and grab my bag.

'See you later,' I say to both Kate and Sadie, and head out of the office before either can reply. I don't want any company. I'm feeling a bit jittery about seeing Josh again. I mean, it's not like I have any *doubts* or anything. Nothing like that. I suppose I'm just . . . apprehensive.

What I'm really not in the mood for is Sadie suddenly appearing beside me as I'm nearly at the tube station.

'You're meeting Josh, aren't you?'

'If you knew, then why did you bother asking?' I say childishly.

'As your guardian angel, I insist that you see sense,' she says crisply.

'Josh is not in love with you, and if you think for a moment he is, you're even more self-deceiving than I thought.'

'You said you weren't my guardian angel,' I say over my shoulder. 'So butt out, old lady.'

'Don't call me old!' she says in outrage. 'And I'm not going to let you throw yourself away on some lily-livered, weak-willed puppet.'

'He's not a puppet,' I snap, then run down the tube steps.

'You don't even love him.' Sadie's voice follows me as I jump onto the tube. 'Not really.'

'Of course I do! Why would I want him back if I didn't love him?'

'To prove to everyone that you're right.' She folds her arms.

This one takes me by surprise.

'That's just . . . rubbish! That just shows how little you know! It's got nothing to do with that! I love Josh, and he loves me . . .' I trail off as I feel the attention of all the travellers in the carriage turning towards me.

I stump to a corner seat, pursued by Sadie. As she draws breath to launch into another speech, I take out my iPod and put it on. A moment later her voice is totally drowned out.

Perfect! I should have thought of this a long time ago.

I suggested to Josh that we meet at Bistro Martin, just to exorcise all memories of that stupid Marie. As I hand in my coat I see him already sitting at the table, and feel a whoosh of relief, mixed with vindication.

'You see?' I can't help muttering to Sadie. 'He's early. *Now* tell me he doesn't care for me.'

'He doesn't know his own mind.' She shakes her head dismissively. 'He's like a ventriloquist's dummy. I told him what to say.'

'Look, you,' I say angrily. 'You're not as powerful as you think you are, OK? Josh is pretty strong-minded, if you want to know.'

'Darling, I could make him dance on the table and sing "Baa Baa, Black Sheep" if I wanted to!' she replies scornfully.

There's no point arguing with her. Deliberately, I barge right through her and head to Josh's table, ignoring her squeals of protest. Josh is pushing his chair back and the light is catching his hair and his eyes are as soft and blue as ever. As I reach him, something bubbles up in my stomach. Happiness, maybe. Or love. Or triumph. Like, a mixture.

I reach up for a hug and his lips meet mine and all I can think is 'Yessss!' After a minute he moves to sit down, but I pull him back into another passionate kiss. I'll show Sadie who's in love.

At last he really does pull away, and we sit down. I lift the glass of white wine that Josh has already ordered for me.

'So,' I say, a bit breathless. 'Here's to us! Isn't it wonderful, being back together again? At our favourite restaurant? I'll always associate this restaurant with you,' I add a bit pointedly. 'No one else. I never could.'

Josh has the grace to look a bit uncomfortable. 'How's work?' he asks.

'Fine.' I sigh. 'Actually, to be honest not that fine. Natalie's pissed off to Goa and left me all alone to run the company. It's been a nightmare.'

'Really?' Josh says. 'That's bad.' He picks up the menu and starts reading, as though the subject's closed, and I feel a tiny pinprick of frustration. I was expecting more of a response. Although, now I remember, Josh never does respond to stuff much. He's so easy-going.

'We should go to Goa one day!' I change the subject.

'Definitely. It's supposed to be great. You know, I'm really into the idea of taking some time off. Like six months or so.'

'We could do it together!' I say joyfully. 'We could both give up our jobs, we could travel round, start off in Mumbai . . .'

'Don't start *planning* it all,' he says, suddenly tetchy. 'Don't hem me in!'

I stare at him in shock. 'Josh?'

'Sorry.' He looks taken aback by himself, too. 'Sorry.'

'Is something wrong?'

'No. At least . . .' He looks confused. 'I know this is great, you and me being back together. I know I'm the one who wanted it. But sometimes I have this flash of . . . what the hell are we *doing*?'

'You see?' Sadie's crowing voice above the table makes me jump. She's hovering above us like an avenging angel. Focus. Don't look up.

'I . . . I think that's pretty normal,' I say, determinedly gazing at Josh. 'We've both got to adjust, it'll take time.'

'It's not normal!' Sadie cries impatiently. 'He doesn't really want to be here! I told you, he's a puppet! I can make him say or do anything! *You want to marry Lara one day!*' says Sadie loudly into Josh's ear. '*Tell her!*'

Josh's look of confusion deepens. 'Although I do think . . . one day . . . maybe you and I should . . . get married.'

'*And have six children!*'

'I'd like loads of kids, too,' he says bashfully. 'Four . . . or five . . . or even six. What do you think?'

I dart Sadie a look of hatred.

'Hold that thought, Josh,' I say. 'I just need to go to the loo.'

I have never moved so quickly as I do across that restaurant. In the

Ladies' I bang the door shut and glower at Sadie. 'What are you doing?'

'Proving a point. He has no mind of his own.'

'He does!' I say furiously. 'And just because you're prompting him to say these things, it doesn't prove he doesn't love me. He probably *does* want to get married to me, deep down! *And* have lots of kids!'

'You think so?' Sadie says scoffingly.

'Yes! You couldn't make him say anything he didn't genuinely believe on some level.'

'You think?' Sadie's head jerks up and her eyes glitter at me for a moment. 'Very well. Challenge accepted.' She zooms towards the door.

'What challenge?' I say in horror. 'I didn't challenge you!'

I hurry back into the restaurant—but Sadie streaks ahead of me. I can see her yelling in Josh's ear. I can see his eyes glazing over.

She vanishes and I approach the table nervously. Josh looks up with a punch-drunk expression and my heart sinks. What's she been saying?

'So!' I begin brightly. 'Have you decided what to eat yet?'

Josh doesn't even seem to hear. It's as though he's in a trance.

'Josh!' I snap my fingers. 'Josh, wake up!'

'Sorry, I was miles away. Lara, I've just been thinking.' He gazes at me with great intensity. 'I think I should become an inventor.'

'An *inventor*?' I gape at him.

'And move to Switzerland.' Josh is nodding seriously. 'It's just come to me, out of nowhere. This amazing . . . insight. I have to change my life. At once.'

I will murder her.

'Josh . . .' I try to keep calm. 'You don't want to move to Switzerland. You don't want to be an inventor. You work in advertising.'

'No, no. You don't understand. I've been on the wrong path. It's all falling into place. I want to go to Geneva and retrain in astrophysics.'

'You're not a scientist! How can you be an astrophysicist?'

'But maybe I was *meant* to study science,' he says fervently. 'Didn't you ever hear a voice inside your head, telling you to change your life? I was just sitting here, minding my own business, when the inspiration came to me.' He's overflowing with enthusiasm. 'Like a realisation. Like when I realised I should be back with you. It's exactly the same.'

His words are like a splinter of ice in my heart. For a few moments I can't bring myself to speak.

'Is it . . . exactly the same?' I say at last.

'Well, of course.' Josh reaches across the table. 'Don't get upset.

Come with me to Geneva. We'll start a new life. And do you want to know the other idea I've just had, out of the blue?' His face glows with happiness. 'I want to open a zoo. What do you think?'

I want to cry. I think I might cry. 'Josh . . .'

'No, hear me out. We start an animal charity. Get some funding . . .'

Tears are welling up in my eyes as he talks. *OK*, I'm saying savagely to Sadie in my mind. *I get it. I GET it.*

'Josh . . . Why did you want to get back together with me?'

There's silence. Josh still has that trancey look in his eyes.

'I don't remember. Something just told me it was the right thing to do. This voice in my head. It told me I still loved you.'

'But *after* you heard the voice.' I try not to sound too desperate. 'Did you feel like all your old feelings for me were kicking in?'

'Well, it was like I heard this voice in my head—'

'*Forget the voice!*' I practically scream at him. 'Was there anything else?'

Josh frowns irritably. 'What else would there be?'

'The photo of us!' I'm scrabbling desperately. 'On your phone. You must have kept that for a reason.'

'Oh. That.' Josh's face softens. 'I love that picture.' He gets his phone out and looks at it. 'My favourite view in all the world.'

'I see,' I say at last. My throat is aching from trying not to cry. I think, finally, I do see. For a while I can't say a word. I was so convinced. I was so sure that once he was back with me he'd realise. We'd click. It would be fantastic, like it was before. But maybe I've been thinking about a different Josh, all this time. There was real-life Josh and there was Josh-in-my-head. And they were almost, *almost* exactly the same, except for one tiny detail. One loved me and the other one didn't.

I lift my head and look at him now as though for the first time. He's still the same person. It's just . . . I'm not the violin to his bow.

'Josh, listen,' I say at last. 'I don't think you should move to Geneva. Or train as an astrophysicist. Or open a zoo. Or . . .' I swallow hard, psyching myself up to say it. 'Or . . . be with me.'

'What?'

'I think this is all a mistake.' I gesture at the table. 'And . . . it's my fault. I'm sorry for pestering you all this time, Josh. I should have let you get on with your life. I won't bother you again.'

Josh looks poleaxed. 'Are you sure?' he says feebly.

'Totally.' As the waiter approaches the table, I close the menu I'm holding. 'We're not going to eat anything after all. Just the bill, please.'

As I walk back to the office from the tube, I feel almost numb. I can't quite process the enormity of what just happened.

I know I did the right thing. I know Josh doesn't love me. I know Josh-in-my-head was a fantasy. And I know I'll come to terms with it. It's just hard to accept. Especially when I could have had him so easily.

'So!' Sadie's voice jolts me out of my reverie. 'Did I prove a point? Don't tell me, it's all over between you?'

'Geneva?' I say coldly. 'Astrophysics?'

Sadie bursts into giggles. 'Too funny!'

She thinks it's all just entertainment. I *hate* her.

'So what happened?' She's bobbing around, her face lit up with glee. 'Did he say he wanted to open a zoo?'

She wants to hear that she was completely right, doesn't she? Well, I'm not going to give her the satisfaction.

'Zoo? No, Josh never mentioned any zoo. Should he have?'

'Oh.' Sadie stops bobbing.

'He mentioned Geneva briefly, but then he realised that was a ridiculous idea. Then he said he'd been hearing this really annoying, whiny voice in his head recently.' I shrug. 'He said he was sorry if he hadn't been making much sense. But the most important thing was, he wanted to be with me. And then we agreed to take things slowly and sensibly.' I stride on, avoiding her eyes.

'You mean you're still seeing each other?' Sadie sounds astounded.

'Of course we are,' I say, as though surprised she's even asking. 'It takes more than a ghost with a loud voice to break up a real relationship.'

Ha. Take that, ghostie.

Sadie glowers at me, and I can tell she can't think of a reply. She looks so disconcerted, I almost feel cheered up. I swing round the corner and into the door of our building.

'There's a girl in your office, by the way,' says Sadie, following me. 'I don't like the look of her one little bit.'

'Girl? What girl?' I hurry up the stairs, wondering if Shireen has come by. I push open the door, stride in—and stop dead with shock.

It's Natalie. What the hell is Natalie doing here?

She's right there in front of me. Sitting in *my* chair. Talking on *my* phone. She's looking deeply tanned and wearing a white shirt with a navy pencil skirt, and laughing throatily at something. As she sees me she demonstrates no surprise, just gives me a wink.

'Well, thanks, Janet. I'm glad you appreciate the work,' she says in her confident, drawling way. 'You're right, Clare Fortescue has hidden her light under a bushel. Hugely talented. She's a cert for you. I was determined to woo her . . . no, thank *you*. That's my job, Janet.'

I shoot a shocked glance over at Kate, who gives me a helpless shrug.

'We'll be in touch.' Natalie's still talking. 'Yeah, I'll talk to Lara. She obviously has a few things to learn, but she's a promising girl. Don't write her off.' She winks at me again. 'OK, thanks, Janet. We'll do lunch. Take care now.' As I stare in disbelief, Natalie puts down the phone and smiles at me lazily. 'So, how's tricks?'

It's Sunday morning and I'm still seething. At myself. How could I be so *lame*? On Friday I was so shocked that somehow I let Natalie take charge of the situation. I didn't confront her. I didn't make any of my points. They were all buzzing round my head like trapped flies.

I know *now* all the things I should have said to her. I should have said, 'You can't just come back and act like nothing's happened.' And, 'Don't you dare take credit for finding Clare Fortescue, that was all down to me!' And maybe even, 'So you were fired from your last job, huh? When were you planning to tell me that?'

But I didn't say any of those things. I just gasped and said feebly, 'Natalie! Wow! How come you're . . . What . . .'

And she launched into a long story about how the guy in Goa turned out to be a two-timing asshole and she'd decided to surprise me and wasn't I relieved?

'Natalie,' I began. 'It's been really stressy with you gone—'

'Welcome to big business.' She winked at me again.

'But you just disappeared! We had to pick up all the pieces—'

'Lara. I know. It was tough. But it's OK. Whatever fuck-ups happened while I was gone, I'm here to put them right. Hello, Graham?' She turned to the phone. 'Natalie Masser here.'

And she carried on all afternoon, moving seamlessly from phone call to phone call, so I couldn't get a word in. As she left for the evening she was gabbing on her mobile, and just gave me and Kate a casual wave.

So that's it. She's back. She's acting like she's the boss and she did nothing wrong and we should all be really grateful to her for coming back. If she winks at me one more time I will *throttle* her.

Miserably I wrench my hair into a ponytail. I'm barely making any effort today. Sightseeing does *not* require a flapper dress. And Sadie still thinks I'm going out with Josh, so she's not bossing me around.

I eye Sadie surreptitiously as I do my blusher. I feel a bit bad, lying to her. But then, she shouldn't have been so obnoxious.

'I don't want you coming along,' I warn her for the millionth time. 'So don't even think about it.'

'I wouldn't *dream* of coming along!' she retorts, affronted. 'You think I want to trail along beside you and the ventriloquist's dummy? I'm going to watch television. There's a Fred Astaire season at the moment. Edna and I will have a lovely day together.'

'Good. Well, give her my love,' I say sarcastically.

Sadie's found an old woman called Edna who lives a few streets away and does nothing but watch black and white films. So she goes there most days now, sits on the sofa beside Edna and watches a movie.

I suggested to Ed that we start off our tour at the Tower of London, and as I come out of the tube station into the crisp air, I feel immediately cheered. Never mind about Natalie. Never mind about Josh. Never mind about the necklace. Look at all this. It's fantastic! Ancient stone battlements, towering against the blue sky as they have done for centuries. Beefeaters in their red and gold costumes, like something out of a fairy tale. How could Ed not even have bothered to come here?

Come to think of it, I'm not sure I've ever actually visited the Tower of London before. But I mean, that's different. I live here. I don't have to.

'Lara! Over here!'

Ed's already in the queue for tickets. He's wearing jeans, and a grey T-shirt. As I draw near he looks me up and down with a little smile.

'So you do sometimes wear clothes from the twenty-first century.'

'Very occasionally.' I grin back.

'I was convinced you were going to turn up in another twenties dress. In fact, I found an accessory for myself. Just to keep you company.' He reaches in his pocket and produces a small, rectangular case made of battered silver. He springs it open and I see a deck of playing cards.

'Cool!' I say, impressed. 'Where did you get this?'

'Bid for it on eBay.' He shrugs. 'I always carry a pack of cards. It's 1925,' he adds, showing me a tiny hallmark.

I can't help feeling touched that he went to that effort.

'I love it.' I look up as we arrive at the head of the queue. 'Two adults, please. This is on me,' I add firmly. 'I'm the host.'

I buy the tickets and a book called *Historic London*, and lead Ed to a spot in front of the Tower.

'So, this building you see before you is the Tower of London,' I begin in a knowledgeable, tour-leader tone. 'One of our most important and ancient monuments. One of many, many wonderful sights.'

'When was it built?' asks Ed.

'Um . . .' I look round for a handy sign. There isn't one. Damn. I can't look it up in the guidebook. Not with him watching me expectantly.

'It was in the . . .' I mumble something indistinct. '. . . teenth century.'

'Which century?'

'It dates from . . .' I clear my throat. 'Tudor . . . er . . . Stuart times.'

'Do you mean Norman?' suggests Ed politely.

'Oh. Yes, that's what I meant.' I dart him a suspicious look. How did he know that? Has he been swotting up?

'So, we go in this way.' I lead Ed confidently towards a likely looking rampart, but he pulls me back.

'Actually, I think the entrance is this way, by the river.'

At that moment a Beefeater stops and gives us a friendly beam. I smile back, ready to ask him the way in, but he addresses Ed cheerily.

''Morning, Mr Harrison. How are you? Back again already?'

What just happened? How does Ed know the Beefeaters?

I'm speechless as Ed says, 'Good to see you, Jacob. Meet Lara.'

'Er . . . hello,' I manage feebly.

'OK,' I splutter as soon as the Beefeater has continued on his way. 'What's going on?'

Ed takes one look at my face and bursts into laughter. 'I'll come clean. I was here on Friday. It was a work team-building day out. We were able to chat to some of the Beefeaters.' He pauses, then adds, his mouth twitching, 'That's how I know the Tower was begun in 1078. By William the Conqueror. And the entrance is this way.'

'You could have told me!' I glare at him.

'I'm sorry. You seemed so into the idea and I thought it would be cool to go round with you. But we can go someplace else. You must have seen this a million times. Let's rethink.' He takes the *Historic London* guidebook and starts consulting the index.

Obviously he's right. He saw the Tower on Friday, so why on earth would we go round it again? On the other hand, we've bought the tickets now. And it looks amazing. And I want to see it.

'I want to see the Crown Jewels,' I say in a small voice. 'Now we're here.'

'You mean you've never seen them?' Ed stares incredulously at me. '*You've* never seen the Crown Jewels?'

'I live in London!' I say, nettled at his expression. 'It's different! I can see them any time I want, when the occasion arises. It's just that . . . the occasion has never arisen.'

'Isn't that a bit narrow-minded of you, Lara?' I can tell Ed's loving this. 'Aren't you interested in the heritage of your great city? Don't you think it's criminal to ignore these unique, historic monuments—'

'Shut up!' I can feel my cheeks turning red.

Ed relents. 'Come on. Let me show you your own country's fine Crown Jewels. They're great. I know the whole deal. The Imperial Crown of State contains an enormous diamond, cut from the famous Cullinan Diamond, the largest diamond ever mined.'

'Wow,' I say politely. Obviously Ed memorised the entire Crown Jewels lecture yesterday.

'Uh-huh.' He nods. 'At least, that's what the world thought until 1997. When it was discovered to be a fake.'

'Really?' I stop dead. 'It's fake?'

Ed's mouth twitches. 'Just checking you're listening.'

We see the jewels and we see the ravens and we see the White Tower and the Bloody Tower. In fact, all the towers. Ed insists on holding the guidebook and reading out facts, all the way around. Some of them are true and some of them are bullshit and some . . . I'm not sure. He has this totally straight face with just a tiny gleam in his eye and you honestly can't tell.

At lunchtime we head to a café nearby serving things like Georgian Onion Soup and Wild Boar Casserole. Ed insists on paying since I bought the tickets, and we find a table in the corner by the window.

'So, what else do you want to see in London?' I say enthusiastically. 'What else was on your list?'

Ed flinches and I suddenly wish I hadn't put it like that. His sightseeing list must be a sore point.

'Sorry,' I say awkwardly. 'I didn't mean to remind you—'

'No! It's fine.' He considers his forkful for a moment. 'You know what? You were right, what you said the other day. Shit happens, and you have to get on with life. I like your dad's thing about the escalator. I've thought about that since we talked. Onward and upward.'

'Really?' I can't help feeling touched. I'll have to tell Dad.

'Mmm-hmm.' He chews for a moment, then eyes me questioningly. 'So . . . you said you had a breakup too. When was that?'

Friday. Less than forty-eight hours ago. Even thinking about it makes me want to close my eyes and moan.

'It was . . . a while ago.' I shrug. 'He was called Josh.'

'And what happened? If you don't mind me asking.'

'No, of course not. It was . . . I just realised . . . we weren't . . .' I break off, with a heavy sigh. 'Have you ever felt really, *really* stupid?'

'Never.' Ed shakes his head. 'Although I have on occasion felt really, really, *really* stupid.'

I can't help a little smile. Talking to Ed puts everything into perspective a bit. I'm not the only person in the world to feel like a fool.

'Hey, let's do something that wasn't on your list,' I say on impulse. 'Let's see some sight that was never in the plan. *Is* there anything?'

'Corinne didn't want to go on the London Eye,' he says at last. 'She's scared of heights and she thought it was kinda dumb.'

'London Eye it is,' I say firmly.

I can't believe I called Ed Mr American Frown. He doesn't frown *that* often. And when he does, he's usually thinking of something funny to say. He pours me some wine and I lean back, relishing the view of the Tower, and the prospect of the rest of the day ahead.

'So, why do you carry cards with you?' I say. 'Do you play Patience the whole time or something?'

'Poker. If I can find anyone to play with. You'd be great at poker.'

'I'd be terrible!' I contradict him. 'I'm crap at gambling and—'

'Poker's not about gambling. It's about being able to read people. Your Eastern mind-reading powers would come in handy.'

'Oh right.' I blush. 'Well, my powers seem to have abandoned me.'

'OK then.' He shuffles the pack expertly. 'All you need to know is, do the other players have good cards or bad? So you look at their faces. And you ask yourself, "Is something going on?" And that's the game.'

Ed deals himself three cards and glances at them. Then he gazes at me. 'Good or bad?'

'Dunno,' I say helplessly. 'I'll go with . . . good?'

Ed looks amused. 'Those Eastern powers really did desert you. They're terrible.' He shows me three low cards. 'Now your turn.' He shuffles the pack, deals out three cards and watches me pick them up.

I've got the three of clubs, the four of hearts, and the ace of spades! I study them, then look up with my most blank expression.

'Relax,' says Ed. 'Don't laugh.'

Of course, now he's said that, I can feel my mouth twitching.

'You have a terrible poker face,' says Ed. 'You know that?'

'You're putting me off!' I wriggle my mouth around a bit, getting rid of the laugh. 'OK then, what have I got?'

Ed's dark brown eyes lock on mine. We're both totally silent and still, gazing at each other. After a few seconds I feel a weird flip in my stomach. This feels strange. Too intimate. Like he can see more of me than he should. Pretending to cough, I break the spell and turn away. I take a gulp of wine and look back to see Ed sipping his wine, too.

'You have one high card, probably an ace,' he says. 'And two low ones.'

'No!' I put the cards down. 'How do you know?'

'Your eyes popped out of your face as you saw the ace.' Ed sounds amused. 'It was totally obvious. Like, "Oh wow! A high one!" Then you looked right and left as though you might have given yourself away. Then you put your hand over the high one and gave me a dirty look.'

I can't believe it. I thought I was being really inscrutable.

'But, seriously.' Ed begins shuffling the cards again. 'Your mind-reading trick. It's all based on analysing behavioural traits, isn't it?'

'Er . . . that's right,' I say cautiously.

'That can't have just deserted you. Either you know that stuff or you don't. So what's going on, Lara? What's the story?'

He leans forward intently as though waiting for an answer. I feel a bit thrown. I'm not used to this kind of attention. If he were Josh, I'd have been able to fob him off easily. Josh always took everything at face value.

Because Josh was never really that interested in me.

It hits me like a drench of cold water. A final, mortifying insight. All the time we were together, Josh never challenged me, barely even remembered the fine details of my life. I thought he was just easy-going and laid-back. I loved him for it. But now I understand better. The truth is, he was laid-back because he didn't really care. Not about me.

I feel like I'm stepping out of some trance. I was so busy chasing after him, so desperate, I never looked closely enough at what I was chasing. I never stopped to ask if he really was the answer. I've been such an *idiot*.

I look up to see Ed's dark, intelligent eyes still keenly scanning me. And in spite of myself I feel a sudden weird exhilaration that he, someone I barely know, wants to find out more about me. I can see it in his face: he's not asking for the sake of it. He genuinely wants to know the truth. Only I can't tell him. Obviously.

'It's . . . quite tricky to explain. Quite complicated.' I drain my glass, and beam distractingly at Ed. 'Come on. Let's go to the London Eye.'

As we arrive at the South Bank, it's buzzing with Sunday-afternoon tourists, buskers and secondhand-book stalls. The London Eye is creeping round like a massive ferris wheel, and I can see people in each transparent pod, peering down at us.

A jazz band is playing an old twenties tune to a crowd of onlookers, and as we pass I can't help meeting Ed's eye. He does a couple of Charleston steps and I twirl some imaginary beads at him.

'Very good!' says a bearded guy in a hat, approaching us with a bucket for donations. 'Are you interested in jazz?'

'We're interested in the 1920s,' says Ed firmly and winks at me.

'We're holding an open-air jazz event in Jubilee Gardens next week,' says the guy. 'You want tickets? Ten per cent off if you buy them now.'

'Sure,' says Ed, after glancing at me. 'Why not?'

He hands the guy some money, takes two tickets and we walk on.

'So,' says Ed after a bit. 'We could go to this jazz thing . . . together. If you wanted to.'

'Er . . . right. Cool. I'd like that.'

He gives me one of the tickets and I put it in my bag a little awkwardly. Is he asking me on a date? Or . . . what? What are we doing?

I reckon Ed must be thinking something along the same lines, because as we join the queue for the Eye, he suddenly looks at me with a kind of quizzical expression.

'Hey, Lara. Tell me something.'

'Er, OK.' I'm nervous. He's going to ask about me being psychic again.

'Why d'you burst into my office? Why d'you ask me on a date?'

A million times worse. What am I supposed to say?

'That's . . . a good question,' I parry. 'And . . . and I have one for you. Why did you come? You could have turned me down!'

'I know.' Ed looks mystified. 'You want to know the truth? It's almost a blur. I can't decipher my own thought processes. A strange girl arrives in the office. Next moment I'm on a date with her.' He turns to me with renewed focus. 'C'mon. You must have had a reason. Had you seen me around the place or something?'

There's an edge of hope to his voice. Like he's hoping to hear something that will make his day better. I feel a sudden, horrible pang of guilt. He has no idea he's just being used.

'It was . . . a dare with a friend. I don't know why I did it.'

'Right.' His voice is as relaxed as before. 'So I was a random dare. Doesn't sound so good to the grandkids.'

I know he's joking, I know this is all banter. But as I glance up I can see it in his face. I can see the warmth. He's falling for me. No, scratch that—he *thinks* he's falling for me. But it's all fake. He's been manipulated by Sadie as much as Josh was. None of this is real, none of this means anything . . .

I feel suddenly, ridiculously upset. This is all Sadie's fault. She creates trouble wherever she goes. Ed is a really, really nice guy and he's been screwed up enough all ready and she's totally messed with him and it's not fair . . .

'Ed.' I swallow. 'You might think you like me. But you don't.'

'I do.' He laughs. 'I really like you.'

'You don't.' I'm struggling here. 'You're not thinking for yourself. I mean . . . this isn't real.'

'Feels pretty real to me.'

'I know it does. But you don't understand . . .' I break off, feeling helpless. There's silence for a moment—then Ed's face abruptly changes.

'Oh, I see.'

'You do?' I say doubtfully.

'Lara, you don't have to soften me with an excuse.' His smile turns wry. 'If you've had enough, just say. It's been fun and I appreciate the time you've taken, thanks very much—'

'No!' I say in dismay. 'Stop it! I'm not trying to bail out! I'm having a really good time today. And I want to go on the London Eye.'

Ed's eyes scan my face. 'Well, so do I,' he says at last.

'Well . . . good.'

We're so engrossed in our conversation, we haven't noticed the gap growing in the queue ahead of us.

'Get on with it!' A guy behind us suddenly prods me. 'You're on!'

'Oh!' I wake up. 'Quick, we're on!' I grab Ed's hand and we run towards the big oval pod. I step on, still hand in hand with Ed, and we beam at each other, all the awkwardness gone.

It's brilliant. I mean, it just is *brilliant*. We've been right up to the top and seen the whole city stretching out below us like the *A–Z* come to life. I've knowledgeably pointed out St Paul's, and Buckingham Palace, and Big Ben. Now I've taken charge of the *Historic London* guidebook. It doesn't have a section on the London Eye, but I'm reading out facts from it anyway, which I'm making up.

'The pod is made of transparent titanium melted down from eye

glasses,' I inform Ed who is gazing through the glass. 'If plunged under-
water, each pod will automatically convert to a fully operational sub-
marine . . .' I trail off. I can tell he isn't really listening. 'Ed?'

He turns round to face me, his back against the glass wall of the pod.

'You want to know something, Lara?' He glances round to check no
one is listening, but everyone else in the pod has piled to the other side,
watching a police boat on the Thames.

'Maybe,' I say warily.

Ed's face flickers with a smile. 'You asked me why I agreed to go on
that first date with you.'

'Oh. That. Well, it doesn't matter,' I say hurriedly. 'Don't feel you
have to tell me—'

'No, I want to tell you. It was . . . freaky.' He pauses. 'I felt as though
something inside my head was *telling* me to say yes. The more
I resisted, the louder it shouted. Does that make any sense?'

'No,' I say hastily. 'None. I've no idea. Maybe it was . . . God.'

'Maybe.' He gives a sudden short laugh. 'I could be the new Moses.'
He hesitates. 'Point is, I've never felt such a strong impulse, or voice,
or whatever it was. Kinda blew me away.' He takes a step forward.
'And whatever instinct it was, it was right. Spending time with you is
the best thing I could have done. I feel like I've woken up from a
dream, or limbo . . . and I want to thank you.'

'There's no need!' I say at once. 'It was my pleasure. Any time.'

'I hope so.' His tone is oblique and I feel a bit flustered under his gaze.

I meet Ed's gaze head on, trying to appear as if nothing's concerning
me at all. Except quite a lot of things are concerning me. The heat rushing to my face. The way Ed's eyes are boring into mine. They're giving
me twinges. Truth is, he's giving me twinges all over the place.

I don't know how I ever thought he wasn't good-looking. I think
I must have been a bit blind.

'Is something going on?' says Ed softly.

'I . . . I don't know.' I can barely speak. 'Is something going on?'

He puts a hand up to my chin and cups it for a moment. Then he
leans forward and pulls my face gently up to his with both hands and
kisses me. His mouth is warm and sweet and his stubble is grazing
my skin, but he doesn't seem to care and . . . oh God. *Yes, please.* All my
twinges have turned into singing, dancing urges. As he wraps his arms
round me and pulls me tighter to him, two thoughts are jostling in my
brain. He's so different from Josh. He's so *good*.

I'm not having many other thoughts right now. At least, you couldn't really call them thoughts so much as ravening desires.

At last Ed pulls away, his hands cradling the back of my neck.

'You know . . . that wasn't the plan for today,' he says. 'Just in case you were wondering.'

'Wasn't my plan, either,' I say breathlessly. 'Not at all.'

He kisses me again, and I close my eyes, inhaling the scent of him, wondering how much longer this London Eye ride has to go. As though reading my mind, Ed releases me.

'Maybe we should look at the view one more time,' he says with a small laugh. 'Before we land.'

'I suppose we should.' I give him a reluctant smile.

Arm in arm, we turn to face the transparent wall of the pod. And I scream in fright. Hovering outside the pod, looking in with searing eyes, is Sadie. She saw us. She saw us kissing.

Shit. Oh, shit. As I quiver in terror, she advances through the transparent wall, her nostrils flared, her eyes flashing, making me back away on stumbling legs as if I really have seen a terrifying ghost.

'Lara?' Ed is staring at me in shock. 'Lara, what's wrong?'

'How *could* you?' Sadie shrieks. '*How could you?*'

'I . . . I didn't . . . it wasn't . . .' I want to tell her I didn't plan all this—

'*I saw you!*'

She gives a sudden huge, racking sob, wheels round and disappears.

'Sadie!' I rush forward and clutch at the transparent wall of the pod.

'Lara! What happened?' Ed looks totally freaked out. I suddenly notice that all the other people in the pod are goggling at me.

'Nothing!' I manage. 'Sorry. I just . . . I was . . .' As he puts his arm round me, I flinch. 'Ed, I'm sorry, I can't . . .'

After a pause Ed takes his arm away. 'Sure.'

We've reached the ground now. Shooting anxious glances at me, Ed ushers me off the pod and onto solid ground.

'So.' His tone is cheerful, but I can tell he's perturbed. 'What's up?'

'I can't explain,' I say miserably. 'Ed, I'm so sorry. I can't do . . . this. It's been a lovely day, but . . .'

'But . . . it didn't go according to plan?' he says slowly.

'No, it's not that! It's . . . it's complicated. I need to sort myself out.'

I look up at him, willing him to understand.

'No problem.' He nods. 'I get it. Things aren't always clear-cut.' He hesitates, then touches my arm briefly. 'Let's leave it here then. It's been a great day. Thanks, Lara. You've been very generous with your time.'

He's retreated into his formal, gentlemanly style. All the warmth and joking between us has ebbed away. He's protecting himself, I suddenly realise with a pang. He's going back into his tunnel.

'Ed, I'd love to see you again some time,' I say desperately. 'Once things are . . . sorted out.'

'I'd like that.' I can tell he doesn't believe me. 'Let me call you a taxi.'

'No. I'll just stay here a bit and wander about, get my head straight.' I muster a smile. 'Thanks. For everything.'

He gives me a farewell wave then heads off into the crowd. I stare after him, feeling crushed. I like him. I really, really like him. And now he feels hurt. And so do I. And so does Sadie. What a mess.

'So this is what you do behind my back!' Sadie's voice in my ear makes me jump and clasp my chest. 'You lying snake. You back-stabber. I came here to see how you were getting on with Josh. With *Josh*!'

She whirls round in front of me, looking so incandescent, I find myself backing away again. 'I'm sorry,' I stutter. 'I'm sorry I lied to you. I didn't want to admit that Josh and I broke up. But I didn't mean for Ed and me to kiss. I didn't mean any of this, I didn't plan it—'

'I don't care whether you planned it or not!' she shrieks. 'Keep your hands off him!'

'Sadie, I'm really sorry—'

'*I* found him! *I* danced with him! He's mine! Mine! *Mine!*'

She's so self-righteous, and so livid, and she's not even listening to what I'm saying. And suddenly, from underneath all my guilt, I feel a surge of resentment.

'How can he be yours?' I hear myself yelling. 'You're dead! Haven't you realised that yet? You're *dead*! He doesn't even know you *exist*!'

'Yes, he does! He can hear me!'

'So what? It's not like he'll ever meet you, is it? You're a ghost! A *ghost*!' All my misery at the situation is bursting out in a vent of anger. 'Talk about self-deluded! Talk about not facing up to the truth, Sadie! You keep telling me to move on! How about *you* move on?'

Even as I'm uttering the words, I'm realising how they sound; how they might be misinterpreted. And I'm wishing beyond anything I could take them back. A tremor of shock passes across Sadie's face. She looks as though I've slapped her. She can't think I meant . . . Oh God.

'Sadie, I wasn't . . . I didn't . . .' My words are all jumbled up in my mouth. I don't even quite know what I want to say.

'You're right,' she says at last, hollow-eyed. All the spirit has gone out of her voice. 'You're right. I'm dead.'

'No, you're not!' I say in distress. 'I mean, OK, maybe you are. But—'

'I'm dead. You don't want me. He doesn't want me. What's the point?'

She starts walking away towards Waterloo Bridge and disappears from view. Racked with guilt, I hurry after her and up the steps. She's already halfway along the bridge and I run to catch up. She's standing still, staring out towards St Paul's Cathedral.

'Sadie!' My voice is almost lost in the wind. 'I wasn't thinking, I was just angry at you, I was talking rubbish—'

'No, you're right.' She speaks fast, without turning her head. 'I'm as self-deceiving as you. I thought I could have some last fun in this world. I thought I could have a friendship. Make a difference.'

'You have made a difference!' I say in dismay. 'Please don't talk like this. Look, come home, we'll put on some music, have a good time—'

'Don't patronise me! I know what you really think. You don't care about me, no one cares about me, some meaningless old person—'

'Sadie, stop it, that's not true—'

'*I heard you at the funeral!*' Sadie suddenly erupts passionately, and I feel a sudden, cold horror. She *heard* us?

'I heard you at the funeral,' she repeats, regaining her dignity. 'I heard all the family talking together. Nobody wanted to be there. Nobody mourned me. I was just a "million-year-old nobody".'

I feel queasy with shame. We were so callous and horrible. All of us.

Sadie's gazing fixedly over my shoulder. 'Your cousin put it exactly right. I didn't achieve anything in my life, I left no mark, I wasn't anything special. I don't know why I bothered living, really!'

'Sadie, please don't.' I swallow.

'I didn't have love,' she continues inexorably, 'or a career. I didn't leave behind children or achievements or anything to speak of. The only man I ever loved . . . forgot about me.' There's a sudden shake in her voice. 'I lived for one hundred and five years, but I didn't leave a trace. Not one. I meant nothing to anybody. And I still don't.'

'Yes, you do. Of course you do,' I say desperately. 'Sadie, please—'

'I've been a fool, clinging on. I'm in your way.' With dismay, I see that her eyes are glimmering with tears.

'No!' I grasp at her arm, even though I know it's useless. I'm almost crying myself. 'Sadie, *I* care about you. And I'm going to make it up to you. We'll dance the Charleston again, and we'll have some fun, and I'm going to get your necklace for you if it kills me.'

'I don't care about the necklace any more.' Her voice wobbles. 'Why should I? It was all nothing. My life was all for nothing.'

To my horror, she disappears over the side of Waterloo Bridge.

'Sadie!' I yell. 'Sadie, come back. Sa-die!' I'm peering desperately down at the murky, swirling water, tears streaming down my cheeks.

'Oh my *God*!' A girl beside me in a checked coat suddenly notices me and gasps. 'Someone's jumped in the river! *Help!*'

'No, they haven't!' I lift my head, but she's not listening, she's beckoning her friends. Before I can gather my wits, people are crowding round the parapet and gazing down at the water.

'Someone's jumped!' I can hear people saying. 'Call the police!'

'No, they *haven't!*' I say, but I'm drowned out. I shout, waving my arms. 'There's been a mistake! Everything's fine! No one's jumped. Repeat, no one's jumped!'

'Then who were you talking to?' The girl in the checked coat gives me an accusing look.

'I was talking to a ghost,' I say shortly. I turn away before she can reply, and push my way through the crowd.

She'll come back, I tell myself. When she's calmed down and forgiven me. She'll come back.

Ten

BUT NEXT MORNING the flat is still and silent. Normally Sadie appears as I'm making a cup of tea, perching on the work surface and making rude comments about my pyjamas. Today there's nothing. I fish my tea bag out of my cup and look around the kitchen.

'Sadie? Sadie, are you there?'

There's no reply. The air feels dead and empty.

As I get ready for work, it's weirdly quiet without Sadie's constant babble. Holding my tea, I go round the whole flat, calling out, but there's no response. God knows where she is or what she's feeling . . . I feel a fresh spasm of guilt as I remember her hollow face.

Anyway, there's nothing I can do about it now. If she wants me, she knows where to find me.

I get to work just after nine thirty to find Natalie already on the phone. 'Yeah. That's what I said to him, babe.' She winks at me and taps her watch. 'In a bit late, aren't you, Lara? Got into bad habits when I was away? Anyway, babe . . .' She swivels back again.

Bad habits? *Me?* I'm seething. Who does she think she is?

'Natalie,' I say as she puts the phone down. 'I need to talk to you.'

'And I need to talk to *you*.' Her eyes gleam at me. 'Ed Harrison, eh?'

'What?' I say, confused.

'Ed Harrison,' she repeats impatiently. 'You've kept him a bit quiet.'

'What do you mean? How do you know about Ed?'

'*Business People!*' Natalie turns a magazine towards me, open at a picture of me and Ed. 'Good-looking chap.'

'I'm not . . . it's a business thing,' I say hurriedly, looking up.

'Oh, I know, Kate told me. You're back with Josh.' Natalie gives a mock yawn to show just how interesting my love life is to her. 'That's my point. This Ed Harrison is a nice juicy bit of talent. Do you have a plan?'

'Plan?'

'For placing him!' Natalie speaks with elaborate patience. 'We're a head-hunting firm. We place people in jobs. That's how we make *money*.'

'Oh!' I try to hide my horror. 'No, no, you don't understand. He's not that kind of contact. He doesn't want a new job.'

'He *thinks* he doesn't,' Natalie corrects me.

'No, really, forget it. He hates head-hunters. He's not interested.'

'Yet.' Natalie winks and I feel like hitting her.

'Stop it! He's not!'

'Everyone has their price. When I dangle the right salary in front of him, believe me, the story will change.'

'It won't! Not everything's about money, you know.'

Natalie bursts into mocking laughter. 'What's happened while I've been away? Have we turned into the bloody Mother Teresa Agency? We need to earn *commission*, Lara. We need to make a *profit*.'

'I know,' I snap. 'That's what I was doing while you were lying on the beach in Goa, remember?'

'Ooh!' Natalie tosses back her head and laughs. 'Miaou!'

She's not remotely shamefaced. How could I have thought she was my best friend? I feel like I don't even know her.

'Just leave Ed alone,' I say fiercely. 'He doesn't want a new job. I'm serious. He won't talk to you, anyway—'

'He already did.' She leans back, looking pleased with herself.

'What?'

'I called him this morning.'

'But he doesn't take calls from head-hunters,' I say. 'How did you—'

'Oh, I didn't give my name at first,' says Natalie gaily. 'Just said I was a friend of yours and you'd asked me to call. We had quite a little chat, as it happens. He didn't seem to know anything about Josh, but I gave him the full picture.' She raises her eyebrows. 'Interesting. Keeping the boyfriend from him for a reason, were you?'

I feel a sudden, rising dismay. 'What exactly did you say about Josh?'

'Ooh, Lara!' Natalie looks delighted at my discomfiture. 'Were you planning on a little intrigue with him? Have I ruined things for you?' She puts a hand over her mouth. 'Sorry!'

I have to talk to Ed. Now. Grabbing my mobile, I hurry out of the office, bumping into Kate on the way. 'Lara! Are you OK?'

'*Natalie*,' I say shortly, and she winces.

'I think she's worse with a tan,' she whispers, and I can't help a reluctant smile. 'Are you coming in?'

'In a minute. I have to make a call. It's kind of . . . private.' I head out onto the street, speed-dialling Ed's number.

'Ed Harrison's office,' a woman's voice answers.

'Hi.' I try not to sound as apprehensive as I feel. 'It's Lara Lington here. Could I possibly speak to Ed?'

As I'm put on hold, my mind can't help travelling back to yesterday. I can remember exactly how his arms felt around me. And then that awful way he retreated into his shell. It makes me flinch just remembering.

'Hi, Lara. What can I do for you?' His voice comes on the line, formal and businesslike. Not one shred of warmth. My heart sinks slightly.

'Ed, I gather my colleague Natalie rang you this morning. I'm so sorry. It won't happen again. And I also wanted to say . . .' I hesitate awkwardly. 'I'm really sorry about how yesterday ended.'

And I don't have a boyfriend, I want to add. *And I wish we could rewind and go up on the London Eye and you'd kiss me again.*

'Lara, please don't apologise.' Ed sounds remote. 'I should have realised you had more . . . commercial concerns. That's why you were trying to let me down. I appreciate that little blast of honesty, at any rate.'

Is that what he thinks? That I was just after him for business?

'Ed, no,' I say quickly. 'It wasn't like that. I really enjoyed our day together. I know things went a bit weird, but there were . . . complicating factors. I can't explain—'

'Please don't patronise me,' Ed interrupts. 'You and your colleague clearly cooked up a little plan. I don't particularly appreciate your methods, but I suppose you have to be applauded for perseverance.'

'It's not true!' I say in horror. 'Ed, you can't believe anything Natalie says. You *know* she's unreliable. You can't believe we planned it!'

'Lara!' Ed sounds at the end of his tether. 'Don't push it. I know you have a boyfriend. The whole thing was a sting. I should've realised the instant you turned up in my office. Maybe you did your research and found out about Corinne and me. Figured you could get to me that way. God knows what you people are capable of.'

His voice is so harsh, so hostile, I flinch.

'I wouldn't do that! I would never do that, never!' My voice trembles. 'Ed, what we had was real. We danced . . . we had such fun . . . You *can't* think it was all fake.'

'And you don't have a boyfriend, I suppose?'

'No! Of course not.' I correct myself. 'I mean yes, I did, but I split up with him on Friday—'

'On Friday!' Ed gives a humourless laugh which makes me wince. 'How convenient. Lara, I don't have time for this.'

'Ed, please.' My eyes are welling up. 'You have to believe me—'

''Bye, Lara.'

The phone goes dead. I stand for a moment, motionless, little darts of pain shooting round my body. There's no point calling back. He'll never believe me. And there's nothing I can do.

No. I'm wrong. There is something I can do.

I fiercely brush my eyes and turn on my heels. As I arrive upstairs, Natalie's on the phone, filing her nails and laughing uproariously at something. I head for her desk, reach over and cut the line.

'What the fuck?' Natalie spins round. 'I was on the phone!'

'Well now you're not,' I say evenly. 'And you're going to listen to me. I've had enough. You can't behave like this.'

'What?' She laughs.

'You swan off to Goa and expect us to pick up the pieces. Then you come back and take credit for a client who I found! Well, I'm not going to put up with it! I'm not going to be used any more! In fact . . . I can't work with you any more!'

I wasn't actually planning to say that last bit. But now I've said it, I realise I mean it. I can't work with her. She's toxic.

'Lara, babe, you're stressed out. Why don't you take the day off—'

'I don't need the day off!' I explode. 'I need you to be honest! You lied about being fired from your last job!'

'I was *not* fired.' An ugly scowl suddenly appears on Natalie's face. 'It was a mutual decision. They were total assholes, anyway, they never appreciated me properly—' She suddenly seems to realise how she's sounding. 'Lara, come on. You and me, we're going to make a great team.'

'We're not!' I shake my head. 'Natalie, I don't think like you! I don't work like you! It's *not* all about salary! It's about the package, the person, the company . . . the whole picture. Matching people. Making it right for everyone. And if it's not about that, it *should* be.'

I'm still half hoping that I might get through to her somehow. But her incredulous expression doesn't alter one iota.

'Matching people!' She bursts into derisive laughter. 'Newsflash, Lara. This isn't a lonely hearts bureau!'

'I want to break up our partnership,' I say, my jaw set. 'It was a mistake. I'll speak to the lawyer.'

'Whatever. But you're not poaching any of my clients. It's in our agreement. So don't get any bright ideas about ripping me off.'

'Wouldn't dream of it,' I say tightly.

'Go on then.' Natalie shrugs. 'Clear your desk. Do whatever you've got to do.'

I glance over at Kate. She's watching us, utterly aghast.

'Sorry,' I mouth. In response, she gets out her phone and starts texting something. A moment later, my phone bleeps and I pull it out.

> I don't blame u. If u start a company can I come? Kx

I text back:

> Of course. But I don't know what I'm going to do yet. Thanks, Kate. L xx

Natalie is ostentatiously typing at her computer as if I don't exist.

My throat is tight as I start packing my stuff into an empty cardboard box. My hole punch. My pen holder.

'But if you think you can set up on your own and do what I do, you're wrong,' Natalie suddenly lashes out. 'You don't have any contacts. You don't have any expertise. All your airy-fairy "I want to give people great jobs"—that's not going to run a business. And don't expect me to give you a job when you're starving in the street.'

I pick up my box, and head over to Kate to give her a hug.

'Bye, Kate. Thanks for everything. You're a star.'

'Lara, good luck.' She whispers, 'I'll miss you,' in my ear.

'Bye, Natalie,' I add shortly as I head to the door.

I push it open and walk to the lift, press the button and heft the box in my arms. I feel a bit numb. What am I going to do now?

'Sadie?' I say out of habit. But there's no reply. Of course there isn't. Sadie's so proud, she'd never make the first move. She'll be waiting somewhere; waiting for me to come and apologise. But where?

The lift arrives at the ground floor, but I don't move. I've left my job. I have no idea what my future is. But I refuse to wallow. Or cry. Or drone on about it. I can almost hear Sadie's voice in my ear. *Darling, when things go wrong in life, you lift your chin, put on a ravishing smile, mix yourself a little cocktail . . .*

'Tallyho!' I say to my reflection in the grimy mirror, just as Sanjeev who works on the ground floor walks into the lift.

'Sorry?' he says.

I summon the most ravishing smile I can. (At least, I hope it's ravishing as opposed to deranged-looking.) 'I'm leaving. Bye, Sanjeev.'

'Oh,' he says in surprise. 'Well, good luck. What are you doing next?'

I don't even pause to think. 'I'll be doing a bit of ghost-hunting,' I say.

'Ghost-hunting?' He looks confused. 'Is that like . . . head-hunting?'

'Kind of.' The doors open, I smile again and head out of the lift.

Where is she? This is getting beyond a joke. I've spent three days searching. I've been to every vintage shop I can think of and hissed 'Sadie?' through the racks of clothes. I've knocked on the doors of all the flats in this building, and called out, 'I'm looking for my friend Sadie!' on the doorstep, loud enough for her to hear. I've been to the Flashlight Club and peered among the dancers on the dance floor. But there was no sight of her.

Yesterday I went to Edna's house and made up a story about my cat being lost, which resulted in both of us going round the house calling 'Sadie? Puss, puss, puss?' But there was no answer.

Looking for lost ghosts is a total pain, it turns out. Nobody can see them. Nobody can hear them. You can't pin a photo to a tree with 'Missing: Ghost' on it. You can't ask anyone, 'Have you seen my friend the ghost? Looks like a flapper, shrieky voice—ring any bells?'

I head out to a café, order a cappuccino and slump into a chair. It's starting to get me down, all this searching. What if I never find her?

But I can't let myself think like that. I have to keep going. Partly because I refuse to admit defeat. Partly because the longer Sadie's gone, the more worried I am about her. And partly because, if I'm honest, I'm clinging onto this. While I'm searching for Sadie, it feels as if the rest of my life is on hold. I don't have to think about the where-does-my-career-go-now? thing. Or the what-do-I-tell-my-parents? thing. Or the how-could-I-have-been-so-stupid-about-Josh? thing.

Or even the Ed thing. Which still upsets me whenever I let myself think about it. So . . . I just won't. I'll focus on Sadie.

Briskly I unfold my list of 'Find Sadie' ideas, but most of them are crossed out. The only entries left are 'Try other dancing clubs?' and 'Nursing home?'

I consider the nursing home for a moment as I sip my coffee. Sadie wouldn't go back there, surely. She hated it. She couldn't even face going in. Why would she be there now? But it's worth a try.

I almost put on a disguise before I arrive at the Fairside Home, I'm so nervous. I mean, here I am, the girl who accused the staff of murder.

Did the police tell them, 'It was Lara Lington who besmirched your good name'? Because if so, I'm dead meat. They'll surround me in a nurse mob and kick me with their clumpy shoes. And I'll deserve it.

But as Ginny opens the door, she shows no sign of knowing I'm the false-accusation-maker. Her face creases into a warm smile.

'Lara! What a surprise! Can I help you with that?'

I'm laden down with cardboard boxes and a massive flower arrangement, which is starting to slip out of my arms.

'Oh, thanks,' I say gratefully, handing her one. 'It's got boxes of chocolates in it for you all. And these flowers are for the staff, too . . .' I follow her into the hall and put the arrangement on the table. 'I just wanted to say thank you for looking after Great-Aunt Sadie so well.'

'How lovely! Everybody will be very touched!'

'Well,' I say awkwardly. 'On behalf of the family, we're all very grateful and feel bad that we didn't visit my great-aunt . . . more often.'

As Ginny unpacks the chocolates, exclaiming in delight, I surreptitiously sidle towards the stairs and look up them.

'Sadie?' I hiss under my breath. 'Are you here?' I scan the upstairs landing, but there's no sign.

'And what's this?' Ginny is looking at the other box. 'More chocolates?'

'No. Actually that's some CDs and DVDs. For the residents.'

I open it and pull out the CDs. *Charleston Tunes*, *The Best of Fred*

Astaire and *1920s–1940s: The Collection.* 'I just thought sometimes they might like to listen to the tunes they danced to when they were young,' I say. 'Especially the really old residents. It might cheer them up.'

'Lara, how incredibly thoughtful! We'll put one on straight away!' She heads into the day room, which is full of elderly people sitting in chairs and on sofas, with a daytime talk show blaring out of the television. I follow, looking all around the white heads for any sign of Sadie.

'Sadie?' I hiss, looking around. 'Sadie, are you here?'

There's no reply. I should have known this was a ridiculous idea.

'There we are!' Ginny straightens up from the CD player. And then it starts. A scratchy, 1920s band, playing a jaunty, jazzy tune.

On the other side of the room, an old man sitting under a tartan blanket with a tank of oxygen next to him turns his head. I can see the light of recognition coming on in faces around the room. Somebody starts humming along in a quavery voice. One woman even begins tapping her hand, her whole self lit up with pleasure.

'They love it!' says Ginny to me. 'What a good idea! Shame we've never thought of it before!'

I feel a sudden lump in my throat as I watch. They're all Sadie inside, aren't they? They're all in their twenties inside. All that white hair and wrinkled skin is just cladding. The old man with the oxygen tank was probably once a dashing heart-throb. That woman with distant rheumy eyes was once a mischievous young girl. They were all young, with love affairs and friends and parties and an endless life ahead of them . . .

And as I'm standing there, the weirdest thing happens. It's as if I can *see* them, the way they were. I can see their young, vibrant selves, rising up out of their bodies, shaking off the oldness, starting to dance with each other to the music. They're all dancing the Charleston, kicking up their heels skittishly, revelling in it . . .

I blink. The vision has gone. I'm looking at a room full of motionless old people.

I glance sharply at Ginny. But she's just standing there, smiling pleasantly and humming along to the CD, out of tune.

Sadie can't be here. She would have heard the music and come to see what was going on. The trail's gone cold yet again.

'I know what I meant to ask you!' Ginny suddenly turns to me. 'Did you ever find that necklace of Sadie's? The one you were looking for?'

'No, I never did.' I try to smile. 'This girl in Paris was supposed to be sending it to me, but . . . I'm still hoping.'

'Oh well, fingers crossed!' says Ginny.

'Fingers crossed.' I nod. 'Anyway, I'd better go. I just wanted to say hi.'

'Well, it's lovely to see you. I'll show you out.'

As the big front door closes behind me my mobile phone rings shrilly in my pocket. I haul it out, and see Dad's number on the ID display. Oh God. Why is Dad calling? He'll have heard about me leaving my job somehow.

'Hi, Dad,' I say.

'Sorry to disturb you at work.' Dad hesitates. 'I know this may sound odd. But I've got something I need to talk to you about and it's rather important. Could we meet?'

This is weird. I'm really not sure what's going on. We've agreed to meet at Lingtons in Oxford Street, because it's central and we both know it. And also because whenever we arrange to meet up, Dad suggests Lingtons. He's unfailingly loyal to Uncle Bill.

As I arrive at the familiar chocolate-brown and white frontage, I'm quite apprehensive. Maybe Dad's got some really bad news to break. Like Mum's ill. Or *he's* ill.

I push open the door and inhale the familiar scent of coffee, cinnamon and croissants. The brown-velvet chairs and gleaming wooden tables are the same as in every other Lingtons around the world. Uncle Bill is beaming down from a massive poster behind the counter.

'Lara!' Dad waves cheerfully from the head of the queue. 'Just in time! What do you want?'

'Hi.' I give him a hug. 'I'll have a caramel Lingtoncino and a tuna melt.'

You can't ask for a cappuccino, it has to be a Lingtoncino.

We wait for our food and then make our way to a table and sit down.

Dad gives me an affectionate look. 'Lara, I want to ask you a question.'

'Absolutely.' I nod earnestly.

'How is your business going? Really?'

'Well . . . you know. It's . . . it's good.' My voice has shot up two notches. 'We've got some great clients.'

'So you feel you made the right decision? You're enjoying it?'

'Yes,' I say miserably. 'I'm enjoying it.' The thing about lying to your parents is, sometimes you really wish you hadn't. Sometimes you just want to dissolve into tears and wail, 'Dad, it's all gone wrooooong!'

'So, what did you want to talk to me about?' I say, to get off the subject.

'No matter. There was an opportunity I wanted to talk to you about.

But I don't want to throw a spanner in the works. You're doing what you love and doing it well. You don't need a job offer.'

Job offer? My heart is suddenly beating fast. But I mustn't give away my excitement.

'Why don't you tell me about it anyway? Just in case.'

'Well, maybe you're right.' Dad takes a sip of coffee. 'Bill called me yesterday. He said you'd been to see him at his house recently?'

'Oh.' I clear my throat. 'Yes, I did pop round for a chat.'

'Well, he was impressed. What did he describe you as, now?' Dad gives that crooked little smile he gets when he's amused. 'Oh yes, "tenacious". Anyway, the upshot is . . . this.'

He takes an envelope out of his pocket and slides it across the table. Disbelievingly, I open it. It's a letter offering me a job in the Lingtons Human Resources department. It's offering me a salary of six figures.

I feel a bit faint. I look up, to see Dad's face glowing. Despite his cool demeanour, he's obviously really chuffed.

'Bill read it out over the phone. Quite something, isn't it?'

'Why did he send the letter to you? Why not straight to me?'

'Bill thought it would be a nice touch.'

'Oh. Right,' I say. But I can't smile. Something's wrong.

'Smile, darling!' Dad laughs. 'It's a wonderful tribute to you. I mean, Bill doesn't owe us anything. He's done this purely through appreciation of your talent and the goodness of his heart.'

OK, that's what's wrong: Dad's nailed it. I don't believe in Uncle Bill's appreciation of my talent. Nor in the goodness of his heart. He's trying to buy me off. OK, maybe that's putting it too strongly. But he's trying to get me onside. I've got under Uncle Bill's skin, ever since I mentioned Sadie's necklace.

'But I don't want this to sway you,' Dad is saying. 'Mum and I are both so proud of you, Lara, and if you want to carry on with your business, we'll be one hundred per cent behind you. The choice is absolutely up to you. No pressure either way.'

He's saying all the right things. But I can see the hope flickering in Dad's eyes, even if he's trying to hide it.

And Uncle Bill knows that. Why else has he sent this letter via Dad? He's trying to manipulate both of us.

'I think Uncle Bill feels rather bad that he turned you down flat at the funeral,' Dad continues. 'He was very impressed at your persistence. And so am I! I had no idea you were planning to go and ask him again!'

'But I didn't even mention a job! I went to ask him about—' I stop hopelessly. I can't mention the necklace. I can't mention Sadie.

I bury my head in my hands despairingly. It's such a preposterous story. It all sounds so unlikely. And now the necklace is gone and Sadie's gone and I don't know what to think . . . or do . . .

'Lara!' exclaims Dad. 'Darling! Are you all right?'

'I'm fine.' I raise my head. 'Sorry. It's all just a bit overwhelming.'

'This is my fault,' says Dad, his smile fading. 'I've thrown you. I should never have mentioned it. Your business is doing so well—'

Oh God. I can't let this charade go on any longer.

'Dad.' I cut him off. 'The business isn't going well. I lied. I didn't want to tell you.' I'm unable to meet his eye. 'But the truth is . . . it's a disaster. Natalie left me in the lurch and we had a big row and I walked out on her. And . . . and I've split up with Josh again. For good.' I swallow, forcing myself to say it. 'I've finally realised how wrong I got everything with him. He didn't love me. I just really, really wanted him to.'

'I see.' Dad sounds a bit shocked. 'Goodness. Well . . . perhaps this offer has come at just the right time,' he says at last.

'Maybe,' I mumble, still staring at the table.

'What's wrong?' asks Dad gently. 'Darling, why are you resisting this? You *wanted* to work for Uncle Bill.'

'I know. But it's . . . complicated.'

I look at Dad, at his straight face, his honest eyes. If I told him the truth he wouldn't believe any of it.

'Did Uncle Bill mention a necklace at all?' I can't help saying.

'A necklace?' Dad looks puzzled. 'No. What necklace?'

'I . . . it's nothing.' I sigh. I take a sip of Lingtoncino and look up to see Dad watching me. He smiles, but I can tell he's troubled.

'Darling, you have a wonderful opportunity here.' He gestures at the letter. 'A chance for you to get your life back on track. Maybe you should just take it. Don't overthink it. Just take your chance.'

He doesn't understand. How could he? Sadie isn't a problem that doesn't exist. She *does* exist. She's real. She's a person, and she's my friend and she needs me—

Then where is she? says a sudden sharp voice in my head, like a knife thumping into a block. *If she exists, where is she?*

I start in shock. I can't be doubting . . . I can't be thinking . . . I feel a sudden feathery panic. Of course Sadie's real! Of course she is! I mean, I saw her. I heard her. We talked together. We *danced* together, for God's sake. And anyway, how could I possibly have invented her? How would I have known about the necklace? I never even met her!

'Dad,' I ask carefully. 'We never visited Great-Aunt Sadie, did we? Except that time when I was a baby.'

'Actually, that's not quite true.' Dad shoots me a cautious look. 'Mum and I remembered that we once took you to see her when you were six.'

'Six.' I swallow. 'Was she . . . wearing a necklace?'

'She might have been.' Dad shrugs.

I met Great-Aunt Sadie at the age of six. I could have seen the necklace. I could have remembered . . . without realising that I remembered.

My thoughts are in free fall. I feel as though everything's turning on its head. For the first time, I'm seeing a new possible reality. I could have made this whole story up in my head.

'Lara?' Dad peers at me. 'Are you OK, darling?'

I try to smile back at him, but I'm too preoccupied. There are two voices arguing in my head. The first is crying out, 'Sadie's real, you know she is! She's your friend and she's hurt and you have to find her!' The second is calmly intoning, 'She doesn't exist. She never did. You've wasted enough time. Get your life back.'

With fumbling fingers I pick up Uncle Bill's letter and read it through again. If I look at it in a different way, there's nothing sinister. He's just a rich guy trying to help out his niece. I could take the job. I'd be Lara Lington of Lingtons Coffee. My memories of Sadie would melt away. My life would feel normal. It would be so, *so* easy.

'You haven't been home for a while,' Dad says kindly. 'Why not come and spend the weekend? Mum would love to see you.'

'Yes,' I say after a pause. 'I'd like that. I haven't been back for ages.'

Home. The word has riveted me. I never thought of that. Sadie could have gone home. Home to where her old house used to be. She refused ever to go back during her lifetime—but what if she's softened? What if she's right there, right now?

I know the sane, sensible move would be to blank out all thoughts about her. Accept Uncle Bill's job. I know this.

But . . . I just can't. Deep down, I can't believe she's not real. I've come so far, I've tried so hard to find her. I have to give it one last go.

And if she's not there I'll take the job and give up. For good.

'So.' Dad wipes his mouth with a chocolate-brown napkin. 'You look happier, darling. Have you decided which way you want to go?'

'Yes.' I nod firmly. 'I need to go to St Pancras Station.'

Eleven

OK. THIS IS THE VERY, very last place I'm looking. This is her last chance. And I hope she appreciates the effort I've made.

It took me an hour to reach St Albans and another twenty minutes in a taxi to Archbury. And now here I am, standing in a little village square, with a pub and a bus-stop and a weird, modern-looking church. I head over to the green. There's a board with a map of the village, and I quickly locate Archbury Close. That's what they turned Archbury House into after it burned down.

I'm heading past the church when something catches my eye. It's a sign on a gate: THE OLD VICARAGE. I suppose that would have been where the vicar lived in the old days. Which means . . . it would have been where Stephen lived. He was the son of the vicar, wasn't he?

I peer over the gate. It's a big old grey house with a gravel drive and some cars parked at the side. There are some people going in the front door, a group of about six. The family living here must be at home.

The garden's overgrown, with rhododendrons and trees and a path leading round the side of the house. I glimpse an old shed in the distance and wonder if that's where Stephen did his painting. I can just imagine Sadie creeping along that path. I wonder . . .

No. She wouldn't be here. No way. She's got too much dignity. She said it herself, she'd never be a trailer. Never in a million years would she hang around an old boyfriend's house. Especially the old boyfriend who broke her heart and never even wrote to her. It's a stupid idea.

Already my hand is unlatching the gate.

This is the very, very, *very* last place I'm looking.

I crunch over the gravel, trying to think of an excuse to be here. Maybe I'm studying old vicarages? Maybe I'm an architecture student?

I approach the entrance and am raising my hand to ring the old bell when I notice the front door is on the latch. Maybe I can sidle in without anyone noticing. I cautiously push the door open and find myself in a hall with panelled walls and old parquet. To my surprise, a woman with a mousy bob and a Fair Isle jumper is standing behind a table covered with books and leaflets.

'Hello.' She smiles. 'Are you here for the tour?'

The tour? Even better! I can wander round and I don't even have to invent a story. 'Er . . . yes, please. How much?'

'That'll be five pounds.'

Five whole *pounds*? Just to see a vicarage? Bloody hell.

'Here's a guide.' She hands me a leaflet, but I don't look at it. I walk swiftly away from the woman, into a sitting room filled with old-fashioned sofas and rugs, and look round.

'Sadie?' I hiss. 'Sadie, are you here?'

'This would have been where Malory spent his evenings.' The woman's voice makes me jump. I didn't realise she'd followed me.

'Oh, right.' I have no idea what she's talking about. 'Lovely. I'll just go through here . . .' I head into an adjacent dining room. 'Sadie?'

'This was the family dining room, of course . . .'

For God's sake. People should be able to take tours of vicarages without being followed. I head over to the window and look out at the garden. There's not a whisper of Sadie. She's not here. I turn round to leave and almost bump into the woman, standing behind me.

'I take it you're an admirer of his work?' She smiles.

Work? Whose work?

'Er . . . yes,' I say hastily. 'Of course. A great admirer. Very great.' For the first time, I glance down at the leaflet in my hand. The title reads: *Welcome to the House of Cecil Malory*. He's a famous artist, isn't he? I've definitely heard of him. For the first time I feel a spark of interest.

'So is this where Cecil Malory once lived, or something?' I ask.

'Of course.' She looks taken aback by the question. 'That's the reason for the house being restored as a museum. He lived here till 1927.'

1927? Now I'm genuinely interested. If he was living here in 1927, Sadie would have known him, surely.

'Was he a friend of the vicar's son? A guy called Stephen Nettleton?'

'Dear . . .' The woman eyes me, apparently perplexed at the question. 'Surely you know that Stephen Nettleton *was* Cecil Malory. He never used his family name for his work.'

Stephen was Cecil Malory? Stephen . . . is *Cecil Malory*?

'He later changed his name by deed poll,' she continues. 'As a protest against his parents, it's thought. After his move to France . . .'

I'm only half listening. My mind is in turmoil. Stephen became a famous painter. This makes no sense. Sadie never told me he was a famous painter. She would have boasted about it. Didn't she *know*?

'. . . and never reconciled before his tragically young death.' The woman ends on a solemn note. 'Would you like to see the bedrooms?'

'No. Sorry, I'm a bit confused. Steph—I mean Cecil Malory . . . was a friend of my great-aunt, you see. She lived in this village. She knew him. But I don't think she ever realised he became famous.'

'Ah.' The woman nods knowledgeably. 'Well, of course, he wasn't during his lifetime. It wasn't until long after his death that interest began in his paintings. Since he died so young, there is of course a limited body of work, which is why his paintings became so prized and valuable. In the 1980s they shot up in value. That's when his name really became known widely.'

The 1980s. Sadie had her stroke in 1981. She went into care. She had no idea what was going on in the outside world.

'Did he work in a shed in the garden?'

'Yes.' The woman's face lights up. 'If you're interested, we do sell a number of books on Malory . . .' She hurries out and returns holding a slim hardback. 'Details about his early life are a little sketchy, as many village records were lost during the War.' She hands me the book.

'Thanks.' I take it from her and start flipping through. Almost at once I come across a black and white photograph of a man painting on a cliff, captioned 'A rare image of Cecil Malory at work.' I can instantly see why he and Sadie would have been lovers. He's tall and dark and powerful-looking, with dark eyes and an ancient, tattered shirt.

Bastard. How could he treat Sadie so badly? How could he go off to France and forget about her?

'He was a towering talent.' The woman is following my gaze. 'His early death was one of the tragedies of the twentieth century.'

'Yeah, well, maybe he deserved it.' I give her a baleful look. 'Maybe he should have been nicer to his girlfriend. Did you think of *that*?'

The woman looks totally confused.

I flip on, past pictures of the sea and more cliffs . . . and then I suddenly freeze. An eye is looking out of the book at me. It's a blown-up detail from a painting. Just one eye, with long, long lashes and a teasing glint. I know that eye.

'Excuse me.' I can barely get the words out. 'What's this?' I'm jabbing at the book. 'Who's this? Where does this come from?'

'Dear . . .' I can see the woman trying to keep her patience. 'You *must* know that, surely. That's a detail from one of his most famous paintings. We have a version in the library, if you'd like to have a look.'

'Yes.' I'm already moving. 'I would. Please. Show me.'

She leads me down a creaking corridor, through to a dim, carpeted room where a large painting hangs over the fireplace.

'There we are,' she says fondly. 'Our pride and joy.'

I can't reply. My throat's too tight. I stand motionless, just staring.

There she is. Gazing out of the ornate gilt frame, looking as though she owns the world, is Sadie. I've never seen her as radiant as she looks in this picture. Her eyes are massive, dark, luminous with love.

She's reclining on a chaise, naked except for a gauze fabric draped over her shoulder and hips. Her shingled hair exposes the length of her elegant neck. She's wearing glittering earrings. And round her neck, falling down between her pale, gauzy breasts, twined around her fingers, tumbling in a shimmering pool of beads, is the dragonfly necklace.

I can suddenly hear her voice again in my ears. *I was happy when I wore it . . . I felt beautiful. Like a goddess.*

It all makes sense. This is why she wanted the necklace. This is what it means to her. At that time in her life, she was happy. Never mind what happened before or after. Never mind that her heart got broken. At that precise moment, everything was perfect.

'It's amazing.' I wipe a tear from my eye.

'Isn't she wonderful?' The woman gives me a pleased look. 'The detail and brushwork is just exquisite. It's painted with such love. And all the more special, of course, because it's the only one.'

'What do you mean?' I say, confused. 'Cecil Malory painted lots of pictures, didn't he?'

'Indeed. But he never painted any other portraits but this one. He refused to, his whole life. He was asked plenty of times in France as his reputation grew locally, but he would always reply, *"J'ai peint celui que j'ai voulu peindre."*' The woman leaves a poetic pause. '"I have painted the one I wanted to paint."'

I stare at her, dumbfounded, taking this all in. He only ever painted Sadie? His whole life? He'd painted the one he wanted to paint?

'And in this bead . . .' The woman moves towards the painting with a knowing smile. 'Right in this bead here, there's a little surprise. A little secret, if you like.' She beckons me forward. 'Can you see it?'

Obediently, I try to focus on the bead. It just looks like a bead.

'It's almost impossible, except under a magnifying glass . . . here.' She produces a piece of matt paper. Printed on it is the bead from the painting, enlarged massively. As I peer at it, to my astonishment I find I'm looking at a face. A man's face.

'Is that . . .?' I look up.

'Malory.' She nods in delight. 'His own reflection in the necklace. He put himself into the painting. The most miniature, hidden portrait. It was only discovered ten years ago. Like a little secret message.'

'May I see?'

With suddenly shaking hands I take the paper from her and stare at him. There he is. In the painting. In the necklace. Part of her. He never painted another portrait. He'd painted the one he wanted to paint.

He did love Sadie. He did. I know it.

'It's . . . amazing.' I swallow. 'Are there . . . um . . . any more books about him?' I'm desperate to get this woman out of the room. I wait until she's disappeared down the passage, then tilt my head up.

'Sadie!' I call desperately. 'Sadie, can you hear me? I've found the painting! It's beautiful. *You're* beautiful. You're in a museum! And you know what? Stephen didn't paint anyone but you. Never his whole life. He loved you. Sadie, I know he loved you. I *so* wish you could see this . . .'

I break off breathlessly, but the room is silent. As I hear footsteps I quickly turn and smile. The woman hands me a pile of books.

'This is all our available stock. Are you a history-of-art student, or simply interested in Malory?'

'I'm just interested in this painting,' I say frankly. 'And I was wondering. Do you have any idea who this is? What's the painting called?'

'It's called *Girl with a Necklace*. And of course, many people are interested in the identity of the sitter.' The woman launches into what's clearly a well-rehearsed speech. 'Some research has been done, but unfortunately no one has been able to identify her beyond what is believed to be her first name.' She pauses, then adds fondly, 'Mabel.'

'*Mabel?*' I stare at her in horror. 'She wasn't called Mabel!'

'I know to modern ears it may seem a little quaint, but believe me, Mabel was a common name of the time. And on the back of the painting, there's an inscription. Malory himself wrote, "My Mabel".'

'It was a nickname! It was their private *joke*! Her name was Sadie, OK? Sadie Lancaster. I'll write it down. And I know it was her because . . .' I hesitate momentously. 'This is my great-aunt.'

The woman gives me a dubious look. 'Goodness, dear. That's quite a claim. What makes you think she's your great-aunt?'

'I don't think she is, I *know* she is. She lived here in Archbury. She knew Steph—I mean, Cecil Malory. They were lovers. It's definitely her.'

'Do you have any evidence?'

'Well . . . no,' I say, a little frustrated. 'But I know it's her, beyond a doubt. And I'll prove it somehow. And . . .' I pause mid-track as something new occurs to me. 'Hang on a minute. This is Sadie's painting! He gave it to her! She lost it for years, but it's still hers. Or, I suppose, Dad's and Uncle Bill's now. How did you get it? What's it doing here?'

'I'm sorry?' The woman sounds bewildered.

I give an impatient sigh. 'This painting belonged to my great-aunt. But it was lost, years and years ago. The family house burned down and no one could find it. So how did it end up hanging on this wall?'

The woman gives me a wary, puzzled look. 'Dear, you do realise this is only a reproduction, don't you?'

'What?' I feel wrong-footed. 'What do you mean?'

'The original is four times the size, and even more splendid.'

'But . . .' I look at the painting in confusion. It looks pretty real to me. 'So where's the original? Locked up in a safe or something?'

'No, dear,' she says. 'It's hanging in the London Portrait Gallery.'

It's massive. It's radiant. It's a million times better than the one in the house. I've been sitting in front of Sadie's portrait in the London Portrait Gallery for about two hours. I can't drag myself away. She's gazing out at the gallery, her brow clear, her eyes a velvety dark green, like the most beautiful goddess you've ever seen.

I must have seen a hundred people looking at her. Sighing with pleasure. Smiling at each other. Or just sitting down and gazing.

I stand up and consult my watch. It's five o'clock. Time for my appointment with Malcolm Gledhill, the collection's manager.

I make my way back to the foyer, give my name to the receptionist and wait until a voice from behind says, 'Miss Lington?' I turn to see a man in a purple shirt, with a chestnut beard and tufts of hair growing out of his ears, beaming at me with twinkly eyes. He looks like Father Christmas before he grew old, and I can't help warming to him.

'Hi. Yes, I'm Lara Lington.'

'Malcolm Gledhill. Come this way.' He leads me up some stairs and into a corner office overlooking the Thames.

'So.' He hands me a cup of tea and sits down. 'You're here to see me about *Girl with a Necklace*?' He eyes me warily. 'I wasn't sure from your message quite what the issue was. But it's clearly . . . pressing?'

'It is quite pressing.' I nod. 'And the first thing I want to say is, she wasn't just a "girl". She was my great-aunt. Look.'

I reach into my bag and produce my photograph of Sadie at the nursing home, wearing the necklace.

'Look at the necklace,' I add, as I hand it over.

Malcolm Gledhill's cheeks turn pink with excitement. His eyes bulge. He looks up sharply at me, then back at the photo.

'Are you saying,' he says at last, 'that this lady here is the "Mabel" in the painting?'

I really have to knock this Mabel thing on the head.

'She wasn't called Mabel. She hated the name Mabel. She was called Sadie. Sadie Lancaster. She lived in Archbury and she was Stephen Nettleton's lover. She was the reason he was sent to France.'

'Do you have any evidence that this is the case?' Malcolm Gledhill asks. 'Any documents? Any old photographs?'

'She's wearing the necklace, isn't she?' I feel a flicker of frustration. 'She kept it all her life. How much more evidence do you need?'

'Does the necklace still exist?' His eyes bulge again. 'Do you have it? Is she still alive?' As this new thought occurs to him, his eyes nearly pop out of his head. 'Because that would really be—'

'She's just died, I'm afraid.' I cut him off before he can get too excited. 'And I don't have the necklace. But I'm trying to track it down.'

'Well. Clearly, in a case like this, much careful enquiry and research is required before we can come to any definitive conclusion . . .'

'It's her,' I say firmly.

'So I'll refer you, if I may, to our research team. They will look at your claim very carefully, study all the evidence available . . .'

'I'd love to talk to them,' I say politely. 'And I know they'll agree with me. It's her.'

'When did your great-aunt die?' he asks.

'A few weeks ago. But she lived in a nursing home since the 1980s, and she didn't know much about the outside world. She never knew Stephen Nettleton became famous. She never knew that *she* was famous. And that's why I want the world to know her name.'

Malcolm Gledhill nods. 'Well, if the research team comes to the conclusion that she was the sitter in the portrait . . . then believe me, the world *will* know her name. Our marketing team did some research recently, and it turns out *Girl with a Necklace* is the most popular portrait in the gallery. They want to expand her profile. We consider her an exceedingly valuable asset.'

'Really?' I flush with pride. 'She'd have loved to know that.' I pause, then say, 'There's another issue I need to talk to you about. I want to know how you got the painting in the first place. It belonged to Sadie. It was hers. How did you get it?'

Malcolm Gledhill stiffens very slightly.

'I thought this matter might arise at some stage,' he says. 'Following your phone call I went and retrieved the file, and I've looked up the details of the acquisition.' He opens a file on his desk and unfolds an old piece of paper. 'The painting was sold to us in the 1980s.'

'But it was lost in a fire. No one knew where it was. Who on earth sold it to you?'

'I'm afraid . . .' He pauses. 'I'm afraid the vendor asked at the time that all details of the acquisition should be kept confidential.'

'Confidential?' I stare at him in outrage. 'But the painting was Sadie's. Stephen gave it to her. Whoever got hold of it didn't have the right to sell it. You should check these things!'

'We do check these things,' says Malcolm Gledhill, a little defensively. 'The provenance was deemed to be correct at the time. Indeed, a letter was signed in which the vendor made all the correct assurances. I have it here.' His eyes keep dropping down to the paper in his hand. He must be looking at the name of whoever sold it. This is maddening.

'Well, whatever that person said to you, they were *lying*.'

'Believe me,' Malcolm Gledhill says, 'I would like to clear this matter up as much as you would. But I am bound by our confidentiality agreement. I'm afraid my hands are tied.'

'What if I come back with police and lawyers? What if I report the painting as stolen goods and force you to reveal the name?'

Malcolm Gledhill raises his tufty eyebrows high. 'Obviously, if there were a police inquiry, we would comply fully.'

'Well, thank you for your time,' I say formally. 'I'll be in touch again.'

'Of course.' Malcolm Gledhill is closing up the file. 'But before you go, would you like to see the letters?'

'What letters?'

'We have in our archive a bundle of old letters written by Malory,' he explains. 'One of the very few sets of documents salvaged after his death. It's not clear if all or any of them were sent, but one has clearly been posted and returned. Unfortunately the address was scribbled out and despite the very best modern technology, we've been unable to—'

'I'm sorry to interrupt.' I cut him off, trying to hide my agitation. 'But could I see them now?'

An hour later I walk out of the gallery, my mind whirling. When I close my eyes all I can see is that loopy script on tiny sheets of writing paper.

I didn't read all his letters. They felt too private, and I only had a few minutes to look at them anyway. But I read enough to know. He loved her. Even after he'd gone to France. Even after he heard that she'd got married to someone else.

Sadie spent all her life waiting for the answer to a question. And now I know he did too. And even though the affair happened over seventy years ago, even though Stephen is dead and Sadie is dead and there's nothing anyone can do about it, I'm still seething with misery as I stride along the pavement. It was all so unfair. It was all so wrong. They should have been together. Someone obviously intercepted his letters before they got to Sadie. Probably those evil Victorian parents of hers.

There's a stream of people walking past me on their way to Waterloo Station, but I don't feel ready to go back to my flat yet. I need some fresh air. I push my way past a group of tourists, and head up to Waterloo Bridge, my mind still lodged in the past. I keep hearing snatches of Charleston music, as though a twenties band is playing . . .

Hang on a minute. A twenties band *is* playing.

I suddenly focus on the scene below me. A few hundred yards away in Jubilee Gardens, people are gathered on the big square of grass. A bandstand has been put up. A band is playing a jazzy dance number. It's the jazz festival. The one they were leafleting about when I came here with Ed. The one I still have a ticket for, folded up in my purse.

For a moment I just stand there on the bridge, watching the scene. The band is playing the Charleston. Girls in twenties costumes are dancing on the stage, fringes and beads flashing back and forth. And suddenly, among the crowd, I see . . . I think I glimpse . . . No.

For a moment I'm transfixed. Then, without allowing a single hope to flicker to life, I turn and start walking calmly along the bridge, down the steps, towards the sound of the music.

There's a trumpeter in a shiny waistcoat on his feet, playing a tricky solo. All around, people are gathered, watching the Charleston dancers on stage, and on a wooden dancefloor laid on the grass, people are dancing themselves—some in jeans and some in 1920s costumes.

I stop dead, my heart in my throat. I was right. She's up by the bandstand, dancing her heart out. She's in a pale yellow dress, with a matching band round her dark hair. Her head is thrown back and her eyes are closed in concentration.

As I watch, she disappears behind two laughing girls in denim jackets, and I feel a dart of panic. I can't lose her again. Not after all this.

'Sadie!' I push my way through the crowd. 'Sadie! It's me, Lara!'

I catch a glimpse of her again. She's looking all around. She heard me. 'Sadie! Over here!' I'm waving frantically.

Suddenly she sees me and her whole body goes motionless. Her expression is unfathomable and, as I near her, I feel a sudden apprehension.

'Sadie . . .' I break off helplessly. I don't know where to start. 'I'm so sorry. I've been looking everywhere for you . . .'

'Well, you can't have looked very hard!' She appears totally unmoved by my appearance. In spite of myself, I feel a familiar indignation rising.

'I did! I've spent days searching! I went all over the place. And I had quite a voyage of discovery. I need to tell you about it.' I'm trying to find a way of edging tactfully into the subject of Stephen, but all of a sudden Sadie says, with a tiny grudging shrug, 'I missed you.'

I'm so taken aback I'm thrown off my stride.

'Well . . . me too. I missed you too.' Instinctively I put my arms out to give her a hug—then realise how pointless that is, and drop my hands down again. 'Sadie, listen. There's something I've got to tell you.'

'And there's something I've got to tell you!' she cuts in with obvious satisfaction. 'I knew you'd come tonight. I was waiting for you.'

'You can't have known,' I say patiently. 'Even *I* didn't know I was going to come. I just happened to be in the area.'

'I *did* know,' she insists. 'And if you didn't appear, I was going to find you and make you come. I've got something really important to show you! There!' She suddenly points in triumph. 'Over there! Look!'

I follow her gaze, squinting as I try to make out what she's talking about . . . and my heart drops in dismay.

Ed. He's standing at the side of the dance floor. He's watching the band and occasionally stumping from side to side to the music as though out of a sense of duty.

'Sadie.' I clutch my head. 'What have you done?'

'Go and talk to him!' She motions me briskly.

'No,' I say in horror. 'I can't talk to him. He hates me.' I quickly hide behind a group of dancers before Ed can catch sight of me. 'Why did you make him come here, anyway?' I mutter at Sadie.

'I felt guilty.' She gives me an accusing gaze, as though this is all my fault. 'I don't like feeling guilty. So I decided to do something about it.'

'You went and yelled at him.' I shake my head in disbelief. 'I thought he was yours, anyway. I thought I ruined everything. What happened to all that?'

Sadie flinches slightly, but holds her head high. I can see her looking at Ed through the crowd. There's a brief, soft longing in her eyes, then she turns away.

'Not my type, after all,' she says crisply. 'He's far too . . . alive. And so are you. So you're well matched. Off you go! Ask him to dance.'

'Sadie.' I shake my head. 'I really appreciate you making the effort. But I can't just make things up with him out of the blue. It's not the right place, it's not the right time. Now, can we go somewhere and talk?'

'Of course it's the right time and place!' retorts Sadie, affronted. 'That's why he's here! That's why you're here!'

'It's not why I'm here!' I'm starting to lose my rag. 'Sadie, I need to talk to you! There are things I need to tell you! Forget about Ed and me. This is about you! And Stephen! And your past! I've found out what happened! I've found the painting!'

Too late, I realise that the jazz band has come to a halt and a guy up on stage is making a speech. At least, he's trying to make a speech, but the entire crowd has turned to look at me, yelling like a lunatic.

'Sorry.' I swallow. 'I . . . didn't mean to interrupt. Please, carry on.' Hardly daring to, I swivel my gaze to where Ed is standing, staring at me along with everyone else.

My skin starts to prickle with mortification as he makes his way across the dance floor towards me. He isn't smiling.

'You found the painting?' Sadie's voice is only a whisper and her eyes seem hollow as she stares at me. 'You found Stephen's *painting*?'

'Yes,' I mutter, a hand in front of my mouth. 'It's amazing . . .'

'Lara.' Ed has reached me.

'Oh. Um, hi,' I manage, my chest tight.

'Where is it?' Sadie tries to tug at my arm. 'Where is it?'

Ed looks as uncomfortable as I feel. His frown is back in place, as deep as it ever was. 'So you came. I wasn't sure if you would.'

'Um . . . well . . .' I clear my throat. 'I just thought . . . you know . . .'

I'm trying to be coherent, but it's almost impossible with Sadie bobbing around to get my attention.

'What did you find out? Tell me!' she says.

'I will tell you. Just wait.' I'm trying to talk subtly, out of the side of my mouth, but Ed is too sharp. He picks up everything.

'Tell me what?' he says, his eyes scanning my face intently.

OK. I cannot cope with this. Both Sadie and Ed are standing in front of me, with expectant faces.

'Lara?' Ed takes a step towards me. 'Are you OK?'

'Yes. I mean, no. I mean . . .' I take a breath. 'I wanted to tell you that I'm sorry I left our date in such a rush. I'm sorry you thought I was setting you up for a job. But I really wasn't. And I really hope you believe me.'

'Stop talking to him!' interrupts Sadie in a burst of fury, but Ed's dark, serious gaze is on mine and I can't tear my eyes away.

'I do believe you,' he says. 'And I need to apologise too. I overreacted. I didn't give you a chance. Afterwards I regretted it. I realised I'd thrown away something . . . a friendship . . . that was . . .'

'What?' I manage.

'Good. I think we had something good. Didn't we?'

This is the moment to nod and say yes. But I don't want a good friendship. I want that feeling back, when he wrapped his arms round me and kissed me. I want him. That's the truth.

'You want me just to be your . . . friend?' I force myself to say the words and instantly I can see something change in Ed's face.

'Stop it! Talk to me!' Sadie whirls over to Ed and screeches in his ear, *'Stop talking to Lara! Go away!'* For a moment he gets that distant look in his eye, and I can tell he's heard her. But he doesn't move. His eyes just crinkle into a warm, tender smile.

'You want the truth? I think you're my guardian angel.'

'What?' I try to laugh, but it doesn't quite come out right.

'You shook me up. You were just what I needed.' He hesitates, then adds, 'You're just what I need.' There's something in his look which is making me tingle all over.

'Well, I need you too.' My voice is constricted. 'So we're quits.'

'No, you don't.' He smiles ruefully. 'You're doing just fine.'

'OK.' I hesitate. 'Maybe I don't need you. But . . . I want you.'

For a moment neither of us speaks. His eyes are locked on mine. My heart is thumping so hard, I'm sure he can hear it.

'Go away, Ed!' Sadie suddenly screeches in Ed's ear. *'Do this later!'*

I can see Ed flinch at the sound of her, and I feel a familiar foreboding. If Sadie messes this up for me, I will, I will . . .

'Leave!' Sadie is shrieking. *'Tell her you'll call later! Go away! Go home!'*

I'm aching with anger at her. 'Stop!' I want to yell. 'Leave him alone!' But I'm powerless. I just have to watch the light come on in Ed's eye as he hears her. It's like Josh all over again. She's ruined everything again.

'You know, sometimes you hear a voice in your head,' Ed says suddenly. 'Like . . . an instinct.'

'I know you do,' I say miserably. 'You hear a voice and it has a message and it's telling you to go away. I understand.'

'It's telling me the opposite.' Ed moves forward and firmly takes hold of my shoulders. 'It's telling me not to let you go. It's telling me you're the best thing that's happened to me and I better not mess this one up.'

And before I can even take a breath, he leans down and kisses me. His arms wrap round me, strong and secure and resolute.

I'm in a state of total disbelief. He's not walking away. He's not listening to Sadie. Whatever voice is in his head . . . it's not hers.

At last he draws away and smiles down at me, pushing a strand of hair gently off my face. I smile back, breathless, resisting the temptation to pull him down straight away for another snog.

'Would you like to dance, twenties girl?' he says.

I want to dance. I want to spend all evening and all night with him.

I shoot a surreptitious glance at Sadie. She's moved away a few feet, her shoulders are hunched over, her hands twisted together in a complicated knot. She looks up and shrugs with a tiny sad smile of defeat.

'Dance with him,' she says. 'It's all right. I'll wait.'

She's waited years and years to find out the truth about Stephen. And now she's willing to wait even longer, just so I can dance with Ed.

'No.' I shake my head firmly. 'It's your turn. Ed . . .' I turn to him with a deep breath. 'I have to tell you about my great-aunt. She died recently.'

'Oh. OK. Sure. I didn't know.' He looks puzzled.

I drag him to the edge of the dance floor, away from the band. 'It's really important. Her name was Sadie and she was in love with this guy Stephen in the 1920s. And she thought he was a bastard who used her and forgot about her. But he loved her. I know he did. Even after he went to France, he loved her.'

My words are spilling out in an urgent stream. I'm looking directly at Sadie. I have to get my message across. She has to believe me.

'How do you know?' Her chin is as haughty as ever, but her voice has a giveaway tremble. 'What are you talking about?'

'I know because he wrote letters to her from France.' I speak across Ed to Sadie. 'And because he put himself in the necklace. And because he never painted another portrait, his whole life. People begged him to but he would always say, *"J'ai peint celui que j'ai voulu peindre"*—"I have painted the one I wanted to paint." And when you see the painting, you realise why. Because why would he ever want to paint anyone else after Sadie? She was the most beautiful thing you ever saw. He loved her. Even if she lived her whole life without knowing it.' I brush away a sudden tear from my cheek.

Ed looks slightly lost for words. One minute we're snogging. The next I'm downloading some random torrent of family history on him.

'Where did you see the painting? Where is it?' Sadie takes a step towards me, her face pale. 'It was lost. It was burned.'

'Did you know your great-aunt well?' Ed is saying, simultaneously.

'I didn't know her when she was alive. But after she died I went down to Archbury, where she used to live. He's famous.' I turn again to Sadie. 'Stephen's famous.'

'Famous?' Sadie looks bewildered.

'There's a whole museum dedicated to him. He's called Cecil Malory. He was discovered long after his death. And the portrait is famous too. And it was saved and it's in a gallery and everyone loves it . . . and you have to see it. You have to see it.'

'Now.' Sadie's voice is so quiet, I can barely hear her. 'Please. Now.'

'Sounds awesome,' says Ed politely. 'We'll have to go see it someday. We could take in some galleries, do lunch . . .'

'No. Now.' I take his hand. 'Right now.' I glance at Sadie. 'Come on.'

We sit on the leather bench, the three of us, in a silent row. Sadie next to me. Me next to Ed. Sadie hasn't spoken since she came into the gallery. When she first saw the portrait I thought she might faint. She flickered silently and just stared, and then at last exhaled as though she'd been holding her breath for an hour.

'Amazing eyes,' says Ed at length. He keeps shooting me wary looks, as though he's not sure how to deal with this situation.

'Amazing.' I nod, but I can't concentrate on him. 'Are you OK?' I give Sadie a worried glance. 'I know this has been a real shock for you.'

'I'm good.' Ed sounds puzzled. 'Thanks for asking.'

'I'm all right.' Sadie gives me a wan smile. Then she resumes gazing at the painting again. She's already been up close to it, to see the portrait of Stephen hidden in her necklace, and her face was briefly so contorted with love and sorrow that I had to turn away and give her a moment of privacy.

'Mabel.' Ed is consulting the guidebook which he insisted on buying at the entrance. 'It says here, "The sitter is thought to be called Mabel."'

'That's what they thought.' I nod. 'Because the painting says, "My Mabel" on the back.'

'*Mabel?*' Sadie looks so horrified I can't help snorting with laughter.

'I told them it was a joke between her and Cecil Malory,' I hastily explain. 'It was her nickname, but everyone thought it was real.'

A movement attracts my attention and I glance up. To my surprise, Malcolm Gledhill is entering the gallery.

'Oh, Miss Lington. Hello. After our conversation today, I just thought I'd come and have another look at her.'

'Me, too.' I nod. 'I'd like to introduce . . .' Abruptly I realise I'm about to introduce Sadie to him. 'Ed. This is Ed Harrison. Malcolm Gledhill. He's in charge of the collection.'

Malcolm joins the three of us on the bench and for a moment we all just look at the painting.

'So you've had the painting in the gallery since 1982,' says Ed, still reading the guidebook. 'Why did the family get rid of it? Strange move.'

'Good question,' says Sadie, suddenly waking up. 'It belonged to me. Nobody should have been allowed to sell it.'

'Good question,' I echo firmly. 'It belonged to Sadie. Nobody should have been allowed to sell it.'

'And what I want to know is, who *did* sell it?' she adds.

'Who *did* sell it?' I echo.

Malcolm Gledhill shifts uncomfortably on the bench. 'As I said, Miss Lington, it was a confidential arrangement. Until such time as a formal legal claim is made, the gallery is unable to—'

'So, let me get this straight,' Ed says. 'Someone *stole* the painting?'

'Dunno.' I shrug. 'It was missing for years, and then I found it here. It was sold to the gallery in the 1980s, but I don't know who sold it.'

'Do you know?' Ed turns to Malcolm Gledhill.

'I do.' He nods reluctantly.

'Well, can't you tell her?'

'Not . . . well . . . no.' Malcolm looks flustered. His eyes flick towards his briefcase.

'Is the file in there?' I say, in sudden inspiration.

'As it happens, it is,' says Malcolm guardedly. 'I'm taking the papers home to study. Copies, of course.'

'Could you do me a small favour and check the date of acquisition? That's not confidential, is it?' I say. A plan has occurred to me.

'It was June 1982, as I remember,' says Malcolm Gledhill.

'But the exact date? Could you have a quick look at the agreement?' I open my eyes innocently at him. 'Please? It could be very helpful.'

Malcolm gives me a suspicious look, but obviously can't think of any reason to refuse. He opens his briefcase and draws out a file of papers.

I catch Sadie's eye and jerk my head at Malcolm Gledhill.

'What?' she says.

'Here we are . . .' He puts on a pair of glasses. 'Let me find the date . . .'

There's the information, open for anyone to read who happens to be of a ghostly nature. And still Sadie is peering at me uncomprehendingly.

'Look!' I mutter, out of the corner of my mouth. 'Look at it!'

'Oh!' Her face snaps in sudden understanding. A nanosecond later she's standing behind Malcolm Gledhill, peering over his shoulder.

'Look at what?' says Ed, sounding puzzled, but I barely hear him. I'm watching Sadie as she reads, frowns, gives a small gasp—then looks up.

'William Lington. He sold it for five hundred thousand pounds.'

'William Lington?' I stare back at her stupidly. 'You mean Uncle Bill?'

Malcolm Gledhill starts violently and clutches the letter to his chest. 'What—what did you say?'

'William Lington sold the painting to the gallery for half a million pounds.' I try to sound firm, but my voice is coming out faint. 'That's the name on the agreement.'

'You are kidding?' Ed's eyes gleam. 'Your own uncle?'

Malcolm Gledhill looks like he wants to burst into tears. 'I don't know how you got that information.' He appeals to Ed. 'You will be a witness to the fact I did not reveal any information to Miss Lington.'

'So she's right?' says Ed, raising his eyebrows.

'I can't say whether or not . . . whether . . .' He breaks off and wipes his brow. 'At no stage did I let the agreement into her view . . .'

'You didn't have to,' says Ed reassuringly. 'She's psychic.'

My mind is going round in circles as I try to get over my shock and think this through. Uncle Bill had the painting. Uncle Bill sold the painting. Dad's voice keeps running through my mind: . . . *put in a storage unit and left there for years. It was Bill who sorted it all out . . . Strange to imagine, but Bill was the idler in those days.*

It's all obvious. He must have found the painting all those years ago, realised it was valuable and sold it to the London Portrait Gallery.

'Are you OK?' Ed touches my arm. 'Lara?'

But I can't move. Now my mind is moving in bigger circles. I'm putting two and two together. And I'm making a hundred million. Bill set up Lingtons Coffee in 1982. The same year he secretly made half a million from selling Sadie's painting.

And now, finally, *finally*, it's all falling into place. It's all making sense. He had £500,000 that no one knew about. I feel light-headed. The enormity of this is only slowly sinking in. The whole thing is a lie. The whole world thinks he's a business genius who started with two little coins. Half a million notes, more like.

And he covered it up so no one would know. He must have realised the painting was of Sadie as soon as he saw it. He must have realised it belonged to her. But he let the world believe it was some servant called Mabel. That way, no one would come knocking on any Lington door, asking them about the beautiful girl in the painting.

'Lara?' Ed's waving a hand in front of my face. 'Speak to me. What is it?'

'The year 1982.' I look up in a daze. 'Sound familiar? That's when Uncle Bill started up Lingtons Coffee. You know? With his famous "two little coins". Or was there, in fact, £500,000 that started him off? Which he somehow forgot to mention?'

There's silence. I can see the pieces falling into place in Ed's mind.

'Your "Uncle Bill" is William Lington of Lingtons Coffee?' he says at last and looks at me. 'This is huge. The whole Two Little Coins story, the seminars, the book, the DVD, the movie—'

'All complete bullshit.'

I'd want to laugh too if I didn't want to cry. If I weren't so sad and furious and sick at what Uncle Bill did.

That was Sadie's painting. It was hers to sell or keep. He took it and he used it and he never breathed a word. How dare he? How *dare* he?

With sickening clarity I can see a parallel universe in which someone else, someone decent like my dad, had found the painting and done the right thing. I can see Sadie sitting in her nursing home, wearing her necklace, looking at her beautiful painting throughout her old age, until the very last light faded from her eyes. Uncle Bill robbed her of years and years of possible happiness. And I'll never forgive him.

'She should have known.' I can't contain my anger any more. 'Sadie should have known she was hanging up here. She went to her death with no idea. And that was wrong. It was wrong.'

I glance over at Sadie. She shrugs.

'Darling, don't drone on about it. *Too* dull. At least I've found it now. At least it wasn't destroyed. And at least I don't look as *fat* as I remember,' she adds with sudden animation.

Sadie meets my eyes and we exchange wary smiles. Her bravado doesn't totally fool me. She's pale and flickery and I can tell this discovery has thrown her. But her chin is up, high and proud as ever.

Malcolm Gledhill is still looking deeply uncomfortable. 'If we'd realised she was still alive, if anyone had told us . . .'

'You couldn't have known,' I say, my anger abated a little. 'We didn't even know it was her ourselves.'

Because Uncle Bill didn't say a word. No wonder he wanted the necklace. It was the only thing left linking Sadie to her portrait. It was the only thing which might uncover his massive con trick. This painting must have been a time bomb for him. And now, finally, it's gone off. I don't know how yet, but I'm going to avenge Sadie. Big time.

All four of us have turned to face the painting again. It's almost impossible to sit in this gallery and *not* end up staring at it.

'I should be going . . .' Malcolm Gledhill has clearly had enough for one night. He picks up his briefcase, nods at us, then swiftly walks away.

I look at Ed and grin. 'Sorry about the diversion.'

'No problem.' He gives me a quizzical look. 'So . . . any other old masters you want to unveil tonight? Or shall we go get some dinner?'

'Dinner.' I stand up and look at Sadie. She's still sitting there, her feet up on the bench, gazing up at her twenty-three-year-old self as though she wants to drink herself in. 'Coming?' I say softly.

'Sure,' says Ed.

'Not just yet,' says Sadie. 'You go. I'll see you later.'

I follow Ed to the exit, then give Sadie one last, anxious look. But she doesn't even notice me. She's still transfixed. Like she wants to sit there all night with the painting. Like she wants to make up for all the time she lost. Like, finally, she's found what she was looking for.

Twelve

I'VE NEVER AVENGED anyone before. And I'm finding it a lot trickier than I expected. Uncle Bill is abroad and no one can get in contact with him. (Well, of course they *can* get hold of him. They're just not going to do so for the crazy stalker niece.) I don't want to phone. This has to be done face to face. So at the moment, it's impossible.

And it's not helped by Sadie going all moral-high-ground on me. She thinks there's no point dwelling on the past, and what's done is done and I should stop 'going on about it, darling'.

But I don't care what she thinks. Vengeance *will* be mine. The more I think about what Uncle Bill did, the more livid I am, and the more I want to phone up Dad and blurt it all out. But somehow I'm keeping control. There's no rush. Everyone knows revenge is a dish best served when you've had time to build up enough vitriol and fury. Ed's already hired a lawyer for me, and he's going to start formal claim proceedings as soon as I give him the say-so. Which I'm going to do as soon as I've confronted Uncle Bill myself and seen him squirm. That's my aim.

To distract myself, I lean against the headboard of my bed and flick through the post. My bedroom is actually a pretty good office. I don't have to commute, and it doesn't cost anything. And it has a bed in it. On the less positive side, Kate has to work at my dressing table, and keeps getting her legs wedged underneath it.

I'm calling my new head-hunting company Magic Search, and we've been running for three weeks now. And we've already landed a commission. We were recommended to a pharmaceutical company by Janet Grady, who is my new best friend. (She's not stupid, Janet. She knows I did all the work and Natalie did nothing. Mostly because I rang her up and told her.) I did the pitch myself, and two days ago, we heard we'd won! We've been asked to compile a short list for another marketing-director job, also in the pharmaceutical industry.

Sadie has proved to be a very quick learner and has all sorts of clever ideas. Which is why she's a valued member of the Magic Search team.

'Hello!' Her high-pitched voice jolts me out of my reverie and I look up to see her sitting at the end of my bed. 'I've just been to Glaxo Wellcome. I've got the direct lines of two of the senior marketing team. Quick, before I forget . . .'

She dictates two names and telephone numbers to me. Private, direct-line numbers. Gold dust to a head-hunter. Sadie winks at me and I grin back. Having a job really suits her. I've even given her a job title: Chief Head-hunter. After all, she's the one doing the hunting.

She's found us an office, too: a run-down building off Kilburn High Road. We can move in there next week. It's all falling into place.

Every evening, after Kate goes home, Sadie and I sit on my bed and talk. Or, rather, she talks. I've told her that I want to *know* about her. And so she sits there, and tells me things. Her thoughts are a bit random but gradually a picture of her life has built up. She's told me about the divine hat she was wearing in Hong Kong when war was declared, the leather trunk she packed everything in and lost, the time she was robbed at gunpoint in Chicago but managed to keep hold of her necklace, the man she danced with one night, who later became President . . .

And I sit there, totally riveted. I've never heard a story like it. She's had the most amazing, colourful life. Sometimes fun, sometimes exciting, sometimes desperate, sometimes shocking. It's a life I can't imagine anyone else leading. Only Sadie.

I talk a bit, too. I've told her about growing up with Mum and Dad; stories about Tonya's riding lessons and my synchronised-swimming craze. I've told her about Mum's anxiety attacks and how I wish she could relax and enjoy life. I've told her how, our whole lives, we've been in the shadow of Uncle Bill.

We don't really comment on each other's stories. We just listen.

Then later on, when I go to bed, Sadie goes to the London Portrait Gallery and sits with her painting all night, alone. She hasn't told me that's what she does. I just know, from the way she disappears off silently, her eyes already distant and dreamy. I'm glad she goes. The painting's so important to her, she *should* spend time with it.

Coincidentally, it works out well for me too, her being out of the way at night. For . . . various other reasons. Nothing specific.

Oh, OK. All *right*. There is a specific reason. Which would be the fact that Ed has recently stayed over at mine a few nights.

I mean, come on. Can you think of anything worse than a ghost lurking around in your bedroom when you're . . . getting to know your new boyfriend better? The idea of Sadie giving us a running commentary is more than I can cope with. And she has no shame. I know she'd watch us. She'd probably award us points out of ten, or say disparagingly that they did it much better in her day.

The phone rings and Kate picks it up. 'Hello, Magic Search, can I help you? Oh. Yes, of course, I'll put you through.' She presses the HOLD button and says, 'It's Sam from Bill Lington's travel office.'

'Oh. Yes, thanks, Kate.'

I take a deep breath and pick up the receiver. 'Hello, Sam,' I say pleasantly. 'Thanks for ringing back. The reason I called is, um . . . I'm trying to arrange a little fun surprise for my uncle. I know he's away, and I wondered if you could possibly give me his flight details?'

'Lara,' Sam sighs. 'Sarah told me that you were trying to contact

Bill. She also informed me that you'd been banned from the house.'

'*Banned?*' I muster tones of shock. 'Are you serious? I'm just trying to organise a little surprise birthday-o-gram for my uncle—'

'His birthday was a month ago.'

'So . . . I'm a bit late!'

'Lara, I can't give out confidential flight information,' Sam says smoothly. 'Or any information. Sorry. Have a good day.'

'Right. Well . . . thanks.' I crash the receiver down. Damn.

'Everything OK?' Kate looks up anxiously.

'Yes. Fine.' I muster a smile. But as I head out to the kitchen I'm breathing heavily with frustration. I flick on the kettle and lean against the counter, trying to calm myself with deep breathing.

'Goodness!' Sadie appears, perched on the stove. 'What's wrong?'

'You know what's wrong.' I haul my tea bag out roughly and dump it in the bin. 'I want to get him.'

Sadie opens her eyes wider. 'I didn't realise you were so steamed up.'

'I wasn't. But I am now. I've had enough.' I slosh milk into my tea. 'I know you're being all magnanimous, but I don't see how you can do it. Don't you want to get back at him? You must be a total saint.'

'Saint is probably a *little* strong . . .' She smooths back her hair.

'It's not. You're amazing.' I cradle the mug. 'The way you don't dwell on stuff. If it were me I'd want to . . . *trash* him.'

'I could trash him.' She shrugs. 'I could go to the South of France and make his life a misery. But would I be a better person?' She hits her slim chest. 'Would I feel better inside?'

'The South of France?' I stare at her, puzzled. 'What do you mean?'

Sadie immediately looks shifty. 'I'm guessing. It's the kind of place he would be. It's the kind of place wealthy people go.'

'Oh my *God*.' I gasp. 'You know where he is, don't you? Sadie!'

'All right.' She looks a little sulky. 'Yes. I do know where he is. I went to his office. It was very easy to find out.'

'Why didn't you *tell* me?'

'Because . . .' She gives a distant, noncommittal shrug.

'Because you didn't want to admit that you're just as mean and vengeful as me! So, come on. What did you do to him?'

'I did nothing!' she says haughtily. 'Or at least, nothing much. I just wanted to have a look at him. He's very, very rich, isn't he?'

'Incredibly.' I nod. 'Why?'

'He seems to own an entire beach. That's where I came across him.

He was lying on a bed in the sun, covered in oil. He looked terribly self-satisfied.' A spasm of distaste passes across her face.

'Didn't you want to yell at him? Didn't you want to have a go at him?'

'Actually . . . I did yell at him. I couldn't help myself. I felt so angry.'

'That's good! You *should* yell. What did you say?'

'I told him he was fat,' she says with satisfaction.

'You told him he was *fat*?' I stare at her incredulously. 'That was it? That was your revenge?'

'It's the perfect revenge!' retorts Sadie. 'He looked very unhappy. He's a terribly vain man, you know.'

'Well, I think we can do better than that,' I say decisively, putting my mug down. 'Here's the plan, Sadie. You're going to tell me where I need to book a flight to. And we're going to get on a plane tomorrow. And you're going to take me to where he is. OK?'

'OK.' Her eyes suddenly brighten. 'It'll be like a holiday!'

Sadie has taken the holiday theme seriously. She's dressed for our trip in a backless flowing outfit made out of orange silky stuff which she calls 'beach pyjamas'. She has on a massive straw hat, is clutching a parasol and a wicker basket and keeps humming some song about being '*sur la plage*'.

'More champagne?' A smiling air hostess appears at my side.

'Oh.' I hesitate, then hold out my glass. 'Er . . . OK, then. Thanks.'

Sadie shrieked at the check-in girl at the airport and I found myself upgraded. And now the hostesses keep plying me with champagne!

'Isn't this fun?' Sadie slides into the seat next to me.

'Yeah, great,' I murmur, pretending to be talking into a Dictaphone.

'How's Ed?' She gets about ten insinuating tones into one syllable.

'Fine, thanks,' I say lightly. 'He thinks I'm having a reunion with an old schoolfriend.'

'You know he's told his mother about you?'

'What?' I turn towards her. 'How do you know?'

'I happened to be passing his office the other night,' Sadie says airily. 'So I thought I'd pop in, and he was on the phone. I just happened to catch a few snatches of his conversation.'

'Sadie,' I hiss, 'were you *spying* on him?'

'He said London was working out really well for him.' Sadie ignores my question. 'And then he said he'd met someone who made him glad that Corinne did what she did. And his mother told him she was so thrilled, and she couldn't wait to meet you and he said, "Slow down, Mom." But he was laughing.'

'Oh. Well . . . he's right. We'd better not rush things.' I'm trying to sound all nonchalant, but secretly I have a glow of pleasure inside.

'And *aren't* you glad you didn't stay with Josh?' Sadie suddenly demands. 'Aren't you glad I saved you from that hideous fate?'

I take a sip of champagne, avoiding her eye. To be honest, going out with Ed after Josh is like moving on to Duchy Originals super-tasty seeded loaf after plastic white bread. (I don't mean to be rude about Josh. And I didn't realise it at the time. But he is. Plastic white bread.)

So really I should be truthful and thank her. Except then she'll become so conceited I won't be able to stand it.

'Life takes us on different paths,' I say at last, cryptically. 'It's not up to us to evaluate or judge them, merely respect and embrace them.'

'What drivel,' she says contemptuously. 'I know I saved you from a hideous fate, and if you can't even be grateful—' She's suddenly distracted by the view out of the window. 'Look! We're nearly there!'

Uncle Bill's mansion is a longish taxi ride from Nice Airport. It's a massive white house with several other houses dotted around the grounds and a mini-vineyard and a helicopter pad. The place is staffed pretty heavily, but that doesn't matter when you have a French-speaking ghost by your side. Every member of staff we come across is soon turned into a glassy-eyed statue. We make our way through the garden without being challenged, and Sadie leads me swiftly to a cliff, into which steps are cut, with a balustrade. At the bottom of the steps is a sandy beach and, beyond that, endless Mediterranean.

For a moment I just stand there, watching Uncle Bill. He's with a personal trainer, doing sit-ups and sweating profusely. I gape, astonished, as he does crunch after crunch, almost howling with pain.

He's so engrossed, he doesn't notice as I quietly make my way down the cliff steps, accompanied by Sadie.

'I still need to work on my abs,' says Uncle Bill grimly, clutching his sides in dissatisfaction. 'I need to lose some fat.'

'Meester Leengton.' The trainer looks totally bemused. 'You 'ave no fat to lose. 'Ow many times must I tell you thees?'

'*Yes, you do!*' I jump as Sadie whirls through the air to Uncle Bill. '*You're fat!*' she shrieks in his ear. '*Fat, fat, fat! You're gross!*'

Uncle Bill's face jolts with alarm. Looking desperate, he sinks to the mat again and starts doing more crunches, groaning with the effort.

I can't help giggling. This is a totally brilliant revenge. We watch him wincing and panting a while longer, then Sadie advances again.

'*Now tell your servant to go!*' she yells in his ear.

'You can go now, Jean-Michel,' Uncle Bill says. 'See you this evening.'

'Very well.' The trainer gathers up all his pieces of equipment, brushing the sand off them. 'I see you at six.'

He nods politely as he passes me, and heads towards the house.

I take a deep breath and start to walk down the rest of the cliff steps. My hands are suddenly damp as I reach the beach. I take a few steps over the hot sand, then just stand still, waiting for Uncle Bill to notice me.

'Who's . . .' He suddenly catches a glimpse of me as he comes down on the mat. Immediately he sits up again and swivels round.

'Is that . . . *Lara*? What are you doing here?'

He looks so dazed and drained, I almost feel sorry for him. 'Yes, it is I,' I say, in the most imposing voice I can muster. 'Lara Lington. Daughter to a betrayed father. Great-niece to a betrayed great-aunt. Niece to a betraying, evil, lying uncle. And I will have my vengeance.' That bit was so satisfying to say, I repeat it, my voice ringing across the beach.

'Lara.' Uncle Bill smiles at me with that old, suave, patronising air. 'Very stirring stuff. But I have no idea what you're talking about, nor how you got past my guards—'

'You know what I'm talking about,' I say scathingly. 'You know.'

'I'm afraid I have no idea.'

So he's calling my bluff. He must think that the anonymous agreement protects him and no one will ever be able to find out.

'Is this about the necklace?' Uncle Bill says suddenly, as though the thought has just struck him. 'It's a pretty trinket, and I can understand your interest in it. But I don't know where it is. Believe me. Now, did your father tell you I want to offer you a job? Is that why you're here? Because you certainly get marks for keenness, young lady.'

'I'm not here about the necklace, or the job.' My voice cuts across his. 'I'm here about Great-Aunt Sadie. And the painting of her that you found,' I carry on coolly. 'The Cecil Malory. And the deal you did with the London Portrait Gallery in 1982. And the £500,000 you got. And all the lies you told. And what you're going to do about it. *That's* why I'm here.'

And I watch in satisfaction as my uncle's face sags in a way I've never seen before. Like butter melting away under the sun.

It's a sensation. It's front-page news in every paper. *Every* paper. Bill 'Two Little Coins' Lington has 'clarified' his story and come clean about the £500,000. The big, one-to-one interview was in the *Mail*, and all the papers jumped on it immediately.

For me, the money really isn't the point. It's that finally, after all this time, he's told the world about Sadie. The quote that most of the papers used is: 'I couldn't have achieved my success without my beautiful aunt, Sadie Lancaster, and I'll always be indebted to her.' Which I dictated to him, word for word.

Sadie's portrait has been on every single front cover. The London Portrait Gallery has been besieged. She's like the new Mona Lisa. Only better, because the painting's so massive there's room for loads of people to look at her at once. (And she's way prettier. I'm just saying.)

As for Uncle Bill's book, *Two Little Coins* has become the biggest object of ridicule since the Millennium Dome. I'm flicking through an editorial about him in today's *Mail*, when my phone bleeps with a text:

Hi I'm outside. Ed.

This is one of the many good things about Ed. He's never late. Happily I grab my bag, bang the flat door shut and head down the stairs. Kate and I are moving into our new office today, and Ed's promised to come and see it on his way to work. As I arrive on the pavement, there he is, holding a massive bunch of red roses.

'For the office,' he says, presenting them to me with a kiss.

'Thanks!' I beam. 'Everyone will be staring at me on the tube—' I stop in surprise as Ed puts a hand on my arm.

'I thought we could take my car today,' he says conversationally.

'*Your* car?'

'Uh-huh.' He nods at a smart black Aston Martin parked nearby.

'That's yours?' I goggle at it in total disbelief. 'But . . . but . . . how?'

'Bought it. You know, car showroom . . . credit card . . . usual process . . . Thought I'd better buy British,' he adds with a wry smile.

'But you've never driven on the left.' I feel a sudden alarm.

'Relax. I took the test last week. Boy, you have a fucked-up system. Don't even get me *started* on your right-turn rules.'

I can't believe this. He's kept this totally quiet.

'But . . . why?' I can't help blurting out.

'Someone told me once,' he says, 'if you're going to live in a country, you should *engage* with it. And what better way to engage than learning how to drive in that country? Now, you want a ride or not?'

He opens the door with a gallant gesture. Still flabbergasted, I slide into the passenger seat. This is a seriously smart car.

'I learned all the British curses, too,' Ed adds as he pulls out into the road. 'Get a move on, you knobhead!' He puts on a Cockney accent and I can't help giggling.

'Very good,' I nod. 'What about, "That's right out of order, you wanker!"'

'I was told, "Bang out of order, you wanker,"' says Ed. 'Was I misinformed?'

'No, that's OK too. But you need to work on the accent.' I watch as he changes gear efficiently and cruises past a red bus. 'But what will you do with it when—' I stop myself before I can say any more.

'What?' Ed may be driving, but he's as alert as ever.

'Nothing.' I was going to say, 'When you go back to the States.' But that's something we just don't talk about.

There's silence—then Ed shoots me a cryptic look. 'Who knows what I'll do?'

The tour of the office doesn't take that long. In fact, we're pretty much done by 9.05 a.m. Ed looks at everything twice and says it's all great, and then has to leave for his own office. And then about an hour later, Mum and Dad arrive, *also* bearing flowers, a bottle of champagne, and a new box of paperclips, which is Dad's little joke.

'It's very smart,' Mum says. 'But, darling, are you *sure* you can afford it? Wouldn't you have been better off staying with Natalie?'

Honestly. How many times do you have to explain to your parents that your former best friend is obnoxious and unscrupulous.

'I'm better off on my own, Mum. Look, this is my business plan.'

I hand them the document, which is bound and numbered and looks so smart I can hardly believe I put it together. If I make a success of Magic Search, my life will be complete.

I said that to Sadie this morning. She was silent for a moment, then to my surprise she stood up with a weird light in her eye and said, 'I'm your guardian angel! I should *make* it a success.' And then she disappeared. So I have a sneaky feeling she's up to something.

'Very impressive!' says Dad, flipping through the plan.

'I got some advice from Ed,' I confess. 'He's been really helpful with all the Uncle Bill stuff too. He helped me do that statement. And he was the one who said we should hire a publicist to manage the press.'

I've never seen my parents so poleaxed as I did when I rocked up at the front door, told them Uncle Bill wanted to have a word, turned back to the limo and said, 'OK, in you go.' And Uncle Bill had got out of the car with a silent, set jaw, and did everything I said.

Neither of my parents could manage a word. Even after Uncle Bill had gone and I said, 'Any questions?' they didn't speak. They just sat on the sofa, staring at me in a kind of stupefied awe. Even now, when they've thawed a little and the whole story is out, and it's not such a shock any more, they still keep darting me looks of awe.

Well, why shouldn't they? I *have* been pretty awesome, though I say it myself. I masterminded the whole press exposé, with Ed's help, and it's gone perfectly. At least, perfectly from my point of view. Maybe not from Uncle Bill's point of view. Or Aunt Trudy's. The day the story broke she flew to a spa in Arizona and checked in indefinitely. God knows if we'll ever see her again.

Diamanté, on the other hand, has totally cashed in on it. She's already done a photoshoot for *Tatler* in a mock-up of Sadie's painting, and she's using the whole story to publicise her fashion label. Which is really, really tacky. And also quite smart. I can't help admiring her for her chutzpah. I mean, it's not her fault her dad is such a tosser, is it?

'Lara.' I look up to see Dad approaching me. He looks awkward. 'We wanted to talk to you about Great-Aunt Sadie's . . .' He coughs.

'*Funeral*,' says Mum, in her 'discreet' voice.

'You haven't done it yet?' I feel a bolt of panic. 'Please tell me you haven't had her funeral.'

'No, no! It was provisionally set for this Friday. We *were* planning to tell you at some stage . . .' He trails off evasively.

'Anyway!' says Mum quickly. 'That was before.'

'Quite. Obviously things have changed somewhat now,' Dad continues. 'So if you would like to be involved in planning it . . .'

'Yes, I would like to be involved,' I say, almost fiercely. 'In fact, I think I'll take charge.'

'Right.' Dad glances at Mum. 'Well. Absolutely. I think that would only be right. Here are the funeral directors' details.' Dad hands me a leaflet, and I pocket it just as the phone rings. I hurry to answer it.

'Hello, Magic Search.'

'May I speak to Lara Lington, please?' It's a woman's voice.

'Speaking.' I sit down on one of the new swivel chairs. 'Can I help?'

'This is Pauline Reed. I'm head of Human Resources at Wheeler Foods. I was wondering, would you like to come in for a chat? I've heard good things about you.'

'Oh, how nice! From whom, may I ask? Janet Grady?'

There's silence. When she speaks again, she sounds puzzled.

'I don't recall who. But you have a great reputation and I wanted to meet you. Something tells me you can do good things for our business.'

Sadie.

'Well, that'd be great!' I gather my wits. 'Let me look at my diary . . .' I open it and fix up an appointment. As I put the phone down, both Mum and Dad are watching with a kind of eager hopefulness.

'Good news, darling?' says Dad.

'Just the head of Human Resources at Wheeler Foods,' I can't help saying, casually. 'She wanted a meeting.'

'Wheeler Foods who make Oatie Breakfast Treats?' Mum sounds beside herself.

'Yup. Looks like my guardian angel's watching out for me.'

'Hello!' Kate's bright voice interrupts me as she bursts through the door, holding a big flower arrangement. 'Look what's just been delivered! Hello, Mr and Mrs Lington,' she adds politely. 'Do you like our new office? Isn't it great?'

I take the flower arrangement from Kate and rip open the little card.

'"To all at Magic Search,"' I read aloud. '"We hope to get to know you as clients and as friends. Yours, Brian Chalmers. Head of Global Human Resources at Dwyer Dunbar." And he's given his private-line number.'

'How amazing!' Kate's eyes are wide. 'Do you know him?'

'No.'

Mum and Dad both seem beyond speech. I think I'd better get them out of here before anything else crazy happens.

'We're going for a pizza,' I inform Kate. 'Want to come?'

'I'll be along in a sec.' She nods cheerfully. 'I just need to sort a few things out first.'

Mum and Dad are just going with the flow. By the time we've all had a glass of Valpolicella, everyone's smiling and the tricky questions have stopped. We've all chosen our pizzas and are stuffing in hot, garlicky dough balls, and I'm feeling pretty happy.

Even when Tonya arrives, I can't get stressed. It was Mum and Dad's idea to ask her along, and the truth is, even though she winds me up, she's family. I'm starting to appreciate what that means.

'Oh my God.' Her strident greeting rings through the restaurant. 'Can you *believe* all this stuff about Uncle Bill?' As she arrives at our table she's obviously expecting a bit more of a reaction.

'Hi, Tonya,' I say. 'How are the boys? How's Clive?'

'Can you *believe* it?' she repeats. 'Have you seen the papers? I mean, it can't be true. It's tabloid rubbish. Someone's got an agenda somewhere.'

'I think it is true,' Dad says mildly. 'I think he admits as much himself.'

'But . . .' Tonya sinks down into a chair and looks around at us all with a bewildered expression. She clearly thought we would all be up in arms on Uncle Bill's behalf. Not merrily tucking into dough balls.

'Here you are.' Mum slides a wineglass across. 'We'll get you a menu.'

I can see Tonya's mind working as she recalibrates the situation. She's not going to stick up for Uncle Bill if no one else is.

'So, who uncovered it all?' she says at last. 'Some journalist?'

'Lara,' says Dad with a little smile.

'*Lara?* What do you mean, Lara?'

'I found out about Great-Aunt Sadie and the picture,' I explain. 'I put two and two together. It was me.'

'But . . . but you weren't mentioned in the papers.'

'I prefer to keep a low profile,' I say cryptically, like a superhero who doesn't need any other reward than doing good. Although, I would have *loved* to be mentioned in the papers. But no one came to interview me. The reports just said, 'The discovery was made by a family member.'

'But I don't get it.' Tonya's baleful blue eyes are on me. 'Why did you start poking around in the first place?'

'I had an instinct something was wrong regarding Great-Aunt Sadie. But no one would listen to me,' I can't help adding pointedly. 'At the funeral, everyone thought I was a nutcase.'

'You said she'd been murdered,' objects Tonya. 'But she wasn't.'

'I had a general instinct that something was amiss,' I say with a dignified air. 'So I chose to follow up my suspicions on my own. And, after some research, they were confirmed.' Everyone's hanging on my words as if I'm a university lecturer. 'I then approached experts at the London Portrait Gallery, and they verified my discovery.'

'Indeed they did.' Dad smiles at me.

'And guess what?' I add proudly. 'They're having the painting valued and Uncle Bill's giving Dad half of what it's worth!'

'No way!' Tonya claps a hand to her mouth. 'How much will that be?'

'Millions, apparently.' Dad looks uncomfortable. 'Bill's adamant.'

'It's only what you're owed, Dad,' I say for the hundredth time. 'He *stole* it from you. He's a thief!'

Tonya seems a bit speechless. She rips into a dough ball with her teeth. 'Did you see that editorial in *The Times*?' she says at last. 'Brutal.'

'It *was* rather savage.' Dad winces. 'We do feel for Bill, despite it all—'

'No, we don't!' Mum interrupts. 'Speak for yourself. I don't feel for him one little bit. I feel . . . angry. Yes. Angry.'

I gape at Mum in surprise. My whole life, I don't think I've ever known Mum actually say she was angry. Across the table, Tonya looks just as gobsmacked.

'What he did was shameful and unforgivable,' Mum continues. 'Your father always tries to see the good side of people; to find the excuse. But sometimes there *isn't* a good side. There *isn't* an excuse.'

'Good for you, Mum!' I exclaim.

'And if your father keeps trying to defend him—'

'I'm not defending him!' says Dad at once. 'But he's my brother. He's family. It's difficult . . .'

He sighs heavily. I can see the disappointment etched in the lines under his eyes. Dad wants to find the good in everyone.

'Your brother's success cast a long shadow over our family.' Mum's voice is trembling. 'It affected all of us in our different ways. Now it's time for us all to be free. That's what I think. Draw a line.'

'It's just an adjustment,' Dad says. 'To realise your younger brother is quite such a selfish, unprincipled . . . shit.' He breathes out hard. 'I mean, what does that say?'

'It says we forget about him,' says Mum firmly. 'Move on. Start living the rest of our lives without feeling like second-class citizens.'

'So, who's been dealing with him?' Tonya frowns.

'Lara's done everything,' says Mum proudly. 'Talked to Uncle Bill, talked to the gallery, sorted everything out . . . *and* started her own business! She's been a tower of strength!'

'Great!' Tonya smiles widely, but I can tell she's annoyed. 'Well done you, Lara.' She takes a sip of wine. I just *know* she's searching for some little vulnerable spot; some way to regain ascendancy . . .

'So how are things with Josh?' She puts on her sympathetic look. 'Dad told me you got back together for a bit, but then broke up for good. That must have been really tough. Really devastating.'

'It's OK,' I say brightly. 'My new boyfriend cheers me up.'

'New boyfriend?' Her mouth sags open. 'Already?'

She needn't look *so* surprised.

'He's an American consultant over on secondment. His name's Ed.'

'Well.' Tonya looks affronted. 'That's great! But it'll be hard when he goes back to the States, won't it?' She visibly brightens. 'Long-distance relationships are the most likely to break down.'

'Who knows what'll happen?' I hear myself saying sweetly.

'I can make him stay!' Sadie's low voice in my ear makes me jump. I turn to see her hovering right by me, her eyes shining with determination. 'I'm your guardian angel. I'll make Ed stay in England!'

'Excuse me a moment,' I say. 'I've just got to send a text.'

I get out my phone and start texting: It's OK. U don't need to make him stay. Where have u been?

'Or I could make him ask you to marry him!' she exclaims, ignoring my question. '*Too* much fun! I'll tell him to propose, and—'

No, no, no! I text. Sadie, stop! Don't make Ed do anything. I want him to make his own decisions. I want him to listen to his OWN voice.

Sadie gives a little harrumph as she reads my message. 'Well, I think *my* voice is more interesting,' she says, and I can't help a smile.

'Texting your boyfriend?' says Tonya, watching me.

'No,' I say. 'Just a friend. A good friend.' I turn away and tap in Thanks for doing all that stuff to help me. You didn't have to.

'I wanted to!' says Sadie. 'It's fun!'

Sadie, I text, u r the best guardian angel EVER.

'Well, I do rather pride myself.' She preens herself.

She floats across the table and sits on a spare chair at the end, just as Kate approaches the table, looking pink with excitement.

'You've had lots of calls, Lara!' she says. 'I've written down all the numbers . . . and the post arrived, forwarded from your flat. I didn't bring it all, but there was one package I thought might be important. It's come from Paris . . .' She hands me a Jiffy bag, pulls out a chair and beams round at everyone. 'Hi, we haven't met, I'm Kate . . .'

As Kate and Tonya introduce themselves, I stare down at the Jiffy bag, feeling a sudden breathless apprehension. Slowly I lift my eyes. Sadie is watching me intently across the table. I know she's thinking the same.

'Go on.' She nods.

With trembling hands I rip it open. I peer inside and see a flash of pale, iridescent yellow. I look up, straight at Sadie.

'That's it, isn't it?' She's gone very white. 'You've got it.'

I nod, then, barely knowing what I'm doing, I push back my chair.

'I just have to . . . make a call. I'll go outside. Be back in a moment.'

I walk to the back of the restaurant where there's a small, secluded courtyard. I head to the far corner, then open the Jiffy bag again, pull out the mass of tissue paper and gently unwrap it.

It's warmer to the touch than I expected. More substantial, somehow. A shaft of sunlight is glinting off the rhinestones and the beads are shimmering. It's so stunning I have a sudden strong urge to put it on. But instead I look up at Sadie, who has just been watching me silently.

'Here you are. It's yours.' Automatically I try to put it round her neck, as though I'm giving her an Olympic medal. But my hands sink straight through her. I try again and again, even though I know it's no use.

'I don't know what to do!' I'm half laughing, perilously near tears. 'It's yours! You should be wearing it! We need the ghost version—'

'Stop!' Sadie's voice rises in sudden tension. 'Don't—' She breaks off and moves away from me. 'You know what you have to do.'

There's silence apart from the steady roar of Kilburn traffic coming from the main road. I can't look at Sadie. I'm just standing there, clutching the necklace. I know this is what we've been chasing and hunting and wishing for. But now we have it . . . I don't want it to have arrived here. Not yet. The necklace is the reason Sadie's been haunting me. When she gets it back—

My thoughts abruptly veer away. I don't want to think about that. I don't want to think about any of it.

Sadie looks up, pale and resolute. 'Give me some time.'

'Yes.' I swallow. 'Sure.' I stuff the necklace into the bag and head back into the restaurant. Sadie has already disappeared.

I can't eat my pizza. I can't make proper conversation. I can't focus when I get back to the office, even though six more calls come in from blue-chip HR managers wanting to set up meetings with me.

I text Ed saying I have a headache and need to be alone. When I get home, there's no Sadie, which doesn't surprise me. I make some supper, which I don't eat, then sit in bed with the necklace round my neck, twisting the beads and watching old movies on DVD and not even bothering to try to sleep.

At last, at about five thirty, I get up, put on some clothes and head out. The soft grey of the dawn is tinged with a vivid, pink-red sunrise.

I buy a coffee from a café, get on a bus and head to Waterloo. By the time I arrive it's nearly six thirty. People are starting to appear on the bridge and in the streets. The London Portrait Gallery is still shut up, though.

I find a wall, sit down and sip my coffee. I'm prepared to sit there all day, but as a nearby church bell strikes eight, Sadie appears on the steps, that dreamy look on her face again. She's wearing yet another amazing dress, this one in pearl grey with a tulle skirt cut in petal shapes. A grey cloche is pulled down over her head and her eyes are lowered. I don't want to alarm her so I wait until she notices me and starts in surprise.

'Lara.'

'Hi.' I lift a hand. 'Thought you'd be here.'

'Where's my necklace?' Her voice is sharp with alarm. 'Have you lost it?'

'No! Don't worry, I've got it. It's OK. It's right here. Look.'

There's no one around, but I glance right and left, just in case. Then I pull out the necklace. In the clear morning light it looks more spectacular than ever. She gazes down at it lovingly, puts out her hands as though to take it, then draws them back.

'I wish I could touch it,' she murmurs.

'I know.' Helplessly, I hold it out to her, as though presenting an offering. I want to drape it round her neck. I want to reunite her with it.

'I want it back,' she says quietly. 'I want you to give it back to me.'

'Now? Today?'

Sadie meets my eyes. 'Right now.'

There's a sudden blocking in my throat. I can't say any of the things I want to say. I think she knows what they are, anyway.

'I want it back,' she repeats firmly. 'I've been too long without it.'

'Right.' I nod several times, my fingers clutching the necklace so hard I think they might bruise. 'Well then, you need to have it.'

The journey is too short. I want to tell the taxi driver to slow down. I want time to stand still. But all of a sudden we're drawing up in the little suburban street. We've arrived.

'Well, that was quick, wasn't it?' Sadie's voice is resolutely bright.

'Yes!' I force a smile. 'Amazingly quick.'

As we get out of the taxi I feel dread clasping my chest like iron. My hand is locked around the necklace so hard, I'm getting cramp in my fingers. But I can't bring myself to loosen my grasp, even as I'm struggling to pay the driver with the other hand.

The taxi roars away, and Sadie and I look at each other. We're standing opposite a small row of shops, one of which is a funeral parlour.

'That's it there.' I point unnecessarily at the sign saying CHAPEL OF REST. 'Looks like it's closed.'

Sadie has drifted up to the firmly locked door and peers in at the window. 'We'd better wait, I suppose.' She shrugs and returns to my side. 'We can sit here.'

She sits down beside me on a bench and for a moment we're both silent. I glance at my watch. Eight fifty-five. They open up at nine. Just the thought gives me a rush of panic, so I won't think about it. Not yet.

'Nice dress, by the way.' I think I sound fairly normal.

Sadie runs her eye over me, then says, 'Your shoes are pretty.'

'Thanks.' I want to smile, but my mouth won't quite do it. 'I bought them the other day. Ed helped me choose them, actually. We went to the Whiteleys centre. They had all these special offers on . . .'

I don't know what I'm saying, I'm just talking for the sake of it. Because talking is better than waiting.

'He's rather good at the old bone-jumping, isn't he?' Sadie suddenly says conversationally. 'Ed, I mean. Mind you, you're not so bad either.'

Bone-jumping? She doesn't mean—

'Sadie.' I turn on her. 'I *knew* it! You *watched* us!'

'What?' She bursts into peals of laughter. 'I was very subtle! You didn't know I was there.'

'What did you see?' I moan.

'Everything,' she says airily. 'And it was a jolly good show, I can tell you.'

'Sadie, you're impossible!' I clutch my head. 'You don't watch people having sex! There are laws against that!'

'I just had *one* tiny criticism,' she says, ignoring me. 'Or, rather . . . suggestion. Something we used to do in my day.'

'No!' I say in horror. 'No suggestions!'

'Your loss.' She shrugs and examines her nails, occasionally shooting me a look from under her lashes.

'All *right*,' I say at last. 'Tell me your genius 1920s sex tip. But it better not involve any weird indelible paste.'

'*Well* . . .' Sadie begins, coming closer. But before she can continue, my eyes suddenly focus over her shoulder. I stiffen and draw breath. An elderly man is unlocking the door of the funeral parlour.

'What is it?' Sadie follows my gaze. 'Oh.'

'Yes.' I swallow.

By now the elderly man has caught sight of me. I suppose I am quite noticeable, sitting bolt upright on a bench staring directly at him.

'Are you all right?' he says warily.

'Um . . . hi.' I force myself to my feet. 'I've come to . . . pay my respects. It's my great-aunt. Sadie Lancaster. Could I . . . see her?'

'Aaah.' He bows his head. 'Of course. Just give me a minute to open up, get a few things straight, and I will be with you, Miss . . .'

'Lington.'

'Lington.' There's a flash of recognition in his face. 'Of course, of course. If you'd like to come in and wait in our family room . . .'

'I'll be in in a moment.' I give an approximation of a smile. 'Just got a call to make.'

He disappears inside. For a moment I can't quite move. I want to stop us doing this. If I don't acknowledge it, maybe it's not really going to happen.

'So, are you ready?' I try to sound light-hearted. 'These places can be quite depressing—'

'Oh, I'm not coming in,' says Sadie nonchalantly. 'I'll sit here and wait. Much better.'

'Right.' I nod. 'Good idea. You don't want to . . .'

I trail off, unable to continue—but also unable to bring up what I'm really thinking. The thought that's going round and round my head.

'So.' I swallow. 'What d'you think will happen when I . . . when . . .'

'Do you mean, will you finally be rid of me?' says Sadie flippantly.

'No! I just meant . . .'

'I know. You're in a tearing hurry to get rid of me. Sick of the sight of me.' Her chin is quivering but she flashes me a smile. 'Well, I shouldn't think it'll work for a moment.'

Her eyes meet mine and I can see the message in them.

Don't lose it. No wallowing. Chin up.

'So I'm stuck with you.' I somehow manage a derisory tone. 'Great.'

'Afraid so.'

'Just what every girl needs.' I roll my eyes. 'A bossy ghost hanging around the place for ever.'

'A bossy *guardian angel*,' she corrects me firmly.

'Miss Lington?' The elderly man pokes his head out of the door.

'Thanks! I'll just be a sec!'

When the door closes I adjust my jacket needlessly a few times, buying myself another thirty seconds.

'So I'll just dump the necklace and see you in a couple of minutes, OK?' I aim for a matter-of-fact tone.

'I'll be here.' Sadie pats the bench she's sitting on.

I take a step away—then stop. I know we're playing a game. But I can't leave it like that. I swivel round, breathing hard, determined that I won't lose it, I won't let her down.

'But . . . just in case. Just in case we . . .' I can't bring myself to say it. I can't even think it. 'Sadie, it's been . . .'

There's nothing to say. No word is good enough. Nothing can describe what it's been like to know Sadie.

'I know,' she whispers. 'Me too. Go on.'

When I reach the door of the funeral parlour I look back one last time. She's sitting bolt upright with perfect posture, her dress skimming her slender frame. She's facing directly ahead, feet lined up neatly, with her hands clasped on her knees. Utterly still. As though she's waiting.

I can't imagine what's going through her mind.

As I stand there she notices me watching her, lifts her chin and gives a sudden, ravishing, defiant smile.

'Tallyho!' she exclaims.

'Tallyho,' I call back. On impulse I blow her a kiss. Then I turn and push my way in with sudden determination. It's time to do this.

The funeral director leads me down a pastel corridor, then pauses meaningfully outside a wooden door marked LILY SUITE.

'I'll let you have a few moments alone.' He pushes the door open a little way, then adds, 'Is it true she was the girl in that famous painting?'

'Yes.' I nod.

'Aaah.' He lowers his head. 'How extraordinary. One can hardly believe it. Such a very, very *old* lady. One hundred and five, I believe?'

I know he's trying to be nice but his words flick me on the raw.

'I don't think of her like that,' I say curtly. 'I don't think of her as old.'

He nods hastily. 'Indeed.'

'Anyway. I want to put something in the . . . coffin. Will that be all right? Will it be safe?'

'Quite safe, I assure you.'

'And private,' I say fiercely. 'I don't want anyone else going in here after me. If they want to, you contact me first, OK?'

He surveys his shoes respectfully. 'Of course.'

'Well. Thank you. I'll . . . go in now.'

I walk in, close the door behind me and just stand there for a few moments. Now I'm in here, now I'm actually doing this, my legs feel a bit watery. I swallow a few times, trying to get a grip on myself, telling myself not to freak out. After about a minute I make myself take a step towards the big wooden coffin. Then another.

That's Sadie. Real Sadie. My 105-year-old great-aunt. Who I never knew. I edge forward, breathing heavily. As I reach forward I see just a puff of dry white hair and a glimpse of dried-out old skin.

'Here you are, Sadie,' I murmur. Gently, carefully, I slip the necklace round her neck. I've done it. At last. I've done it.

She looks so tiny and shrivelled. So vulnerable. All the times I wanted to touch Sadie, to squeeze her arm or give her a hug . . . and now here she is. Real flesh. Cautiously I stroke her hair and pull her dress straight, wishing beyond anything she could feel my touch. This frail, ancient body was Sadie's home for 105 years. This was really her.

As I stand there I'm trying to keep my breathing steady; I'm trying to think peaceful, suitable thoughts. Maybe even a couple of words to say aloud. I want to do the right thing. But at the same time there's an urgency beating inside me, growing stronger with every moment I stay here. The truth is, my heart isn't in this room. I have to go. Now.

With trembling legs I reach the door, wrench the handle and hurtle out, to the obvious surprise of the funeral director.

'Is everything all right?' he says.

'Fine,' I gulp, already walking away. 'All fine. Thank you so much. I'll be in touch. But I must go now. I'm sorry, it's rather important . . .'

My chest feels so constricted I can barely breathe. I have to get out of here. Somehow I make it down the corridor and through the foyer, almost running. I reach the entrance and burst out onto the street. And I stop dead, clutching the door, looking straight across the road.

The bench is empty.

I know right then. Of course I know. But still, my legs take me across the road at a run. I look desperately up and down the pavement. I call out, 'Sadie? SADIE?' till I'm hoarse. I brush tears from my eyes and look up and down the street again and I won't give up. At last I sit down on the bench, gripping it with both hands. Just in case. And I wait.

And when it's finally dusk and I'm starting to shiver . . . I know. Deep down, where it matters.

She's not coming back. She's moved on.

Thirteen

'LADIES AND GENTLEMEN. Thank you so much for being here today at this occasion of sadness, celebration, festivity . . .' I survey the massed faces gazing up at me expectantly. Rows and rows of them. Filling the pews of St Botolph's Church. '. . . and above all, appreciation of an extraordinary woman who has touched us all.'

I turn to glance at the massive reproduction of Sadie's painting which is dominating the church. Around and beneath it are the most beautiful flower arrangements I've ever seen, with lilies and orchids and trailing ivy and even a reproduction of Sadie's dragonfly necklace, made out of the palest yellow roses set on a bed of moss.

I honestly didn't intend this event to be such a massive deal at first. I just wanted to organise a memorial service for Sadie. But then Malcolm at the London Portrait Gallery suggested they announce the details of the service on their website for any art-lovers who wanted to come and pay their respects. To everyone's astonishment, they were besieged by applications. In the end they had to do a ballot. And here they all are, crammed in. People who want to honour Sadie.

'I'd also like to say, great clothes. Bravo.' I beam around at the vintage coats, the beaded scarves, the occasional pair of spats. 'I think Sadie would have approved.'

The dress code for today is '1920s' and everyone has made a stab at it of some sort. And I don't *care* if memorial services don't usually have dress codes, like that vicar kept saying. Sadie would have loved it, and that's what counts.

All the nurses from the Fairside Home have made a spectacular effort, both with themselves and also with all the elderly residents who have come. They're in the most fabulous outfits, with headdresses and necklaces, every single one. I meet Ginny's eye and she beams at me.

It was Ginny and a couple of other nurses from the home who came with me to Sadie's private funeral and cremation, a few weeks ago. I only wanted people there who had really known her. It was very quiet and afterwards I took them all out for lunch and we cried and drank wine and told Sadie stories and laughed, and then I gave them a big donation to the nursing home and they all started crying again.

Mum and Dad weren't invited. But I think they kind of understood.

I glance at them, sitting in the front row. Mum is in a disastrous lilac drop-waisted dress with a headband which looks more seventies Abba than twenties. And Dad's in a totally non-1920s outfit. It's just a normal, modern single-breasted suit, with a silk spotted handkerchief in his top pocket. But I'll forgive him, because he's gazing up at me with such warmth and pride and affection.

'Those of you who only know Sadie as a girl in a portrait may wonder, who was the person behind the painting? Well, she was an amazing woman. She was sharp, funny, brave, outrageous . . . and she treated life as the most massive adventure. As you all know, she was muse to one of the famous painters of the twentieth century. She bewitched him. He never stopped loving her, nor she him. They were tragically separated by circumstances. But if he'd only lived longer . . . who knows?'

I pause for breath and glance at Mum and Dad, who are watching me, riveted. I practised my whole speech for them last night, and Dad kept saying incredulously, 'How do you *know* all this?' I had to start referring vaguely to 'archives' and 'old letters' just to keep him quiet.

I sneak a tiny glance at Ed, sitting next to Mum, and he winks back. 'She lived to 105, which is quite an achievement.' I look around the audience. 'But she would have hated it if people just thought of her as "the 105-year-old". Because inside, she was a twenty-three-year-old all her life. A girl who lived her life with sizzle. A girl who loved the Charleston, cocktails, shaking her booty in nightclubs and fountains, driving too fast, lipstick, smoking gaspers . . . and barney-mugging.'

I'm taking a chance that no one in the audience knows what barney-mugging means. Sure enough, they smile back politely, as though I've said she loved flower-arranging.

'She loathed knitting,' I add, with emphasis. 'That should go on the record. But she loved *Grazia*.' There's a laugh around the church, which is good. I wanted there to be laughter.

'Of course, for us, her family,' I continue, 'she wasn't just a nameless girl in a painting. She was my great-aunt. She was part of our heritage. It's easy to discount family. It's easy to take them for granted. But your family is your history. Your family is part of who you are. And without Sadie, none of us would be in the position we are today.'

I can't help shooting Uncle Bill a steely gaze at this point. He's sitting next to Dad. It hasn't been a great month for him. He's been constantly in the news pages *and* the business pages, and none of it good.

'We should honour her. Which is why I've set up the Sadie Lancaster Foundation. Funds raised will be distributed by the trustees to causes of which she would have approved. In particular we will be supporting various dance-related organisations, charities for the elderly, the Fairside Nursing Home and the London Portrait Gallery.'

I grin at Malcolm Gledhill, who beams back. He was so chuffed when I told him.

'I would also like to announce that my uncle, Bill Lington, wishes to make the following tribute to Sadie, which I will read on his behalf.'

There is no way on earth I was letting Uncle Bill get up on this podium. Or write his own tribute. He doesn't even know what I'm about to say. I unfold a separate piece of paper and begin.

'"It is entirely due to my aunt Sadie's painting that I was able to launch myself in business. Without her beauty, without her help, I would not find myself in the privileged position I occupy today. During her life I did not appreciate her enough. And for this I am truly sorry."' I pause for effect. '"I am therefore delighted to announce today that I will be donating £10,000,000 to the Sadie Lancaster Foundation. It is a small recompense, to a very special person."'

There's a stunned murmuring. Uncle Bill has gone a kind of sallow putty colour, with a rictus smile fixed in place.

'I'd sincerely like to thank you all for coming.' I look around the church. 'Sadie was in a nursing home by the time her painting was discovered. She never knew quite how appreciated and loved she was. She would have been overwhelmed to see you all. She would have realised . . .' I feel a sudden rush of tears. No. I *can't* lose it now. After I've done so well. Somehow I manage a smile. 'She would have realised what a mark she made on this world. She's given so many people pleasure, and her legacy will remain for generations. As her great-niece, I'm incredibly proud.' I swivel to survey the painting briefly for a silent moment, then turn back. 'Now it simply remains for me to say . . . To Sadie. If you would all raise your glasses . . .'

There's a rustling and clinking as everyone reaches for their cocktail glasses. Each guest was presented with a cocktail as they arrived: a gin fizz or a Sidecar, mixed by two barmen from the Hilton. (And I don't *care* if people don't usually have cocktails at memorial services.)

'Tallyho!' I lift my glass high, and everyone obediently echoes, 'Tallyho!' There's silence as everyone sips. Then, gradually, murmurs and giggles start to echo round the church.

The organ crashes in with the opening bars of 'Jerusalem' and I make my way down the podium steps to rejoin Ed, who's standing next to my parents. He's wearing the most amazing vintage 1920s dinner jacket, which makes him look like a black and white movie star.

'Good job,' he whispers, clutching my hand. 'You did her proud.'

I look round at the flower-laden church, and the beautiful outfits, and all the people gathered here. So many diverse people, from different walks of life. Young, old, family members, friends from the nursing home . . . people that she touched in some way. All here for her. *This* is what she deserved. All along.

When the service finally ends, the organist launches into the Charleston (I don't *care* if memorial services don't usually have the Charleston) and the congregation slowly files out, still clutching their cocktail glasses. The reception is being held at the London Portrait Gallery, thanks to lovely Malcolm Gledhill.

But I don't rush. I can't quite face all the talking and chatter and buzz. Not just yet. I sit in my front pew, waiting till it's quieter.

'Darling.' Mum's voice interrupts me and I see her approaching. Her cheeks are flushed and there's a glow of pleasure all around her as she slides in beside me. 'That was wonderful. *Wonderful.*'

'Thanks.' I smile at her.

'I'm so proud of the way you skewered Uncle Bill. Your charity will do great things, you know.'

I gaze at Mum, intrigued. She hasn't worried about a single thing today.

'Mum . . . you're different. You seem less stressed. What happened?'

There's silence as Mum adjusts her lilac sleeves.

'It was very strange,' she says at last. 'A few weeks ago, something strange happened. It was almost as though I could hear . . .' She hesitates, then whispers, 'a *voice in my head.*'

'A voice?' I stiffen. 'What kind of voice?'

'I'm not a religious woman. You know that.' Mum glances around the church and leans towards me. 'But truly, this voice followed me around all day! It wouldn't leave me alone. I thought I was going mad!'

'What . . . what did it say?'

'It said, "Everything's going to be all right; stop worrying!" Just that, over and over, for hours. I got quite ratty with it, in the end. I said out loud, "All right, Mrs Inner Voice, I get the message!" And then it stopped, like magic.'

'Wow,' I manage, a lump in my throat. 'That's . . . amazing.'

'And ever since then, I find things don't *bother* me quite as much.' Mum glances at her watch. 'I'd better go, Dad's on his way round with the car. Do you want a lift?'

'Not just yet. I'll see you there.'

Mum nods understandingly, then heads out. I lean back, still a bit blown away by Mum's revelation. I can just see Sadie trailing after her, pestering her, refusing to give up. All the things that Sadie was and did and achieved. Even now, I feel like I only ever knew the half of it.

The music eventually comes to an end and I rouse myself, pick up my bag and get to my feet. The place is already empty.

As I head out of the church into the forecourt, a ray of sunlight catches me in the eye and I blink. I find my gaze drifting upwards to the sky. As it does so often. Still.

'Sadie?' I say quietly. 'Sadie?' But of course there's no reply.

'Well done!' Ed suddenly descends on me from nowhere and plants a kiss on my lips, making me jump. 'Spectacular. The whole thing. It couldn't have gone better. I was so proud of you.'

'Oh. Thanks.' I flush with pleasure. 'So many people came!'

'It was amazing. And that's all down to you.' He touches my cheek gently and says more quietly, 'Are you ready to go to the gallery? I told your mom and dad to go on.'

'Yes.' I smile. 'Thanks for waiting. I just needed a moment.'

'Sure.' As we start walking he threads his arm through mine and I squeeze it back. Yesterday, out of the blue, as we were walking to the memorial rehearsal, Ed told me casually that he was extending his London secondment by six months, because he might as well use up his car insurance. Then he gave me a long look and asked me what I thought about him staying around for a while?

I pretended to think hard, trying to hide my euphoria, then said yes, why not? And he kind of grinned. And I kind of grinned.

'So . . . who were you talking to just now?' he adds carelessly. 'When you came out of the church.'

'What?' I say, a little thrown. 'Nobody. Um, is the car nearby?'

''Cause it *sounded* . . .' he persists lightly, 'as if you said "Sadie".'

There's a beat of silence while I try to arrange my features in exactly the right mystified expression.

'You thought I said *Sadie*?' I throw in a little laugh to show exactly what a bizarre idea this is. 'Why would I say that?'

'That's what I thought,' Ed says, still in the same conversational manner. 'I thought to myself, "Why would she say that?"'

He's not going to let this go. I can tell.

'Maybe it's the British accent,' I say in sudden inspiration. 'Maybe you heard me saying Sidecar. "I need another Sidecar."'

'Sidecar.' Ed stops walking and fixes me with a long, quizzical gaze. Somehow I force myself to look back with wide, innocent eyes. He can't read my mind, I remind myself. He *can't* read my mind.

'There's something,' he says at last, shaking his head. 'I don't know what it is, but there's something.'

I feel a fierce tug in my heart. Ed knows everything else about me, big and small. He has to know this too. After all, he was part of it.

'Yes.' I nod at last. 'There's something. I'll tell you about it. One day.'

Ed's mouth twitches into a smile. He runs his eyes over my vintage dress, my swingy jet beads, my marcelled hair and the feathers bobbing over my forehead, and his expression softens.

'Come on, twenties girl.' He takes hold of my hand with the firm, sure grasp I've got used to. 'You did great by your aunt. Shame she didn't see it.'

'Yes,' I agree. 'It's a shame.'

But as we walk away I allow myself one more tiny glance up at the empty sky.

I hope she did.

Sophie Kinsella

Like most modern women, Sophie Kinsella is used to juggling a number of different roles in her life. Wife. Mother. Sister. Friend. Headmaster's Wife. Author. 'It's like wearing lots of different hats,' she told me when we met recently. 'And luckily, I'm a girl who just loves hats!' she laughs. 'It hasn't helped that I've written books under two different names: my real name, Madeleine Wickham, and as Sophie Kinsella. But to some extent, I guess, all authors are a little schizophrenic. We lead most of our lives in solitary confinement, living and breathing the books that we're writing. Then it's out into the world to meet and greet and promote the book.'

As Sophie is an author who writes about shopping and fashion so successfully, especially in her series of *Shopaholic* novels, it is no surprise to me that she looks absolutely amazing, wearing a vintage 1960s polka-dot dress with gorgeous flat pumps—'They came in a goody bag from *Glamour* magazine when I won their Writer of the Year Award'—and the most fabulous Prada handbag. 'I saw this when I was on the set of the *Confessions of a Shopaholic* movie. We were filming in Prada and there it was and it was like instant love. There was a waiting list of about fifty people but, magically, I managed to get it.'

The last twelve months have been a whirlwind for Sophie and one in which her multi-faceted personality became a necessity, as she jetted between home and the movie set where her *Shopaholic* novels were being filmed. 'Being a novice in the film world, everything seemed exciting: watching the first scene I wrote over ten years ago come to cinematic life as Becky Bloomwood—played by Isla Fisher—gazes at her Visa bill in horror; seeing the designer name I invented, Denny & George, emblazoned on shop windows on Fifth Avenue; filming all night in Barney's department store. Then, in an instant, I was on a plane and boom! back home at the boarding prep school where my husband, Henry, is headmaster, and attending chapel service . . . and back to planning the next book.'

The next book was *Twenties Girl* and Sophie had got the idea for it from her American editor. 'She suggested some years ago that I write a ghost story. It was just an off-the-cuff remark but I remembered it and thought it would be fun to try. But I'm not really into the supernatural, I'm into comedy. So, for me, it was a question of whether I could make a ghost a strong enough character. I knew that I wanted a very bolshy, demanding, bossy ghost who would wreak havoc in the life of the person she was haunting. I absolutely love the Twenties period and thought by having a flapper as a ghost, the comedy could come through the culture clash between modern girl Lara and 1920s Sadie.'

With the idea now firmly in place, how does she actually begin? 'It all starts with what I like to call my "coffee shop stage". I have a very full loyalty card at Starbucks! I love to sit around, watching and listening to the world go by, losing myself in my characters, and plotting and writing notes. Planning takes a couple of months. I don't rush it. By the time I am ready to start writing, the story is all there and I am dying to tell it rather than feeling my way cautiously. I find the writing process is a little bit like acting—I laugh, I cry, I get so wrapped up in the story. At the end of the day I can come downstairs and Henry will ask me something, like, "Have we any bread?" "Bread?" I'll wail. "How can you worry about *bread* when Lara and Sadie have just had a terrible fight?"

One question I had to ask Sophie is whether or not she has learned to dance the Charleston? 'Yes, I had a go, but learned would be an overstatement! You must check out the Charleston on YouTube. They have some amazing original footage and a step-by-step guide and everyone should have a go. I tried but wouldn't say it was a success—I put my lack of brilliance down to needing a shiny dance floor, the right ambience, lots and lots of cocktails and the perfect dress, of course.'

After all the glamour of the film world and hard work at the computer, what does Sophie do to relax? 'Relax? What's that? I love to just hang out with Henry and my kids. In the winter months, Saturday night's *X-Factor* has become an absolute must—it's old-fashioned family viewing. But, basically, spending time with Henry and my boys is me wearing my most favourite hat of all.'

TELL ME
NO SECRETS

JULIE CORBIN

Two years ago, I was given a writing
assignment: Write an autobiographical piece
and insert three lies.
I wrote about an experience I'd had at Guide
camp, and suddenly one of those *What if?*
moments struck me.
What if one of the girls did something awful?
What if she covered it up? And what if it came
back to haunt her in later years?
As I pondered the answers to these questions,
the first seeds of *Tell Me No Secrets* were sown
and began to grow, forcing me to realise how
guilty secrets can poison our lives and change
our destinies for ever . . .

Julie

They say that everybody has a secret. For some, it's a stolen extramarital kiss on a balmy evening after two or three glasses of wine. For others it's that girl, teased mercilessly about the shape of her nose or the whine in her voice until she has to move school. Some of us, though, keep secrets that make liars of our lives. Take me, for example. The skeleton I fear isn't hiding in my closet. The one I fear lies underground. Her name was Rose and she was nine years old when she died.

I'm not going to make excuses for what I did. I'm going to tell my story as it is and as it was.

This isn't the beginning but it's a good place to start . . .

1

I LIVE IN SCOTLAND, on the east coast a few miles beyond St Andrews. The east of Scotland is flatter than the west, the scenery less spectacular. We don't have the craggy peaks or brooding glens dour with dead men's stories. We have instead a gentle roll and sway of land and sea that lifts my spirits the way a mountain never can.

And the weather isn't great. After a couple of sunny days we're punished with the haar that rolls in off the North Sea, thick and cold until you can't see the hand in front of your face. But this evening it's exactly as I like it and when I've finished preparing the evening meal, I stand at the sink and watch a couple walking along the beach, their faces turned up to enjoy the last of the day's sunshine.

The phone rings. I dry my hands and lift the receiver. 'Hello,' I say.

'Grace?'

I don't reply. I feel as if I recognise the voice but at the same time,

I don't. There's a tingling under my scalp and it spreads to my face.

'Grace?'

Still I don't reply. This time because I know who it is.

'It's me. Orla,' she says.

I put down the phone and return to the sink. I drain the spaghetti, toss it in oil and cover it with a lid, and then bend down and open the oven door. The juice from the berries has bubbled up through the crumble, running scarlet rivers over the topping. I turn off the oven and walk to the downstairs bathroom. I lock the door behind me and vomit so violently and repeatedly that I taste blood on my tongue.

The front door opens and then slams shut. 'Mum?' I hear Daisy drop her school bag in the hallway and walk towards the kitchen. 'Mum?'

'I'm in here.' My voice wavers and I clear my throat. 'Give me a minute.' I splash my face in the basin and look at myself in the mirror. My eyes stare back at me, my pupils huge and fixed. My face is colourless and there is a relentless drumming inside my skull. I swallow two ibuprofen with a handful of water and count slowly, from one to ten, before I open the door. Daisy is sitting on the bottom stair with our dog Murphy's head on her knee. She's crooning to him and rubbing the backs of his ears. 'How was school?' I ask.

Daisy looks up at me. 'You look hellish. Is it a migraine?'

'Must be.' I try to smile but my head hurts too much. 'Where's Ella?'

'Walking back with Jamie.' She rolls her eyes, stands up and kicks off her shoes. 'I don't know what she sees in him. What's for tea?'

'Spaghetti bolognese and fruit crumble.' The thought of food makes me want to be sick again. I lean into the wall and try to calm myself but I hear her voice: *It's me. Orla.*

I follow Daisy into the kitchen where she's taking a spoonful of sauce from the pot. 'It's good!' She smiles at me, reaches forward and kisses my cheek and then wraps her arms round my shoulders. She's a couple of inches taller than me now. 'Why don't you have a lie down, Mum? Tea can wait.'

'I've taken some painkillers. They should kick in soon.'

'If you're sure.' She rubs my back. 'I'll go and change.'

I tilt my head and give her what she calls my Oh-Daisy smile. Her tie is skewwhiff and her tights have a hole in them.

'I don't do uniforms,' she tells me, her cheeks dimpling.

I run my hand through her cropped hair and she leans against it for a moment before I push her away. 'Go on, then, back into the combats.'

She leaves the room, calling to Murphy who pads along beside her, his tail thumping the air. I sit on a chair and try to think of nothing.

By the time Paul's car tyres crunch over the gravel on the driveway, I feel almost calm again. I hear the muffled sound of his voice and then Ella's in reply. 'I didn't mean it like *that*, Dad!' she says. 'It's a play on words like two martyrs soup, tomato soup.'

Paul laughs. 'Don't tell me one of my daughters is developing a sense of irony. Whatever next!'

They come into the room; Ella is hanging on his arm. Paul bends to kiss me. 'Darling, are you OK?' He runs a hand over my cheek.

'I'm fine.' I stand up and rest my head against his neck. Immediately, tears flood the back of my eyes and I pull away. 'How was your day?'

'Usual procrastination at the departmental meeting but otherwise—' He stops talking. He is watching me. I am making tidy piles of the bills and letters that are on the sideboard. He pulls me back towards him. 'Grace, you're shaking. What's wrong?'

'Just a headache.' I press my fingertips round my eyes so that he can't see the expression in them. 'It'll pass. Combination of tiredness and dehydration.' I smile. 'You know me—I never drink enough water.'

'Well, if I've told you once . . .'

'. . . you've told me a hundred times.' I manage to look into his eyes and see nothing but straightforward concern: no suspicion or irritation, just humour and a gentle kindness that comforts me. I risk leaning into his neck again. 'Thank you.'

'For what?'

I kiss below his ear and whisper, 'For being you.'

He squeezes me tight and then releases me. 'Daisy home?'

'She's upstairs changing.'

'How's my dad been today?'

'Fine. He went into St Andrews to the hardware store. Came back with a bootload of supplies to repair the fence with.'

'No forgetfulness?' He tries not to look worried.

'Not that he mentioned. Let's not cross bridges.'

He gives me a tight smile. 'I'll call him through.'

He goes outside to the small apartment that connects to our house and I mix some dressing for the salad.

'Are you getting tea?' Ella is eyeballing me over the glass she's holding up to her lips, swigging back a huge mouthful of juice until her cheeks puff out.

'Yes. And it's ready so please don't eat anything.' I drizzle oil and lemon juice over the green salad. 'Are you going to change?'

She looks down at herself. She is wearing exactly the same uniform as Daisy but somehow on Ella it looks stylish. She never has holes in her tights and her tie is always lying off centre. 'I'm not changing. I'm fine as I am.' She stuffs a piece of cold ham into her mouth and lifts the carton of juice, slurping it back in exaggerated gulps.

I say nothing. My head still hurts, my nerves are strung tight—*It's me. Orla*—and, anyway, I pick my battles carefully with Ella. I edge past her and take the warm plates from the oven.

Ed comes into the house with Paul. 'What's for tea tonight then, Grace?' he shouts, rubbing his hands together. 'Best part of the day, this is.'

I smile at him. I love my father-in-law. He's one of life's gentlemen.

We sit down to eat. Paul and Ed are at either end of the table and the girls are opposite me. My stomach contracts at the sight of the food but I spoon spaghetti into my mouth and eat automatically, preoccupied with what's going on inside my head. Memories hatch like chicks in an incubator: Orla does handstands in the sun, her hair brushing over my bare feet as I catch her legs; arms round each other's back, running the three-legged race, giggling; summer afternoons, rolling up and over the dunes; cookery classes, the rolling pin a weapon in her hand; trying on shoes, tops, trousers, skirts before finally parting with our pocket money. And then the last time we were alone. The hard slap of her hand on my cheek.

'Is there any more, Mum?' Daisy is holding her plate towards me.

'Sure.' I load some onto her plate.

'Wait till you girls leave home,' Ed is saying. 'You'll appreciate your mum's cooking then. Won't you just.'

'I already do,' Daisy says, looking sideways at her sister.

Ella seems not to have heard and, pushing her plate away, looks around the table at us all. 'So guess who got the lead in the play?'

'Now what play would that be?'

'*Romeo and Juliet*, Granddad.'

'Ah!' Suddenly, like a cloud drifting over the sun, Ed's eyes glaze over. Then, looking around him, he says, 'Where's Eileen?'

'Eileen's not here right now, Granddad, and we're all having tea,' Daisy says.

'Of course we are. We're all having tea.'

He looks worried and I sense his rising panic. I rest my hand on his. How to tell him that his wife has been dead these last five years? In the beginning we tried to orientate him to the present but all it did was make him relive his grief, acutely as a knife through flesh.

'Mum's busy, Dad,' Paul tells him. 'You're eating with us this evening.'

'Yes, right.' He nods to himself, trying to make sense of it, hanging on to the words. He looks at me. 'Is there pudding, Alison?'

'Coming right up,' I tell him. In these moments he often mistakes me for his daughter and I don't correct him.

'Anyway,' Ella says, turning to her father. 'I got the part.' She gives a broad, excited smile that lights up the whole table.

'Congratulations!' Paul and I say, both at the same time.

'That's fantastic! And who's playing Romeo?' I ask.

'Rob.' She shrugs. 'He wouldn't be my choice.'

'And how many girls auditioned for Juliet?' I say.

'About twenty.'

'And you were the best. Well done.' Paul reaches over and claps a hand on her shoulder.

'It's because she's good at flirting,' Daisy comments under her breath.

'I heard that,' Ella says. 'For your information there's more to acting than meets the eye and at least *I* have boyfriends. Maybe if you didn't dress like a dyke—'

'Maybe if you weren't such a fashion victim, you wouldn't always be borrowing money from me.'

'Well, maybe if you were a better sister you'd be pleased for me,' she bites back. Her eyes well up with angry tears and she pushes back her chair and flounces from the room, banging the door behind her.

Daisy watches her go. 'With acting like that, is it any wonder she gets the parts?'

'Daisy! Be careful of sour grapes,' Paul says. 'It's not worthy of you.'

'Why would I be jealous of her? We're identical twins. Capable of exactly the same achievements.'

'And that's why winding each other up makes no sense. I appreciate that you might have wanted the part—'

'I didn't audition,' Daisy tells him. 'I don't like acting.'

'Is that any reason not to support Ella?'

'I do support Ella. More than you know.'

'Well, it doesn't look that way to me.'

His tone is mild, but Daisy is bristling. She finishes her pudding and gives me the bowl. Her hands are steadier than her eyes and as she leaves the room she murmurs, 'What's the point?'

'Daisy!' Paul calls after her but she ignores him and he offers me an apologetic smile. 'Sorry, love. You've cooked a lovely meal and now they're both upset. I don't know what gets into them sometimes.'

'They're sisters.' I shrug. 'That's what sisters do.'

'You're right. Whoever said being a parent was easy?' He leans over and kisses my cheek. 'We'll get there. We have each other. That's the most important thing.' His eyes meet mine. Soft, the grey of dove's wings, they are both wise and calming and it makes me want to tell him about the phone call. And more. But I can't. Not now, not ever.

He looks to the end of the table. 'How about a game of Scrabble then, Dad, eh?'

Ed, quietly finishing his crumble, brightens immediately and they both go through to the living room, leaving me to stack the dishwasher. While my hands do the work, my mind is elsewhere. Orla. Until this evening, I hadn't heard from her for over twenty years. So successfully have I locked away her memory that I have barely even thought of her. As young teenagers we were best friends. And then, the year we both turned sixteen, everything changed. Rose died. And though we had our chance to be truthful, we didn't take it. We lied; each lie feeding the next until we had created a huge, irreconcilable secret.

The doorbell rings and I jump, then I make my way to the front of the house. I have a horrible feeling that Orla will be standing there. But when I open the door, I'm relieved to see that it's Jamie, Ella's latest boyfriend. His hair is gelled up in spikes across the top of his head and he smells strongly of deodorant.

Ella clatters down the stairs and elbows me out of the way. She's wearing a tight, short denim skirt and a top that shows off her midriff.

'Ella, you'll freeze. Please wear something more substantial.'

'I'll keep her warm,' Jamie volunteers and Ella giggles. He licks his lips and I think of my beautiful daughter under his sweaty, adolescent body. I want to push him back through the door.

'Is it just the two of you?' I say.

'No.' She shakes her head. 'Sarah, Mat, Lucy, Rob. The usual.'

'Where are you meeting?'

'Di Rollo's.'

I watch them walk away, their hips touching. His hands slide down her back and they kiss up against a lamppost. I turn away. Daisy is beside me putting on her boots. 'You know your dad didn't mean to get at you,' I tell her, stroking the top of her head.

'I know, Mum.' She shrugs and texts a quick message on her mobile. 'I'm going out for a bit. I'll be home before dark. And don't worry about Ella,' she shouts back over her shoulder. 'She's going to be careful.'

She's going to be careful? Unease creeps along my nerve endings. I want to call after Daisy but she's already along the end of the street. I shut the door and rest my back against it, then I climb the stairs and go into Ella's room. The floor is a muddle of clothes, clean and dirty mixed up. Schoolbooks are dumped in the corner. I open the drawer of her bedside cabinet and see a half-empty foil strip sitting on top of her hairbrush. I pick it up and read the name. The pills are called Microgynon and each one is labelled a different day of the week.

I try to line up straight, coherent thoughts. I can't. All I keep thinking is that she's too young for the stuff of adult life: sex, choices and consequences. Rationally, I accept that she is hardly a child. She is in fact the same age as I was when Orla and I last saw each other: in the police station, both of us bedraggled, wrapped in blankets, complicit.

I put the pills back into the drawer. I'll talk to Paul. He is more levelheaded than I am; his parenting skills are more assured.

The mobile in my pocket starts to chirrup like a budgie. I look at the name flashing on the screen: Euan.

'Hi, Grace. Is Sarah there?'

'No. They're all down at Di Rollo's.'

He sighs. 'Great. She hasn't come back from school yet and she needs to revise for her history tomorrow.'

'You could always go down and collect her but—'

'Might be more than my life's worth. What happened to only going out on Friday and Saturday nights?'

'Like when we were young?'

'Aye.' He starts to laugh. We have this conversation often. It goes along the lines of: When we were their age we wouldn't have dared . . .

'So how are things?' he asks. 'I missed you at work today.'

'I took some samples over to Margie Campbell in Perth,' I say, closing my eyes against thoughts of Orla and what she knows about me. 'She's commissioning me to paint the view from her family home in Iona.'

'Great stuff. You're becoming quite the local celebrity.'

'Euan—' I stop. 'Remember Orla?' I say in a rush.

'Yeah?'

Tears collect behind my eyes. 'She called me earlier.'

'Shit.' He whistles. 'What did she want?'

'I don't know. I cut her off before she had a chance to tell me. The sound of her voice, it freaked me out. I thought I'd never hear from her again. I *hoped* I'd never hear from her again.'

He turns from the mouthpiece and I hear him talking to Monica, his wife. 'She's down at the beach. OK, you go. Yup.' He speaks back into the receiver. 'I wonder why she would call you after all this time.'

'Twenty-four years bar six days,' I say. 'I counted.'

'Grace. Don't,' he says. 'Don't go over old ground.'

'Do you remember when we were kids?' I'm whispering now. 'Do you remember how Orla always managed to get her own way?'

'Yes, I remember.' He's silent for several seconds and I wonder whether he's thinking what I'm thinking. 'Are you coming into work tomorrow?'

'Yeah.'

'See you then . . . and, Grace, don't worry. Chances are she was feeling a bit nostalgic; spur-of-the-moment call and she won't repeat it.'

I wish I could believe that. 'But how did she get my number? Do you think she's been talking to Monica?'

'Monica hasn't mentioned it and I think she would have. She never liked Orla. She would have asked you before giving out your number.'

I'm sure he's right. As children they were out-and-out enemies. I finish speaking to Euan and stand by the door watching Ed and Paul play Scrabble. Paul laughs along with Ed. He is a good man, an excellent husband and father and I love him more than I am able to express. The thought of living life without him is unthinkable. I wonder how much he could take before he was unwilling to stand by me. I wonder just exactly how far and wide his love for me stretches. I wonder but I don't want to find out.

June 15, 1984. Rose shoves her way to the front. The other girls don't grumble because Rose's mother died recently and Miss Parkin, Rose's teacher, has ordered us all to be extra kind to her. 'Rose is in your patrol, Grace, because I know I can rely on you,' she tells me.

I'm bored but trying not to show it. Almost sixteen and desperate to leave the Guides, I promised to go on one last camping trip. There are five girls in my patrol, all of them under twelve, and Rose, the youngest, has just had her ninth birthday. That makes her a year too young for the Guides but Miss Parkin has allowed her to join early.

The girls are all waiting for their instructions. 'Go and find some sticks,' I tell them. 'Hang on, Rose.' I point to her laces trailing on the ground. 'You need to tie those up before you trip over them.'

Her eyes look anxiously towards the other girls who are disappearing into the trees.

'Don't worry, you'll catch them up.' I bend down to help her.

'Thank you, Grace.' She smiles. 'I can't do double knots.'

'You'll learn.' I stroke her hair. 'Off you go, then.'

Orla comes over. 'Have you got rid of your shadow at last?'

'She's just desperate to get everything right. We were like that.'

'You maybe! I never was.' She pulls cigarettes and a lighter out of her pocket. 'Her dad's a bit of all right though, isn't he?'

'For God's sake!' I hiss. 'His wife's not long dead.'

'So?' She gives a careless shrug. 'That doesn't stop him being attractive. You coming?' She waves the cigarettes at me.

I shake my head.

'Suit yourself.' She throws me a dirty look. 'Some friend you are.'

She stomps off, her boots kicking up the earth, and I hesitate, almost go after her, but decide not to. For the last few weeks she's been acting weird. I don't know what's wrong with her and she won't tell me. I suspect it might be to do with her parents. They are having marriage problems and Orla, as an only child, ends up in the middle of it.

I walk through the trees towards the campfire. The air smells sweeter than newly baked bread or Euan's baby nephew when he's been bathed and talcumed, and a cool breeze is blowing through the branches. The other patrol leaders are gathered in the clearing and we stand chatting for ten minutes before Miss Parkin comes to give us our orders. Her hair is sticking up all over her head and her blouse is crushed.

Orla is back looking cheerful again. She sidles up to me and speaks into my ear: 'Give her another day and she'll be completely demented.'

'Always talking, Orla!' Miss Parkin barks, her glance including me. 'Both of you, see to the sausages.'

The sausages are wrapped in greaseproof paper, more than a hundred of them, tight and shiny in their skins.

'What does this remind you of?' Orla asks me. She positions one of them in front of her shorts, points it upwards and waves it around.

'Callum when Miss Fraser bends over at the blackboard,' I say at once and we both dissolve into hysterics, a sloppy tangle of weak legs and arms.

Miss Parkin slaps the backs of our bare legs as we fall. 'You should be setting an example to the younger ones,' she tells us. 'Now get on with it or there will be no marks for either of your patrols.'

The fire is lit and we place the sausages over the makeshift grill. My job is to turn them and I do so carefully, shaking off burning sparks that fly up onto my arms. Orla works around me, organising plates and cutlery. Monica and Faye, heads together, are deep in concentrated effort. One splits oblong rolls with a bread knife, the other pours wavy lines of ketchup along the spines. As usual, Monica looks perfectly groomed as if she's just stepped out of the hairdresser's. I wonder how she does it.

Orla takes one of the sausages and bites the end off it. 'How about we sneak off and join the boys tonight?'

I don't answer. The youth club is camping about 300 yards away, through the trees and beyond the pond. Several boys from our school are there, including Euan, whom I've been going out with for five weeks and six days. He's my next-door neighbour and we've known each other for ever but that hasn't stopped me falling for him. The thought of joining him in his tent sends my heart racing but I don't want Orla there as an audience.

At last we sit down to eat and for the first time that day we are all quiet. The sausages, wrapped in white bread rolls, taste like a small piece of heaven. Dusk is creeping through the trees, casting shadows behind us and blowing a cold wind over our tired bodies. When Miss Parkin's back is turned, Orla reaches for the ketchup bottle, tips it up and makes words on the tray. I sit up to read what she's written: *Rose! Mummy wants to talk to you.*

I meet her stare. She is bold and brazen as a wolf on the hunt. Without shifting her eyes from mine, she nudges Rose with her feet. Rose, already half asleep, is curled up like a kitten at my side.

'What?' she says, rubbing at her cheek.

'There's a message for you, Rose!' Orla shakes her fully awake. 'Look! It's from the spirit world.'

I grab a sausage and before Rose reads the words, I swirl it through the ketchup until all that's left is a mix of half shapes and splodges.

Orla glares at me. 'Spoilsport,' she says.

Next day I stay in bed until almost seven, hugging into Paul's back, lingering in the intimacy of the night before. As soon as the game of Scrabble was over and Ed went through to organise himself for bed, I told Paul about finding out that Ella was on the pill. His reaction was, as I expected, more measured and less fearful than mine. He reminded me that she is, after all, being responsible. Nothing would be gained by taking a hard line but something could be gained by chatting quietly about how she is feeling and what her plans might be. We agreed that I would speak to her after school, including Daisy in the conversation so that Ella doesn't feel as if I'm picking on her.

Then the girls came home from their evenings out and we all retired to bed. Paul and I lay side by side talking about the possibility of a sabbatical in Australia. For the last fourteen years, Paul has been professor of marine biology at St Andrews University but he is due some research time and has applied for a position at the University of Melbourne. Fingers crossed he will be successful and in two months' time we will up sticks and move to Victoria. Paul's sister and family have lived there for over fifteen years and are looking forward to welcoming us all.

Paul and I spent time planning and imagining where we'll live and how we'll enjoy the holidays and then, moments later, we were making love, the sort of married sex that takes ten minutes but leaves behind a residue of sweetness that endures for days.

Daisy is out of bed first and then I follow, prepare breakfast and see them all out of the door before I set off myself. I'm lucky. I can walk to work. I call Murphy and walk to the end of our street and down to the waterfront. The harbour is empty this morning and the tide is going out. The fishing boats have already left for the deeper waters of the North Sea where they catch shellfish and crabs. The harbour wall stretches for over 200 yards; its top is almost four feet thick and I walk along the inside edge of it, enjoying the strength of the wind that comes in off the sea and tries to blow me backwards.

When the wall ends, I drop back down onto a single-track road with yellow gorse on one side and a sandy beach on the other. I breathe in a lungful of salty air and then look up to the sky where clouds scud across the blue towards the far horizon. It's an optimistic sky and I feel like an optimistic me. Thoughts chase around my head—Orla, Ella, Ed, a triumvirate of worries—but I don't hang on to them. Instead I enjoy the walk, one foot in front of the other, Murphy at my heels and the sea breeze buffing my cheeks.

As I turn the last corner I see Monica placing her briefcase and jacket into the boot of her car. Monica is one of those women who illuminates my own inadequacies. She is a successful and popular GP. She dresses beautifully; she runs marathons; she is organised. Her children never forget their lunch boxes or PE kit and she isn't confused about how to bring them up. She knows exactly what they need: love, guidance and opportunities.

We have a long history together, beginning in primary school when I stood, brand-new and alone, in the dinner queue.

I wanted to cry. Monica made room beside her on the bench. She patted the space and I felt gratitude swell up through my chest. Then she told me that my shoes needed cleaning and I should make sure I did it that evening. Perhaps I even needed new ones?

That's Monica. What she gives with one hand she takes away with the other.

As I draw close she turns to me, smiling into the sun. 'Hi, Grace. Congratulations are in order, I hear. Euan tells me you have another commission.'

'Oh, that.' I nod as if I'm just remembering. 'Margie Campbell.'

'She's a great one, Margie. Has a real sense of community. She likes to support local artists.' She looks up at me. 'For better or worse.'

'Mmm. She does.' I smile straight back at her.

'Tom's off school today. He was sick last night so he's upstairs in bed.' She opens her car door. 'Don't let Euan forget about him.'

'I won't.'

'And the window cleaner will be here around eleven. His money is on the kitchen counter.'

I wave back over my shoulder and walk round the side of their house, following the winding path of steppingstones to the bottom of the garden. Euan is an architect and he and I share a workspace. He designed it himself, soon after they moved back from London. The cabin is modern, built from Scandinavian pine, and is all soft angles. There are two rooms: one we work in and the other is a guest bedroom.

I can see Euan through the side window as I walk towards the door. He is working on a barn conversion and is standing in front of his drawing board. I push open the door. Murphy barks and runs over to Euan. Meanwhile Euan's dog, Muffin, has come over to me. She is also a Labrador, a gentler, calmer version of Murphy. She and Murphy settle down into their dog bed in the corner, resting their heads on each other.

'Good walk over?'

I nod. 'It's the best sort of day out there. So Tom's not well?'

'Temperature, headache, up all night vomiting. What can I say?' He sits down. 'Any more calls from Orla?'

I shake my head. 'I've been thinking. What's the worry? What motive could she have for digging up the past? What could she possibly have to gain?' I let out a breath. 'Coffee?'

'Please.'

'I don't think she'll ring again, but if she does, I'm going to make it clear that I don't want to hear from her. We're grown-up women, for God's sake. What's she going to do? Stalk me? You know what? I think I overreacted. She's probably embarrassed by the whole thing and—'

Euan cuts in. 'She was never that easily embarrassed.'

'She might have changed.'

'Have you? Have I? Don't be fooled. You know what she's capable of.'

I think back to some of the lies she told and the people she hurt and I give an involuntary shiver. 'Do you think she's intending to come back to the village?' I swallow the lump in my throat. 'Do you think she's going to say something about Rose?'

'I don't know.' His face is concerned. 'But unless she's had a personality transplant, I think that anything is possible.'

It's not what I want to hear. 'So what should I do?'

'Act friendly. Find out what she wants.'

'Keep your friends close and your enemies closer?'

'Exactly.'

'You really think she might be my enemy?'

'Think about it. Think about how she used to behave. She had you dancing to her tune.'

'Not always,' I say slowly. 'Sometimes it felt like a tug of war between the two of—'

The boards in the hall creak. Somehow Tom has managed to come through the door without either of us noticing.

'Grace, I'm not well.'

'Poor you.' I give him a sympathetic look. 'Do you want to sleep down here?'

'Is that OK, Dad? It's lonely in the house.'

'Sure.' Euan claps him on the back and I walk him through to the bedroom. The bed is already made up and I pull back the covers.

'Climb in, laddie,' I say, adopting a nurse's jollity. 'Sleep is the best medicine.'

'It's a shame this bed never gets used.' He throws himself onto it, grabs a pillow to hug. 'Whenever we have guests they always sleep at the house. I'm hoping that Dad's going to let me have the cabin as a bachelor pad when I'm eighteen. I'll be needing my own space by then.'

'You might find Sarah trying to beat you to it, Tom,' I say, tucking the covers round him. 'She has two years on you.'

'She's not going to hang around at home. She'll be straight off to uni. Mum gets on her nerves.' He gives a yawn. 'I feel really hungry.'

'I'll make you some lunch when you wake, I promise.'

'Thanks, Grace. You're wicked.'

I stroke the top of his hair flat. His lashes are long and rest on the crest of his cheeks and freckles scatter across his nose. He looks so much like Euan did at fourteen that it makes my heart ache.

I arrive home after the girls. They are in the living room. Ella is lying on her front on the sofa, her eyes closed, her face resting sideways on a textbook. Daisy sits in one of the easy chairs, a science book on her lap.

'Girls!' I smile at them. 'I thought this might be a good time for the three of us to have a chat.'

'Sure.' Daisy closes her book.

Ella gives a laboured sigh and hauls herself up into a sitting position. 'If this is about the state of my room then I'll tidy it up at the weekend. I don't need a whole lecture about it.'

'No, it wasn't about that,' I say, sitting on the arm of the chair. 'It was more about boyfriends. You know, like you and Jamie and what your intentions might be.'

'Oh Jesus! You have to be kidding.' She stands up and folds her arms across her chest. 'I bet you were a sweet little virgin until you were eighteen.' She laughs. 'What could you possibly have to tell us about boys?'

I bite my tongue and take a breath. 'The point is, Ella, that you're growing up fast and . . .' I pause, trying to find the right words.

'And?'

'And it isn't always a good idea to rush the process,' I say. 'Sometimes we want to be grown up before our time and that's when we might get into trouble.'

'We? Who's we?' she snaps back.

'You, Ella. You.' I stand up alongside her. 'The fact is that you are only fifteen.'

'Sixteen on Saturday. We're having a party, remember?'

'The fact *is*,' I continue, my voice sharpening, 'you are *my* daughter, living in *my* house and I would like you to behave like a decent girl.'

Daisy shifts in her seat and starts to click her tongue.

It distracts Ella, but only for a second, and she looks at me with a brittle stare. 'You've been snooping in my room.'

'I have been in your room but I don't believe I was snooping.' I watch her face move from incredulous through hurt and then anger. 'You're my daughter and I love you. All I want is what's best for you.'

She's still glaring at me when the phone rings and Daisy jumps up to answer it. 'Time out, you two,' she says, holding the phone out to me. 'Mum, it's for you.'

I whisper. 'Who is it?'

She shrugs and I look back at Ella. 'We'll talk more later?'

She doesn't answer. She throws me one last filthy look and then I watch her retreating back and hear her feet hammering on the stairs as she goes up to her room.

I take the phone from Daisy's outstretched hand. 'Hello?' I say.

'Your daughter sounds nice.'

Hearing Orla's voice again makes my stomach tighten and all my earlier resolve evaporates quicker than drops of water on a hot griddle.

'Grace?'

I hang up and, taking the phone with me, walk through the kitchen and down the three steps into the utility room. Within seconds it's ringing again. I don't answer. I turn the ringer off and watch the display flash like a beating pulse and then stop. Within seconds the display is flashing again until the call times out. The cycle is repeated several times and it becomes obvious that she isn't going to stop. When the pulse starts up for the tenth time I answer it.

'What do you want?' I sound calm but my knees are wobbling.

'To catch up,' Orla says lightly. 'What else?'

'I'd rather not,' I tell her. 'Please stop calling me.'

'Grace, don't be like that.' There's bewilderment in her voice. 'Why can't we spend some time together? Weren't we friends once?'

'Once,' I agree. 'Twenty-four years ago.'

'But we *were* friends. I want us to meet up,' she says, more definite this time, and I sense steel behind the apparent friendliness.

'Well, I don't,' I say firmly. 'And I don't want you ringing me again.'

'Just once. Meet me just the once. For old times' sake.'

'What old times would they be exactly?'

'Are you saying that we didn't have any fun together? Does our whole relationship have to be coloured by what happened at the end?'

I think about Rose. How much she trusted me. I feel the familiar sadness ripen inside me like a bruised, inedible fruit. 'Yes, I think it does.'

'Grace, I've changed.' Her voice drops to a whisper. 'I have. Truly, I have. I can't explain it all to you over the phone. It sounds dumb and I don't think you'll even believe me.' She laughs. 'I know how this must seem, me getting in touch after all this time, but, please, just listen. I'm back visiting my mum. She's living in Edinburgh now. In Merchiston. My dad, you know, he passed away a few years back.'

'I'm sorry.' I mean it. 'I liked him. He was always very kind to me. And your mum.' I think for a moment. 'I liked her too.'

'I know. It was sad. Dad was very sick and was in a lot of pain but towards the end he was peaceful and, well . . .'

'How is your mum?'

'She's happy with her new husband. Murray Cooper.'

I think about what Euan said: *Find out what she wants*. 'Why do you want to meet me?'

'It's a long story. And better told face to face. Relax, Grace. It's not what you think,' she says darkly, her tone edged with mirth. 'How about I drive up tomorrow?'

'No,' I say quickly. 'I'll come to you. And not tomorrow. Thursday? I need to shop for supplies in Edinburgh: brushes, acrylics, that sort of thing.'

'There's a small restaurant, halfway up Cockburn Street on the left-hand side. One o'clock?'

'Fine.'

As the line goes dead, so do my legs, and I crumple down onto the floor. I sit in a heap for five minutes or more, trying to work out how scared I should be. Thinking back, it doesn't take long for me to come to the conclusion that even if she is only half as reckless and manipulative as she used to be then I should be very afraid. I have to tread carefully. I can't let her back into my life. She is a living, breathing reminder of what happened all those years ago and I don't want her near Paul and the girls—not least because of what she knows about me.

June 1978–82. Orla's mother is French. She wears neat black suits with fitted skirts. She wears patterned silk scarves that she wraps three times round her neck. She wears stockings, not tights, and slides her feet into shoes with three-inch heels. Her lipstick is red and she keeps it in the fridge. She strokes my hair as if I am a cat; kisses me on both cheeks whenever I come to visit. She has flashes of anger, stamps her foot, says '*merde*'. Then, in the next second, she will laugh as if the world is once more a happy place. When Orla's father comes home from work she kisses him on the mouth and strokes her hand down the front of his trousers just as she strokes my hair.

'She's a right selfish madam,' my mother says.

'God knows what Roger sees in her,' my father says. 'She's as flirty as a flea in a bottle.'

I think she's wonderful. I am allowed to call her by her first name. 'On-je-line,' I say. To Angeline, I am clever, I am pretty and I am the best friend her daughter could ever have.

Both Orla and I are only children, but whereas I am often kept at home or weighed down with 'too dangerous', 'be careful', 'mind you don't fall', 'you'll catch your death out there', Orla is allowed to swim in the sea in winter, dance in puddles, camp outside under the night sky.

Angeline is a Catholic. Sometimes my mum allows me to go to church with her and I watch her pray as if her life depends upon it.

At home we eat plain food. 'Get that down you,' my mother says, passing me a steaming plate of stovies. Angeline wrinkles up her nose at the mention of corned beef and cabbage or mince and tatties. She says haggis is hardly fit for dogs. She travels to Edinburgh once a week to buy courgettes, aubergines and peppers, olive oil and anchovies. Sometimes they eat in front of the television.

Orla spends a lot of time ignoring her mother. 'I'm more of a daddy's girl,' she says. By the time we're both teenagers, they have out-and-out screaming matches. Orla swears and shouts in rapid, hectic French. She throws cups and glasses until her mother grabs her wrists and shakes her. It's at times like this that Orla turns up at my house, unannounced, just barges in as if she lives here and has hysterics. My mother calms her down, then my dad drives her home. If it was me, I'd be told to stop the nonsense, but Orla gets away with it. 'She's highly strung,' my mother pronounces. 'It'll be the French blood in her.'

When I'm fourteen, I'm on a trip to Edinburgh with my grandmother. Gran is in the toilet in Jenners store and I am waiting for her. I walk a few yards into the lingerie department and run my fingers through a rack of silk nightdresses with lace round the bodice.

I see Angeline. My heart lifts and as I open my mouth to shout hello, a man walks towards her. It's Monica's father. I wonder why he's there. I watch him as he wraps his arms round her from behind and she leans back into him so that he can kiss her neck. She sees me and one of her eyebrows arches just a little. She places a finger vertically over her lips and leaves it there until I raise my own to mimic her. Then she smiles and blows me a kiss. I don't know what to think.

There is no one in the graveyard but me. Windswept trees afford some shelter from the briny air that evaporates up from the sea, but still many of the headstones have fallen and others are faded or covered in moss, succumbing to weather and neglect. But not this one. This one is upright, gold lettering legible on a background of pink marble.

Rose Adams
1975–1984
Safe in God's hands

The grave is well tended. I have brought some delicate yellow roses. I put them in the vase and pull a few small weeds from the ground. Then I kneel down, clasp my hands together and close my eyes. Guilt, regret, sorrow and remorse: over the last twenty-four years I have known them all. But now, with Orla's phone call yesterday, I am mostly afraid. Afraid of being found out. I try to come up with a prayer, but God and I have never been close and I don't feel I have any right to call on Him now. Instead, I speak directly to Rose. *Please, Rose. Please. I have done my best. Please.* It's not much but it's all I can think of to say to her.

Orla's voice is still in my ears. I am disappointed with myself for falling in with her plans, but I am not sure what else I could have done. She wasn't about to give up. All I can do is listen to what she has to say and hope that she will leave again without causing any damage.

On the way to my car, I pause in front of Euan's mother's gravestone.

Maureen Elizabeth Macintosh
1927–1999
Beloved wife, mother and friend

Mo was the original earth mother, universally loved and as much involved in my upbringing as my own parents were. She gave birth to six children of her own: four boys and two girls. My own parents, on the other hand, tried for a baby for almost twenty years before they quietly gave up. Mo and her husband Angus lived next door and their children, a healthy, happy brood, spilled over the fence and into my parents' lives. A balm of sorts, perhaps. My mother would bake cakes with the girls while my father taught the boys how to work with wood. So it was in the giving up that somehow I came into being and I was born on my parents' twenty-first wedding anniversary.

But my mother found that the reality of a child was often more than she could take. So when I refused my dinner again or ran away from the potty only to wet myself, Mo scooped me up and took me next door where I was absorbed into the crowd. I was propped up in the pram alongside Euan, her youngest, and just three months older than me, or in the playpen in the kitchen.

When I started nursery school, my mother went back to work. Every day I escaped the intensity of parental interest that shadows the only child and walked home with Mo and Euan to spend the afternoon with them and any other stragglers who needed a place to go.

I wish I'd brought two sets of flowers: one for Mo's grave too. She's been dead almost nine years but I can remember her voice. *Some things we're not meant to know, Grace. Some things we're meant just to accept.*

I wonder at the things I accepted and the things that I didn't and I hope that wherever she is, she understands the choices I made.

I'm two minutes from my parents' house and I drop in on them on my way back from the church. My dad is up a ladder. He's closer to ninety than eighty but he won't slow down.

I keep the ladder steady and shout up to him. 'Hello, up there!'

He looks down between the rungs. 'Oh, it's you, hen. What brings you here?' He climbs down, putting one careful foot after the other. 'Of course, it's the birthday cakes. For the party.' I follow him over to the bench where he throws himself down. 'Look at that view.' His breathing is hoarse and he pulls a handkerchief from his pocket and coughs into it. 'No amount of money can buy a view like that.'

My dad has the bench positioned on the crest of the hill with an uninterrupted view of the sloping land and the water beyond it. The air is crisp and clear and, out at sea, an oil tanker tips over the horizon. The wind whips the waves into frothy white peaks that wash the rocky shoreline clean, while up above gulls cry, flock and hover on the wind.

I breathe in deeply and smile. 'I love it here,' I say, then I notice that a small red stain is spreading across his handkerchief. 'Is there blood on that hanky, Dad?'

'What's that?' He pushes the evidence deep into his trouser pocket. 'You're as bad as your mother. Looking for problems.' His face contrives innocence but behind it his eyes flicker with anxiety.

I want to hug him to me, but I don't. I am on the edge of my own tears, ready to blurt out my own problems. 'Shall I get us a cup of tea?' I say. I lay a hand on his shoulder then go into the house. My folks have dozens of photos in the hallway: Euan and me sitting end to end in a Silver Cross pram; me and my dad holding up a shelf I'd just made; and, at the end of the row, Orla and me aged thirteen, grinning like mad. Our arms are wrapped round each other's back, our riding boots and jodhpurs splashed with mud. I remember the day well. We were both competing in the village pony trials and managed to come home with four rosettes and two cups between us.

I bend down and scrutinise the photo. There is no mistaking that we are the best of friends. Looking at her face, the black curly hair, dark eyes and open smile, I feel something unexpected. I feel happy. Tomorrow, for the first time in twenty-four years, we will lay eyes on each other. With a few chosen remarks to the right people she could blow my world apart, and yet there is a small corner of me that is looking forward to meeting her.

I stand up, shocked, and remind myself that there is no room for sentiment. I can't afford to make a mistake with this.

I take the photograph off the wall and go into the kitchen where my mother is spreading pink icing over the surface of a twelve-inch cake. As I open the door, she looks up, startled.

'Oh, it's you, Grace,' she says. 'What on earth are you doing here?' She gives me a perfunctory hug. 'If you've come for the cakes then I haven't finished them yet.'

'I know they won't be ready until Saturday. I'm not here to rush you.' I show her the photo. 'Do you mind if I borrow this?'

'Of course not.' She waves the palette knife. 'Keep it. Wonder how Orla's doing now,' she adds casually.

I shrug. 'No idea. She just upped and disappeared.'

'She did write to you, Grace.' She gives me a sharp look. 'You were the one who let it slide.'

There's no arguing with that. I lift a couple of mugs off the hooks. 'I've just been chatting to Dad. I came in to get us a cup of tea. Why don't you stop for a minute and join us?'

'No, no, no! I'm busy with the finishing touches.' She examines the smoothness of the icing from several angles. 'You go and talk to him. Lunch will be ready soon. You're staying, I take it?'

I hesitate, putting tea bags in the mugs. 'Only if it's convenient.'

She frowns at me. 'Since when have I given my own daughter the impression that her visits are inconvenient? Not those tea bags, Grace! Give him some peppermint. He's been having trouble with his stomach.'

'What sort of trouble?' I try to sound casual, add the boiling water to the mugs and look her full in the face. 'Mum, is Dad not well?'

'Oh, you know your father.' She breezes past me and takes another knife from the drawer. 'Always in denial.'

I wonder whether to mention the blood on the hanky, but she's left the kitchen. I take the tea outside and sit down on the bench beside my dad. 'I hear your stomach's giving you gyp? Why not have the doctor check you over, Dad? One of those well man clinics, you know?'

'I know I'm getting old, toots. That much I know. No point in digging around. It'll only stir it all up.'

'Please?' I take hold of his hand. 'Please, Dad. For me.'

'Well . . . I don't know, lass.' His face moves through reluctance and irritation. 'You were always one for getting your own way.'

'I'll take that as a yes, then,' I tell him, smiling.

'So how are the girls? Keeping you busy?'

'The girls are great.' I nod. Since I confronted her yesterday, Ella is acting as if I don't exist. I have yet to resume the conversation about 'boys' and I know that when I do it will be an uphill struggle. 'Ella has the lead part in *Romeo and Juliet* so that will be one for your diary.'

'I'll look forward to that.'

A car draws up next door and a young couple climb out. We all wave. They walk up the path and my dad pulls his chest up and sighs. 'It's never been the same since Mo and Angus passed on. Spring comes around again and the house changes hands.'

'I'll never get used to it either, Dad.' I rest my head on his shoulder. 'I'm going to Edinburgh tomorrow. Is there anything you want?'

'What would you want to be going all the way to Edinburgh for?'

'I like to browse the art shops and galleries. Gives me ideas.' I pause. In my head I say the words: *Remember Orla, Dad? She called me twice. She wants to meet me. I don't know why, but I do know that I'm scared. How much do you love me, Dad? How much?* I want to blurt it out and I almost do, but just then my mum sets a tray down in front of us.

My mother knows how to make a good sandwich and, when I leave, my stomach is full. It's already two o'clock by the time I round the path to work. Euan is on the phone and watches me as I come in. 'Sure. No bother. We'll catch up next week.' He puts the phone back onto the cradle. 'Morning off?'

'I was taking photos. Then the churchyard. Had lunch with my mum and dad.' I drop my bag down on the floor. 'Is Tom well?'

'Yeah. He's fine now. Back at school.'

I walk over and sit on the edge of his desk. 'She called again.'

His eyes widen. 'Did you ask her what she wants?'

'She wouldn't say. She said she has to tell me face to face. I'm meeting her in Edinburgh tomorrow. She said it wasn't what I thought.'

'She'd say that to get you to go.'

That thought has been at the back of my mind and my heart sinks to hear Euan say it out loud. 'But there's really nothing else I can do, is there? I have to go. And when she finds out who I married . . .'

'She's trouble, Grace. She always was.' He lays a hand on my arm. 'Do you want me to come with you?'

'No.' The palm of his hand feels warm, his fingers firm around my upper arm. Safe. I shrug him off. 'I'll be fine. I'll manage.'

'I might be better at talking her round than you.'

'I doubt it, Euan. She never liked you. I think I can do it.' I take a purposeful breath. 'I know I can do it.'

June 1976. Euan and I are playing in our den at the edge of the forest. He's just joined the Scouts; he's been practising his knots and I have both my wrists tied together and then the string is looped round the trunk of the tree. 'I'm going to go back home and get us something to eat,' he says, running off. 'Wait for me.'

I wait for him. There's not much else I can do, tied up as I am, so I rest my head against the bark and drift off into the gap between sleep and wakefulness, and the next thing I hear is my mother's voice.

'What in God's name?'

I jump guiltily. 'Euan's coming back in a minute.'

My mother wrestles with the knot. 'What sort of a game is this, Grace? Look at the state of you!' My skirt has ridden up almost to my waist and she yanks it down. When the knot comes loose, she shakes me roughly, grips my arm and marches me back up the road.

Mo answers the doorbell, wiping her hands on her apron. The smile dies on her face as my mother speaks. 'I have just found Grace.' She jerks me forward. 'Tied to a tree down at the far end of the field. By herself. Her skirt practically up round her neck. *Anyone* could have found her. *Anything* could have happened to her.'

Euan appears at Mo's side. 'I was going back.' He holds up a bag of sandwiches and two bottles of lemonade. 'I've got the supplies.'

'Next time, Euan, bring Grace back with you,' Mo says.

'But I was guarding our den,' I say.

'Yeah.' Euan is frowning. 'We weren't doing anything wrong.'

'He had her tied to a tree, Mo.' My mother is shouting now.

'Now, Lillian, a wee bit of freedom doesn't do them any—'

'*You* have the cheek to tell *me* how to raise a child? With Claire hanging out with the local boys and George drunk of an evening—and Euan! What of Euan? Never out of trouble!'

Mo's face turns whiter than her freshly laundered sheets that buffet and bounce on the line.

My mother looks down at me. 'You're not to play with Euan any more.' She looks back at Mo. 'I'll be making other arrangements for after school.'

My mother turns and I am half walked, half dragged down the path.

At school the next day, Euan won't speak to me. 'I'm a bad influence on you. Mum says I have to give you a wide berth.'

I am mortified and I try to explain that I'll win my mother round. He's not interested. I feel angry and then unbearably sad.

I spend the next month going to Faye's after school. She won't play outside or climb trees. She doesn't have dogs or chickens or a goat.

We have tea at five but I won't eat. After a couple of weeks of this, I grow tired and listless and my mother has to do the thing she hates most—take time off work—because I can't go to school.

I move three peas on top of a pile of potato and pat it down with my fork. 'I hate Faye,' I say. 'I'm not going there any more.'

'How about the new girl, Orla?' my mother asks, in a too-bright voice.

I shake my head. 'I don't know her yet.'

'How about Monica? She's a lovely, clever girl.'

I scream so loudly that my father comes through to the kitchen from the living room. 'What's going on in here?'

My mother is scouring the pots. 'She's acting up again.'

'Then perhaps we should listen,' my father says to my mother's stiff back. 'What sense is there in all this misery?'

'Misery? Who's causing the misery? Always wanting her own way.'

'Lillian!' my father bellows. 'She's eight years old. She's making herself ill. Now climb down from that high horse of yours and go to Mo.'

'I will not!' my mother shouts back, turning round at last. 'I will not, Mungo! She will *not* run this house with her tantrums and her temper.'

Before my father has a chance to reply, I bolt from the table and up the stairs to the bathroom, where I sit with my hands over my ears.

Minutes later, the kitchen door bangs shut. I run to the back window and watch my mother walk down the path and into Mo's garden. I can only hear snatches of words. Mo gives her a handkerchief and my mother blows her nose then comes back to the house. I hold my breath. She comes into my room. She doesn't speak, just looks at me. I clutch her round the waist, tight as I can, and then run down the stairs, out through the gate and into Mo's arms.

She laughs and pushes me away. 'You'll be knocking me over next.'

I jump up and down. 'Where's Euan?'

'Down by the cove. And don't forget your bucket!' she calls after me.

Still running, I lift the pail and shout back, 'I love you, Mo,' then head off down the beach. The wind whips at my dress, my hair.

I see him along the shore bending to look at something in a rock pool. When I reach him I can barely speak I'm so excited and I jump up and down and turn round on one leg. 'Euan! Euan! Guess what? We can play again! My mum gave in. I went on hunger strike like they do in Ireland and my mum gave in!'

He squints up at me. His face has sand stuck all over it in little clumps. 'Who says I want to play with you any more?'

I stop, deflated, feel tears sting at the back of my eyes. 'But you do,' I say. 'Because we're best friends.'

'Maybe. But no more crying and no more showing your knickers.' He grins at me. 'Unless you want me to pull them down.'

'That's rude!' I push him and he pushes me back. I fall over and he sits on top of me, holding my arms.

'Do you submit?'

'Never!' I struggle and push as hard as I can but he holds my wrists.

'Do you submit?'

His weight is pressing down on my stomach. 'All right, all right!'

He climbs off and lies beside me, lining up his head with mine. We stay together, catching our breath, squinting up at the clouds.

'Those big round ones that look like cauliflowers'—he points up— 'are called cumulus and those ones over there, see, really high up, are called cirrus and they're made at thirty thousand feet from ice needles.'

'Who told you that?' I ask him.

'Monica.'

'Monica!' I turn to face him and giggle. 'You played with Monica?'

He shrugs. 'She kept on following me around. She knows a lot of stuff. She even knows about fishing.'

I pinch him hard on the arm.

'Ow!'

I jump up and start to run.

'I'll catch you,' he shouts. 'I will.'

2

I TAKE THE LATE-MORNING train through to Edinburgh. Waverley Station is buzzing with people and the hum echoes up into the steel rafters high above my head. I have five minutes to spare and I go into the bookshop to choose a book for Paul's birthday, which falls just two weeks after the girls'. I know the one to buy: an autobiography by a famous musician. I pay for the book and walk out into the wind, stopping for a minute to fasten my jacket and look up at Edinburgh Castle. Sometimes it is sunlit and benevolent, today it is brooding.

I dodge a throng of tourists heading towards Princes Street Gardens, and make a slow climb up Cockburn Street. I'm about ten feet away when I spot her, just inside the doorway of the restaurant. I'm surprised by how she looks. She isn't wearing any make-up, her black curly hair is pulled back in a band, highlighting the grey that spreads at her temples, and her clothes are simple. Up in the castle, the one o'clock gun goes off and it startles me so that I automatically step towards her and she sees me, calls my name, rushes forward and kisses me on both cheeks.

'You look wonderful,' she tells me, standing back and holding on to my elbows. Our eyes are level; hers are deep brown, almost black, like cocoa-rich chocolate. 'You haven't aged a bit.' She laughs and looks me up and down. 'Adult life suits you, Grace. Come!' She gestures behind her and starts to walk backwards. 'I've bagged us a table in the corner.'

We sit down. I feel happy, sad, nervous, but most of all I feel awkward. She looks so much like herself and yet the spark is missing. Even at fifteen she was glamorous, mischievous, sexy. Boys trailed behind her, bug-eyed and tongue-tied, and she would flash them smiles so sultry, so promising, that they would melt into puddles of hormones.

She takes a breath and gives me a playful smile. 'Let's play catch-up. Last twenty-odd years.' She leans her elbows on the table and her chin on her hands. 'Start wherever you want.'

Her stare is piercing and I pick up the menu to occupy my eyes while I think of a reply, but before I have a chance to read it, she snatches it from me and says, 'I've ordered for us. I hope you don't mind.'

I do mind. It's presumptuous of her. She has automatically assumed the right to make decisions for me, just as she did when we were children. I debate with myself whether to take a stand and insist on choosing my own lunch but decide not to. I want to get to the crux of the meeting as soon as possible.

'So how have you been?' I say.

'Good.' She gives me a Gallic shrug that reminds me of her mother. 'I've lived all over: Far East, Australia, Peru, Italy, Mumbai, all for three years or so, and then time in Canada where I settled for twelve years.'

'And is there a man in your life?'

She rolls her eyes. 'Let's not go there. Me and long-term relationships—always a disaster; until now, that is.' Her face softens.

Maybe this is why she's come back. 'Are you in love now?'

'I suppose.' She grows thoughtful. 'Yes, I am. But please! Now you! Tell me about your children. How many? How old are they?'

'I have two girls, identical twins but Daisy has short hair and Ella's is long. Daisy is good at science and likes to make things with her own hands. Ella loves to act. She's more outgoing than Daisy.' I stop talking while the waitress places a salad in front of us: buffalo mozzarella, melon and watercress. 'They'll be sixteen on Saturday.'

'Sixteen? Wow!' She shakes out her napkin. 'Are they having a party?'

'Yes. In the village hall. We've hired a DJ.'

'Do you remember my sixteenth?'

I nod. 'I was thinking about it yesterday. First the fight with your mother and then all that business with Monica.'

'I never did forgive my mother.'

'What, even now?'

She wrinkles her nose. 'She always had to be the centre of everything.' She finishes her salad and pushes the plate away. 'So, two girls? Almost grown-up.'

'Well, Ella would like to think so.'

'Is she difficult? Like her mother?'

'I was never difficult.' I give her an appraising look. 'I would have had to work hard to catch up with you.'

'I did have my moments, didn't I?' she concedes. 'Thank God we don't stay fifteen for ever.' The waitress clears our plates and Orla reaches down into her bag and brings out her mobile phone. 'I need to make a quick call,' she says and steps outside the restaurant.

It's a good opportunity to watch her and I do. She looks completely harmless. There's not a hint of the conniving or spite that she used to be capable of and I'm beginning to wonder what I was nervous about. She's not the dangerous, impulsive Orla that she once was. She's a calmer, more civilised version, I think.

She comes back to her seat. 'So what about the old gang? Monica, Euan, Callum, Faye.' She reels them off. 'What happened to them?'

The restaurant is in full lunchtime swing. The waitresses weave between the tables, plates held high above their heads. Our main course is red mullet with spring vegetables and I take my first mouthful before answering. 'Tastes good,' I say.

'My mother comes here. You know how fussy she was . . . and is.'

'Is she well?'

'Yes, very. In her element. New husband, lots of money, busy social scene.' She shakes her head. 'I wonder why my father put up with her for all those years. She was the reason we left the village, you know.'

'No, I didn't.' I had always thought it was because of Rose, because Orla and I could never have lived together in the same village, looking each other in the eye day in and day out, after what we'd done.

'Did you think it was because of Rose?'

I nod. She was always in the habit of second-guessing me.

'It wasn't.' She looks beyond me. Her eyes are still her most stunning feature. A cocoa and caramel blend. 'Anyway, tell me about the gang.'

'Faye lives on the Isle of Bute. She married a sheep farmer. Callum runs his dad's business now. Employs half a dozen people on the boat and in the fish shop. Hasn't changed. His son Jamie is Ella's boyfriend. Euan is an architect and Monica is a GP.'

'So Euan's still in the village?'

'Mmm.'

'You didn't marry him, did you?' Her eyes widen. 'Tell me you did!'

'No!' I look at her as if she's mad. I knew this was coming. 'God! That would have been like marrying my brother.'

'Grace, you don't have a brother and the looks you used to give each other had nothing to do with sibling love.'

'Really, Orla.' I fake a bored expression. 'That was a hundred years ago. He married Monica.' I say it casually.

'Euan and Monica? *Are married?* That just doesn't make sense!'

'Love doesn't always, does it?'

'Euan didn't even *like* Monica.'

'Well, sometimes that's the way it is, isn't it? You think you don't like someone, in fact you positively dislike them, and then wham!' I bang my hands together. 'Cupid's arrow strikes and you're lost.'

'You didn't feel jealous? You were inseparable!'

'No, we weren't. You and me.' I point to her and then back to myself. 'We were inseparable. I was happy for him!'

'Euan loved you,' she says quietly. 'Even at sixteen I could see that.'

I laugh. This is harder than I thought. 'As I said. We were like brother and sister. Still are.'

'So who did you marry?'

'Paul. He works at the university. He lectures in marine biology.'

'Would I know him?'

Our desserts have arrived and I swallow a spoonful of pavlova, sweet meringue breaking into the sharp taste of the raspberries. It occurs to me to make something up but my marriage is not a secret; she can easily find out for herself. And I'm hoping that Euan is wrong. If she intends to tell the truth about Rose's death, then this will surely stop her. 'I married Paul Adams.'

She stares at me. I watch as her jaw slackens and drops open. I don't look away. I am prepared for this. I have rehearsed it. I knew she would take issue with my choice of husband. She's not the first.

I stare her down and at last she looks away, lifts her glass of water to her mouth. Her hand is shaking and she tries to steady it with the other one. She lets out a breath. 'The same Paul Adams?'

'Yes.'

'Rose's dad?'

'Yes.'

She sits back and pulls at her hair. 'I just don't know what to say.'

'Why? Because of what happened to Rose? We fell in love. We got married. We have the girls. I love him—still. That's it.'

'You're happy?'

'Yes. I am.'

She smiles at me. 'Then I'm glad,' she says. 'I am, really. You deserve to be happy. We all do.'

I can't believe she means it. I wait for her to throw something else my way but it doesn't come. We finish our desserts.

'Are you staying with your mum?'

'No. At a convent in the Borders.'

'A convent? A Catholic convent? With *nuns*?'

'Yes.'

'Never!' I laugh. 'Your mother couldn't get you to church for love nor money. At twelve, you were calling yourself an atheist, weren't you?'

'Mmm, I was. But I've changed. I'm joining the order as a novice. I want to become a nun.'

'Great . . . good.' I shrug and smile as though I mean it. I realise I do mean it. It seems out of character, but I want to wish her well. 'Surprising, but good.'

'More surprising than you marrying Paul Adams?'

'What?'

'You expect me to say nothing? You drop a bombshell like that and I'm supposed just to smile and congratulate you?' Her voice grows harsh. 'Paul Adams? What the fuck possessed you? *Rose's father*?'

I sit back in my seat and fold my arms. 'Interesting language for a would-be nun,' I say quietly. 'But then I have been wondering when the old Orla was going to make an appearance.'

'Well? I've found God, not so unusual for someone our age. While you . . .?'

'You know very little about the grown-up me, Orla, as I know very little about you.' I feel tired suddenly. 'So how about we just stop the pretending and you tell me exactly why you got in touch.'

'OK.' She takes a breath. 'You're not going to like it, but I want you to remember that I bear you no malice.'

'Just spit it out.'

'I need to put my wrongs to right. And I need to make peace with those people I hurt.'

Ice starts in my fingertips and freezes a path beneath my skin, travelling inwards until I shiver. 'What exactly are you saying?'

'I've made my confession to the priest. Now I need to confess to the people who were affected by my actions.' Her tone is light as candy floss. 'What happened to Rose: it was cruel. What we did was wrong and then we compounded it by lying to ourselves and to the police.'

'You're telling *me*?' I don't know whether to laugh or cry. 'Since when are you entitled to take the moral high ground?'

'Don't be angry, Grace.' She tries to take my hand. I pull away. 'This is not about you and me. This is about doing what's right.'

'I have paid my dues, Orla. I have.' I keep my voice low. 'I may not have been honest with my family or the wider community but I have'— I pause—'I have made good any sin that I committed.'

'There is a penance to be paid.'

'I'm not a Catholic,' I remind her. 'And this isn't about religion for me. This is about doing the right thing.'

'Me too. I need to do the right thing. Surely you can see that?'

'And what would that entail, exactly?'

'Telling Paul.'

'Why? Why on earth would you do that?'

'To give him some closure.'

'At the expense of his marriage? His daughters' happiness?' I am horrified. 'We agreed to keep this a secret.' I bang my fist against my chest. 'Paul is my husband. We have two girls together. If you tell the truth about what happened that night, you will ruin all of our lives. Is that really what your priest, your God wants?'

'Put yourself in my shoes.' Her voice is silky smooth, her eyes black and shiny as hot tar. 'I need to join the convent with a clear conscience.'

I stand up. 'I knew you hadn't changed. You are your mother's daughter. Everything is always about you.' I rummage in my bag, find my purse, pull out thirty pounds and slap it down. 'Go back to where you came from, Orla. Stay away from me.'

As I turn from her she grabs hold of my wrist. 'Ten days. That's all you have. Either you tell Paul or I do. The choice is yours.'

I wrench her off me and, careless of the other lunchers, say loudly, 'You come near my family and I will have you, Orla.' I hold her eyes for several long seconds. Her look is fearless. 'I won't hesitate to hurt you.'

I leave the restaurant and hurry along the road back to the station. I realise that I've forgotten the book I bought for Paul, but I can't go back for it. I know that I'm crying, but I don't care. I board the first train back home and wonder what the hell I'm going to do now. Always, always, I knew. I knew that this would come back to haunt me. I drive home from the station, rigid, gripping the wheel.

By the time I pull into the driveway my head is so full of fear, remorse and what-ifs that I want to bang it against a wall. Instead I open a bottle of Pinot Grigio and watch it glug-glug into the glass. I drink one full glass down then pour myself another, and another. My life, my girls, my husband, my house, my dog, I'm going to lose all of it.

Ella comes into the kitchen. 'Drinking already? It's only four thirty.'

My head is starting to fuzz over. A blessed distance is opening up between myself and the words in my head. Sure, Orla is a bitch but I will find a way to shut her up. I will. Perhaps Euan will help me. I wasn't entirely truthful with Orla. After Rose died, we made a pact not to tell anyone, but I did. I told Euan. I couldn't keep it to myself.

My limbs feel heavy and loose and I roll my head round on my neck to ease the tension in my shoulder muscles.

'So?' Ella is watching me. 'What's with the drinking?'

'Ella.' I smile. 'We still need to talk.'

She leans back against the counter and folds her arms across her chest. 'So you know I'm on the pill and you don't like it and you don't like Jamie. Big deal!' she sneers. 'And, by the way, it was Daisy who suggested I go on the pill. She's not as perfect as you think.'

'That's great. I'm glad you girls have been giving each other advice. Sisters should support each other.' I wave the glass at her. 'Why should it matter what I think? You go right ahead! Do what you want.'

I pour my fourth glass of wine, toss the empty bottle into the bin and when I look back at her I see that disquiet is edging in at the corner of her eyes, forcing her to speak. 'What's the matter with you?'

I laugh. 'I'm tired of your attitude. You want to be an adult? I'll treat you like one.' I turn my back to her and scrabble about in the back of the cutlery drawer until I find what I'm looking for.

'You *smoke*?' She is incredulous.

'What? You think you have a monopoly on that too?' I light up the cigarette and inhale.

'You've been crying, you're smoking, knocking back the wine like there's no tomorrow? Jesus, Mum, are you ill? Shall I call Dad?' A tear trickles down her right cheek.

I wave her away. The wine is making me want to confess but I look at my daughter and know that she must never find out. Never. 'Really, I'm fine. Just wallowing in a little self-pity.' I shrug. 'It happens.'

She hugs me hard and I feel her woman's body press against mine.

'All part of being an adult.' I make an apologetic face. 'Every so often you feel a failure or a bitch and wish you'd done something differently.'

'But you *never* do anything wrong, that's why you get on my nerves!'

she says. 'You're always patient with me, even when you should be grounding me. You never lose it with Granddad even when he's confused as hell and you're kind and you laugh and you can paint—and you look good!'

Somehow I'm being allowed to stroke her hair. 'So will you come and visit me in prison?'

'Oh, Mum, stop it! Like you ever did anything wrong!'

June 15, 1984. Lightning wakes up the sky. It's raining so hard that the water stings my cheeks. I pick my way over exposed roots and fallen branches. It takes me only a couple of minutes, but by the time I reach Orla my hair is plastered to my head and my boots are sopping wet. She is waiting for me close to the pond, which is out of bounds because it's less than 100 yards from where the boys from the youth club are camping. Somewhere, just beyond the trees, Euan, Callum and several other boys from our year are in their tents, most likely getting drunk.

'This had better be good,' I shout to Orla as I draw within earshot. 'Parky will have our guts for garters if she catches us out here.'

'Live dangerously, Grace, why don't you?' she shouts back. 'What's the worst she can do? Throw us out of the Guides?'

I don't share Orla's 'fuck-em' approach. I wish I did, but I am burdened by expectations. I am the apple of my parents' eyes. I am polite. I never make trouble at school. I always do the right thing.

It's close to midnight and, as the clouds blow across the sky, the moon is revealed, full and bright as a silver coin. But still the rain pours down.

'So what, Orla? What?' I shout to her. 'What did you want to tell me?'

She comes right up beside me and whispers loudly into my ear. 'It's about Euan. I tried him out for you.'

I frown, confused. 'What do you mean?'

'I tried him out for you. He could be a better kisser but otherwise . . . otherwise he was a pretty good shag.'

I stare at her, my stomach hollow as if scooped out with surgeon's metal. I am wet through and yet still a fire sparks up in my throat.

'What's with the face?' She laughs. Water drips off the end of her eyelashes, nose, hair and off the end of her smile which is both knowing and sly. Sleekit, my father would say. 'You look like your dog's just died.' She pushes me on the shoulder and my feet slip on the muddy bank. I fall down on to my knees and catch myself just before my face hits the ground. The wet earth smells bitter. I stand upright again, reach forward, grab her and pull her towards me.

'You had sex with Euan?' Her eyes look straight into mine. I see spite, anger and something else that I don't recognise. 'How could you, Orla? You could have anyone! *How could you?*'

'He's nothing,' she says to me. 'Shag him and get it over with.'

I feel someone tugging at my back. I keep hold of Orla and turn round. Rose is standing there. Her lips are moving and I hear the words 'lost' and 'sleep', but I have trouble making out what she is saying.

'Go back to the tent, Rose!' I bawl into her face and she is startled, draws away but doesn't let go of my jacket. I turn back to Orla.

'He doesn't matter! Forget him!' she shouts. She is laughing. I realise she is enjoying this. She has chosen this exact moment to tell me. We're in the middle of nowhere. I have no one to turn to.

'You bitch.' I say the words so quietly I can't even hear them myself. Rose pulls at me again and I turn and push her hard, backwards, down the muddy bank away from me, and swivel round to face Orla again. 'You bitch. You fucking, fucking bitch!' I slap her hard. She reels sideways but doesn't slap me back. She lets me hit her over and over until my hands are sore and the strength is gone from my arms.

I head back to the camp, tripping over boulders and fallen branches. Monica is standing outside the supplies tent. 'I thought it would be better to put these under cover,' she tells me, shifting plastic boxes and cooking utensils under the awning. 'You can help, if you like.'

I ignore her, unzip my tent and feel my way through the darkness to my sleeping-bag. I take off my wet clothes, dry myself and climb into my pyjamas. In my sleeping-bag, curled up like a foetus, I think about what just happened. Orla is—was—my best friend. We were friends, weren't we? How could she? And Euan? How could *he*?

Sophie, the community psychiatric nurse, is coming for a visit this morning, so neither Paul nor I have gone into work. Paul is marking papers and I'm making flapjacks. I can't get yesterday out of my head: the disastrous lunch in Edinburgh; Orla and her revelation. Of all the unlikely people in the world, Orla has decided to take holy orders. As a teenager, not only was she irreligious but she was also a consistent bully and often a liar and a cheat. Looking back, I am amazed that I remained friends with her for as long as I did.

Ten days. I have ten days to tell Paul how Rose died otherwise Orla will come and do it for me. But I have no idea how to tell him. The optimist in me hopes that she'll reconsider without persuasion. Before we met yesterday, she didn't know that I married Rose's father. Surely that will change her mind? I know it would change mine; but then the pessimist in me reminds me that I'm not Orla.

I try to focus on the positive—somehow Ella and I ended the evening closer than we've been in ages. She and Jamie haven't got as far as actually having sex but she was worried that it might happen and wanted to be careful.

'I admire your frankness,' I told her. And we laughed as if we were the best of friends.

I don't expect it to last, but it's such a leap in the right direction that I want to enjoy it. And, because of Orla, I can't. I know that I dealt with her badly: losing my temper and walking out of the restaurant was not the best idea. And now everything is left hanging.

Through the kitchen window I can see Ed weeding one of the flowerbeds. I admire his courage and his sheer bloody-mindedness. One day at a time is his maxim. At the moment it seems like a good one.

Paul comes into the kitchen and starts to mend the broken toaster. I stop what I'm doing and watch him. He is twelve years older than me, but aside from the fact that we grew up liking different music, I can't say the age difference has ever been an issue. Like most couples, our marriage has had its share of ups and downs, but through it all I have never doubted my love for him or the choice I made to marry him.

When he puts the toaster back, I grab both his hands. 'Why don't we go to Australia early? Now?'

He laughs. 'I haven't had word from the university yet.'

'But there's no way you'll be turned down. The acceptance letter is only a formality.' Suddenly it seems like the easiest solution. Surely Orla wouldn't follow us to Australia? 'Let's be spontaneous! Just think! We could live out all those dreams we've been sharing.'

'And we will! But the girls haven't finished the school year and Ella has yet to dazzle us with her performance as Juliet. Also, you have Margie Campbell's painting to complete and we have to rent out the house.' He puts his hands to my face and kisses me. 'And I have to finish up at work. There are all sorts of ends to tie up, aren't there?'

'Paul. I . . .' I stop, not sure what I'm going to say next. After all these years, I can't just come out with it. When I was first married, I had this theory that I would be able to tell him about what happened to Rose and that we would be close enough for him to forgive me. There would be a moment, an opportunity, an opening up in time and space, a redemption gap for me to slide into. But, of course, although we talk about Rose, that moment of truth never comes.

He is waiting for me to speak, his look unhurried. I remember reading once about the necessary attributes for a lasting marriage: patience, humour, kindness . . . and forgiveness. I know that Paul is blessed with the first three. But forgiveness is a tall ask and I know how he feels about responsibility. He has always wanted to know who was responsible for Rose's death and I know that if he ever found out, he would want that person taken to task. What I don't know is what he would do if that person was me.

'What's up? I can see you're worried about something.'

'Paul . . .' I hesitate, remind myself that once out in the open, the truth can never be put back. My marriage will be over, my life will change for ever and the girls—what about them?

'Grace?'

I have to say something but I'm not sure what. I can't risk telling him about Rose and my part in her death, yet somehow I have to warn him about Orla. 'There's a threat—not to our lives,' I assure him quickly, knowing how he feels about the girls' safety. 'But to our happiness.'

He smiles uncertainly. 'What sort of a threat?'

'The past. Something from the past.'

'What?'

'Just a moment. A moment in time when I did the wrong thing.'

He thinks about this. 'You're not secretly in debt, are you?'

'No. I—'

He tips my chin up. 'And you're not having an affair?'

'No. I'm just . . . Well . . . hypothetically, if someone came to talk to you about me,' I say in a rush, 'to tell you something bad about me, something you didn't know and hadn't imagined, would you listen?'

He starts back. 'Is this a serious question?'

'Yes.' I lean against the worktop and wait for him to think. He is a scientist. He thrives on facts, proof and evidence. I haven't given him much to go on but still he does me the courtesy of thinking about it.

'So, hypothetically?' He raises his eyebrows and I nod. 'Someone comes to tell me something that you did when?'

'A while ago. Before we met.'

'Is it an offence? In the eyes of the law?'

'Probably.'

'But you got away with it?'

'Yes . . . actually, no!' I say quickly. 'I didn't get away with it. It might look that way but I do believe that I have made up for it.'

'Then that's good.' He strokes the back of his hand down my cheek. 'And, no, I wouldn't listen to what anyone has to say. If you choose not to tell me then I respect that.' He shrugs. 'I find it odd though, Grace.' His smile is confused bordering on hurt. 'I didn't think we had any secrets from each other.' He gives a definitive nod of his head. 'Still, it happened before we met and so I respect your right to privacy.'

'Thank you.' My eyes well up and I blink to keep away the tears.

'Just one thing.' He frowns. 'You don't have to give me the details but I'm interested to know why—why can't you tell me?'

His eyes are gentle, encouraging. We have been together for more than twenty years and I can count on the fingers of one hand the times we have wounded each other. There was the day I lost Ella on the beach in France and he was angry at my carelessness, and then there were the months following our move back to Scotland when I sank into a depression and I would catch him watching me. 'I can't tell you,' I whisper. 'Because I'm afraid you won't love me any more.'

Immediately, he reaches for me and I cleave to him like a barnacle to the hull of a fishing boat. 'Listen, I know you. I know you are a good person. I will never stop loving you. Never.'

His words slide deep into the well inside me and for a moment my fear is diluted, but almost at once I know that the feeling won't last.

He looks beyond me towards the front of the house. 'Sounds like Sophie's car. Are you up to her visit?'

'I'll be fine.' I give him a watery smile. 'Sorry to make such a fuss.'

He gives me a quick hug. 'Let's just forget it.'

He walks away from me, leaving a cold space where he stood. I splash my face in the sink, take a couple of deep breaths and have a smile ready for Sophie when she comes into the kitchen.

'So how's it been, Grace?' Sophie is small and dark and exudes calmness and capability. She pauses. 'Are you all right? You're looking flushed.'

'I'm fine. Nothing to do with Ed. Trials and tribulations of raising teenagers. You know how it is.' I feel guilty blaming the girls but it's the easiest thing to say.

'How are you, Sophie?' Ed comes in through the door and holds out a hand to her. 'Just been finishing a spot of gardening.'

We all sit down and Sophie takes Ed's details from her bag. 'Now, last month we were discussing the memory lapses and different strategies you could use to help.'

'Yes.' Ed takes his notebook from the back pocket of his trousers. 'I keep notes so that I remember who's been to see me, what's been said. What to do before I go to bed, switching off the television, locking up, that sort of thing.'

'And have you been getting out and about?'

'Yes. I play bowls.' He looks at me. 'I have a lot to do here.'

'Ed is invaluable to our family,' I say. 'Gardening, handles on doors, helping with the shopping—he fills in all the gaps.'

Ed smiles gratefully and Sophie writes a few words in his file. 'And how have you found your memory?'

'Well, I have lapses, of course, but, mostly, I think I'm managing. Adding up is difficult and sometimes I don't know who people are.'

'We play Scrabble most evenings,' Paul chips in. 'That helps Dad's confidence with words.'

'And we have Australia to look forward to,' Ed says.

Sophie starts to ask questions about Australia and I tune out, find I can smile and nod in the right places without really listening.

Trying to tell Paul was a mistake that I can't repeat. It's automatic for me to seek comfort from him but this is not something he can help me with. I have established that he loves me and is completely on my side but it is cold comfort because the fact is that I am deceiving him. Were he to know the nature of my secret, I am sure he would feel horrified and betrayed. It's doubtful that he could ever forgive me. Instead of reassuring myself of his love, I have made myself feel worse than ever. Compounding one deception with another—I feel as if I am on a slippery slope and I have to haul myself to safety before it's too late.

June 16, 1984. One of the junior girls lands on my head. 'Ow! Angela!' I push her away from me and massage my scalp.

'Sorry, Grace.' She starts to giggle. She has one leg in and one leg out of her trousers. 'I'm just trying to get my jeans on.'

'Well, sit down then before you land on someone else.' I take some clothes out of my rucksack and put them on. Lynn is asleep. Mary and Susan are getting dressed. 'Where's Rose?'

'She must have gone to the toilet,' Angela tells me.

My face feels puffy, my skin tight with dried-on tears and I grab my wash bag, unzip the tent and go outside where the sun is beginning to warm the ground. The heavy rain has left puddles all through the campsite. It's already seven o'clock and most of the patrol leaders are up. Last night seems unreal. Could I have imagined it? I look around for Orla. Somehow she's found dry wood and is building a fire. She looks up. Her face has the beginnings of a bruise over one cheek. I didn't imagine it, then. My stomach lurches as her words come back to me. *I tried him out for you.*

I feel as if I want to start crying all over again and am grateful when Miss Parkin blows her whistle. 'Fall into patrols, please, girls. Who's on breakfast duty?'

Faye's patrol raise their hands.

'Bacon butties all round, I think. Get started. You'll find everything you need in the supplies tent.' She eyes the rest of us. 'Sandra, your shirt should be tucked in. Angela, stop giggling. Grace? Where's Rose?'

I notice for the first time that she isn't part of the circle. That's odd because she has stuck to me like glue since we climbed into the minibus. And then the details of the night before come back to me. I remember ignoring her when she came to speak to me. And I pushed her. I remember now. Quite hard. Maybe she's in a huff somewhere.

'I'll go and find her, Miss Parkin.' I move out of the circle.

'Be quick about it, Grace. Orla, you go with her.'

I'm already at the edge of the wood. 'I can go myself,' I call back.

Orla runs to catch me up. 'Wait!'

She's almost alongside me. 'Fuck off, Orla.' I push her backwards.

'For God's sake!' She rights herself and grabs hold of my arm. 'I was just winding you up! I didn't really have sex with him. He fancies you!'

I fold my arms and face her. I want to believe her but on countless occasions I've watched her lie: to teachers, to parents and to other children. She does it seamlessly. 'How do I know you're not lying?' I say.

'Because we're friends. Best friends.' Her hair is wild around her shoulders, curls jump out all over her head. She looks miserable.

'We can talk about this later. We need to find Rose. I'll look over by the pond.'

I trudge off over the squashed ferns and tangled brambles and Orla holds up her hands on either side of her mouth and shouts, 'Rose!'

My chest feels lighter and I take some deep breaths. I'm not totally convinced that she's telling the truth but it doesn't look as black as it did last night. I decide to give my face and hands a quick wash, so kneel down at the edge of the pond and take my soap out of the bag.

My mother has packed me off with Yardley's Lily of the Valley: *With no proper facilities you'll want something that smells nice.*

I dry myself on my T-shirt and sit back against a rock. All is quiet apart from Orla's voice and the intermittent calls from one blackbird to another as they busy themselves in the trees. The air is unusually still.

About twelve feet into the water ahead of me I spot a jacket. I can't see the front of it but it looks like one of ours. We all have the same navy-blue waterproofs with the Girl Guide motif.

Orla pushes through the woods behind me. 'She isn't out in this direction.' She stops beside me. 'What's that nice smell?'

'Lily of the Valley soap.' I touch my wash bag with my foot. 'You know my mum—good at the details.'

'Unlike mine,' Orla says, her expression cloudy. 'She won't even notice I'm gone this weekend.'

I point ahead of us. 'One of the girls has lost her cagoule.' I pick up sticks and discard the shorter ones until I find one long enough. 'I think I can reach it with this,' I say. I take off my shoes and socks, roll up my jeans and wade in. The stick catches at the body of the jacket. I try to give it a tug but it doesn't shift. 'It's lodged on something. I'll have to go in deeper.' I come back out and take off my jeans.

'You really hurt my face, you know.'

'Serves you right. You shouldn't go around making up stuff like that.' I throw my T-shirt down on top of my jeans and wade in some more. The cold water reaches up past my knees and makes me gasp. 'I hope whoever's jacket this is appreciates it.'

'We'll make her scrub the pots,' Orla says.

When the water hits my thighs I stop. The movement in the water sets up a small wave. The arm of the jacket slides out to the side. I go to grab it with the stick then stop, blink once, twice, three times. There are fingers coming out of the end of the jacket.

'Hurry it up!' Orla is growing impatient.

I turn back. 'Orla, in . . . I . . .' My voice gives out.

'What?' She frowns and looks to the end of the stick. 'What the . . .' She splashes in behind me and we grab the body, haul it back to the bank then up onto the flat ground.

When we turn her over we both scream. It's Rose. Beautiful, blonde Rose. Her face is greyish-blue and bloated, her hair tangled with weed.

'Fuck, fuck, fuck. Grace!'

She is stiff and cold. I roll her onto her side and press down on her back to expel the water from her lungs. Some dribbles out. I roll her onto her back again and thump her heart once. Then I begin cardiac massage. I pump her chest, counting as I go . . . five, six, seven . . . and then blow air into her mouth. 'Get Miss Parkin, Orla!' I say between breaths. 'We need help.'

'Grace! She's dead.' She pulls me away from her. 'Can't you see?'

I frown, back off, stare at Rose, now merely a body. Her eyes are blank, empty. I can't think. I look round at Orla.

'It was you.' Orla claps a hand over her mouth. 'It was you.'

'What are you talking about!' I am horrified.

'When you pushed her!'

'What?'

'Was she in the tent when you went back?'

'I don't know.'

'Think, Grace.' Her eyes are wide and feverish. 'Think.'

I think back. I didn't check that Rose was in her sleeping-bag. I didn't check on any of them. I was too upset. And before that, the memory of Rose's hands on the back of my coat. I see myself turn round on the very spot we're standing on now. She was trying to tell me something but I couldn't make out the words.

I look down at my hands. 'Christ! I pushed her. I pushed her down the bank.'

Orla moans and starts to pace. 'Think, think, think.' She is banging her head with her fist. 'We have to get our story straight.'

There's a singing in my ears. 'She's dead.' I realise the enormity of what I've just said and I throw up.

'We have to stay calm.' She holds my shoulders, her fingers gripping my skin. 'You could be done for murder.'

'Murder?' My insides drop, my legs give way.

Orla catches me, then pushes me back against a tree.

'But it was an accident. Jesus, Orla. It was an accident,' I tell her. I look down at Rose's body on the ground. 'I would never do something like this.' A tremendous pressure builds in my chest, leaving no room for air. I start to choke, hold my neck and try to cough but I can't.

Orla slaps me hard across the face. My teeth bite into my tongue and I wince, then cry out with the pain.

Orla shakes me. 'Listen! You can still be prosecuted. Say nothing about last night. Nothing. Grace?' she hisses. 'We saw nothing. We heard nothing. Do you hear me?'

3

THE DJ IS SET UP at one end of the room. Lights flash behind him, change colour and make shapes on the ceiling. Daisy is in jeans and a plain black halter-neck top. Ella is wearing a pair of faux leopardskin footless tights, flat gold shoes and a black pelmet skirt. Her T-shirt is a shocking pink and says 'Super Bitch' on the front in sparkly letters. They are both surrounded by friends and are opening presents. Daisy folds the wrapping next to her on the table; Ella throws it by her feet.

I leave them to it and arrange the food onto plates next to bottles of drink and paper cups. Then I take a bag of rubbish outside and light up. I'm halfway through the cigarette when I hear Euan's voice.

'What? You haven't started again?'

'Only in moments of stress,' I tell him.

He comes down the steps to join me and I offer him the packet and the lighter. He takes one out, lights it and looks up into the sky. It's bursting with stars. 'So, what happened in Edinburgh?'

'It was bad,' I say. 'Think of the worst-case scenario and double it.'

'She's going to tell Paul how Rose died?'

'Yup.'

I feel him recoil. 'Shit.'

'I know.' I shrug as if it's hopeless. 'It's all part and parcel of clearing her conscience. She's becoming a nun.'

He gives a dry laugh. 'That's bullshit.'

'Probably some nuns do start out as troublemakers.'

'She was more than a troublemaker. She was cruel and bitchy and dangerous. She was dangerous, Grace.' He points his cigarette at me. 'And she was always the girl you could have behind the bike sheds.'

I turn to him. 'You had Orla behind the bike sheds?'

'I might have done.'

I jerk up straight. 'You *might* have done?'

He has the wits to look sheepish.

'Well, did you or didn't you?'

'I think I might have. Well, not behind the bike sheds . . .'

'You *think* you might have?'

He sighs. 'I did. It meant nothing to me and even less to her, believe me.'

'You never told me that. God, Euan! When did you have sex with her?'

'It was twenty-odd years ago! I was a virgin. I was horny.'

'When exactly, Euan? Was it before Rose died?'

'I don't remember.'

'Well, *try!*'

'What is this?' He reaches for me, strokes the goose bumps on my arm. 'What's going on?'

'Please.' I force myself to stay calm. I wonder why Euan and I have never discussed this before. And then I know. Because I believed her the next day when she said she had made it all up. 'Just try.'

He thinks for a few seconds. 'It was when we went potholing in Yorkshire for Geography O level. We stayed in tents in a field next to the youth hostel. Usual thing, no mixing with the opposite sex after lights out but we did and then'—he raises an eyebrow—'somehow Orla and I fell onto the sleeping-bags together.' He stops. 'She seemed to know what she was doing. Guided me inside her. It was—'

'She planned it,' I tell him. 'She knew how much I liked you.' I start to pace up and down. 'So, in March you turned sixteen. In April you went potholing. On May the 5th we started going out. Rose died on June the 15th.' I sit down on the bottom step because my legs are not going to hold me up. 'Why didn't you have sex with me?'

'You didn't do geography.'

'I don't mean then *exactly*,' I say. 'I mean at any time. Back then.'

'Grace.' He looks at me sadly, reaches his hand towards me but I am too far away and it drops into the space between us. 'When Rose died? That was it.' He shrugs. 'You were off on a mission.'

He's right, but it hurts to hear it out loud. I can't look at him. Why is it that the course of my life ended up hovering on such a mundane decision: geography or history? If I had been there, Euan wouldn't have slept with Orla. I'm sure of that. And then there would have been nothing to argue about.

But even if he had, what about the night Rose died? If it hadn't been raining so hard, I'd have heard the splash as she fell into the pond and I'd have dragged her out again. If Miss Parkin had put her in another girl's patrol, Monica's or Faye's, for example, she wouldn't have come looking for me. If I'd had flu—it was doing the rounds—and missed the camp, Rose would still be alive.

A series of incidents, a series of choices, and finally a consequence so appalling that it has haunted me the whole of my adult life.

'We were arguing about you,' I tell Euan. I rest my head back against the cold stone of the wall. 'She said that she'd had sex with you. And then the next day she denied it. Said she'd only been winding me up.'

'She was always a good liar.'

'I tried to tell Paul yesterday.' The memory fills me with a new sort of terror and I start to hyperventilate. 'I couldn't bring myself to say it, but if I can't change her mind then I'll have to tell him before she does.'

'Don't. Don't even think about going down that road. First we have to talk to her.'

'You know what? Maybe it's time for me to stand up and say I made a horrible, horrible mistake. I pushed a little girl over and she died.'

'She may not have died because you pushed her, Grace.' He's said this to me before and like all the other times I wish I could believe him.

'I'm just so tired of hiding this. Really and truly, I am.' I stand up and start pacing again. 'Don't you think Paul deserves to know the truth? She was his daughter, Euan. His *daughter*.'

'Confession may be good for the soul but it's not always good for your relationships. Think. You love Paul, don't you?'

'Yes.'

'So you have to preserve your marriage,' he says flatly. 'Your love for him and his love for you. The girls' happiness. Your family.'

He is right and it does me good to hear it. I nod, pull my shoulders back and take a few breaths. 'So how can I stop Orla?'

'Let me help you. Two heads are better than one.'

Relief floods my bloodstream and is quickly followed by a reminder. Euan and me: we're not always good for each other. 'You're sure?'

'Yes.' He stands beside me and says softly. 'We're friends, aren't we?'

His leg is touching mine and I move away at once. 'We have to keep this kosher.' I try to make my voice light. 'You know—'

'I know,' he cuts in and his eyes narrow. 'We had an affair. But that was years ago. It's all behind us now. Orla is threatening you and you need help. That's it.' He shrugs again. 'That's all. No ulterior motives.'

'Then I appreciate your help. Thank you.' I give him a quick hug and then I catch the sound of Paul's voice behind me. I shift away and start to tie a bin bag, my shaky hands more thumbs than fingers.

'I think she's just outside. Yes, here she is! Grace!' He's smiling broadly. 'Look who I found.'

Orla appears out of the back entrance of the hall. I stop breathing and stare at her. She is smiling down at us, and then she runs down the steps, has her arms round me, hugging me to her as if we are long-lost sisters. 'Grace! It's so wonderful to see you!'

I keep my arms flat to my sides and say nothing. Truth is I am too shocked, too completely blindsided to have any idea what to say.

She lets me go and throws her arms round Euan. 'Euan Macintosh!' she says. 'You haven't changed a bit!'

'Orla? What a surprise! What brings you to the village?'

'Oh, you know how it is. I've always loved a party and I was passing through, reacquainting myself with old haunts, when I met Daisy outside. One look at her and I knew she had to be Grace's daughter!' She lets go of Euan and grabs hold of my hands. 'It seems like only yesterday that *we* were both sixteen.'

I pull my hands away. There is bitter saliva in my mouth. I can't look at her. I know that if I do I will grab her hair and shake her, rattle her until her teeth fall out and her spine is reduced to jelly.

Paul searches our faces, sensing the tension. 'So, I'll leave you three to catch up, shall I?' He looks at me enquiringly.

I look back. I want to protect him. I take hold of his arm and push him ahead of me. 'I'm coming inside, too.' We climb the steps and find the girls milling around in the kitchen.

Ella gives a shriek when she sees Paul. 'I wondered where you were! Come on, Dad, you're allowed a dance.' Ignoring his protests, she drags him off and Daisy, already flushed from dancing, turns to me.

'Your old friend seems really nice, Mum.' She drinks back a glass of Coke. 'Dad's invited her to lunch Sunday week.'

'He's *what?*'

'Well, she kind of invited herself really. She said something about wanting to catch up with you and perhaps we could all have a meal together and Dad said she was welcome to pop in some time and then she said how about Sunday and Dad said OK.'

I can hardly believe it. Orla has wheedled her way into an invite to Sunday lunch and that will be exactly ten days since we met in Edinburgh. She means it. She means to tell Paul about that night. Dizziness spreads through me in a powerful wave and I fall back on my heels, bump my head on the cupboard door.

Daisy pulls me upright again. 'What's up with you, Mum?'

'I'm sorry.' I take a deep breath and make myself smile. 'Dad and I are going to walk back home soon. Leave you both to it.'

'Cool. Want to come for a dance first?'

'No, you go on, though. Give your dad a run for his money.'

I follow behind her and stand in the shadows watching her join Ella and Paul. The girls hold one of Paul's arms each and begin to teach him some dance steps. I want to join them but I can't. I don't deserve them. This is my family. I am a wife and a mother but I am hiding a secret so huge that if it comes out it will negate everything good I have done these last twenty-four years, and to expect Paul's forgiveness would be to expect the moon to drop onto my doorstep.

I watch them and I know, in this moment, that I will do anything to preserve this. I go to the back of the hall to find Orla again. She is in the kitchen with Euan and Callum, who was at school with us.

'But what about marriage and children?' Callum is saying. 'Won't you feel like you're missing out?'

'My spiritual life is everything to me. I really feel like I've found myself.' Orla laughs self-consciously. 'I spent a lot of time roaming,' she continues. 'I was lost. I lived with men who were . . .' She pauses, looks at Euan as she searches for the right word. 'Unsympathetic. But now, at last, I have a fit. In the convent.' She has the same look on her face that she had in the restaurant. As if she's in love.

'So what about sex?' Ordinarily a shy, amiable bear, I'm guessing Callum is emboldened by a couple of Special Brews.

She gives him a motherly look. 'There's more to life than sex.'

'I'm not saying it's the be-all and end-all. But it's an important part of life. Expressing yourself as an adult. What do you think, Euan?' He turns to Euan and winks. 'Back me up here, pal.'

'I think it's up to the individual,' Euan says. He is standing to the left of me. 'You never struck me as someone who would be attracted to a life of self-denial, Orla.' He shrugs. 'But each to his own.'

'I know!' She gives a giddy, girlish giggle. While not exactly flirting—she's not quite the old Orla—she's clearly loving the attention. 'I've finished with all that worldly striving and competing.'

'Having a faith sets you free from all that?'

'Yes, I think it does. It's real.' She clutches her chest. 'Don't you believe in God, Euan? Don't you feel there's a power behind all this?'

'I believe in personal responsibility.'

'Really?' Her voice is light and I almost don't catch her next words. 'Personal responsibility and integrity go hand in hand, don't they?'

'I live my life as best as I can. Keep moving forward.'

She glances at me, then at Euan. 'No looking back, huh?'

'The past can't be relived, Orla. Nothing that was broken can be fixed. Nothing done, undone. What use is raking over old ground?'

'Reparation . . .' She thinks for a bit. 'Redemption.'

'Can redemption be healing when others are hurt by it?'

She leaves his question to hang in the air until it grows heavy around our heads. I find it increasingly difficult to breathe in.

'Am I missing something here?' Callum smiles uncertainly at them.

'Callum, I think the DJ needs a strong arm to help him with some boxes,' I say, finding my voice at last.

'That'll be me then.' He heads for the door. 'Back in a mo.'

'Twenty-four years have gone by, Orla. We're not the people we were. If you carry out your threat you'll not only ruin Grace's life but you'll take her family down too. Can you live with *that* on your conscience?'

The only sound in the room is the fan in the corner of the kitchen. Her eyes tilt and meet mine. 'Still your knight in shining armour?' I don't answer. She meets his eyes again. It's a look that says, Do you really want to take me on?

Euan doesn't falter. He stares right back at her and I love him for it.

'So what's to be done, Euan? What's to be done?'

I jump in: 'You leave and never come back. I'm taking back Paul's invitation to Sunday lunch. You're not welcome in my house.'

'Is it yours to take back?' She lifts her handbag off the floor. 'This is not going to go away, Grace.'

She leaves the kitchen and I follow her, watch as she walks straight onto the dance floor towards Paul and the girls. Within seconds she is moving in time with the three of them and they are all laughing together as if they've known each other for years. Then, arms in the air, she shimmies in front of Paul, blatantly provocative.

'A lap-dancing nun,' Euan says in my ear. 'I've seen it all now.'

Anger cranks up the heat in my stomach and I move forward.

'Don't.' He holds my wrist. 'She wants you to make a scene. Don't give her the satisfaction.'

I grit my teeth and wait for the music to finish. When it does, she kisses them all on both cheeks, saving Paul for last, and then she clasps his hands, cleverly letting go of them just before he begins to look uncomfortable. She heads for the door and I follow her out and down the steps to her car.

'What happened that night will stay between the two of us,' I say.

'Or would that be the three of us?' She looks back to where Euan is standing in the shadows. 'You told him, didn't you?'

I don't reply.

'Euan knows you did it. Am I right? And he's still fighting your corner. Or is it more than that?' Her voice lowers. 'He gave you a look just now. What kind of a look was it?' She muses for a bit. 'I know! Hungry. That's what it was.'

My teeth are clenched tight. 'You should set off. Even at this time you can meet traffic on the bridge.'

'Honesty really is the best policy. Set down your burden.'

'Oh, please!' I'm fast approaching breaking point. 'Cut the sanctimonious crap! When you make your confession to Paul, what *exactly* do you think is going to become of my marriage?'

'Paul is a reasonable man. I think you underestimate him.'

'And I think you should stop messing with my life!' I am shouting.

'What makes you think you can stop me?' She unlocks the door. 'My reasons are for the best, Grace. While yours? Can you say the same?'

'Yes, I can. This is about my family.' I look away, distracted for a moment by Monica. She's watching us from the other side of the road.

'Sooner or later children have to learn that their parents are fallible.'

'Oh, really?' My eyes are back with Orla. I'm nodding. 'Is that what this is about? Fallible parents? *Your mother?* Is that it, Orla? Is it *my* fault your mother slept around? Is it *my* fault you went into competition with her? Just exactly how many boys did you shag in fourth year?'

She flinches.

I don't stop. 'There was Dave Meikle, Angus Webb, Alastair Murdoch.' I count them off on my fingers. 'Oh, and then of course there was Euan, wasn't there? That one was just for me.' We are right in each other's face. 'If you want to take the blame for Rose's death, you go right ahead, but you are not dragging me into it.'

'I don't have to drag you into it. You're already in it and I'm going to tell the truth whether you like it or not.' She opens the door with a flourish and climbs into her car. The engine starts up and she drives off.

'What is *she* doing here?' Monica has crossed the road and is standing beside me. She is pale, her eyes wide open and anxious. 'What did she want? Why are you mad with her?'

I want to say, *What's it to you, Monica? What's it to you?* But I say breezily, 'You know Orla. Always likes to wind everyone up.'

'Me for sure,' Monica says. She is visibly trembling. 'We hated each other's guts. But you were her friend.'

'Well, not any more.' I walk away. 'You coming inside?'

June 16, 1984. Miss Parkin is sitting on a wooden bench. 'She must have got up during the night to go to the toilet.' She shakes her head and more tears run down onto the collar of her blouse. 'I thought we were far enough away from the pond. I thought we were.' She keeps repeating this over and over. 'I knew she couldn't swim but I thought we were far enough away.'

Sergeant Bingham rests a hand on her shoulder. 'I'm sure you did your best, Miss Parkin. Accidents will always happen. Tragic, for sure. Absolutely tragic.'

We're in the police station. Orla is on the bench opposite me, Miss Parkin is to the right. They've wrapped us in blankets. Orla has shrugged hers off but mine is still tight around me because I can't stop shivering. Rose, sweet little Rose, is dead. And I've killed her. I'm holding my jaw tight, jamming my teeth together but it doesn't stop them from chattering. I want to collapse and let the words pour out, just tell the truth and take my punishment, but Orla holds me with her eyes. Her will is like iron. Every time I feel myself falter, she draws my gaze back to her and encloses us both in her determination.

My parents arrive and my dad gathers me up in his arms. He hugs me tight, rocking me backwards and forwards.

'Your daughter and her friend Orla found the younger girl's body,' Sergeant Bingham tells them.

My mother gasps. 'How could such a thing happen?' she says.

'A tragic accident,' the policeman tells her. 'Your daughter did a sterling job of trying to resuscitate Rose but it was to no avail. Most likely she had been in the water all night. I'm afraid Grace is in shock.'

'Sarge?' A policewoman sidles up to him. 'Rose's father is here.'

I don't want to see his face but something makes me look. He is standing completely still. Sergeant Bingham breaks the news and I will never forget what happens next. Mr Adams drops to his knees and when Sergeant Bingham tries to lift him to his feet again he resists and starts to bang his head on the floor. The sound is loud and hollow like the crack of an air rifle. 'Mr Adams. Please. Let's help you up, sir.' Rose's dad is beyond hearing him. He has started to cry; gut-wrenching sobs that find an echo in my own chest.

The story is covered in the local paper. GIRL DROWNS ON GUIDE CAMP, the headline screams, in inch-high bold print. And underneath:

Nine-year-old Rose Adams, only child of Paul Adams, drowned in a deep pond last night in a picturesque woodland close to St Andrews. Rose was out of her tent in the middle of the night. It's thought that, upset by the thunderstorm, she must have stumbled into the pond some time after midnight. Rose's body was discovered early this morning by Grace Hamilton, 15, and Orla Cartwright, 16. The girls made a valiant attempt to resuscitate Rose but were unsuccessful.

Miss Parkin, who leads the unit, said, 'I knew that Rose was a non-swimmer but I felt we had taken the necessary precautions. I am deeply upset by this tragedy and my sympathy is with Mr Adams.'

This is a double tragedy for Mr Adams, a newly appointed lecturer in marine biology at St Andrews University, whose wife died last year.

I lie in bed. I can't get up. I try but I feel dizzy. This goes on for over a week. My mum tries to persuade me to make an effort, have a bath, come downstairs for tea—but I can't.

On the eighth day, Mo comes to my room. She cradles me in her arms. 'What's all this about you not getting up?'

'I can't, Mo. When I walk I fall over.'

'That's because you've hardly been eating anything. I made you some cheese and onion scones.' She holds out the goodies towards me. 'Smell that and tell me you're not hungry?'

She's right. Hunger knocks my reluctance sideways.

My mum appears at the door with a tray of tea. 'Any luck?'

'She's just tucking in now, Lillian,' Mo says, standing up. 'Shall I send Euan through later to cheer you up?'

'What an excellent idea!' my mother says, all bright and breezy.

'Yes,' I say to Mo. 'Please ask him to come through.'

Euan and I started going out on the night of Orla's party back in May. He's knocked on the door every day since the tragedy but my mother has told him I'm asleep. I'm not but it's easier to pretend. I am afraid to sleep because every time I do, the nightmare starts; every night the same one, the same outcome.

I know that I can't lie in bed for the rest of my life but neither can I go back to my old life and act as if nothing has happened. I know that when I explain what I need to do, Euan will be on my side.

'And Orla called in several times this week,' my mum is telling Mo. 'Grace was sound asleep but we chatted for a bit. She's putting it behind her and getting on with her life.' My mother glances over at me. 'She left you another letter, Grace. Have you read it yet?'

I don't answer. It's the fifth letter she's written to me. I've ignored all of them—I'm not even reading them now—but she still hasn't got the message. I don't want anything to do with her. It's not that I blame her, but Orla is a reminder of the worst person I can be.

I finish eating, have a bath and wait for Euan. As soon as I see him, my heart fills. I jump out of bed and throw myself against his chest.

He hugs me to him. I'm wearing a cotton nightie, not very thick. I am suddenly shy, knowing that he can feel every part of my body through it. I slide under the covers again, pull them up to my chin.

'I brought you some sandwiches.' He sits down on the bed and passes me one, egg mayonnaise and pickle, and bites into the other one himself. We eat in silence for a few minutes. When we're finished he leans over to kiss me. I hold his shoulders.

'I did it.' I say it quickly before I lose my courage.

'Did what?'

'I killed her.'

He frowns at me. 'Who?'

'Rose.' I remember that there has been no suggestion that Rose's death was anything other than accidental. 'It was my fault.'

'Just because you were her patrol leader it doesn't make it your fault.'

'No. I did it. I actually did it. It was a mistake. I pushed her, Euan. I pushed her hard and it was raining and she was tiny.'

He pulls away.

'The ground was slippery, the pond was deep and she couldn't swim.'

He's staring at me as if I've lost my mind.

'I didn't know she'd fallen into the water. It was dark and Orla and I were arguing and—' I stop, remembering what we were arguing about. I climb out from under the covers, kneel on the bed and start from the beginning. I give him all the details: the depth of the pond, her hand on my jacket, me turning round, unable to make out what she's saying, bawling into her face, then pushing her hard, down the bank, going back to my tent, not checking that she was there. I tell him everything except what Orla and I were arguing about.

When I'm finished he says nothing for a few seconds and then, 'That doesn't prove you did it.' His lips tremble as he speaks. 'It doesn't, Grace. There are other scenarios that are just as logical. You pushed her away and she went back to the tent. Then later on, when you were asleep, she got up and went out again.'

'Why would she do that?'

'Because she wanted to talk to one of the other girls, because she was looking for something, because she was sleepwalking!'

I want to believe him but I can't. I know what I did.

'If I didn't do it, then why would she be visiting me?'

'Visiting you?'

'Every night since it happened, I have dreamed about her.' I screw up my fists and keep my voice steady. 'And every night when I wake up, she's standing at the bottom of the bed trying to tell me something.'

'For fuck's sake! This is bollocks.' He grabs hold of me. 'You're upset. You're imagining it. It isn't real!'

I start to cry. I can't do this on my own. 'Listen, Euan, please. I need the dream to stop. You have to help me.'

'Help you how?'

I tell him.

Twice he draws away from me, once he says quietly, 'This is mad, Grace. Totally bollocks.' But he strokes my hair as he says it, and I know that he will help me.

He leaves soon after and for the first night in over a week I am able to fall asleep without dreading it. The nightmare comes as it has every night since I found her body. I'm standing beside a river. The sky above me rumbles and rain buckets down, but somehow I never grow wet.

I wait for her, patiently, until suddenly she's there in front of me, wet through. She is trying to tell me something, but as she talks she slides away from me. I catch hold of the tips of her fingers . . . for a second I have her . . . and then she slides down the bank and into the water.

I throw back the covers, sweating. Rose is standing at the bottom of my bed, water dripping from her hair. Her mouth moves. I lean forward, try to lip-read, but still I can't make out what she's saying. This time, though, I'm able to tell her something. We watch each other for the longest moment and then I blink and she is gone.

'**W**asn't it funny Orla turning up like that?'

I don't answer. I'm round at Monica's. I'm returning the food containers she brought to the girls' party. We're in her kitchen. The work surfaces gleam. Utensils hang in regulation rows. There's an absence of dust, of clutter, of spilt milk or peeling paint. It's like a show house. And Monica is perfect to show it off. Her hair is always sleek and her make-up carefully applied, her smile the same.

'Ground control to Grace.' Monica hands me a cup of freshly brewed coffee. 'I said wasn't it funny, Orla turning up like that?'

'I didn't ask her, if that's what you're implying.'

'What does Orla have on you?'

'I'm sorry?'

'If looks could kill, I'd have been certifying her death.'

'She gate-crashed the twins' birthday party. I didn't appreciate it.'

'You didn't know she was coming? Really?' She's trying to read me, catch hold of the lie and wring its neck. I guess it's part of the training. Doctors are used to patients being evasive.

'Has my dad made an appointment to see you?' I say, suddenly remembering about the blood on the hanky.

'If he had I wouldn't tell you,' she says. 'Patient confidentiality.'

'I realise that, but maybe you could prompt him into coming? I'm worried about him. When I was with him the other day he coughed some blood onto his hanky.'

She gives a reassuring nod. 'I'll have a word.'

'Thank you.' I look around the pristine kitchen and sigh. 'Are you up in the middle of the night cleaning? Seriously, Monica, I don't know how you do it. You put the rest of us to shame.'

'I wasn't brought up like you.' She sits down opposite me. 'You were spoiled. You had a surfeit of everything. I had to bring myself up. My parents' marriage was a shipwreck for as long as I can remember.'

'I'm sorry.' I take a mouthful of coffee. 'I didn't know.'

'And it wasn't just your own mother who looked after you like you were a princess.' She's glaring at me now. 'But you had Mo, as well. Mo. Everybody loved her.' She stops talking, looks into the middle distance and says quietly, 'I was glad when she died.'

'What?' That wakes me up and I jerk upright, watch the coffee rise in the air like a wave and spill down onto the walnut worktop.

She looks at me blankly. 'How could I ever have competed with her?'

'You couldn't possibly have wished her dead!'

'I didn't say I wished her *dead*,' she shouts. 'I said I was glad when she *died*. No.' She holds up her hand. 'I wasn't *glad* when she died, but I wasn't as bothered as I should have been. Oh, I don't know what I'm saying.' She starts to cry. 'Jesus, don't tell Euan. He'd be gutted. Please.'

'I won't.' I'm genuinely shocked not just by what she's said but by the way she's breaking down. I haven't seen her lose control since Orla's sixteenth birthday party. 'I think you need to rest more.'

'Listen!' She grabs my hands and looks at me with the kind of desperation that I associate with myself. 'Orla is bad news. I know that you were friends with her but you have to keep her away from the village.' She's squeezing my hands and I try to wriggle them free but she tightens her grip. 'I want you to know that if you need any help dealing with her then I'm willing.'

I have a sudden and intense urge for a cigarette. 'Please, Monica,' I say. 'Let me have my hands back.'

She lets go immediately, sits back and takes a few breaths. 'You know about Orla's mother and my father? I saw them in Edinburgh together. He was kissing her. It took me a while to put two and two together.'

'You saw them? Where? When?'

'I was fourteen. I know that for sure because my gran took me to Jenners for afternoon tea. It had been going on for about a year before I found out then.' She sits back in her seat, her cheeks streaked with tears. 'You'll understand now why I hate her so much.'

'But that wasn't Orla. That was her mother.'

'She's tarred with the same brush.'

'Monica, you're a doctor. That's hardly scientific!' I have to shout after her because she's left the room and is climbing the stairs. I stand by the back door and look down the garden. I can't see the cabin from here but I know it's there. I want to kick off my shoes and run down the path, lock myself inside and never come out.

'This is the three of us.' Monica is back, holding out a photograph. 'I keep it beside my bed.'

I take it from her. It's black and white and is in a polished, silver frame. She is sitting on her father's shoulders, her hands resting on his head. His right hand is holding her feet and his left arm is round her mother's waist. Monica is laughing. They are all laughing. 'You look happy,' I say, passing it back to her.

'I was seven. We were in North Berwick on holiday.' She stares at the photo. 'Angeline took that away from me.'

'It doesn't do any good to dwell on the past. Your parents are both dead, Monica.' I shake her gently. 'And Angeline lives in Edinburgh now. She can't hurt you any more.'

'Secrets are destructive, Grace. You know?'

I feel prickles of discomfort hurtle down my spine. I, of all people, understand the eroding nature of secrets. I wave my thumb in the direction of the front of the house. 'I need to get back.'

'Sure.' She follows me along the corridor. There's a chart beside the coat rack with the children's timetables on it: their music lessons, sports practice and coursework deadlines. I stop to admire it.

'We could do with one of those,' I say.

'It keeps us right.' She's rubbing her hands together. She's nervous suddenly. It's coming off her like radiation. 'Grace?'

'Mmm?'

'I'd rather you didn't mention this to Euan. Any of it.'

It's on the tip of my tongue to say, 'I thought you were tired of secrets,' but I don't because I am seeing parallels between her and me. 'I won't tell him,' I say.

When I climb back into the car, I don't drive off straight away. I sit with my head back against the rest and my eyes closed. For the first time in years, I've seen a side of Monica that makes me remember she's human: flesh and blood, like me. We're not natural friends; we never have been. But adultery respects no one, and when Euan and I were having the affair, I went out of my way to avoid her. It was easier to do that than acknowledge how hurt she would be if she found out. And Paul. What is the matter with me? I have been the worst sort of wife. I have deceived him and I have cheated on him.

There's a knock at the window and I look up, startled. It's Euan. He climbs in the passenger side. 'What brings you here?' he says.

'I took some food trays back to Monica.' I give him a half-smile. 'Thank you for yesterday. I appreciate your help. I do.'

'Pity about the argy-bargy at the end though.' He raises his eyebrows.

'I'm sorry. I am. But she really winds me up. She's so up herself. Do you think she really intends to be a nun?'

'Not for one moment. She's not doing this for the sake of her conscience; she's doing it to make trouble.'

'I suppose.' I take a big breath. 'I've been thinking. I can't just sit here and wait for her to turn up again. I'm going to go to Edinburgh this afternoon and see whether I can have a chat with her mother. Angeline always liked me. She might be willing to fight my corner and change Orla's mind. They often battled over Orla's behaviour, but in the end Orla always did what her mother wanted.'

'Do you have her address?'

'Not exactly but I know she's married to a man called Murray Cooper and that they live in Merchiston. Can't be that hard to find them.'

'It's worth a try.' He sighs. 'Raking over old ground will mean everyone has to relive the whole thing. That won't be good for any of us.'

I shiver. 'It's Paul's reaction I'm worried about.'

Thinking about Paul is difficult. I am so afraid that he will end up hurt by this, so deeply hurt that he will question everything: our love, our marriage, our memories, and he will look ahead and see an impossible future. Despite my secrets, I believe that we have a strong and loving partnership. Could I stand up in court and convince a jury of my peers? Could I take the jury on a journey that would make them understand my actions and so forgive my mistakes?

I think I could.

September 1984. It's over two months since Rose died and I'm back at school. I quickly realise that I have to pretend to be over it otherwise people watch me and whisper about me. So I do. I pretend to everyone around me but not to myself. Me, myself, I remember everything: her bloated face, waxy skin and staring eyes. And I remember the reality of her father's grief: gutted. Literally. As if someone had emptied him out.

At the start of the new term, I find out that Orla has left the village. Her father has moved to the London branch of the company he works for and they will now be living in Surrey. I didn't see her or speak to her but I overheard my mother and Mo talking about how Orla didn't want to go and locked herself inside the house. I'm glad that she's gone. I'm glad I'll never have to see her face again. She sent me a letter with her new address on the back of the envelope. I tore up the letter without reading it. Five more have arrived. I tore them up too.

Euan is fed up with me. He thinks it's time to move on from 'all this mithering on about Rose'. I understand why he feels that but I can't move on until it's sorted, because if I do, the dreams will never stop. And when I wake she'll be there, watching me.

I have been reading about ghosts and how they can be laid to rest. A ghost will stick around and haunt the living until satisfied that justice is done and that their loved ones will be fine without them. Rose won't leave me alone until I make amends. I'm sure of it.

So what to do? I can't bring her back and I can't go to the police.

My plan is to find someone for Mr Adams. In less than a year, he has lost the two people who mean more to him than anyone else in the world: Rose and, before that, his wife Marcia. Euan found this out for me. Two evenings a week he washes dishes in Donnie's Bites, the restaurant opposite the university. Mr Adams and Rose were regulars there.

'I'm not doing any more spying,' Euan says.

'I'm not asking you to spy. Not exactly.'

We're sitting on the bed in my room. My mum and dad think he's helping me with my Biology Higher. I've had to make decisions about what I want to do when I leave school and I said nursing and the careers officer was pleased. She wrote that down and told me what subjects I needed and where I should be applying to.

Truth is I have no idea about what I will do when I grow up. I can't think beyond the shadow of Rose at the bottom of my bed.

'He looks fine. He's back at work now. He came into the restaurant last night to have something to eat.'

'On his own?'

'Lots of people eat on their own and anyway'—Euan kisses me just below my ear—'I'm giving up that job. There's one going on reception in the community centre. Better perks. I'll get to use the gym for free.'

'Have they replaced you yet?'

'No and no.' He shakes his head. 'I know what you're going to say and I won't put you forward for the job. You don't need a job. You get more than enough pocket money as it is.'

'Yes, but—'

His mouth stops mine. I let him kiss me for a few seconds and then I pull away. 'I won't ask you for anything else, ever again. I promise.'

'For fuck's sake!' He stands up. 'How long is this going to go on?'

'I just want to make it right.'

He sighs and stares at his feet. 'Mr Adams will be fine. He's a good bloke. He won't have any trouble finding another wife and having more children. All in good time. You have to let this go.'

I don't answer. I am locked into it. Euan can walk away. I can't.

'Fine, then. I give up.' Resigned, he turns the door handle and looks back at me. 'See you around.'

I jump up from the bed. 'Are you chucking me?'

His face is set hard. 'There's no talking to you.' He closes the door behind him. I hear him say good night to my parents and then he's gone.

Over the next few days I persuade myself that Euan and I are just on hold and I persuade my parents to allow me to apply for the job.

The dishwashing job is gone, Donnie tells me, but he can go one better. I can be a waitress.

The first time I serve Mr Adams he looks at me twice and says, 'Grace? Grace Hamilton?' He shakes my hand. 'How are you?'

'I'm fine.' I feel embarrassed and ashamed. 'I'm sorry. I never properly said . . . I'm so sorry.' My face flushes and my lips begin to tremble.

There is a sadness in his eyes that makes my throat catch. 'Rose was delighted to be in your patrol. She looked up to you. You have nothing to be sorry for.' He points to the blackboard on the wall. 'So what would you recommend from Donnie's specials this evening?'

'The mussels are popular,' I tell him. 'And treacle tart for pudding?'

I find myself watching him from the shadow of the corridor that leads to the kitchen. He is even more handsome than I remember. He has high cheekbones and soft grey eyes, and when his mouth smiles, they smile too. I also remember that Orla wasn't the only girl in the Guides who had a crush on him. Much younger than all the other dads, he affected us all, to varying degrees. He was always friendly, without being overly so, and had the ability to tune in and listen to us in a way that most adults didn't.

Days become weeks and I begin to call him Paul. Sometimes he eats with colleagues, but occasionally a woman called Sandy joins him. If he is alone and business is slow, I sit down beside him and we chat about school and his work at university. I keep my eye out for women to introduce him to, teachers at school who're single, and other customers in the restaurant, but no one seems special enough and, truthfully, the few times he is joined by Sandy I feel jealous and find every reason not to like her.

The dreams become less frequent—I must be doing something right—and my life settles into a rhythm. Euan does a good job of avoiding me and I let him and then, after the October half-term, he doesn't come back to school. I ask my mum whether he's sick.

'Not that I know of,' she says, and then hesitates before adding, 'He's moved down to stay with his uncle in Glasgow.'

I go next door to Mo. I haven't spoken to her for a few weeks and she spends the first minute hugging me and asking me how I am. When she takes a breath I say, 'Where's Euan?'

'He's in Glasgow with family. Better for him down there.'

'He didn't even say goodbye.'

'It all happened fast.'

'Could I have his address?'

'Best leave it, Grace,' she says. 'How about a lemonade?'

'But, please, Mo. He's my friend. I want to write to him.'

'No,' she says. 'That won't be possible.'

'Why not?' Tears are already filling my eyes and I blink them away.

She sighs and looks at me sadly. 'He doesn't want to hear from you.'

My solar plexus pulls inwards as if I have been punched. I run out of the front door and keep running until I get to the playground. I can't believe it. Euan has left. He doesn't want any contact with me.

I sit on a swing for over an hour. I come to the conclusion that there's nothing I can do about it. If he doesn't want to talk to me then that's that. Macintosh is too popular a name for me to try to look for him. But he'll have to come back and visit and then we can talk. I'll keep myself busy. I'm in the restaurant three evenings a week and working hard with my schoolwork. My art teacher thinks I should study art at the college in Edinburgh. She writes a letter home to my parents.

'What do you want, Grace?' my dad asks.

I want it to be like it was. I want to go back to June the 15th, 1984, and live it differently. 'I'm not sure, Dad,' I say at last.

'In that case stick with nursing,' Mum says. 'Don't go changing your mind at this late stage. You don't know what type of people you'll end up mixing with if you go to that art college.'

By the end of fifth year we're all seventeen. To my knowledge, Euan has not been home. Not once. But I do find out that he's been accepted at university to study architecture. I have enough Highers to start my nursing course but I'm not yet seventeen and a half so I decide to stay on for sixth year at school.

Sixth Year Studies biology is harder than I thought. I've been serving Paul for over a year now and feel brave enough to ask, 'Do you ever do extra tuition? I'm struggling a bit.'

He looks up from the paper he's reading. 'I'd be happy to help you.'

Paul coaches me in his lab at the university. Soon it becomes the highlight of my week. He is easier to be with than anyone I know. Every so often we talk about Rose and one day as we're finishing up he tells me about his wife Marcia. They met at university when they were both eighteen. She fell pregnant by accident and neither of them was comfortable with the reality of an abortion. So they married. When Rose was born he fell in love with her, he said. She was the perfect baby, a sweet and cheerful bundle. To lose them both was the hardest thing.

'Anyway, enough about me.' His hand shakes as he locks the lab behind us. 'Have you applied for your nursing course yet?'

'Not yet. I have the application forms. I just haven't filled them in.'

'What's stopping you?'

'I'm not sure I want to be a nurse. I don't like the sight of blood.'

He laughs. 'That could make it tricky then.' He presses the button for the lift. 'Your drawings are beautiful, you know. The details included in your field-work report show exceptional talent.'

'I like drawing and painting,' I acknowledge. 'I had thought about art college but my mother thinks I'll end up mixing with hippie types and be smoking pot and having rampant sex with all and sundry.'

'It's a mother's job to worry. Don't be too hard on her.'

I punch his shoulder. 'How do you know that I'm hard on her?'

'It's that look you get on your face sometimes—don't-mess-with-me-or-else.' We step into the lift and he glances at me sideways. 'Feisty.'

'Feisty?' I hold up both fists. 'Who's feisty?'

I start to think of him at night, in my bedroom. I'm still a virgin. I wish I wasn't, I'm almost eighteen, but it was always going to be Euan and now he's gone and not one letter, not one. I start to think about Paul, to fantasise about him kissing me, making love to me.

I don't dream about Rose any more. Being close to Paul has lessened the guilt. I'm not over it. There is no way to reconcile killing a child, but I am able to function and smile and even laugh again. I have to avoid certain triggers: I've never been back to the Guides, I don't go anywhere near the pond and I cannot abide the smell of Lily of the Valley soap.

Towards the end of the school year I'm having my last lesson with Paul and feeling desperate. He's so much a part of my life now that I don't know what I'll do without him. We cross over the road to Donnie's Bites. I'm taking him for dinner, as a special thank you.

We're eating our starters, prawn cocktail with Donnie's spicy sauce, when he tells me he's planning to go to Boston for a couple of years.

My heart plummets. 'I'll miss you.' I blurt it out, just like that.

'And I you, Grace.' He looks at me kindly. It's a look he always gives me: tolerant, understanding, fatherly. I hate it.

'I'm not a child,' I tell him. 'You always look at me as if I'm a child. I'm not.' I take a mouthful of food. 'I'm eighteen next month.'

'I know.' He pauses. 'I am well aware of you.'

'You are?'

'Of course I am. You're a very attractive young woman.'

'You find me attractive?' My heart is swelling like a balloon.

'Grace.' There's that look again. 'Don't.'

'Why not? Because of the age difference? Paul, it's only twelve years.'

'Not just that. I've had too much tragedy. You're young. You have your whole life ahead of you. It would be wrong of me—'

'What happened was terrible,' I butt in. 'To lose Marcia and Rose. But please. Give me a chance.' I take his hand. 'Please.'

It's three months until he leaves for America and he agrees that we can spend some of that time together. He is working on a PhD—toxicology and disease in marine mammals—and I join him in the lab, either helping set up experiments or working on a project of my own: a portfolio for art college. Although I've yet to tell my parents, I've decided that I can't possibly be a nurse. It's the thought of having to encounter death. I can't do it. I know it would remind me of Rose and what I did to her. And that hurts too much.

Three days a week, after the lab work, Paul teaches me how to play squash. We go to the cinema together and find we have similar tastes in movies and books. He introduces me to his close friends and I find I can hold my own. I know enough about Paul's work to talk with confidence and I find his friends impressed by my own growing conviction that I can paint. As time passes, I see Paul looking at me differently. I become less of a teenage girl and more of an equal and finally, towards the end of the summer, he kisses me and I know that at last he is seeing me as a woman. 'What man could resist loving you?' he says.

Before he goes to Boston he asks me to marry him. I tell my parents. My mother's mouth falls open into an O shape. My father clears his throat. 'It'll be a long engagement?'

'No, Dad. Paul starts work in America next week. I want to be married by Christmas so that I can go out and join him.'

'What? What is this madness, Grace?'

'Lillian.' My dad stands up. 'Grace, as you know, we are very fond of Paul, but he is a man who has suffered two great losses.'

'But that's the thing, Dad. I can make him happy again. I love him.'

'Then I'm asking you to wait. Just wait a little while.'

'But I want to join him in America.'

'If he loves you then he'll be happy to wait.' My dad walks towards the telephone. 'I'll have a word with him.'

'No!' I shout. I have a horrible feeling he will put Paul off. 'Paul makes me happy. I thought you would understand that.'

'Grace.' My dad rubs his forehead. 'What about Euan? I always felt that you two would end up together.' He looks pained.

'But I haven't seen Euan for ages and I haven't even thought about him in weeks.' That isn't entirely true. I think of Euan most days. It isn't deliberate. It's just that he pops into my mind. I eat a sandwich and I think about how Euan doesn't like tomatoes. I play some music and I remember the concert we went to in Edinburgh. But Euan is gone. I'm eighteen now and ready to get on with the rest of my life.

My father insists that Paul comes to have a word with him. Paul agrees to wait for a year but I do not. I insist, persist, push and pull until we all make up our minds to a compromise—six months.

Paul and I are married on April 15, 1987. When I see him standing at the altar, all the love songs in the world fall short of what I feel. The ceremony is profound, permeated with the love that passes from his eyes to mine and back again. The reception is small—just close family and friends. Mo and Angus are there but Euan is not. He is at university in Bristol studying architecture. 'But he sends his good wishes,' Mo tells me.

I can see in her eyes that this isn't true but still I smile because, strangely, it doesn't hurt. I belong to Paul now. And he to me. For the first time since Rose died I believe I have a future and that, at last, I am truly making it better.

4

BY THE TIME I GET to Edinburgh it's already well past midday. A search through the telephone directory confirms that there's only one Murray Cooper living in Merchiston, in a detached, early Victorian house. I park on the street and walk up a gravel driveway The front door is part wooden, part stained glass in the style of Charles Rennie Mackintosh; my fingers feel along the copperfoil squares at the edges of the panel before I ring the doorbell. A balding man with ruddy cheeks steps into the porch, closes the inner door behind him and opens the outer one.

'I'm sorry to disturb you but I'm looking for Angeline,' I say.

'And you are?'

'Grace Adams. My maiden name was Hamilton. I was a friend of Orla's.'

'Ah.' He points towards an estate car in the driveway. 'I'm off for a round of golf but I expect that Angeline will be free for a chat. Come in.'

I follow him into the hallway. Black and white tiles stretch to the bottom of the wide stairs and beyond.

'You say you were a friend of Orla's?'

'As children, yes.'

'I expect she's alienated you too, then, has she? With all her antics? I can't imagine what Angeline did to deserve such a daughter. But judging by the father I suppose it's hardly a surprise.'

I wonder whether I've heard him correctly but, before I can ask, we are interrupted. 'Murray?' The voice is melodic but with a commanding undertone, unmistakably Angeline. 'Do we have company?'

'Indeed we do.' He holds on to the walnut banister and calls up. 'A young lady friend of Orla's. Grace is her name.'

'Grace?' Angeline comes to the top of the stairs and stands there. 'Grace?' She takes the steps quickly, elegantly. Her face lights up. 'Look at you!' She throws out her arms and kisses the air either side of my cheeks. 'Aren't you looking fine!'

I can't help smiling. She looks almost exactly as I remember her and I'm catapulted back to ten years old again: chumming Orla home from school; dressing up in Angeline's old blouses and scarves; singing and tap-dancing our way around the house, Angeline leading the way; chopping vegetables in the kitchen, learning how to make ratatouille, how to roast a duck and make authentic fish stock for bouillabaisse.

She is still beautiful. Her clothes are classic, understated. Delicate pink pearls lie round her throat. Her lipstick, though, is bold, the same pillar-box red that I remember.

'You've met Murray?' She gestures manicured nails towards him. 'We've been married five years now. Are you still living in Fife, Grace?'

I nod. 'Still in the village.'

'Fife has some excellent golf courses.' Murray purses his lips. 'Would like to move up that way myself but Angeline has too many unhappy memories.' He pats her hand. 'Not all men are meant to be faithful.'

I try to catch Angeline's eye but she is busy with the collar of Murray's polo shirt. What has she been saying? Roger, with his tartan braces and endless patience for the low-key rhythms of family life—I can't imagine any man less inclined to adultery. 'I don't follow,' I say.

She turns her back to me. 'Murray, my darling, enough chatter! You will be late.' She bundles him outside and he allows himself to be settled into the car, hair smoothed down, both cheeks kissed.

I watch them and think about Roger, salt of the earth, hard-working. He was kind, respectful, a quiet man who was bowled over by his exotic wife—a wife who never held back when it came to showing off. She waves Murray to the end of the drive and then comes back inside.

'Roger wasn't unfaithful, was he?'

'There is more than one way to be unfaithful, Grace.' She offers me her knowing look. 'He didn't give me the life he promised me.'

I look around. This property has to be worth more than a dozen of mine. 'Because he didn't earn enough?'

'I like powerful men, Grace. Men who are successful. Money is a part of that. I make no secret of it. Is it a crime for a person to reinvent herself? Or is the crime success itself, perhaps?'

'I don't mean to criticise,' I say, backtracking now, mindful of why I'm here. 'It's just that I remember Roger as a good man.'

'But memory can be faulty, don't you find? And there are so many things that children don't see.' She walks ahead of me and I follow her into a square sitting room with French doors leading into the back garden. 'So, what brings you here?' she says.

'I had lunch with Orla earlier in the week and last night she came to the village to see me.' I sit down on a cream leather sofa that swallows me into its middle. 'I came here to ask you about her.'

She sits opposite me on a high-back chair. 'Why?'

'She could potentially make a lot of trouble for me. She knows something about me that could ruin my life. She is planning on telling the one person who will be most hurt by it.'

'Your husband?'

'Yes.'

She inclines her head. 'She knows that you are unfaithful to him?'

'Worse than that.' I briefly close my eyes. 'Much worse than that.'

She is frowning. 'You have children?'

'Two girls.'

'A mother will do anything for her children. I stuck with Roger because of Orla. Whatever my mistakes—and there were many—I tried to be the best mother I could.'

'I'm sure you did, Angeline.' I'm not about to argue that point. 'I just wondered whether you could help me understand Orla. Why does she want to rake up the past? She is coming to the village next Sunday and says she will tell my husband what I did. I can't stress how damaging this will be for my family. Is there any way you can talk to her for me?'

'No.'

'Angeline. I would never have come here if I wasn't desperate. I'm appealing to you as a woman and as a mother.'

She looks at me through eyelashes that are long and sleek and curled up at the ends. They have to be false. 'Shall we have coffee?'

'Please.' When she leaves the room, I stand up, start to walk the floor, moving around occasional tables and ornaments. A grand piano has pride of place close to the French doors. Photograph frames are arranged across its lid. There's Murray and Angeline's wedding: people all around them, sunshine, a horse and carriage, electric smiles. I look closely at the family and friends' faces but Orla isn't there.

Angeline comes back with the coffee on a tray.

'Orla isn't in your wedding photos,' I say, this time sitting on a hard-backed chair to the side of Angeline.

'No.' She pours coffee. 'She wasn't able to make it.'

'Oh?'

'Life is a series of choices, Grace. Sometimes we go right and some-times we go left. But always we need to be moving forward. Orla does not have a talent for this. She made an enormous fuss when we left Scotland. She wrote to you, you know, but you never wrote back.'

I say nothing. I refuse to feel guilty about that too.

'Does she have any proof?'

I keep my tone light. 'Proof of what?'

Angeline takes a sip of her coffee, returns the cup to the saucer and draws her back up straight. 'You strike me as a woman of experience, Grace. Would you say honesty is always the best policy?'

I don't answer straight away. I wonder how much she knows. Would Orla, all those years ago, have told her about Rose? Unanswered letters, a new school, a dearth of friends, would she have been pushed to confide in her mother? I doubt it. And, likewise, I'm not going to be pressured into saying something I'll regret.

Angeline watches me. She's waiting for a sign of weakness. I'm not about to buckle. 'So, when you left Scotland, Orla was unhappy?'

'She had a breakdown. She made a foolish mistake, had to have an abortion and as if that wasn't bad enough'—she forces a sigh—'when she was admitted to hospital, she threw herself from a window, ended up with concussion and a fractured femur but still very much alive.'

I wonder why she's telling me this—and with quite such frankness. I feel a rush of questions—*Abortion? Suicide attempt? Why? What happened?*—but I keep my face impassive. I have a feeling that if I push too hard for answers, Angeline will clam up and I will be dismissed. 'That must have been a worrying time for you.'

She dismisses it. 'It was a dramatic stunt, nothing more.'

'What happened to Roger?'

Her eyes dart to mine.

'Orla told me he died.'

'Roger isn't dead!' She is bristling now. 'I divorced him ten years ago.'

'Orla lied?' Why would she do that? I can almost hear Euan's voice: *She wanted you to meet her and she was prepared to lie to get you there.*

'Perhaps she lied, perhaps you misheard her.' Angeline is unconcerned. 'It's of no importance. What *is* important is that my daughter was forty this year and what does she have to show for it? No husband, no children, no property, just debts and addiction and . . .'

'Addiction?' I say quietly.

'Yes, Grace. My daughter is a drug addict . . . *was* a drug addict,' she corrects herself. 'But then we only have her word for that. What does it matter what happened years ago? Bad things happen. It's how we deal with them that counts.'

That resonates with me. Rose died twenty-four years ago and how have I dealt with it? By keeping it covered up.

'How are *you* anyway?' She treats me to an open smile. 'Tell me about your husband and children.'

Her mood has shifted again but I can't match it. 'My family are well and happy. I'm here to ensure it stays that way.'

'Your tone is harsh.' She pauses, lets the air freeze. 'Must I remind you that you have come to see me? That this is my home?'

Her expression seethes with hostility and I feel uneasy, afraid even. 'You're playing with me, Angeline. I don't appreciate it.'

She laughs at this. It's deep and throaty and involves her tossing her head back with a younger woman's abandon. 'Grace! *Tu es si grave!*'

'This *is* serious.'

Her eyes heat up. 'Very well.' She settles her mouth back to neutral. 'Perhaps the truth will enable you to help both my daughter and yourself. She liked you once. Perhaps you can like each other again. Orla has spent several years in prison. She has been free for four months.'

Everything inside me stops. 'Prison?'

'She has yet to find her bearings. All this business with the nunnery. Nonsense.' Angeline brushes the palms of her hands together. 'She could do with a friend, someone to help ease her back into society.'

'What was she in for?' I blurt out. 'Was it serious?'

'I will leave her to tell you herself. But, really, Grace! I think we've spent enough time catching up, don't you?' Arctic smile. She starts a brisk walk to the front door and I follow her. 'It's for the best that you don't come here again. I've moved on with my life. Perhaps you need to too. Delving back into the past is never a good idea.'

'But we're all a product of our pasts, are we not?' My legs are shaking as I go down the front steps.

She chooses to ignore this. 'Orla's married name was Fournier. Quite a scandal.' She half closes the door. 'And, Grace?'

'Yes?'

'All this nonsense about the convent? I'm sure that were they aware of her past, she would be shown the door.' Her eyes are blank. 'So now you have what you came for?'

I turn away before she does—a small victory—and just about manage to resist the urge to run down the driveway. I climb into the car, start the engine, drive about 200 yards then pull into a parking space and just sit there, thinking, trying to make sense of everything.

Orla's life is all much more dramatic than I expected. I wonder how much Angeline is twisting the truth, making brutal statements about Orla while leaving out any details that might help me make sense of her. It strikes me that even Orla's memory isn't loved; no photos, no tender words. Angeline's fine speech about a mother doing anything for her children? I don't believe it. Not this mother.

I ring Euan. 'Can you talk?'

'Give me a sec.' I hear him walk outside. 'How was it?'

'Worrying. If Angeline's to be believed, Orla sounds like a loose cannon. But then Angeline is no doting mother. Utterly ruthless. If I ever complain about my mother again just remind me of Angeline.'

'That bad, huh? But did you find out anything useful? Anything that might persuade her to back off?'

'Maybe. Are you near a computer?'

'I'm walking down to the cabin. Why?'

'According to Angeline, Orla had an abortion, then tried to kill herself, was a drug addict and was in prison.'

'Shit. What the hell for?'

'I don't know. Angeline wouldn't say. I wouldn't be surprised if she was exaggerating. Downright lying, even. Are you there yet?'

'Yes. I'm just switching on.'

'And talking of lies, Orla told me that her father was dead and he isn't. How weird is that?'

'Sounds like a woman who'll use anything to get what she wants.'

'Can you Google her? Her married name was Fournier.'

I think about the threads that link one event with another. When did it start to go wrong for Orla? With Rose? Or was it before that?

I hear Euan typing. 'Nothing's coming up so far. I'll keep trying. You coming into work tomorrow?'

'Yeah.'

'See you then. And, Grace. Don't worry. We'll fix it.'

May 5, 1984. 'You will be coming to Guide camp, won't you, Grace?' Miss Parkin says. 'With Rose recently joining your patrol, it will be such a boon to have you there. I know she's very young but she really is a sweet child and her father is a wonderful man. Very handsome too.' She looks wistful. 'He won't stay a widower for long.'

Miss Parkin is round at our house because my dad is making her a rocking chair. It's bad timing for me because I had hoped to avoid the Guide camp in June, but now, with my mother breathing down my neck, it's impossible to say no.

'Grace will be happy to come along, won't you, Grace?'

I nod and then try to smile. 'I'm off to Orla's.'

It's a ten-minute walk to Orla's house. It's early evening and I'm going round to hers so that we can get ready for her sixteenth birthday party. This last couple of days she's been moody or distant and I'm hoping that she'll be back to her old self.

When I knock on the door I hear Orla and her mother arguing. That's not unusual, but this time it sounds particularly fierce. I ring the bell and, seconds later, Orla throws the door wide, doesn't acknowledge me but turns back to her mother and continues her rant. The French is so rapid I can barely make out what they're saying. I catch phrases like 'none of your business', 'how dare you!' and 'your father is a gentleman' from Angeline while Orla hurls insults: *Salope! Putain!*

I don't stop in the hallway. I know there's no point in getting between them. I tried that before and ended up catching the tail end of a punch.

Instead I climb upstairs to Orla's room, sit on her bed and read an old copy of *Jackie* magazine until Orla comes crashing into the bedroom, banging the door so violently that a shelf of books tilts to one side and drops onto the bed beside me. The right side of her face is red where her mother has slapped her.

'Jesus, Orla!' I put *Jackie* aside and start to gather the books into a tidy pile. 'What on earth were you fighting about this time?'

'You couldn't follow it?' She pushes me aside, scoops at the books with her arm and tips them all onto the floor.

'I don't think those were the sort of French words Madame Girard would normally teach us,' I tell her, trying to straighten the shelf.

'Will you leave that!' She grabs the corner of the wood and hurls it across the room. It hits the edge of the windowpane and cracks the glass. Several jagged lines fan out from the crack.

'Orla!' I hold on to her shoulders and shake her. 'Calm down! You'll end up not being allowed to go out. You can't miss your own party.'

'My mother is a bitch, a *putain*, a whore!'

'Look, everybody hates their mother sometimes.'

She looks at me and I see there are tears in her eyes. My own eyes automatically fill up in response. I have rarely seen Orla cry. She is fierce and feisty and will take anyone on, suffer anything. It's part of the reason I like her.

She looks away, picks at the wallpaper and says quietly, 'You don't know the half of it. My father is an arse for putting up with that bitch.'

I am reminded of Edinburgh, standing in Jenners department store and watching Orla's mum, her lipsticked smile, her body leaning into Monica's dad. 'Orla, it's your birthday!' I reach forward and hug her. 'Let's just forget all this and have a great time.'

By the time we get to the village hall she's back to her old self. The disco is set up and we spend the first ten minutes dancing, and then we stand back with some Irn-Bru to watch the others.

'Shall we get some fresh air?' Orla says. 'I've hidden some vodka under the second bush past the phone box.'

We go outside just as Monica comes round the corner. She is positively shimmering with animosity. She stops in front of Orla. 'I want to talk to you.'

'Not *now*, Monica.' Orla gives a weighty sigh of boredom.

'Your mother is a filthy French whore.'

'Monica!' I move in front of Orla. 'What the hell? Go away!'

'This is between me and Orla,' she shouts. Her eyes are wild and her hair is standing up on end as if she is possessed. 'Out of the way.'

'It's OK, Grace,' Orla says, shrugging. 'We've already had a run-in about this. She's come back for some more punishment.'

'Don't think you'll get away with this.' Monica points a shaky finger into Orla's cheek. 'May you rot in hell, Orla Cartwright. May your whole family rot in hell! Every last one of you.' She finishes it off by spitting on the ground at our feet.

As she turns away, Orla's hand moves out and grabs the back of Monica's blouse. It all happens quickly and I am slow to react. By the time I try to separate them Orla is sitting across Monica's back and is pulling her hair. The screaming and swearing is louder than my entreaties to stop and I can't match Orla for strength. I need Euan's help. I know where he'll be—down at the harbour with Callum.

I run as fast as I can. They are sitting on one of the two picnic benches opposite the harbour wall.

'Come quickly!' I am puffed. 'Monica and Orla are fighting.'

They both jump up and we run back together to the village hall. Callum hauls Orla off while Euan helps Monica to her feet. There's blood trickling down the side of her cheek. She touches it with her fingers. 'I think it's just superficial,' she tells him. 'I want to be a doctor, you know. I'm going to get out of this place.'

'Right.' Euan takes a few steps backwards to stand level with me.

Monica's face twists. She looks a complete sight.

'I'll walk you home,' Callum volunteers.

Monica looks him up and down. 'Don't bother,' she says. 'Enjoy your party.' Her eyes fill up. 'Don't let me stop you.' She lurches off.

'Show over.' Euan takes my elbow. 'Fancy a dance?'

We all go back into the hall. Orla wipes the back of her hand over her bloodied lip but otherwise she seems to be none the worse for wear. She starts slow dancing with a boy from fifth year. Euan takes my hand and leads me onto the floor. He puts his arms round me.

'I don't want to stay,' I tell him. I pull away. 'I think I'll just go home.'

'I'll walk with you,' he says.

I put my arm through his and we go down to the beach so that we can walk home along the shore.

'What was the fight about?'

'Orla's mother and Monica's father are having an affair.'

'Shit.'

'I know. Monica's never been my friend but I feel sorry for her.' I lean my head against his shoulder. We're close to the water's edge where icy waves stalk us, stretch out and cover our shoes, splashing our ankles. 'It's freezing!' I shriek and pull him towards the sand dunes.

His arms circle my waist and he kisses me gently on the lips.

'What was that for?'

'Because you're the prettiest girl I know. Do you want to go out some time?' His voice is low. 'Grace?'

'We're always together.'

'I mean out. Out together. Properly.'

I frown. 'Like a date you mean?'

'Yeah.' He waits.

I think about it. Euan and me. Me and Euan. A couple. 'OK then.'

When Paul leaves for work and the girls for school, I take Murphy for a quick run on the beach and then drive to work. Euan is already there. 'Was there anything on the web about Orla?' I say as I come in the door.

'Nothing.'

'Shit.' I start unbuttoning my coat. 'I was hoping we'd find out what she'd done.' I think back to Angeline's words. 'I thought she said her married name was Fournier but maybe I heard her wrong.'

'I'll try other spellings later. In the meantime, I've found the convent she's staying in,' he says. 'St Augustine's. It's close to Hawick. Shall we go?'

'To the convent?' I stare at him. 'Now?'

'Why not? Like you said—we can't just let her make all the moves.'

'Are you sure? It's a long drive. We'll be gone the whole day.'

'I wasn't planning on doing much work this week anyway.' He's already putting on his jacket. 'I won't say much. I promise.' He takes hold of my elbow. 'But I'll be there if you need me.'

He locks the cabin behind him and we start off up the path and past the house. Visiting Orla when she least expects it seems like a good idea and I'm glad that Euan is prepared to come with me. The clock is ticking, the seconds, minutes and hours bearing down on me.

We travel in Euan's car and while we drive I tell him about Angeline. 'She behaves with complete authority. Like she's some sort of monarch. And she has no sympathy for Orla.'

'Well, neither have we.'

'Yes, but Angeline's her mother! You'd think she'd at least express some love or understanding. Take the abortion for example. She described the pregnancy as a foolish mistake and Orla's suicide attempt as a dramatic stunt.'

'Lots of women have abortions. They don't throw themselves out of windows afterwards.'

'Yes, but it was obviously traumatic for her!'

'Grace, don't go down the road of trying to understand her.' His tone is harsh. 'She's as manipulative as her mother. She's a conniving bitch.'

'I know. I know.' I'm surprised by his vehemence. 'It's just that if her mother had been—' I stop and think about my own girls, how I would move heaven and earth to protect them. Orla is a real threat to their happiness. There's no room for weakness. 'You're right. No sympathy. None.'

The convent grounds are close to the English border, off a long, straight road with rolling hills either side. When we see the sign, ST AUGUSTINE'S ROMAN CATHOLIC CONVENT, we leave the main road and drive down a narrow single track, until we come to the front of a red-brick wall. The wall is upwards of thirty feet high and has a huge wooden door, shaped like the jawbone of a whale, positioned halfway along it. A smaller, person-sized door is cut into the bigger one. We use the iron knocker three times, then stand back to wait.

Less than a minute later, there is the distinctive sound of someone dragging back the bolts, then the door swings open, wide enough for us to see a smiling nun. She's short, five feet at the most, and her frame is as delicate as a child's.

'I'm sorry to bother you. My name is Grace and this is Euan. We need to speak to Orla Fournier. Urgently,' I add.

'Fournier?' she repeats, pursing her lips.

'Cartwright,' Euan says, and looks at me. 'She's using her maiden name. It's an emergency. Family business.'

'Orla is here on retreat. She will be leaving us on Friday. Could your business wait?'

'I'm afraid not,' Euan says. 'Time is of the essence.'

'In that case you must come inside.' She pulls the door open wider. It creaks on its hinges before coming to rest against the back of the bigger one. 'I'm Sister Bernadette.' Her handshake is firm. 'Welcome.'

We step into a cobblestone courtyard with a grass square at its centre. The grass is neatly trimmed and edged with rosebushes. We walk round the square and through an open archway in the building diagonally opposite. We are shown into a room with three long windows facing south. Two well-used sofas face each other, and a solid oak coffee table is positioned to one side. Several books lie on the table.

'A little "make do and mend" in places but we're here for the Lord's work.' Sister Bernadette smiles, and we both smile back. I'm so tense, my face feels as if it will crack.

'Now to find Orla. At this hour she may well be helping in the dairy.'

'Before you go, Sister,' I say, my hand skimming her sleeve. 'I'm wondering—do you think Orla will join you permanently?'

'As a novice, you mean?'

I nod.

'There's been no suggestion of that. I think Orla's feet are very firmly planted in the outside world.' She gives me a conspiratorial nudge. 'A life of prayer is not part of her aspiration.'

Sister Bernadette leaves and we are left alone.

'You were right,' I say to Euan. 'Another lie.'

'It should make it easier,' he says. 'If she's not doing it as a matter of conscience then we have a better chance of changing her mind.'

Five minutes pass and, finally, Orla walks in. Euan is standing by a window and I am sitting on the arm of one of the sofas, skimming through an edition of *The Imitation of Christ* by Thomas à Kempis.

'Grace. Euan.' She does a good job of smiling. 'This is a surprise. Take a seat.' She sits down opposite, crosses her legs and waits. I am immediately reminded of Angeline. Both mother and daughter have a rock-hard stillness that radiates outwards like a force field.

'Orla, I've come here to ask you not to visit my house on Sunday.'

She raises one eyebrow. 'You don't think Paul will be relieved to have some closure?'

'Paul accepted the pathologist's verdict.'

'He must have had questions?'

'It was an *unfortunate accident*,' I stress. 'Most likely caused by a combination of factors: the storm, unfamiliar ground, a child's natural curiosity putting her at risk.' As I'm speaking a memory comes back to me: Paul, several years ago, visiting Rose's grave, grief talking. *Why did she go into the water?* I blink the memory aside. 'Your story would be—'

'My story?' she interrupts. 'The truth is not a story. The truth is the truth. Wouldn't you agree, Euan?'

All this time Euan has been standing by the window but now he comes and sits down beside me, his thigh resting against mine. 'The time for the truth was then, Orla.'

'The truth will out,' she says. It's almost a whisper.

'Dredging it up won't help anybody.'

She laughs. 'It will help me! Aren't my feelings worth considering?'

'Orla, we had our chance to be truthful,' I butt in. 'Now time has moved on and Paul and I'—I bring my hands together—'our destinies are linked. We have two children.' I'm managing to keep my tone even but only just. I take a few breaths, wait for Orla to answer.

She doesn't. She stares at Euan, then at me, and then back to Euan again. 'Let's be clear.' She leans towards me. 'I am going to tell Paul about that night whether you like it or not. What you think or feel is irrelevant.'

'But, Orla, you didn't even push her! It was me!'

'I was there. Right next to you. It might as well have been my hand.'

'But it wasn't your hand. You were simply a bystander.'

'I see.' She looks up to the ceiling and then back at me. 'So a blind man is walking along the street. There's a manhole in the road but the cover has been left off. I see him walk towards it. I watch as he falls down into the hole. Who is to blame, Grace? The person who left the cover off? Or is the fault mine for watching him fall?'

'That's hardly the same thing,' Euan says. 'Nobody saw Rose drown.'

'So you're saying Grace is innocent?'

I hold my breath. I expect him to tell Orla what he's been telling me all these years, that there's no hard-and-fast evidence it was me.

But he doesn't cast doubt on my guilt, instead he says, 'Accidents happen. Tragic accidents that can't be undone.' He shrugs.

Orla gives Euan the full benefit of her stare. 'We killed someone,' she says flatly. 'We killed a child.'

'It was dark, Orla!' I shout. 'We didn't know she'd fallen into the water.'

'And the next day when we found her? What about then?'

'Well, it was too late, wasn't it? She had been dead for hours.'

'We could have owned up.'

'We could have . . .'

'But I stopped you saying anything.'

'But I didn't have to listen to you!'

'Of course you did! You always listened to me.'

'I had free will. I chose not to exercise it. That doesn't make it your fault.'

'We wouldn't even have been there if it hadn't been for me.' She tips her head to one side and says softly, 'Seriously, though, how have you lived with it all these years?'

'With difficulty,' I admit. 'And believe me—that's an understatement. But always, *always* I try to make things better whenever I can.'

'She was a child. We were cruel and careless and she ended up dead.'

'I know that, Orla!' I shout.

Euan puts his hand on my arm.

I swallow, lower my voice and say, 'Believe me, there has not been one single day when I haven't thought about Rose and wished that I'd done it differently—but it happened. Confessing to Paul and dragging my family through the mud will not change the fact that Rose died.'

'It keeps you stuck in the past though, doesn't it?'

'What do you mean?'

'You're stuck, Grace. You're on a rubber band looping backwards. You're continually pulled right back to that night and the horror that followed. You even married her father.'

'I fell in love with him. I told you that already. I love him still.' My tone is staccato and my fists are clenched. I want to pull her to the ground and stamp some sense into her. It's not an emotion I'm used to and my face is heating up from the effort involved in staying still.

She gives me a satisfied smile and I realise that getting me riled is exactly what she's after.

'You know what, Grace?' She laces her fingers together and raises her arms straight up above her head. 'I think you'll feel much lighter when we get this out in the open.' She looks at Euan. 'I think we all will.'

I lean forward. 'You have to see how impossible my life would become.'

'But think what it would be like if you no longer had anything to hide.' She also leans forward. 'What would it feel like?'

I almost fall into her eyes. I can't help it. In direct sunlight they are smoky, large, fluid and soft as cashmere. I think about what it would be like to live life without fear of discovery. Wonderful. And impossible.

'You know Euan thinks there's a distinct possibility that I didn't kill Rose,' I say.

She glances across at him. 'Does he now?'

'He thinks there are other explanations. She could have been sleep-walking, she could have been out looking for something—'

'Euan wasn't there. He was off getting drunk with Callum and co.'

I grab her arm. 'We just automatically assumed that it was me.'

'I know what happened to Rose.' She shakes me off. 'There is absolutely no doubt in my mind. None.'

The room is growing darker. The sun is now fully hidden behind clouds that cover the sky and cast murky shadows on the walls. 'What happened to your husband?'

She shrugs. 'It didn't work out.'

'How come?'

'We weren't suited. Sometimes that happens, doesn't it?' Her voice thickens. 'It seemed like we were compatible. We were both half French. We both loved rock music. He was sexy.' She pauses. 'We were together a year before it dawned on me that he wasn't all he seemed.'

'And the drugs? And the prison sentence?' I say quietly.

She starts back but recovers almost immediately. 'Congratulations. You really have done your homework. Euan's idea, was it?'

'No, it was my idea. And your mother helped.'

She flinches. 'You went to see her?'

'Yesterday.'

She is visibly rattled, her foot shaking. 'I've no doubt she took great delight in telling you about all the bad men I've chosen. The drug abuse. And then there's my stint in prison. Did she visit me, I hear you ask?' She raises her eyebrows. 'Not once.' She laughs. It's a discordant sound that makes me recoil. 'Kept you away from Murray, did she?'

'He went out for a round of golf. He's under the impression your father was unfaithful.'

'I know. My mother as a victim?' Her tone is acerbic. 'Can there be anything less likely?'

'Lying about your dad's death. That was . . .' I try to find the right word. 'Cheap. It was cheap and it was callous.'

'So? It got you to meet me, didn't it?' She says it without emotion. Her mood has oscillated from pent-up agitation to disengagement. She has the most disconcerting stare—knowing and yet compassionless. It makes me realise that she's not the girl she was. I thought I was dealing with a grown-up version of the girl I once knew—a girl who was impulsive and headstrong, who could lie and cheat but underneath it all had a beating heart. This isn't that girl.

'I don't remember you like this.' I reach across and shake her knee. 'What has happened to you?'

'We all have to choose sides.'

'What sides?'

'Right and wrong. If someone does wrong they should be punished, shouldn't they? What do you think, Euan?' she says loudly.

'Rose's death was an accident,' he says. 'Punishment doesn't always have to be public or direct. There are many ways to make good.'

'And I have,' I say. 'I make Paul happy. I do.' I change direction. 'You're not becoming a nun then?'

'Says who?'

'Sister Bernadette. No suggestion of it, she said.'

Orla shrugs. 'So what?'

'So what you're a liar? So what you're a meddler? So what you don't give a shit about anyone except yourself? What is this about, Orla? Twenty-four years later and you turn up to set the story straight. Why?'

She shrugs again. 'Memories. Past lives. You know how it is.'

'No. I don't. I don't know how you get from that to this.'

'I don't have to explain myself to you. Either of you.'

In my handbag, I still have the photo I took from my parents' wall, the one where Orla and I are dressed in jodhpurs and riding boots, splashed in mud, happy with our rosettes. For six years we were best friends. Surely that's still worth something.

'I brought a photo with me.' I dig around inside my bag to find it. 'Do you remember this?' I stretch to put it in her hands.

I watch her eyes roam over the picture.

'We both won that day.' I point to the rosettes. 'You over the jumps, me on the cross-country.'

'Bobbin never had the patience for cross-country.' She hands it back to me. 'We had some good times.'

'We did. We really did.' I smile, watch her face harden.

'But, in the end, we weren't such great friends, were we?'

'Orla—'

'The letters I sent after Rose died. You didn't read them, did you?'

She's right, I didn't. I simply binned them.

'I was trying to make it up to you. You should have read them.'

'Orla . . .' I hesitate. 'I was really upset. I couldn't get out of bed. I could barely stand. I'm sorry I wasn't there for you but I wasn't even there for myself! I was like a zombie. Wasn't I, Euan?'

Her eyes flick upwards. 'Why do you do that? Why do you look to him for verification?'

'He was there! He has seen me go through it.'

'I bet he has.'

'Look! You're not the only one who has a conscience. But telling the truth won't change the outcome. There is nothing to be gained.'

'I'm looking for redemption. And I will have it.' She stands up. 'That night, what happened to Rose? It wasn't all about you. We could have helped one another. If you had shown me the slightest concern . . .'

I stand up opposite her. 'You're doing this to me because twenty-four years ago I didn't read some letters that you sent?' I almost laugh. 'Christ, Orla! I'm sorry I hurt you.' I clutch my chest. 'But—'

'It's too late. I don't need your permission to tell the truth. Or yours.' She throws Euan a malevolent stare. 'Now fuck off, both of you.'

She leaves the room. Euan is on his feet and after her before I have a chance to react. When I find them in the corridor, he is holding her arm just above the elbow. He is talking quickly, urgently, and she listens and then she laughs, spits in his face and says something. He reaches for her throat and pushes her back against the wall. I hear the thud of her head as it ricochets off the stone.

'Euan!' I try to pull him away from her but it's as if I don't exist.

Their eyes are locked. She doesn't try to remove his hand. And she doesn't look scared. In fact, weirdly, she is smiling. After a few moments he lets her go, turns and walks towards the front door.

I am stunned by his sudden aggression. 'Orla?'

Her eyes are glowing, bright and lively, as if she's having the best time. It is so at odds with what has just taken place that I back away and at once her attention shifts to Sister Bernadette who is coming towards us from the other direction. 'I'm so looking forward to Sunday lunch,' Orla says loudly, pulling me into her. She kisses my cheek and murmurs, 'You're not fooling me with your I-love-my-family-more-than-anything crap.' She gestures towards Euan's retreating back. 'Just think yourself lucky I don't tell Paul about him too.'

April 1996. I open the door. Euan is standing on the step. He is wearing a dark brown leather jacket and has the collar pulled up round his ears. His hair is longer now and is being blown by the wind. Curls drift across his forehead and back again.

'Grace,' he says, and smiles at me.

I stare at him. His eyes are so blue that I see the summer sky in them.

'Can I come in?' he says.

I move aside and he climbs the steps. As he passes me I breathe in deeply and shut my eyes. He smells of the wind and the sea but mostly he smells of himself.

'Grace?'

I look into his eyes. 'You smell the same,' I tell him. I consider him. I drink him in. 'You look the same.'

'As I did twelve years ago?'

I nod. We haven't seen each other since we were both sixteen and he went to live in Glasgow.

'I have some lines now around my eyes.' He smiles. 'See?'

I nod again.

He walks through to the kitchen and I follow him. 'Mum tells me you have twin girls. Are they here?'

'Paul's taken the girls up to his parents in Skye,' I tell him. 'They're due back tomorrow morning. He's very good with them,' I add.

He looks at the mess of paper across the table, lifts one of my charcoal pencils and puts it down again.

'I was drawing. I was thinking.' I stop, breathe, and try again. 'I was hoping to draw. I was thinking of organising myself to paint. I want to paint again,' I finish, helpless in front of him.

He leans back against the worktop and crosses his arms. 'Haven't you been painting?'

I don't answer.

'You were good. What happened?'

I clear the papers into a tidy pile and shrug. 'Life, babies.'

'Do you enjoy your life?'

'Do you?'

He nods. 'Yeah. For the most part, I do.'

I avoid his eyes, switch on the kettle, empty spoons of coffee into two mugs. I fill them with boiling water, top up with milk and slide along the bench seat, hugging my mug. He sits down opposite me.

'I'm sorry I don't have any biscuits,' I say. 'I was going to bake some this afternoon but—' I stop. 'Truth is I'm not much good in the kitchen.' I think about the mess in the rest of the house. 'I'm not much of a housewife.' I laugh; it sounds shrill and I frown.

'Do you have any help?'

I screw up my face. 'Why would I need help? It's perfectly simple. I just have to apply myself.'

'So why don't you?'

'Because . . . because . . . I'm tired.' I shrug as if it should be obvious.

'The girls. They're almost four now, right? Do they sleep?'

I nod. Then I shake my head. 'It's not the girls.'

'What is it then?'

'What is what?'

He doesn't answer straight away. He just looks at me as if he's disappointed, as if I should be pouring my heart out, then and there.

'You look thin,' he says finally.

I try to laugh. 'Thin is good, isn't it?' I feel as if I'm choking and I cough into my hand. 'So why have you come to see me? I was under the impression you were avoiding me. Mo's kept me up to date, of course. Congratulations on your children, by the way.'

He is looking me up and down. 'You don't look well on it, Grace.'

I am hurt, devastated even. I know what he means, of course. I am a mess. My hair is unkempt. Fingerprints pattern my clothes. Four little hands. I never seem to be able to keep them clean. And I'm thin, I know. But his words hurt because I want him to see me as I was.

He's waiting for me to give him some explanation. What? That I can't be bothered eating? That I'm too tired to eat? That, anyway, I can't taste anything? And worst of all, that I don't see the point?

'Are you visiting your folks?' I say at last.

'Yes and no. I'm moving back to the village with Monica.'

I stop my hands shaking by sliding them under my thighs. 'Why? I thought you couldn't wait to get away from here?'

'Well, we decided it wasn't so bad here after all. Sarah is almost four, Tom just two.' He looks out of the window to the sandy beach. 'What better place is there to raise children? Monica has been offered a position in a GP's practice up in St Andrews.'

'She's done well,' I say, wondering how she managed it with two small children. 'But then she was always the organised one.'

'Monica was always more willing to apply herself than you or me.'

'But you're an architect?'

'Yes, but not a very ambitious one.' He laughs as if it might be a sore point. 'So we're coming home. I will start a part-time business that fits around the children. Monica will work full-time.'

I can hardly breathe. My head is buzzing, light-hearted and joyous; I imagine having him in my life again, the delicious possibility, years of bumping into him in the newsagent's, Sunday lunches in the pub, PTAs, our girls becoming best friends, New Year parties.

'So, Grace, twelve years, huh? How's life? Do you enjoy being a wife and mother? How are you?'

I pick up a pile of tumble-dried children's clothes and fold them. I'm on my fourth T-shirt when he stops my hand with his.

'How are you?'

I don't take my hand away. He feels so warm, so overflowing with heat that I want to take off my clothes and sunbathe.

'Tell me.'

Of late I have been feeling bloodless, as if there's nothing in my veins, but now colour floods my cheeks. 'I'm managing,' I say at last.

'Look at me. Tell me,' he says.

I shake my head.

'Grace? I'm your friend. Tell me,' he says.

'I don't lie to you,' I tell him. 'I don't lie. Not to you.'

'Oh, Grace.'

That's all he says—*oh, Grace*—and then he reaches across the table and I begin to weep. He stands up and lifts me off the bench, rests his back against the wall and holds me against his chest while I weep his shirt wet. He says nothing, just holds me, and when I'm finished he leads me into the living room and sits me on the sofa. He gives me tissues, hunkers down in front of me and rubs my knees.

'You're freezing,' he says. He pulls the blanket off the back of the sofa and wraps me in it, swaddling me up like a baby so that in spite of myself I giggle.

'You're a good dad,' I tell him.

'Mostly. Not always.' He smiles at me, smooths his fingers over my swollen eyelids. 'So tell me. What's going on with you?'

'I see her,' I say at once. 'I see Rose. Mostly in my dreams and she's drowning and I can't save her but then other times I see her on the beach or in the garden and in my girls—I see her in my girls. I was fine until I came back to Scotland.'

'You're tired, Grace.' His face is solemn, his jaw tight. 'That's all. Ghosts don't exist. You're exhausted from young children. You don't eat enough. Listen!' He holds my face close to his. 'I would bet all the money I had that Rose didn't die by your hand.'

'You would?'

'Yes. I would. You're a good person. There is no one I know who is a better person than you. I mean that.' His tone is compassionate and urgent. It feels like balm, like forgiveness. 'You have to let this go. Otherwise it will destroy you. And it will affect the girls and Paul.'

I nod. 'I can't tell Paul. I've never been able to tell him. The doctor says I have depression.'

'You don't.' He looks fierce. 'You just need to be kind to yourself. You need to move on and you need to eat.' He goes into the kitchen. I listen to him as he opens the fridge and cupboards. I rest my head against the back of the sofa and for the first time in years I feel as if I can just be.

Euan comes back. He's made scrambled eggs for us both. 'Now don't say you don't like them,' he tells me. 'Because I know you do.'

I take the plate from him and swallow the saliva that fills my mouth. I sit the plate on my knee and look at it. The eggs are sunshine yellow from our own chickens. The toast is granary. It looks perfect but I don't want to eat it. Instead, I toy with rearranging it so that the eggs sit neatly on the toast and the sprig of parsley is dead centre.

The room is so quiet I can hear the ticking of my own watch. I turn my fork round in my hand. He's waiting for me to start. 'Tuck in,' I say.

'Not until you do.' He lifts the fork to my mouth.

I take a breath. I close my eyes and open my mouth. I want to spit it out but I don't. I chew it. Slowly. It tastes good.

When I've finished my eggs, I lean back and puff out my cheeks. 'That was good. I never knew how hungry I was.'

He touches my arms, runs his hands the length of them and clasps my hands in his. 'OK, Grace, here's the deal,' he says. 'You're going to let go of Rose and start remembering stuff. You're going to remember that we're friends and that you can draw and paint. Do you promise?'

'Yes.'

'I can't hear you.'

'Yes, yes, yes.' My insides are smiling. 'I promise.'

We talk and we talk, about everything and nothing: what it's like being parents, whether he still listens to the radio in the dark, whether I still have to draw everything I see. He leaves around midnight. We hug on the step. 'Meet you down on the harbour wall tomorrow? Two o'clock? Bring the girls. It's time I met them. I'm practically their uncle.'

I watch him walk to the end of the street and then I come inside. My heart is floating behind my rib cage and my face is sore from so much smiling. Euan is the closest I've ever had to a brother. He makes me feel good about myself. And as the only other person who knows about Rose, he is a counterpoint to my own fear. Having him back in the village will be a gift. All my Christmases and birthdays rolled into one.

I rise early in the morning, shower, wash my hair and dry it into something that resembles a shape. I rummage through my make-up tray and find eye shadow, an almost dried-up mascara and a lipstick. I pour some muesli from the container and cover it with milk. I lift my spoon and hesitate, close my eyes, take a deep breath. I eat slowly and carefully. I finish a whole bowl and want to cry with relief. Instead I stand in front of the mirror and smile at myself. I'm still too thin, too tired-looking, but behind that there is a light in my eyes that I haven't seen in a while. If I had to give it a name I would call it hope.

When my family arrives back home I'm drawing—simple, charcoal sketches of the girls, partly from memory, partly from photographs.

Paul comes into the kitchen alone; the girls have fallen asleep in the car, and I hold the drawings up for him to see. 'What do you think?'

'I love them.' He examines each one. 'Can I keep them?' He looks at me. 'I'd like to have them framed.' He hugs me suddenly and speaks into my hair. 'I've been so afraid that we might have lost you,' he says, his voice thick with emotion.

I pull up my head so that I can look into his eyes. 'Paul, I know I haven't been the best wife and mother lately. But I think I can change.'

He starts to kiss me and I lean into him, relax my body against his, breathe in his familiarity and close my eyes to everything except the feeling that I am loved and wanted much more than I know.

Just before two o'clock I load the girls into the buggy. They're old enough to walk but still Ella insists on having her own place to sit. I give them each a bag of breadcrumbs for the gulls and we head off along the path to the harbour. It's a beautiful day. The sea is calm, its surface like polished glass broken by gulls as they dive for fish.

When I reach the beginning of the harbour wall, I stop. I don't really expect him to be here. I wonder whether I've imagined the whole of the previous evening; a kind of intense wish-fulfilment brought on by an empty stomach and a lack of sleep. I look along the curve of the wall. He's standing about fifty yards away, talking to a group of fishermen who are mending their nets. He glances up and sees me, climbs up on-to the wall and jogs towards me, one leg perilously close to the outside edge. When he reaches me, he looks as if he's going to topple over backwards and I scream, grab hold of his trouser leg.

'Chicken.' He grins at me and jumps off the wall down beside us. The girls are regarding him with cool, serious eyes.

'Man being silly,' Ella says, pointing at him.

'Out of the mouths of babes. I'm Euan and you must be?' He waits, his eyebrows raised quizzically.

Neither of them deigns to answer him.

'This is Daisy.' I gesture in her direction. 'And this is Ella.'

'Is this for the gulls?' He reaches for Ella's bag of bread and she pulls it tight into her stomach. He turns my way with a help-me-out face.

I giggle and shake my head.

'I know!' He rubs his hands together. 'Who wants an ice cream?'

'Me!' they both cry out at once.

'Shouldn't we feed the seagulls first?' he asks them.

'No,' Ella shouts, fingers working at the straps round her shoulders.

'She takes after her mother,' I say, bending to help her and then Daisy. 'No patience.'

They both run off along the path to Di Rollo's. Euan lifts my arm and puts it through his and pushes the buggy with the other hand. We get to the shop as Ella is pointing to the largest cone.

'It will be melted before you can eat it,' Gianluca is telling her. 'And look who is here!' He shakes hands with Euan. 'You back for a visit?'

'Coming back here to live,' Euan tells him. 'Can't get a decent ice cream in London.' He looks down at Ella and Daisy. 'So what will it be?'

Ella jumps up and down. 'Chocolate chip, chocolate chip!'

Gianluca loads two scoops of ice cream onto a cone and passes it to Euan who hands it down to Ella. 'Daisy?'

Euan lifts her up and she leans on the glass and frowns down into the trays then, overwhelmed, looks at me uncertainly.

'You usually have mint,' I remind her. 'Like Daddy.'

She nods and Euan puts her down. She runs to stand beside me, wraps her arms round my legs and pushes her thumb into her mouth.

'Daisy is the shy one,' Gianluca says, giving Daisy her cone. 'And there is nothing wrong with that, huh, *bambina*?'

We say goodbye and go back out into the sunshine. We walk over to the fishermen and sit down, like they are, on upturned boxes.

'Business good?' Euan asks Callum.

'Can't complain.' He threads the needle through the netting. 'As many lobsters and crabs as we can catch, we can sell. For all those fancy restaurants down your way.'

'Not any more,' Euan tells him. 'I'm coming back here to stay.'

'Well, good on you, pal. Come to his senses at last, eh, Grace?' He looks over at me. 'What do you think to that? Euan's coming back where he belongs, north of the border.'

'I think it's great.' It's an understatement so huge that I tremble with a kind of bottled-up hysteria, like a fizzy drink that's been shaken and is about to pop.

I follow Euan out of the convent. He is fuming. His hands and legs shake as he climbs into the car. Neither of us speaks until he overtakes a lorry too close to a bend and I ask him to slow down. He says nothing, just pulls into a lay-by. Clouds gather on the horizon ahead of us.

'Look, this isn't your battle.' I rub his left hand through mine. 'I don't want to drag you down with me. Maybe you should cut me loose.'

He gives a short laugh. 'How would I go about doing that? You're more a part of me than my own sisters. Letting go of you isn't an option. I think we have to outmanoeuvre her.'

'How?'

'Say we were with each other on the night Rose died. Brazen it out. She doesn't have any proof. Look at her history—mental illness, drugs, prison. Who's going to believe her?'

'But if we say we were with each other that will be perjury.'

'It won't go to court, Grace.'

'But still.' I think about it. I'm not sure I could pull it off. In spite of the way I've lived for the last twenty-four years, lying does not come easily to me. The fact is, I was never properly questioned about Rose's death. It was presumed that her death was an accident, unseen, unheard. I have never had to defend my position and I am absolutely sure I couldn't stand in front of Paul and fake innocence.

I sit back and chew on my nails, frustrated and dismayed with the turn of events at the convent. Nothing either of us said made any difference. In fact, it seemed like the opposite. The more Orla saw I wanted her not to tell Paul, the more determined she became to do it.

Outside the heavens open. We both stare through the windscreen. Water pours down from a heavy sky, flattening grass and making quick puddles in the hollows.

I rub my hands over my face. 'I wish I'd read those bloody letters.'

'This isn't about letters,' Euan says. 'It's about control and revenge.'

'Revenge for what? I honestly don't get why she would come back after all this time.'

'It's like that sometimes for people, isn't it?' He turns to look at me. 'Grievances fester for years. Then a catalyst comes along and bingo.'

I turn sideways too so that our faces are close. 'What did you say to her? Just now. Before you had her by the throat.'

'To back off. Crawl under the nearest stone.'

'And what did she say?'

He shrugs. 'Nothing worth repeating.'

'The bit that made you really mad? When she spat at you?' I say.

He shakes his head. 'Swearing. Nonsense. She isn't rational.'

I have to agree with him. Her eyes, just before we left, were lit with an unhealthy euphoria; the kind that speaks of madness rather than joy.

'Rain's easing off,' Euan says. 'We should head back.'

'I'm not going to let her anywhere near Paul on Sunday,' I say.

'One step at a time.' He turns the key in the ignition. 'It's not over yet.' We rejoin the road and he settles to a reasonable speed.

I try to relax back in my seat, silent, prey to my own thoughts. I feel as if the past has caught up with the present. I'm right back where I started. I've just killed Rose. I am the fifteen-year-old me in the body of a woman. I feel panicked and ready to jump from the car and run.

I look at Euan; his loss of control back at the convent—that wasn't Euan the husband, father and upstanding member of the community, that was Euan at sixteen, impulsive and headstrong.

Neither of us speaks until we drive across the bridge and into Fife.

'Do you want to stop for something to eat?'

I look at my watch. It's just gone three o'clock. 'I mustn't. I have to get started on the piece for Margie Campbell. I'm already days behind.'

When we get inside the cabin I sit down behind my desk and immediately stand up again and start to pace. Euan has the kettle on and is making tea in the small kitchen between the workroom and the bedroom. I walk towards him and blurt out, 'Orla was right, you know, about me living in the past.'

Euan glances at me quickly then away again.

'Do you know what she said to me when we were leaving just now? She said I should think myself lucky that she doesn't tell Paul about us.'

He stops pouring milk into a cup and gives me his full attention.

'How can she know about us? How can she know we had an affair?'

'She doesn't know!' He shakes his head at me. 'She's just taking a punt and no doubt the look on your face told her she was right.'

'It's not just *my* face that gave it away. At the girls' party she said you gave me a hungry look. That's what she said.'

He throws out his arms. 'So what if I did?'

'We had an agreement.' I bang my hand on the work surface.

'I haven't broken any agreement.' He moves to the sink. 'Look at yourself! She winds you up and you're off across the floor like a tin soldier.'

'Well, she had you pretty bloody wound up by the end! You had her by the throat. You could have hurt her!'

'Would you care, Grace?' He is speaking quietly, his face up close.

I think of how angry she makes me. Was my threat in the restaurant to hurt her an empty one? I can't answer that. Would I step forward and save her? No, I wouldn't.

'I just want her out of my life,' I say lamely.

'Well, that won't happen unless you take measures to stop her. Wake the fuck up.'

I flinch. 'Don't swear at me. You sound nasty. You don't sound like yourself.' I press my fingers against my temples. I feel as if it's only a matter of time before my head shatters completely.

'Come here.' Euan puts his arms round me and at once I feel something else: something sweet and familiar, deadly, to be avoided. I push him away from me.

'Don't,' I say.

He draws back, sighs.

'I'm sorry,' I say quickly. 'I'm confused. I don't know what to do.'

'Well, when you make up your mind, let me know. In the meantime, I'm having something to eat.'

He goes through and sits down behind his desk and I try to stop pacing, shaking, going over the same worries—but I can't. My head is full of fear and reproach. There's some whisky at the back of the cupboard. I pour some into a glass and swallow several mouthfuls down. Within minutes a comfortable fuzz swells through my skull and I am able to shut out the noise and tune into quieter thoughts: a memory.

I am seven years old and my dad and I are out on our bicycles. It's summertime and every evening we come to the neighbouring field to feed the horse carrots and then his favourite Polo Mints. He comes running across and lets me stroke his velvet muzzle. But this day, just as we arrive, we witness the horse being shot in the head. The instant the bullet makes contact with his skull, he drops to the ground, the sound splits the air and crows scatter and cry up into the sky. I fall off my bike and start to scream. My dad helps me up and then speaks to Mr Smith, the owner, and to the vet.

'He was sick, Grace,' my dad explains to me. 'The vet had to put him out of his misery.'

I have nightmares. I see blood and guts and things that didn't even happen. The only person who comforts me is Euan, not by anything he says, just by letting me sleep beside him in his bed. For three nights I lie beside him, my sore heart soothed by the sound of his breathing.

I go through to the room and look at Euan. What I am about to do is wrong but I truly believe that I am doing it for the right reason.

'Remember when Smithy's horse had to be shot?' I know my lips are moving but my voice sounds far away. 'You let me sleep in your bed.'

'What age were we?'

'Seven.'

'I didn't take advantage of you then?'

I resist the temptation to banter. 'On the fourth night you got fed up and kicked me out because I was making you hot, but for those three nights you were everything to me.' I move closer. 'And when Rose died you were the only person I could tell.' Closer still. 'And when you came back to Scotland, you set me right again. I know we're married to other people and I know I shouldn't be saying this, but you've always known how to fix me. Always.'

His face softens. 'Grace?' He stands up.

I tune in to the detail on his shirt. I focus on the buttons. The top one is undone. I unbutton the next one and slip my hand inside. My face follows my hand. He smells like ginger biscuits and warm chocolate and something else that makes me feel crazy. Relief. I kiss the quickening pulse in his throat and whisper, 'Please.'

He says my name again but this time it isn't a question and I feel the last of my inhibitions fall away. He turns me round so that my back is against his chest. I look through the window back up the garden where Muffin is lying full stretch in a patch of sunshine. When Euan starts to kiss my neck, I close my eyes. His hands travel up my back, unhook my bra and cup my breasts. He pulls my trousers down, slides his hand to the inside of my thighs and separates me with his fingers. I gasp, lean forward, and when I hear him unzip his jeans I start to moan. At first he moves in short, shallow strokes and when I ache for more he pushes hard and deep until I tell him I'm coming and he stops and kneads the back of my shoulders, waits for me. I am relaxed to my fingertips and smile from the relief and wonder of it.

He backs away from me and into the bedroom, where he sits on the bed and I ease myself down on top of him. 'I've missed you.'

'More.' He looks at me quickly, holds my hips and pulls me to him. 'I've missed you more.'

We don't rush. We linger and prolong the moments and then, when we're both satisfied, we lie back on the bed. After several minutes, Euan says quietly, 'We have to decide what to do about Orla.'

Memory crawls up from the pit of my stomach and bites me. 'We do.'

'We could buy her off?'

'I don't have any money.'

'I do.'

'No.' I frown at him. 'I'm not taking your money. Not that. God knows I take everything else.'

'Don't be daft.' He kisses my fingers. 'If she's about to wreck your life and money will keep her quiet then let's just give it to her.'

I am grateful to him. I climb out of bed and pull his shirt on. 'I would pay you back.' I nod my head. 'I would.'

He smiles. He looks relaxed, free, like the boy I remember.

I lean forward and kiss him. 'I'll get us a drink.' I go through to the kitchenette, fill a pint glass with ice and orange juice then go back to bed. 'When I was in the graveyard the other day,' I say, 'I was trying to work out what Mo would think of all of this.'

'My mum was a practical woman. If she'd known a phrase like "damage limitation" I think she would have used it.' He looks at his watch and stands up. 'Let Orla come to Sunday lunch. Get Paul out of the village. All of you, the whole family, should go out for the day.'

'And when she turns up?'

'I'll meet her,' Euan says. 'I'll offer her money.' He bends down to pick up his clothes. 'I'll get rid of her.'

I stand up alongside him. 'But what if—'

He puts his hand over my mouth. 'Trust me,' he says. 'I'll deal with her. Then we can all go back to normal.'

Normal. Normal is good. Normal is fine. Normal means we return to nothing more than childhood friends, grown-up workmates. Normal is Paul never imagining that I know anything about Rose's death. Normal is going off to Australia for a year, more, for ever.

'Euan?' I bite my lip. I haven't told him about Paul's sabbatical in Australia. I haven't told him because I had a feeling he would try to talk me out of it and now that we are intimate again it's even more important that I go away.

'Yeah?' He is half dressed, disappearing back into his clothes. And then he'll be gone. It makes me want to push him onto the bed.

'Thank you.' I pull his shirt off, over my head, and hold it out to him. 'This is yours.'

He looks me up and down, slowly. I watch his eyes move and focus. I wait. And when he pulls me into him, I breathe into my relief.

'Forget the shirt.' His hands are everywhere, roaming, along my spine, my neck, my hair and down again. I don't resist and an hour later when he leaves me at the gate, I look up and down the street, don't see anyone and risk turning my head back for a last kiss.

My family are at home. They all shout hello as I come in.

Paul goes to stand up but I wave him down again. 'I've had a hectic day. Do you mind if I go straight up to bed?'

He looks concerned. 'Can I bring you anything?'

'No, thank you.' I drop my head as if I'm tired. 'I just need to sleep.'

I say good night and go upstairs, shower and then lie in bed and stare at the ceiling. My body is still resonating with the aftershock of what I've done. Self-loathing lurks in the background—I haven't forgotten that adultery is a sure road to misery—but, for now, I feel as if I've been rinsed through with honey.

Hours later, when Paul comes to bed, I'm still awake. I love him—that has never been in any doubt—but at the moment he can't help me.

June 19, 1984. It's three days since we found Rose's body and I'm in bed. I've spent the day lying here, hardly moving. Whenever my mum or dad come into my room I close my eyes and deepen my breathing, make it long and slow. Shortly before teatime I hear Orla at the front door. My mum tells her I'm asleep and then says, 'But join us for tea! I'm sure Grace will get up when she knows you're here.'

No, I won't. I absolutely, bloody won't.

Orla says no, she can't come in. But she's written me another note—her third since it happened. My mum brings it in with my tea.

Dear Grace,

    Please! I'm so worried about you. Please stop ignoring me. I'm upset too. I'll drop in again tomorrow at four o'clock. I have something to tell you. I think we'll be able to help each other.

Love, Orla xxxxx

When my mum leaves the room I tear the note into tiny pieces.

Just before seven thirty the doorbell rings again.

'I'm so sorry to disturb you—'

'Mr Adams,' my dad says. 'Please come in.'

I lie completely still in my bed. I daren't blink or move a muscle.

'First,' my dad says, his tone grave, 'my wife and I wish to express our heartfelt condolences for the loss of your daughter.'

'Indeed.' My mother has joined them in the hallway. 'We are so terribly sad for you.' Her voice catches.

'Come through,' my dad says. 'Sit with us for a moment or two.'

They leave the living-room door open but although I strain my ears, all I can hear is the slow murmur of Mr Adams's speech and my parents making sympathetic noises. I get out of bed, creep down several steps, and sit just above where the banister starts.

'And I want to thank Grace for trying to save Rose.'

'We'll pass on your message, Mr Adams.' It's my father who's talking. 'Unfortunately, Grace is not up to visitors at the moment.'

'I was hoping she could help me understand why Rose was out of her tent.'

'She's told the police everything she knows,' my dad says.

'Of course, and I wouldn't want to bother her. Not at all. Rose was delighted to be in her patrol. The night before she left, it's all she could talk about, how kind Grace was and how much fun they all had.'

I wince, draw up my knees to my chest and press hard to stop myself from crying.

'Shock affects people in different ways. She's not saying much.'

'I understand,' Mr Adams says. 'There're just so many unanswered questions. You see, Rose couldn't swim. She was afraid of water. She would never have gone into it without a very good reason.'

'It was the middle of the night. She must have slipped.'

'Yes, but why would she be out of her tent? She was nine years old. She was a good, obedient girl.'

'Perhaps she needed the toilet and didn't want to disturb anyone,' my dad says. 'And then she must have lost her way in the dark.'

'She wasn't in the habit of getting up to the toilet during the night. She must have been out of her sleeping-bag for another reason.'

'Why don't I make us some tea?' my mum says with forced lightness.

As she walks below me to go into the kitchen, I sit further back on the step and hug into the wall. Mr Adams has thought this through. Like me he is obsessed by the detail—detail he doesn't and can't ever know. For how can I tell him? Tell him that Rose was out of bed at midnight because she had something important to say to me. Tell him that I wasn't interested in what she had to say. Tell him how she ended up in the water. I imagine walking downstairs to the living room and announcing, 'It was me! I killed Rose. I pushed her into the pond.' I imagine the ruckus it would cause. Orla and I questioned again by the police. Both of us branded as cruel and heartless—the worst sort of girls.

My mother comes back with the tea and I am still glued to the stairs. It's too late for honesty. There is no going back.

'Have you got someone looking after you?' my mum asks him.

'My parents have come to stay.' The teacup rattles on the saucer. His hands must be shaking. 'They live in Skye, close to Portree.'

'They must be devastated too. Their little granddaughter.'

'Yes. Rose meant a great deal to them. We spent a lot of time up there, especially after my wife died. I wish I'd never let her go to Guide camp. I wish I'd been there,' Mr Adams says, sounding distressed. 'She was young and vulnerable and I wasn't there for her.'

My dad murmurs something soothing and then there is an awkward silence, a full minute or more, until Mr Adams clears his throat and says, 'I won't keep you back. Perhaps if Grace is ever able to talk about what happened, you might get in touch with me.'

'Of course,' my dad says.

As soon as they all stand up, I sneak back upstairs, pull back the edge of the curtain and watch Mr Adams climb into his car. He doesn't drive off straight away. He sits there in the dark, and I know that, like me, he is tormented with thoughts of Rose's last moments. Did she struggle and fight before she slid under? When her lungs filled with pond water instead of air, were the pain and fear overwhelming? Did she drown because she became tangled in the weeds or did her body float and settle there after she was dead?

Finally, Mr Adams starts the car's engine and drives off, slowly.

5

THE VILLAGE I LIVE IN is tranquil and slow. Nothing much happens here beyond the simple activities of daily living: shopping, cooking, raising children. When we were young, the village felt constrictive and boring and we used to fantasise about moving to the lively streets of Edinburgh or Glasgow, but now I love it. Every day, come rain or shine, wind or sleet, I walk along the cliff path and enjoy the sensation of salty air in my lungs and the wind cutting in from the North Sea.

But my life as I know it is under threat. Why couldn't I, all those years ago, have done the right thing? Fifteen was surely old enough to face up to what I had done. Old enough to recognise that the consequences of keeping such a hulking great secret would far outweigh the pain of confessing at the time.

My body is aching for Euan and a repeat of yesterday afternoon but I'm ignoring it and I'm ignoring him. He called me twice this morning. I didn't answer so he sent me a text: I know you're avoiding me. Come to work. I'm barely there this week anyway. Nothing will happen.

I know him and I know myself. If I go to the cabin today we will make love. Once was an emergency, a last-resort bid to escape the chaos in my head—and it worked. I feel clearer, less afraid, more able to see a way through this. But twice would start a pattern and lead us both back into an affair. I've been there before, and for the love of Paul and my girls I've worked long and hard to haul myself back from it.

The sign reads *Mind yer heid!*. I duck obediently and walk through the doorway into Callum's fish shop.

'My favourite customer,' he says. 'Much mess after the party?'

For a moment I wonder what he means. The twins' party seems like weeks ago. 'No, it was fine. We had it cleared up in no time.'

'So what was Orla doing turning up?'

'You tell me. I didn't know she was coming.'

'You were good mates once, you two.'

'Once. Yes. Many moons ago.'

'No love lost there then, eh? The aggro was fairly brewing. Thought Euan and I might have to separate you both.'

'Even worse, Paul invited her to lunch this weekend.'

'Just tell her she can't come! Simple, innit? Make something up. White lie never did anybody any harm. So what are you after?'

'I was thinking of making crab pâté. Family picnic.' *For Rose. In her memory. Remember her, Callum? I killed her. Me. How can that be?*

'Just want the white meat then?'

I nod and he starts preparing the crabs.

Tomorrow is the anniversary of Rose's death. It's twenty-four years since she died. Since the girls were small our routine is to take a photograph of Rose up to the cemetery and remember Paul's daughter and the half-sister the twins never met.

'Euan got a lot of work on?'

'He's working on a barn conversion, for the Turners.'

'Thought he might fancy a fishing trip. There's some good salmon to be caught up near Inverness.'

'He's doing a lot with the school this week. They're having organised activities for the fourth years.'

'Jamie's signed up for sailing right enough. Teenagers, eh?'

He starts telling me about his son's wasted opportunities and I nod in the right places. Fishing? It sets me thinking. It's a while since Paul and Ed have been to Skye. The house Paul grew up in is still in the family. I'll suggest it. The girls and I can go down to Edinburgh for a shopping spree. They never turn down an opportunity to shop. Orla will still come to lunch but she will meet Euan instead of Paul.

Callum hands me the crab.

'Cheers. Put it on my tab, will you?' I say as another customer comes into the shop behind me: Mrs McCulloch, a good friend of my mother's; we exchange hellos.

'Give me that piece of haddock there, Callum.' She turns to me. 'Of course! You'll remember her, Grace! Roger Cartwright's daughter. Bonny girl, her mother was French.'

My heart skids to a halt. 'Orla?'

'That's her! The run-down cottage at harbour's end—the one that's inaccessible by car—she's renting it.'

Suddenly the smell of fish threatens to make me vomit.

'Apparently she came up the once, about three months ago, to have a recce round. She didn't stop by to see you then?'

I push through the door, not caring that my hasty exit will be seen as something to speculate about, and run home. Once inside, I lock myself in the downstairs bathroom.

So. Orla is moving back into the village. Came three months ago to have a look round. If Angeline is to be believed, that would have been soon after she left prison and weeks before she called me. She has clearly been planning this. I wonder how much she knows about us. I would bet every last penny I have that when I met her in Edinburgh, she knew exactly who Euan and I had married and more besides. She must have known my married name when she first rang me. She has played us both for fools. I ring Euan's mobile. 'It's me. Can you talk?'

'Mum!' Daisy giggles. 'I have Euan's phone. He's windsurfing. It's really funny actually 'cos—' She breaks off. More giggling.

I hear a boy's laughter in the background. 'Daisy? Ask Euan to call me when he has a moment, will you?'

'Yup.' She's still laughing when I hang up.

I come out of the bathroom. Ella is lying on the sofa watching MTV. She is eating her way through a packet of custard creams, scraping the cream in the middle out with her teeth and giving the biscuit to Murphy. She sees my face. 'I only like the creamy centre.'

'It's not good for him.'

She leans her cheek on his furry back. 'Doesn't she just spoil every-one's fun?'

I grit my teeth. As I thought—our getting along was short-lived. 'Did you stack the dishwasher?'

'I'm going to Sarah's in a minute. Monica's giving us twenty quid to clean out her attic this week.' Her mouth drops down in a huffy pout. '*She* doesn't expect slave labour.'

I have an almost overwhelming urge to hit her: for her insolence, her carelessness and her don't-give-a-shit attitude. I flex my fingers and call on Murphy. I'm better off outside.

I walk briskly, the coastline stretching ahead of me to St Andrews. I try to walk my thoughts into some sort of order but it doesn't work. There is no way to reconcile this. Orla can't live here. She has to be made to see that.

There's a figure walking along the sand towards me. It's Monica. 'I forgot how strong this wind can be,' she shouts to me, holding her hair down into her neck. 'Do you mind if I walk with you?'

'No.' My face is smiling. Yesterday, I made love to her husband but somehow I'm behaving normally. She falls into step beside me. 'Ella tells me she's going to help Sarah clean out your loft.'

'With Euan off doing activities this week, I thought I'd take a couple of days off myself and clear out the junk. Some of it's his stuff. He can't possibly want it after all this time.'

We are at the end of the sandy beach and we climb up and over the grassy hillocks that border the pathway to a ruined cottage. I turn to breathe in the view that stretches out before us. The pewter sea roars, yawns and bites at the shore.

'This place is so *depressing*,' Monica says. 'Dark, brooding. Everything I hate about the Scottish character is reflected in the landscape.'

'Hardly!' I turn towards her profile. 'It's exciting and dramatic and when the sun comes out there's nowhere like it in the world.'

She grabs my arm and propels herself round to face me. 'Do you believe history repeats itself, Grace?'

I take a moment to think. Monica waits. Her eyes are wide and seem to reflect my own sense of foreboding.

'I believe that, eventually, what goes around will probably come around,' I say at last.

'Did you know that my father killed himself?'

'Well . . .' I suspected as much. When I was sixteen, I overheard a whispered conversation between Mo and my mum.

'My father committed suicide and my mother drank herself to death. Do you think there's a suicide gene?'

'I don't know.' I'm out of my depth with this. 'Neither of your parents was able to cope with their lot but that doesn't mean it will happen to you.' I remember that, like me, she is an only child. She lost her father at sixteen and her mother at twenty. How hard must that have been? I reach for her hand. 'Look, Monica, I feel for you, I do. And I wish I had done something to help you when we were young.'

She turns blank eyes to mine. 'Orla didn't care that her mother was destroying my family.'

'I think she did, you know. On the evening of her sixteenth birthday party she had a huge fight with Angeline. She really didn't approve of what her mother was doing.'

'Angeline had my father under her spell.'

'She didn't hold him against his will,' I say quietly.

'As good as! Women like Angeline have no respect for family or commitment. My dad was a decent man and an excellent husband and father. And then Angeline turned his head.' She tears some grass into long strips. 'We were the perfect family until Angeline came along.'

I know that this isn't true. Monica's mother and mine were in the Women's Guild together. I have clear memories of my mother telling my dad how negligent Peter was, how he was never there for his daughter and how he never gave Margaret enough money to run the house.

'My dad went round to help Angeline with her accounts for that beauty business she started.' Monica tilts her head towards me. 'Lots of small businesses relied on him. You ought to have seen all the cards we received when he died! Praising his care and his attention to detail. But Angeline, she mesmerised him.'

For Monica, life becomes bearable when her father is blameless. Angeline was the whore and the wrongdoer. All her father suffered from was being too trusting to see it coming. Because a man who chooses his mistress over his wife and child is not a man who loves his family and can ever be loved in return.

Euan and me. The parallels are obvious. But we will never fracture two families. And we do love our partners and our children. Paul will be accepted for his sabbatical in Australia and then I will leave the village and temptation will cease.

'It's important to understand why things happen, Grace.'

'That's not always possible.' This whole conversation feels too close to home and I am only just holding myself together. 'Sometimes it's just bad luck and worse judgment but it doesn't have to cloud the good times and the day-to-day commitment.' *That's what I tell myself, anyway.*

'You're right.' Monica smiles at me. 'My father did his best. My mother? Well.' She shrugs. 'She was drinking long before the affair.' She looks upwards and breathes deeply. 'Orla isn't a threat to me. I expect that's the last we'll see of her.'

If only. I realise I have to tell her. She'll only find out from someone else. 'Orla is moving back to the village.' I watch her smile wilt.

'She can't!' She grabs my wrist. 'She can't do that.'

'She can and she is. She's renting a cottage.'

'I have to stop her.'

'Monica!' I shake her gently. 'I know she brings back memories of your parents and I know that hurts, but now, in the present, you have nothing to fear from Orla.' Her eyes say otherwise and as she looks into mine I see that she is close to telling me something. 'What is it, Monica? What is it?' My scalp tingles. 'Is it about Rose?'

Her eyes glaze over. 'I was warned about this. I was warned—'

'What are you talking about? Warned by whom?'

'Grace!' she hisses. 'Do you have any idea how much damage she could do? Orla is dangerous. She will cause havoc and then she will leave. We have to stop her.'

'Believe me, I don't want her around either.' I take her hand. 'Tell me what's troubling you.'

'I can't.' She pulls free. 'I can't break a confidence.' She takes a few steps backwards. 'Can you find out what Orla wants? Can you do that?'

I already have. 'I'll do my best.' I try to look optimistic.

'Good.' She recovers her composure and gives me an awkward hug. 'I may not have been popular at school, my home life was in meltdown, but hey!' She looks around her, takes in the sea and the sky and all the space in between. 'I have a great career, two wonderful children and I married the man I love. I consider myself very lucky. Well, he's lovely, isn't he?' She smiles. There isn't a trace of guile on her face. 'But then I don't need to tell you that, Grace, do I?'

May 14, 1999. I've been sharing space in Euan's cabin for over a year now. It's cold outside and the heating is on. When I arrive, I peel off my coat and then stand opposite my half-finished canvas and warm myself over the radiator. I look at my canvas, then across at the photographs I'm working from: the sky at dusk, clouds gathering over the sea, an epicentre of swirling black clouds rising up from the horizon. When I look back at the canvas I see immediately where I'm going wrong. The painting is taking shape but the contrast between light and shade is poorly defined and I've lost all sense of the encroaching storm.

Euan arrives. He's whistling. ''Morning,' he says.

'What is your eye drawn to in this picture?'

'This here.' He points to the edge of the canvas. 'What is it?'

'At the moment just a splash of red but it will become the slate roof of a house.' I shake my head. 'There's no movement in it.'

'In the house?'

'In the painting. There should be movement, drama, with the storm at the centre. The light's all wrong.'

'Coffee?'

'Please.'

Euan hands me coffee then sits down behind his desk and leans back. 'Grace? Do you ever imagine us making love?'

He says it, just like that, as if it's a perfectly normal Monday morning question to ask of a workmate. I take a breath in but have trouble letting it out. I don't answer.

'Do you ever think about us making love?' he repeats. He comes over, stands beside me. 'Grace?'

'I'd rather not answer that,' I tell him.

'Why not?'

'Because'—I wave my hands around the room—'we're making this work. Why spoil a good thing?'

'Be honest. Please.'

'Why?'

'I want to know what to imagine.'

I stare up at him. The simple truth is that I can't deny him anything.

'Yes, I think about it,' I say quietly.

'Do you know why I came back to live here?'

'Euan, please.' I think I know where this is coming from. Mo died less than three months ago. It's taken its toll on the whole family. 'We've all had a difficult time lately. You more than any of us.'

'This isn't about Mum.' He takes hold of both my elbows. 'I came back to live here because of you. I came back for you.'

I want to cry. In all my life I can't remember anyone ever saying anything that meant so much to me.

'I think about making love to you all the time. I just want you to know that.' He drops my arms, turns away and walks back to his desk.

I stand still. I feel as if the air is alive and if I move I'll push my life in a certain direction and I don't know which way to go. I swivel round. 'That's it? You drop a bombshell like that and just sit down?'

'It's hardly a bombshell.' He takes a drink of coffee. 'It's been running between us for months, years, decades.'

'But you've just crossed a line by talking about it,' I point out. 'Now we can't put it back. We work in such a close space.' I look round the room. 'How are we expected to carry on now?'

'This room is over five hundred square feet and anyway'—he shakes his head—'I'm not going to make a move on you.'

'Why not? Why bring it up just to do nothing about it? Because we're married? Because you don't want to spoil a good friendship?'

'Do you want me to make love to you?'

'No.' I lean back against the desk, purse my lips, fold my arms. My heart's pounding but I'm angry as hell. I expect him to back off, apologise. But he doesn't. 'What's brought this on, Euan?'

'We're a long time dead.'

I hold his eyes, see desire in them and tenderness and a flicker of fear. I walk over, stop in front of him. Inside me a voice screams: *What the hell are you doing?*

'If I could go back in time I would do things differently,' I say. 'When you went to Glasgow I thought about looking for you. I imagined myself turning up at your uncle's house and surprising you. I imagined you walking away from me—'

'I wouldn't have walked away from you.' He pulls me onto his lap and starts to kiss me. My skin sings. I reach my hands up under his shirt. His chest is warm and I tangle my fingers in the hairs.

So it begins.

We make love that first time and all the waiting, the wondering and the imagining ignite with the touch of our bodies like oxygen to a flame. I am shameless. He takes me so completely that I feel my body is his. My feelings for him stretch to the corners of myself and back again.

The minute I leave the cabin to go home for the evening, the guilt starts. Why did I do it? *Why?* I love Paul, I love my children. In the end I put it down to a flash of pure lust. It won't happen again.

I don't go into work the next day. At ten o'clock Euan calls me.

'Are you coming in?'

'No.' I screw my eyes up tight. 'I'm too scared.'

'You have one hour and then I'll come and get you.'

I go. We do it again and again. We take risks but we minimise them. We never send texts to each other. We don't email. We limit ourselves to once a week. We double-check that Sarah and Tom are not likely to arrive home unexpectedly.

Sometimes I dig and push. 'Why did you marry Monica?'

'Monica's a good person, Grace. She works hard. She's loyal and kind. I love her for that.'

'More than me?'

'Different.'

I can't stop. 'But if you had to choose one of us?'

'I don't know. She's the mother of my children.'

'Does that mean you'd choose her?'

'It means I don't know.'

I still can't stop. 'In your heart me or her?'

He looks at me for a long time. I wait and in the waiting it comes to me that I don't want to know the answer. 'I'm sorry,' I say.

'I think we need some rules.' He takes my wrist, kisses the back of it. 'We don't talk about our partners. Ever. That has to be a boundary.'

It's not the nineteenth century. We could leave our families and start afresh together. It would be messy, nasty even, but that doesn't stop a lot of people. We talk about it. Just the once. But I can't do anything else wrong. Having an affair is wrong, I know that, but it's the lesser of the wrongs than splitting up two otherwise happy families.

After eight months we agree to give each other up. There is no future in it. I know that it's the right thing to do but I feel utterly desperate, incomplete, raw inside. I can't sleep and spend the small hours doubled up on the bathroom floor. Euan is no better. He looks drawn, fatigued, snaps at his clients and sighs for no reason. We still work in the same space but keep our backs turned and our heads down.

It gets easier. I work from home more and Euan has a huge project in Dundee that keeps him in the office on site. We manage this for four years. And then one day, I'm feeling low. Paul's mother has died and Ed has been diagnosed with Alzheimer's. I'm at work, Euan and I reach for the kettle at the same time and our hands touch and hold. I start to cry. He takes me into the bedroom and we spend the whole day in bed.

Three weeks of loving each other again and then a jolt, a near miss. Sarah and Ella are moments away from catching us in bed together. We stop again. It's difficult and painful but we do it. Another four years pass and then Orla comes back.

I have a recurring nightmare and whenever I'm stressed, it visits me with a religious vengeance. There's a knock on the door. Two men are on the doorstep; they both pull out ID and hold it up to my face. 'Are you Mrs Grace Adams?'

I nod.

'Would you be good enough to accompany us to the station?' one says. 'We have reason to believe you were involved in the death of a young girl back in 1984. Ring any bells, Mrs Adams?' He has a leering, jeering face that morphs into a demon with horns and burning coal for eyes.

When I wake, my hands are covering my face. I don't want to disturb Paul so I slither out of bed and go downstairs. It's two o'clock in the morning and I'm wide awake. I know there's no point in me going back to bed yet so instead I go into the kitchen and make the pâté, set out the picnic cutlery and glasses.

Orla was right—I am stuck. Just as she said, forever sliding backwards, remembering Rose, reliving that night, catching hold of Euan, seeing myself in his eyes; the self that existed before Guide camp. I have tried to assuage my guilt with a life of family and love and commitment. I have made Rose's father happy. Paul loves me and I love him. And yet what have I really been doing all these years? Delaying the moment when I have to pay for what I did.

And Euan. When he returned my call yesterday, he already knew that Orla was living in the village. Monica told him immediately after I met her on the beach. I asked him why Monica was so upset. He didn't know or didn't want to talk about it. He asked me when I was coming into work. I said I thought we shouldn't be alone together. I told him that we couldn't repeat Monday. He said, of course not. He knew that.

But we should talk about Orla. I told him that Paul and Ed are going away for the weekend fishing and the girls and I will go to Edinburgh. So that leaves Sunday free for him to meet Orla and bribe her? Persuade her? Leave that to me, he said, and we both hung up.

When the picnic is organised, I go back to bed, turn towards Paul and shape myself round the curve of his spine. It's only two hours until I have to get up and tackle the day and when I finally nod off, my sleep is fitful. I wake up as Paul leaves the bed.

'I thought we could go up to the graveyard for eleven, Grace.'

'No problem. I'll make us all some breakfast first.'

The day is warm. The family join me for breakfast and afterwards we all climb into the car. Ed sits in the middle of the girls. For the last day or so he has been avoiding me. I don't know whether it's something to do with the Alzheimer's. I tried to have a word with him about it but when I asked him what was wrong, he gave me a withering look and said, 'If you don't know, then I'm not the one to tell you.'

We gather in front of Rose's grave. Paul, the girls and I sit on the grass. Ed is busy digging up the small plot in front of her headstone and is arranging some bedding plants in the newly turned soil. Emotions swirl around inside me like a sea gathering to a storm. Coming to the graveside reminds me that my whole life revolves around Rose and what happens next is dependent on keeping what happened a secret.

'Mum!' Daisy calls. 'You keep drifting off. Is everything OK?'

Paul is watching me. Everybody is. 'I'm fine.' I pull my lips back into a smile. 'I'm sorry, what were you saying?'

'How did you two end up getting married?' Daisy says. 'You never really told us.'

'We met in La Farola a few months after Rose died,' Paul says. 'Well, it wasn't La Farola's then. It was called Donnie's Bites. Your mum was a waitress. She wore a dinky little uniform that showed off her legs.'

'Do you still have it, Mum?' Daisy says. 'It might come in handy for fancy dress.'

'It's probably in the attic somewhere.'

'It's my birthday coming up,' says Paul. 'As a special treat, perhaps?'

I laugh and Ella screws up her face. 'Do you *mind*?'

'So?' Daisy says. 'Did you eat there a lot?'

'I had nothing to go home for. And, as you know, I'm not much of a cook. I spent a couple of nights a week in there. We got talking.' He looks at me and smiles. 'We found out that we had a lot in common.

We started to play squash together, went for long walks, your mum would bring her sketchbook, I always had a camera with me.'

'Not the most exciting of courtships then?' Ella says. We ignore her.

'And were Granny and Granddad OK about you marrying so young, Mum?'

'They didn't take much persuading.' Paul holds my eyes. 'When they saw how much we loved each other'—he leans over and kisses my lips—'any reservations they had melted away.'

'Can we go easy on the mush?' Ella says. She is pulling the petals off a buttercup. 'And anyway, shouldn't we be talking about Rose?'

'I remember Rose,' Ed says, swivelling round on his knees. 'She had her own little set of garden tools. She loved to help me in the garden.'

I stand up to stretch my legs while Paul takes up the story. The path ahead is clear, all the way to where the land slopes down to the sea. In the other direction is the church. It's stone-built and weather-worn and has stood on the hill, battling the elements, for more than 200 years. It's the church I was married in and in my mind's eye I can still see Paul standing at the altar, turning round to take my hand, holding my gaze all through the ceremony. I loved him so completely then. And I love him still. But it isn't the same. And I was the one to spoil it, not him. When Euan came back into my life, part of me was reborn. I can't explain it, even to myself, but he gives me something, a feeling, a love, an affirmation that is nigh-on impossible to live without. How can I love two men at once?

As I turn to walk back towards my family, I notice that someone else is there—a woman. The way she is standing, the tilt of her head, jolts me back into the past. Angeline? But this woman can't be Angeline—she is too young. Her hair is straight and lies loose around her shoulders—that's why I don't recognise her immediately. She's straightened it. As I draw closer, I see that today she is wearing make-up. Her eyes are grey across the lids, her lashes long and curled with black mascara. Daisy and Ella are both admiring her shoes and she holds on to Paul's arm as she slides them off her feet. Ella immediately puts them on and starts to parade up and down.

'You look fantastic in them!' Orla exclaims. 'I can tell you the name of the shop where I bought them.' She claps her hands. 'Even better! Why don't I take you both on a shopping trip? Now that I'm home to stay, your mum and I can be friends and I can be—'

'Like a surrogate auntie?' Ella says, handing the shoes to Daisy.

'Exactly!'

'Mum?' Daisy spots me watching them. 'What do you think?' She walks towards me. 'She could come with us on—'

'Orla! What a surprise,' I say, interrupting Daisy before she mentions Sunday's shopping trip. 'Back in the village.'

'Where else?' She turns a full circle, her arms out, eyes closed. 'There's nowhere quite like it.'

'We felt the same when we came back.' Paul looks towards me. 'We lived in Boston when we were first married, didn't we, Grace?'

'Yes.' I am tightlipped, both hot with fury and cold with a steely, focused anger that I have never experienced before.

Orla reaches forward and hugs me, brushes my hair aside with her fingers and whispers, 'Relax! I won't tell him. Not yet.'

I hold myself still, stop short at pushing her away.

'A picnic!' she exclaims. 'How wonderful! Is this a special day?'

'It's the anniversary of Rose's death,' Paul says.

'Of course. I'm so sorry.' She lays a hand on Paul's forearm. 'How stupid of me.' Her expression is solemn as she looks around at all of us. 'I'm intruding on family time.'

'Not at all,' Paul says. 'We were just about to walk down to the beach and enjoy our picnic. Why don't you join us?'

'I couldn't possibly. I really don't want to intrude.'

'You won't be intruding,' Paul says, looking to me for confirmation. 'Grace has packed more than enough, haven't you, love?'

'I'm sure Orla is busy with her move,' I say. 'Perhaps another time.'

'Grace is right. The cottage will need a lot of work doing to it before I can call it home.' She sighs happily. 'But I'm not planning on moving anytime soon so I have all the time in the world.'

I don't react. She really is laying it on thick, each comment set to scare me further. But it isn't working. I feel strangely powerful.

'Rose was such a lovely child,' she says, her eyes on Paul. 'Grace and I enjoyed looking after her at camp, didn't we?'

I say nothing. Ed and the girls start to drift down towards the beach and I follow them with my eyes.

'Yes, we must be off,' Paul says, lifting the picnic basket up off the ground. 'Did you mention Sunday lunch, Grace?'

'I haven't but I will.' I put my arm through Orla's. 'I'll walk you to the gate,' I say, steering her uphill and out of my family's earshot. 'About Sunday,' I continue, determined that she should still keep the lunch appointment and come up against Euan instead of Paul and me. 'We were wondering whether you have any dietary considerations: peanut allergy, wheat allergy. That sort of thing.'

'Really?' She crosses her arms.

'Yes, really.' I match her body language. 'Do you have any?'

'No.' She tips her head to one side. 'The clock is ticking, Grace.'

'Is it money? Is that what you want?'

'You think I'm doing this for money?' Her laugh is derisive.

'Why then, Orla?' I'm right in her face. 'Why are you doing this?'

She thinks for a moment. 'Because I can.' She looks down to the shore. 'I had a lot of time to think when I was in prison. One of the first things I did when I came out was to come back to the village—just the once—to check up on you. I saw you and Euan walking on the beach together. And you looked so'—she searches for the right word and her face is twisted with a manic look that is unsettling—'so fucking happy.'

I take a step back. 'This is about me and Euan?'

She doesn't answer me. I watch her. Her eyes are black, fathomless. I can see her playing a memory through her mind. I know that this is it. If she doesn't level with me now she never will.

'You know what? I hope that when Paul discovers the truth, he chucks you out onto the streets. I hope your girls never want to see you again. I hope that you are shunned by everyone. And I hope the regret eats away at you until there's nothing of you left.'

'You hate me that much?'

'I don't hate you. I despise you.' Her saliva spits onto my face.

I wipe the back of my hand over my cheek and keep my face lowered as anger swells in me. 'You need to stop now before this gets out of hand.'

'Are you threatening me?'

'It's more of a warning.'

'Are you going to set Euan on me?' I wonder how she is always able to work out our next move. 'Is he going to have a quiet talk with me? And if that doesn't work, will he progress to not-so-gentle persuasion?' Her eyes sparkle. 'I know! Why not kill me?' she whispers.

'I don't want you dead,' I say flatly. 'I want you gone.'

'Euan was always good at doing what had to be done, wasn't he?' She paces around me, leaning into my body as she speaks. 'You can hold me down and Euan can do the deed. You've lived with one death all these years. Hell! Why not make it two? I won't struggle.' She crosses her heart with her fingers. 'I promise.' Then she walks away, laughing.

November 1983. 'This is a critical year for all of you. The make-or-break year. Time to separate the wheat from the chaff.'

We're in assembly. We're fifteen going on sixteen. It's our O-level year. The headmaster has been talking for fifteen minutes.

'Hard work is of the essence. No lateness to lessons. Homework in on time. Have we all got that?' Nobody answers. 'Good,' he says.

The home-time bell can't come soon enough. Orla and I sit together on the bus. It's a twenty-minute ride back to the village and we talk about the upcoming school disco; what we're going to wear, who we're going to dance with. At the village hall we all spew out onto the pavement. Orla goes one way, me the other. I promise to call her later and then run to catch Euan up. He's walking uphill towards our houses, cracking his fingers, one by one, left hand and then right. It's something he does when he's anxious or in trouble.

'Macintosh!' a voice roars from behind us.

I look back. It's Shugs McGovern, the boy everyone fears.

'Don't turn round, Euan,' I say.

But Euan does turn round. Stops. Waits. I wait too. Shugs catches us up. Acne spots are dotted across his face. 'You're claimed, Macintosh.' He moves an index finger across his own throat and then points at Euan. 'After footy.' And then he goes back towards the village hall where half a dozen boys are waiting for him.

My heart freezes. 'I'll tell my dad and your dad and they'll go to the police,' I say in a rush.

'No way!' He looks scathing. 'That will only make it worse.'

'You can't fight him!' I hiss. 'He'll kill you.'

'Just leave it.' He points a finger at me. 'Don't tell anyone. I knew it was coming and I know what to do. I'll get him before he gets me.'

'But, Euan . . .' I grab the lapels of his blazer. 'You can't let him hurt you.' My voice is muffled. I wipe tears into his shirt.

'It's just the way it is. If I don't do it now, I'll have to do it in a month or in a year. I might as well get it over with.' He puts his arm round me and we walk the rest of the way home like this, leaning into each other. When we get to his gate, he lets me go.

'I'll come with you.'

'No. You mustn't.' He rubs my hands. 'You might get caught up in it. I'll be fine.' He walks up his front path and shouts back, 'Nice that you care though.' As he goes through his front door he smiles at me.

I'm convinced that's the last time I'll ever see him smile. I'm sure he'll end up brain-damaged or, at the very least, all his teeth will be knocked out. Shugs is known for violence. If he's not torturing small animals then he's picking fights and in trouble with the police, most recently for giving a boy a broken collarbone. And last year he was suspended from school for drug dealing and spent two months in Edinburgh, in what my mother euphemistically calls 'the home for bad boys'. Since he got back, he's been settling old scores—he thinks Euan told on him—and when Shugs claims you for a fight, refusal isn't an option.

Youth club football starts at seven o'clock. By nine o'clock I'm on tenterhooks and when the doorbell rings I hurtle down the stairs and almost knock my mother over. It's Euan. I join him outside, scan his body and see that he is intact. I even feel along his face and arms and torso just to be sure.

'I should get in a fight more often.' He is laughing.

I hug him hard and he doesn't even wince. 'What happened?' I stare at him in wonder. 'You're not hurt at all!'

'Like I said, I got him first. When he was bending down to do up his boots, I brought my knee up into his face. One shot. Got him hard. Felt his nose break.' He swivels on the balls of his feet. 'Fancy an ice cream?'

'You felt his nose break?' I am disgusted. 'Shit, Euan.'

'It was me or him. I did what had to be done,' he says.

I grab my coat and we walk down to the village, arm in arm. Callum is already there and he's telling everyone about what happened. It sounds like Shugs has been badly hurt, but, in the dog-eat-dog way that boys have, Euan has earned his respect, so there won't be any reprisals.

I feel proud of Euan but at the same time I see there is a side to him that I don't know anything about; a ruthless side that is foreign to me.

When we're walking back home he says, 'You were really worried about me.'

'I was scared. You're like a brother to me.'

'A brother?'

'Not exactly a brother,' I say, backtracking. 'But more than just a friend.'

'In that case'—he adopts a bashful swagger—'you can kiss me if you want.'

I'm not sure I want to kiss him. The story of the fight has unsettled me. It's not the Euan I know. I didn't want him hurt but I didn't want him doling out violence either. Anyway, I kiss him because he's been brave and he's happy and if I don't kiss him I think he'll find some other girl who will. And I don't want that.

6

It's Thursday. One week since I met Orla in Edinburgh. And though it's already three o'clock in the afternoon, I haven't been in to work. I have been walking Murphy and thinking about the past and the present, trying to join the dots between what happened then and what is happening now. But I need more information and there's only one place to get that. I call Murphy and we go back to the car. I drive along the coastal road back to the village. The cottage Orla is renting is positioned on the headland looking out towards the North Sea. I stop some distance from the obvious parking spot, noticing as I do that Orla's car isn't there. Good. I pat Murphy goodbye, lock my car and walk the hundred yards or so down the grassy bank to the front door.

From the outside, the house looks as if it has suffered years of neglect. The stonework is crumbling at the corners and under the windows. Roof tiles have slipped and the garden is overgrown. I bang hard with the door-knocker. No answer. I put my hands up either side of my face and peer through the dirty window. I can't see anyone inside.

I have never broken into a house. I wouldn't know how to go about it. In any event, I don't have to because the key is in a similar place to where Orla's mother used to leave it when we were children: underneath a medium-sized stone beside the front step.

The interior is just as dilapidated and gloomy as the outside suggests. There is a stale, dank smell, wallpaper is peeling off and there are brown stains from water leaks running across the ceiling. The living-room curtains are hanging by only a few hooks; the fireplace is obscured with dust and grime and looks as if it hasn't been lit for many years. It's made of cast iron and has two child-unfriendly spikes at either end of the plinth.

There has been no attempt made at homemaking. There are no pictures or photographs, no personal items spread over the dining table, no keys or magazines. Nothing. The sum total of recent habitation amounts to two empty whisky bottles and the remains of a carry-out.

I come out of the living room and into the kitchen. The old-style porcelain sink is tea-stained, the cooker thick with grease. I have a cursory look in the bathroom and then open the door of the last room: the bedroom. What I see stops me short. I blink several times and tell myself that I must be imagining it. I even close the door and then open it again, expecting to see something different, but I don't. Orla has re-created her teenage room. The duvet is a faded blue-and-yellow flower print that I remember us choosing from a catalogue, likewise her slippers, and her bedside cabinet is the very same solid-oak unit with three drawers and a cupboard. Even the bedstead is the one she had as a teenager, with stickers placed randomly across it.

I walk into the room feeling as if I am stepping through a hole in time. The posters are the same ones she had on her walls back then: Tears for Fears, Guns N' Roses. My legs feel hollow and I fall back into a sitting position on the bed. I can't believe she kept all this stuff.

The house is completely silent, eerily so. It feels creepy, sitting amid all these memories: creepy and dangerous, as if being here will surely invite disaster. I stand up with the intention of leaving but the heel of my shoe catches on the handle of a suitcase and pulls it out from under the bed. I bend down to take a look inside. It doesn't contain clothes or a wash bag. It contains a large and expensive digital camera with a hefty zoom lens. Next to it there are half a dozen A4 manila envelopes. I don't hesitate. I look in the first one. It contains a wad of twenty-pound notes. I put it back and look in the second envelope. Three brand-new syringes and needles still in their cellophane wrapping and a small packet of brownish powder. Heroin? I don't know. I wouldn't know what it looked like. The third envelope contains photographs. I see myself and Paul, Euan, Ella and Daisy; Euan and me with the dogs, Paul outside the university, Ella and Daisy coming out of school, crossing the road, smiling.

I know that Orla visited the village some months ago but to see it like this . . . It makes me feel sick to my stomach. This isn't just run-of-the-mill spite, this is a sustained obsession. She has been secretly, stealthily plotting and gathering information.

I empty another envelope onto the floor. Newspaper clippings. I pick up one. It's from a Canadian newspaper, dated seven years ago. The article is in French. The gist of it seems to be that a man was arrested for the murder of another man. The murdered man is called Patrick Vornier. I scan the text for Orla's name and see it halfway down. She is the dead man's wife. As I thought, I misheard Angeline, thinking she said Fournier when in fact she said Vornier, hence the reason Euan found no record of Orla's crime on the Internet. I see that she was arrested for being a *complice de meurtre*—an accomplice to murder.

As I'm trying to translate the next sentence, I sense the blur of a shadow dart past the window. Immediately, I put everything back where I found it, apart from two of the newspaper clippings, which I put into my pocket. Then I jump to my feet and look outside. I can't see anyone. Satisfied, I turn back into the room just as a face jerks into view, filling the small window. I scream. It's a man. He is grinning. Two of his teeth are missing and the others are twisted and rotten. His head is shaved and he has a row of earrings from his left ear lobe, upwards around the rim. It is Shugs McGovern, looking just as menacing as he did when we were teenagers.

I run through the house and try to get to the front door before he does. I don't make it.

'All right, Grace?' We meet in the hallway. He comes inside. His voice is a croak and his right eyelid ticks repetitively. 'Looking for someone?'

'Orla.'

'Still a friend of yours, is she?'

'Not exactly,' I say, wondering what gives Shugs the right just to walk inside. As a child Orla hated him. And then the reason jumps out at me. 'Delivering drugs, are you?' The words leave my mouth before I can stop myself.

'She's been telling me a thing or two about you.' He is closer now. 'You're not quite the prissy little wife you pretend to be, are you?'

My stomach turns over. I give him what I hope is a vague, unconcerned smile. 'I'm leaving now.' I walk purposefully towards the door but he stands his ground between me and the only way out.

'Where are you going?' He barges me with his shoulder and I lurch back against the wall. 'Oops!' He widens his eyes in pretence of an apology and then takes hold of a handful of my hair. 'Still a natural blonde?' Snake tattoos wind down his forearms and round his wrists like rope. His fingers, like the rest of him, are squat and strong. He runs them through my hair from my scalp to the ends. 'You always thought you were better than the rest of us, didn't you, Grace?' He is right up close. He smells of stale beer and cigarettes. I want to gag. 'Snooty bitch.' His face is in my neck and he whispers, 'Time for me to get my share. How about a kiss for Shugsie?'

The horror of his mouth on mine galvanises me. My knee comes up into his groin and he groans, doubles over. I'm through the door and up the hill as fast as I can. I get to my car and lean on the bonnet, catch my breath and look back at the cottage. Shugs hasn't followed me. He is standing outside the door lighting up a cigarette.

As I go to open my car I notice that the window has been smashed and broken glass is scattered across the seats. 'Shit!' I say out loud and look back down at Shugs who is leaning up against the wall outside. 'Bastard,' I say, under my breath this time, and then I see a small patch of blood on the floor. Murphy. He isn't in the car. 'Dear God.' I spend the next couple of minutes whistling and calling, but he doesn't appear. 'What have you done with my dog?' I scream at Shugs but my voice is lifted away in the air and he makes no sign that he has heard me.

Murphy knows this area and could find his way home from here except that he has no traffic sense. I have visions of him lying bleeding by the roadside and I quickly brush the broken glass off the driver's seat onto the floor and start the engine. I drive home at a snail's pace, scanning the pavements and the side streets, the grassy patches and the shop fronts. Wind blows through the space where the window should be and I gulp back the tears, grateful for the sea air cooling my face.

When I get home, I park haphazardly and go inside to get help. But as I run through the hallway to the back of the house I see Murphy lying on the kitchen floor, Daisy on one side of him and Ella on the other. I fall down onto him and rub my face in his coat. 'You came home!' He licks me appreciatively. 'Clever, clever boy.'

'We tried calling you but your phone is off.' Paul comes over to greet me. 'Did Murphy run away from you? What happened?'

'My car was broken into.' I lean back on my heels to look up at him. 'The window was smashed and there was blood inside. Is he hurt?'

'Your car was broken into?' Paul touches my forehead. 'Are you OK? Did they take anything?'

'I'm fine and no, they didn't take anything. Murphy must have escaped through the window.'

'He just has a small cut on his head but it's stopped bleeding now. Wasn't it lucky that Orla found him?' Daisy says and my spine snaps up straight. 'He could have been run over.'

I get up quickly, turning as I do so. She is standing there. She is wearing a summer dress, off-white, off the shoulder. She looks fresh and flirty. She is holding one of my best crystal glasses. She goes to the dresser, takes out another glass, fills it up and hands it to me.

'Champagne,' she says. 'I wanted to celebrate my return to the village. I hope you don't mind?'

Anger is rising inside me like a geyser. She is in my house, fraternising with my family, pretending to have saved our dog. She must have come back to the cottage for her meeting with Shugs and seized the opportunity to break into my car and steal Murphy. The knife block is to the right of me. I could reach it without even moving my feet. I could grab the biggest one; I could push the blade into her until her blood flows. I wonder what it would feel like. I wonder whether she would scream. 'Where did you find Murphy?'

'Out on the pavement.' She takes a sip. 'Lost.'

'How did you know he was our dog?' My tone is flat, unfriendly. I feel Paul and the girls looking at me and then looking at each other.

'He has a collar with your surname and phone number on it.'

'Well, thank you.' I take the glass from her hand. I think about the photos of my family in her bedroom. 'You can go now.'

'Grace!' Paul laughs uncertainly. 'I invited Orla to stay for a drink.'

Orla touches Paul's arm, lightly, almost a stroking movement. 'I don't want to cause any trouble.' She makes wide eyes at him, manages to look both innocent and vulnerable.

As I watch Paul's face soften, a bitter taste washes through me. 'You really are a piece of work.' I make a decision. I know I'm risking her upping the ante—if I take a stand against her then she might shout out the truth about Rose's death—but what I've just seen in her bedroom, the damage to my car and the way she's worming her way into my family's affections, feels more urgent than a twenty-four-year secret. I point to the front door and say quietly, 'Get the fuck out of my house.'

'Grace!'

'Mum!'

Paul takes my arm and leads me into the hallway. 'What on earth has got into you?'

'Orla is not our friend,' I tell him. 'She's dangerous and she's, she's'— I think of an appropriate word—'unstable. She's unstable, Paul. She is twisted and evil and would happily have killed our dog. She will destroy our family without batting an eyelid.'

'What?' Paul is incredulous. 'Where is this coming from?'

'She smashed my car window. She hurt Murphy.'

'How can you know that? Did you see her?'

'No. But I know what she's capable of and there's no one else it could be,' I say, agitated now. 'And Shugs McGovern was at her house. He had gone there to sell her drugs.'

'That seems remarkably far-fetched.' He is struggling to believe me. 'How would you know that?'

'I know this seems ridiculous. I know it looks as if I'm making it up but I'm not, Paul. I'm really not. Please trust me. Will you?'

He starts back and then half smiles at me. 'Of course, I trust you.'

'Then, please, ask her to leave.'

He holds my eyes for a couple of seconds. 'OK, I will.' He sighs. 'But let's try to do it politely.'

We both go back through to the kitchen. The girls have recovered from my outburst.

'Look, Mum!' Ella is holding up a patterned T-shirt. 'Look what Orla bought us!' Daisy has one too, a different colour and design but the same expensive cut.

'Belated birthday gifts,' Orla says, brazen as a vulture. 'And for you, Paul.' She kisses him and holds out a book-shaped package. 'I was going to bring this on Sunday to thank you for your hospitality but'— she gives me a pointed look—'I bumped into Grace's mum this morning and she told me you're going fishing.'

So she has found out that Sunday lunch is off? No problem. Euan and I will arrange some other time to meet her, deal with her.

'Well . . .' Paul doesn't take the present from her. 'I appreciate your generosity, Orla, but we have things we need to press on with here.'

'What things?' Ella says. 'Just open it, Dad!' She takes it from Orla's hand and tries to put it into his. 'It's a present!'

I have an almost overwhelming urge to grab the package, push it back at Orla and bundle her out onto the pavement, but I daren't because I have to let Paul handle this and he has asked me to be polite.

Ella, impatient with the delay, tears the wrapping off the package. His present is the autobiography I bought for him and mistakenly left underneath the table in the restaurant in Edinburgh. 'That's such a good choice!' Ella says. 'Dad wanted this book, didn't you, Dad?'

I catch Orla's eyes as they light up with triumph.

'I did,' Paul acknowledges and Orla preens herself in front of him, managing to look both coquettish and angelic.

'And this is for you, Grace.' She tries to hand me a box. 'For old times' sake.'

I push her aside. 'I'm not prepared to accept it.'

'But it's just right for you! Here.' She removes the lid and holds it up to my face. As soon as the scent hits the back of my nose, it jump-starts a memory so intense that my heart stops and my stomach turns over.

'Is it OK? It was always your favourite, wasn't it?' She acts stricken. 'Lily of the Valley. I haven't got it wrong, have I?'

I'm next to the pond; Orla is screaming; Rose is lying on the ground, her face bloated, limbs dense, chest still, eyes staring at nothing. Dead. Because of me.

Dizziness closes down my thoughts. For a few seconds I lean forward with my hands on my knees and then I snatch the box of soap from her, open the patio door and throw it out into the garden.

When I turn back into the room, Paul is addressing Orla. 'I don't know what's going on here but clearly you are upsetting Grace and I'd like you to leave now. Girls, give me the tops and go upstairs.'

'But . . .' Ella clutches hers to her chest. 'Do we have to?'

'Give them to me and go upstairs.' This time his tone is stern and both girls respond at once. He holds the gifts towards Orla. 'Take these and leave now.'

Orla doesn't move. 'What do you say to that, Grace?'

I can do no more than stare at her. Paul, impatient now, takes her by the shoulders and marches her out of the front door. I wait for her to shout out the truth but she doesn't. She lets him lead her out onto the front step and close the door behind her.

My legs are wobbly and I collapse down onto a chair.

Paul pulls another one up opposite me, sits down, takes both my hands in his. 'So, are you going to tell me what's going on?'

'Orla is a bad person,' I say slowly. 'When we were young she was involved in all sorts of stuff—'

'Last week,' he interrupts me. 'Is Orla the one who knows something about you?' I freeze. 'You don't have to tell me,' he says. 'But it might be easier if you did.'

I can't look at him. The room is silent. I remember one of the phrases from the newspaper clipping. 'Recently . . . well . . . she's been in prison. She was an accomplice in her husband's murder.'

He tilts back in his seat. 'Honestly?'

I nod. 'It was in the newspapers. And—' I stop. I don't want to tell Paul about the bedroom. I stand up. 'I'll go and clean the glass out of my car and take it along to the garage to be mended.'

'Sweetheart, I'll do that for you.' He takes the brush and dustpan from the kitchen cupboard and goes outside.

I sink onto the chair, think about what just happened. She's smart, Orla. Everything she's doing, she's doing for a reason. Just now, she had the chance to tell Paul all about Rose, but she didn't take it. Clearly she has something else in mind for me.

May 1982. 'Shugs McGovern is a weirdo,' I say.

We're lying in the sand dunes, sheltering from the winds.

'He's worse than a weirdo, he's a psychopath,' Orla replies. 'Being cruel to animals—it's one of the first signs. I read about it.'

'Faye's going to tell her dad so he'll do something.'

'We should do something.'

'What?' I think of the poor cat, his tail set alight, and I shiver. Then I jump up and wipe the sand off my shorts. 'If we're quick we'll have time for an ice cream before the café closes.'

'Fuck's sake, Grace! This is important. Sometimes you have to have principles, stand up for what's right.'

Since Orla turned fourteen she's taken to swearing a lot. I look around, scared someone is going to hear us. Callum and Euan are running across the sand, kicking a football between them. When they're close enough, I shout to Euan, 'Do you know if Faye's told her dad about Shugs McGovern and the cat?'

'Not yet.' He comes over and throws himself down next to Orla. 'Her dad's still out on the rigs. He won't be home till next week.'

'It'll all be forgotten by then.' Orla is sitting up and putting on her shoes. 'We have to do something now!'

'I'm up for that,' Callum says. 'I've wanted to give him a doin' since Primary Three when he dobbed me in for breaking the window.'

'We're not resorting to beating him up, Callum,' Orla tells him. 'If he's to learn his lesson then we have to hurt him long-term.'

'Two wrongs don't make a right,' Euan says. 'We should just report him to the police. Let them deal with it.'

'Like that's going to work!' Orla is scathing. 'He'll tell the police it wasn't him and they'll believe him and that will be that. He'll know he's got away with it. Where's the justice in that?'

At school next day, Orla seems to have forgotten all about Shugs. Our first lesson is English. When class is over, we climb the two flights of stairs to the science labs together. When we get to biology, both teachers are standing at the blackboard with their hands in front of them. Miss Carter looks as if she's been crying.

'Everyone sit down, quickly and quietly,' Mr Mason orders. He is visibly shaking. We slide onto our stools and wait. 'This morning when I came in to work I found Peter dead. His throat was cut.'

A couple of girls gasp and then there's complete silence. Peter is the class rabbit. We have three guinea pigs, a snake and half a dozen gerbils. Mr Mason likes to bring biology to life.

'Only this class has access to the room before school begins. Only this class feeds the animals. Only this class knows the combination to the animals' cages. Who fed the animals this morning?'

Breda Wallace stands up. 'It was me, sir.'

'Was Peter alive?'

'Yes, sir.' Her voice trembles. 'When I left he was eating a carrot.'

'Sit down, Breda.' He paces backwards and forwards, his fists clenching and unclenching. 'Does anyone have anything they want to tell me?'

Seconds tick by. No reply.

'Turn out your bags.'

The tension is palpable. We look at Mr Mason, then at each other, and then we do it. Books, pencil cases, lunch boxes and gym kit spill across the science benches. We shake every stray penny and empty crisp packet out of the bottom of our bags. A commotion breaks out on the back row and we all turn round.

'I didn't do it, sir. Honest!' There's a knife in front of Shugs. 'That's not my knife!'

Mr Mason uses a tissue to pick it up. 'You're saying this isn't yours, McGovern? And yet it was in your bag?'

'I don't have a knife like that!' He looks at the boys either side of him for verification. 'Somebody must have put it in my bag.' Nobody comes to his defence. Even worse follows.

'You set fire to that cat's tail, though,' the boy to his right says.

I glance over at Orla. She seems to be as shocked as the rest of us.

Mr Mason takes Shugs by the arm and brings him to the front. 'We'll see what the police have to say about this.' He leaves with Shugs, who is all the way protesting his innocence, and the rest of us repack our bags and open our books.

As soon as the lesson's over and we're on our way out I grab Orla's shoulder and swing her round to face me. 'You didn't kill Peter, did you, Orla?'

'Me?' Her eyes are obsidian, like black marbles. 'Of course not! For heaven's sake, Grace!' She jumps down two stairs at a time and then looks back up at me. 'It was good he got caught though, wasn't it?'

Once more I sleep fitfully. My dreams are full of Orla and Rose. By the time I get up in the morning, I feel no more rested than when I went to bed. And to make matters worse, Paul is genuinely worried about the threat Orla poses to our family. When he comes back with a hired car for me to use while my broken window is being fixed, he tells me that he will cancel the fishing trip to Skye. I try to persuade him that we will all be fine, but he is not prepared to leave us. So I promise him that we will join him and Ed at the cottage.

I'm still mulling everything over: *Why didn't Orla seize the opportunity to tell Paul yesterday?* And I've yet to translate the newspaper clippings. Euan's French is much better than mine and I decide to meet him later and ask him to help me.

As I chivvy the girls to have breakfast, the post arrives; Paul has been accepted for his sabbatical. We leave for Australia in less than two months. I couldn't be happier if we'd won the lottery.

The girls go off for a day's sailing with the youth club, Paul and Ed are packed and ready to set off to Skye, and I'm desperate for some time alone to think. The three of us are having a late breakfast.

'I'm sorry, Grace,' Ed says. 'My knife is not quite equal to this bacon.'

'I have overcooked it, haven't I?' I put my own knife and fork together and take both our plates away. 'More coffee?'

'It's not that bad, love.' Paul drinks some water.

Ed's face is serious. He frowns across at Paul. 'Where's your mother?'

'She's not here right now, Dad. Busy, I expect.'

Ed looks up at me. 'You're not my daughter. You're not Alison.'

'I'm Grace. I'm married to Paul, your son.'

He laughs. 'Not a bit of it. Aren't you married to that young man I saw you kissing along Marketgate? It was the other day when I was on my way to bowls. You were standing by his gate.'

Instantly it hits me that this memory is true and the air around me thickens. It was on Monday, after we'd made love. I looked up and down the street but saw no one. Then we kissed. Ed must have been passing by. That's why he hasn't been speaking to me. *If you don't know, then I'm not the one to tell you.* He didn't say anything then but now the memory has spilled out.

I don't look at Paul. I don't need to. I can sense that he has straight-ened his back and is now perfectly still and waiting. I shake my head. 'Couldn't have been me, Ed,' I say. 'I'm married to Paul.'

'It was you all right!' Ed chuckles. 'And if you're not married to that young architect then you should be!' He helps himself to more coffee. 'Passionate embrace if ever I saw one.' He looks down the table at Paul. 'Took me back to the days when your mum and I were courting.'

Paul is still waiting. I feel his eyes on my face. My face flushes up red and guilty as the sin I have committed.

Ed looks up. 'Have I got it wrong? I'm so sorry.' He looks from one of us to the other. 'What have I been saying?'

'Nothing, Dad.' Paul stands up. His face has turned a greyish colour and his mouth is trembling. 'Why don't you start packing the car? The tackle's in the front porch.'

Ed walks off whistling and Paul turns to me. 'Grace? Were you kiss-ing Euan?'

'No. Not like that! Of course not! We were hugging,' I admit. 'Yes. Because I have a new commission and he was congratulating me.'

'A new commission? Since when? You didn't tell me.'

'A friend of Margie Campbell's.' I try to breathe but even to my own ears my breath sounds ragged and panicked. 'She heard what I was doing for Margie and called me on my mobile.'

'What's her name?' he fires quickly.

'Elspeth Mullen. She lives outside Glasgow.'

'Why didn't you tell me?'

'I don't know.' I shrug. 'It wasn't at the forefront of my mind.' He doesn't believe me. Ironically, it's partly true: the commission part. But, in fact, I hadn't told anyone, not even Euan, because I had more impor-tant things on my mind.

Paul folds his arms. 'So if I was to ring Euan, he would know about this Elspeth Mullen?'

'I'd prefer that you believed me.' My voice sounds weak. I can't look at him. I'm digging myself in deeper and I feel sick and ashamed.

'I've always tolerated—' He stops, drums his fingers on the dining table, thinks. 'Not tolerated, encouraged. I've always encouraged your friendship with Euan because I know how much you like each other but so help me God, Grace, if you are having an affair with him . . .' He balls his fists. 'If you are jeopardising our family life for—'

This is not a good moment to find out that when push comes to shove I can't lie to my husband. I just can't. I lift a hand to my chest. 'Paul, you have to know that I love you.'

'Would that be with all your heart?' He is icy. 'Or just part of it?'

'I . . . I'm not—'

'Is this why you wanted to keep Orla out of the house?' His voice cracks. 'Because she knew about you both?'

'No! It's not. Everything I said about Orla was true!'

'So this is something else, is it?' He is leaning over me and he is white with anger. 'Something else you can't tell me?'

'Please, Paul, let me—'

'Stop there.' He puts his hand up in front of him. 'I think you've said enough.' He turns away, walks through the door, slams it behind him.

I open the door and follow him. 'Paul, please!' When I reach the car, he's already revving the engine and he drives off. I go back inside. It's not yet midday but I pour myself a whisky. I think. I think about my family, my mistakes, my guilty secrets. I am appalled by the mess I have made. And then I do the only thing I can do. I ring Euan.

'I'm about to go out on the water. You at work?'

'Euan.' I take a deep breath. 'Ed saw you kissing me on Monday. When we were standing at the gate. He blurted it out at breakfast just now.' I start to cry. 'I'm in so much trouble and this is just the beginning.' I pull a tissue from my pocket and blow my nose. 'Paul's furious with me and now they've gone to Skye.'

'Christ.' I hear voices in the background shouting Euan's name. 'Grace, I have to organise these kids. Come and meet me at the end of the day, will you?'

'Yes. And I have to talk to you about Orla,' I say, my free hand feeling for the newspaper clippings that are still in the pocket of my jeans.

We say our goodbyes and I put down the phone, lean my head on the table. Paul and I have been married for over twenty years and in all that time I have never wanted to be without him. I know I am duplicitous. I know that Euan and I should never have started our affair. Some would say that I want to have my cake and eat it. I would say that without Paul I have no place in the world. He is my family, my every day.

And Euan? He anchors me to myself. When he looks at me, he sees me as I am. Not the Grace who is a mother, a wife or a daughter but the Grace who is . . . just Grace. Is he a luxury? It doesn't feel that way. He feels essential to me, like my own arms and legs.

But the affair is the lesser of the evils. Orla's news on top of this will surely break Paul. I, of all people, know that he has never forgotten Rose. To find out that his own wife is not only unfaithful but was involved in his daughter's death—I don't know what that will do to him.

September 1995. When do things start to go wrong? I can't answer that. The first years of our marriage we live in Boston, the girls are born there, we are happy. And then we come back to Scotland. It is not good for me. I feel tired. I suffer from one bout of flu after another. I start to feel Rose's presence again. I start to watch out for her, to sense her in the room or on the pavement ahead of me. I know I need help but I have no one to confide in. I love Paul. He is kind and funny, easy-going, an excellent husband and father, but I am never able to tell him about Rose and I come to accept that there is a part of me that I will have to keep hidden, no matter what. I become watchful, afraid that I will be exposed for what I am: a fraud and a liar. We've been back in the village eight months, the girls are barely three and I am anorexic and withdrawn.

And the more I watch, the more I see that I am not the only one who is keeping secrets. Paul isn't a man prone to unexplained absences. He is a family man, one hundred per cent. But when we're back living in Scotland, I realise that there are times when Paul doesn't go straight to work; and sometimes when he returns home, the car's wheels and sides are mud-splattered, yet there are no dirt roads between our house and the university. And it's always on a Tuesday, when he has a free lesson first thing. Clearly, he's spending time elsewhere. Is he having an affair? Is he gambling? What?

I sit on my curiosity for months, feel it grow into anxiety and then decide that I will settle it. Tuesday comes round, I kiss Paul and wave the girls goodbye as usual. Then I start my car and follow him. I see him deliver the girls to their nursery. When he's in his car again, I shadow him up to the main road but instead of turning right to the university, he turns left. We travel away from the sea, into the countryside. We drive for five miles and when he turns into an unmade road I drop my speed, hang back, park in a space fifty yards behind him. Then follow him, on foot, along the path to the pond. When I get to the water, I stop a discreet distance away, my body concealed by the trunk of a pine tree. Paul is sitting on a rock, the very rock I sat against before I noticed the jacket in the water. In all these years I have never been back here.

My husband is completely still. He is looking across to the far end of the pond where a stream trickles in. Above the trees' reach, the sky is turquoise blue and blackbirds call to one another, their tune high and clear, a late summer melody. Nowhere is there any suggestion that a child died here.

Paul pulls a book from his jacket pocket and starts to read aloud. I can't hear the words but his tone is tender and humorous. Now, suddenly, it seems obvious. All those months of wondering where he was going. My suspicion is shameful. Of course, he would come here to sit and remember. How could I ever have imagined that he was over this?

I have a sudden horror of being seen and I retrace my steps as quickly as I can. When Paul comes home from work he is as he always is and so am I. Nothing is said. When I wake at three in the morning, as I do most nights, I get up and go downstairs. I take the book from his jacket pocket. It's a hardback exercise book. I open the first page. Paul's unfussy hand has written a title: *Letters to Rose*. He has written her a letter most weeks since her death. I read no further, close it and put it back where I found it. Rose is his secret just as she is mine.

Paul and Ed have been gone for almost four hours. My insides are doing somersaults with the fear of impending catastrophe. Orla, unhinged and determined, is going to reveal the secrets of that fateful evening at Guide camp. What of my marriage then? Could I even go to prison? How can the girls love a mother who cheats on their father? Worse still, how can they love a mother who is careless enough to push their half-sister to her death? I don't know what to do next. I feel as if I am walking a tightrope in the dark. I've tried Paul's mobile six times. He hasn't answered and so finally I send him one text and then another, asking him to call me . . . please. I need to speak to him. I don't know what I'll say but I can't bear that I have hurt him.

I spend the day marking time and then, at last, it's late afternoon and I drive to the sailing club to meet Euan. I pull into the car park, choose a bay that faces down to the beach. The sailing boats are back. They are small, two-man vessels. I remember learning to sail with Euan on something similar myself, never enjoying the experience much. I could never get the hang of it.

When I climb out of my car, Callum comes up alongside me. 'I thought I was giving the girls a lift home today? Paul brought Jamie home yesterday.'

'I was passing,' I say. 'I need to speak to Euan. Work stuff.'

'They've had a good day for it. Sea's set to whip up a storm tomorrow.

Some fierce weather moving in from the north.' We walk down onto the sand where the boats have been pulled up onto the beach. 'Euan's over there, look!' Callum points his finger. 'Somebody's bending his ear.'

Euan is about fifty yards away. One of the boys is talking to him.

Ella and Jamie are entwined outside the storage hut. His hands are on her backside, pulling her into his groin. I avert my eyes.

Callum has none of my qualms. 'Shouldn't you two be helping pack up the equipment?' he asks pointedly. They reluctantly separate their faces. He gives Jamie a hefty nudge. 'There's work still to be done.'

Callum and Jamie walk off towards the shore. 'We did go sailing, if that's what you're thinking,' Ella says.

'It wasn't.'

'We came in a bit earlier.' She bangs sand off her trainers and looks up through her hair. 'When Monica dropped Sarah off she was asking me about Orla. She doesn't like her either. She *really* doesn't like her.' Her eyes widen. 'What's so bad about her anyway?'

'She's a troublemaker,' I say. 'You have to stay completely away from her, Ella.' I hold her shoulders so that she's forced to look at me. 'It's very important that you understand that.'

'Fine.' She shrugs me off. 'Whatever.'

I want to say more but I don't want to scare her. 'And did you do a good job of cleaning out Monica's attic?' I try for a bright tone.

'I did and by the way, don't throw a fit, but I have a box of stuff to bring back home.'

'Ella, not more for your bedroom! Not now that we're going to Australia.'

'Well, it won't seem real until I can start telling everyone.'

'And you will. After the weekend. Just like we said.'

'It's torture,' she moans. 'I hate keeping secrets from Jamie. He is going to be allowed to come out and visit me, isn't he? And Sarah?'

'Of course,' I say. Although it's unlikely Sarah will ever come. As Euan's daughter—how would that work? In my heart I feel that I will be saying goodbye for good and I wonder how it will feel to leave all this behind. I will miss it: my friends, the beach, the sky, I will even miss the weather. And Euan: losing Euan will be almost unbearable but I stand to gain too—peace of mind, for one thing.

And then there are my parents. I was hoping they would come for an extended stay at Christmas. Then—who knows? They might like it well enough to live with us for ever. But if Dad's not well . . .

'Ella, you and Daisy should still go back with Callum,' I say, taking my mobile from my pocket. 'I'm going to ring Gran and then I need to talk to Euan.'

'OK.'

I dial my parents' number and my mum answers at once. When we've got through the usual pleasantries, I ask about my dad.

'Well, funnily enough, the doctor called him in to the surgery. He was seen this morning.'

I mentally remind myself to thank Monica.

'The doctor thinks it might be a stomach ulcer. He's sending him for one of those things where they put the camera down.'

'That's good, Mum,' I say. 'Doesn't sound too serious.' I almost tell her about Australia but don't want to tempt fate—after all, Paul might not want me to come and first we have to deal with Orla. I say goodbye to her and start walking towards the boathouse. Euan is inside packing up. 'I was thinking just now about how you taught me to sail,' I say.

'It was an excuse to touch you.'

'We were thirteen. You didn't fancy me then.'

'I've fancied you since I was about—I dunno, nine? When I had you tied to the tree.'

'We were eight,' I say, thinking back to those days. 'We had fun then, didn't we?'

'Didn't we just.' He looks at me properly for the first time since I walked into the boathouse. 'You heard from Paul?'

I shake my head.

'Have you seen Orla again?'

I nod. 'She was at my house yesterday when I got home.' I tell him the story. 'I think Shugs was there to supply her with drugs,' I say, following Euan to the back of the boathouse. 'Ironic when you think how much she hated him when we were kids.'

'Drugs, prison, violence. They have a lot in common.'

'Talking of which.' I tell him about the bedroom, the photographs, the money, the drugs and the newspaper clippings. 'Here.' I bring the clippings out of my pocket. 'I understand some of this but you have a try. I misheard her surname. That's why you couldn't find anything.'

He takes the papers from my hands and starts to read, translating as he goes. 'Medical experts have begun a post-mortem examination on a man murdered over the weekend in downtown Quebec. Patrick Vornier, thirty-one, was found dead in his bedroom. Police told reporters that a man named Sucre Gonzalez and Mr Vornier's wife Orla have already been arrested in connection with the death. Mr Vornier is thought to have been stabbed in the chest. There is speculation that Mr and Mrs Vornier may have been using heroin on the night he died.'

Euan rolls back on his heels, says, 'Bloody hell,' and then translates the next article. Orla is cited as an accomplice to Gonzalez and is sentenced to six years in prison. 'So Angeline wasn't exaggerating,' Euan says. 'This proves Orla's capable of just about anything.'

I nod. 'I think she's building up to something spectacular. She has this crazy idea that we should be punished. And she hates that we're happy. Not that I am any more.' The memory of this morning, Paul leaving, comes back to me in a wave of shame and anxiety. 'Paul thinks I only wanted her out of the house because she knew about you. I was going to take the girls and drive up to Skye to join him and Ed later.' I shrug. 'But now I don't suppose I have to.' I look down at my feet. 'Euan, I can't let her tell Paul about Rose. I simply can't. Orla knows Paul is going fishing so she won't be coming round on Sunday.'

'OK. Then I'll go round to her place tomorrow.'

After what we've just found out I feel scared for him. I take his hand and hold it. 'Euan, you mustn't put yourself in any danger.'

He laughs. 'She doesn't frighten me.'

'But what if she comes at you with a knife? Shugs might even be there.'

'Shugs won't get involved. He won't risk prison again.'

'So what time will you go tomorrow?'

'Afternoon probably. I'll text you. You can be my alibi.'

I have to ask. 'What will you say to her?'

'You don't need the details, Grace. I will deal with her.'

'You're not going to do anything'—I hesitate—'definite, are you?'

'I have to do something definite or she won't go away, will she?'

'Kill her,' I say in a rush. 'You're not going to kill her, are you?'

'What do you take me for?'

'So why the alibi then?'

'In case something goes wrong, but you're right. Don't worry about the alibi.' He gives me a cocky smile. 'I won't need it.'

I remind myself that Euan is doing this for me and that if Paul finds out I killed Rose, albeit accidentally, life as I know it will be over. 'I'm sorry. Of course I'll give you an alibi. I'm not meaning to sound like I doubt you.'

'I need to check on the boats.' He puts his hand on the nape of my neck and gives me the briefest of kisses. 'I'll call you tomorrow.'

I watch him walk away from me and then I drive home.

When I come in through the back door both girls are already there. Ella has the stuff from Monica's attic spread over the kitchen table. There are dusty, hardback books and bits of old clothing, a box of buttons and some old postcards. 'I thought I could sell some of it on eBay,' Ella says.

In among the junk, there is a silver charm bracelet. The chain is delicate and is joined at either end by a heart-shaped lock. Six charms hang at regular intervals round the chain: a tiny fan; a Welsh dragon; a spinning wheel; a rose; a Viking boat; and a gondola. Somewhere in the back of my mind I have an idea that I've seen the bracelet before but I can't place it. 'Did Monica say you could have this?'

'Yes.' Ella is rummaging in the fridge. 'Can we have money for chips?'

I finger the cool silver charms. 'Help yourself to money from my purse. Take enough for a fish supper each.'

The girls slam the front door behind them and I sit down with the bracelet on my lap. It's still niggling me. Where do I remember it from? I begin to doze, drifting off into the mesmerising gap between sleep and wakefulness. I roam through splinters of memory: the girls as babies; a weekend in New York, Paul's hand holding mine as we skip along 42nd Street, late for a play; Euan sitting in the pram opposite me; Ella and me winning the mother and daughter's three-legged race. Backwards and forwards through my life until finally I land where I need to. I reach for the memory, grasp it and make the connection. My eyes snap open. The bracelet—I know where I've seen it before.

April 1987. Paul and I honeymoon on the New England coast. We base ourselves in Cape Cod where the weather is kind to us. We stroll along the wide sandy beaches, cycle up country paths and visit the numerous lighthouses that stand guard over the coastal waters.

We talk and we laugh and every morning and evening we make love. At first I'm shy, but soon I learn to let go and my body wakes up to his. I want our honeymoon to last for ever. I want to trap the moments in aspic and jump in alongside them so that I can relive the sense of completeness where all desires are met and past mistakes wiped clean.

We both love living in Boston. Paul studies at the State University and we are welcomed into a circle of friends. Within the year I have a place at art college and start to live out my dream of becoming an artist.

We've been married for four years when we start trying for a baby. First month, nothing, second month, I'm two weeks late. Then I wake up and immediately throw up. I'm pregnant: happily, deliriously, unbelievably pregnant.

When I tell Paul he falls to his knees and hugs me, strokes my belly and I giggle. He is a model expectant father. He does all the shopping and cooking; he comes with me for the first scan.

'Well, well, well!' the doctor says, grinning at us both. 'There's one heartbeat and then there's another! Two for one.'

'Twins?' We both look at each other and then laugh, incredulous.

I love being pregnant. I feel as if I'm incubating a miracle, two miracles, in fact. Time passes, the babies are born, and Daisy becomes as summery as butter with cheeks as round as red apples. And she is content. She's in no hurry to grow up. Ella wants to be mistress of her own fate. She reaches all the milestones first. She smiles first, crawls and walks first. Her first word is dada; her second is dog.

'I think we should live in the country,' I tell Paul. 'On a farm and—'

'Well! There's the thing, Grace. It's time for me to apply for a professorship. And guess what? There's a post coming up in St Andrews of all places.' He takes my hand. 'Wouldn't you like to go back home?'

I don't answer. Going back? I'm not so sure. We've made a life for ourselves in New England. I'm a different person here.

'So what do you think?'

He is excited. He holds both my hands and waits, smiling. I want to please him. After all he has given to me, I want to give him something back. 'If it's the job you want then we should go for it,' I say.

While Paul's at work, I pack. I'm sorting through some boxes when I find it. It's a close-up photo of Paul and his first wife, Marcia. They are both grinning, showing off their wedding rings. Around Marcia's wrist is a silver charm bracelet. I can clearly see two of the charms: a Viking boat and a gondola. When Paul comes home from work I ask him about it.

'The Viking boat was to remind her of her gran who lived on the Shetlands.' He points to the gondola. 'We went to Venice in the spring before we got married,' he tells me. 'I bought that charm for her at one of the markets in the square. Had to haggle a bit on the price.'

'It's a beautiful bracelet. What happened to it?'

'I'm not sure,' he says. 'When Marcia died I gave it to Rose. She took it everywhere with her but the catch was loose. She had it with her at Guide camp.' He shrugs. 'She must have lost it somewhere there. I went back several times to look for it but I never found it.'

7

'WHAT'S GOING ON?' Ella is standing at the bottom of the ladder staring up at me. 'The hall is full of junk.'

It's the next morning and I've already turned out the under-stairs cupboard. 'I'm looking for something.'

'If you're trying to compete with Monica, I'd give up now. We've got ten times as much junk as her.'

'Do you want to help me?'

She makes a face and goes into her bedroom. I climb up the ladder into the attic and survey the scene. We have more boxes of books and paraphernalia than I would have thought possible. Almost every inch of space is taken up with a box or binbag of stuff. I need to find the photograph of Paul and Marcia's wedding. I have to make sure that my memory isn't making links that don't exist. And if it is the same bracelet, how did Monica get it? And why has she kept it all these years?

I start working through the bags and boxes, trying not to be distracted by everything else I come across. Wind is whistling through the roof space from west to east. The final cluster of boxes I come across look as if they could well have been there for some time. Since we moved back to Scotland? As soon as I open the first one, I have the feeling that I've struck lucky. It's all the photographs that Paul took before I met him. I scan through the ones on top and then decide to look through them downstairs, away from the draught.

Ella has just come out of her bedroom and jumps as I drop the box of photos close to her feet. She looks into it, her nose wrinkling at the cobwebs and dust. 'You're just so random,' she says.

I pick up the box and go downstairs.

She follows me. 'I'm not putting all that stuff back under the stairs.'

She points a plum-coloured fingernail in the direction of the emptied-out cupboard. The hallway is now almost impassable: tennis rackets, raincoats, old shoes, a dozen boxes full of the twins' old school books.

'I'm not expecting you to,' I tell her.

I climb over everything and sit down on the couch. I turn out the box on the floor, looking at each photo until at last I come to it. It's a professional one. Paul and Marcia grinning in front of the register office. I position the bracelet on the table next to the photo and examine them carefully. Identical. It's what I expect but how did Monica get the bracelet? Why didn't she hand it to the police? Why has she never in all these years given it back to Paul? When I went back to the tent after the argument, Monica was still up. What if Rose went to bed after I pushed her? I may even have unconsciously registered that all the girls were there. She may have got up later, just as Euan has always said.

Could it be that I wasn't the last person to see Rose alive?

The doorbell rings and Ella answers it. 'I have to warn you,' I hear her say. 'She's in a strange mood today.'

The living-room door opens. It's Euan. I slip the bracelet into the back pocket of my jeans. He looks around at the mess. 'Are you OK?' he says.

'Yeah.' I shrug, aim for nonchalance.

'Has Paul been in touch?'

'No. I've left messages but he hasn't answered them. At least he's out of Orla's reach,' I say, trying to see the upside. 'But I'm not sure what he'll do when he does come back home; maybe he'll come to see you.'

I expect him to look worried but he doesn't. He gives me a half-smile, resigned. 'It was bound to come out sooner or later.'

'Are you going to tell Monica?'

'One thing at a time. Are you still OK about the alibi?'

'Yes.' I can't pretend that I haven't had some second thoughts but bottom line: Orla has to be stopped and I trust him completely.

'I'll text you.'

'Euan.' I pause. The bracelet is burning a hole in my back pocket. 'Has Monica ever said anything about Rose's death?'

'Why would she?' He's whispering. We both are.

'Well . . . I'm not telling you this to make trouble, but Monica was out of bed that night too. I saw her when I was going back to my tent.'

'So?'

'When Orla turned up at the girls' party last week, Monica saw me arguing with her and was pretty freaked out about it.'

'Grace, have you eaten anything recently?'

'Well, no, but—'

'This has got nothing to do with Monica and everything to do with us.' He shakes me gently. 'You have to stick to the point. Leave Monica out of it. I mean it. No one will ever find out what really happened to Rose. It's a dead end.' He leads me through to the kitchen. 'You should eat something and then you should rest.' He takes cheese and ham, butter and pickle from the fridge, slices some bread, then puts his arms round me and makes the sandwich with me standing in between.

I shut my eyes and lean into his neck. I could show him the bracelet but I don't want him to come up with a rational explanation. I want to hang on to what I know: Monica had a bracelet that belonged to Rose. She has been on the edge of her nerves since Orla came back to the village. It does add up to something.

Euan hands me the bulging sandwich and I offer him half back. He shakes his head. 'I'm meeting Callum in the Anchor for a pub lunch.'

'That's nice.' I take a bite.

'Grace? Monica had nothing to do with Rose's death. Just remember who's the enemy here. I'll text you late afternoon.'

I follow him into the hallway and watch from the window. When his car turns the corner, I go outside, start up my own car and drive off in the other direction. I should be able to have it out with Monica before Euan gets back from the pub.

Monica opens the door and stares at me. She looks as if she's been crying, as if she's suddenly aged ten years. 'You'd better come in.'

The house smells of burnt toast. I follow her through into the kitchen and sit down on one of the stools. The kitchen is a mess. I have never seen it like this before.

I want to blurt out, *What's going on, Monica? What happened to Rose?* But something inside me says to slow it down, slow it right down. I don't want Monica to clam up on me. 'Is everything OK?'

She stares at me. Her eyebrows are raised as if it's a stupid question and she's waiting for the next one. She might just deign to answer that.

'Is this about what happened when we were all sixteen?'

Nothing. Just that look.

'That year, 1984?' She still doesn't answer so I answer with another question. 'This?'

I bring the bracelet out of my pocket and lay it on the breakfast bar. She glances at it and then walks over to the kettle. 'Coffee?'

'If you like.'

She puts a cup of coffee down in front of me. 'We never really escape our pasts, do we?'

'We all have regrets. Things we would change.'

She laughs. 'What regrets can you have, Grace? You always seem so perfectly well adjusted, perfectly happy with Paul and your girls and your painting.'

'We all have our dark times.' I tap my finger next to the bracelet. 'This bracelet. I've come about this.'

She looks at it again. 'I don't know anything about that.'

'Pick it up. Look at it closely.'

She does. 'It's tarnished but still very pretty. However, there are much more pressing matters on my mind.'

'It was in your loft,' I say lightly. 'Ella said you let her have it.'

She shrugs. 'So?'

'It belonged to Rose.'

'Paul's Rose?'

I nod.

'Well, I have no idea how it came to be with my stuff.'

'She had it on the Guide camp.'

'Well, it must have got mixed up in my camping gear.'

'But you weren't even in her tent.'

She looks exasperated. 'What do you want me to say? That I took it?'

'Paul always wondered what had happened to it. She was never without it. It belonged to her mother. She kept it on her at all times.'

'Well, I will go and see Paul and apologise to him.' Her tone is impatient. 'But in the meantime can we please talk about Orla?'

'I have spent the last twenty-four years thinking that I was the last person to see Rose alive,' I say quietly. 'Thinking that if I'd only listened to what she was saying I might have been able to prevent her death, thinking, Monica, *thinking*, that when I pushed her away, she fell into the water and drowned.'

'What are you talking about?'

I stand up and come alongside her. 'Orla and I had an argument that night. Rose came to me for help. I pushed her away. The next day I found her in the water exactly where I had pushed her.'

Monica is tapping her foot. 'Have you been drinking?'

'No!'

'You think you killed Rose? This is what Orla has on you?'

I nod.

'Christ!' She topples backwards, catches hold of the worktop and looks at me as if I'm mad.

'I know.' I hold up my hands. 'It's horrendous. But just recently, well, something isn't adding up and I need to get it clear in my head. The sequence of events. Did you see Rose that night? Did she come to you?' I point to the bracelet. 'Why did you have her bracelet?'

Monica's eyes look past me as she winds back the clock. 'So around midnight when I was putting away the supplies and you came back to the tent—'

'I had already pushed her.'

She gives a perfunctory shake of her head. 'Then you didn't do it. Rose came back to the tent about ten minutes before you did.'

For a second I am completely still and then I grab Monica by the shoulders and say loudly, 'You're absolutely sure about this?'

'Yes! Otherwise I would have told you that one of your patrol was out of bed.'

Ever-practical Monica. Of course she would have made sure the girls were in their tents before she settled down for the night.

I start to tremble. My knees give way and I sit down hard on the stool. *I didn't do it. I didn't kill Rose. It wasn't me.* 'Are you absolutely sure?' I say again.

'Yes. For heaven's sake! I told the police that at the time.'

'You did?' On the one hand I feel an elation, a need to shout my innocence from the rooftops. On the other, I feel a crushing, debilitating sense of loss. Years of guilt and reproach and all for nothing. If only, at the time, I had gone to the police, they would have told me that it couldn't possibly have been me.

'Grace, Rose must have got up later and then fallen in the water. These things happen.' Monica sits down opposite me. 'Now, please! Can we talk about Orla? She must not be allowed to stay in the village.'

'Why not?'

She hesitates. 'Do you promise this will just be between you and me?'

I nod, hardly breathing. I hear my phone beep with a text message but I ignore it, primed for what's coming next.

She looks beyond me. 'I love Euan, Grace. Even when we were at school, I loved him. He has always been, and still is, the only man I've ever wanted. History repeats itself. When I was young, Angeline wrecked my family, and now Orla will do the same to my children.'

'I don't understan—'

'She's come back for Euan,' she says quickly.

'She's come back for *Euan*?' I almost laugh. I think of his face at the convent. He is not attracted to Orla. Not at all. I know he isn't. I hold Monica's shoulders. 'Euan and Orla? Never in a million years! If that's what you're worried about then I honestly think you've got the wrong end of the stick.'

She breathes deeply. 'I know we've never really been friends but I need you to help me look out for him.'

To my shame, I nod. The irony of Monica asking me to look out for her husband is not lost on me but I want this conversation to be over. I want time to accelerate a month, six months, whatever it takes for me to get past this moment. I want to think and to appreciate and to bask in the knowledge that I didn't kill Rose. I want to make it up to Paul and I want to live in Melbourne and enjoy being with my family.

Monica is still talking. 'She could ruin Euan's life. And for what?' Her mouth is trembling. 'It was Mo who told me. She said to me, "I have a bad feeling about that girl. This isn't the last you'll see of her." And Mo was right, just as she always was.'

In a distant part of my brain a bell goes off. 'What was Mo right about?'

'Orla being a threat. Coming back for Euan. Not letting it drop.'

'What drop?' The house is so quiet I can hear the sound of the sea.

'When she was sixteen—' She stops. Tears spill onto her cheeks. 'When she was sixteen, Orla had an abortion. The baby was Euan's.'

I am too shocked to speak. At first I don't believe it, and then connections start to form in my head: Euan being so sure Orla's intentions were spiteful, their heated exchange in the convent, Orla spitting in his face. Slowly it sinks in. This isn't just about me. She is taking her revenge on Euan too. 'When did she have the abortion?'

'The end of August 1984.'

Euan told me he'd only slept with her the once, when they went potholing for Geography O level. That was towards the end of April. By August, she would have been more than sixteen weeks pregnant. That would explain her erratic behaviour at Guide camp. And I suppose that's what was in the letters. The ones I never read.

'Euan has always been convinced that the baby wasn't his,' Monica says. 'That was one of the things that set Orla off. The fact that he wouldn't believe her. You know she attempted suicide?'

I nod.

'Do you remember when Euan went off to live with his uncle? Orla was causing him loads of problems, phone calls, letters, turning up at the door. They moved to England but still it carried on. She sent him pictures of dead babies in the post, wrote to the headmaster at school. So Euan went to Glasgow where she couldn't reach him.'

I am speechless. How could I not have known about this? I can hardly believe it and yet, at the same time, it rings true. Orla is out to punish both of us because neither of us helped her.

No secrets. For the first time in twenty-four years I have nothing to hide. I didn't kill Rose.

I sit on the step outside Monica's house and stare straight ahead. The air smells salty and wet. The wind is whipping in from the sea and I pull my coat around me. I didn't do it. My adult life has turned on an event that didn't happen. I walk back to my car and settle into the seat. I say it out loud. 'I didn't kill Rose.'

It's impossible to describe how much of a weight has lifted and I'm enjoying the feeling of light and air inside me. My marriage is still in trouble—I haven't forgotten—but adultery is the lesser crime.

Euan. I can't believe that he didn't tell me about the abortion. I don't understand it. He was only sixteen: the age for mistakes. I would have helped and supported him. For almost two weeks now, I have been banging on about Orla and motives and the fact that this was my problem, not his, and all the time he was keeping a hefty secret of his own.

Before I start the engine, I remember to look at my phone. There's a text from Euan. Forty-five minutes ago. I try to phone him but his mobile is switched to message service so I drive to Orla's house. Euan's car isn't there but there are lights on inside. It's only three in the afternoon and yet the sky is dark with clouds. It's raining a few miles out to sea. Wind heralds the rain's approach and the waves are jumping skittishly as if they know what's to come.

I knock on the door. Orla answers it. 'Well! Look who's here!'

She is dressed up to the nines. She is wearing a red satin dress that grips tightly over her breasts and hips and has a thigh-high split up one side. I wonder whether she knew Euan was coming.

'I'm not here to see you,' I say. 'I need to speak to Euan.' I can see him standing beyond her.

He doesn't look pleased to see me. He comes outside and we move away from the house a few feet. 'What are you doing here?'

'I found something out just now. It was Monica who told me. I couldn't possibly have killed Rose,' I say breathlessly. 'She came back to the tent before I did. She was in her sleeping-bag when I climbed into mine.' I expect him to be pleased but he shows no emotion. It's as if he hasn't heard me. 'Euan?' I shake him. 'Did you hear me?'

His face is expressionless. 'Is Monica sure?'

'Absolutely! She was there. She remembers it clearly. And you know Monica; she doesn't get stuff wrong. Isn't it brilliant?' I shake him again.

'Yeah, it is.' He says it without enthusiasm and looks beyond me to where the storm is gathering pace, coming across the sea towards us.

'Don't you see what this means?' He is still staring at the horizon, preoccupied. 'We can both walk away from this.'

No response.

I reach for his hand. 'You could have told me.'

His eyes snap back to mine.

'The abortion,' I say. 'I wish you'd told me.'

His jaw relaxes. If I didn't know better I would think it looked as if he was relieved.

'I didn't think we had any secrets from each other. I'm the last one to criticise anyone for keeping secrets but I never had any from you.'

He clears his throat. 'It was a long time ago and I never really believed the baby was mine. I wasn't the only boy she had sex with.'

I nod. 'I understand.' I pause. I have a feeling there's something he's not telling me. 'You know . . .' I hesitate. I feel spots of rain land on my hair. I'm tired and I'm desperate to go home. I want to get right away from Orla, but first I need to tell Euan that it has to be over between us. 'I have always loved you and a part of me always will.' I hold his hand. 'I want to stay married, Euan. I want to make things right again.'

'This sounds like goodbye.' He tries to laugh. 'What's going on?'

'We have to move on.'

'From each other?' His expression merges hurt and scepticism. 'We've tried that before.'

'Monica loves you and you love her. I know you do. This thing between us?' I shake my head. 'There's nowhere for it to go.' I breathe in. 'I'm hoping that Paul will forgive me. He's taking a sabbatical year in Melbourne. We'll be moving there in August.'

He steps towards me. 'Grace—'

'When we were young we had our chance, Euan. We didn't take it.'

Wind is whistling around our ears. I lean in towards him. 'If we sleep together the guilt eats away at us and if we see each other every day but don't sleep together then it's a different sort of torment. We have to get right away from each other.'

'Grace.' He puts a hand under my chin. 'I love you.'

It would be a lie to pretend that I'm not tempted. But I can't leave Paul, I love him; and anyway, I don't want Euan if he has to break Monica's heart to be with me. I want to start over in a new country.

The rain is falling heavily now and he pulls me inside Orla's cottage. 'You have to let me go, Euan.'

'Lovers' tiff?' Orla is watching us. She has her shoulders against the wall but is pushing the rest of her body forward provocatively. 'Is she trying to dump you, Euan?'

'Mind your own business,' I tell her.

'Isn't it time we told her?' she says, her voice like warm treacle.

'I already know about the abortion,' I say to Orla. 'I'm sorry you had to go through that but—'

'She's sweet, isn't she?' She moves towards us and runs her fingers down my wet cheeks. 'Sweet and innocent.'

'And I also know that I didn't kill Rose.' I try to hold her eyes but she seems to be having trouble focusing and her gaze slides sideways out of reach of mine. 'She was in the tent when I went back there.'

She shrugs. 'That's only the half of it.'

'So you have nothing on me,' I finish. I feel strong. 'Game over, Orla.' I open the front door. 'Time for you to go off and bother someone else.'

'Don't you want to find out what really happened to Rose?'

I turn back to them both just in time to catch a look that passes from Euan to Orla. It's a warning look, a don't-you-dare glance that makes my scalp tingle and my stomach turn over. And then he cracks his fingers, one by one, left hand and then right. 'Euan?' His face has shut down again.

'Shall we give her a clue?' Orla says.

'Go home, Grace.' Euan grasps my elbow and tries to urge me through the door but I push him away from me. His eyes beseech mine.

I look from one of them to the other. My instinct is to trust Euan. Orla is poisonous, unhinged, malevolent. But still.

'No.' I close the door and walk back into the living room.

They both follow me. We stand together in the centre of the room. A triangle. Orla is beaming; this is what she's been waiting for.

'So tell me, Orla,' I say. 'Let's just get this over with.'

'Well, when you went to bed,' she says, her eyes wide open and staring, 'I stayed by the pond for a while. I'd arranged to meet Euan there. We were going to talk about the baby.' She gives a laugh. It's as brittle as smashed glass. 'I was hoping he was going to support me, but no! He accused me of trying to trap him.'

'You were promiscuous,' I say. 'You had sex with loads of boys.'

'Lying about the baby's father? Do you think I would do that to a child?' She shudders. 'My child?'

'Yes, I do. I think that—' I stop talking as thoughts collide in my head: Euan was there that night; Rose's bracelet was found in the loft; Monica said Euan had stuff up there too. I take the bracelet from my back pocket and throw it to him. He catches it. He can't look at me.

'Ella came home with that. It was in your loft.' I lurch to one side and then say quietly, 'Please, Euan. Just tell me it wasn't you.' I'm so afraid of the answer that I keep my eyes tight shut.

Seconds tick by and still he doesn't speak. I open my eyes and look at him. 'Just tell me what happened,' I say. 'Please.'

He wants a reprieve. He doesn't have to ask; it's written all over his face. But we're not kids any more and I'm losing patience. 'Just get on with it,' I say curtly.

He stares up at the ceiling. 'I had a lot to drink. I saw Rose twice. First time I saw her she told me she had lost her bracelet. I said I would look out for it and less than five minutes later I found it in a patch of grass. The storm started up, I drank some more vodka and then I met Orla by the pond.' He shrugs. 'It didn't go well. She was determined to have the baby, tell my parents—'

'Don't blame me,' she cuts in.

'Shut up!' I swivel towards her. 'This isn't about you.'

'Second time I saw Rose, Orla was hassling me, following me. It was late and I was well on the way to paralytic,' Euan continues. 'I was trying to find my way back to my tent but I was too drunk to realise I was going round in circles. She asked me again if I had seen her bracelet and I said I had found it but—' He stops. His mouth is trembling. 'It was a case of finders keepers. That's what I said to her: "Finders keepers, losers weepers", and I kept on walking.'

I flinch. 'Euan, the bracelet belonged to her dead mother.'

'I know.' I watch years of self-reproach flood into his eyes. 'And that's not the worst of it. I told her that if she wanted it, she'd have to find it and I pretended to throw it into the pond. I didn't for one moment think that she would go in after it.'

I feel incredibly still inside as if the blood has stopped flowing in my veins. 'And did she?'

'I honestly don't know. Eventually, Orla left me alone and I found my way back to my tent. I didn't think about it again until you said you thought you'd done it and slowly I started to remember that night. Weeks later, when I finally emptied out my rucksack, I found the bracelet and knew that what I barely remembered had actually happened.'

'So all these years you've known she didn't die because I pushed her?'

To his credit, he looks me in the eyes when he answers, 'Yes.'

My heart contracts to a tight fist. I drop into a chair. I start to rock myself backwards and forwards. Euan. I trusted him. Implicitly. I have made love to him, cried for him, held him, defended him, longed for him. God help me, I have even thought of running away with him. I have hurt Paul and threatened my girls' happiness and all this time he knew I had nothing to do with Rose's death.

I look up at him. 'Why didn't you tell me?'

'I tried.'

'Well, not hard enough.' Rage peaks inside me and I stand up, slap him across the face, once and then again. He doesn't defend himself. 'You shit! You spineless shit,' I hiss. 'You're as bad as her.'

'You have every right to be angry—'

'I'm not angry,' I shout. 'I'm furious and hurt and betrayed and—'

'When would have been the right time to tell you?'

'Any time was the right time!' I stalk round him. 'When I couldn't get out of bed and was plagued by nightmares, when I was ill and you came back to Scotland. Hell! Even just two weeks ago when Orla turned up. But not like this, Euan. Not me finding out from her.'

Orla lights a cigarette and walks towards me. 'He really has betrayed you, Grace. Hasn't he?' She tries to lay an arm on my shoulder.

'Get off me!' I push her roughly and she wobbles on her heels. 'Do not touch me.' I look at Euan. 'Either of you.'

I stand by the window. The sky is almost completely dark now; the storm is directly overhead. Hailstones are hammering against the windowpane, on and on like an extended drumroll.

'I fully intended to tell you before I went to university,' he says. 'But Mum told me you were engaged. I thought you had moved on. Like loving Paul had wiped it out somehow.'

'And when you came back to live in Scotland?' I turn back to him. 'Why not then? You saw the mess I was in.'

'You were ill. I didn't—' He stops, sucks in his cheeks.

'Christ! You were afraid I would tell on you?'

'Look, I'm not proud of this.'

'His mother didn't help.' Orla saunters over to stand beside us again. 'Ruthless when it came to protecting her boy.'

'Mum, she—'

Another penny drops. 'Mo knew?'

'I had to tell someone.'

Like a pendulum swing, I lurch from anger back to grief again. It catches in my throat and I moan. Mo knew about this. She also let me down. It's too much to take in.

'She didn't know that you thought you'd done it,' Euan says quickly. 'She wouldn't have chosen between us.'

I want to believe him but I can't. It's not that I blame Mo for putting Euan first—of course she would choose her own flesh and blood over me—I just wish that she had told me. 'Why did you keep the bracelet?'

'I always intended to give it back.' He looks apologetic, desperate even. 'I wanted to tell you. At Mum's funeral—'

'It's too late,' I say sharply and turn to Orla. 'Did you see Rose go into the water?'

'Don't be ridiculous! I would have stopped her. I was following Euan.'

'And next day. When we found Rose's body. You knew it couldn't have been me, didn't you?'

'Yes.' She makes a petted lip. 'I'm sorry about that but I was protecting Euan. He was the father of my child. Then later, when I realised he wasn't going to support me, I wrote to you but—'

'So both of you knew.' I look from one to the other. If it wasn't so tragic it would be funny. 'My boyfriend and my best friend.'

'Well, what could I do?' Orla shrugs. 'I had to put Euan first.'

'And the best way to do that was to pin it on me?' Anger spikes inside me. 'You were the one who told me I'd killed her.'

'And you might have done it. You did push her after all. If you'd read the letters—'

'Fuck the letters!' I'm shaking with rage. 'You convinced me that I was guilty. You, Orla.' I point my finger into her face. 'I have spent twenty-four years thinking I killed a little girl.'

She smiles, triumphant, delighted with her own deceit. I want to slap her hard but my anger is being sapped by a profound sadness. Rose died because none of us helped her, and while Euan's actions were more final than mine, I know that I also let her down. Perhaps, if I had listened to her, I could have changed the course of events. I feel drained. 'I never want to set eyes on either of you again.'

'But you're missing an opportunity!' Orla throws an arm out towards Euan. 'He's the villain here. Why don't we give him what's coming to him? You and me? What do you say?'

'I say'—I lean towards her—'I say you're a manipulative, twisted bitch who needs psychiatric help.'

She flinches at this. 'I expect you agreed to let him deal with me.'

'We're not killers.'

'But I saw you thinking about it.' Her eyes are piercing. 'The knife block in your house. You imagined sticking a knife in me, didn't you?'

'I did.'

'So why didn't you?'

'I've told you.' I raise my voice. 'Unlike you, I'm not a killer. I can walk out of here with a clear conscience.'

She throws back her head and laughs at this. It's a mirthless sound that echoes the mania in her eyes. 'I'll destroy you, Grace. I'll tell Paul you've been having an affair.'

I'm tired of this. I'm not blameless; I know that. But I've had enough of Orla's games. 'You're too late. Paul already knows. You have no control over me.' I start moving towards the door and she follows me.

'You are not going to walk away from me!'

'Oh, yes, I am.' I'm inches from her face. 'I'm going to find Paul and I'm going to grovel and beg and hope that he has enough compassion to forgive me.'

Her mouth is crippled with an ugly smile. 'I'll come after your girls.'

'Why?' I shake my head. 'Why pursue me?'

'Because you can't just throw me off like this.' Her tone is adamant. She flashes a glance across at Euan. 'I spent a lot of time in prison thinking about you both, and then when I came back to Scotland and found out that you were playing happy families, I made up my mind not to let you get away with it. You think you deserve to have perfect lives when I have nothing?'

Her eyes are bright with enmity. Her hand is round my throat and she pushes me back against the wall. She is surprisingly strong, strong enough to stop me breathing. Panic overwhelms me. I struggle against her, digging my nails into her hand and kicking out with my feet. My lungs are fit to burst. I see Euan pull her away from me, hard. She falls back, her arms windmilling, her eyes wide with surprise. Her head strikes the cast-iron fireplace. The sound is like nothing I've ever heard before: a cross between the thud of a football against a wall and the cracking of a very large nut. I don't move and neither does Euan. Her eyelids flutter once and then stay closed.

A weighty silence swells to fill the space around us and then Euan crouches down beside her. 'Orla! Can you hear me?' He lays his ear against her chest. 'She's not breathing.' He starts mouth to mouth, then pushes hard where her heart should be. Just as I did for Rose. Fifteen compressions and two breaths, over and over.

Time slows right down. I watch Euan and I watch Orla. Blood is leaking onto the floor. Her skull has been opened up by one of the cast-iron points at the edge of the fire surround. Blood and a spongy, grey mess is oozing from a deep cut in the base of her skull. I put my fist in my mouth. The air around me judders. I'm on the floor. Someone is whimpering. Me. My head pounds and I cough and then immediately wince. My throat feels as if it's lined with cut glass. I crawl round Orla's body and grab hold of Euan's trousers. 'Her head,' I say.

Euan leans over her body. He feels the back of her skull. There is blood all over his hands. The smell is cloying and I retch. I crawl back towards my handbag and my mobile phone. I will call an ambulance. They might be able to save her. But hard as I try, I can't press the numbers. My hands are shaking and my vision is blurring. I start to cry, hacking sobs that shake me inside out.

I don't know how much time passes—one minute or five, I can't say—but finally I get up onto my feet again. Euan is standing now and is looking down at Orla's body. 'Is she dead?'

He nods.

I steel myself to look at her. Her body is eerily still. Her dress has risen up at one side and I can see marks on the inside of her thigh.

'Track marks,' Euan says. 'From where she's been injecting heroin.'

He sits down in the armchair and I sit on the floor close to his feet. What now? Orla is dead. It's over. My stomach shrinks. It's as she said in the graveyard: *Euan was always good at doing what had to be done.*

I twist round to face him. 'Did you mean to kill her?'

He looks hurt and then says flatly, 'I didn't know the spike was there and even if I had, I could hardly have judged it so accurately.'

I consider this and then say, 'Why did you never tell me about Rose?'

He raises his eyebrows. 'Cowardice.'

I shake my head. 'You're not a coward.'

'Then you pick a reason.' He stands up. 'For now we have to deal with this.' He points to Orla's crumpled body. 'This is what you have to do. Go back to your car and wait there. If anybody comes down the path to her cottage call me. Can you manage that?'

'What will you say to the police?'

'We can't call the police.'

'Why not?'

'I could end up being prosecuted.' He looks stern. 'We both could.'

'We can't cover this up!' I stand up beside him. 'It was an accident! Self-defence. She was trying to strangle me and you stopped her.'

'Maybe so but it doesn't look good. There will be an inquiry and the police will discover that we had reason to shut her up.'

I almost agree with him and then I think about the years stretching ahead of me. Fearful. Looking over my shoulder. What if someone has seen my car and tells the police I was here? What if Orla told someone that she thought we were going to harm her? What if Euan, years down the road, decides to blackmail me? He's not someone I can trust any more. He's almost as much of a snake as she was.

I reach for my mobile.

'Stop! Think,' he says, urgent now. 'Think about the girls and Paul.'

'No.' I shake my head. 'I've been down this road before. I can't keep another secret. Not again.' I call emergency services and ask for the police. I expect Euan to take the phone from me but he doesn't.

'What are you going to tell them?'

'I'm going to tell them the truth.'

'All of it?'

I don't answer.

'We have to tell the same story,' he says. 'Grace?'

I turn away and when I see the lights of the police car arrive at the top of the footpath, I walk out into the rain to meet them.

Once more a police station. Once more I am wet and have a blanket round me, but this time Orla is not opposite me. Orla is dead. Euan and I are taken to separate rooms and questioned. I tell the truth. It isn't the whole truth: I don't mention Rose and I don't mention the fact that I thought about killing Orla, albeit only for moments. I always give them the same answers: she was obsessed with me and my family and with her teenage self. She had been hounding me for almost two weeks and I came to the cottage to try to reason with her. She attacked me. I have bruises from her fingers round my throat. I confirm Euan's story that all he did was pull her off me and that she fell awkwardly.

Paul and Ed return from Skye at once. Paul stays beside me, supporting me through the questioning and the speculation that inevitably follows. To all intents and purposes he is one hundred per cent on my side but when we are alone, I see and hear how he really feels. 'I'm doing this for the girls,' he tells me. 'You, Grace.' His eyes are shot through with betrayal. 'I will never understand why you were having an affair with Euan or why you didn't tell me about Orla's obsession with you.'

'I couldn't—'

'But you could tell Euan?' he snaps back.

I say nothing. Nothing I can say will make it better. I truly believe that there is nothing to be gained from telling Paul the exact sequence of events that led to Rose's drowning. It's too late to help Rose and it will reopen an old wound for Paul. I don't feel as if I'm protecting Euan and I don't feel as if I'm protecting myself. I feel as if I'm doing the only thing I can do by accepting that what happened all those years ago can never be made right and I have to live with that.

Daisy and Ella are both visibly horrified when they find out about Orla's obsession with me. Ella fluctuates between tears and being over-protective of me. Daisy is confused. 'I don't understand,' she keeps saying. 'Why did she want to hurt you? She seemed nice.'

I worry that Shugs will come forward to give the police another angle, but he never does. I worry that fellow diners in the Edinburgh restaurant might read about the case, recognise Orla's photograph and come forward to say that they heard me threaten her, but that doesn't happen either.

Two weeks after Orla's death, the police come to the house to inform me that neither Euan nor I will be prosecuted. There's the bedroom—evidence that her obsession was a real and powerful one. Her history of poor mental health, her drug addiction and her conviction for the part she played in her husband's murder. (I find out that while she didn't actually wield the knife, she paid the man who did and then stood watching as her husband died.)

When the police leave, my feeling of relief is tempered by the growing rift between Paul and myself. We are to move to Melbourne but gone are the shared decisions. Paul makes all of them himself. He no longer includes me in his thoughts. We don't make love any more.

I throw myself into packing up and one morning, when I am at the front of the house emptying the garage, a car pulls up. My stomach turns over when I see Murray and Angeline climb out. I meet them halfway along the front path and see at once that Angeline has changed. She is immaculately dressed, as always, but her walk is less confident.

'Grace.' She stops a pace away from me. 'It seems I misjudged you.'

'I'm sorry for your loss, Angeline.'

'Are you? Are you really?'

'Yes, I am.' I keep my voice steady.

She leans towards me. 'Look me in the eye and tell me that neither of you wanted my daughter dead.' I look her in the eye but before I speak she says, 'I thought as much.' She starts to shake with rage. 'I will not forget this. You may have fooled the police but you have not fooled me.'

'Angeline.' Murray takes her left elbow and as he does so she lifts her right arm and slaps me so hard across the face that my teeth shift in my jaw. Murray turns Angeline round and they go back to the car.

I go inside, my face stinging with pain. I pull Murphy up on the sofa beside me and stay there for the rest of the afternoon, dry-eyed and empty inside. No one disturbs me. The girls are not coming home until late evening because they are rehearsing *Romeo and Juliet*—Daisy has found her niche backstage. Ed isn't due to come home either. He has been staying with my parents since Orla died. All three support me unreservedly. 'Don't you worry about us—we're all rubbing along well together,' my mum tells me. 'And we're looking forward to Australia.'

I'm pleased that my mum and dad are coming out with us. My dad's stomach has settled since he started a course of treatment and they are planning 'an adventure', my mum says. 'We won't come for the whole year; just to see you settled. And then we might do a spot of travelling.'

Just after six Paul comes through the front door and Murphy goes to greet him. I stand up and touch him on the arm. 'The table is set,' I say.

He doesn't look at me. 'Give me fifteen minutes.'

When Paul comes to the table I sit opposite him and dish up. When I take the first forkful I realise that I can barely swallow.

'Are you going to tell me how you got that mark on your face?'

The sound of his voice makes me jump. 'Orla's mother.'

'She came here?'

I nod.

He leans across the table and tenderly touches my cheek. 'My God, she really hit you. Why didn't you call me?'

'I thought you would think . . .' My voice gives out. I try again. 'I thought you would think that I deserved it.'

His jaw tightens and then he gives me a small, sad smile. 'No, I don't think that.' He runs his hands across my hair and down my shoulders.

At once I start to tremble and then to cry. 'Please, Paul,' I whisper. 'Just tell me that there's a chance you'll forgive me.'

'Of course there's a chance.' He pulls me into his chest and holds me there. 'Give me time, Grace.'

It's more than I could have hoped for and I can barely breathe for fear that he will change his mind and push me away. But he doesn't. He keeps his arms round me and I tell him how sorry I am, how much I love him, and how hard I will work to make our family happy again.

The evening's performance of *Romeo and Juliet* is just days before we leave for Melbourne. We collect my parents and Ed and go in to St Andrews to watch the play. Just before the performance starts, my dad realises he has left his glasses in the car. I take the keys from Paul and go back through the foyer. I find Dad's glasses and head straight back inside, only to bump into Monica and Euan. I haven't spoken to either of them since the day Orla died.

There are an awkward few seconds while we each appraise one another. Monica has hold of Euan's arm in such a way that makes it look as if she is the one keeping him upright. Clearly, he hasn't shaved and there is a tremor in his jaw. I don't know what goes on in their private moments but, in public, Monica has behaved like Paul. She has stayed by Euan's side, warding off gossip and nosy neighbours. I don't know whether she knows about the affair, but if she does, she hides it.

'It hasn't started, has it?' she asks me.

'Just about to, I think.' I sidle past them both.

'Grace?' His voice sounds sore. I turn back and find that I can look him in the eye without hating him, without loving him, without, in fact, feeling anything at all. 'I'm sorry.'

I don't answer. I walk back down the centre aisle, just as the curtain begins to open, and slide into my seat next to Paul.

'Did you get talking to someone out there?' he says.

'There's nobody out there.' I rest my head against his shoulder. 'Nobody at all.'

Julie Corbin

Tell Me No Secrets takes place on the east coast of Scotland, close to St Andrew's. Is this an area you know well?

No, I was brought up in Edinburgh, but I wanted to set the story in a fishing village on the east coast of Scotland that wasn't too close to either Edinburgh or Glasgow, and so not in commuting distance of either city. I'm very fond of the east coast and I went to Crail and walked around, and I really felt that it was the right place. But then I found there wasn't an ice-cream shop there and there *had* to be one in my story, so I created my own village. That's the joy of writing fiction!

Did you grow up in the same kind of close-knit community that Grace knew?

Yes, I did. And, as I wrote in the introduction, like Grace, I did go to Guide camp when I was fourteen and no longer wanted to be a Girl Guide—at that time I was always thinking about one particular boy—and I did have a friend who wasn't as bad as Orla, but she was a very difficult girl.

Were you inspired to write by a particular teacher when you were at school?

I'd always been a voracious reader and I was twelve when I first realised that I might enjoy writing, too. There was a Miss Durkin (who I have called Miss Parkin in the novel), who taught me English and also took the Guides, and she got me writing stories, one of which she secretly entered in a competition and it won!

Did you ever think about pursuing a career in publishing or becoming a writer?

I think perhaps I should have done, but at the time I was worried about studying for a degree that didn't lead directly into a job. I'd always had a thing about working in a hospital and my careers adviser told me about a course at Edinburgh University where I could get a BS with Nursing qualifications.

Did you find your nursing career fulfilling?

Yes, I did, and as a writer it has been a great help because it has given me good insight into people. I worked in various specialities from community to intensive care, and then thirteen years ago, a short while after we moved to Sussex, I took on the management of the medical department in a local prep school. I've really enjoyed my time with the children, and I've made many good friends, but last summer term was my last in that post and I'm now a full-time writer!

When did you make the decision to give up your 'day job' to become a novelist?

Six years ago I decided to take writing seriously and so I signed up for two creative-writing classes, where I made some good 'writing friends'. After that I signed up for a university course and formed a writing group. We meet every two weeks, read each other's work and say positive things. You have to be quite robust to take major criticism. Some people just give up and that's no good.

How did you make the leap from aspiring writer to published author?

In 2007, my first draft of *Tell Me No Secrets* was shortlisted in *The Daily Telegraph* First 1,000 Words of a Novel and the A.C. Black First 10,000 Words competitions. I sent the synopsis and three chapters off to three agents and one of them contacted me, saying, 'I love the set-up, can you send me the rest?' Then I received detailed feedback from him telling me why the story didn't work! I went to meet him in London and that meeting was probably the most exciting and overwhelming of my life. He was treating me like a writer and really understood my writing. When I got home I burst into tears and kept doing that for two days! My husband said, 'Come on, Julie, if this is making you unhappy you mustn't do it.' And I said, 'No, I'm just so scared he'll change his mind!' The fourth draft was taken by a publisher.

Are you currently writing your second novel?

Yes, and it's almost done. I found it very hard to leave my first set of characters behind, and so I've made a very deliberate decision to make the protaganist in this new story absolutely honest. This book is all about loss. Yesterday I was writing an emotional scene and I ended up making myself cry, and I thought, 'Oh, that's perfect!' because I actually felt the pain of the character.

What do you do to unwind after a day spent planning or writing your book?

I walk my dog every day in Ashdown Forest and I do yoga. And my husband and I have just signed up for dancing classes. Having watched *Strictly Come Dancing*, we've decided it's time. So, Ballroom, Latin, and by March we'll be Salsa experts!

Sheila Roberts

Love in Bloom

Hi one and all!

I'm very proud of my book, *Love in Bloom*, which features Hope Walker, a young woman who owns *Changing Seasons*, a popular flower shop in the fictional town of Heart Lake. When it comes to love and relationships, Hope is able to work magic through her expert flower arranging . . . for everyone but herself. But when she stakes a plot of ground at Heart Lake's community garden, magic happens. Hope discovers that a woman can grow all kinds of things there: flowers, herbs, vegetables—and even friendship. Amber Howell and Millie Baldwin share neighbouring plots, and as the three women become friends, Hope realises they can all learn from each other—not only about gardening, but about life. And love. I hope when you read this you'll be inspired, like Hope, to get out there and live life to the fullest.

Sheila

One

'I NEED FLOWERS, dead ones. Have you got any that are starting to wilt?'

'Excuse me?' Hope Walker stared at the woman standing in front of her. She looked like she could scorch a pansy at twenty paces. This was a new one for Changing Seasons Floral.

'I want to send flowers to my dog,' the woman explained.

Hope frowned and ran a hand through her hair—all those curls, still hard to get used to. 'Excuse me?'

'My ex has custody, so I don't want anything pretty sitting on his doorstep. And I want the card to read, "These aren't for you, they're for the dog. Condolences, Schatsi, on getting stuck with Daddy." I'll pay for it with MasterCard.'

For everything else, there's MasterCard. But not for this.

'I'm afraid I can't help you,' said Hope with a smile of faux regret. 'All my flowers are fresh.'

'Well, you must have something,' snapped the woman.

What to say to someone like this? Hope arranged flowers for happy: weddings, graduations, birthdays. She arranged flowers for sad: funerals, hospital stays. And she arranged flowers for love and sex, and probably not always in that order. But what she didn't arrange flowers for was bitter, angry or vindictive, and this woman could qualify for all three.

OK. This was a business. 'How much do you want to spend?'

'Whatever it takes.'

Whatever it takes? That was something a woman said when she was hurt and angry and, deep down, hoping that one desperate gesture would work magic and take her to a Hallmark happy ending.

Now Hope knew these flowers weren't for the dog. She also knew the message this woman really wanted to send. 'All right,' she said crisply. 'I think I can help you. But you need to allow me creative licence.'

'Do whatever you want,' said the woman.

There it was. Permission to do what she did best: speak what was in someone's heart with her flowers. She took the credit card information and Schatsi and Daddy's address, then Hope sent the woman on her way with a shamrock plant to make her feel better.

Hope slipped behind the thick velvet curtains that hid her work area at the back of the shop and got busy. She combined red carnations, which symbolised an aching heart, with red roses, for love, remembrance and passion. Ferns made the perfect green because they symbolised sincerity. On the card, she wrote the message behind the message: 'Schatsi, I wish things could be different.' She added a note explaining the symbolism of the flowers. She'd wait a day before delivering. The flowers wouldn't be wilted, but they wouldn't be fresh, either. It felt like a good compromise.

She emerged with her masterpiece and looked round her shop, all gussied up in anticipation of Easter, with baskets brimming with tulips and daffodils, Easter egg trees and pastel egg garlands. 'Well, everyone,' she said, 'you heard. She insisted. And this will accomplish so much more than what she originally wanted.'

The little bell over the shop door jingled and Clarice, her girl Friday, walked in, ten minutes late as usual, a vision in retro hippy clothes, maroon hair and ear piercings. Clarice was nineteen and very creative. 'Who are you talking to?'

Hope shrugged. 'Just myself. I had the weirdest order. A woman wants to send a wilted bouquet to her dog.' Hope pointed to the bouquet.

'Those don't look wilted to me.'

'By tomorrow when we deliver, they'll be as close as I can get. If she's not happy, I'll refund her money.'

Clarice frowned and shook her head. 'It's a good thing you've got the touch with flowers, 'cause you suck at business.'

'Look who's talking,' Hope retorted. 'I swear if you ever get a real job, you'll get sacked the first week.'

Clarice dumped her bag behind the counter with a sigh. 'I know I'm late. I overslept. I met the most amazing guy last night.' She hugged herself and closed her eyes.

A teeny weed of jealousy popped up in Hope's heart. She gave it a mental yank. Just because she would probably never find a man didn't mean that she had to resent it when someone else got lucky.

Another weed. Yank, toss. Sigh.

The bell over the door jingled again, and in walked the Hunk of the Century.

'Wow,' breathed Clarice, speaking for both of them.

Hope shot her a look, then asked, 'May I help you?'

He looked a little embarrassed, whether from Clarice's unbridled admiration or the fact that he was in a flower shop. He was tall, with an Arnold Schwarzenegger chest. Dressed in jeans, a denim shirt and work boots, he had sandy hair and brown eyes and the tanned skin of a man accustomed to working outside.

'I need to order some flowers,' he said, stating the obvious.

Hope walked over to him. He smelled of sawdust and aftershave. 'Do you have anything in mind?' She asked. She did, but it had nothing to do with flowers.

'I don't know. Some kind of arrangement.'

'For your girlfriend?' chirped Clarice from behind the counter.

The customer shook his head. 'My mom. It's her birthday.'

A hunk who loved his mother. The man had to have a flaw somewhere. Hope walked over to the wrought-iron café table where she kept the book with pictures of all her arrangements and flipped it open. 'Would you like to look at some samples?'

'Uh, I actually have to get back to work. My company's doing the renovations on this building.'

The renovations on the building that housed her flower shop, Something You Need Gifts, and Emma's Quilt Corner had made the sound of hammers and saws familiar background noise as builders shored up some of the sagging structure at the back of the building. So she'd heard him before she'd seen him.

'Maybe you can just pick something out,' he suggested.

Hope hated it when people said that. Flowers had a language all their own, and every arrangement should say something special that reflected the heart of the giver.

'Flowers are so personal,' Hope said. 'Does your mom have a favourite?'

'She likes roses.' His brows knitted together. 'She doesn't live in Heart Lake. She's closer to Lyndale. Do you deliver that far?'

Hope nodded. 'No problem. How much did you want to spend?'

'Cost doesn't matter.'

'Dark pink roses symbolise appreciation. You could add some daffodils, and the colour contrast would be striking.'

'Do those symbolise something?'

'Every flower does. Daffodils symbolise respect.'

He snapped his fingers and pointed at her like she'd just come up with something brilliant. 'Perfect. Add those.'

'All right then,' she said. She moved to the counter and he followed her, pulling out his wallet. She brought up an order form on her computer and took the name and address of the recipient. 'And how would you like the card to read?'

'"Happy birthday, Mom"?' he guessed.

Clarice snickered and Hope frowned at her.

'Words aren't exactly my specialty. I appreciate words though,' he added. 'I'm open to suggestions.'

Hope loved this part of her job. She enjoyed helping people with the little cards that accompanied their gifts almost as much as she enjoyed creating floral arrangements. 'Since you're picking such symbolic flowers, it would be nice to tell her what they mean. So, how about, "Roses for gratitude, daffodils for respect".'

'I like it,' he said with a nod. 'And sign it, "Love, Jason". Wait. Make that, "Love and gratitude". How's that?'

He was looking at Hope as if waiting for her approval. 'That says it all,' she said. *You're perfect.* For some other woman, not for her.

He handed over his charge card. She looked at the name on it. Jason Wells. It was a nice, solid-sounding name to go with those nice, solid muscles. *Oh, stop already.*

Their business done, he gave her a nod and a smile and an easy 'Thanks,' then left the shop.

Hope watched him go.

'Great butt,' Clarice said, echoing her thoughts. 'No wedding ring. I wonder if he's got a girlfriend.'

'Didn't you just meet Mr Amazing last night?' Hope teased.

Clarice made a face. 'Not for me, for you. He's probably at least thirty. That's your age.'

'Me?' Hope shook her head. 'He's not my type.'

'A man like that is anybody's type.'

Not anybody's, thought Hope. A man like that needed a perfect woman, not one who was scarred and had an implant where her left boob used to be.

Two

Seventy-six-year-old Millie Baldwin felt like the Invisible Woman. What did it take to snag a boy's attention these days? 'Guess what I did while you were in school?' she asked her twelve-year-old grandson.

No response.

'I stole the Liberty Bell.'

Eric gave a grunt and pressed the controls on his video game.

'I buried it in the neighbour's backyard,' Millie continued. 'That's just temporary, till I can find a buyer.'

'Oh, man, he killed me!' cried Eric in disgust.

Millie sighed and let him go on with his game: something called 'Halo' that he played on-line. Maybe if she had expressed an interest in killing virtual people when she first came to stay with Debra, she and her grandson would be spending more time together now. Maybe they would talk. Maybe when she talked he would listen. Probably not though. Who wanted to listen to an old woman?

She had tried to figure out the game one afternoon, thinking it would be fun to surprise Eric and challenge him to a duel when he got home, but she'd been unable to even make the game start, let alone decipher the purpose of the buttons on the controller.

'I think I'll just scoot out to the kitchen and make myself a cup of tea, plan my next heist.'

'Whoa!' he hooted.

'Would you like something to eat, Eric?' she offered.

'Fritos,' he said.

Millie fetched the bag of chips, then dropped it on the coffee table in front of Eric. He reached for the chips while simultaneously punching the game controls.

'You're welcome, dear,' she prompted.

'Oh, yeah. Thanks, Gram.' He shot her a quick grin. He was a cute boy. They used to have fun together when he and his sister came out to visit, playing games like Sorry and Steal the Pack. But here, those quiet games couldn't compete with the action on the TV screen. Neither could she.

Back in the kitchen, Millie put the kettle on to boil and stood looking out of the window. She saw a drizzly Pacific Northwest day and a stark landscape, dotted with a few ornamental bushes. Her daughter claimed it was restful. How could a yard with barely any vegetation be restful? And if it was so restful, why was Debra always so tense?

That, of course, was a rhetorical question. Debra was a single, working mother with a stressful job and spoiled children who required the latest of everything.

Fourteen-year-old Emily bounced into the kitchen, home from school and ready to forage for food. She planted a quick kiss on Millie's cheek. Like Eric, Emily was a beautiful child, with golden hair and blue eyes. She was two years older than her brother and just as skinny. She also had an equally never-ending appetite.

Right now Emily was searching the fridge and talking on her shiny, pink cellphone.

'I did not say that about her,' Emily snarled into her phone.

'I made oatmeal cookies this afternoon,' offered Millie.

'Cool, thanks.' Emily grabbed a yogurt and piled two cookies on top. 'Well, I didn't say that and you need to tell Rachel I didn't say that.' She sailed out of the kitchen.

The phone rang. Millie checked the caller ID and saw that it was her dearest friend, Alice Livingston, calling from Connecticut.

Alice barely gave her time to say hello. 'You ready to come home yet?'

'This is my home now,' Millie said firmly.

Alice gave a snort. 'Living in your daughter's house?'

'I like it here,' Millie insisted. All right. Perhaps she had made a hasty decision, but at the time it seemed like the perfect solution for both her daughter and herself. Debra needed help, and Millie needed a home. All those unexpected medical expenses had really upset her financial apple cart. She and Duncan had been the poster couple for why all Americans over the age of sixty should have long-term-care insurance. She was sure that, in the end, Duncan had willed himself to pass on to save what little they had left for her.

'Oh, you cannot be serious,' Alice said, her voice dripping scorn. 'Going from your own home to being a dependent.'

Millie said stiffly, 'I contribute.' Not only did she do the laundry, help with the cooking, and clean up the kitchen after meals, she paid Debra rent from her social security cheque. Debra had baulked at taking the money at first, but Millie had insisted.

'You should have moved in with me,' Alice said. 'We could have had so much fun.'

Just thinking about her happy life in Little Haven was enough to bring a sigh—tea parties with her friends of forty years, gardening, attending St. Mark's Church, where Debra had been married.

'It's not too late. You could come back,' Alice coaxed.

'No,' Millie said firmly. 'Going back is never a good idea. I need to move forward.' She was needed here. And that was better than mouldering in the past. 'Now, dear. I have to go start dinner.'

'Debra's going to work you into an early grave.'

That made Millie smile. Secretly, Alice was jealous. She and her daughter weren't on speaking terms. 'I'll talk to you soon,' Millie said, and hung up.

She lifted the kettle from the hob. The phone rang again. It was Debra. That meant one thing. 'Do you have to work late?'

Millie had thought when she moved out here they'd have more time to talk, do things together. That hadn't quite worked out.

'Sorry, Mom. But don't worry about making dinner. I can pick something up on the way home. The kids don't mind eating late.'

That was the trouble with life at Debra's house if you asked Millie: no routine. 'You have leftover chicken in the refrigerator. I can make a pot pie.'

'No, that's OK. Just leave the chicken. I'm going to make chicken curry with it on the weekend. I'll bring something home. I should be there by quarter to seven.'

Millie wished her daughter well with the rest of her day and hung up. She fixed her tea and then stood in front of the window.

Most of Heart Lake was pretty, with its tall evergreens, its homey downtown and converted summer homes. Even the newer houses on the lake had a casual feel that suited the area, and were landscaped in a way that blended with the firs and pines and alders. But the development where her daughter lived was made up of ostentatious mansions, bulging like squatting monsters over their small lots.

Perhaps Alice was right. Millie didn't fit here. She shouldn't have let Debra persuade her otherwise. At least in Little Haven she had familiar surroundings and good friends. And a lovely garden.

'Mom, you could live with Randall or me,' her son Duncan Jr had told her. 'You don't have to move there just because Deb wants you to.'

'I know, dear. But she needs help with the children.'

'She needs help. Period. When she's not working you to death, she'll take over your life and boss you around. That's what she did to Ben. That's why he left. She's high maintenance, Mom.'

'I'll be fine,' Millie had assured him. Debra was the youngest of her three children. Perhaps she'd spoiled her just a little.

The old house in Little Haven had felt too big for her to rattle round in alone. But this house felt too small. There was no room for her to squeeze into the lives of the people occupying it. Her daughter barely had time for her; her grandchildren ignored her.

Millie longed to feel cheered by an English garden with flowers spilling everywhere, a garden she could stand in the middle of and smell the fragrance of new life in bloom.

'It doesn't do any good to mope,' Millie told herself. 'I need to make some changes.'

She took her tea, settled at the kitchen table, and began to look through the weekly edition of the *Heart Lake Herald,* determined to find something with which to build a new life.

She suddenly found what she'd been looking for. GARDEN SEASON IS HERE AGAIN, proclaimed the headline. Millie smiled as she read on. The Heart Lake Park and Recreation Department is currently reserving plots for all interested gardeners at the community garden at Grandview Park.

Heart Lake had just given her a get out of jail free card.

Three

'I NEED TO LEAVE EARLY,' Clarice told Hope as they stood removing thorns from the roses the wholesaler had delivered that morning.

Hope cocked a finger at her. 'April Fools, right?'

'No, for real.'

She'd come in late and now she wanted to leave early? Hope combed her fingers through her hair. 'Do you have to?'

'Look on the bright side. It's an hour you don't have to pay me.'

'I'd rather pay you,' Hope said. 'Clarice, I depend on you.'

Clarice had the grace to look guilty. But only for a moment. 'You can handle things on your own for the last hour, can't you?'

'Barely. We're getting busier all the time.'

Word was spreading. Hope Walker was the Picasso of flowers. Between her flower arrangements and the inspiring words she helped customers put on the gift cards, she had probably saved a dozen relationships and cemented another twenty since Valentine's Day. She was already booked for two weddings. This morning alone she'd had a dozen calls for arrangements for everything from birthdays to new babies. And with Heart Lake High's Junior Class Spring Fever Dance coming up on the weekend, orders for corsages and boutonnières were pouring in. That was all good, but it was all even better when her help actually stuck around to help.

'I promised I'd make dinner for Borg.'

Mr Wonderful. Of course, she should tell Clarice that she was going to have to make a choice. But that was easier said than done. Clarice had been Hope's first employee. Her only employee. Who would she get to replace Clarice?

Hope put on her sternest expression. 'Look,' she began. Clarice was making a pitiful, pleading face. 'You can't cook.'

'I know,' Clarice moaned. 'That's why I need to get off early. It's going to take me hours to figure out how to make spaghetti.'

'Buy frozen meatballs, canned sauce, and boil some pasta and you're good to go. Trust me.'

'And the place is a mess. Come on, Hope. Haven't you ever been in love?'

Hope gave up. She still believed in love, if not for herself, then for other people. 'Oh, all right. But don't do this again. The dance is Saturday, and with all the other orders, we'll be swamped.'

Clarice beamed. 'I'll be here. You can count on me.'

Her words rang mockingly in Hope's ears when, on Thursday with forty-three corsages to make, the clock hit 11 a.m. and there was still no sign of Clarice. Hope had tried Clarice's home phone and her cellphone only to get her voice mail.

She had finally broken down and put in a desperate call to her younger sister. Bobbi was a disaster in heels, but she had artistic flair and a way with flowers that couldn't be taught. Hope just had to keep her sister away from the phones and the computer. Nobody could screw up an order like Bobbi. Nobody had a heart like Bobbi, either. When someone needed help, Bobbi came at a run.

The phone rang for what felt like the millionth time. Hope said calmly, 'Changing Seasons. May I help you?' Then she heard the voice on the other end of the line. 'Clarice! Where are you?'

'I'm in Vegas. I'm married!'

Hope blinked and gaped at the receiver. 'To Borg?'

'I am totally in love. He is amaaaazing.'

No, amazing was that Clarice could run away to Vegas with someone she'd known a week. And leave her boss stuck up to her neck in flowers. 'Why didn't you at least call me and let me know you were going?'

'Well, it was kind of sudden.'

Kind of? There was an understatement.

'Borg got laid off and was going down there to check out working at his cousin's garage. And he found this great deal on Travelocity, so we figured, what the hell.'

What the hell.

'We're staying at the Bellagio,' Clarice continued. 'Borg used his whole last pay cheque for this. Isn't that sweet? This whole place is awesome. I'm so happy,' Clarice ended on a squeal.

Hope couldn't help smiling. 'Well, I wish you both the best.'

'Thanks. You're the best. And, Hope?'

'Hmm?' Hope said absently.

'Go for it. Find somebody and just . . . go for it.' Then the line went dead.

The bell over the shop door jingled and a familiar voice warbled, 'I'm here to save the day.'

Thank goodness. Help. 'I'm in the back,' Hope called.

The red velvet curtains partitioning off the work room parted and through them stepped her little sister, the reincarnation of Scarlett O'Hara, only with blonde hair and bigger boobs. She was wearing jeans, boots and a black leather jacket over layers of style.

She blew over to Hope and hugged her, enveloping her in a mist of perfume. Bobbi never could put on perfume with a light hand. The parade of men who chased her never seemed to mind.

Normally Hope wouldn't, either. But when she was going through chemo the smell of perfume had made her sick. It still did a little. She pulled away and tried not to make a face.

'What?' Bobbi's eyebrows rose with sudden understanding. 'The perfume? You can smell it?'

'Um.'

'Sorry. I'll wash it off.'

Hope nodded. 'Thanks. I hate to cramp your style.'

'Nothing cramps my style,' Bobbi said with a grin and went off to de-scent herself.

'Thanks for bailing me out,' Hope said, when she returned.

'No problem. When you're working nights, you're home all day with nothing to do but fold your laundry and eat.'

Who was Bobbi kidding? She was always out, either having coffee with a friend or lunch with some man she'd met at the Last Resort, where she worked as a cocktail waitress while she tried to figure out what she really wanted to do with the rest of her life.

Bobbi plopped her handbag under the work counter. 'So, how many million corsages do we have left to make?'

The phone rang. 'Ask me after this call,' Hope said, and took the order. 'We're going to be here till midnight,' she groaned when she hung up.

'You're going to be here till midnight,' Bobbi corrected her, starting on a corsage. 'By midnight, I'll be serving drinks and dodging losers trying to cop a feel.' She heaved a sigh. 'I don't know how long I'm going to last over there.'

When it came to careers, Bobbi tended to have a short attention span. In fact, when it came to most things she didn't have a very long attention span. She started books but never finished them (unless they were romance novels), and she tried on different hobbies like they were shoes. So far she'd tried hiking, cycling and French cooking. Her relationships didn't last long, either—not surprising, considering the undependable guys she picked.

'What we don't get done today, we'll finish tomorrow.' Bobbi put a hand over her heart. 'I pledge to make sure that no Heart Lake High School dance queen goes without her flowers.' She gave a stack of pink tissue paper a dramatic tug and knocked over a container of carnations. 'Oops. Don't worry, I'll get it,' she said.

Maybe calling her sister for help hadn't been such a good idea.

'Don't worry,' Bobbi assured Hope. 'I'll get into the rhythm here in a minute. So, have you heard from Clarice yet?'

'She eloped to Vegas.'

'Oh, fun!' cried Bobbi. 'I so need to go to Vegas. I hear the shopping there is incredible.'

'You wouldn't go with someone you'd known only a week would you?'

'You don't need years to know if it's right.'

This coming from the woman who'd had one starter marriage and six boyfriends in the last three years. Talk about starting your twenties with a bang. 'Sometimes you worry me, Bobs.'

'I know what you're thinking,' Bobbi said. 'Even though my relationships haven't worked out, I still believe in love at first sight. I just have this way of killing it before it can grow.'

'I hate it when you talk like it's all your fault that things didn't work out with those bozos,' Hope said. 'You just haven't found the right man yet.'

'I need someone who's nice. And responsible.'

The shop bell summoned Hope to the front of the shop, and she found Jason Wells, the hunk, hands shoved into his jeans back pockets, looking at her premade arrangements. Her body had an instant high-voltage reaction. What cruel joke of fate was this, anyway? Of all the flower joints in the world, he has to walk into mine.

'You're back,' she said. *Real professional, Hope.*

He smiled at her. It was a friendlier smile than the day before, maybe even a mildly interested smile. 'The flowers for my mom were a hit. Now I need something to make a woman feel better.'

Was he kidding? All he'd have to do was walk into a room. 'Can you give me some details?'

'You can deliver flowers to another state, right?'

'Sure. That's no problem,' Hope said, moving to her computer. 'What's the occasion?'

'They're for . . .' He stopped mid-sentence.

Hope didn't have to turn around to see what he was looking at. She knew. Bobbi had that effect on men.

'Hi,' she said from behind Hope. What was Bobbi doing out here anyway? Why wasn't she in the back room where she belonged, toiling away at corsages?

Jason closed his mouth and managed a feeble, 'Hi.'

Hope tapped the keyboard impatiently with her fingers. 'The flowers are for?' she prompted.

He cleared his throat. 'My . . .' He shook his head as if trying to restart his brain. 'They're for my sister.'

'What a nice brother,' cooed Bobbi.

For a flash, Hope had thought he'd just made up an excuse to come in and see her again. Maybe he had. But now he only had eyes for her sister. She could feel a weed of jealousy growing in her. *Yank that out right now.*

'She broke up with her fiancé,' Jason said. He moved closer to the counter where Bobbi stood next to Hope. 'I bet you've never had that problem.'

Bobbi shrugged. 'It always hurts to break up.'

Hope inserted herself into the conversation. 'How much would you like to spend?'

'This man looks like he's got a big heart. I bet if it's for his sister, he doesn't care,' said Bobbi, and Jason's face took on a slightly red tint. His embarrassment didn't stop him from smiling at Bobbi. It was the kind of smile ignited by intense sexual attraction.

'I just want something nice that will make her feel good,' he told Hope. 'Have you got a flower for that?'

'Let's see,' she said, trying to ignore the sudden desire to give her attention-stealing sister poison ivy. You can't have him, she reminded herself, so why not let Bobbi have him? Because even though he wouldn't want Hope, she wanted him.

But it was a shameful reason, especially since Bobbi had never done anything but look up to her. And chauffeur her to chemo, and buy her pretty scarves and hats to cover her bald head. Hope felt hot with shame.

She redirected her brain to the business of selecting just the right flowers for the occasion. 'Lily of the valley would be nice. It signifies a return to happiness.'

He nodded enthusiastically. 'That'll do.'

'Now, how about something for your wife?' said Bobbi.

He shook his head. 'I don't have a wife.'

'Girlfriend?' persisted Bobbi.

Another head shake. 'Nope.'

'How do you want the card to read?' asked Hope.

'She loves poetry. How about something . . .'

'Poetic?' Hope teased. She loved poetry too. 'Hmm. How about this one? *Though lovers be lost love shall not.*'

'That's good. It sounds familiar. Who's the poet?'

'Dylan Thomas,' said Hope.

'Love him,' Bobbi gushed. The only Dylan she'd ever heard of was Bob Dylan and she was barely familiar with him.

Jason nodded approvingly. 'I like him, too. That'll do great.' He produced his charge card and they finished the deal.

'Come back again,' Bobbi said.

'I will.' He smiled at both of them, but when his gaze finally picked one to settle on, it picked Bobbi.

Hope felt a sharp stab deep in her chest. She felt like all the happiness she ever would have just rushed away. She needed to send herself some lily of the valley to remind herself every day that she should always be happy just to be alive.

'That man is amazing,' said Bobbi.

'He's OK,' said Hope. She sighed inwardly. She wouldn't have gotten this man anyway; she knew that. But it was going to be really hard to watch him fall for her sister.

Hope was wilted by the end of the day. 'I owe you big time,' she told Bobbi, giving her a hug.

'Yes, you do owe me,' Bobbi said with a sly grin.

Hope knew what that meant. They'd spent most of the afternoon brainstorming ways that Bobbi could interest Jason Wells, and Bobbi had finally come up with the perfect plan, one that involved her older sister.

'Oh, not now,' Hope moaned. 'Can we do this tomorrow?'

'I want to do this today, while he still remembers me.'

Hope couldn't help smiling. 'He's not going to forget you.'

'I promise I'll be quick.' Bobbi produced the grocery bag full of guy junk food she'd picked up at the store. 'I can put the gift basket together. I just need you to help me with the card. I don't want him to think I'm an airhead.'

'He won't care.' That hadn't sounded right.

'Come on, you promised you'd help me. This guy looks like a keeper. I need to impress him.'

'Bobs, you already did.'

'No. I need to impress him with my brain. I want him to think I'm amazing.' Bobbi's gaze dropped. 'I've got to brainwash him early, before he finds out I'm just a cocktail waitress.'

'There's nothing wrong with being a cocktail waitress,' Hope argued. 'It's an honest living. You shouldn't put yourself down.'

Bobbi pulled out a bag of corn chips and nestled it in her basket of shredded paper next to a jar of salsa. 'I'm not you.'

Hope gave a disgusted snort. 'You don't want to be, believe me.'

Bobbi whirled round. 'Just because you were sick . . .'

'And am now Franken-boob.'

Bobbi pointed an admonishing finger at her. 'Don't go there. There's more to you than your boobs.' She smiled. 'Just like there's more to me than my body.' She sprinkled a bunch of Hershey's Kisses around the basket. 'Now, what kind of flower should I add?'

Hope arched an eyebrow. 'White mums?'

Bobbi looked at her. 'That means something bad, doesn't it? I can tell by looking at you. What do they stand for?'

'Truth.'

'Just because I'm having you coach me on my card doesn't mean I'm not being truthful. I picked the stuff for the basket. And, if I do say so myself, it's genius.'

'The oysters are subtle.'

'Never mind the oysters. What about the flowers?'

'What about yellow acacia,' Hope suggested, 'for secret love.'

'Oh, I like that!' cried Bobbi. 'Do we have any acacia?'

'Yeah, silk ones.' Hope started to get up.

'I'll get 'em,' said Bobbi. 'Which ones are they?'

'They're over in the corner of the west wall. They're the pouffy yellow blooms with the feathery leaves.'

'Um, which wall is the west wall?'

'Never mind. I'll get them,' said Hope.

Bobbi trailed her. 'I could have found them.'

'Never mind,' Hope said again, and plucked a spray.

They returned to the back room and arranged the flowers in the basket, then wrapped it in blue cellophane.

'That looks awesome,' Bobbi said with an approving nod. 'Now I just need the card.'

'What do you want to say?'

'That I think he's hot and I want to go out with him.'

Hope handed Bobbi a pen. 'It should be in your writing.'

'OK, help me think. The sooner you help me the sooner you can go home.' Bobbi gave her a playful nudge.

Hope sighed. 'OK. Why don't you make a mystery of it? How about "Every flower has a meaning, every petal speaks a word."'

'Oooh, that's so pretty!' gushed Bobbi. She wrote down the words. 'Are you going to make a rhyme out of it?'

Hope drummed her fingers on the counter. 'Hmm. Add: "But unless you speak their language, something special goes unheard." Then add: "If you learn what this yellow acacia symbolises, you'll be halfway to solving the mystery of this basket."'

'Oh, I love that!' Bobbi stopped writing. 'But that doesn't tell him who sent it.'

'It's coming from this shop. We were talking about the meaning of flowers earlier today. He'll figure it out.'

'Great.' Bobbi slipped the card in an envelope. Then she scooped up the basket. 'I'll deliver this on my way home.' She hugged Hope. 'I can help you tomorrow, too, if you want.'

That was Bobbi, generous to a fault. She deserved a great guy like Jason Wells. 'You are amazing.'

'Aw, you're just saying that 'cause it's true,' Bobbi quipped. She gave Hope another hug. 'Go home and rest. You look rotten.'

'Thanks.'

Bobbi left and Hope locked up the shop. Then she drove home, wondering if Bobbi had been able to deliver her basket in person. She made herself some green tea and ran a bath, filling the tub with extra bubble bath. She picked up her well-worn copy of Jane Austen's *Mansfield Park* and climbed into the tub to drink tea and read more about the adventures of her favourite heroine, Fanny Price. Fanny was plain and quiet. But she had a good heart, and in the end Miss Austen rewarded her goodness by giving her the man of her dreams. Hope liked that.

But tonight Fanny seemed insipid and undeserving. What man in his right mind would want a Fanny when he could have a Bobbi?

Jason Wells sauntered into Changing Seasons Floral on Saturday. If a fish going after a lure could smile, it would look like that, Hope thought. He was wearing jeans, a T-shirt and a windbreaker, and once again he started those attraction tremors in her.

'Hi. Back for more flowers?' she asked, playing dumb.

'Back to solve a mystery,' he replied.

'Oh?' So, Bobbi hadn't found him when she made her gift basket delivery. But, from the look on Jason's face it was clear that this love rocket was already launched.

'So, what can I do for you, Sherlock?'

'I got an interesting gift basket from here yesterday. I'm thinking you might know who's responsible for it.' He looked past her shoulder and nodded in the direction of the workroom. 'Would the person who sent it be back there by any chance?'

'Sorry, Bobbi's running some errands right now, but she should be back in an hour.'

He grinned. 'I'll be back.'

He was just turning to go when the door flew open and in blew Bobbi, looking adorable in jeans, a pink sweater and a red leather jacket. 'Well, hi,' she said.

'Hi,' he said.

The way they were looking at each other, Hope felt like she was watching a movie.

'I got a cool basket,' Jason said to Bobbi. 'Did you have something to do with that?'

Bobbi smiled. She was the queen of the flirty smile.

Hope slipped into her workroom, turned on the radio, and began sweeping stems and ribbon off the counter into the garbage, trying to ignore the burble of voices drifting in.

The bell over the shop door jangled and a moment later Bobbi was dancing into the workroom. 'He loved the basket. And the card.' Bobbi hugged Hope. 'You're a genius!'

'Yes, I am.'

'We're going out to lunch next week at the Family Inn.'

'Great,' Hope said encouragingly.

Bobbi was suddenly quiet. That wasn't normal.

'OK, what's wrong?'

'I didn't tell him why I couldn't go out for dinner.'

'He's going to find out what you do for a living eventually.'

'I know, but meanwhile . . . . He, um, thinks I work here.'

'Well, you've sure been doing a lot of work the last couple of days. That qualifies.' Why was Bobbi looking so guilty?

'He thinks we own this shop together.'

'What?'

'Please, don't be mad. I couldn't tell him I'm a cocktail waitress. I mean, he runs a construction company. I didn't want him to think I'm a nobody,' Bobbi said.

'You're not a nobody,' Hope insisted. 'What's the point of dating someone if you don't let him know who you really are?'

'I will,' Bobbi said. 'As soon as he gets to know me better. So, can we please, for a little while, let him think I'm somebody?'

'You are somebody,' Hope told Bobbi, 'but if you need this shop to prove it, that's OK.'

'Oh, thank you,' Bobbi gushed. 'You're the best sister in the whole world.'

Not really, but she wanted to be.

And she kept reminding herself of that as she moved through the rest of her day, as she drove home, as she entered her apartment. She'd made it cosy, filling it with books, plants, souvenirs from trips, and framed photos she'd taken on hikes in the Cascades. But it was still lacking something. Testosterone.

She plopped down at her vintage yellow Formica table and opened up the night's issue of the *Heart Lake Herald*. And then, like a gift from the flower gods, she found it. Garden therapy. She'd call first thing Monday and reserve a plot at the community garden.

Four

THE HEART LAKE PARK and Recreation offices opened at 9 a.m., Monday through Friday. At 8:50 on Friday, Millie Baldwin climbed into her Buick LeSabre to go and stake her claim on a garden plot.

She was pleased with her new car, a nice solid used model. Debra didn't see the need for it. Not, she said, when she had a perfectly good car and could take her mother anywhere she needed to go.

But Millie had shown Debra otherwise. One of the first things she'd done when she arrived in Heart Lake had been to insist her daughter drive her to the nearest used-car lot. Millie was going to have her own car and drive it, and she was going to have a life of her own, and a garden of her own, thank you very much.

She smiled as the park came into sight. This was a lovely park. She could easily picture herself spending mornings in a small corner of it in a cosy patch of flowers.

Grandview Park not only offered a peekaboo view of the lake, it came with a view of the Cascade Mountains. Forty acres of land, it had been put to good use, and now the community enjoyed a soccer field, a play area for children, tennis courts, a sand volleyball court, and a section of small plots for gardeners.

Every parking space was full except for one. She hoped all those cars didn't represent people wanting a garden plot.

She had already pulled into the space when she noticed it was for handicapped parking. There was nothing to do but find another spot. She put the car in reverse, turned the wheel, and started to reverse. And suddenly crashed into something unyielding. This couldn't be good.

She let down the window and peered out. Oh, dear. Just as she had suspected, she had backed into a parked car. She put a hand to her chest and took a deep breath. Calm down, she told herself.

She turned off the engine and got out of her car to inspect the damage. She had managed to effectively crunch both cars. This probably wouldn't be good for her insurance. She could almost hear her daughter pointing that out.

Well, there was nothing to be done but go and see whom she had hit. The sky was blue, but Millie walked into the Park and Recreation offices under a black cloud.

The office was cheery, panelled in pine. Three women sat at desks in a work area behind a long counter. The counter held a pile of catalogues for spring classes and community activities, a bowl of candy, and a pot full of pens. A young woman wearing jeans and a sweatshirt was conducting business with one of the employees. At her side, a little boy who looked about four hung from the counter.

Millie cleared her throat. 'Excuse me? Does anyone own a white car, rather small? It's parked outside.'

The young woman turned round. 'A Honda?'

'I'm not sure about the make,' Millie said, 'but it's the only white car out there.'

'It's mine, then,' said the woman.

'I'm terribly sorry, but I'm afraid I've hit it.'

The young woman's questioning smile dissolved.

'I'm so sorry. Naturally I'll pay for all repairs. I do have insurance,' Millie assured her.

'Hey, it could happen to anyone,' the woman assured her back. 'The way my luck's been running, I'm not even surprised it happened to me.'

'I think it would be best if we called the police,' Millie suggested. 'I don't have a cellphone,' she told the clerk.

The clerk smiled kindly at her. 'Not a problem. Jean,' she said to one of the secretaries manning a desk, 'can you ask Tom to send someone out here?'

The secretary nodded and got on the phone.

'Maybe I'd better look at it,' the young woman decided. She left the office for the parking lot, the little boy skipping along beside her. Millie followed them out.

'I feel just terrible,' Millie told her when they reached the cars.

'Don't,' said the woman. She was a pretty thing, with long brown hair and big brown eyes.

'I was in a big hurry to come in and reserve a garden plot,' Millie said, disgusted with herself all over again.

'Are you a gardener?' The woman's look turned hopeful.

'I am,' said Millie.

'I just reserved a plot. We're going to grow our own food, aren't we, Seth?'

The boy nodded. 'We're gonna grow punkins for Halloween.'

'That sounds pretty special,' she said to the child.

'They still have several plots left,' the woman told her. 'Would you like to sign up for one while you're waiting?'

'All right.' It was, after all, what she'd come here for.

'Are you a good gardener?' the woman asked as they walked back to the office.

Millie couldn't remember a time when she hadn't gardened. 'I certainly have done a lot of it.'

'I'm afraid I'm not very good,' confessed the woman.

'Maybe I can give you some gardening tips,' Millie offered.

The woman nodded. 'Thanks. Can you put her next to me?' she asked the clerk as Millie reserved her plot.

'Sure.'

'Hello, neighbour,' said Millie, offering her hand. 'My name is Millie Baldwin. I'm new to the area.'

The woman smiled. 'I'm Amber Howell. I'm still new here, too. I work at the bakery in town.'

'Ah. Perhaps I could buy you and your son a treat there.'

'I want a treat,' piped the child, jumping up and down.

Little boys didn't like to sit still at bakeries while grown-ups talked.

'Perhaps we could buy something there and then visit that little lake-front park,' Millie suggested.

'I want to go to the park!' Now the boy was really bouncing.

'I guess that settles it,' said Amber, just as a young man in a blue police uniform walked into the office.

It was embarrassing having to explain to the officer how she had managed to bang into poor Amber's car, but he was very helpful.

As if sensing Millie was still shaken, Amber offered to drive to their picnic. They made a stop at the bakery for three bottles of juice and half a dozen oatmeal cookies, then went to the park where they enjoyed the sunshine and watched Seth play on the slide.

'What brought you to Washington?' Amber asked.

'My daughter lives here. I moved out to help her.'

'Lucky her,' Amber said. 'I left my mom in California.'

It was always hard for a woman to leave her family. 'How did you end up here?'

'My husband came up for a job. He's a chef. But the restaurant went belly-up.' Amber shrugged. 'We found a little place on the lake to rent.'

'Has your husband found a new job?' Millie asked.

Amber's face tightened. 'No.'

'I'm sure he will.'

'Until he does, we've got my part-time job at the bakery, and cheap rent. And growing our own food should save us money.'

Millie thought of all the money she'd spent over the years on her gardens and wisely kept her mouth shut.

'So, we'll see you at the garden next month,' Amber said an hour later, as she returned Millie to her car.

'Sooner than that,' said Millie. 'You'll want to fertilise before you plant, get your soil ready. Chicken manure works well.'

'Chicken manure,' repeated Amber.

'Just turn it under.' Millie gave Amber's arm a pat. 'You'll be an expert gardener in no time. You'll see.'

'Obviously, I need help. With everything,' Amber added. 'But, hey, I've got my own garden guru now. I have a feeling my luck is going to change.'

'Luck is a lot like the weather this time of year,' Millie said, giving Amber an encouraging smile. 'It changes often.'

Amber nodded. 'Thanks. I like you.'

'I like you, too,' Millie said.

Amber returned home to find her husband, Ty, right where she'd left him, his wiry frame sprawled on a chair in their tiny living room in front of the TV. Ty hadn't even bothered to shave yet.

Seth ran over and climbed in his lap. 'We got a garden. We're gonna grow punkins. And carrots. Mommy said.'

'All right, bud.'

'And Millie came with us to the park,' Seth continued.

'Who's Millie?' he asked Amber.

'A woman I met when we went to sign up for our garden plot. She backed into our car.'

'What next?' muttered Ty. He grabbed his coat and started for the door to inspect the damage.

'It's not bad,' Amber said, following him. 'You can still drop off job applications.'

'Thanks,' he said sarcastically, making her wish she'd bitten her lip. Nagging didn't help. It only made him defensive. Outside, he inspected the car and shook his head in disgust. 'Just great.'

'It could have been worse,' Amber said. 'Seth and I could have been hurt. There are worse things than losing your job, you know.'

He scowled. 'Thanks for the reminder.' He opened the car door.

'Where are you going?' she demanded.

'To look for a job,' he snapped as he drove off.

She doubted he'd go look for job. These days, all he wanted to do was sit around and mourn the fact that they were broke and going nowhere. She'd gone along with the dream to own a restaurant. She'd signed those loan papers, too. But when things had started to sour, the team had dissolved. He turned a deaf ear to her pleas that they try to find a buyer and get out before they got completely burned. He kept telling her she was worrying for nothing.

And nothing was what they wound up with. Ty's confidence and hard work hadn't been enough to save them from disaster. They lost the money their parents had invested and they had to sell their house to pay off their small-business loan.

Now they were racing towards forty and were broke. Failures. At least that was how Ty saw it. And he couldn't get far enough away from everyone who had witnessed the whole ugly mess. The job in Seattle had provided the perfect escape. But then it dried up, and they moved further north.

At least she had her job at Sweet Somethings, the bakery at the centre of town. She hoped someday she'd be baking there, but for now she was making lattes and ringing up customers. Still, she loved her job. Even though she was new to Heart Lake, Amber could already tell it was a great community.

And she loved this run-down summer cabin that they'd found to rent. Right on the water, it had a little porch to sit on and enjoy the view. Watching that lake comforted her, especially on a day like this, with the promising spring sun spreading a bright sheen on the water. Given time, she could be happy here. Maybe that wouldn't be with Ty, though, not the way things were going between them.

Millie's sunny mood lasted until afternoon when her grandchildren came home from school.

'Gram, someone creamed your car,' Eric informed her.

Millie looked up from her crossword puzzle. 'I know, dear. It's all taken care of.'

'Gram, what happened to your car?' Emily asked later.

'I had a little accident,' Millie said, and continued calmly peeling carrots.

'Are you OK? Did you get whiplash or anything?'

'No. I'm fine.' She was exhausted from all the excitement.

Emily peered over her shoulder. 'What are you making?'

'Carrot cookies,' said Millie.

Emily made a face. 'Gross.' And with that she was gone.

Debra had a little more to say, however. They sat at the table after dinner. 'Mom. There comes a time . . .'

'Well, it hasn't come yet,' Millie said, cutting her off. 'I'm only seventy-six.'

'Seventy-seven in June,' Debra reminded her. 'Anyway, I still don't get why you need a car during the day.'

Millie frowned. 'Is that what you envisioned when you invited me to come stay with you, that I would simply rattle round here alone all day, with no life of my own?'

'You have a life, with us. And the bus stops right down on the corner. Or I can drive you.'

'I am perfectly capable of driving a car,' Millie said irritably.

'Perfectly capable of wrecking a car,' her daughter muttered.

'You don't need to worry about me. And now, if you'll excuse me, I'm going to go read my book.' Millie marched from the kitchen, enjoying the satisfaction of having the last word.

But that satisfaction quickly wore off. Was she that bad a driver? She leaned on the dresser in her bedroom and regarded the woman staring back at her in the mirror. 'I'm not too old,' she told herself. That old face was the outside Millie. The inside Millie was still thirty, and the inside Millie wasn't ready for a rocking chair yet. She had lots of good years left in her, and she intended to make the most of them.

Bobbi arrived at the Family Inn for her lunch date with Jason dressed to kill. She was wearing her favourite top, the black one that showed a hint of cleavage, and her short denim skirt. She'd drenched herself in Vera Wang Princess, her perfume du jour. Before lunch was over Jason Wells would be madly in love with her.

She smiled in anticipation. She had finally found her perfect man. He was hunkalicious, he was kind, and he was in construction, which meant he would know how to fix anything, a skill that would come in handy when she finally had a house. All that remained was to find out if Jason liked kids and if he liked to dance. She simply couldn't be with a man who didn't dance.

She found him waiting in the reception area. The food here was far from five star, but the price was right. She didn't want to give the impression that she was high maintenance.

He turned and his eyes lit up at the sight of her. She had that effect on men. Still, she always seemed to find herself stuck with losers. Not this time though. She knew Jason Wells was a keeper. And she was going to keep him no matter what it took.

'You look incredible,' he said.

And you are incredible, she thought.

The hostess led them to a window table with a view of thick shrubs and bushes, and beyond that, a duck pond.

The best view was sitting in front of Bobbi. Jason's shirt hung open over a blue T-shirt that draped perfect pecs.

'You know, the guys are still talking about that basket,' he said. 'You've got flair. Were you an art major in college?'

College? Which one? She'd done a quarter at Mount Vista Junior College where she'd flunked Math Skills and Science 101, and gotten two marriage proposals. She'd managed a semester's worth of classes at the Northwest Business College where she half-mastered typing and flunked her filing test.

'I should have been an art major,' she decided. Why hadn't she thought of that? But did she really want to study dead artists who painted cherubs on church ceilings?

She liked making things look pretty. Maybe she should become an interior decorator. Or sell pretty house things on the home party plan. She loved parties. She could probably make a fortune.

'So, how'd you end up with a flower shop?' Jason asked.

'It was a good thing to do with my sister,' she said.

'I'll bet you two have a great time together.'

'We do. She's awesome,' Bobbi said. 'She's always been there for me.' She still was.

The waitress came and gave them their menus.

Jason opened his. 'What's good on the menu?'

'Not much,' Bobbi answered. 'But you can't go wrong with the pizza.'

'OK, pizza it is,' Jason decided. 'What do you like on yours?'

'Anything but anchovies.'

He grinned and ordered a deluxe large and two Cokes. 'And we'll do the salad bar,' he added, smiling at Bobbi.

'How did you know?'

'You don't exactly look like the kind of woman who pigs out on pizza.' He shrugged. 'But I guess I could have been wrong. When I first saw you, you didn't strike me as the kind of woman who'd be into poetry.'

'I'm no expert,' she said, stretching the truth. She had never in her life, of her own volition, picked up a book of poems.

'I'm not much of an expert myself,' said Jason. 'But I've got my favourites.'

They were creeping onto dangerous ground. If she asked him who his favourite poet was, he was bound to ask hers. What to do?

When it came to men, Bobbi's mind was a computer. She inputted her questions and the answer quickly came back: look interested. Ask him about poems.

'So, what's your favourite poem?'

'I like a lot of stuff. I really like Robert Service,' he said.

'Who?' *Way to sound dumb, Stupid.*

'He wrote about life in the Yukon. His most famous poem is 'The Cremation of Sam McGee.' Ever hear of it?'

'Eeew. No.'

Before he could ask her who her favourite poet was she stood up, saying, 'Let's check out the salad bar.'

But as they moved along the salad bar, he picked up the conversation again. 'My dad turned me on to Robert Service. I think he figured it would be a good way to whet my appetite. Mom's an English prof and she insisted my brother and I be well rounded, so even though we'd rather have watched football or worked with Dad on construction sites, she forced us to read poetry and go to musicals. I was even in one once.'

'Only once?'

He shook his head. 'Once was enough. Anyway, sports took most of my time.'

She hoped he didn't like outdoor sports like hiking. She said, 'I like musicals. My favourite is *Phantom of the Opera*.'

'Most women like the Phantom,' he said. 'Hard to understand why though. I think it must be the mask.'

She smiled. 'Women like secrets.'

'So do men.' He gave her a look that just about set her on fire. 'I found out what those flowers stand for.'

The acacia. She'd already forgotten.

'That was an awesome message on the card. You're quite a poet.'

'Oh, not really,' Bobbi said, searching her brain for a new topic.

'So, got a favourite?'

'Oh . . .' Her mind was a blank. What kind of guy asked questions like this? Oh, yeah. One who wanted to know more about her, who wasn't a bad boy, one who was perfect. *You have to impress this man.*

She should tell him the truth right now, about how she hadn't paid attention in English class, how she'd jumped from school to school and job to job trying to decide what she wanted to be when she grew up. She tried to pull up some poet's name from her mental computer, but this was hard. She blurted out, 'Jane Austen.'

His eyes widened in surprise. Uh-oh. 'I didn't know she wrote poems. You learn something new every day.'

'Yeah,' Bobbi agreed. Where had she heard of Jane Austen?

Too late to retrieve her misstep now. And he was on to new conversational territory. 'I bet you're into those movies they made out of her books.'

Now she remembered: Jane Austen wrote books. Hope loved her books. Well, Jane probably wrote poems, too.

'My sister is big into those movies,' Jason was saying. 'Too slow for me. I'm more of a *Die Hard* man.'

Finally, something she knew. 'Me, too,' she agreed. 'Didn't you love the last one?'

'Oh, yeah. I like action.'

She knew they had a ton in common. 'Me too.'

He cocked his head. 'I've never met anyone quite like you. You're beautiful, talented, smart—just too good to be true.'

'That's me,' she said lightly, and vowed to work on getting smart as soon as she found her library card.

After lunch with Bobbi Walker, Jason went to see how things were going at the site of the two duplexes A-1 Construction was building on the outskirts of town. Duke Powers, his right-hand man, looked up from his clipboard and greeted Jason with a jealous smirk. 'So, how was it?'

'Great. Did you get hold of Barrett? Are they delivering the rest of those two-by-fours today or not?'

Duke frowned. 'Not. He claims they're short on guys.'

'The only thing those clowns are short on is brains.'

'Speaking of brains, what's the verdict?'

Jason smiled. 'This one's got 'em.'

'So, it looks like you've finally graduated from bimbos,' said Duke. 'Think you can bring this one home to Mom and Dad?'

'Oh, yeah.' This woman had keeper written all over her. She was perfect: easy on the eye just like her sister, fun and smart. And obviously the driving force behind the flower shop.

'Hey, if things don't work out and she wants a real man . . .'

Jason looked round. 'Where? Anyway, there's no way I'm introducing her to you. She'll take one look at you, see what kind of friends I have, and dump me before we even have a second date.'

'That I'll bet you already set up.'

Jason smiled. 'Sunday.'

'Sunday? What's wrong with Saturday night? Does she turn into a werewolf or something?'

'Sunday night is some kind of dancing at the Grange Hall.'

'Dancing? Since when do you dance?'

'Since now.'

Duke shook his head. 'A hot chick going out with a klutz-foot like you. Man, what a waste.'

'She doesn't think so.'

'And that makes me think this chick isn't as smart as you think she is,' Duke said with a grin.

Five

EASTER WEEKEND had been wet, so Amber opted out of the annual egg hunt at Grandview Park, instead giving Seth a hunt inside their tiny cabin. Ty had taken the car in to get fixed on Monday, then it had rained again Tuesday and Wednesday.

But this was Thursday, she didn't have to work, and Heart Lake was getting a sun break. So, she and Seth began their garden adventure with a visit to the Trellis, the town's nursery.

There was something calming about walking past all those bushes and trees, and trays of flowers. Amber spotted a line of little red wagons and got one for Seth. 'You can pull the wagon for our seeds and things. OK?'

She got a grown-up wagon so she could carry their heavier purchases. It didn't take long to find the things she needed. Amber watched the mounting total as the clerk rang up her purchases and tried not to panic: garden gloves, seeds, chicken manure and two spades—one for her and one for Seth. Yikes! It sure cost a lot of money to save money on food. At least she already had an old shovel. It would do fine for working fertiliser into the ground.

As she handed over her charge card, she reminded herself what a good thing this garden was going to be: fresh air, organic food, something fun to do with Seth. And it was better than hanging round the house watching Ty mope.

Seth bounced ahead of her as they made their way back to the car, singsonging, 'We're gonna garden, we're gonna garden.'

This will be fun, she told herself, trying to work up to her son's level of enthusiasm. But it wasn't fun, really. The fertiliser bags were heavy and a real pain to haul to their garden plot. And the stuff was stinky. And, good grief, who'd have thought it was such hard work shovelling dirt? The earlier rains had made the ground sodden, and it felt like she was working cement. It wasn't work for Seth. He was having a great time using his new spade to fling soil and manure everywhere.

A fat raindrop hit her nose. 'We'd better hurry,' she told Seth.

Taking her at her word, he began to toss spadefuls of dirt in the air. The rain was really coming down now. Suddenly, something splattered the side of her head, getting in her hair and on her face.

'Enough, Sethie,' she cried. 'It's time to go home.'

'No,' protested Seth, his voice suddenly tearful.

'We'll come back.'

In about a million years. At the car, she loaded up the shovel and spades and threw the gardening gloves into the trunk after them. The pouring rain pelted her and she could feel a river of dirt trickling down her neck. Ick, ick, ick!

This was insane and she was going to stop the insanity now. She would see if she could get some more hours at the bakery, or she'd make cookies and sell them at the farmer's market and use the extra money for groceries. But the garden thing was not happening.

'Can we go tomorrow?' asked Seth from the back seat.

His cheeks were rosy. He looked so cute in his yellow rubber boots. She felt like a rat for not wanting to ever see that stupid garden again. 'We'll see,' she said.

They got back and Seth ran ahead of her into the house. Ty was already making lunch for them. It was something he'd started doing on the days she worked, and the part-time lunch service had evolved into an everyday offering. It was one of the few things he did that showed her deep inside he hadn't lost hope, that he wasn't completely ready to give up on life. On them.

He sent Seth to his room to peel off his muddy clothes. Then he took a look at Amber. 'Whoa. New look?'

Ha, ha. 'I've got chicken poop in my hair,' she informed him, and kept moving to the bathroom, pulling off her jacket.

Ty followed her in. 'What happened?'

'We were shovelling in the chicken manure. Seth got carried away. I hate gardening!' She pulled off her sweatshirt. 'And I spent a ton of money,' she finished on a wail.

'Hey, at least you're doing something.'

Next thing she knew Ty was pulling her to him to comfort her— something he hadn't done since those early days when they first saw trouble looming outside their little restaurant.

It made her cry all the harder, for what they'd had and lost, for where they were now.

'It's OK,' he said. 'Forget the garden.'

'Mommy?' Seth stood in the doorway, stripped down to his Spider-Man underwear, his round little face tight with worry.

She and Ty pulled apart like they'd been caught doing something wrong. 'It's OK, sweetie,' she said to Seth. 'Go let Daddy feed you lunch while Mommy takes a shower. OK?'

'Come on, bud,' Ty said, steering Seth out of the room.

She piled her dirty clothes on the floor and charged into the shower. After three shampoos, she almost felt normal. But normal these days wasn't necessarily that good. She put on clean clothes, and joined the boys in the kitchen.

Ty had made panini with some day-old bread she'd brought home from the bakery. This particular sandwich was one of Ty's creations—a panini with mozzarella, red onions, tomatoes, a dash of Dijon mustard and some basil.

She sank her teeth in and felt instantly consoled. 'This is great.'

'Thanks,' he said.

Another bite restored her equilibrium. 'I can't quit.' She'd already invested in seeds and gardening tools and put down her deposit on the garden plot.

He cocked an eyebrow. 'Sure you can. There's nothing wrong with quitting. Isn't that what you told me?'

The bit of sandwich she'd just swallowed stuck in her throat.

He got up, took his plate into the living room, and turned on the TV. She followed him.

She sat down on the couch opposite her husband, who was staring at the TV screen. 'Are you comparing a garden to that restaurant?' she demanded, her voice low. *That restaurant.* Bad choice of words. She could see his jaw tighten.

'Don't start,' he said.

This was pointless. She went back to the kitchen and Seth. 'After lunch, we'll take a rest and then when we wake up we'll colour. How does that sound?'

Seth smiled and nodded.

She couldn't let her life keep getting away from her like this, she just couldn't. She grabbed a pencil from the jar of pens and pencils she kept by the phone on the kitchen counter, then picked up a yellow legal pad. She plopped on the couch and drew a big square. Over it she wrote: Amber's Garden. Then she began to plan.

By one on Saturday afternoon, all of the Heart Lake High students had been in to pick up their flowers for the dance. Hope expected the afternoon to be relatively quiet, so she gave her sister some money and set her free to enjoy a much-deserved break.

'Are you sure?' Bobbi asked. 'I don't mind staying.'

'You have to work tonight. Scram.'

'You talked me into it. I'll see if Jason likes coffee.'

Bobbi was barely out the door when a young couple entered the shop. Even before she saw the ring on the woman's finger, Hope knew they were engaged. Everything about them said it. They were here to order flowers for their wedding.

'We've heard you're the best,' said the groom-to-be.

'I do love doing flowers for weddings,' Hope told them, and seated them at her little wrought-iron table. She fetched her laptop and joined them. 'What are your colours?'

'Red and orange,' said the bride.

Well, there was a new one. 'We could do your bouquet in red and orange roses,' she suggested.

'Oh, I like that,' said the bride. 'Roses are my favourite flower.'

It didn't take long to settle on flowers for the boutonnières, the tossing bouquet, the chapel and the reception.

Her customers left, beaming, and she smiled as she put their deposit cheque in her cash register. 'Life is good,' she reminded herself. She happened to look out the window to see Jason Wells walking down the street, talking into his cellphone. He was smiling. Was he talking to Bobbi?

She would be happy for them if they fell in love. Jason would never have a dull moment with Bobbi, and Bobbi would have a dependable man. And Hope would have a nice brother-in-law: a win-win situation for everyone. So, she should feel like a winner. She drummed her fingers on the countertop. It wasn't even two yet and she always stayed open until four on Saturdays, but she needed garden therapy right now, today, or her heart would explode.

She turned the sign on her door to Closed.

Then she drove to the Trellis and bought basil, coriander, dill and nasturtiums, which would give her pretty orange blossoms to use in salads. She enjoyed growing garden goodies for cooking, and now that her appetite had returned she was looking forward to spending time in the kitchen again. Others, like the baby's breath and the root beer plant, she'd dry and use for flower arrangements.

She left the nursery with a feeling of anticipation. It was sunny and warm. It would be the perfect day to start her garden.

Hope arrived at the community garden to find that she had neighbours. Their plots were to the east of hers, side by side. It looked like they were already on their way to becoming friends: an older woman and a woman who looked around Hope's age. The younger woman had a little boy beside her, playing in the soil. She was slim, clad in jeans and a black sweatshirt. She had long, brown hair and brown eyes and full lips. She looked familiar.

The older woman was slender and delicate. She was wearing the kind of smile that said, 'You want me for your grandma.' She was also wearing purple slacks and a floral blouse topped with an ancient-looking lavender sweatshirt. A straw sun hat shaded her eyes.

Hope walked over and set down her armload of goodies. 'Hi,' the younger woman greeted her.

'We were wondering who our neighbour might be,' said the grandmother.

Hope introduced herself.

'I'm Millie Baldwin,' said the grandmother, 'and this is Amber Howell.'

'And this is Seth,' Amber said, pointing to her son.

The little boy managed a happy hello.

'You look familiar,' Hope said to Amber.

'Ever come into the bakery?'

'Of course. I've seen you behind the counter.'

Amber nodded. 'That's me. I'm a lot more at home in the bakery than in the garden, let me tell you. Thank goodness I met Millie. She's going to be my garden guru and cure me of my disease.'

The word made Hope's heart catch. 'Disease?'

'Gardenus ickus.' Amber raised a hand, thumb up. 'I've got the world's biggest black thumb.'

Millie chuckled and Hope allowed herself to breathe again.

'The only difference between you and me, my dear, is that I've had more practice,' Millie told Amber. She smiled at Hope and peered at her box. 'And what are you growing? Oh, I see herbs!'

Hope ran a finger over a feathery dill plant. 'I like to cook. And I'm a florist. Some of these I'll dry.'

'Do you work at that florist shop downtown?' asked Amber.

'Actually, I own it.'

'How lovely!' cried Millie. 'I always thought it would be fun to have a flower shop. But between my family and my garden and my church activities, I wouldn't find the time. Owning a business is a lot of work.'

Amber's smile shrivelled, and Hope couldn't help wondering what nerve Millie had accidentally hit.

Millie obviously saw the change, too. 'Well,' she said briskly, 'now, thanks to Amber, I can get started planting. Although you really didn't need to turn the soil for me. I could have done it.'

Amber brought back her smile. 'I needed the exercise.'

The women set to work laying out their gardens. Hope felt soothed by the sun and the sound of Millie's voice as she coached Amber. 'I think your pumpkin and zucchini would do better if you plant them in little hills. Yes, that looks about right. Now, make six little holes round the mound. Lovely. Drop in the seeds. You'll be able to make wonderful zucchini bread with your harvest.'

As the day moved on, Hope learned a lot about the other two women. Millie had moved to Heart Lake from back east and was helping her daughter with her two children. But she seemed lonely, happy to have other women to talk to.

'I miss being near my mom,' said Amber.

'Me, too,' said Hope. Florida sometimes felt like the other side of the world. 'Do you and your daughter do a lot of cool stuff together on the weekends?' she asked Millie.

'Debra is awfully busy,' Millie hedged. 'Anyway,' she added, 'a woman should always have a life of her own, no matter how much she loves her children.'

Hope could see Amber frowning in disapproval. Their gazes met and an unspoken agreement flashed between them. They would make sure this woman felt wanted and appreciated. That wouldn't be hard. Millie was a sweetie.

Millie was the first to quit. 'Well, I think it's about time to go home,' she said, straightening and stretching out her back. 'I'm afraid I don't have the stamina I did at seventy.'

'You're older than seventy?' asked Amber.

Millie smiled. 'I'll be seventy-seven come June.'

Hope vowed right then to make Millie a birthday bouquet.

'Wow. You're amazing,' Amber said. 'I hope I'm in as good shape as you when I'm your age.'

'I'm sure you will be,' Millie said. 'You young girls all work so hard at staying fit.'

Millie said her goodbyes, and the two women watched as she climbed into a big boat of a car with a dented bumper and sailed off.

'Mommy, I want to go home,' said Seth. 'I'm hungry.'

'OK. Let's go see if Daddy's got dinner ready.'

'Your husband cooks for you?' asked Hope.

'Sometimes.'

'Lucky you.'

'Yeah. Lucky me.' Amber's smile was tinged with melancholy. 'OK, Sethie. Pick up your truck. Nice meeting you,' she said to Hope. 'See you next weekend?'

Hope nodded and watched as Amber led her son away. Interesting neighbours she had here at the community garden.

That night Hope dreamed about her garden. The dill grew waist high, and some of Millie's English garden seeds migrated to her plot and produced a wondrous flower chorus.

She woke up with the morning sun kissing her cheek. With a dream like that, she simply had to have a wonderful day.

It began with a favourite ritual. On Sundays Bobbi wandered down from Apartment 302 in the Lake Vista Apartments to have lunch with Hope in number 103. Hope always made a soup or salad and served it with wholewheat bread from the bakery, and Bobbi brought dessert. Today's offering was chocolate from the Chocolate Bar, the new chocolateria in town.

'Tonight's the night,' Bobbi said, setting out a pink box of truffles. 'We are going line dancing at the Grange.'

No need to ask who the 'we' was. Hope reached for a chocolate. She'd have just one. 'So, he's already getting the dance test.'

'Why not? Anyway, we couldn't exactly go out last night.'

'Did you give him a reason for why you couldn't go?'

Bobbi took a truffle. 'I played it mysterious and said I had plans.' She closed her eyes and sighed. 'He is gorgeous.'

'Amen to that,' Hope said. She needed another truffle.

'We talked on the phone for an hour yesterday.'

Hope remembered watching Jason, smiling as he talked into his cellphone. She popped another truffle. 'What did you talk about?'

'Just silly stuff. Where we grew up, what we like to do for fun.' She frowned. 'He likes to hike. That is not a plus.'

Bobbi watched Hope put a fourth truffle in her mouth. 'Are you on a chocolate bender or something?'

Hope looked at the box. There was only one left. She took that and ate it, too. 'No. Just in the mood for chocolate. Life's uncertain; eat dessert first.'

'Not funny,' Bobbi said. 'Not after what we just went through with you.'

'Sorry. I guess I should have said that I'm just trying to live life to the fullest like you're always telling me to do.'

Bobbi grinned. 'Better your hips than mine.' She looked at her watch. 'I'd better get going. I need to clean my place.'

No need to ask why. Of course she'd invite Jason over after they were done dancing. Well, good for her.

Then Bobbi was gone and the apartment was quiet. The sun was out, the air was spring warm, and Hope was on chocolate overload. Time for a walk.

She grabbed her sweatshirt and took off, her destination the Grand Forest, a nineteen-acre stretch of land that had been bought by the Heart Lake Land Trust. Walking through stands of Douglas fir, red cedar, hemlock and broadleaf maple trees always restored her equilibrium. Sometimes she'd see a deer regarding her cautiously from a clearing. And sometimes she'd meet other people, walkers with a dog on a leash, joggers. Today, she encountered . . . oh, good grief.

Jason Wells stopped in front of her. 'Well, hi,' he said.

'Hi,' she said. 'Nice day to be out,' she added.

He looked around them, smiling. 'Yeah. This is a pretty cool place. Your sister's not with you?'

Hope shook her head. 'No, she had some things to do. I believe she's getting ready to turn you into Patrick Swayze.'

'I think I'm in trouble.'

'Don't worry,' Hope teased. 'She'll make it painless.' Suddenly, she was out of words. She managed a breezy 'I'd better get going,' and started backing away.

Next thing she knew a sneaky branch had reached out and tripped her. She went over a log with a yelp, landing with her feet in the air. Getting upright was easier said than done.

Jason reached a hand towards her. 'Here, let me help.'

She took his hand and he pulled her to her feet.

'You OK?'

'I guess I need to get my steering checked,' she said, making him smile. 'I'm not normally clumsy,' she added.

'You sure you're OK?'

'I'm fine. Thanks. Nice running into you,' she stammered.

He grinned. 'Same here.'

She started walking—forwards this time. She could hear him striding away.

Get a grip, she scolded herself. Hope realised she was suddenly tired. What she needed was a cup of herbal tea and a good book. No Jane Austen today. A murder mystery, a gory one.

In his jeans, white shirt and boots, Jason Wells looked like he was born to dance. Boy, are looks deceiving, thought Bobbi. Even simple steps eluded him. But he was good-natured, laughing as he turned the wrong way or bumped into someone.

'I think I need private lessons,' he said as they sat back down at their table and dived into their lemonades.

'I think that could be arranged,' she said coyly.

'Tonight?'

She hadn't cleaned her apartment for nothing. 'Maybe.'

Half an hour later they were on their way to her place. 'I was walking not far from here today,' he said as he parked his truck. 'In your Grand Forest.'

'Oh,' she said, trying to sound interested.

'I ran into your sister.'

That wasn't surprising. Bobbi had never understood what Hope found so exciting about wandering around in the woods.

'I thought maybe I'd see you with her. Do you like to hike?'

'Who doesn't?' There. She hadn't lied.

Inside her apartment, she settled Jason at the kitchen table, then set out milk with cookies from the bakery.

'These are good,' he said, holding up a half-consumed ginger cookie. 'Did you make them?'

'I love to bake.' She slid the plate towards him. 'Have another.'

He swallowed the last of his cookie and got up slowly. 'So, how about that dance lesson?'

'OK.' She led him to the living room. 'Maybe we should try it without music first so we can go slow.'

She placed herself by his side, ready to help him master the concept of heel-toe, but he caught her round the waist and pulled her to him. 'What if I don't want to go slow?'

'We could speed things up a little,' she said with a smile. She let him kiss her. And that was the end of the dance lesson.

By the time he left, Bobbi was dizzy with love. This man was perfect. Well, other than the fact that he had two left feet and that he liked to stomp around in the woods, they were a perfect match.

On Monday at Changing Seasons Floral, Hope had the Easter inventory to mark down, a cooler case to stock and orders to fill. And it seemed like everyone in Heart Lake wanted to stop in to visit.

'The flowers you did for my mom's ninetieth birthday were gorgeous,' said Judy Lyle, one of her favourite customers.

'And was the party a big hit?' Hope asked.

'With my chocolate-fudge cake? How could it not be?' Judy produced a foil-wrapped package. 'I saved you a piece.'

The last thing Hope wanted was more chocolate. She'd give it to Bobbi—restitution for eating all the truffles. 'That was really sweet of you. You're great.'

Judy smiled, looking like a senior-citizen pixie. 'I know.'

She left the shop and two more customers wandered in. 'It's so gloomy out today. We need flowers,' said one.

'Tulips,' said the other.

'Tulips are perfect for a gloomy day,' Hope said with a smile.

'Especially if they come from Changing Seasons. I swear, your flowers last forever.'

'Only if they're silk,' Hope quipped.

Bobbi arrived at noon, ready and willing to work. But first . . . 'I want to send a card,' she said. The front of the card was a collage of flowers. The inside was blank. 'What would you say to a man if you'd had an incredible evening together?'

Hope swallowed a little bud of envy. 'The possibilities are endless. So, you had a good time. Does that mean he can dance?'

Bobbi made a face. 'Barely.' Her expression turned dreamy. 'But he has no problem with slow dancing.' She scrabbled in her handbag and came up with a pen.

'Hmm.' Hope tried to focus. '"Two bodies swaying."'

'Oooh, that's good,' Bobbi approved, and began to write.

'"Two hearts feeling the same beat, moving as one."' Hope closed her eyes and got a vision of herself in Jason's arms.

'That's good. What next?'

'I don't know. I'm out of ideas.'

'You're never out of ideas. Come on. Let's come up with something that says I want to see him again.'

'Hmm. OK, how about this? "We're just learning the steps, we've barely begun."'

'Oh, yeah. It rhymes! That's great.'

'And maybe sign it, "Let's keep dancing."'

Bobbi was just stuffing the card in the envelope when the shop door jangled and in walked Jason. She hid the card behind her back.

'You look like a woman with a secret,' he teased.

Bobbi produced the card and handed it to him. 'I was going to mail you this.'

'Yeah?' He opened the envelope, pulled out the card and read, a grin spreading across his face. He pointed a finger at Bobbi. 'You've really got a gift. You know that?'

Her cheeks turned rose-petal pink. 'Oh, not really,' she said. 'So, what brings you to the shop?'

He tapped his watch. 'Lunchtime. I thought maybe you could take a break.' He smiled at Hope. 'How about it?'

He was asking her to join them? Of course she'd be a good sister and turn down the offer. But her spirits lifted all the same.

'You wouldn't mind watching the shop for an hour, would you?' he continued. 'I promise I'll bring her back by one.'

Of course he hadn't been inviting her along. What had she been thinking? 'No problem,' she said. 'Have fun.'

They barely heard her as they sailed out of the door.

'So, how about going out with me this weekend?' Jason asked Bobbi as they sat in Sweet Somethings, digging into sandwiches made of freshly baked sourdough bread.

'How about Sunday?' Bobbi offered.

'Friday,' he countered. 'We could catch a movie.'

'I'm kind of booked Friday.' Now he'd try for Saturday. No chance of getting Saturday night off. *Take Friday.* If you turn him down for both days, he'll want to know why. 'But I think I can change my plans,' she added. She'd find someone to cover for her.

'Great,' he said.

'That new movie, *Bomb Squad*, is opening,' Bobbi suggested. She could tell by his expression that she'd hit it on the nose.

'Works for me,' he said. 'How about lunch tomorrow?'

She was making it too easy for him. 'Sorry. I've got plans.'

'I guess I'll have to wait till Friday then.'

Anticipation was a good thing. Men loved the thrill of the hunt, and she didn't want to deny him that. Funny, she was so good at hooking men, but keeping them on the hook was another matter. Probably because she never seemed to find the perfect man.

This time you have, she reminded herself.

Jason was certainly hooked Friday night. He had no desire to end their date with just a movie—a very good sign.

But his choice of how to continue the evening nearly gave her a heart attack. 'How about going over to the Last Resort for a drink? I've been meaning to check the place out.'

All she needed was to go in there with Jason and have the other waitresses asking her how she was enjoying her night off. 'I've got a better idea,' she said. 'How about coming back to my place? I've got chocolate cake.'

'That's even better,' he said with a smile.

She was feeling pretty smug about how she'd dodged that bullet, and watching him devour the cake she'd picked up from the bakery, when he pointed to her *People* magazine and idly observed, 'So, you like to read?'

'Oh, yeah.'

He looked round the apartment. 'Where are your books?'

Books? *Umm.* 'They're still in boxes,' she improvised.

'Oh, you haven't been here that long?' He looked confused. Probably wondering how she could be new in town and own a flower shop.

'Not in this apartment.' That was no lie. This apartment had become available and the idea of being neighbours with her sister had sounded like fun. 'I need to get a bookcase,' she added.

'I could make you one. I make all kinds of stuff.'

'Well, then, I'll take one. Thanks. That's so sweet.' What was she going to fill it with?

Saturday morning found Bobbi at the Heart Lake Library for the Friends of the Library book sale, frantically stocking up on books to supplement her meagre supply. So far she'd found a money management one for dummies (she needed that), two fitness books, a Martha

Stewart tome on decorating, and a great cookbook that was nothing but chocolate recipes. She'd even picked up a Jane Austen novel—*Pride and Prejudice*.

'That will be six dollars,' said the woman taking the money.

'A steal,' said a deep voice behind Bobbi.

She gave a guilty start and turned to see Jason. He was wearing baggy shorts, a sweatshirt with the sleeves ripped off and tennis shoes. He looked like he was getting ready to go running or work out at the gym—both preferable to being here, catching her buying props for her apartment.

'I see you're taking advantage of the sale,' he said.

'Absolutely.' She nodded vigorously. 'You, too?'

'Yep. I was on my way to the gym when I saw the sign outside. By the way, your bookcase should be done by next Saturday. Want me to come over and help you fill it?'

'Sure,' she said. What she had here was not going to fill a bookcase. Then she remembered Hope had just filled a box to donate to the library. Maybe a few of those books could take a little detour to Bobbi's apartment.

Bobbi left Hope's apartment after lunch on Sunday carrying a box of books and vowing to read every one.

'Do you really think you can sit still long enough?' Hope teased.

'I can try,' Bobbi replied with a grin.

Hope shut her apartment door with a sigh. Bobbi needed to just be herself. If the man didn't like Bobbi for who she was then he wasn't the right one. It was silly to build up a false image.

Hope thought of her fake breast. That was different, she told herself. She wasn't trying to get a man. The second operation after the complication of a capsular contracture had gone better, but it wasn't hard to spot which boob was the patch job and which one was the original. Still, she wasn't out to do any false advertising. She was just trying to get her life back.

And she was glad to be alive. Glad. To prove it, she got her gardening tools and drove to the community garden.

She arrived to find Millie Baldwin there. Millie pointed to Hope's pale green sweatshirt. 'That's almost too pretty for the garden. And such a flattering colour.'

Millie made it sound like Hope really looked special. That was stretching it. Even before the cancer she'd been just OK. She had nice eyes to make up for the snub nose she hated, an OK mouth. Good legs. But stand her next to Bobbi and she disappeared.

'Thanks,' she murmured. 'Are all your flowers planted now?' She motioned to the little stakes capped with empty seed packets.

'Almost. I'd love to plant lavender, but it's silly to plant a perennial in a community garden, in case I have to swap plots or something. Such a shame, though. I have the best recipe for lavender cookies.'

'If it's any consolation, you can get lavender sugar at Kizzy's Kitchen,' Hope said.

'I'll remember that,' said Millie. 'Although I'm not sure lavender cookies will go over big with my grandchildren. Carrot cookies certainly didn't. Maybe I'll give the recipe to Amber, our resident baker,' Millie added. 'I'd love to be able to pass it on to someone.'

'I'm sure Amber would love the recipe, and so would I.'

As they chatted, Hope felt her frustrations slipping away. A couple of mothers had brought their children to the play area, and the sound of laughter danced on the air and lulled her.

And then the lull ended. 'I imagine a pretty girl like you has got a boyfriend waiting for you to finish up here and go do something with him,' said Millie.

'No boyfriend,' said Hope. 'I'm too busy with my shop.'

'Oh.' Millie appeared nonplussed.

Hope could feel Millie studying her. 'I . . .' She had no idea how to finish her sentence.

'It's none of my business,' Millie said quickly.

Now Millie thought she was a loser. She didn't want that. 'I'm still putting my life back together. I was sick.'

'Oh, I'm sorry,' Millie said, her voice filled with concern. She offered a gentle smile. 'You look the picture of health now.'

Hope shrugged. 'So far, so good.'

'I hope it's not something that can come back.'

'It could. Right now I'm in remission.' Hope regretted the words the minute they slipped out. Such a dead giveaway. And what was she doing sharing personal stuff with someone she hardly knew?

'What kind of cancer did you have, dear?'

'Breast.'

Suddenly, bitter words wanted to spill out of Hope's mouth. It wasn't fair. Who in her twenties got cancer? That happened to older women,

women who'd had a chance for husbands and children and . . . Hope bit her lip.

'You've been very blessed,' Millie said. 'You're still here. God must have important things for you to do in that flower shop.'

Millie's gentle reminder sweetened the bitter waters. Hope wasn't sure about many things, but the fact that she was doing something good with her life was one she was sure of.

'And someone very special waiting in the wings.'

Right. To want someone with a scarred body and a questionable life span, the guy would have to be way beyond special. Hope shook her head. 'I don't know about that.'

'I do,' Millie said, a smile in her voice. 'You'll see.'

Six

APRIL BOWED OUT to May, which entered Heart Lake bearing perfect weather. Amber came home from work one day to find her son with an overload of energy needing to be burned, and her husband ready for a break. She decided to take Seth to check their garden.

They arrived to find Millie already there, digging away in the damp earth with her garden spade.

She smiled and waved at the sight of Amber and Seth.

'How are our gardens?' Amber looked at her plot. Lots of little green things were popping out. 'Look at all the veggies we've got growing!'

'I'm afraid many of those are weeds,' Millie informed her. 'And it looks like the slugs have gotten some of your crop.'

Amber looked close and saw nibbled-down greens.

'Bring some of the grounds from those coffee drinks you're making and sprinkle them round your plants,' suggested Millie. 'That will keep the slugs away.'

'Really?'

'I got my truck,' Seth announced before Millie could say more. He held up his prized Tonka truck for her to see.

She nodded. 'Very handy for hauling away weeds.'

He beamed. But then he cried out, 'Look, Mommy, a bunny!' and ran towards it.

The rabbit took off, and Seth began peering under bushes.

'He's a sweet child,' Millie commented. 'And all those lovely golden curls. Does he take after his father?'

'Well, in looks. Thank God that's all,' Amber said, and immediately felt like a heel. 'I shouldn't say that. Ty's not a bad guy. Right now he's not much fun to be around. He still hasn't found a job.'

'Well,' Millie said thoughtfully, 'didn't you tell me that your restaurant closed down?'

'Yeah. And we were supposed to come up here to make a new start. The only one really making any kind of new start is me. Oh, he makes lunch every day. Big whoop.'

'Considering how depressed he probably is, I think it might actually be a big whoop,' Millie said thoughtfully.

Amber protested, '*I'm* at the bakery three days a week at eight a.m. *I'm* growing the garden. I'm even going to start selling cookies at the farmers' market.' With each word she could hear the anger building. 'Ty only went out to look for a job once last week.'

'Maybe because he's battle weary and he's lost his armour.'

Surely Millie wasn't comparing Ty to a knight in shining armour. 'Oh, come on.'

'I know it sounds corny, but every man wants to provide for his family and protect them. Your husband is no exception. He's failed at both. That has to have hit him pretty hard.'

'But that's no excuse for doing nothing.'

'Of course not,' Millie agreed. 'But it is an explanation. It's hard for a person who is depressed to motivate himself to do anything.'

'Hey, I'm depressed, too,' protested Amber.

'There are some things we women simply don't understand about our men. They need to be able to provide for us, even in this day and age. If a man can't provide for his family, he doesn't feel like a man. It's as if he's gone to war and lost a limb.'

'Lots of men learn to cope without an arm or leg.'

'Yes, they do. But I suspect what your husband really needs before he can fight the world again is his armour.'

That again. 'Well, tell me where the nearest shining armour shop is and I'll be happy to get him some.'

Millie beamed at her. 'Well, it's quite simple really. The armour is your faith in him, your encouragement.'

That wasn't fun to digest. Amber spent the next ten minutes stabbing the dirt, pulling weeds and brooding. Millie wisely kept quiet. 'I don't see why I have to be the one to make all the effort,' Amber said at last. 'He needs to man up.'

'It's been my experience that men sometimes need help with that. What was your husband like before your restaurant failed?'

Amber took in a deep breath of spring air. The fragrance of newly mowed grass drifted their way along with the hum of the mower. She could close her eyes and remember other smells—the smells in the kitchen of their little restaurant: garlic and seared beef and salmon. She could almost hear the hiss of the pots on the big stove, and Ty's laughter.

His grandfather had been a chef who'd owned his own restaurant. Ty had inherited his grandfather's flair for food. His dad had become a teacher, but he loved the idea of his son owning a restaurant. In fact, both families had been more than happy to support them. In spite of all the hands willing to catch them, the fall from that lofty, hopeful high had been humiliating.

Amber took in a deep breath. 'He was a happy man. Lots of big dreams, you know. He was fun to be around. Everybody liked him.'

'Including you.'

'Including me. I don't like him much right now, though. In fact, I don't even know if I love him any more.'

'Well, it seems to me that love is ninety-nine per cent doing. If you keep doing love, the feeling might grow back.'

Seth came over with a handful of what Amber hoped were weeds. 'Look at all the weeds I got, Mommy.'

'Good job, Sethie,' she told him.

Millie let out a sigh and checked her watch. 'Oh, look at the time. I need to get going. Don't forget about the coffee grounds.'

'I won't. And thanks. For everything.'

Millie smiled at her. 'You're going to be fine, dear. I know it.'

Amber stayed at the community garden a little longer, idly pulling weeds and thinking about the man she'd married. Things couldn't get much worse. Did she have enough energy to try just a little harder to make them better?

They returned home to find Ty brooding on the couch, scowling over an old issue of *Bon Appétit*.

'Daddy, we saw a bunny today,' Seth announced.

Ty rubbed a hand across his stubbled chin. 'A rabbit, that'll be good for your garden.'

His negative words didn't do much for Amber's new determination to take Millie's advice. She had to force herself to walk over to the couch. She pulled out the memory of their first night back from their honeymoon and in their new apartment, envisioned Ty and herself making chicken for their first dinner, then eating it while they unpacked boxes. And kissed. They hadn't eaten much that night, and they didn't get very many boxes unpacked. But after she went to bed, he had stayed up half the night setting up her kitchen for her.

She bent down and kissed him on the cheek.

'What was that for?' he asked suspiciously.

'Just a thank-you for being a good man.'

He looked at her with eyebrows raised. 'Uh. Thanks.'

She didn't say anything more. She simply went to the bedroom to change. She hadn't exactly given her husband an entire emotional suit of armour, but it was a beginning.

It dawned on Millie when her grandson came home that it wouldn't hurt her to take some of her own advice.

When he plopped on the couch to play his video game, she plopped right next to him. 'You know, that looks like fun,' she lied. 'How about showing me how to play?'

'Sure,' he agreed. He plugged in a second set of controls and walked her through the intricate how-tos.

So many buttons to push, so much to remember! It seemed she barely got her man on the screen when Eric killed him. 'Eric the Punisher strikes again,' she moaned, making him laugh.

The game was ridiculous, but she didn't care. She was sitting beside her grandson, doing something together. That was priceless.

Emily came in with her best friend, Sarah. 'Gram, what are you doing?'

'Just playing a game,' Millie said.

'OK,' Emily said dubiously. They disappeared up the stairs.

At five o'clock the phone rang. Millie knew before she answered it that it was Debra, calling to say she'd be home late.

'Some of the women in my department are going out for dinner. Ben won't be coming to get the kids until tomorrow. Do you mind keeping an eye on things tonight?'

'Not at all. You need to get out.'

Although Debra hadn't been home much at all that week. She had to work late. She had to run errands. She had to get her hair cut. She had to go shopping. Home was not a place of refuge for her daughter. It was a reminder of failure and responsibility to be borne alone. Not totally true, since her ex-husband took the children every other weekend. But he wasn't there in the trenches with her every day.

'Thanks,' said Debra. 'Oh, and Emily had asked if Sarah could spend the night, but if it's going to be a problem having an extra kid around, you can tell her no.'

'That's not a problem,' said Millie.

'Thanks, Mom. I really need this. Love you.'

Millie could hear the gratitude in her daughter's voice and it made her feel good that she could help. Still, she hung up with a sigh. Debra was another garden that needed serious tending.

Debra was grumpy on Saturday morning, refusing the offer of pancakes and yelling at Emily, who was chasing her friend up and down the stairs in pursuit of the pink cellphone that held treasure—a boy on the other end of the line. Millie watched with concern as Debra poured herself a cup of coffee, then leaned against the kitchen counter gripping her cup like it held the elixir of life.

'I know I'm a grump. I had too much to drink last night.'

It wasn't a hangover that was responsible for her daughter's mood. Debra's ex-husband was due to pick up the children for the weekend. Millie made a wide berth around that subject.

Debra had been such a pretty girl. But this morning, with the dark circles under her eyes and the deepening frown lines between her brows, the prettiness was slipping away. 'But you had a good time?' Millie prompted.

'It was OK,' Debra said. She rubbed her forehead. 'I'm going to shower. Ben should be here soon.'

'I'll clean up,' Millie said.

'Thanks, Mom,' Debra said, and kissed her cheek.

It was a small, daughterly gesture, but it warmed Millie's heart.

She had just finished in the kitchen when the doorbell rang. It was Sarah's mother coming to collect her.

Next, Debra's ex arrived. 'Emily, your father's here,' Millie called up the stairs. Debra was still nowhere in sight.

Ben followed Millie into the living room and they took up positions on opposite ends of the couch.

Millie hadn't seen her son-in-law without the buffer of other people since the divorce. 'Would you like some coffee?'

'No, thanks.' He cleared his throat. 'Are you settling in out here OK?'

'Oh, yes.' And then, she couldn't help herself. 'Ben, I'm so sorry you and Debra couldn't work things out.'

'Maybe if she was more like you, we could have,' Ben said.

'Yeah, and maybe if you weren't a bastard, I would be more like my mother,' came an angry voice from the stairs.

Ben stood. 'I see you're your normal happy self.'

Debra walked into the room. She'd put on make-up but her angry expression ruined the effect.

Emily thumped down the stairs, dragging an overnight bag. 'Daddy!' she cried; she left the bag at the bottom of the stairs and ran to her father for a hug.

'Hey, Princess,' he said. 'Ready for some fun?'

'Oh, yeah.'

Eric was equally glad to see his dad.

This, Millie decided, was not the place for her. She slipped away to the kitchen. Five minutes later, the children were gone and Debra was in the kitchen, too. 'I'm going to run some errands,' she said.

'Why don't we do something fun today, maybe go out for lunch?' Millie offered.

'I can't, Mom. I've got too much to do,' Debra said as she left the kitchen. 'I don't know when I'll be back.'

A moment later, Millie heard the front door shut, and she was standing alone in the empty kitchen. What was she doing here? She threw the sponge in the sink and went to put on her garden clothes.

Amber was already at the community garden when she arrived. She greeted Millie with a smile.

'You look happy,' Millie said to her. 'Where's your son?'

'Home, playing with Dad.' She suddenly got busy examining her garden gloves. 'I probably didn't seem real open to advice yesterday, but I'm glad you gave it anyway. In fact, if you keep counselling me, you may just save my marriage.'

Just a few words, but they acted like soul vitamins. Someone appreciated her. Millie still wasn't sure what she was doing at her daughter's house, but she knew why she was here at this garden.

Seven

At 11 A.M. on Saturday morning, Jason was on Bobbi's doorstep with the bookcase he'd made, a cedar, contemporary ladder style where she could put both books and plants. She opened the door and gave him a real feast for the eyes: tight jeans, blonde hair caught up in a ponytail, and lips tinted pink, waiting to get kissed.

He was ready to learn more about how her mind worked. So far they'd been having a great time together. But he wanted more, he wanted depth. Those cards she kept giving him told him it was there somewhere under all that froth. Helping her load up her new bookcase was going to give him the perfect place to look.

Bobbi stepped onto the porch and ran a hand along the surface of the top shelf. 'It's gorgeous,' she breathed.

He could feel himself puffing up like a bullfrog. 'I'm glad you like it. Let's see what it looks like with your books on it.'

She stepped aside so he could carry it up to her apartment.

'I thought it might look good on that wall over there, by the window.' She pointed to where a box of books already sat. Next to that he saw another small stack of books.

As he settled the bookcase in its new home, Bobbi turned round and began to dig books out of the box. 'I hope they'll all fit.'

'If not, I'll just have to make another bookcase,' he said, and reached into the box. 'Do you have a particular order you want these to go in? Alphabetical? By category?'

'Just, well, um.' She began digging out books.

'You've got a lot of books on gardening,' he observed.

'There's a community garden at Grandview Park.'

Gardening and reading were solitary pursuits. Somehow, he had a hard time matching those hobbies with the vivacious Bobbi. She was a people person, a real party girl.

He flipped open a book. Inside he saw the name Hope Walker. 'This has your sister's name in it.'

She shrugged and said, 'We borrow back and forth a lot.'

He scooped up a trio of self-help books on time management and goal setting. 'Which one of you read these?'

Bobbi snatched them away. 'I was going through a phase.'

'A good phase to go through when you're starting a business,' he observed. 'So, got your whole life mapped out?'

'I wish,' she said. 'I'm just not sure what I want to do.'

'You mean the flower shop isn't what you want to do?'

'Oh, I love the shop,' she said quickly. 'I mean, well . . . it's complicated. Life is like that, isn't it?' she added breezily, shutting the door on the topic.

Now, that was interesting. Why didn't she want to talk more about her complicated life? Women always wanted to talk about their problems. He picked up another handful of books. Here was one on herbal medicine. And *Beating Breast Cancer with a Positive Attitude.* Whoa. Was this what she meant by complicated? Had Bobbi had breast cancer?

He studied Bobbi as she burrowed in the box. She was so sexy and full of energy. Jason thought it was pretty cool that she owned her own business, but maybe after having survived the disease she was re-evaluating her life. It was too early in the relationship to ask all the details, but he hoped she'd tell him soon.

The doorbell rang and Bobbi ran to get it.

She opened the door and there stood her sister, Hope, holding a cardboard box. 'I found some more books.' She caught sight of Jason. 'Oh, sorry. I didn't know you had company already.'

'Come on in.' Bobbi turned to Jason. 'We were just . . .'

'Putting together donations for the library,' Hope finished.

Jason took the box from Hope. 'So, you live nearby?'

'Thanks. Just downstairs.'

'Where do you want this?' Jason asked Bobbi.

'Put it by the bookcase. I'll sort through it later. Don't you love the bookcase Jason made?'

Hope moved to the bookcase. 'It's gorgeous. You've got a real talent,' she said to Jason. 'What else have you made?' She knelt in front of the books and began separating them into piles.

He joined her. 'I made a bed for my sister, and a rocking chair for my mom. I've done some wood carving.'

'That's amazing,' said Hope.

She was so earnest. Jason liked earnest in a woman. 'Thanks.'

'I love a man who can use his hands,' added Bobbi, plopping down next to Jason.

He tried to look modest. 'Everybody's got talent. You ladies work magic in that flower shop of yours.'

'We try,' said Hope, and Bobbi smiled at her.

These two were close. Had Hope been there for Bobbi when she had cancer? Probably. 'Looks like you've got a system going here,' he said, pointing to the piles in front of Hope.

'I like to sort books by category and then author,' she said. 'It's easier to find what you're looking for that way.'

'Great idea,' said Jason.

'That's how I like to do it, too.' Bobbi picked up a book.

'How about putting that one over here with your fiction?' Hope suggested.

Bobbi nodded and handed it over. 'I was just going to do that. You know, I think we should have some lunch,' she decided, jumping up. 'I've got pizza in the freezer. I'll throw it in the oven.'

'Oh, I can't stay,' Hope said. 'I've got things to do.'

'Are you sure?' asked Bobbi.

Jason could tell it was halfhearted, and he couldn't help smiling. Bobbi didn't want to share. He liked that.

'Yeah. Nice to see you,' Hope said to him, and smiled. She had a nice smile. It was quiet and warm.

'Same here,' he said, standing and lifting a hand in salute.

He settled back on the couch as Bobbi walked her to the door. Pizza for lunch sounded good. The sun was shining. Maybe he could parlay lunch into an afternoon hike in the Grand Forest.

'So,' he said later, 'what do you think about working off that pizza?'

'What did you have in mind?' she asked.

'How about a hike in the Grand Forest?' The smile died from her eyes. 'You like to hike, right?'

'Well, I have to be somewhere tonight and . . .'

Where did she have to be tonight, and with whom? It was still too early to be asking those kind of questions. But that didn't mean he wasn't dying to know who his competition was. 'Tonight is a long way away,' he said.

'You're right.' She stood up like a woman who had made a decision and was ready to act on it. 'Let's do it.'

It wasn't quite as good a response as 'Cool' or 'Sounds like fun,' but it was still a yes, so Jason decided he was good with that.

As they meandered along various trails under tall firs and cedars, Bobbi plied him with questions about the different hikes he'd done. Had he ever seen a bear? Had he ever been stung by bees? Did he ever worry about getting mugged? Not exactly the conversation of a seasoned hiker.

Suddenly, a vision of his encounter with her sister came to mind. Hope had been smiling, walking on the trail, lost in the experience.

Bobbi started chewing her lip as if working on a big decision. 'I should tell you, I haven't gone hiking since I got stung by bees.'

Hmm. She'd led him to believe she was into this kind of thing. Well, maybe she had been before she got stung. 'You can get stung by bees in the garden, too,' he pointed out.

'Not a whole nest of them.' She shuddered. 'But this is nice,' she added in a small voice. 'I'm having a good time.'

He smiled down at her. 'I'm glad.' He gently pulled her to him and kissed her.

Half an hour later they had reached the end of the trail. 'I think you helped me conquer my fear of bees,' Bobbi told him, giving him a smile.

'Good. How about we go out to dinner tonight and celebrate?'

She shook her head. 'I'm sorry. I've got a commitment.'

'Every Saturday?'

'For a while. But I'm free on Sunday. Want to try your hand at line dancing again?'

Not really, but for her he would. 'Why not?' he said.

He was about as excited over that as he was at having nothing to do on a Saturday night. Maybe he should have just come right out and asked Bobbi if he had competition.

'Still can't make the A-list, huh?' teased Duke when Jason called to see if he wanted to go out for a beer.

'You're funny,' said Jason.

Duke said amiably, 'Why dontcha come check out the action at the Last Resort? Those cocktail waitresses are hot.'

Jason wasn't interested in hot cocktail waitresses, not when he'd found the perfect woman. But he wasn't interested in sitting round watching TV on a Saturday night, either. So, nine o'clock found him threading his way through a sea of tables to where Duke sat.

'Hey, man,' Duke greeted him.

Jason sat down and looked round. The bar took up the far end of the room. The dance floor wasn't big. The place was packed with a mix of twenty-something couples and singles looking to end up as a couple before the evening was over. Two women sat at a table nearby nursing drinks as they checked out the neighbouring tables.

Duke smirked. 'I might give 'em a thrill. After I get this chick's phone number.' He nodded at the approaching waitress, all decked out in a short black skirt and a plunging halter-neck top. 'Don't get any ideas about this one. She's got Duke written all over her.'

Jason stared at the waitress. 'What the hell?'

Bobbi had been approaching the table at a good clip. She put on the brakes and stared at Jason. She made a fast recovery though, smiling at him and closing the distance. 'Fancy meeting you here.'

Her recovery was quicker than his. All he could do was gawk at her, his brain frozen. He turned to Duke as if his friend somehow had an explanation for why his perfect woman was slinging drinks in the local pickup place instead of . . . what? At least he now knew there wasn't somebody else.

'You guys know each other?' Duke asked.

'Yeah,' Jason said slowly. 'Why didn't you just tell me you worked on Saturday nights?' he asked Bobbi.

'This is the Sunday-night chick?' Duke asked, dismayed.

'I thought you wouldn't be real impressed if you knew I was a cocktail waitress.' She lifted one shoulder in an embarrassed shrug. 'But . . . I've got bills.'

Jason remembered the book on cancer he'd seen at her apartment. The poor kid was moonlighting to pay off medical bills. 'How do you manage to do this and work at the shop every day?' This woman needed someone to step in and take care of her.

She smiled her dimpled smile. 'Working at the shop's not working. That's fun.' And then she turned the thousand-watt charm on Duke, too. 'So is working here. What can I get you?'

'Heineken,' said Duke.

'I'll have a Hale's Pale Amber,' said Jason.

'Coming right up,' she said and hurried off.

Duke was frowning. 'I can't believe that's the woman you've been seeing. I thought you said she owned a flower shop. What's she doing working here?'

'You heard her. She's got bills.'

'What, she's got a shopping addiction?'

'She's got medical bills. I was helping her set up her bookcase today. She had a book on cancer.'

Duke let out a soft whistle. 'I can't believe it.'

'Me, neither,' said Jason. 'She's got so much energy.'

They both watched as Bobbi stopped at other tables, collecting empty glasses and fresh orders. Neither one said anything more until after she'd returned with their beers.

'I don't know,' Duke said as she walked away. 'It can't have been breast cancer. Those are real.' He took a swig of beer. 'I can't believe my cocktail babe is your flower chick.'

She'd known this was coming. Sooner or later, Jason had to come here. He'd been too polite to say anything rude, but Bobbi had seen his shocked expression. Everyone thought cocktail waitresses were dumb. But she had a brain and she'd prove it to him. She was going to read that Jane Austen book when she got home.

She went to turn in her orders to Don, the owner, who was tending bar. Anna Lane, another one of the waitresses, was frowning as she loaded up her cocktail tray.

'If that creep puts his hands on my butt one more time . . .'

'After this, I'm cutting him off,' Don said.

'Why don't you let me take that table?' Bobbi offered.

'No, I can handle him,' Anna said.

Bobbi wasn't so sure, so she kept an eye out as she served her tables. If that slimeball made one false move . . .

And there it was. Anna leaned over to lay a drink in front of his friend and got her butt patted in the process.

Anna straightened and said something. Slimeball held up both hands, feigning innocence.

Bobbi sailed off across the lounge, riding to the rescue.

She arrived at the table just in time to hear Anna say to the slimeball, 'You did, too, touch me.'

'You apologise to her right now,' Bobbi demanded.

'Whoa, it's Wonder Babe.' He picked up his drink.

'Yeah. Wonder Babe meets Slimeball.' Bobbi still had a drink on her tray. She dumped it into his lap.

Her surprise attack made him jump up. In the process, he bumped the table and sent his drink flying into a tipsy woman sitting with him and his friends.

'I want an apology,' yelled Slimeball.

'Maybe you should learn how to give one before you ask for one,' Bobbi retorted.

'Hey,' said his friend. He made a grab for Bobbi.

'Oh, dear,' gasped Anna.

Suddenly, there was another player. Jason had Bobbi firmly by the arm and was trying to lead her away, saying, 'My friend and I are ready for another drink.'

But the tipsy woman caught her other arm. 'Where do you think you're going? I want an apology.'

Two more guys from a neighbouring table joined the fray, and suddenly they had a major testosterone spill at the Last Resort, with male fists starting to fly in all directions.

'I think it would be a good idea if you went home sick,' Jason said, urging Bobbi along. She could hear a police siren.

Jason's friend was with him now, running interference. Brawlers bounced off him as Jason hustled Bobbi towards the door.

They were about to go out when the police came in.

'Just as well,' Jason's friend told her. 'You can tell the cops what happened. We saw everything. We'll back you up.'

And they did, which was good enough for the cops. But not good enough for Bobbi's boss.

'Bobbi, we need to talk,' Don told her when things settled down.

She knew what that meant.

'You know I like you,' he began. 'But if the cops come one more time, I'm out of business.' Don scratched his head. 'I wish I didn't have to let you go, but I've sunk everything into this place and I can't lose it. And that guy you dumped the drink on . . .'

Uh-oh. 'Someone important?'

'The mayor's kid.'

'I'm sorry, Don. I'm really sorry.' If only she'd known.

'Me, too,' Don said. 'But I still have to let you go.'

Bobbi nodded, tears slipping down her cheeks. 'I understand.'

Your boss is a moron,' seethed Jason's friend as they walked her to her car. 'You're the reason I come in there. They're not getting my business any more.'

Bobbi blew her nose into the tissue he'd offered and tried to smile her thanks. That muscle-filled black T-shirt, those black jeans and the leather jacket just cried bad boy. And now here he was, being a bad boy with a good heart.

'That's sweet of you to say,' she managed, her voice quavering.

'At least you still have the flower shop,' Jason said.

It was the final straw. Her stream of tears became a river. What, oh, what was she going to do? How was she going to pay her rent?

'**I** know exactly what you're going to do,' Hope said when Bobbi told her the news the next day. 'You can move in with me and work for me full time.'

'You can't afford that,' Bobbi said.

'Sure, I can. Clarice handed in her notice. I was paying her to work there four days a week, and what's one more day? The way the business is growing I really need the help. And, now that you're not working nights, you could take a course and become a floral designer.'

'Wow,' breathed Bobbi. 'You'd really do this for me?'

'It's not much compared to how you saved me when I was sick,' said Hope.

'It's a lot to me,' Bobbi assured her. She jumped out of her chair and hugged Hope. 'I've got to go.'

'Where are you going?'

'I have to start packing, sign up for my first class . . .' Her words echoed behind her. A moment later, the door shut, leaving Hope smiling. She'd done a good thing.

Millie had tried to convince her daughter to go to church with her in the morning, but Debra had insisted she wasn't up to it.

Millie sighed. She felt suddenly tired, but she was going to church. And then she was going to spend some time in her garden, where things wanted to grow.

By the time she got to the community garden, Amber and her son were already there. Amber sat in the spring sunshine pulling weeds, while Seth squatted in front of some bushes looking for the rabbit.

Millie stepped through her garden gate and set down the containers of pansies she'd picked up.

'Look,' Amber said, pointing to the coffee-grounds fence she was building round her plants. 'No slugs. You're a genius, Millie.'

Seth came running back. 'Mommy, I saw the bunny.'

'Did you leave him the carrot?'

Seth nodded eagerly.

'They like the greens,' said Millie. 'I do think you're going to have to add that chicken wire.'

'This garden is going to cost me a fortune,' said Amber.

'Think of it as an investment,' Millie told her. 'You get so much from a garden, things that you can't put a price on.'

'I did the farmers' market yesterday,' Amber announced.

'Oh? And how did that go?'

Amber gave a shrug. 'OK. I didn't realise how many people would be there selling. A lot of people selling baked stuff.'

'So, the competition was fierce?' guessed Millie.

'You could say that. I think I need to sell something besides banana bread and oatmeal cookies. Got any suggestions?'

'As a matter of fact, yes,' Millie said slowly. 'What about trying something unique? Take advantage of the garden season. So many flowers are edible and they make lovely decorations.'

'Great idea! I could sugar them, and put them on cupcakes,' said Amber, catching on.

'There you go. And I have a wonderful recipe for lavender cookies I could give you, if you'd like it,' Millie offered.

'I'll take it,' said Amber with a decisive nod.

'I'll copy it for you, and you can come by this week and pick it up. I'll make tea. How does that sound?'

'That sounds like a deal,' Amber said, beaming. 'Um. We're not growing any lavender, are we?'

'I'm afraid not,' Millie said. 'But Hope says that little kitchen shop in town sells lavender sugar.'

'Perfect. I'll make a batch of cookies to sell this weekend.' Amber smiled at her. 'Millie, you're amazing.'

They worked on, Seth chattering happily. At last Amber sat back and sighed. 'I never thought I'd like being in the garden, but I feel like I'm building my own world here.'

Millie smiled at her.

'Here comes our neighbour,' Amber said, pointing to Hope Walker, who was striding their way, resplendent in jeans and a sleeveless pink top, and carrying a little basket full of gardening tools. 'It's about time you got here,' Amber greeted her. 'We've been at this for hours.'

Hope waved her hand in salute. 'I'll bet.'

'How's life?' asked Amber.

'Crazy,' said Hope. 'My sister's moving in with me. And I have a new employee.'

'Really. Who?' asked Millie.

'My sister.'

'Wow, that's a lot of togetherness,' Amber observed. 'How did all this stuff with your sister happen?'

Hope set down her gardening basket. 'Well, she lost her job.'

Amber got suddenly quiet, leaving Millie to carry on the conversation. 'It's really sweet of you to help her out.'

'She'd do the same for me,' Hope said. 'In fact, she's done a lot for me. I owe her big time. But that's not why I'm doing this,' she added quickly. 'I love my sister. Bobbi does gorgeous arrangements. And people love her. She'll be wonderful with the customers. And the shop's getting busier all the time, so I need the help.'

Millie set down her spade and studied Hope. 'Taking on a full-time employee is a big step.'

'But it's a good step. If I get sick again . . .'

Amber looked questioningly at Hope. 'Were you sick?'

Millie kept quiet. It wasn't her place to say anything.

'Not that it's any of my business,' Amber said quickly.

'No, that's OK. It's just . . . I had cancer.'

'Gosh, I'm sorry,' said Amber. 'You've had it tough.' She lowered her gaze. 'It makes losing our restaurant seem like nothing.'

Hope looked at her in surprise. 'You had a restaurant?'

'Once upon a bad time.'

'That couldn't have been easy,' said Hope. 'I can't imagine losing my business.'

Millie regarded the two women working companionably alongside her. Debra could learn something from them. She was probably at the mall, engaging in what she called retail therapy.

If you asked Millie, this was true therapy. Enjoying the company of women who were working hard to make their lives better, listening to a child's laughter.

Amber returned home carrying a heart full of hope. She loved it here at Heart Lake. She loved her new friends. And she loved gardening. It all worked like some magical tonic.

She and Seth came into the house to find Ty stationed at his usual post in front of the TV.

'You should come to the garden with us,' said Amber.

He held up a hand in a no-thanks gesture. 'That's OK.' Then, 'Are you hungry? I've got stuff cut up for stir-fry.'

'That sounds good,' she said. What she'd really wanted to say was, 'So, have you been looking for work?' But she didn't.

'This is good,' she said later as they ate.

He shrugged. 'I just threw in a bunch of stuff.'

'You throw good,' she said with a smile. 'And pretty soon we'll have spinach from our garden to cook with, won't we, Sethie? Spinach salad, spinach quiche, spinach pie,' she added, tickling Seth and making him giggle.

'You've actually got things growing?'

Amber frowned. 'Yeah, as a matter of fact, I do.'

He acknowledged her accomplishment with a grunt.

She let it go without saying anything, but inside she fumed. At least she was doing something. What was he doing?

The next morning Amber woke feeling tired and grumpy. She needed mommy R & R. 'I've got some errands to run,' she told Ty.

'Are you taking Seth?' he asked.

She shook her head. 'You guys are on your own.'

'I was going to drop off some job applications.'

Sure he was. 'I'll be back by noon,' she said. If she didn't return to find him camped in front of the tube, it would be a miracle.

Her first stop was Kizzy's Kitchen to look for lavender sugar to use in her baking. Kizzy, the shop owner, was happy to help her. In her red apron she looked like she should be on a cooking show.

'Are you new in town?' she asked. 'I could have sworn I knew every baker in Heart Lake.'

'I am. And I love to bake. If these cookies turn out, I'm going to sell them at the farmers' market.'

'Maybe you should be making them at Sweet Somethings Bakery. Sarah Goodwin is a friend. I could speak to her.'

'How about telling her to give me a raise?' Amber joked. 'Right now I'm ringing up orders and making lattes.'

'You come up with some good stuff and she'll have you chained to the oven in no time, I can guarantee it,' Kizzy said, handing over the bag with Amber's purchases. 'Let me know how those cookies turn out.'

Millie's house was Amber's next stop. She had to double-check the address when she pulled up in front of the place. What kind of bad karma was this? The house was big and boring, and it had no yard. Millie belonged in a little English cottage, or a farmhouse with flowers everywhere. No wonder she was at the community garden so much.

Millie was ready for her. 'I've got the water on,' she said, leading the way to the kitchen.

Amber followed her through a living room with big, leather furniture and a flat-panel TV.

'These used to be the hit of my garden club meetings,' Millie said, handing over a sheet of paper with a beautifully scripted recipe. 'I'm so happy a whole new generation is going to be enjoying them. I'll give you my carrot cookie recipe, too. People will love those and come back for more.' Millie nudged a plate in her direction. 'Have a carrot cookie.'

Amber took a cookie and bit into it. And was pleasantly surprised. 'You're right. People will love these.'

Millie poured tea into their cups. 'They're perfect with a nice cup of tea. I think tea is very comforting.'

'I could use some comfort,' Amber said.

Millie leaned across the table and placed a hand on her arm. 'Be patient, dear. These difficult times always feel like they'll never end. But trust me, they do.'

Amber could feel the tears rising. 'I'm such a baby.'

'No, you're not.' Millie patted her arm. 'And this will all work out, you'll see.'

'How do you know?'

'Because I'm going to pray about it,' Millie said firmly.

'Well, good luck with that,' Amber said.

Millie took a sip of tea. 'I have a feeling it's about time for some good things to happen in your life. Your life is like your garden. You plant your seeds, but it takes time for them to germinate. You don't see vegetables or even the promise of vegetables for a while, but they're still busy growing beneath the soil, getting ready to produce something wonderful for you. I think life is like that.'

'Is that how it's worked for you?' Amber asked. If so, why did Millie look kind of sad all of a sudden?

'That's how I try to make it work,' Millie said.

'Well,' Amber said with a sigh, 'all I can do is keep planting, I guess. I've got too much invested to quit.'

She thought of Hope Walker, working hard to turn her back on a scary past and seed her life with new, good things. And here was Millie, making friends in a new place. If they can keep working at it, so can I, she told herself.

Eight

JASON STOPPED BY the flower shop on Tuesday.

'So, you're doing OK?' he asked Bobbi.

'Absolutely.' She slung an arm over Hope's shoulder. 'Who needs the Last Resort anyway? I'm happy here with my sis, making art.' She turned to Hope. 'That's what we're doing, isn't it?'

Hope nodded.

'And my money problems are solved,' Bobbi went on. 'We're going to be roommates.'

Jason smiled at that. 'I tried being roommates with my brother. It lasted two months.'

'That's not going to happen to us,' Bobbi insisted. 'We're not just sisters, we're best friends.' She gave Hope a squeeze.

'Absolutely,' Hope agreed, and squeezed back.

The phone rang. 'I'll get it,' Bobbi said.

While she talked on the phone, Jason turned to Hope and asked in a low voice, 'Is she going to be OK?'

'She'll be fine,' Hope assured him.

He drummed the counter, calling Hope's attention to his hands. They were big and work roughened. Strong hands. He looked to where Bobbi stood, busy on the phone. 'I don't want to rush her to share personal stuff with me, but if she's got a problem, if she's got a bill she can't pay . . .'

Thanks to her skill with a charge card, Bobbi always had bills, but they weren't anything she couldn't handle. Hope shook her head, confused.

'Hospital bills?' he prompted.

'Hospital bills?' Hope repeated. What could her sister have told Jason to make him believe she had hospital bills? Someone in this shop had them, but it sure as heck wasn't Bobbi.

'Look, I saw a book when we were helping her load her bookcase, the one about cancer. When I saw her Saturday, she talked about having bills to pay. I assumed . . .'

Hope felt her cheeks warming. She wasn't about to step forward. But she couldn't let him think Bobbi had had cancer. 'It wasn't her. It was . . . someone else in our family. Bobbi was helping her.'

Jason looked at Bobbi like he was watching a saint in action. 'Is this person OK now?'

'She's doing fine,' Hope said.

Bobbi hung up and announced, 'We just got an order for a fiftieth birthday.'

'Well, I'd better get back to work. Just thought I'd see if you needed anything,' Jason said.

'As a matter of fact, I do,' said Bobbi. 'I need your body.'

That got his interest.

'And any other help you can find. Bring your friend. This Saturday is moving day. I'll feed you,' she added.

A corner of his lip lifted. 'Food is good.'

'OK, then. Ten a.m.?'

'Ten a.m.,' he repeated, and left the store.

Bobbi beamed at her sister. 'There. Jason's got a really cute friend. Maybe he'll bring him.'

'Getting greedy?' Hope teased.

'Not for me, for you.'

'I'm not interested,' Hope said, and slipped behind the velvet curtain to the work area.

Bobbi followed her. 'You'll have the hots for this guy, trust me.'

'Speaking of trust,' Hope began, 'Jason saw one of my books. The one on cancer.'

'Oh.' Bobbi gave her lower lip a good gnawing.

'I told him someone in our family had it, so I don't think he'll bring up the subject again. But don't tell him it was me.'

Bobbi nodded, her face serious. 'Don't worry. I won't.'

The day drifted pleasantly by. The sisters got their orders filled and, that afternoon, while Hope was doing paperwork, Bobbi delivered them. Bobbi wasn't the world's best driver, but she made it back, mission accomplished, and Hope decided she didn't need to worry so much. This was all working out beautifully.

Hope was at Bobbi's apartment on Saturday, helping Bobbi finish packing her dishes, when the moving team showed up. Jason was his usual delicious self. The other guy was even more muscled, with swarthy skin, dark hair and Johnny Depp eyes. The newcomer was wearing black jeans and a ripped grey T-shirt, partially covered by a black leather jacket, and black boots.

Duke gave Hope a genial smile, but when he looked at Bobbi, lightning flashed. He quickly looked away, but not before Hope spied a dangerous answering flicker from her sister. Oh, no. This was not good. Her sister needed to stay on track, especially now that she had Mr Right's heart in the palm of her hand.

'We've got my truck outside,' Jason said.

Bobbi set the men to work loading her couch. As soon as they were out of the apartment, Hope gave Bobbi a low-voiced third degree. 'What are you doing?'

'What do you mean, what am I doing?'

'I saw how you looked at Jason's friend.'

Bobbi stared at her, faking affront. 'I just looked at him. There was no *how* to it.'

'What happened to picking Mr Right?' Hope hissed.

'I have picked Mr Right. I don't want Duke.'

'You just remember that,' Hope warned.

By five o'clock, all Bobbi's possessions were either in storage or at Hope's apartment.

'OK, time for burgers,' Bobbi said, and went to the kitchen of her new home. 'And we've got beer.'

'I could definitely use one of those,' said Duke.

Hope watched as Bobbi smiled up at him. 'I'll make some oatmeal cookies,' Hope offered.

Both Duke and Jason were underfoot the minute the cookies came out of the oven.

'Hey, these are good,' Duke said.

'You're a good cook,' Jason told Hope.

'I'm good at a lot things,' she said coyly, and turned to pull salad makings from the fridge. Now, where had that come from? Shades of the good old days when she actually dated.

'All right, we're ready,' Bobbi announced, and set out a platter piled with burgers.

Duke moved to her side, like one of Pavlov's dogs. 'These look good,' he said, but Hope couldn't tell if he was talking about the burgers or the view down Bobbi's top.

Jason seemed oblivious. He was helping himself to another cookie. Well, he was either confident or clueless.

As they ate, Hope tried to gently interrogate the newcomer. 'So, have you got family round here?' she asked.

'Nope,' Duke said, and took a swig from his second beer. 'I'm really up here because Jase convinced me the area's growing. Lots of work.'

'How do you two know each other?'

'We went to high school together,' Jason said.

'Yeah, then I split for California. Did the beach bum thing, played in a band.'

After they'd eaten, they found enough energy to play Spoons, a wild card game that involved diving for and fighting over a limited supply of spoons. Bobbi managed to gouge both men with her fingernails before the game was over. Hope was the first one out and it gave her a chance to observe Bobbi. She laughed and flirted with both men, but the way she looked at Duke made Hope nervous.

Still, Hope breathed easier when the guys finally stood by the front door, ready to leave, and Bobbi hung on Jason's arm. 'Thanks for being so awesome,' she told him.

'That's what we do best,' Duke answered for him, and sauntered out of the door.

At least he'd had the grace to leave. Hope did the same.

A moment later, Hope heard Jason's big truck roar into life, and the front door shut. Bobbi came into the living room, wearing the smile of a woman who had just been thoroughly kissed. Good. Her sister was back on track. She could quit worrying.

Hope's first customer on Monday was Amber Howell.

'I need to order an arrangement,' Amber announced. 'It's for Millie. I owe her big time.' She reached into her handbag and pulled out a fist-ful of notes. 'Thanks to her lavender and carrot cookie recipes, I am rolling in dough, and I need to thank her.'

'How about yellow roses. They symbolise joy and friendship.'

'Perfect! Can we tell her that in the card?'

'Absolutely,' said Hope.

Amber was barely out the door when Bobbi entered, bringing coffee. 'So, was that an order?'

'As a matter of fact, it was. You are going to be a busy bee today. We've got a lot of important orders to deliver.'

They worked companionably for the next two hours.

Hope finally said, 'OK, let's get this finished, then we can load up the wagon.' The wagon was a used PT Cruiser, yellow with *Changing Seasons Floral* scripted on its side in green.

'OK now, remember, drive carefully,' Hope cautioned as Bobbi slipped in behind the wheel.

They had a lot of inventory stashed back there: three birthday arrangements, one anniversary special, something to celebrate a new baby, a delivery to welcome a newcomer to Heart Lake and Amber's thank-you gift to Millie. The most valuable thing in the truck was a showy arrangement for a booksellers' reception Hope's friend Erin Rockwell was in charge of.

Bobbi gave a snort of disgust. 'Of course I'll drive carefully.'

Hope nodded. She'll be fine, she told herself.

Really, Bobbi thought as she tooled along Lake Way, Hope was such a worrywart. Bobbi decided to make the new baby delivery first since that was furthest away, on a road off one of the curves at the top end of the lake. Heart Lake was shaped like a two-mile-long valentine, and, at this end, the roads tended to be a tangle.

Bobbi was relieved when she finally found the address.

The new mommy's eyes lit up like Bobbi was holding out a tray of diamonds instead of an arrangement of blue carnations and baby's breath. 'For me? Thank you.'

'For sure. Happy baby.'

Bobbi hopped back into the car, then bumped her way back down the potholed drive. She'd gone a mile when her cellphone rang.

She did a quick look to see who it was. Even as she was looking at the phone, she saw an old dog limping out onto the road. She stomped on the brakes. The Cruiser fishtailed, the phone went flying. And, in the back of the Cruiser, things were going thump, thump, thump. When the car came to a stop, she was on the shoulder of the road. Where was the dog? She jumped out of the car. Her anxious gaze swept the road.

There went the old guy limping off into the bushes. She leaned against the car and let out a sigh of relief. And what about the flowers? She ran to the back of the Cruiser and pulled it open.

Flowers lay everywhere, their little boxes upended. Many of them had slid right into the side of the car and the little plastic forks that held the gift card envelopes had been snapped. Rivulets of water snaked towards three cards that had managed to get dislodged.

Bobbi scooped up the envelopes and began righting the arrangements. Hope was going to fire her, for sure. Fired twice in one week, and once by your sister. Did it get any worse than that?

Thank goodness, no vases had broken. A couple of the hyacinths had taken a beating. A rose had suffered a broken neck. It followed the hyacinths into a gully. There, that took care of that. She coaxed the arrangements back into place. Good as new. She'd stop by the gas station and refill the vases.

And now, the cards. What went where? Some she knew, like the showy arrangement for the reception. Some . . . She got her clipboard from the front seat. It gave her only names and addresses. There'd been no need to note who was getting what, not when the cards with the recipients' names on them were in the arrangements.

The cellphone was singing again. Bobbi knew she had to answer.

'How's it going?' asked Hope.

'Oh, fine,' Bobbi said, forcing her voice to sound carefree.

'The customer from the bank called and wants to know when we're getting there with the flowers. They're right in the middle of the birthday party.'

'They're next.' They were now. Bobbi looked at the card envelopes in her hand. One of these belonged on flowers destined for the bank. But which one?

'OK,' Hope said. 'I'll tell her that Linda will have her lavender roses in what, ten minutes?'

Bobbi sighed inwardly with relief. 'Absolutely.' She snapped the phone shut and hurried back to the flowers. Bobbi propped the card among the flowers. That took care of Linda.

Now, what about the two remaining mystery arrangements? Neither one of them were orders that Bobbi had taken. One was a gigantic wicker basket of plants. The other was an arrangement of yellow roses. She studied the clipboard. Who did we have to choose from here? Millie Baldwin and Altheus Hornby. So, which of these looked like a Millie and which one looked like an Altheus?

And then she remembered. Hope had met Millie at the community garden. So, of course, the plants had to go to Millie the gardener. Whew, that was a close one.

Now, the next challenge was to get the Cruiser safely backed up. She restarted the car and backed up very slowly. Just when she thought she was going to have a nervous breakdown, the wheels grabbed onto dirt. She stopped as soon as all four wheels were safely on the road again, leaned her head back against the seat, and let out her breath. OK, she'd be fine. Everything would be fine.

At the gas station, she gave the flowers a drink and cleaned up before she went into the bank.

While everyone was busy raving over Linda and the flowers, Bobbi slipped back to the Cruiser. The rest of her deliveries went just fine. Hope would never have to know. Except then, right as Bobbi was pulling away from the last house, Hope called.

'I just had a call from Amber. Millie called her to thank her for the plants. But Millie was supposed to get yellow roses. Is there something you need to tell me?'

The jig was up. Bobbi confessed. 'I had an accident. I almost hit a dog. I stopped just in time. And the car's fine,' she added. 'I got everything put back together and everything's fine.'

'Then how did you wind up delivering Altheus Hornby's plants to Millie Baldwin?'

'It was the dog. I had to stop suddenly. The flowers just got a little, um . . . mixed up.'

Hope expelled a breath. 'Oh, no. What did they look like?'

'Don't worry. I got them all fixed back up, good as new.'

'And delivered two to the wrong place.'

'I'll go back and redeliver right now.'

'No. It's OK. It's taken care of.'

Hope was trying to sound forgiving, but Bobbi could hear frustration in her voice. 'You're mad.'

'No. Well, sort of.'

'I'm sorry,' Bobbi said. 'I should have told you. I was just so afraid you'd be mad at me. I thought I could fix it.' But she'd only made things worse. 'You should fire me now and get it over with.'

'No. We're there for each other. But I really need you to tell me when something is going wrong. Then we can fix it together.'

'And we'll tell each other the truth, no matter what,' Bobbi vowed.

'No matter what,' Hope agreed. She hung up the phone and mentally added, *but only if one of us asks*. Wanting your sister's boyfriend was another matter altogether.

Millie Baldwin settled the basket of plants on the back seat of her car. Hope had been embarrassed when she called to apologise for the delivery mix-up, but Millie assured her that it was not a problem. It was also not a problem for Millie to take the flowers to their rightful recipient and make an exchange. In fact, she insisted.

She didn't tell Hope, but she wanted to get out. She'd tidied up the kitchen and finished her book, and then found herself at a loose end. The children wouldn't be home for another hour.

It had taken a great deal of persuading to convince Hope to give her an address and some directions and let her play delivery girl, but at last Hope had relented.

It was drizzly, and Millie drove carefully, paying attention to street signs. This house was off North Lake Drive, which meant it was right on the lake. She was to look for Loveland Lane and a big camellia hedge, then, past that, a set of mailboxes. Just beyond those, she would see the driveway.

This is lovely, she thought. In between the undeveloped wooded lots, big yards with houses gave her glimpses of the lake. This was what she'd envisioned when her daughter had first told her she'd moved to some place called Heart Lake.

Oh, there was Loveland Lane. And the camellias. And there were the mailboxes. She turned down the gravelled drive. The road widened and she saw an old yellow Victorian with a wraparound porch. At the back of it, she caught sight of a dock slipping out into the lake. Whoever owned this house was one lucky woman.

Not the best gardener, though, judging from the weeds.

Millie stopped the car and took the plants out of the back. She looked to the house and saw that a man had opened the front door. He was tall, with a thick mane of grey hair and a square jaw. Looking at him stirred up flutterings Millie hadn't felt in years.

She didn't get far before he reached her and took the basket. 'Here, let me. You must be Millie. The flower shop called and told me you were on your way. I'd have been happy to come to you.'

'Oh, nonsense,' said Millie. 'It's a nice day for a drive.'

He held out a hand. 'Altheus Hornby. I'm new here.'

'So am I,' said Millie as they shook hands. 'Is your wife enjoying it here?' It would be nice to make a friend her own age.

His smile got smaller. 'I'm afraid my wife's no longer alive. I lost her three years ago.'

'Oh, I'm sorry,' said Millie. 'It's hard to lose a mate.'

'I miss her a lot, but I know she's in a better place.'

Millie nodded. 'That is a comfort.'

He motioned her towards the house and they began walking.

'This is a lovely house,' Millie said as they reached the porch.

'I like it,' he said. 'I have your flowers inside. Would you like to come inside?'

She looked at her watch. She should get home.

'Your husband is probably expecting you back,' he said.

'I'm a widow.'

'Oh. I'm sorry,' he said, but he looked . . . interested.

She was being silly. 'I'm living with my daughter. My grandchildren will be home pretty soon.'

He nodded, polite resignation on his face.

'But I'd love to see some of the house before I go.'

That made him smile. 'Great. Come on in.'

The house had a reverse floor plan, with the living room at the back to take advantage of the view of the lake. She stood in front of the window. 'Isn't this a lovely view!'

Altheus stood next to her. 'It's what sold me on the house.'

'A wonderful place for a gardener,' Millie mused.

'My wife was the gardener,' said Altheus. 'I don't know what to do with all this. Maybe you'll help me,' he said, with a twinkle in his eye.

'Oh.' She was blushing. 'I should probably be going.'

'Sure, the grandkids. Well, let me carry your flowers for you.'

'My, they are lovely,' Millie said when she saw them.

'Someone here cares a lot about you,' said Altheus. 'I imagine you have lots of admirers.'

He was flirting with her. At her age, a man was flirting with her.

He escorted her to her car and carefully installed the box containing the vase on the back floor.

'Thank you so much,' she told him.

'No, thank you for driving all the way over here. Say, I was just thinking. How about letting me really thank you for your trouble? Would you like to have lunch with me tomorrow?'

Why not? 'I'd love to,' she said.

Before she knew it, Altheus Hornby had her phone number and address, and they had plans for him to pick her up at noon. 'I'll take you to the Two Turtledoves. It has a great view of the lake.'

'That sounds wonderful,' said Millie.

She got home and carefully carried her flowers into the house, settling them on the dining room table. The card she'd put in her scrapbook. Amber had written, 'You've really been there for me, and I just wanted you to know how much I appreciate it.'

She had just tucked away Amber's card when the kids came home, each bringing a friend. Millie shifted gears and got busy making cookies.

'Who sent flowers?' Debra asked when she got home.

'A friend of mine.'

'Oh.' Debra sounded disappointed. Millie decided not to share the news about her lunch date with her daughter.

But it was no fun keeping it to herself, so the next morning she called Alice. She hadn't spoken to her friend in a while.

'Alice, I met someone.'

'Met someone?' Alice echoed. 'You mean, a man?'

'Yes. We have a date for lunch today,' Millie said, and explained how she met Altheus Hornby.

'That is simply amazing,' Alice said. 'And I'm jealous. Ask him if he's got a brother. And Millie, don't play too hard to get. At our age there's no point wasting time.'

Millie chuckled and rang off, then went to make the all-important decision of what to wear. She settled on her navy blue slacks and a white turtleneck, with her favourite red blazer, accessorised by the red, glass bead necklace Duncan Jr had given her for Mother's Day.

Altheus arrived promptly at noon. He looked her up and down and grinned. 'Millie, you're quite a dish.'

'Oh, don't be silly,' she said.

'I've got to tell you,' he said after he'd helped her into the car, 'I've been looking forward to this since yesterday. I was beginning to think I'd made a mistake moving up here.'

'What did bring you here?'

'I needed something new,' he said as they drove off. 'I'd been in a rut since my wife died. So I let the kids have the other house, bought a new car, and headed north. I've still got lots of miles left.'

Oh, dear. She was out with a younger man.

The restaurant looked expensive. Millie took in the linen tablecloths and crystal, the jacket-clad waiters. She tried to find something reasonably priced on the menu.

Altheus said, 'Please, order anything you want. I'd like this to be special.'

'Simply being out with a new friend is special.'

'I hope it's going to be the first of many times,' he said.

Millie ordered vegetables in puff pastry, the most inexpensive thing she could find. And Altheus ordered wine for them. Wine with lunch, it was so extravagant.

'Now,' he said. 'Tell me all about yourself.'

By the time they'd finished their salad, Altheus had heard all about her gardening addiction, her love of books and her penchant for crossword puzzles.

'I do them, too,' he said. 'Keeps the mind sharp.'

Millie wondered how sharp her mind would stay if that waiter kept filling her wineglass. Before she knew it, Altheus had heard about her children, her concerns over Debra, and even worse, had learned that she was almost seventy-seven.

'I'd never have guessed,' he said gallantly. 'I like older women,' he said with a wink.

By the time they finished dessert, two hours had slipped by.

'How about a drive round the lake?' Altheus suggested.

The way he drove, he should have offered her a race round the lake. But Millie wasn't ready to go home to that big, quiet house yet, so she said yes. Thankfully, Altheus drove at a more sensible speed. The sun came out, turning the lake a dark spring blue.

'Look,' Altheus said and pulled the car off the road. 'I'm thinking of buying this piece of land as an investment.'

'It's like a wooded fairyland,' Millie said, taking it all in. 'I certainly admire you for being so daring.'

'Not daring, just business. I'm a working stiff, Millie.'

'What kind of work do you do?'

'I buy and sell real estate. And,' he continued, 'I can even manage to foot the bill for a nice meal. So, next time I take you out to eat, you don't have to find the cheapest thing on the menu.'

'Next time?'

'There will be a next time, Millie, and soon.'

And, to prove it, he called her the next night. Debra got to the phone before Millie. The surprised look on her daughter's face told Millie who it was. 'It's for you,' she said.

'Thank you,' Millie murmured.

'How about dinner with me tomorrow night?' Altheus suggested. 'And a movie after.'

'That sounds wonderful,' she decided.

'Then I'll pick you up at five thirty.'

'I'll be looking forward to it,' she said.

'Looking forward to what?' Debra asked.

'I'm going out with a friend tomorrow night,' Millie said.

'I don't even have a life yet,' Debra protested. 'How could you? And where did you meet a man?'

'Quite by accident.'

'I wish I was accident-prone,' Debra muttered. 'Just be careful,' she added. 'You don't know anything about this man. I don't want to have to worry about you.'

'Don't worry about me. I think you have your hands full worrying about yourself,' Millie said crisply.

Millie dressed carefully for her date, putting on her favourite black skirt and pink rayon blouse. Then, she gathered up her handbag and coat and went downstairs.

Emily looked up from where she and Eric lay sprawled on the couch watching TV. 'Are you going out?'

'Yes, I'm going out to dinner with a friend,' Millie told her.

Emily cocked her head, studying Millie. 'You look nice.'

'Well, thank you,' Millie said. This was high praise indeed, coming from a teenage girl.

The doorbell rang, and that brought Debra out from the kitchen. But Millie beat her to the door.

There stood Altheus. He smiled at the sight of her. 'Well, well. You look good enough to eat.'

'Oh, really. Come in,' she said. 'This is my daughter, Debra.'

He shook Debra's hand. 'You're just as lovely as your mother.'

Debra was underwhelmed by his gallantry. 'Thanks.'

'And these are my grandchildren,' Millie said, and made introductions to Eric and Emily.

Altheus nodded. 'Hi there.'

They smiled. 'Hi.'

'Well, shall we go?' Altheus said to Millie. He took her coat and helped her into it. 'Nice to meet you,' he said to Debra. He opened the door and whisked Millie out, saying, 'I don't know about you, but I'm hungry.' Once they were in the car, he said, 'I have a feeling your daughter wants to know my intentions.'

'I'm not sure she's excited that I've found a friend.'

He shrugged. 'One thing I've learned, kids sure don't like their parents to get a life.'

After an enjoyable evening of fine food, and fine conversation, he returned her to her doorstep. 'I hope you'll let me take you out again,' he said.

She smiled at him. 'I would love that.'

'And I hope you'll let me kiss you good night,' he added.

Millie's heart began to race. 'Oh, Altheus, I don't know.'

'I do,' he said, and pulled her to him and kissed her.

She felt a jolt as if someone had applied those emergency-room paddles to her chest. She pulled away, completely frazzled. 'Really, Altheus, I'm seven years older than you.' *And I haven't kissed a man other than Duncan in fifty-four years.*

'It doesn't matter to me,' Altheus countered. 'You're an attractive woman, Millie, and I enjoy being with you. And I certainly enjoyed kissing you just now.' He put a finger under her chin, forcing her to look at him. 'Don't you miss this?'

With her husband gone, one of the things she missed most were those little moments of closeness—the hugs in the kitchen in the morning, the soft kiss good night before they turned out the lights. She had to nod and murmur, 'Yes, I do.'

He gave her a hug and another kiss, this time on her forehead. 'I think we've got something good going. Let's enjoy it.'

She smiled up at him. 'I think you're right, Altheus.'

Nine

IT WAS SATURDAY, and Slugfest, Heart Lake's annual spring festival named after the Northwest's famous pest, was in full swing. The downtown section of Lake Way had been cordoned off and packed with everything from bouncy castles and climbing walls to sidewalk chalk art. Every restaurant, local church and club had set up a food booth along the street, which was packed with revellers. Amber and her family walked along, taking it all in.

Amber had saved up her cookie money so she could spring for eats, and now they were sampling hamburgers from the Family Inn.

Ty frowned at his. 'This is a case of *E. coli* waiting to happen.'

He gathered their burgers and handed them back to the cashier. 'You wanna cook these a little longer?'

She looked at him like he had a problem, but nodded and took the gut-rot burgers.

'If all their food is this bad, they're in trouble,' said Amber.

Had Ty checked with this restaurant? They could sure use help. Should she even bring up the subject? Well, what the heck. 'Did you ever drop off an application here?'

He shook his head.

She wanted to push him to at least check it out. WWMD? (What would Millie do?) It was as if Millie was whispering in her ear, 'Give him some armour.'

'They'd be lucky to get you,' she said. 'And, who knows? You may save them from going out of business.'

He gave a nod. 'Maybe I'll check it out next week.'

It was such a small thing. A maybe. But it was progress. She smiled at him and gave his arm a squeeze as they started walking towards the bouncy castle. Halfway there she spied Millie, strolling along next to a big man with grey hair, each of them eating candy floss.

'There's my friend, Millie. Let's go say hi,' she said.

Ty heaved a sigh and let Amber tow him through the crowd, calling to Millie as they went.

'Well, Amber, hello,' said Millie, lighting up at the sight of them. 'Isn't this fun?'

'It is,' Amber agreed and introduced Ty.

'I've heard so many nice things about you. It's nice to finally get to meet you in person,' Millie told him.

Ty looked questioningly at Amber. *What nice things?*

She ignored him. 'I don't think we've met,' Amber said to Millie's companion.

'No, we haven't,' he agreed, 'but I'll bet you're one of the garden girls. Millie talks about you a lot.'

Millie made the introductions, referring to Mr Tall, Grey and Handsome as 'my friend' Altheus.

Well, those weren't platonic looks Amber had been seeing these two giving each other. She guessed love could blossom at any age.

It could die at any age, too. Your love's not dead, she told herself. It was sick, wilted, but not dead. All they needed was to get a little bit of sunshine back in their life.

'Have you eaten?' Millie asked. 'Altheus and I were talking about stopping by that Family Inn booth. My treat.'

Ty spoke up. 'I wouldn't waste your money. We just tried the burgers. They're bad.'

Millie's eyebrows shot up. 'Really?' She turned to Altheus. 'I guess that's not surprising, is it?'

He shook his head. 'I met Charlie Thomas, the owner. He's having a hard time finding a decent chef.'

'Really?' Ty said, his voice speculative.

'It is hard to find good chefs,' Millie said. 'I'm trying to remember. Didn't your wife tell me you're a chef? Mr Thomas might want to steal you from your current employer.'

As if Millie didn't know Ty was unemployed. Amber could almost feel the warmth from her husband's red cheeks. 'He is a great chef,' she said.

'Can we bounce?' Seth asked, pulling on Amber's arm.

'We'll take a rain check on the food,' Amber said to Millie.

'That's fine. You enjoy yourselves,' she said.

'So, what *did* you tell her about me?' Ty asked Amber as Millie and Altheus strolled off.

'Not much,' Amber lied. 'Just that you're a good cook. And a good man.'

There. Husband armoured up. And, who knew, maybe next week, Ty would feel equipped to enter the job-hunting battle again.

And, speaking of jobs, why had Millie suddenly wanted to get something to eat when she and Altheus were already snarfing down candy floss? Had she known the owner of the Family Inn was in need of a chef? Amber had to hand it to Millie. She was smooth.

Bobbi was insistent that Hope come to Slugfest. 'You need to get out and have fun. Just come for a while,' Bobbi pushed. 'When you've had enough, you can take my car home and I'll have Jason bring me back.'

'OK. But just for a while.'

'Great!' Bobbi picked up her cellphone and punched in a number. Not hard to figure out who. 'OK, Hope's coming.'

The little beast! 'You already had this planned,' Hope accused.

Bobbi ignored her. 'We'll meet you by the beer garden.'

'You can meet him at the beer garden.'

Bobbi stuck a finger in her ear. 'What?' Now she was grinning. Hope knew from experience that this didn't bode well for her. 'Great. Thanks. See ya later.'

'What's great?' Hope demanded as her sister hung up.

'You have to stick around, at least for part of the dance. Duke's coming. We're double-dating.'

A million thoughts swarmed Hope like angry bees. How dare Bobbi set her up on a date without asking! This had all been a trick.

'I don't want to date Jason's friend.'

'Oh, come on,' Bobbi pleaded. 'It will be fun.'

'No, it won't. I don't even like Duke.'

'He's hot,' Bobbi protested.

'He's not my type.' Hope remembered the looks she'd caught shooting between him and Bobbi. This man wasn't coming along because he wanted her.

'Just for a while,' Bobbi pleaded. 'Come on.'

Hope gave up. 'OK. But I'm not staying for long.'

Bobbi grinned. 'Great. Now, let's get gorgeous.'

Getting dressed turned out to be a production. Bobbi took one look at Hope's jeans and her favourite figure-hiding top and shuddered. 'Oh, no. I'm not going to be seen with you in that.' She grabbed Hope's arm and hauled her to her own bedroom.

Before Hope knew it, she was in a soft pink sweater with a white camisole under it.

Too clingy. 'No, that won't work.'

'We're not done yet. Here, put this on.' Bobbi handed over a denim jacket. 'Wear it open.'

Hope slipped it on and looked in the mirror. She looked normal, cute even. Behind her Bobbi was indulging in a knowing smirk. 'Told you. Now here, put on these earrings.'

Hope slipped on Bobbi's favourite garnet drop earrings. They looked great. Next, the tennis shoes she'd been about to wear got traded for pink pumps Bobbi declared were too big for her.

'Now, let's do something about your make-up.'

Make-up, too? Hope hadn't worn make-up since she was first diagnosed with cancer. What was the point? 'Let's not bother. I'm fine like this. Anyway, I'm not going to . . .'

'Not going to what?' Bobbi asked. Then understanding dawned in her eyes, followed by concern. 'Of course you're going to find someone. You don't want to go through your life alone.'

'Yes, actually, I do.'

Bobbi threw up both hands. 'You have got to stop doing this to yourself. So, you've got some scars. So, you're not perfect and you've got an implant. Half of Hollywood has implants.'

Stop acting like such a thistle. It's one date, and a group date at that. Anyway, it was easier to let Bobbi have her way than argue.

'Ha! I'm amazing,' Bobbi crowed when she'd finally finished. She pulled Hope off her bed and planted her in front of the mirror. 'There. Do you look great or what?'

Hope looked in the mirror. Her face had changed. Had her lips always been that full or had she simply forgotten? And her eyes were big and her lashes were thick and sexy. She looked . . . alive. And healthy. 'Wow,' she breathed.

'Now you look the way you used to,' Bobbi approved.

Hope did a turn in front of the mirror. 'I can't believe it's me.'

'I can,' said Bobbi. 'Now, we so have to go. I'm starving.'

Ten minutes later, without giving Hope any further chance to protest, Bobbi slid out of the car, taking the keys with her.

She stuffed the keys in her pocket. 'You gotta eat something and dance at least three dances before you get to go home.'

'Boy, are you bossy,' Hope muttered.

'I'm pretending I'm the big sister,' Bobbi cracked, and gave her a hug. 'Oh, the band is already playing. Let's move it.'

Hope could hear a guitar screaming and, under it, the pounding of drums and the thumping of a bass. The smell of grilling onions and candy floss drifted on the air, making her mouth water. She took a deep breath and followed her sister to the party.

It wasn't hard for Jason to spot Bobbi Walker in the crowd, not in that red leather jacket. Under it she was wearing a black top and tight jeans. Her blonde hair gently caressed her shoulders as she walked. She looked like a model. But she wasn't the only one.

'Check her out,' said Duke, standing next to him.

Dressed in pink, Hope looked soft and feminine, and made Jason think of cupcakes. As they got closer, he saw she was wearing make-up. It made her whole face come alive.

'Not bad at all,' said Duke.

Jason wasn't sure he liked the way his friend was checking out Bobbi's sister. Duke was a connoisseur of women, a no-commitment gypsy. This hadn't bothered Jason before. It had seemed like a good idea when Bobbi suggested a double date, but now he realised he'd just served up a dove on a platter to a wolf.

Bobbi caught sight of them and waved. 'We're here,' she announced. 'The party is on.'

'I'm down with that,' said Duke.

The wolf had a big appetite. Duke was doing an X-ray thing with Bobbi now and not trying to hide it. That was going to earn him a fist in the nose.

Then Jason caught the way Bobbi looked back and felt like he was the one who just got punched. Sucker punched. But when she smiled up at him, he decided he was imagining things.

'Let's get something to eat,' she said. 'I'm starving.'

'We can't have that,' said Duke. He put an arm round Hope. 'Whaddya say to something . . . hot?'

She slipped out of his easy embrace. 'Maybe we'd better start with something cold.'

That made Jason snicker. OK, this woman could take care of herself. He didn't need to worry about her.

They filled up on barbecued ribs and corn on the cob, washed down by beer from Brewsters, the local brew pub. Then Bobbi led them to the big, inflatable bouncy castle.

They were the only grown-ups in there, but Jason couldn't help laughing as he bounced round like a human spring. And then everything went downhill. Hope lost her balance and fell into him. He tried to keep her upright but down they went, Hope landing on top of him. The groin-to-groin contact was a double whammy, but she turned it into a triple when she wriggled to get off of him, muttering, 'Sorry.'

He wasn't, and that, naturally, made him feel guilty. He got to his feet just as Bobbi moon-jumped over to him and threw herself into his arms, taking him over backwards again.

By the time they left that big bubble of trouble, Jason was sweating, and it wasn't from exercise. He wished it was just him and Bobbi here tonight. It got dark and the dancing began in earnest. And suddenly, Duke and Bobbi were dancing together in a way that should have burned off their clothes.

'I'm gonna kill him.'

'Oh, I don't think you need to go that far,' said a soft voice at Jason's elbow. 'Just cut off his feet.'

He turned to find Hope standing next to him, watching her sister. 'Bobbi loves to dance,' she explained.

'I've figured that out,' he said sourly. Well, it was caveman manners to stand there and not ask the woman next to you to dance. 'I could use a lesson,' he said to Hope. 'Wanna teach me?'

He took her hand and led her to a corner of the crowded floor. They had barely started moving when the band stopped. She smiled at him and shrugged, indicating he was off the hook.

But now the band was going into a slow song, and Duke had already whirled Bobbi into some kind of showy, slow dance.

Jason forced himself to put murder on the back burner and said to Hope, 'I think my feet will do better at this speed.'

'Oh, that's OK. You don't have to.' She looked flustered.

He was making her nervous, which was weird. There was no need to be nervous round him. It was Duke she had to watch.

Jason drew her to him. She had longer legs than her sister and it made her just about the right height to fit him perfectly. He reminded himself that this woman could wind up as his sister-in-law and put a brotherly distance between them.

'After this, we should find Bobbi,' Hope said. 'I know she looks like a flirt, but she's not really. She's just bubbly, full of energy.'

'If I had a two-by-four handy, I'd hit Duke with it. He's supposed to be your date.'

'That's OK. Duke's not my type,' Hope said.

Somehow, he'd known it. He should never have listened when Bobbi suggested he bring Duke along.

'So, what is your type?' Jason asked, making conversation.

She cocked her head, considering. 'Oh. I like men who think about more than the next party. Who think, period.'

'What? Guys don't think?' he teased.

'Some do. I get the impression you do.'

'I try,' he said, flattered. 'So, what else?'

'I like a man who enjoys nature.'

'Hiking?'

Her cheeks turned pink as soon as he'd said that, and Jason remembered their trail encounter when she'd landed on her back.

'Sorry. I didn't mean to embarrass you,' he said.

'I'm really not a klutz like that.'

'Everybody has klutzy moments,' he said. The music ended and he felt something soft under his right foot. Hope's toe.

He quickly removed his foot as she said, 'Yeah, I guess everybody does.'

She was grinning. He found himself grinning, too.

'You two are having fun,' said Bobbi, now back at his side.

They were. Hope would make a great sister-in-law.

If he and Bobbi got together. She'd seemed so perfect. But a perfect woman didn't leave a guy to go off dancing with his friend.

'Let's get something to drink,' Bobbi suggested.

'I think I'm going to go home,' Hope said. She turned to her sister and held out a hand. 'Keys?'

Bobbi made a face. 'Oh, come on. Not yet.'

Hope shook her head. 'I really need to get going. Sorry.'

Bobbi gave up the keys and Hope said her goodbyes. 'Thanks for the dance,' she said to Jason.

'I enjoyed it,' he told her. And he had.

Hope left and the trio went to the beer garden for more beer. And then Bobbi went to the bathroom, leaving Jason and Duke together for a little talk.

'OK, you jerk,' Jason growled as soon as she'd left. 'What's the idea of dancing off with my woman?'

Duke looked surprised. 'Hey, we were just dancing.'

'You had someone to dance with.'

'She wasn't into me.'

'Well, neither is Bobbi.'

Duke levelled him a get-real stare. 'Yeah? I hate to say it, man, but I don't think she's that into you.'

'The hell she's not,' Jason snarled.

'Hey.' Duke stabbed a finger at him. 'She asked me. You got a problem with that, maybe you need to talk to her.' Before Jason could rip his head off, Duke left the table, calling over his shoulder, 'I'm out of here.'

Jason fell back onto his chair. Bobbi asked Duke to dance. Why was she asking Duke to dance? Bobbi was his date, not Duke's.

She returned to the table, all smiles. She was so damned cute, so fun. Jason was ready to forgive her.

Until she opened her mouth. 'Where's Duke?'

'Missing him already?'

Her smile ran out of energy. 'Just curious. Are you OK?'

'Just wondering how my date wound up dancing with another guy.'

She lowered her eyes, unable to meet his gaze. 'That was tacky. I just love dancing with really good dancers. So, when he made some crack about giving the women a treat on the dance floor, I had to ask if he knew how to dance and he said he did and I said, "Yeah? Show me," and then . . . he did.' Bobbi looked at him earnestly. 'I'm sorry. Let me make it up to you.'

'I can't dance like Duke,' Jason said grumpily.

She grinned at that. 'But you can be taught.'

OK, she'd said she was sorry. He stood up, managed a smile, and held out his hand to her. 'Let's dance.'

And they did. Mostly slow dances and some shaking around to the fast numbers. She tried to show him a couple of steps, but his brain and feet refused to cooperate.

'You'll get the hang of it eventually,' Bobbi promised.

As the evening wore on, Jason realised he was not having fun. Finally, he said, 'How about taking a break?'

She looked wistfully at the other dancers, but said, 'OK. Let's bag it for the night. Want to come back to the apartment and watch a movie? It's still early.'

Hope was at the apartment when they arrived. She'd changed into sweats and was curled up on the loveseat with a book.

'We thought we'd watch a movie,' Bobbi said to her. 'Want to join us?'

'Don't let us chase you off,' Jason added. 'Stay.'

'I just got the new James Bond from Netflix,' Bobbi said, pulling Oreos from a cupboard. 'Come on,' she urged her sister.

Hope surrendered, positioning herself in a chair and leaving the loveseat for Jason and Bobbi. Bobbi set the cookies on the coffee table. Jason idly picked up the Jane Austen book sitting on it. The bookmark hadn't moved since the last time he was here. It was still on page two.

'You guys are going to love this movie,' Bobbi said, and snuggled in next to Jason.

Maybe he would have loved it, but he kept thinking about that bookmark. And his and Bobbi's dance incompatibility. And, after the movie, after she'd walked him to the door and given him a kiss that should have fried his memory chip completely, he walked to his truck thinking about something else: the look he'd seen flash between her and Duke.

Bobbi flopped on the loveseat and helped herself to another cookie. 'I swear, I could have eaten this whole packet, but I didn't want to look like a pig in front of Jason.'

Hope was looking at her disapprovingly. 'Now you think about what you look like in front of Jason?'

'What's that supposed to mean?' Deep down she knew.

'Maybe you shouldn't be looking at his friend like you're on a diet and he's Boston cream pie.'

'I was not looking at him like that,' Bobbi protested. She could feel her cheeks flushing.

'Jason saw it, too,' Hope said. 'And I don't think he was very happy that you left him to dance with Duke.'

'We got that all straightened out. I said I was sorry.'

Hope shrugged, and returned the cookies to the kitchen.

Bobbi could feel panic starting to rise in her. She couldn't afford to lose the perfect man. Why did Duke have to come along and make her mess up? This was silly. Things were fine with Jason.

Still, insurance would be good. 'I'll write him a letter and go put it in his truck,' Bobbie decided. She sat down at the Formica table with paper and pen. 'What can I say?'

'That you're sorry,' Hope suggested.

She picked up her book and started for her room, and that made Bobbi panic all the more. 'Don't leave me,' she begged.

Hope turned back and slumped on the loveseat, closing her eyes.

Bobbi held her breath, waiting for magic to happen.

And then her sister, the good fairy of love, spoke. 'What about this? "Rhythm and music and feet aren't the real dance. The real dance is when two hearts move together."'

Her sister was amazing. 'I couldn't do that in a million years.' Bobbi buried her face in her hands. 'This is like cheating on a test. I shouldn't be doing this.'

'Well, then, you come up with the last part.'

Bobbi heaved a sigh. '"My heart wants to dance with you!"'

Hope nodded. 'Only maybe change the *you* to *yours*.'

Bobbi scrawled out the sentence. There. She wasn't a fraud. She folded the paper and jumped up from the table. 'I'm going to go put this under his windshield wiper so he'll find it tomorrow.'

Bobbi drove to the duplex Jason was renting. She slipped her offering under his wiper. There. Now everything would be fine.

On Sunday, the sisters' usual Sunday lunch together was more torture than fun for Hope. Bobbi kept up a constant stream of fretting. 'Do you think he got the letter yet?' . . . 'Does it sound like I wrote it?' . . . 'I need retail therapy. Let's go to the mall.'

Hope needed garden therapy.

'I should really run over to the garden for a while.'

Bobbi looked disappointed. 'OK.' She sat bolt upright. 'I should just go over to Jason's.'

'Good idea,' Hope said. Bobbi would go over and fall into Jason's arms. And then they'd live happily ever after.

Hope shot out of the apartment as soon as Bobbi left and drove to Grandview Park. Garden therapy, garden therapy.

Millie and Amber were both already there when she arrived, and were busy putting chicken wire round Amber's veggies.

'Welcome to the Bunny Produce Mart,' Amber greeted Hope. 'That stupid rabbit got into my garden and ate my lettuce. I should have listened to you earlier, Millie.'

'Better late than never,' comforted Millie.

Amber looked to where Seth sat by the bunny's favourite camping spot, inching a carrot under the bushes. 'I doubt he needs that, well fed as he is,' she said.

'The animals have to live, too,' Millie reminded her.

'I don't know why they can't learn to live on things we don't want to grow, like dandelions,' said Amber.

'It's the Murphy's Law of gardening,' said Millie.

That made Hope chuckle. Just being here with these women sloughed off her bad mood. The sun was warm and the air smelled of earth and growing things.

'We were just talking about how much fun the Slugfest was,' Millie said to Hope. 'It looked like you were having fun. I saw you dancing as my friend and I were leaving.'

Hope felt her stomach clench. Oh, no. No talking about Jason here. That would be pathetically un-Zen.

'Millie's *male* friend,' added Amber, her voice teasing. 'He's a hottie, Millie.'

Relieved to have the topic turned away from herself, Hope asked, 'Who's the friend?'

'Actually, it's the man I met when the flower deliveries got mixed up,' said Millie.

'Is this someone special?' Hope asked. As if they couldn't tell simply by Millie's smile.

'He is,' Millie admitted. 'He's a widower, new to Heart Lake.'

'Millie's the welcoming committee.' Amber quickly added, 'Seriously, I think it's great that you've got a boyfriend.'

Millie suddenly got very busy weeding. 'Well, I am enjoying his company. Life is short, girls. It's foolish not to take advantage of every good thing that comes along.'

Amber grinned wickedly. 'Have you taken advantage of Altheus yet?'

Millie shook a gloved finger at her. 'You are a naughty thing.' She sat back on her heels, admiring her handiwork. 'A garden is such an amazing thing, isn't it? There it is, the whole cycle of life played out for us every year—death, then resurrection, new buds, new life, new beginnings.' She returned her attention to Hope. 'Speaking of new beginnings, dear, tell us about that handsome man you were dancing with.'

'There's nothing to tell, really. I was just having a dance with my sister's boyfriend.'

'Your sister's boyfriend,' Millie said in surprise. 'You two looked like you were meant to be partners.'

'Jason wants Bobbi. And that's just as well.'

'Why is that?' asked Amber.

Hope gave a shrug. 'She's the pretty one.'

'You're not exactly unattractive, either,' said Amber.

'I am naked.' Hope regretted the words the second they slipped out of her mouth.

'Is it the fallout from the cancer, dear?' said Millie.

Suddenly, Hope watched in horror as her tears seeped into the soil. 'No man wants a woman who's scarred.'

Amber left her garden patch and came into Hope's, sitting her down and sitting next to her, and putting an arm round her. 'Hey, come on. That's not true. A real man cares more about what's inside than what's outside. And it can't be that bad.'

Hope shook her head. 'It is. Trust me.' She ran a hand through her hair. It was getting longer all the time, the curl slowly loosening its hold as her hair remembered it had once been straight. 'This is so embarrassing. I don't know what's wrong with me today.' But, of course, she did. It was the same thing that had been wrong with her since Jason Wells first walked into her shop.

Millie joined them and sat on the other side of Hope.

'You had reconstructive surgery, right?' Amber pressed.

Hope nodded. 'It's not the same.' She could barely speak.

'Think of how many women are walking round with implants and leading perfectly normal lives,' Millie said.

'I am leading a perfectly normal life,' Hope insisted.

'A life where you turn your back on love is not perfectly normal,' Millie gently chided.

'It's better than trying to build a future with someone when I don't even know how much of a future I'll have,' Hope said, her voice barely above a whisper. 'Getting cancer this young, my chances are so much higher that . . .' Her voice broke.

'None of us has any guarantee,' Amber said, hugging her fiercely. 'You can't just give up and sit on the sidelines.'

'Live your life to the fullest,' Millie added. 'Take advantage of every good thing that comes into it.'

'Like Millie's taking advantage of Altheus,' cracked Amber, easing them into a lighter mood. 'So, when *are* you going to take advantage of Altheus?' she added.

Millie blushed. 'Now, don't be asking nosy questions. Anyway, he's seven years younger than me.'

'Sweet. A toy boy,' said Amber, clapping her hands.

'We're just friends,' Millie said firmly.

Amber cocked an eyebrow. 'After that lecture you just gave Hope, we don't want to hear you didn't go for it because of a little thing like age.'

'A little thing like age is why I don't have to be in a hurry to go for it,' Millie replied crisply. 'I think that's enough serious conversation for today. But let's take a lesson from our flowers. They seek out the sun. How can we do less than these sweet flowers?'

'I'm going to remember you said that,' Amber warned her.

'You must have gone to the Grange,' Hope said when Bobbi walked into the apartment later that evening.

'Yeah,' Bobbi said listlessly.

'I take it you didn't see Jason?'

'No.' Bobbi frowned. 'But, you know, I don't need a man around all the time.'

Hope looked cosy, curled up on the loveseat with a book. Bobbi settled in with her Jane Austen book and a glass of wine. She could be cosy, too.

She lasted an hour. 'Want to watch a movie?'

'Sure,' said Hope, and set aside her book.

The movie didn't really help, either. Bobbi kept thinking about Jason. He had to have read her letter by now. Why hadn't he called?

Hope was at the shop early on Monday. By nine the phone was ringing. She should have had plenty to keep her mind busy, but the sawing and hammering on the site next door kept luring her thoughts to Jason.

'You have to stop this,' she scolded herself.

And she almost had when, out of the blue, he wandered into the shop. He had sawdust in his hair. 'Hi.'

'Hi,' she said.

He rubbed his chin as if he were trying to remember what he was doing in her flower shop. 'Is your sister in yet?'

'Not yet. I'll tell her you came by.'

'You don't have to do that,' he said quickly. 'Look, can I ask you a question? About Bobbi?'

'Sure.' Maybe he wanted advice on rings.

'Does your sister like to read?'

'Excuse me?'

'Never mind. See you later.' He turned and left.

What on earth was that all about?

Ten

TY DROPPED OFF an application at the Family Inn on Tuesday. On Wednesday, Charlie Thomas, the owner, called him in for an interview that afternoon. Amber bit off every fingernail as she waited for Ty to come home. She even prayed.

She heard the crunch of tyres on gravel and tensed.

The door opened. Seth hopped up and ran to greet his dad. Amber was afraid to even look in Ty's direction. What would she do if she saw failure on his face again? How could she handle it?

She heard Ty say, 'Hey, buddy.' Was there a new energy in his voice or was she imagining it?

She forced herself to look in her husband's direction.

A smile. 'How'd it go?'

'You're looking at the Family Inn's new chef.'

She jumped up with a squeal and ran to Ty and threw her arms round him, and now he was twirling her in the air and Seth was clapping and giggling. It was like they had just stepped out of a big, dark cocoon. God had been listening.

'This calls for a celebration,' she said. There wasn't anything much to celebrate with other than popcorn, but she put a scented candle on the table and presented the treat with much fanfare. And the guys were pleased.

'The place is a disaster,' Ty said, digging into his bowl. 'Their chef quit two weeks ago and the owner has been trying to do it all. He says the cooking isn't really his thing.'

'Then why on earth did he open a restaurant?'

'He did it for his kids. His daughter had just finished cooking school; his son needed work. But then his daughter got pregnant and decided on a career change and his son moved to L.A. The guy's heart's just not in it now.'

Her husband had been hired by a man who didn't know what he was doing, to work in a restaurant that was going down. This was not what Amber had in mind when she asked God for help.

'But here's the cool part,' Ty went on. 'Thomas might be willing to sell down the road.'

Amber stared at him. She felt suddenly sick. 'Why don't you just feed me poison now and be done with it.'

Ty's smile reversed direction. 'Hey, hear me out.'

No. No hearing out, no talking. 'Sethie, you want to watch *SpongeBob SquarePants*?' She picked up his bowl of popcorn.

'My popcorn!' he protested.

'You can eat it while you watch cartoons. OK?' She settled Seth in front of the TV, then went to the bedroom.

Ty followed her in. 'You didn't let me finish. I'd be the head chef, run the kitchen for the next five years, and Thomas would stay in. I'd get a percentage of the profits and that would go towards buying the place. That would give me time to turn it around.'

Was he crazy? They hadn't been able to get their first restaurant going, and now he wanted to turn around one that was in trouble.

She threw up her hands. 'Why can't you be happy to just be the head chef?'

'You can lose a job.'

'You can lose a business, too. Or have you forgotten?'

He stiffened. 'No. You won't let me.'

'Why is everything my fault?' she cried. 'Why is it always about you and what you want and never about me? When does it matter if I'm hurting?' Thoughts that had been backing up in her brain for months spilled out. 'Ty, what have I done to deserve the moping and the emotional disconnect? Where does it say I get to carry everyone in this family on my back?' Ty was staring at her in horror. And that made her all the more berserk. 'When do you start remembering that there are two other people in this family?'

She turned her back on him, buried her hands in her face, and burst into bitter tears. He didn't try to comfort her.

A moment later she heard the front door slam. She fell on the bed and kept on crying. What was she going to do?

She was going to go see Millie.

She went back out into the living room. Seth, fortunately, had gotten sucked into cartoons. She looked out of the window and saw the car still parked outside. Ty had taken off on foot. Well, good.

She called Millie and didn't bother with small talk. 'I need help. Can I come over?'

'Of course,' said Millie. 'I'll make tea.'

Amber loaded Seth in the car and took off. They hadn't gone far when they passed Ty, storming down the road. Amber stepped on the gas and floored it past him.

'There's Daddy!' cried Seth.

'Yes, Daddy's taking a walk.'

Millie's house, which had been quiet the last time Amber was there, was now a hotbed of noise. A boy sat on the couch, playing a noisy video game on TV, and a young teen was on her cellphone, talking. Seth took it all in, wide-eyed.

'Hi, Seth,' Millie said. 'I've got some apple slices for you. Would you like to eat them out here with Eric?'

Seth nodded, staring at the TV.

Millie set the plate on the coffee table and settled Seth on the couch next to Eric, then she led Amber into the kitchen.

'Sit down,' said Millie. 'I'll have tea in a minute.'

Amber fell onto a chair. 'Ty got a job.'

'But that's wonderful.' Millie poured hot water into a china teapot. 'I guess there's a downside here, but I'm not seeing it.'

'The man is talking about selling the restaurant to Ty.'

Millie stopped pouring. 'Oh.'

'Yeah, oh. This guy's got a lemon on his hands he wants to unload and in walks Ty, with "Sucker" written on his forehead.'

Millie brought the teapot to the table. 'I assume you and Ty discussed this.' She set a cup and saucer in front of Amber and one in front of the chair opposite and sat down.

'I'm not sure "discussed" is exactly the word. Oh, Millie, what am I going to do?'

Millie poured tea in each of their cups. 'Surely the owner didn't expect Ty to come in and buy him out immediately, not when he only came in looking for a job?'

Amber shook her head. 'No. Ty said something about doing this over the next five years. Millie, I don't want to own another restaurant. I don't want to lose everything I have.'

'You've already lost a business and a house. What more could you lose? Except your family?'

Amber's fingers clenched round her cup. 'Ty's the one who's going to lose the family. I can't do this again.'

'What if he sees this as a second chance, an opportunity to save his family?'

'What if he sees this as a chance to save his pride?' Amber countered. Really, Millie was not helping at all.

'Well, dear, I certainly can't tell you how to live your life, but if I were in your shoes . . .'

Amber made a face. 'You'd be perfect.' Why had she come over here, anyway?

Millie shook her head. 'I was far from perfect, both as a wife and a mother. Maybe if I'd been a little more assertive, especially in financial matters, my life would be different now.'

'Then I shouldn't just go along with this?'

'I didn't say that. I think you need to look beyond the immediate future.'

Amber stared into her cup. 'I just feel like no matter what, I lose. If I get behind Ty and say, "Go for it with the restaurant," then we'll probably lose our shirts. If I don't, then we'll probably lose our marriage.'

Millie gave a deep sigh. 'That is a hard choice. I guess you have to ask yourself which is more important.'

If she were to be honest, Amber would have to admit that right now security and peace of mind were what she wanted more than anything. 'I'm just so sick of struggling. I want to be past this.'

'I felt like that when Duncan was ill,' said Millie. 'In fact, I felt like that so many times.'

'Yeah? When?'

'When the boys were little, Duncan lost his job. He developed a . . . problem.'

'What kind of problem?'

'He drank.' Millie looked embarrassed. 'But he got over it. He was a member of Alcoholics Anonymous for years.'

'So, how'd you manage that?'

'I didn't manage it, although God knows I tried,' Millie said with a shake of her head.

'OK, then what happened?'

'It was Christmas Eve. He was still out of work and he'd been out job hunting. He stopped off for a beer and didn't come home. I took the children to my mother's and spent the night.'

'That sounds good to me,' Amber said.

'Being separated from my husband wasn't what I really wanted,' said Millie. 'But I was prepared to do it if I had to.'

'I guess it worked.'

'You could say that. But it wasn't as if I had a plan. It was more a case of Duncan finally coming to his senses. He came to the house Christmas morning with a note he'd written promising no imbibing in the New Year. He never touched another drop of liquor.'

'And, obviously, he got a job.'

'In Little Haven. It turned out to be the best thing that ever happened to us. We had a very nice life.'

'But—' Amber began.

'Yes, I know. Now here I am living with my daughter. We made some mistakes and paid for it. It happens. Life doesn't always go smoothly. What Duncan and I learned together in those early hard years was what helped us survive all the bumps that came after.'

'I could survive the bumps better if my husband wasn't the one making them,' Amber muttered. 'I can't take much more of this.'

Millie took a sip of tea. 'You're a strong girl. You'll sort everything out.'

Amber looked at the wall clock. Five thirty. 'I'd better get going so you guys can have your dinner,' she said, and stood.

'Oh, don't worry. Debra won't be home for another hour.'

Seth's laughter drifted in from the living room.

'If I don't get my son out of here pretty soon, he's going to start spinning round the room like a flying saucer.'

They went into the living room. 'Come on, Sethie,' Amber said. 'We need to go and see if Daddy's back from his walk yet.'

The front door opened and in walked a woman in her late thirties. She was slender like her mother and had the same blue eyes, but there the resemblance ended. She was like a psychic porcupine, sending out sharp, angry vibes.

'Debra, you're home early,' Millie said.

'I've got a migraine starting.'

'You should probably go right to bed,' Millie told her.

'Sorry to be rude,' the woman murmured to Amber, but she didn't look all that sorry.

'This is my friend, Amber,' Millie said.

'We were just leaving,' Amber explained. She gave Millie a hug. To Debra she said, 'Your mom's the greatest.'

'Yes, she is,' agreed Debra, and managed a smile.

'Come on, Sethie,' Amber said. 'Let's go.'

Ty was nowhere to be seen when Amber got home. That was just as well she decided, as she made burritos for her and Seth. She didn't want to talk to her husband anyway, not if they were going to talk about starting another restaurant.

She put Seth in the tub, leaving the door open so she could hear him. She was cleaning up when Ty finally showed up. And what was this? Flowers? 'I walked into town,' he said. 'I thought you might like them.'

'What are these for?'

'I'm sorry I got so pissed off. I was mad because . . .' He shifted his gaze out of the kitchen window to the lake, which was slowly darkening in the twilight. 'I want you to believe in me. But I haven't given you any reason to, so I guess I can't blame you. Anyway, you were trying to make a celebration and I ruined it. You've been trying hard. I've been nothing but a loser.'

She felt her throat tightening. 'Oh, Ty.' She slipped her arms round his waist. 'I'm so scared. We lost everything. And then, I lost you. I just . . . want to feel safe.'

He didn't say anything, but his arms came round her.

She began to cry. 'I don't want to lose anything more.'

He was rubbing her back now. 'I know. I'm sorry.'

She hated herself for not being a Millie, not being willing to gamble everything for her man, but she couldn't. 'Can we just wait for a while and see how this place does? I need to be able to stop holding my breath.' As soon as the words were out, she realised what she'd done. She'd opened the door to the dangerous possibility that they'd risk it all again.

He hugged her close. 'We can wait.'

'And what if I don't want to buy the restaurant, what if I never want to?' She looked up into his face.

'We have to both want it or I won't do it.'

'You mean it?' Could he really do this?

'I want my own place, but I'm not going to throw us under the bus again. For now, I can be happy to be working.'

'Thank you,' she whispered. Maybe they hadn't lost everything. Maybe they still had each other. To see, she kissed him.

He kissed her back. Really kissed her.

'Mommy, I'm done,' Seth called from the bathroom.

They broke off the kiss. Ty was smiling. 'We'll finish this later.'

And later Amber realised they weren't going to be finished for a long time.

Amber called Millie the morning after her visit. 'I can't talk long,' she said, 'but I just wanted to tell you that we have had a major breakthrough over here. It's like a miracle.'

'I'm so happy for you,' said Millie.

'Thanks for being there. You're better than a shrink. I'm working tomorrow. Come on in and have a thank-you latte on me.'

Millie couldn't help feeling glad, both that her young friend was doing well now and that she'd been able to help. It was good to be needed, good to have someone want to hear what you had to say.

'Who was that?' Debra asked, coming into the kitchen. She was in her bathrobe, but she looked better than she had the day before.

'Just a friend,' Millie said. 'Are you feeling better?'

Debra nodded. 'I'm glad I called in sick though.'

'Since you're home, would you like to do something fun today?'

Debra nodded thoughtfully. 'Why not?'

By eleven thirty, Millie and her daughter sat with the early-lunch crowd, sampling the quiche at Sweet Somethings.

Debra took a sip of her tea. 'It feels good to take the day off.'

'You've been going awfully hard,' Millie said.

Debra set down her mug. 'I hate my job.'

'Maybe you should look for a new one,' suggested Millie.

'Mom, I can't just quit. I've got bills. It's not like it was for you. I can't just say, "Oh, I want to stay home and play in the garden."'

Millie wasn't sure she liked the implication that her life as a wife and mother had been one long garden party.

'Life is all about choices, Debra,' she said firmly. 'If you don't like your life, make it different.'

Debra blinked in surprise. Then her features soured. 'I didn't choose to be divorced, Mom.'

'Yes, you did,' Millie said with a sigh. 'You probably made a million little choices that brought you to this point. But that's water under the bridge. If you want to go somewhere better, you're going to have to start picking some new paths.'

Millie realised she should have given her daughter this kind of a tough-love pep talk years ago. She and Duncan had treated their baby like a hothouse flower. Whenever Debra got in trouble at school, Millie and Duncan took her part, something they'd never done with the boys. When she overspent her allowance in college, they bailed her out. When Debra and her husband fought, Millie always took Debra's side. If she'd been able to be as impartial as she'd been when giving advice to Amber, would Debra still be married? Who knew? But it hadn't helped that she'd never built in her daughter the endurance for weathering hard times. What a painful thing to have to admit!

But Millie began to take hope that maybe her pep talk had done some good. On Sunday, Debra announced she was going line dancing at the Grange. 'You don't need a partner to dance,' she told Millie. 'They have a beginner class at five. You don't mind feeding the kids, do you?'

'They don't want to go with you?' Millie asked. She'd actually planned to go out with Altheus.

'They wouldn't be interested.'

'I'll make something,' Millie promised. She also promised herself that next time she had plans, she wouldn't cancel them.

So when Debra called on Tuesday asking if she could run Eric to his five thirty dental appointment, Millie said, 'I'd love to, dear, but I have plans.'

'With Altheus?'

'Yes,' Millie said, determinedly pleasant.

Debra gave a disgusted snort. 'I thought you moved here to help me.'

'I did,' Millie said, her voice less pleasant. She could feel her blood pressure rising, along with her ire. 'I also moved out here so we could enjoy spending more time together, something which we've done very little of. I didn't move out here to become your au pair. Things like dental appointments and Little League games are your department, Debra, and I wouldn't dream of depriving you of the satisfaction of being able to do those motherly duties.'

Debra was still sputtering when she hung up, and that made Millie feel a little guilty. But not guilty enough to break her plans with Altheus. Debra wasn't the only one who needed a new life.

Eleven

JUNE HAD FOLLOWED a wet Memorial Day weekend. Other than meeting for coffee, Bobbi hadn't seen much of Jason. She could have. Her note had worked wonders and he was securely in her pocket now. He'd invited her to go camping over the weekend. She'd invented a big wedding and claimed she couldn't possibly leave Hope to fill the order single-handed, so Jason's brother went with him.

And now he was back, it was Friday, and they were going dancing. Everything was going according to plan.

Until someone wandered into the flower shop: Mr Not-Perfect. Bobbi stared at Duke and swallowed hard in a feeble attempt to water her dry mouth. 'What are you doing here?' she blurted.

He frowned. 'I came to order some flowers.'

'You've got a girlfriend,' she accused.

'No, they're just for someone I wish was my girlfriend.'

Ouch. What did she care, though? She didn't want Duke. She wanted perfect, stable, sweet, boring Jason. Boring? Where had that come from?

'What kind of flowers do you want?' Bobbi asked.

'I'm not sure.'

'It's hard to help you if you don't know what you want.'

'Oh, I know what *I* want.'

The way he was looking at her was not good. Neither was the way she was feeling. Well, actually, it was very good. But this wasn't supposed to be happening with Duke.

Bobbi bit her lip. 'I'm dating Jason.'

'Lame.'

He leaned closer. 'So, Jase tells me you guys know what flowers mean. What flower says you belong with me?'

'I don't know.' The words came out as a squeak.

'Well, find out and then send yourself some. And let my boy off the hook. You guys don't belong together.'

'Yes, we do,' she called as Duke left the shop.

Jason returned from problems at the new house they were building on the lake to discover one of his workers at the downtown project was demolishing the wrong wall. The day went downhill from there. By the time he'd put out half a dozen more small fires, Jason was fried. He was seeing Bobbi that night, and he'd promised he'd take her dancing. All he wanted to do was crash in front of the TV.

He called her on his cellphone as he drove home to shower.

'Hi, Jason,' she said, chipper as always.

He felt even more tired. 'Hey, do you mind if we just watch the tube or something tonight? I've had a hell of a day.'

'OK,' she said. 'Come on over and I'll order a pizza.'

He didn't even want to drive. 'How about you come over here and I'll order the pizza?' The privacy would do them good.

'OK,' she agreed. Suddenly, her enthusiasm was underwhelming.

Even though he was shot, he did a quick detour by the Safeway to pick up some Ben and Jerry's chocolate fudge brownie ice cream, her favourite.

She arrived at his place at seven. 'What happened at work?' she asked. 'Did somebody drop a hammer on your foot?'

'Somebody damn near dropped a whole building on my head. And that was just for starters.' He pulled her to him and said, 'I'll make it up to you, I promise. I just needed some peace and quiet.'

She did settle in and enjoyed the action flick he'd rented. And she really enjoyed the ice cream. Watching her lick her spoon, Jason realised he wasn't so pooped any more. 'Come here.' He pulled her in close for a kiss. And another, and another.

Then, suddenly, she was pulling away. 'I know we've been dating awhile now.'

'Yeah?' he prompted. He put an arm round her and leaned in to nibble on her neck, but she slipped out of his embrace and left the couch, saying, 'This is wrong. I can't do this.' She snatched up her handbag and started for the door.

'What? Where are you going?' he protested.

'I have to go home and think.'

He was off the couch now. 'What?'

She shook her head. 'I have to go.'

What was she doing? There she'd been, kissing Jason and thinking of Duke. How sick and wrong was that?

Now she didn't have any doubt at all. She knew for sure she couldn't keep Jason. They weren't right for each other. She had to tell him they were through. Right now.

In less than four minutes, she was back on his porch, banging on the door. He yanked it open.

'I can't see you any more,' she blurted.

'What? Here, come on in.'

He joined her in the living room where she sat on the couch.

'Bobbi, if it's about not going dancing tonight . . .'

'No. It's about us not being a fit. We don't have anything in common.'

His brows knitted together. 'We don't?'

'I think you'd better sit down.'

He sat on the other end of the couch. 'OK.'

'I'm a fake. I hate hiking. And I'm not that into books.'

'But all those books?' he protested.

'Belong to my sister. Well, except Jane Austen. I like to read magazines and romance novels. And I don't own half the flower shop. I just work there. My sister gave me the job when I got fired.'

'What about the cards, the letters?'

'My sister wrote them for me. I couldn't think of what to say. I know it was wrong,' Bobbi rushed on. 'I wanted to impress you. I thought you were the perfect man. But the problem is, you're not the perfect man for me. And I'm not the perfect woman for you.'

'I can't believe this.'

'I'm sorry. I never meant to hurt you.'

He shook his head. 'What an ass I am. And your sister went along with this?'

'Don't blame Hope,' Bobbi begged. 'I made her do it. Anyway, she only wanted to help me.' She managed one more 'I'm sorry,' then fled, crying.

She was still crying when she stumbled into the apartment. Hope shot up from the loveseat where she'd been reading. 'What's wrong? What happened?'

'I broke up with Jason,' Bobbi wailed.

Hope looked at her like she'd just confessed to vehicular manslaughter. 'Why?'

'Because I couldn't do it any more. I'm a phony.' She went to the refrigerator. 'I need more chocolate.'

She pulled out a pint of ice cream, got a spoon, and plopped down at the table. 'It was terrible. But I had to get everything off my chest.'

Hope sat down opposite her. 'Everything?'

Bobbi spooned a heap of ice cream into her mouth. 'He even knows I don't own the shop. He even knows about the cards. I told him you wrote them.'

Hope took Bobbi's spoon and the ice cream and shovelled herself a big mountain of it. 'We'll never see him again.'

'Like I want to?' Bobbi said.

'Oh, Bobs,' Hope said, and left the table.

'Hope!' Bobbi cried after her, but Hope shook her head, went into her bedroom and shut the door.

All Saturday morning, Hope kept watching the shop door, hoping Jason would come in, maybe wanting to hear her side of the story. But he never did.

She was doing some bookwork when Amber stopped by. 'Don't forget you're sneaking out early today for Millie's birthday.'

Hope had forgotten. 'I'll do her arrangement right away.'

'And I'm bringing the birthday cake. It's a lavender cake from Sweet Somethings and it's now my all-time favourite. And look what I found.' She opened a pink paper bag and pulled out a little plaque which proclaimed, 'Friends Are For Ever.'

'She'll love it,' said Hope. She reread the words. This was what mattered, her friends. As long as she had them, she'd be fine.

She finished Millie's bouquet, then left Bobbi in charge of the shop and went to the community garden. Amber had been waiting on the side of the road, and now drove behind her into the park. As usual, Millie was already there, tending her flowers.

Amber pulled a picnic basket from the back seat of her car and gave it to Seth, then got out a Tupperware carrier with her cake. 'OK, let's go make her day.'

'We're gonna have a party,' Seth informed Hope.

'Yes, we are,' Hope said, smiling.

'What's this?' Millie said as their little parade approached.

'It's a garden party,' said Amber, 'for your birthday.'

She started singing 'Happy Birthday'. Hope and Seth joined in.

'Oh, girls, you shouldn't have,' Millie protested.

'Of course we should have,' Hope said, presenting her with the birthday bouquet. 'We just want you to know we love you.'

Millie put a hand to her chest. 'I'm overwhelmed.'

'You better not be too overwhelmed to eat this lavender cake,' said Amber.

'Lavender? Oh, how lovely!'

Amber cut pieces of cake and they sat in Millie's garden plot among the flowers, eating cake and drinking bottled juice.

'This cake is wonderful,' said Millie.

'You saved my marriage,' Amber said to Millie. 'I owe you cake for life.'

Millie brushed away her gratitude with a wave of her hand.

'What are you doing for your birthday?' Amber asked.

'Well, let's see. Debra's coming home from work early Monday and making birthday dinner and, on Tuesday, Altheus is taking me to the Family Inn.'

'I thought he'd take you someplace really nice, like the Two Turtledoves,' said Amber.

'Oh, he offered. But I told him I wanted to go to the Family Inn. I hear they have a wonderful new chef there.'

Amber beamed. 'Yes, they do.'

'Let's open the present,' said Seth, tired of grown-up talk.

Amber dug their gift out of the picnic basket. 'It's from Hope and me.'

'And me,' piped Seth.

Millie lifted the plaque out of its tissue paper bed, and her eyes filled with tears as she read it. 'You girls, you shouldn't have.'

Just then a butterfly swooped down and landed on one of Millie's cosmos. 'Look, a butterfly!' cried Seth.

Millie smiled. 'We used to say butterflies mean good luck.'

'He must be here for one of you guys,' Amber said. 'I've already got mine.'

'Then it must be you, Millie,' Hope said. It sure wasn't her.

Bobbi sat at the order desk looking out of the window at the shoppers. She wished someone would come into the shop. She'd finished *People* and now she was totally bored. What to do?

She'd tidy up. She went into the workroom and wet a paper towel, then came back out and started to wipe down the counter. Bobbi even moved the computer so she could clean behind it.

And what was this? A little piece of paper with Hope's writing.

I teach the steps. She dances. I wish I could dance. With him.

Bobbi got that it was a poem, and not a happy one. But who was the she? Hope? And what him?

She sat at the counter and stared at the poem.

The bell over the door jingled and in walked Duke. Bobbi's heart started doing the happy dance at the sight of him.

'When do you close?' he asked.

'In about an hour. Why?'

'Because in an hour, you're getting on my motorcycle and we're going to the lake to celebrate.' He held up a bottle of sparkling wine.

'Celebrate what?'

'Your freedom. It's about time,' he added.

She slumped down at the counter. 'I hurt him.'

'He'll get over it. You guys weren't a match. Trust me, I know.'

She couldn't resist asking, 'How do you know?'

''Cause you're right for me.' He leaned over the counter and gave her a kiss that had so much heat, it should have wilted every flower in the place.

She sighed. 'I still feel bad though. And not just for Jason. Look what I found.' She held out the paper.

Duke took it, read it, and frowned. 'It's a poem.'

'I know that. I just don't know what it means.'

'Do you know who wrote this?' Duke asked.

'My sister. It's her handwriting.'

He studied the poem some more.

'You're the she. Your sister's jealous of you.'

'What?' Bobbi picked up the paper. 'That's impossible. She doesn't have a jealous bone in her body.'

He shrugged. 'She did when she wrote this.'

'Oh, it's got to be something else. How could she be jealous when she thought Jason was perfect for me?'

Duke snorted. 'How well does your sister know you, anyway?'

'No, you don't understand. I tend to pick losers.'

'Used to pick losers,' Duke corrected her.

Bobbi rewarded him with a smile, then returned to the subject of Hope. 'She thinks I blew it and she's not happy that we'll never see him again.'

'We?'

'That's what she said.' Bobbi remembered it clearly. A light bulb suddenly clicked on. 'Oh, my gosh. All this time Hope's been in love with Jason.' Bobbi ran round the counter, grabbed Duke's hand, and started running for the door. 'Come on.' She flipped the sign to Closed and shut and locked the door.

'I thought you had to stay open,' he said.

'Not now,' she said. 'We've got an emergency.'

The Sticks and Balls was a rundown tavern on the outskirts of town. The regulars knew what the place was about. It was man haven, a hangout where guys could have a beer, shoot some pool and shoot the bull.

Jason watched warily from the corner where he was playing a solitary game of eight ball as Bobbi hurried towards him with his so-called friend right behind her. Duke hadn't wasted any time.

'You need to know something,' Bobbi greeted him.

'I think I know all I want to know.' Jason took aim and launched the cue ball at the two. It hit its target with a resounding clack and the two jumped into the corner pocket.

'About my sister.'

Jason lined up his next shot.

'I think she's in love with you.'

He missed the cue ball entirely. He straightened and frowned at Bobbi. 'That's nuts.'

'No,' she corrected him, 'that's Hope. She'd never take you for herself if she thought I wanted you. In fact,' Bobbi added sadly, 'she'd never take you for herself at all.'

He shook his head and turned his attention back to the balls.

'I know I messed up,' Bobbi said. 'But I didn't mean to. I was so sure you were perfect for me. That's how everything started with Hope. She's the smart one, and I thought if I got her to help me, then I could really impress you.'

Jason focused on his next shot. Maybe if he ignored her long enough, Bobbi would give up and leave.

A small hand slipped into Jason's field of vision, setting a piece of paper on the green felt. 'I just found this. Hope wrote it.'

'I've read enough of your sister's writing.'

'You need to see it. She's been in love with you all along.'

'Right.' Jason sent another ball tumbling into a corner pocket. 'How about you two beat it and leave me alone?'

Duke took Bobbi's arm and led her away. 'Come on. You tried.'

After he was sure they were gone, Jason read the hastily scrawled words. Then he reread them. He folded the paper and stuffed it in the pocket of his shirt, where it rode round for the rest of the afternoon and that evening, as he worked on a wood carving.

He cut deeper into the wood than he'd intended and swore. He gave up, flipped the TV on to the fight, then sprawled on the couch and glared at the boxers. He didn't care how smart Hope Walker was. She was a sneak, just like her sister.

So then, why, on Monday, did he find himself wandering into the damned flower shop?

Hope was standing at the counter, taking an order over the phone. She saw him and her face suddenly looked like she'd gotten a three-hour sunburn. 'We'll get that out today,' she said weakly. 'No problem. Thanks for calling.' Then she hung up and looked at him like he was a giant Venus flytrap about to swallow her. She cleared her throat. 'I'm sorry things didn't work out with you and Bobbi.'

'Did you think they would? Everything about her was a façade, and you built it.'

Hope got busy straightening the counter. 'Bobbi isn't good with words. She wanted to impress you. It got out of hand.'

Jason gave a disgusted snort. 'Do ya think?'

'Nobody meant to hurt you. And you can hardly blame my sister for realising you two weren't a fit and stopping it before it went any further. She felt like a fake.'

'She also felt like taking up with my best friend.'

Hope sighed. 'There is that.' She looked at him with regret in her eyes. 'A heart's not like a car. You don't drive it. It drives you.'

'Nicely put,' he conceded sourly.

She has a way with words, whispered the little paper in his pocket. *Maybe you should ask her about me.*

'Look,' Jason said, softening his voice. 'I just want some clarification.' He pulled out the paper. 'Did you write this?'

She looked confused, so he handed it over. She read it and the blood drained from her face. 'Where did you get this?'

'I found it.'

She closed her hand round the paper, crumpling it, and took a step back. 'It's just a poem. I was doodling one day.'

'Who's it about?'

She took another step. 'I don't remember.'

Like hell.

'I've got an order to fill and I'm sure you've got to get back to work.' Another step. 'I'm sorry you got hurt. I'm sorry for everything. Next time you want to send flowers, it's on the house.' Then she disappeared behind the velvet curtains.

But the words on the paper stayed with him. And they invited a crowd of memories: Hope sorting through piles of books like they were treasure, Hope falling on him in the bouncy castle at Slugfest, Hope making oatmeal cookies. Hope in his arms at the street dance.

A heart's not like a car. You don't drive it. It drives you.

Twelve

ON MONDAY NIGHT, Debra came home from work early and made birthday dinner. And she and Emily baked a chocolate cake. It wasn't from scratch, but Millie pretended it was wonderful because she was so thrilled that they'd gone to the trouble. She didn't have to pretend to appreciate the music box Debra gave her or the little pots of marigolds from Emily and Eric.

Then it was just Millie and Debra at the kitchen table. 'Thank you for a lovely birthday,' Millie told her.

'I do appreciate you, Mom. I want you to know that. And we'll spend more time together, I promise.'

Except on Tuesday, when, as Millie was getting ready to go out with Altheus, Debra called to say she'd be late getting home. Would Millie mind starting dinner?

'Well, I don't mind making some sandwiches,' said Millie, 'but that's all I have time for. I'm going out to dinner.'

'You are?' Debra sounded a little miffed.

'Altheus is taking me out for my birthday.'

'Oh.' This was followed by a moment of silence.

'And doesn't Eric have a Little League game tonight?'

A martyr's sigh drifted from the phone. 'I'll find him a ride.'

'Debra, he'd probably love it if you came to the game,' Millie said. 'These years go so fast and then the children are gone.' And have their own lives and no time for their parents.

'I know, Mom,' Debra said. 'I've got to go.'

Millie hung up with a sigh. When it came to life lessons, her daughter was a difficult pupil.

Altheus could tell immediately that Millie was bothered. 'Trouble on the home front?' he asked as they drove to the restaurant.

'I do worry about Debra,' she confessed. 'I'm afraid she's very . . .' How to phrase it?

'Self-absorbed?' he guessed. He took her hand. 'She'll sort things out.' He gave Millie's hand a squeeze. 'She's your daughter, Millie girl. Sooner or later she'll figure that out and want to be more like you.'

'Oh, Altheus,' Millie said. 'That's so sweet.'

'Now we're going to focus on you. OK? And we're going to live it up tonight!'

He made good on his promise, taking her to the Family Inn where they enjoyed grilled salmon in some exotic sauce and a salad of greens, blueberries and feta cheese. The staff all sang 'Happy Birthday' to her and presented her with a little carrot soufflé, compliments of the chef. Embedded in the top, she found a ring with her birthstone, alexandrite, centred among a cluster of diamonds.

She gasped, 'Oh, Altheus. I can't accept this.'

He grinned. 'Sure, you can. I'm hoping you'll wear it on your left hand. I guess you could say it's a proposal.'

'But we've only been seeing each other a short time.'

'Millie, I knew I wanted to spend the rest of my life with you from the first day we met,' he said, making her heart flutter. 'Didn't you?'

'Well, I just can't . . . I mean, really—' she sputtered.

'What's wrong with two people finding happiness? At our age, don't you think that's a good thing?'

He was smiling at her like she was the most beautiful woman in the world. Who would have thought? 'Oh, Altheus.'

'Does that mean yes?'

'I'm seven years older than you.'

'Well, you don't look a day over sixty-nine,' he assured her. 'Say yes. I'd hate to unbook that cruise.'

'Cruise?' she repeated.

'I've booked an Alaskan cruise. For next week.'

'Oh, my.' Millie's heart began to race. What would Debra say about this? 'I don't know.'

'Yes, you do.'

'And a cruise. That's so much money.'

'Millie, my dear. I promise you I can afford a cruise. And I can afford to give you a comfortable life. You'll have your own garden,' he added, sweetening the deal.

She had a sudden vision of herself as mistress of her own home again. She could see Altheus sitting with her on the porch of that charming house on the lake, could envision the flower beds all weeded and prettied up.

He reached across the table and took her hand. 'You've given me a new lease of life.'

He had done the same for her, but still. 'There's so much we don't know about each other.'

'We know we share the same politics, and we like church services where they sing hymns. We know we both like to get up early. We know you like to garden and I like to play golf. We both like Gin Rummy and an early dinner.' He waggled his eyebrows. 'And we like the taste of each other's lips.'

That made her blush. 'You do make it hard to say no.'

'That's because I want you to say yes. Put on the ring, Millie girl. Let's enjoy our golden years together.'

She slipped the ring onto her right hand, over the gold wedding band Duncan had given her many years ago. When she had moved that gold band to her right hand, she had thought she'd be a widow the rest of her life. But now, the rest of her life could be really special with Altheus.

Still, it was a big decision. 'Give me a couple of days to think about it,' she said.

'I'll give you one to get used to the idea,' he said, and raised her hand to his lips, making her heart flutter.

Oh, my!

Debra was doing something on her laptop computer when Millie finally came home. 'Did you have fun?'

'Yes, I did.'

'Good.' Debra continued looking at her computer screen.

Was this a good time to tell her daughter her news? There probably was no good time. 'Altheus gave me a ring.'

Debra looked up from her computer. 'A birthstone?'

'It has my birthstone in it.' Millie showed off her new jewellery.

'That's a lot of diamonds. This isn't just a birthstone, is it?' Debra asked, her voice laced with suspicion.

'Well, no,' said Millie. 'Altheus would like it to be an engagement ring.'

Debra gave a disgusted snort. 'You're seventy-seven.'

Millie frowned. 'I didn't know there was an age limit on love.'

'Love! You hardly know this man.'

'I know him well enough to know he's a wonderful man.'

'What would Daddy say?' Debra protested.

'I hope he'd say he was glad I'd found someone to love.'

'You have someone. Me.'

'Yes, and your brothers. But I think there's room in my life for one more person.'

'Mom, you can't just marry some person you hardly know,' Debra said. 'Go out with him, go to the movies, but don't go crazy.'

Millie said stiffly. 'You're busy. I'll let you get back to work.'

'Where are you going?' Debra demanded.

'I'm going to bed,' snapped Millie.

'I'm calling Duncan Junior,' Debra threatened.

Well, let her tattle to the boys. They'd probably tell her to mind her own business. Wouldn't they? She'd tell them the same thing she told Debra: there was no age limit on love.

Millie got into bed and frowned at the new ring on her right hand. She moved it to her left hand.

It was prom week and the phone was ringing off the hook at Changing Seasons Floral. Hope loved doing corsages and boutonnières for dances. She loved seeing the high schoolers come in to pick up their orders. The boys came in alone or by twos, venturing into the shop like nervous explorers checking out a foreign world. The girls always came in groups, giggling and excited. Prom night was always magical.

So, now, to help with the magic, Hope and Bobbi made each prom offering with special care.

The bell over the shop door jingled. 'I'll get it,' Hope said.

But when she emerged from behind the curtain and saw Jason Wells, she wanted to run into the back room. Why was he here?

She forced herself to look calm. 'Can I help you?'

He nodded. 'I want to order some flowers.'

He was taking advantage of her peace offering. Good. She nodded. 'Who are they for?'

'My grandmother. It's her birthday tomorrow.'

She opened up an order document on her computer. 'What would you like to send?'

'She likes chrysanthemums. What do those stand for?'

Hope felt her face flaming. 'Truth.' She looked up to see him cocking an eyebrow at her and hurried on, 'It's still just a little early for those. How about a pot with herbs—sage for wisdom, rosemary for long life, thyme for strength and courage.'

He nodded. 'That'll do. Where'd you learn all this, anyway?'

'I found a book at a garage sale years ago.'

'All those books I made the bookcase for were yours.' He didn't necessarily say it accusingly—more like a discovery.

Hope bit her lip and nodded.

'Well, I'm glad it's getting used.' He stood there for a moment, looking almost as awkward as she felt. Then he said, 'My grandmother's in Oregon. You can see she gets that by tomorrow, right?'

'Of course.'

He pulled out his wallet. 'Put it on my MasterCard.'

'No. This one's on the house. Remember?'

'You can't stay in business that way,' he said, pushing his charge card at her.

Hope kept her hands firmly on the computer keyboard. 'My business is fine.' It's my life that's a mess.

He set the charge card on the counter. 'I insist.'

'Take your card when you go. You don't want someone stealing it,' she said as she walked into her back room.

She practically trampled Bobbi, who was jumping away from the curtain. 'Were you spying on me?' Hope hissed.

The phone rang and Bobbi grabbed the workroom extension. Saved by the bell. 'It's for you,' she said, handing Hope the receiver.

'Were you with a customer?' asked Millie.

'No. This is a perfect time, especially for my sister.'

'Well, I'm calling to ask a favour.'

'Sure. Name it.'

'I'm hoping you'll keep an eye on my garden. I'll be gone for a few days.'

'Oh? Where are you going?'

'On a cruise.' Millie's voice trembled with excitement.

'A cruise? With who?' Then Hope knew. 'Altheus, the toy boy.'

'Not exactly,' Millie corrected her. 'Altheus, the husband.'

'You're getting married? Oh, my gosh. That's fabulous!' Hope said. 'Does your daughter know?'

'No. We're eloping.'

Eloping at seventy-seven. Hope couldn't help grinning. 'It sounds really romantic.'

'It is. He is. I'm so happy. I feel like a girl again.'

'And I'm happy for you. When did this all happen?'

'Tuesday night. He gave me a ring for my birthday.'

'And you're just now calling?' Hope teased.

'I've been so busy. We had announcements to send to our friends, and Altheus insisted on buying me a trousseau. I swear, I'm almost over-whelmed. I didn't get out of bed until an hour ago.'

Millie in bed all morning? That wasn't like her. 'Are you feeling OK?' Hope asked.

'I'm more than OK.'

Being more than OK couldn't happen to a better person. 'When are you leaving?'

'Tomorrow,' Millie said breathlessly.

'You tell Altheus to come in this afternoon then. I'll have something for both of you.'

'Thank you, dear, that's terribly sweet of you.'

'My pleasure,' Hope said. 'And I really am happy for you.' Not to mention inspired. If Hope ever reached that age, would she be a Millie, always reaching out for something new?

Millie called Debra at work on Friday morning from the deck of the *Amsterdam*, using the new cellphone Altheus had given her. 'Hello, dear. I'm sorry to bother you at work, but I thought I should let you know I won't be home for a few days, so you and the children are on your own.'

'Mom, where are you?' Debra demanded.

'Well, right now, I'm on a cruise ship, and we're about to depart for Alaska.'

'Alaska!' Debra shrieked. 'We who?'

'Altheus and I. The captain of the ship is marrying us this afternoon.'

'Mom, you can't just run off and marry this man. Get off that boat. I'll come and get you.'

'No, you won't, and yes, I can,' Millie said, and smiled at Altheus, who hugged her. 'Don't worry about my things. I'll come and pack them and take them to the new house when we get back. You'll love Altheus's house, by the way.'

'Mom!'

'I have to go now,' Millie said, and hung up on her daughter.

On Monday, the shop bell jingled. Hope looked up from where she and Bobbi were stocking the cooler case to see Jason. What was he doing here?

'Hi, Jason,' Bobbi managed.

He nodded at her, then said to Hope, 'I need some flowers.'

'You just bought flowers last week,' she reminded him.

'I need some more, for my secretary. Secretary's Day.'

'That's in April,' Hope informed him.

'I forgot. I have to make it up to her.' He grabbed a beribboned pot brimming with Gerbera daisies. 'I'll take these.'

'OK,' Hope said, moving towards the cash register.

'So, what do these mean?' he asked.

'They can symbolise several things,' Hope said, double-checking the price on the pot. 'Innocence, purity.'

'Scratch that. She's gone through two husbands.'

'They also symbolise loyalty and cheer.'

'I guess they'll work,' he said.

'They should. Everyone needs cheer,' Hope said.

He had his charge card out now. 'I'm paying this time.'

'I probably owe you flowers for life.'

He half-smiled and shook his head. 'Somebody does,' he said, looking in Bobbi's direction.

Bobbi, who had been shamelessly eavesdropping, turned red and got back to work stocking the cooler case.

He scooped up the flowers. 'Thanks. I guess I'm done here.'

'I guess so,' Hope agreed.

'Come back any time,' Bobbi called after him as he left the shop.

Hope leaned on the counter and watched, mentally drooling, as he walked past the window.

'He's interested in you,' said Bobbi.

'That's ridiculous. He was just interested in you.'

'So? Men are like dogs. They're easily distracted.'

'Look who's talking,' said Hope.

Bobbi made a face at her. 'I know I made a mistake with Jason,' she said. 'I got confused because he looked right. But Duke, he feels right. I could spend my whole life with that man. And I don't have to worry about being what he wants. I just am.'

'That's as good a description of love as I've ever heard,' Hope admitted. 'But is he a commitment kind of guy?'

'He is now.' Bobbi's smile was smug. 'How long do you think a person should wait to get married?'

'You barely know the guy,' Hope protested.

'I know, but I think he's the one. You know, Mom and Dad are coming in August.'

'To look for a summer home on the lake.'

'There's nothing wrong with killing two birds with one stone.'

Hope pointed a stern finger at her. 'Don't even think it.'

What a strange flower love was, Hope thought. Maybe finding the right person was like looking through a flower shop and trying to decide what to purchase. Maybe Bobbi wasn't so much fickle as simply shopping.

Maybe Jason was shopping, too. But interested in her? No.

Yet, the next day, there he was again. 'My secretary wanted to know what kind of flower that was. I forgot.'

'Gerbera daisy,' Hope said. She grabbed a piece of scratch paper and wrote it down. 'Here, so you can remember.'

He slipped it in his pocket. 'Thanks.' He looked at his watch. 'It's almost lunchtime. Are you hungry?'

Her? Suddenly, she could barely breathe.

'Why do you want to go out to lunch?' she blurted.

He looked at her. 'Because I'm hungry?'

'OK.'

Jason escorted her out of the shop and down the street to the bakery. They ordered sandwiches made with freshly baked bread, then moved on to order their drinks. Hope felt her cheeks warming under Amber's speculative look as she set their colas on the counter.

They took the last vacant table. Jason crooked an arm over the back of his chair and regarded her. 'So, are you ever going to tell me what that poem was about?'

He said it teasingly, so she forced her voice to be light. 'Just thoughts about love and life.'

'Whose love and whose life?' he countered.

'Who knows?' she said.

'You're an interesting woman,' Jason said. 'You and your sister are polar opposites.'

'I guess we are,' she mused. 'I wish I were more like her.'

'Yeah? How?'

So many ways. 'Oh, her looks, her charm, her energy.'

He shrugged. 'You're not so bad yourself, you know.'

Which is why the minute you saw Bobbi I became invisible? Hope kept her mouth clamped shut.

He leaned forward. 'OK, I'll admit, when I saw your sister, all my brains fell out,' he said. 'But you want to know something?'

'What?'

'I'm not sorry things ended with us. And no hard feelings. Even though you two did a number on me, I think I get why you did it.'

He did? Hope forced herself to close her dropping jaw.

'I helped my brother cheat on a test once.'

He was comparing her helping Bobbi write clever poems and cards to him helping his brother cheat? 'I don't think—' she began.

'Civics. He was flunking it. And he was getting Ds in everything else. Never turned in his homework—had being a teen real bad. All of a sudden, it dawned on him what a jerk he'd been. He wanted to graduate. This one teacher was the only one who wasn't going to cut him any slack. It all hinged on this one test. He ended up acing the test, went to junior college and brought up his grades. Then he transferred to a four-year college and graduated *cum laude*.'

'The end justifies the means?'

'Only when you want to help somebody you care about,' Jason countered. 'It was wrong. I shouldn't have done it. At the time though, it seemed like the right thing to do.'

'I'm not sure that you can equate helping your brother cheat on a test with me helping my sister write some poems.'

'Did you help her or write them for her?' he countered.

'She just didn't want you to think she was dumb.'

'I don't. She's pretty smart, really. She should have gone into advertising.'

'Where people lie for a living?' Hope translated.

'Where people are good at creating an illusion, so other people will buy what they're selling,' Jason amended.

'I guess we all do that,' Hope said.

Which was what she was doing right now. She was out with this man, pretending they could advance from a truce to a relationship. They couldn't. At least not the kind he'd want. No man was ever going to see her naked.

Their sandwiches were ready and Jason went to pick them up, but Hope no longer had an appetite.

'Speaking of advertising,' he said, as he set her plate in front of her, 'you don't advertise at all. What's with that?'

She shrugged.

'*Many a flower is born to blush unseen?*' Jason wondered.

'*And waste its sweetness on the desert air,*' she finished. 'I'd forgotten that poem.'

'Me, too, until just now.' He studied her. 'So, is that you?'

She shook her head, trying to ignore the sudden heat in her cheeks. 'I don't think my life is wasted.'

'Maybe not so much wasted as not finished,' he suggested. 'You spend a lot of time worrying about other people. What about you?'

'I'm fine. I'm happy just the way I am.'

He let the subject drop with a nod.

After that, they stuck to small talk, chatting about hiking and books. That was fine, until Jason said, 'My folks would love you. You're the real deal,' and she knew it was time to end lunch.

She pushed her chair back. 'I've got to get back to work.'

'You know, I'm running out of people to buy flowers for,' he said as they walked back to the shop.

'You'll have to switch to chocolates.'

'So, I'm thinking maybe you should just go out with me this weekend. Not dancing,' he quickly added.

'Thanks, but no. I think we're better off not starting anything.'

'I wasn't asking you to marry me.'

'I know.'

'I just thought you might like to hang out,' he persisted.

Men weren't into being friends. They always wanted to be friends with benefits. 'I don't think that would be a good idea.' She added, 'I don't have time in my life for someone.'

He frowned, but he said, 'OK.'

Good. That settled it.

Thirteen

JASON DIDN'T SEEM TO GET the concept of taking no for an answer. He came into the shop every day that week, each time with some new flimsy excuse.

'You can't afford this,' Hope informed him as he set an iced coffee on the counter for her.

'I think I can manage an iced coffee.'

'You know what I mean,' she said. 'All these flowers?'

'Why don't you want to go out with me? Give me one reason.'

'My reason is none of your business, OK?'

He shook his head and said, 'I don't get you.'

'You're right, you don't,' she said. And he never would because she couldn't bring herself to share the intimate details that made up this new and far from improved Hope Walker.

He threw up his hands. 'OK, I give up.'

Still, she didn't say anything.

Instead, she watched him leave, tears in her eyes. All the flowers seemed to wilt. She went into the back room and had a big pity party.

Which she was enjoying immensely until Bobbi came in and crashed it. 'What's wrong?' she cried, rushing to Hope's side.

'Nothing,' Hope insisted, brushing at the corners of her eyes.

'Did you and Jason have a fight?'

'No. And will you please quit trying to matchmake?'

'But he's perfect for you,' Bobbi protested.

'Well, I'm not perfect for him,' Hope said bitterly.

Bobbi studied her a moment. 'Are you going to let cancer take away your life?'

This was totally crossing the line. Bobbi didn't know what it was like to wonder if you'd be around to see another Christmas. She had no idea what it felt like to hold your breath when you went to the doctor, to look at your body and want to cry.

'Don't you tell me how to run my life. You haven't been where I've been and you have no way of knowing how I feel.' Hope grabbed her handbag and brushed past her sister.

'Wait. Where are you going?'

'Away. You can close up.'

Swiping at bitter tears, Hope walked to the downtown lakefront park, marched to the end of the dock, and sat down, dangling her feet over the water. She looked across the lake at the Cascade Mountains in the distance, stretching in rugged grandeur toward an endless blue sky. She was just a tiny speck in this great painting.

She sighed. She'd been happy as a tiny speck until Jason Wells had walked into her shop. Now she wanted to jump to a different spot in the picture. But it didn't work that way. She had to learn to be happy where she was.

On Sunday afternoon, working next to Amber at the community garden, Hope could almost convince herself that, deep down, when she wasn't getting distracted by handsome men who could quote poetry, she was perfectly content.

'I love it here,' Amber said with a sigh. 'I don't know what I'm going to do when winter comes and we can't be out here.'

'We'll plan our gardens for next spring,' Hope told her.

'And wrangle more recipes out of Millie,' Amber added. 'Hey, and speaking of Millie.' She pointed to a white Prius pulling up at the edge of the garden path.

Inside sat a beaming Millie, cuddling up to Altheus. They shared a kiss and she slipped out of the car. He waved at Amber and Hope, and the car purred off.

'Welcome back,' Amber greeted her. 'You look like married life agrees with you. Except you're moving kind of slow.'

'I'm a little tired,' Millie admitted, stepping into her plot. 'I got all my things from Debra's yesterday.'

'I bet that was fun,' Amber said.

'Well, Debra is a little unhappy about the suddenness of everything,' Millie admitted.

'She'll come round,' Hope predicted.

'So, I suppose you worked yourself to death trying to get everything organised at the new house,' said Amber.

'Altheus won't let me work too hard,' said Millie.

But as they weeded, Hope noticed that Millie was becoming increasingly quiet. The late June weather was warm, but not warm enough to justify the profuse sweat on her face. She straightened and massaged her temples.

'Are you OK?' asked Amber.

Millie frowned. 'I have such a headache.'

'Maybe you should quit for the day,' Hope suggested.

'Maybe,' Millie agreed. 'I just feel so . . . I don't feel well,' she finished weakly and sank down on the ground.

'Millie,' Hope said, fear making her voice sharp.

Amber left her plot immediately, coming round to sit next to Millie, putting an arm round her shoulders. But Millie hardly seemed to notice her. She sat breathing as if it was the only thing she could focus on.

'Tell us exactly what you're feeling.' Now Amber sounded as scared as Hope felt.

'I don't know,' Millie fretted. 'I feel like I'm going to faint.'

Hope began to add up the symptoms. Sweating, light-headedness, anxiety. She pulled her cellphone out of her jeans pocket and dialled 911. 'I'm calling from Grandview Park,' she said as soon as someone came on the line. 'I think we've got a woman here having a heart attack.'

'No,' Millie whimpered, and Amber hugged her, stroking her hair and chanting, 'It'll be OK, it'll be OK.'

At last the ambulance arrived, sirens wailing, lights flashing. Seeing it, Millie became agitated. 'Oh, dear!'

She clutched at Amber, who was pleading, 'Stay calm, Millie.'

It only took a couple of minutes for the paramedics to decide Millie needed to go to the hospital. Then they loaded her into the ambulance and carried her off. Amber and Hope got into Amber's car and followed.

At the hospital, Amber told the nurse at the desk that she and Hope were Millie's granddaughters and the nurse promised to let them see Millie as soon as it was possible. 'We're the closest thing she's got,' Amber rationalised as they waited.

'Altheus doesn't know,' Hope realised. 'We've got to call him. And what's her daughter's name? Her last name?'

Amber shook her head.

'Well, let's hope Altheus knows.'

Amber nodded grimly.

Hope hurried outside to call. Altheus answered the phone with such a hearty hello she wanted to cry. She nearly did as she broke the bad news to him.

'I'll be right there,' he said, grimly.

Why did this have to happen to Millie just when she'd found real happiness? It wasn't right.

Hope returned to the waiting area. 'No news yet?'

Amber shook her head.

At last the doctor came out and informed them that Millie had, indeed, had a heart attack.

They were finally allowed to see her. Millie lay propped up in a typical hospital bed. She looked old and frail, like someone else. She smiled and held out a hand to each of them and they took up positions on either side of the bed. 'Thank you, girls, for taking such good care of me.'

'We're just glad you're OK,' Amber said.

Hope couldn't speak, so she squeezed Millie's hand.

'I'm just so sorry I caused you girls all this trouble,' Millie said.

'Yeah, you're a regular drama queen,' Amber teased.

'But we love you anyway,' Hope added.

Millie chuckled.

Hearing it, Hope felt comforted.

Millie started to speak, but instead her features contorted into a look of pain and confusion.

'Millie!' cried Hope.

Amber rushed to the door and called, 'We need a doctor!'

Hope stayed next to Millie, holding her hand tightly.

Altheus arrived at the hospital in time to learn that his wife had had a heart attack and then a stroke. 'I'm very sorry. This happens sometimes,' the doctor said.

'I'm so sorry,' Hope said to Altheus.

He swallowed. 'She was feeling tired by the end of the cruise, but then we'd been going pretty hard. I wanted her to take a day and rest when we got back, but she insisted on going to her daughter's. I offered to help her pack, but she wanted to do it all herself.'

'And I can guess why,' Amber said quietly to Hope as they set up headquarters in the little waiting room of the critical-care unit. 'She was probably afraid to let him near her daughter.'

Just then Debra marched in. Hope and Amber had ringside seats, right near the nurses' station, and it was easy to hear every angry word spilling out of her mouth.

'Why didn't someone from the hospital call me?' she demanded. 'Where is my mother now?'

'She's in room two-oh-four. They're getting her settled,' the nurse said. 'You can see her in just a minute.'

'I'll see her now,' Debra snapped, and marched into the room. They heard her cry, 'Mom! Oh, Mom!'

At the sound of the commotion, Altheus started for Millie's room. Hope and Amber exchanged looks and followed him.

'This is all your fault,' Debra accused Altheus as they entered the room. 'What were you thinking, hauling her all over the place like she was thirty?' She scowled at Hope and Amber. 'This is a private room.'

'These are my wife's closest friends,' Altheus said calmly. 'She would want them here.'

Debra covered her face and burst into tears.

On Monday, Hope left Bobbi to man the shop during lunch hour and went to the hospital.

As she entered Millie's bedroom, it struck Hope that her friend was beginning to disappear. This wasn't the Millie Hope knew. Altheus sat slumped on one side of the bed holding Millie's hand.

He motioned Hope over next to him. 'Come over here where she can see you.'

Hope forced herself to smile as she took her place by Millie's side. 'How are you doing?'

Millie's voice was slurred. It sounded like she said, 'Fine.'

'Don't worry about your garden,' Hope told her. 'We'll take care of it while you're busy getting better.'

Millie mumbled something and shut her eyes.

'She'll be better tomorrow,' Altheus said.

By mid-week, when Hope and Amber came to visit, Millie was eating. Her speech was still slurred, and she was paralysed on one side, but Altheus insisted that, with some physical therapy, she'd soon be right as rain.

'If you girls will excuse me, I have some places to check,' he said. 'The hospital is kicking her out soon.'

'That's wonderful news,' Amber said as he left. 'By the way, your garden is doing great. Everything's blooming.'

Millie managed a smile. 'I think my . . . gardening days are over.' Hope had to swallow a lump in her throat.

'But you can recover,' Amber insisted.

Millie shut her eyes. 'I've had a full life. You'll be fine now, dear. Hang onto that husband.' She fell silent. Just when Hope had decided she was asleep, she spoke again. 'Hope?'

'I'm here,' Hope said, squeezing her hand.

'No Shasta daisies at my funeral. Those . . . smell awful.'

'Millie, that's not funny,' Hope scolded.

'And find . . . someone to love.'

Where had that come from? 'Oh, Millie.'

'Don't let the past steal from the future. Life is . . . short. But it can be sweet.' A moment later she was asleep.

Amber and Hope sat with her all afternoon, but she never woke up. Two days later, she suffered a second heart attack and died.

After getting the news, Hope drove to her favourite hiking spot in the Cascades and spent the day wandering along forest trails, looking for new growth. Once she spotted a lady's slipper. The delicate woodland flower was a rare sighting, and she knelt and took a picture of it. 'You look like you belong in Millie's garden,' she told it.

Life is short.

Hope stood and sighed. Yes, and right now it wasn't very sweet.

Millie's memorial service was set for Wednesday afternoon, July 2. Hope worried that the funeral wouldn't be well attended. Millie hardly knew anyone.

She was surprised when orders for flowers started coming in: from Altheus, of course, and Amber, but also from the Lakeside Congregational Church, and the teller at the bank. And then the orders started flying in from out of town. Millie's friend, Alice, wanted a hydrangea that Altheus could plant in his wife's honour. Millie's old garden club sprang for a basketful of plants, also to go to the new husband. The parade of names continued.

'The church is going to look like a garden,' Bobbi said that morning as they finished the last of the orders.

'Millie will like that.' Hope could feel the tears coming. 'Now, let's get these arrangements finished.'

Bobbi drove the little PT Cruiser very carefully to the church. All the way, she kept thinking about her sister. Why did Hope insist on working so hard to make other people's lives good, and then let her own go untended? All the way back, Bobbi chewed on how she could manage to get Hope a life. There was only one way to do it. Someone had to tell Jason what Hope's problem was.

'Oh, boy,' Bobbi muttered. She parked at the back of the shop and sneaked the few feet to where Jason and his crew were working.

Except Jason wasn't there. 'Where is he?' she asked Duke.

'He's over at the Smith job on the lake,' said Duke. He frowned. 'Whaddya need to see him for?'

'I have to tell him something important about Hope.'

Duke was still frowning, but he rattled off an address.

She kissed him and scampered back to the Cruiser. Hopefully, with all the banging and sawing, Hope hadn't heard her pull up. It would be hard to explain why she left with an empty delivery car.

She found Jason at the site, talking with a man holding a blueprint. When Jason saw Bobbi, he detached himself and walked over to where she stood. He asked politely, 'Did you need something?'

'Not me,' she said, 'but my sister does.'

That got him curious. 'Oh?'

'She needs you.'

Jason rolled his eyes and started to turn away.

Bobbi caught his arm. 'Seriously. You have to know why she doesn't want anything to do with you.'

Now she had his full attention. 'I'm listening.'

'She had cancer.'

His features took on an oh-no look. 'The book on cancer. It was hers. I should have figured that out. God,' he added softly. 'What kind?'

'Breast. She lost one.'

He stood there staring at Bobbi.

'Did you get that?' she asked, giving his arm a shake.

'Yeah. Yeah, I got it. Is she OK?'

'She's as OK as a woman can be who's had two surgeries: one to get a fake boob, the other to make it look good. It still doesn't as far as she's concerned. It's why she doesn't want things to go any further with you, even though she's in love with you.'

Jason clawed his fingers through his hair. 'Why didn't you tell me this earlier?'

'You think she would have let me? You think she even knows I'm here now? The only reason I'm telling you this is because I think you and my sister belong together. And you'd be lucky to get her,' Bobbi added. 'So, now you know. Don't tell her I told you. I want to live to see thirty.'

'What am I supposed to tell her?' Jason held out his hands, the picture of male helplessness. Really, women had to do all their thinking for them.

'Tell her you put two and two together. Do something romantic with flowers. That'll help. Oh, and first hypnotise her and convince her she's pretty.' With that, she left. It was up to Jason now.

The sanctuary wasn't packed, but it was respectably full. Next to Hope, Amber was sniffing into a big ball of tissue. Debra and her children and two men who were probably Millie's sons sat up front in a separate pew, leaving Altheus to grieve alone. 'That woman will be lucky if anyone comes to her funeral,' Amber hissed.

The minister commanded everyone to rise and sing Millie's favourite hymn, 'Amazing Grace'. How appropriate, thought Hope. She was all about extending grace.

The minister summed up Millie's life, finishing with, 'We're all a little better for having known Millie.'

Hope closed her eyes and saw Millie standing in her garden, wearing her purple outfit, waving. 'Don't forget,' she called. 'Go and find someone to love.'

'At this time, the family would love it if some of you would share how much Millie meant to you,' said the pastor.

Amber didn't hesitate to stand. 'We just moved here this spring and I didn't know anyone. Millie adopted me. She shared recipes and taught me how to garden. She was awesome.' Amber finished on a sob and sat down.

Another person stood up, an older woman. 'I still remember Millie bringing me chicken soup when I was sick.'

'She came to my baby shower and brought me flowers from her garden,' said a woman. 'My baby had colic. She showed me how to carry him so he'd feel better. I wish I'd known her better.'

On and on the testimonials went. Finally, the pastor said, 'Let's close with Millie's other favourite song, "Nearer, My God, to Thee".'

'I should have said something,' Hope told Amber as they stood.

'You did,' Amber said, and pointed to the huge arrangement of flowers from Hope sitting by Millie's picture.

The churchwomen had put together a salad buffet, and so everyone trooped to the fellowship hall. Debra had positioned her brothers and herself near the doorway to accept condolences. Her children stood beside her. Poor Altheus hovered over by a table on the far side of the room.

'I'm going to go give him a hug,' said Amber. 'You deal with the princess. You'll be nicer.'

Hope started out as nicely as she could. 'Your mom was an amazing woman,' she said to Debra.

Debra was a wreck. She yanked back a sob. 'I just can't believe she's gone. I feel so alone,' she added.

'Well, you don't have to be,' Hope said. She took Debra by the arms and turned her so she could see Altheus on the far side of the room. 'He loved her, too, and he's all alone. Just like you.'

Debra's eyes widened, then narrowed.

Hope wasn't done. 'Maybe if you start working at it now, you can be like her someday and make her proud. You could start by being nice to the man she loved.'

Debra was staring at her in shock. Hope was a little shocked herself. Had all that just come out of her mouth? 'Uh, sorry for your loss,' Hope said, and made a hasty retreat.

'What did you just say to Debra?' asked Amber as Hope hugged Altheus. 'She looked like she was about to go into conniptions.'

'I was just offering my condolences,' said Hope.

On the way home, the two of them stopped by the garden and had their own little ceremony. They picked some of Millie's pansies and sprinkled the petals over both their gardens, and they each cut a flower to take home and press.

'We love you, Millie,' Amber murmured. 'We always will.'

'Look,' said Hope, pointing to the zinnias. There sat a swallowtail butterfly, gently fanning its wings. It left the flowers and swooped past them, then off and away.

'Goodbye, Millie,' Hope whispered. 'See you in heaven.'

Back at their cars, Amber asked, 'How about coming with me to the Fourth of July parade? I promised Seth we'd go and Ty has to man the Family Inn booth. I'd like the company.'

Hope didn't feel like being by herself, either. 'OK.'

She got back to the apartment to find a flower on her doorstep. The little primrose wasn't from her shop—too plainly packaged. Hope picked it up and the envelope that had been lying under it. What on earth?

She opened the envelope and pulled out a small sheet of paper. She read, *It's from the competition, but it says what needs to be said. Since you know what flowers mean, you should get the message.* It was signed with the letter *J. Jason.*

Primroses said, 'I can't live without you.'

So he thought. Still, she'd take this offering and treasure it. She set the little pot on her kitchen windowsill to remind her that, even in desert times, a girl could always find flowers.

The next day at the shop was quiet, with only a couple of arrangements to make for Fourth of July parties. 'Let's close up early,' Bobbi suggested. 'We can get drinks at Organix and go to the city park and sit on the dock.'

'Good idea.'

They were just getting ready to leave when the phone rang. 'Oh, for Pete's sake,' grumbled Bobbi as Hope answered it.

The female voice on the other end was subdued. 'I'd like to order some flowers. Could you possibly send them today?'

'If it's local,' Hope said.

'It is. I hear you do flowers that have special messages.'

'I can,' said Hope. 'What would you like to say?'

The woman's voice caught on a sob. 'Sorry.'

'That's OK. Take your time.'

'No, that's what I want to say.'

'Well, purple hyacinths say "I'm sorry", but they're not in season right now. All I have at the moment are silk ones.'

'Oh.' The woman didn't sound excited by artificial flowers. 'I need it to be special. I haven't been very nice to someone.'

'Maybe you want something that signifies a new start,' Hope suggested. 'Pink roses can stand for friendship.'

'That will work.'

'OK. What would you like the card to say? Maybe, "Let's start again"?'

'Please.'

'OK.'

'No, I mean add "please". And you'll tell him what the flowers mean?'

'Of course. Who is this going to?'

'Altheus Hornby.'

Altheus? 'How would you like to sign it?'

'Just, I don't know. Sign it "Debra".'

Hope nearly dropped the phone. Amber would never believe this. 'Would you like to add "Your daughter-in-law"?' she asked.

'Oh. How did you know? Have we met?'

Maybe they didn't want to go there. 'Briefly, at the funeral. Your mother was a friend of mine. She was quite a woman.'

'Yes, she was. I miss her so much.'

'She'd be glad to know you're letting new people into your life,' Hope said. 'I'll get those roses out right away.'

She took Debra's charge-card information, then hung up.

Bobbi had been leaning on the counter, listening. 'So, Millie's daughter is sending flowers to the guy she was mad at?'

'That about sums it up,' Hope said. 'I guess she can be taught. Life is short. What's the sense in wasting it?'

'Yeah. What's the sense?' Bobbi gave her a meaningful stare.

A picture of the primrose on the windowsill danced into Hope's mind and echoed, 'Yeah. What's the sense?'

Fourteen

THE FOURTH OF JULY was a scorcher, but downtown Lake Way was packed with throngs of people. Hope, with Amber and Seth, looked for the perfect kerbside seat from which to view the parade.

'Millie would have loved this,' said Amber.

'Yes, she would,' Hope said. As she settled on the hot sidewalk, she found herself wishing she'd gotten another drink before they moved to the parade route.

'Water?' asked a male voice.

She knew that voice. She turned to see Jason squatting behind her. He was wearing flip-flops, shorts and a red Hawaiian print shirt, which hung open over his bare chest. His well-muscled, tanned, bare chest. She grabbed the bottled water he held out. It was even hotter out here than she'd realised.

'Hi.' Amber was all stares. 'Haven't I seen you at the bakery?'

Of course she had, and she'd called Hope wanting the scoop on him. Hope had assured Amber he was just a friend. But the way Amber was looking from Hope to Jason as Hope introduced them, it was clear she was getting a whole new message now.

'We're gonna see a parade,' Seth informed him.

'Cool. Can I sit with you?' Jason asked him.

'Sure,' said Seth, but before he could make space for Jason next to him, Amber scooted them both over, making room between her and Hope.

Jason plopped down on the kerb, his leg grazing Hope's in the process and making her feel like someone had set off a sparkler inside her chest. 'How're you doing? I'm sorry about your friend.'

'Me, too. I already miss her.'

He nodded and they sat in silence. She wanted to thank him for the primrose he'd left on her doorstep, but if she did, then they'd have to talk about what that flower symbolised, and things would really get awkward.

'You all going to watch the fireworks tonight?' Jason asked.

'After we go home and have a nap,' Amber replied, ruffling her son's hair.

'How about you?' Jason asked Hope. 'Hey, why don't you come with me? We can talk about flowers.'

Hope took a long swallow from the water bottle.

He took that for a yes. 'Good. I'll pick you up around eight.'

And, if that wasn't bad enough, when the parade finished, Amber decided to play Cupid. 'You know, I think Ty's going to need the car. Do you think you could find another ride home?'

'My truck's just around the corner,' Jason offered.

It was too far to walk. Hope resigned herself. 'OK.'

Once in the truck, Jason started the air conditioning going and she fell back thankfully against the seat. 'Better?' he asked softly. 'You were starting to look a little wilted there.'

'Yes, thanks,' she murmured.

'You mind if I make a quick stop?' he asked as they drove by the Gas 'n' Go.

She shook her head, figuring he needed gas. But instead, he pulled up in front of the little grocery store and ducked in. He came out carrying some small chilled bottles and a big bag of chips.

He stowed them in back of the truck, then got in. 'So,' he said casually as they wound their way round the lake. 'Want to talk about primroses?'

'Jason, I already told you . . .' she began.

'I know what you told me, but you left out some details, like the little one about you having had cancer.'

She bit her lip and looked out of the window at the fir and alder trees along the road.

'That's why you don't want to go out with me. Right?'

'It wouldn't be fair.'

'Maybe it's not fair to decide for someone whether or not you get to be together.' Instead of going towards the apartment, he turned the truck down a bumpy private road edged with woods.

'Where are you going?' She just wanted to get home.

'I need to check something at this site. You don't mind, do you?'

They emerged from the woods to a view of the lake, sparkling in the afternoon sun and, off to the side, a framed-in house—two-storey with a deck. He turned off the engine, saying, 'I think we should get in the lake and cool off.'

This was all slipping sideways. 'I thought you had to check on something,' said Hope.

'I can multi-task.'

'I'm not dressed for swimming.'

'We can work round that,' he said easily, and opened his door. 'Stay put. I'll open the door for you.'

She watched, heart racing, as he walked round the back of the truck and picked up the snacks he'd purchased, along with an old army blanket. She'd have to tell him everything. After a drink, maybe she'd have the nerve.

'Is it OK to be here?' she asked, looking around them as they walked across the property.

'The owners won't care. They're in California.'

He spread out the blanket on the porch.

She sat down on it and tried to concentrate on the view instead of the man sitting on the blanket next to her. The other side of the lake was fringed with trees and dotted with houses, some with lawns running like green skirts to the lake's edge.

'Beautiful here, isn't it?' he said. He opened a strawberry daiquiri cooler, and passed it to her.

'Did my sister tell you this is my favourite drink?'

He shook his head and opened a bottle for himself. 'Just a lucky guess.' He clinked bottles with her.

Hope watched the muscles in his throat work as he drank. Was there anything about this man that wasn't sexy?

He caught her watching him and smiled like he knew what she was thinking. 'I don't know why I didn't see how perfect you were right from the start.'

Hope took a drink. 'You don't know me that well.'

'I'll bet I know you better than you think. I've had a lot of chances to get to know you: when I was with you and your sister, when I've talked to you in the shop, when we went to lunch, when I read what you wrote to me in those cards.'

'I was writing for Bobbi,' she insisted.

'Were you?'

His intense scrutiny felt like the sun's rays through a magnifying glass. She took another drink. 'You know, you can't be in love with my sister one minute and chasing me the next.'

'Bobbi's fun, but I wasn't in love with her. And I never slept with her,' he added. 'Look. You've got what I want.'

'I need another drink,' Hope decided.

He opened another bottle for her and handed it over. Then he reached up and began playing with the last of her curls. 'Where'd you get these, from your mom or your dad?'

'From my oncologist. This is how it grew in after the chemo.'

She didn't look at him, but she could feel the charming smile smothering under the heavy dose of stark reality. 'God.'

That about summed it up. 'I said that a lot myself, mostly in prayers. *God, please let me live through this. God, why did I get this?*' She offered him a smile to ease the awkward moment. 'Mostly now, though, I simply say, *God, thanks that I'm alive.*'

'You're amazing.'

He was looking at her like she was some kind of saint. 'No, I'm not. I get grumpy and ungrateful and jealous, and . . .' Loose lipped. She looked at the half-empty bottle in her hands.

'Jealous of who?'

'You know, I think I need to cool off,' she decided. She hopped up and ran for the lake.

'Good idea,' said Jason, coming after her.

He caught up with her at the water's edge and she saw he'd shed his shirt. And he was closing the distance between them like a man with a purpose. 'Come here, you,' he teased.

She stumbled backwards and went down, tangling herself in the water lilies. She came up sputtering and he caught her.

He brushed her wet hair out of her face and chuckled. 'I'm beginning to wonder if you're accident-prone.'

'Only around you,' she managed.

She opened her mouth to tell Jason she needed to go home. But he pulled her to him and kissed her. Good and thoroughly, and all she could think about was how much she wanted this man.

Five minutes later, he was scooping her up and carrying her out of the water, lying her down on the bank. And then his hand was sliding up her thigh, turning her into a one-woman Fourth of July fireworks display.

When his hand started creeping up her midriff, the fireworks stopped instantly and she sat up. 'I can't.'

'Oh. Too soon. You're right.'

'No, it's not that.'

'Well, what then?' He sounded completely puzzled.

She kept her eyes firmly on the lake. 'I lost a breast.'

'OK.'

He said it like he wasn't tracking. She let out an angry hiss. 'You don't want to see me naked.'

'How do you know?'

She inched away from him. 'I had replacement surgery. It didn't go well the first time. The second wasn't much of an improvement. I'm scarred and imperfect.'

He let out a big sigh and sat up next to her. 'Look at me.'

She shook her head and kept her face averted.

He took her by the chin and turned her face to his. 'Maybe I haven't made myself clear. I'm looking for the whole package in a woman.

I don't want just a pretty face and a hot body. And who cares about some scarring?'

'I do,' Hope insisted. She wanted to cry.

He gave her neck a gentle rub. 'Hey, you want to talk scars.' He pointed to a long, white lightning bolt of a scar running along his upper arm. 'I got that when I was eleven. Ran through a sliding glass door.'

'It's not the same.'

Now he frowned. 'The hell it's not. People get hurt or sick all the time. Then we need to get patched up. So, you had to get patched up. The important thing is, you're here.'

'But I don't know if it's gone for good.'

'Well, I don't know if I'm going to fall off a roof tomorrow and end up in a wheelchair,' he said. 'But I'm sure not going to let that stop me from living my life right now. Here.' Suddenly, he had the bottom of her shirt and was easing it up.

She tried to pull away. 'What are you doing?'

'We're going to settle this right now.'

'No!' Panic swamped her. 'Someone will see.'

'OK, then.'

He stood and pulled her up after him. Then he led her back to the house and inside. 'Now,' he said gently. 'Come here.'

There was no sense postponing this. Hope shut her eyes and let him pull the top over her head. She squeezed her eyes shut, feeling the tears sting her cheeks as he slipped off her bra.

'Hope.'

He said it gently. He was going to let her down easy.

Her eyes shot open in amazement as he bent and kissed her scarred breast.

'I want you,' he said.

And then she cried.

And then she took his face in her hands and kissed him, putting her whole heart and soul into it. It was a perfect kiss.

And a perfect beginning.

Jason proved how much he wanted Hope when he proposed to her in August as her family picnicked on the site of what was going to be her parents' summer home.

'It's about time,' said Bobbi, hugging them both. 'I want to do the flowers for the wedding.'

But when they got married two weeks later, they didn't need flowers, other than the elaborate bouquet Bobbi and Jason planned together. The ceremony took place at the community garden, with family and friends gathered round. Altheus surreptitiously wiped his eyes as Hope stood among the blooms with Amber and Bobbi as her bridesmaids. Duke and Jason's brother served as groomsmen, and the looks flashing between Duke and Bobbi spoke of another wedding soon to follow.

The minister asked Jason if he took Hope to be his wife in sickness and in health, and Jason smiled at her and said, 'Absolutely.'

They picnicked in the park, their feast of scones and tea sandwiches catered by Ty and Amber. They were about to cut the lavender cake when Amber nudged Hope and said, 'Look.'

A butterfly perched on the nearby vase of lavender, fanning its wings.

'I think Millie approves,' Amber said.

'I think so, too,' Hope said with a smile. Millie was right, life was short. And she was going to live hers to the fullest.

Sheila Roberts

Can you tell me just a little about yourself, your family and where you live?

I live in Washington State, in America's Pacific Northwest, one of the prettiest corners of the world. I am happily married and have three wonderful children.

How do you write? Do you have a routine?

I write every day, usually starting around mid-morning. I am careful to build my writing life around my social life though. My faith, family and friends are very important to me. I love to write, but I don't want it to take over my life.

Where did you get the idea for _Love in Bloom_? Did it come to you as a complete story, a character, or a theme?

It started as a theme. My editor thought it would be fun to write about women who become friends in a community garden. That sounded like a good idea to me . . . except, when I first started this book, I had the world's most un-green fingers. There's a wonderful quote by poet Alfred Austen: 'Show me your garden . . . and I will tell you what you are like'. Well, at the time mine would have said, 'clueless'. So it was rather ironic that I wound up with a book about gardeners. I will say that I have since caught the gardening bug. We built a house on a small man-made lake and did all the landscaping ourselves. I am now the queen of the daisies!

Did you do a lot of research on the feelings of women who have had a mastectomy?

Yes, actually. Hope's character required some research. And her journey hits close to home for me. I have two friends who are cancer survivors and they are an inspiration. My friend Kema was especially helpful, reading the manuscript to see if I'd got Hope's character right. I truly felt for Hope. It's hard to feel good about yourself when you've come out of a life-and-death battle looking ravaged and scarred. But, as my friends who have gone through this will attest, our true loves always see us as beautiful.

In this novel you tell the stories of three women, Hope, Amber and Millie. Do you like to explore the different stages of life? Which one did you identify with most?

Hmmm. Good question. Probably all three. I identified with Amber because, like her, I wasn't much of a gardener. I identified with Hope because of the whole body image thing. Been there, done that. And I identified with Millie because of her love for life. Millie reminds me of many of my older friends who are busy living life to the fullest. I want to be a Millie when I'm old. Heck, I want to be a Millie now.

You must love flowers? What are your favourites and why?

I do love flowers, and it has been so much fun to see my garden come to life. Our landscaping is really starting to mature now and I've tried to plant an English garden (Yes, I'm an Anglophile!), full of Lady's Mantle, lavender, Brown-eyed Susans, Nigella and pansies. We have a fairly large lot and I've filled it with everything from roses to blueberries. This year we added a vegetable garden and I have currently got zucchini overload!

Which man do you think you would have gone for—steady Jason or badboy Duke?

I think I'm a Duke kind of gal—although I'm married to an awesome Jason.

Your website, www.SheilasPlace.com, mentions that you once owned a singing telegram company. How did that come about?

The company was the brain baby of my best buddy from high school. We had stayed in touch over the years, and one year I arrived at her office and sang happy birthday to her. She and her co-worker decided this might make a fun business. So we all put our heads together, and next thing I knew I was in business. I wrote all the songs and was the main singer until we hired more people. I sang to Mickey Mouse on a destroyer once—that was fun!

What music do you most like to listen to?

I love country music. Before I became a writer I was trying hard to make it as a songwriter. When I'm working I love to listen to Sting, Johnny Logan, and Astrud Gilberto, Gerry Rafferty or Chris Tomlin. That's my standard line-up.

Do you have any particular ambitions you'd still like to fulfil?

Yes! I'm dying to go on *Dancing with the Stars* as I just love to dance. Now, I just have to convince someone that writers are stars.

What is your idea of a perfect day?

Getting together with family and friends and playing all day long.

MONOGRAPHS OF THE SOCIETY FOR RESEARCH IN CHILD
DEVELOPMENT, SERIAL NO. 219, VOL. 54, NOS. 1–2, 1989

CONTENTS

ABSTRACT

MALATESTA, CAROL Z.; CULVER, CLAYTON; TESMAN, JOHANNA RICH; and
SHEPARD, BETH. The Development of Emotion Expression during the
First Two Years of Life. With Commentary by ALAN FOGEL and MARK
REIMERS and by GAIL ZIVIN; and a Reply by CAROL Z. MALATESTA,
CLAYTON CULVER, JOHANNA RICH TESMAN, and BETH SHEPARD. *Monographs of the Society for Research in Child Development,* 1989, **54**(1–2, Serial
No. 219).

This study examines the course of emotion expression development
over the first 2 years of life in a sample of full-term and preterm children. 58
mother/infant pairs were videotaped at infant ages of 2½, 5, 7½, and 22
months, recording face-to-face interaction involving play and separation/
reunion sessions. The tapes were coded on a second-to-second basis using
Izard's facial affect coding system. Data analysis focused on (1) differences
in expressive behavior at 22 months as a function of risk status, gender,
attachment status, and patterns of earlier maternal contingency behavior;
(2) stability of specific emotional expressive patterns across assessment periods; and (3) the relation of expressive behavior and security of attachment
at 2 years to qualities of earlier affective interchange.

Mother's contingency behavior (both general level and specific contingency patterns) appeared to have a material effect on the course of emotional development, as did birth status and gender. Prematurity was associated with differential socioemotional development well into the second year,
much in contrast to the "catch-up effect" observed in linguistic and cognitive
functioning. Discrete emotions analysis of attachment groups yielded differentiation along a broad negative/positive dimension, but it also showed that
insecurely attached children can be characterized as showing inhibited anger
expression.

The results of this study are discussed within the framework of organizational models of infant affective development; attachment theory and
discrete emotions approaches were found to yield different yet equally informative data on the course of socioemotional development.

I. THEORETICAL ISSUES AND APPROACHES

Almost all theories of infant emotional development acknowledge that emotional expressions undergo transformation with age, and much contemporary research has been directed at documenting the normative changes that occur in development (e.g., Demos, 1986; Izard, Hembree, & Huebner, 1987; Oster, 1978, 1984; Stenberg, Campos, & Emde, 1983). As a result of this work, we now know that certain emotional expressions are present at birth whereas others enter the behavioral repertoire somewhat later in development (Izard & Malatesta, 1987). We also know that infants' emotional expressions become more graded, subtle, and complex beyond the first year of life (Demos, 1986) and that instrumental control of facial expressive behavior occurs during the preschool years (Cassidy & Kobak, in press; Cole, 1985), if not sooner. Although this body of descriptive research has been crucial in documenting important developmental trends, it is still quite limited as it is confined to descriptions of only certain classes of emotional behaviors and early periods of development.

Most recently, researchers have turned their attention to the question of individual differences in emotional development. Research has begun to focus on how characteristics of the child (gender, temperament) interact with particular socialization influences (styles of parental tuition, aspects of parental personality, presence or absence of siblings) to alter the basic maturational trajectory.

The present study applies a close lens to the course of socioemotional development over the first 2 years of life. In this *Monograph*, we attempt to enlarge on the already existing literature on normative expressive development as well as define the contribution of certain individual difference variables that have been hypothesized to influence socioemotional development in significant ways. Before proceeding to a presentation of these data, it will be helpful to address the theoretical assumptions that guided our choice of methods and informed our interpretation of the data. To this end, we provide a general theoretical background to the area, highlighting basic

1

approaches as well as debates and controversies in the field. We then proceed to a specification of our own theoretical assumptions.

HISTORICAL AND THEORETICAL BACKGROUND

Against the backdrop of over a century's worth of thought and debate concerning emotion as a psychological faculty or system, the relative poverty of theory concerning emotional *development* that has prevailed at least until fairly recently is somewhat of an enigma given the rich history of developmental psychology itself (Cairns, 1983; Senn, 1975). Nevertheless, in recent times there have been several contributions in the theoretical domain that promise to compensate for the delayed attention to this crucially important developmental topic.

Although it is beyond the scope of this *Monograph* to cover the history of theory and research in the field in very great depth (for excellent general-theoretical and developmental-theoretical summaries, see Campos, Barrett, Lamb, Goldsmith, & Stenberg, 1983; and Izard, 1977) or to discuss theoretical debates at any great length, it will be helpful, as a point of departure, to mention some of the key turning points in the history of the field.

Most early theories of emotion were patently nondevelopmental (Cannon, 1927; Darwin, 1872; James, 1884). The important issues in the latter part of the nineteenth century and the opening decades of the twentieth were those involving the causation of emotion, the significance of the emotion expressions, and the ordering of physiological events. In general, there was little concern for developmental issues per se, with two notable exceptions. John Watson's investigation of early infant emotional expressions and Katharine Bridges's studies of the expressive behavior of infants in a hospital and of older children in day care were among the earliest experimental and observational studies of emotion in early development.

Watson (1919; Watson & Morgan, 1917) proposed that the young infant is innately endowed with three primary emotions—rage, fear, and love. All other emotional responses and subsequent personality development were said to arise from this basic substrate following the particulars of an individual's conditioning history. A small flurry of studies appeared in the literature following Watson's assertions, but these proved largely nonconfirmatory. Thus, the case for innate, discrete emotional expressions was quickly laid to rest (prematurely, as it turns out), and the issue did not surface again until fairly recently.

Somewhat later, Bridges spent several years observing the emotional behaviors of infants and young children and was led in the course of her work to formulate one of the first models of emotional development in infancy and early childhood (Bridges, 1931, 1932). Her observations of infants led her to conclude that infant emotion expression is originally un-differentiated rather than discrete and that individual emotions such as fear and anger appear only after a period of differentiation from more general states. Observations beyond infancy led Bridges to conclude that emotional development consists of a decrease in the frequency of intense emotional responses, the progressive transfer of responses from socially disapproved to socially approved stimuli, and a gradual change in the nature of the overt responses. These changes were conceived to occur as a function of both maturation and the cumulative effect of social conditioning.

Although the influence of Watson's and Bridges's work was short lived in their own day, they provided us with some of the earliest formulations on emotional development, and the debate concerning discrete versus undif-ferentiated emotions can still be discerned within contemporary theories. The one feature of these two early models that seems to have been aban-doned is the idea that emotional development consists of a process of rela-tively straightforward conditioning. Instead, as we shall see, classic S-R mod-els of emotional development have all but fallen by the wayside. Although various writers do not deny that some social learning theory principles play a role (e.g., observational learning), the most distinctive revolution in our thinking about emotional development during this century has been the emergence of various "organizational" models of development, including those of discrete emotions theory, cognitive/constructive theory, and ethol-ogy. Here the stress is on the functional and adaptive qualities of emotions and the central role they play in the regulation of individual and interper-sonal behavior. Emotions are not "stimuli" or "responses" but central, or-ganizing features of personality and behavior. Before we proceed to exam-ine some of these more recent models, it will be helpful to identify two major axes along which they can be seen to differ. Broadly conceived, these affect theories can be differentiated according to whether they stress the "dimen-sional" (degree) or the "typological" (type) aspect of emotion and whether they take a more nativist or a more constructivist stance with respect to the origin of emotions and their development.

Dimensional approaches emphasize the general degree of activation, almost to the exclusion of its qualitative aspects; such approaches flourished during the days of activation theory (see, e.g., the work of Duffy, Lindsley, Schlosberg). More recently, typological approaches (including differential emotions theory and other discrete emotions positions), which are inclined to focus on the differences in emergence, function, and phenomenology among types of emotion, have received a good deal of attention. The dimen-sional and typological approaches are not mutually exclusive; indeed, most contemporary typological approaches, including the one adopted in the current investigation, are concerned with the degree of arousal (intensity) and activation (rate) as well as with the particular type of emotion (fear,

3

anger, happiness) that is elicited. In general, typological approaches also recognize that, despite the heuristic and practical value of distinguishing among different types of emotions (say, among the several emotions of fear, sadness, anger, happiness, and interest), discrete emotions are also subsumable along dimensional axes of hedonic tone, with fear, sadness, and anger falling along the dimension of negative emotion and happiness and interest along that of positive emotion. With respect to contemporary developmental theories, the prevailing approach can be characterized as more typological than dimensional, although dimensional elements are not excluded from consideration.

A less readily reconcilable difference among different theoretical approaches concerns the distinction between constructivist and nativist positions with respect to the origin and development of emotions over time. Models that have a nativist orientation tend to stress that emotions are part of a common mammalian heritage, endorse the view that certain emotions are not only present but functional at birth or shortly thereafter, and, somewhat less frequently, maintain that there is an original isomorphism between expressive behavior and feeling states. Most representative of this tradition is Izard's differential emotions theory, a developmentally oriented neo-Darwinian, discrete emotions model. In contrast, theoretical approaches with a constructivist orientation tend to ignore or de-emphasize the innate aspects of emotions (i.e., their evolutionary, preadapted nature) and focus instead on emotions as products of cognition. Among contemporary developmental theories, those of Kagan (1978, 1984), Lewis and Michalson (1983), and Sroufe (1979) come closest to the constructivist position, although none deny the original preadapted, neurophysiological underpinnings of emotion. Campos and Barrett's goal-organizational theory (1984), Emde's psychoanalytic theory (Emde, 1980a, 1980b), and contemporary attachment theory fall somewhere in between with respect to degree of emphasis on the biological versus the cognitive. In its pure form, the distinction between nativist and constructivist approaches is merely one of heuristic contrasts; no existing theory takes such an either/or stance, recognizing that emotions are clearly both neurophysiologically based and affected by circumstances of social ecology and cognitive maturation. The differences lie rather in degree of emphasis on the neurophysiological versus the sociocognitive and in the conceptualization of the way in which the two interact.

In the following section, we examine emotional development from three perspectives—those of discrete emotions theory, cognitive/constructivist theory, and ethological theory—and draw on the most representative theorists in each tradition. We also compare these theories with respect to their stance on several issues that are related to the nativist/constructivist polarity: namely, (1) whether some innate, discrete (vs. undifferentiated) emotions are functionally present at or around the time of birth; (2) the infant's ability to experience emotional feelings; (3) the role in emotional experience assigned to facial expression and other expressive gestures; (4) the degree of concordance between facial expressivity and feeling state both originally and in development; (5) the processes by which emotion is socialized; and (6) how emotion relates to personality functioning.

CONTEMPORARY THEORIES OF EMOTIONAL DEVELOPMENT

Discrete Emotions Theories

Discrete emotions theories (Ekman, 1984; Izard, 1971, 1977; Plutchik, 1980; Tomkins, 1962, 1963) reflect Darwin's original formulations concerning the origin of the basic human emotions, their significance for biological and social adaptation, and the value of discriminating among types of emotion. One of the most representative and developmentally oriented theories in this tradition (and the one that most closely expresses the underlying theoretical assumptions of the present investigation) is Izard's differential emotions theory.

In 1971, Izard published an important volume, *The Face of Emotion,* which not only chronicled the history of the study of emotion over the past century but also introduced his own "differential emotions theory," which was grounded in the original formulations of Darwin (1872) and Tomkins (1962, 1963). The theory derives its name from an emphasis on a limited number of discrete, differentiated, fundamental emotions that are said to have distinct phenomenological, motivational, and signal properties. Each of the primary emotions is thought to affect broad domains of behavior in distinctive and characteristic ways. Because discrete emotions have individual signal properties (i.e., different facial, vocal, and gestural features), they provide important communicative links between individuals. In early development, facial and vocal expressions of emotion figure prominently in the child's ability to communicate needs and establish affective bonds with the caregiver.

Development of the emotion system is said to occur as a product of the maturation of the nervous system, of changing adaptational needs, and of cognitive development; the specifics of the theory are spelled out in Izard and Malatesta (1987) and will not be elaborated here. Instead, we concern ourselves with the stance that this theory takes with respect to the six key developmental issues that we listed earlier, issues that form the sum and substance of the sharpest current theoretical debates.

Differential emotions theory stresses that emotions are neurophysiologically grounded behaviors; consequently, much early affective behavior is innate and stereotyped, although socialization rapidly exerts influence on its subsequent development. According to the theory, there are distinct neural circuits for the basic emotions that govern the form of expression (facial, vocal, bodily). Certain emotions are said to be functionally present at birth, whereas others require maturation and adaptational demands before they become manifest. In fact, research indicates that virtually all the component muscle movements of adult facial expressions needed for encoding different emotion states are present at or before birth (Oster, 1978), that patterns of infant emotion expressions typically resemble those of adults (Izard, 1979), and that at least some expressions are functionally adaptive at birth (e.g., the disgust expression seen in the expulsion of distasteful substances; for a review, see Izard & Malatesta, 1987). Most recently, Camras (1988) videotaped the facial expressions of her infant daughter over the opening months of life. She found that almost all the basic emotions (happiness, sadness, anger, distress, and surprise) can be reliably observed within the first few weeks under reasonable incentive (eliciting) conditions, although the elicitors do not always correspond to those of adult emotion expressions.

Affective expressions themselves are said to mediate crucial adaptive functions in individual development through a sophisticated signaling system that provides vital information to the self and others. With respect to the role of facial expressions as self-informing signals, differential emotions theory maintains that there are distinct neurophysiological processes subserving each of the fundamental emotions and that these processes and their corresponding neuromuscular efferents are activated by biologically and psychologically meaningful stimuli. Patterned feedback from sensations generated by facial and other neuromuscular responses yields the distinctive subjective experiences that we recognize as different qualities of feeling state. The theory also assumes that there is an innate expression-to-feeling concordance in the young infant (e.g., distress crying is accompanied by distress feelings). Over time, this close relation between feeling and behavior becomes less reliable as the child learns how to dissociate or uncouple the two through various strategies.

The argument that expressive behavior and feeling states are originally concordant rests largely on the notion of functional preadaptation. According to Carmichael's (1971) law of anticipatory function in prenatal neurogenesis, many structures and systems (and presumably links between the two) that are needed in later adaptation are functionally mature at birth or before. It is hard to conceive of other kinds of behavior, other than those involved in central vital functions, that are more immediate to survival than the young infant's ability to signal her internal states (hunger, distress, pain, pleasure) for crucial caregiver interventions. In the context of her altricial status and in the absence of alternative systems for signaling feeling states (e.g., language), much depends on the infant's nonverbal expressive behavior, and a certain degree of congruence between behavior and state seems necessary for reliable and appropriate caregiver interventions. This is not to say that infants experience feelings identical to those of adults in similar circumstances and with similar facial/vocal configurations; given the differences in cognitive capacities and exposure to life's experiences, it is almost certain that they do not. However, the theory assumes an underlying identity between the ways in which adults and infants experience emotion. While the experience of joy is different from that of anger, the experience of joy, for example, is fundamentally the same for both adults and children.

Although this theory emphasizes innate wiring, preadaptation, and an early stereotypy of response patterns, it also has a good deal to say about other sources of influence in later development. Beyond early infancy, it is assumed that the child develops certain self-regulatory processes as a function of maturation (e.g., through cortical inhibitory controls) and socialization experiences. It is a fundamental fact of social life that emotions must be regulated in the service of goal-directed behavior and interpersonal harmony. This means that the intense and unregulated expressions of infancy must give way to expressions that are more modulated. Among the formal aspects of emotion expression that seem to undergo change with age are the frequency, range, discreteness, and integrity of the expression (Izard & Malatesta, 1987). The existing literature indicates that with age emotional expressivity becomes less frequent (Emde, Gaensbauer, & Harmon, 1976; Malatesta, Grigoryev, Lamb, Albin, & Culver, 1986; Malatesta & Haviland, 1982), less variable and more conventionalized (Saarni, 1979), less discrete (Demos, 1982a, 1982b), and more miniaturized (Malatesta & Izard, 1984; Zivin, 1982).

Another major developmental milestone revolves around the child's mastery of the ability to uncouple expressive behavior from feeling state, for example, to smile despite intense displeasure or to mimic distress that is not really felt. Expressive behavior can be uncoupled from feeling state and managed in several ways. Ekman (1982) has identified four categories of expressive transformation: intensification or exaggeration, deintensification or minimization, neutralization (putting on a poker face), and masking (concealing an internal emotional state by adopting a noncongruent facial expression). There does not yet exist a systematic corpus of research concerning when and under what conditions stereotyped emotion expressions undergo transformation, nor is there much information on when and how children acquire the various transformational capacities. However, the existing literature suggests that there may be some (nonconscious) modulation of affect during the first year of life—for example, when cries become less intense because of expectancies derived from response-contingent behaviors of caregivers.

Emotion modulation involving maneuvers other than deliberate (conscious) expressive control has been observed in infants as young as 3½ months of age (Demos, 1986); the use of thumb-in-mouth in self-soothing is one such example. Conscious, voluntary control over affective expression is not expected until the second year, when the child becomes capable of more intentional planning. Some recent research indicates that children are capable of understanding "display rules" (i.e., what is expected in terms of affect modulation) as early as 2 years of age (Lewis & Michalson, 1983). Cole (1985) has found evidence of conformity to gender-appropriate display rules as early as ages 3 and 4. Demos's (1986) naturalistic observation of two girls during the first and second years of life provides evidence that some degree of affect modulation through control of facial musculature (intensifying and deintensifying negative expressions) is possible in the second year. Van Leishout's (1975) longitudinal study of distress between 18 and 24 months of age is also germane. In this study, infants in the presence of their mothers were confronted with conditions designed to produce frustration; girls but not boys showed a decrease in negative displays over time. Neutralization of expressive behavior (i.e., the deadpan face) has been observed in preschoolers (Cole, 1983) and may even occur as early as 12 months of age (Grossmann, 1981).

In contrast, the ability to mask emotions appears to be a relatively late developmental phenomenon. One of the commonest means of masking negative emotion is to pretend pleasure or happiness by adopting a smile (Ekman & Friesen, 1975). Preschoolers can apparently enact happiness on request if there is no underlying competing negative state (Cole, 1985); however, even school-age children have difficulty simulating pleasure while experiencing negative affect (Saarni, 1979).

In summary, it appears from these observations that the earliest forms of expressive control involve intensification and deintensification (miniaturization) of expressive behavior related to ongoing states. Some degree of skill in this area is achieved during the first year of life. When deintensification of affect is taken to the limit, it results in neutralization, a behavior that can be observed in preschoolers. Developmentally, the most difficult feat appears to be masking. In the light of the foregoing observations—and if, as Izard has argued, state (feeling) and behavior (expression) are relatively congruent in early development—expressive behavior should remain a fairly reliable index of feeling state until the third year, although the intensity of felt emotion may be somewhat exaggerated or minimized.

The specifics of how, and in what form, modulation will be accomplished in any one individual are apparently mediated by culture and familial experience, although it is assumed that certain general principles apply, including contingency learning (Watson, 1972), observational learning, desomatization through symbolic representation (Izard, 1971), and self-regulation (Wilson, Passik, & Faude, in press). With respect to the latter, self-regulation may involve either a primitive organismic reaction oriented toward the avoidance of negative affect (Haviland & Lelwica, 1987; Tomkins, 1962) or more self-conscious and deliberate adjustments, that is, active impression management.

In addition, given that expressive behavior is inherently linked to feeling states, that minimization of negative affect is a basic human goal (Tomkins, 1962, 1963), and that control of expressive behavior is an option, it follows that self-regulation of unpleasant emotional states will likely entail a suppression or minimization of negative affect. A corollary of this assumption is that such suppressive activity may be accompanied by a real reduction in felt level of distress.

For Izard, personality development is intimately linked to the course of emotional development. In early development, repetitive experience and expression of emotion are said to establish particular kinds of responses from others. These responses, in turn, generate certain kinds of interactions that, over time, inevitably produce distinct and significant personality characteristics. Personality, in its established form, is described in terms of patterns of "affective-cognitive structures," which are trait-like psychological organizations of affect and cognition deriving from repeated interactions between a particular affect or pattern of affects and a particular set or configuration of cognitions. These structures then govern the individual's goal-directed motivations and social experiences in ways that are related to the particular motivating properties of particular emotions. The development of these affective-cognitive structures is related to early temperamentally based thresholds for emotion as well as to the form of affective interaction experienced with caregivers.

A more explicit set of formulations concerning the socialization of affect and personality development is found in Tomkins's affect theory (Tomkins, 1962, 1963), which also takes a discrete emotions position. Tomkins distinguished four kinds of emotional organization or individual "affect theories": (1) a monopolistic type, in which a single emotion tends to dominate the affective life of the individual (as, e.g., in the distress- or anger-prone individual; (2) an intrusion type, in which a minor element in the general structure of personality intrudes and displaces a dominant affect under specific conditions; (3) a competition type, in which one emotion-based structural aspect of personality perpetually competes with others in the interpretation of information; and (4) an integration type, in which no single affect theory is permitted to dominate the personality in a monopolistic way.

According to Tomkins, the most developmentally favorable outcome—the integration type or affectively balanced personality—results when affect socialization is "rewarding" rather than "punishing." Affect socialization is rewarding when social agents permit or encourage the child to maintain positive affective states and help her reduce or attenuate negative affect

9

states when they occur. The attenuation of negative affect states is achieved when the caregiver shows little of a particular negative emotion toward the child or others; helps the child attenuate negative affect when it occurs by de-emphasizing rather than amplifying the experience; communicates tolerance of the negative affect within the self and in the child; shows affective engagement with the child or adult having negative affect, both verbally and nonverbally (nonverbal engagement being especially important); shows consistency among ideological posture, action, and affect with respect to the emotion; and helps the child cope with the sources of negative affects so as to avoid their unnecessary provocation. Teaching the child to avoid the occasion of unnecessary negative affect is not to be confused with teaching her to avoid the *experience* of negative affect, which would result in suppression or repression of the emotion. Tomkins suggests that parents should teach tolerance rather than avoidance of negative affect experience.

"Punitive socialization" of affect leads to less than optimal personality formation (i.e., the formation of monopolistic, intrusion, or competitive affect organizations). This occurs when the caregiver amplifies negative affect rather than helping reduce it; provides an ideology that teaches the child to screen the world for stimuli capable of eliciting negative affect; behaves and expresses emotion in a way that is consistent with this ideology; and fails to help the child cope with her suffering.

In summary, Tomkins gives us a complex set of formulations about the nature of affective organizations and their socialization. The implied principles of parental socialization are empathy, modeling, induction, and sensitive as well as consistent verbal and nonverbal communication about affective states of both the parent and the child. Classical behavioral principles do not apply in the expected manner. For example, although amplifying negative affect is "punishing," this kind of punishment does not serve to reduce or temper the negative affect; rather, it results, paradoxically, in its monopolization of the personality. Furthermore, the principle of "extinction training"—that is, ignoring negative affect—is not advocated by Tomkins as a means of reducing it. Instead, monopolistic affective organizations are avoided if parents assist children in the sympathetic experience and reduction of negative affect, that is, if they attend to their children's affect sensitively and show integrity with respect to their own feelings, behaviors, and ideology.

It is clear that for both Izard and Tomkins emotion serves an important organizational role in the life of the individual. In early development, affects, as primary motivations, elicit and sustain interactions with others in the social environment. These interactions, which include assisting the child in the regulation of affective states, effect subsequent personality development and lead to the adoption of local cultural ideals of expressivity as well as the development of personal styles of behavior and affective/cognitive structures. Particular patterns of affective-cognitive structures then contribute to particular patterns of goal-directed behaviors, perceptual and cognitive biases, and behavioral preferences (Malatesta & Wilson, 1988).

The Cognitive/Constructivist Position

Before we outline the cognitive/constructivist approach, let us reiterate that the distinction we have drawn between theoretical systems as more nativist or constructivist is intended as a heuristic rather than as a representation of a genuine dichotomy. In fact, although there are a few sharp divergences on some of the key issues we raised earlier, the differences are more a matter of focus and emphasis.

Sroufe's (1979) theory of socioemotional development, which advances a differentiation theory of emotion based on Bridges's (1931, 1932) observations of early infant affect, Spitz's genetic field theory, and Piaget's theory of cognitive development, is representative of the cognitive/constructivist position. In Sroufe's view, affects begin as undifferentiated precursor states of distress and nondistress and differentiate into specific emotions only gradually. Differentiation occurs in a stage-like way as a function of major developmental reorganizations. Cognition is an all-important variable in his developmental scheme and acts as a central mechanism in the growth, elaboration, and differentiation of the emotions.

Sroufe's position with respect to the six key issues outlined earlier is generally at variance with Izard's. First, he discounts the existence of discrete emotions during the opening weeks of life, instead referring to what appear to be emotional behaviors as "precursor" affects. Differentiation does not begin until about 2–3 months of age; the emergence of "true" emotions requires the prior establishment of elementary forms of cognitive activity promoting consciousness—the sine qua non for feeling states. The experience of emotion also depends on the ability to differentiate the self from others. Other theorists whose work falls within the cognitive/constructivist camp defer the emergence of feeling states until even later, into the second half of the first year of life or beyond (Emde, Kligman, Reich, & Wade, 1978; Kagan, 1984; Lewis & Brooks, 1978).

As we have already noted, recent research has been instrumental in documenting the existence of a range of discrete emotional expressions in early infancy (Izard & Malatesta, 1987). Although such findings would seem to challenge Sroufe's position concerning the lack of early emotional differentiation, they actually damage only the thesis that affect expression is undifferentiated; there is still no way of ascertaining with any degree of certainty whether affective experience (or feeling) is differentiated. Izard's theory assumes that differentiated facial expressions imply differentiated

11

affect expression. Sroufe's does not; instead, as indicated above, emotional experiences are said to be instigated by such cognitive factors as recognition and appraisal and to be dependent on level of cognitive development.

Sroufe has less to say about the relation between facial activity and feeling states beyond early infancy, except to suggest that facial expressions may lag behind the capacity for emotional experience (since emotions are dependent on cognitions, not facial expressions). Nevertheless, he leans toward the possibility that facial expressions may often index states and that the addition of expressive behavior may further amplify and sharpen the experience.

Sroufe's views on the socialization of emotion and his treatment of individual differences in the development of personality are closely linked with the outcome of attachment. Individual differences in competence and styles of adaptation in later childhood are sequelae of the early affective bond that is established between caregiver and child. Since this view coincides with ethological (attachment) theory, which we describe in more detail in the next section, we defer a discussion of this position until then.

A somewhat more extreme cognitive/constructivist position with respect to the relation between state and behavior is entertained by Lewis and Michalson (1983). According to these writers, there are three stages of expression development. During earliest infancy, there is an absence of coordination between internal states and expressive behaviors; socialization experiences involving tuition about what kinds of expressions go with what kinds of feeling states are important in establishing the connection. During the second stage, there is greater synchrony between facial expressions and emotional states, and expressive behavior is a more reliable sign of feeling state. Later, other socialization experiences foster learning how to dissimulate or uncouple state and behavior; at this point, emotion expressions serve more as symbols than as signs of underlying state. Lewis and Michalson do not provide a general timetable for the achievement of these stages; moreover, they suggest that different emotions achieve synchrony (and dissynchrony, one assumes) at different points in development. Emotions that emerge from an undifferentiated state, they assert, will probably reach a period of synchrony earlier than those emotions that appear later; thus, after a certain point, facial expressions provide little guide to emotional states. These authors also obviously do not subscribe to a facial feedback theory. Within their framework, facial expressions, sui generis, have little to do with generating, sustaining, or amplifying emotional experiences. Instead, emotional experience is largely the product of cognitive activity and of socialization by caregivers and others concerning what and how to feel.

The writings of Lewis (1988; Lewis & Michalson, 1983) provide one of the more fully elaborated treatments of affect socialization from within the cognitive/constructivist school. Personality outcomes are viewed as the products of socialization experiences and the child's cognitive constructions. Among the socialization processes that are thought to play a role in the development of more mature forms of emotional behavior are reinforcement principles (reward and punishment); imitation; incidental learning; parental tuition about the use of affect labels to encode experience; and the acquisition of emotional scripts, which are learned by "figuring out" the lawful principles governing others' behavior.

Attachment Theory

The third approach to affective development to be discussed is that of attachment theory. Like the two preceding theoretical frameworks, attachment theory is concerned with organizational aspects of behavior and with the role of affect in the development of social relationships and personality. Over the past 15 years, it has been one of the most influential theories to evolve within the developmental literature.

As is now well known, the theory originated with John Bowlby's attempt to synthesize principles from psychoanalysis and ethology in order to illuminate the nature of the young child's attachment to the parent. A review of the original theory (Bowlby, 1969, 1973, 1980) and a summary of attachment research to date can be found in Bretherton (in press) as well as in an earlier *Monograph* (Bretherton & Waters, 1985). Consequently, we present only a synopsis here, highlighting aspects of the theory and research that are most relevant to the six key developmental questions specified earlier.

In brief, Bowlby proposed that the child's tie to the caregiver arises in the context of the activation of a preadapted, biologically based, goal-corrected, motivational system. In the earliest stage of development, the young child is said to be innately predisposed to engage in behaviors that will ensure proximity to the caregiver. Of special significance are specific attachment behaviors that act as signals in promoting caregiving behavior, most notably crying, clinging, tracking with the eyes, smiling, and babbling. In a complementary fashion, caregivers are said to be biologically predisposed to respond to such signals. It is in the context of these early attachment behaviors and reciprocal interactions that the child comes to develop an attachment bond to the caregiver. At the emotional level, attachment connotes "felt security"; the child discriminates the caregiver from others and prefers to be in this person's presence, especially under conditions of threat. Later, the focus of attachment shifts from maintenance of physical proximity to achieving a balance between attachment and exploratory needs and, ultimately, to an elaboration of an internal working model of that relationship and of interpersonal relationships in general.

Research on attachment theory began with Ainsworth's (1967, 1972) observations first of Ugandan infants and later of a sample of Baltimore

13

mothers and children. In Uganda, Ainsworth spent most of her time study-ing the normative aspects of infant attachment, but eventually she became more interested in those infants who displayed more atypical patterns. As her work progressed, she was led to propose that differences in the ways mothers responded to the emotional signals of their infants early in life might influence the outcome of attachment. Subsequent research employing a laboratory-based assessment (the "Strange Situation") led her to codify differences in attachment at 12 months and to relate them back to the mother's level of sensitivity as observed during feeding sessions in the open-ing months of life. Both Ainsworth (Ainsworth, Blehar, Waters, & Wall, 1978) and Bowlby (1969) have defined sensitivity in terms of the caregiver's ability to read and respond appropriately to the infant's nonverbal behav-iors. The thesis that maternal sensitivity is linked to the outcome of attach-ment first appeared supported by the findings of Ainsworth's Baltimore study. Since then, there have been several replication studies indicating that maternal sensitivity is indeed a factor in the development of attachment, although infant characteristics such as temperament also play a role (Gross-mann, Grossmann, Spangler, Suess, & Unzner, 1985; Miyake, Chen, & Campos, 1985).

Originally, three types of attachment pattern were distinguished: avoidant (A), secure (B), and ambivalent (C), with both the A and the C types reflecting insecure attachment. A fourth classification, D, was added later to encompass those children who showed varying degrees of avoidance and ambivalence, but this type still remains to be validated against home observations during the first year (Bretherton, in press). Subclassifications have also been distinguished; however, attempts to establish their discrimi-nant validity have been generally unsuccessful (Campos et al., 1983). The most common grouping factor for much attachment research has been the A/B/C distinction or the designation of a secure (all B types) versus an insecure group (A and C groups combined).

Over the past several years, a great deal of research has been devoted to assessing the stability and predictive validity of attachment classifications. A good summary of this literature appears in Bretherton (1985). In brief, the literature indicates support for the stability of pattern over time, at least in terms of major attachment classifications. It also indicates that the predictive validity of classifications is best for the broadest grouping factor, that is, grouping on the basis of secure versus insecure attachment status.

Most recently, work on the attachment construct has focused on Bowl-by's (1973) notion of internal working models as an explanatory force for the observed continuity of attachment patterns. Bowlby hypothesized that the infant begins to construct working models of the world, the self, and attachment figures during the second year of life. These working models are affectively imbued representations that help the child summarize her experiences with attachment figures and make predictions about future behavior and relationships. We have little to say about internal working models ourselves since our research is limited to the first 2 years of life and since we did not attempt to assess this aspect of the child's development. Most research on internal working models has been with older children or adults since assessment typically requires that language functions be fairly mature. Bretherton, Ridgeway, and Cassidy (in press), however, have had some success in assessing working models in 37-month-olds.

With this overview as a backdrop, we turn to what attachment theory has to say vis-à-vis the six developmental questions that were the focus of our previous discussion. To begin with, attachment theory does not specifically address the question of whether there are innate, discrete expressions of emotion early in development. The theory does assume, however, that the infant is preadapted to display a number of differentiated signals that are activated by appropriate stimuli and that typically elicit different kinds of responses from caregivers. Three of the signals present at birth or shortly thereafter are crying, orientation, and smiling. It is of moment that these same three behaviors are regarded as emotional displays by discrete emotions theory. It is also interesting to note that Bowlby (1969) opened his chapter 7—"Appraising and Selecting: Feeling and Emotion"—with a quotation from Darwin on the role of expressive movements as the first means of communication between the mother and her infant. Attachment theory, at least as formulated by Bowlby, thus occupies a middle ground between discrete emotions theory and the cognitive/constructivist position with respect to this question. It specifies the existence of innate signals that have a distinctly emotional tone. The signals are discrete rather than graded (i.e., they vary in quality, not just in intensity), but they also seem to fall along a continuum of hedonic tone, that is, from positive to negative feeling, with smiling at one end and crying at the other.

With respect to questions of the infant's ability to have feeling states and of the relation between facial or other expressive gestures and emotional experience, it must be admitted that Bowlby did not emphasize the experiential aspect of attachment in his discussions of infancy. As Bretherton (1987) has noted, at the time Bowlby began writing about attachment he was more concerned with demonstrating the usefulness of the evolutionary-ethological approach in explaining the adaptive (i.e., survival related) function of the infant's attachment to her caregiver. A second reason was the absence, at that time, of a formal corpus of theory concerning the emotions and their role in early development. When Bowlby did discuss emotions, he linked them with aspects of the appraisal process. Individuals make affective appraisals of their environment, and these appraisals may or may not be felt (i.e., consciously experienced). Whereas some theorists assume that emotions must be consciously experienced to qualify as emotions, Bowlby allowed for "unconscious feeling." In this sense, his position is rather close to that taken by Izard (1984; Izard & Malatesta, 1987), who holds that emotional experience can and does exist in the young infant at the level of organic sensation and that this level of feeling can and does motivate behavior.

Bowlby was less equivocal about the relation between overt (expressive) behavior and internal feeling states. It is significant that the quotation he selected from Darwin expresses the view that there is an "intimate relation which exists between almost all the emotions and their outward manifestation" (Darwin cited in Bowlby, 1969, p. 104). Bowlby himself accepts the position that there is a fairly reliable link between feeling and behavior, acknowledging that feeling states are "usually accompanied by distinctive facial expressions" (1969, p. 105). It is no accident that Bowlby endorses this view. The integrity of his theory depends on such a position since the very formation of the attachment relationship requires both readability of infant signals and appropriateness (i.e., signal specificity) of caregiver responses. The argument was further buttressed, Bowlby thought, by the observation that expressions are good indices of response predispositions—our interpretations of others' emotional states are far more often correct than incorrect.

On the issue of emotion socialization, attachment theory provides us with little in the way of any explicit formulations. Emotions are not seen as requiring socialization per se, although emotional milestones do occur in the course of development. In the first year of life, the infant forms an attachment relationship with a primary caregiver. In the majority of cases, the attachment is accompanied by positive affect and affectionate feelings, and the child achieves felt security. The attachment process unfolds naturally as a function of an evolutionarily based, preadapted program. Despite the lack of theoretical focus on the issue of emotion socialization, research on attachment has documented that the manner in which caregivers respond to their infants' communications is associated with different emotional profiles and patterns of expressivity (Bretherton, in press). For example, Cassidy and Kobak (in press) describe the avoidant behavior of infants classified as A as concealing an underlying hostility, implying that these children suppress or neutralize felt anger. Similarly, a study by Grossmann, Grossmann, and Schwan (1986) indicates that insecure infants are significantly less likely to communicate their distress to their caregivers when in an unhappy mood.

The attachment literature has had far more to contribute with respect to the issue of personality development, although as originally formulated attachment was viewed not as a personality configuration but rather as an index of a biologically based, goal-corrected, motivational system oriented toward maintaining homeostasis. However, as research on the characteristics of A, B, and C children accumulated, and as the attachment construct began to take on more and more trait-like qualities, the resemblance to personality constructs could not be ignored. Indeed, many workers have come to regard A, B, and C typologies in the same way that personologists have treated different personality types.

Differences in the quality of attachment are said to be linked to variations in mother-infant interaction during early development, especially along the dimension of maternal sensitivity to infant signals. Although Bowlby (1969) himself referred to sensitivity as an important factor facilitating the attachment process, the concept was first formalized and tested by Ainsworth and her coworkers. Ainsworth, Bell, and Stayton (1971) defined the component parts of maternal sensitivity as consisting of the mother's awareness of the signals, her ability to interpret them accurately, her tendency to respond appropriately, and the promptness (i.e., contingency) of her response.

Three other maternal difference variables thought to affect the development of attachment include the mother's degree of acceptance or rejection, her degree of cooperation or interference, and her accessibility or ignoring. An accepting mother, according to Ainsworth's scoring system, is characterized as having an open emotional awareness of both her positive and her negative feelings toward the infant and as having the ability to integrate these feelings so as not to suppress awareness of either. (To the extent that this description applies to the mother's general functioning and not just her attitude toward the infant, the accepting mother would appear to possess a balanced affective organization of the sort described by Tomkins's integration model of personality.) The cooperating mother attempts to guide rather than control her infant's behavior. The interfering mother, in contrast, has been described as trying to "train" her infant, that is, to shape it to fit her own concept of a good baby. She also tends to be constantly "doing something to the baby" and in some cases overwhelms it in a physical sense. Thus, infants of interfering mothers may experience their interactions as aversive and overstimulating. Ignoring mothers are described as tending to neglect their infants. These mothers may perceive their infant's signals adequately enough but not acknowledge or respond to them. For example, an infant may cry, but the mother may not know the cause and therefore do nothing because she does not know what to do.

Assessments of each of the four maternal difference variables are based on global ratings involving nine-point scales. The dimension of maternal sensitivity has been found to be highly correlated with each of the other three (Ainsworth et al., 1971).

As indicated earlier, maternal sensitivity ratings do appear to predict the quality of attachment relationship; in turn, the child's attachment classification status (securely or insecurely attached) tends to predict individual differences on a number of personality and social dimensions, including tolerance for frustration in problem-solving situations (Matas, Arend, & Sroufe, 1978), quality of affect during free play (Main, 1973), curiosity, and ego resilience (Arend, Gove, & Sroufe, 1979).

There is also a corpus of literature on maternal personality characteristics—in addition to, or overlapping with, sensitivity to infant signals—that may contribute to the formation of insecure attachments. Some of these have a bearing on emotional expression patterns. For example, Gaensbauer et al. (1985) found that mothers of infants classified as very insecure were rated as angrier, more fearful, less curious, and less happy than mothers of infants classified as securely attached. Main, Tomasini, and Tolan (1979) reported that, during free play, mothers of insecurely attached babies were angrier and less expressive than mothers of securely attached infants; these mothers also communicated their affect less openly when greeting a somewhat familiar woman as she entered the playroom. In both studies, assessments of expressivity were made on the basis of general rating scales rather than through the use of validated facial emotion coding systems.

Summary

It is clear that the three theoretical approaches to emotional development have points of divergence as well as of consensus. All three positions agree in according emotions a central organizational function in human development. When they differ, it is mainly with respect to the issue of the relation between experience and behavior (i.e., between feeling states and facial and other expressive gestures) and in the degree to which emotional behavior is perceived as being guided by either cognitive or evolutionarily grounded, biologically based control systems and maturation during early development.

II. THEORETICAL ASSUMPTIONS OF THE CURRENT INVESTIGATION

The theoretical assumptions that guided the present investigation come closest to those of differential emotions theory and of attachment theory. Although we do not deny the importance of cognition in human development and in the child's active construction of social reality, we take issue with the cognitive/constructive position with respect to the six key developmental questions that formed the basis of our comparison among theories. We believe that, for phylogenetic considerations alone, one must assume that emotional behavior is part of an evolutionarily adapted behavioral system. As such, there is a compelling argument for assuming that a good deal of emotional behavior in human infants is prewired and preadapted. Specifically, we assume—as do Izard and Bowlby—that there is an inherent link between expressive behavior and emotional experience, especially in early development. However, we also acknowledge that it is one of the more important developmental tasks of infancy and childhood to learn how to modulate affective state and transform the original, preadapted, innate expressive displays into the more variable forms used in a variety of social communicative functions. As far as that process is concerned, one cannot deny the important contributions of maturing cognitive abilities and socialization in shaping socioemotional development. Indeed, our examination of expressive development during the first 2 years of life gives us an opportunity to learn something about when cortical inhibitory control systems may first exert an influence on overt expressive behavior. It also gives us an opportunity to examine what kinds of social experience may foster individual differences in such behavior. A secondary reason for our focus on overt behavior rather than on the constructive aspect of the infant's emotional development is methodological; the tools for assessing the infant's cognitive constructions are less well developed than is the technology for examining expressive behaviors (Bretherton et al., in press).

Another assumption that we make as a reasonable extrapolation from the empirical literature is that, during the first 2 years of life, expressive behavior may be a fairly reliable index of underlying state. There is little evidence that 1- or 2-year-olds have the capacity to dissimulate or mask intense emotional experience. They may, however, deintensify or dampen their emotional expressions in an attempt to master painful affect, or, conversely, they may intensify or exaggerate them to protest separations, to gain comforting, or to achieve other instrumental purposes.

We also assume, as does each of the three theories discussed in the previous chapter, that infant personality development is forged within the context of relationships. We furthermore assume that it is within the context of close interpersonal interactions that children acquire the ability to modulate state and also develop idiosyncratic styles of expressive behavior. On the basis of attachment theory and Tomkin's affect theory, we expect that maternal sensitivity to affective signals will have a crucial influence on this process. Attachment theory also leads us to believe that the child's interactive experiences along the broad dimension of positive versus negative affective tone will discriminate different developmental profiles. Beyond this, Izard's theory leads us to expect that the kind of affect (i.e., differential emotion) communicated by the mother may be of particular importance in the development of unique emotional profiles. Not only does the present investigation provide detailed descriptive data on infant expressive development over the first 2 years of life, but it does so by tapping the relationship context that is said to provide the foundation of affective and personality development.

FOCUS OF THE PRESENT INVESTIGATION

This study is concerned with describing normative patterns of expressive development during the first 2 years of life as well as with accounting for the development of individual differences in emotional profile. We take our cue from two early developmentalists. Charlotte Buehler, one of the first psychologists to break ground in the experimental study of children's social development, insisted in her chapter in the first edition of the *Handbook of Child Psychology* that aspects of socialization "must be regarded from two different points of view, first the developmental aspect, and secondly, the point of view of individual differences" (Buehler, 1933, p. 375). Her husband, Karl Buehler, was to draw attention to the fact that social development took place within the context of a mutual accommodation and regulation in the exchange of signals, or what he called "gegenseitige Steurung" (Buehler, 1929).

In deciding to study both normative and differential development, our choice of individual difference variables was guided by the previous literature. Three variables were of particular interest: maternal contingency, infant temperament, and gender of the infant. Our rationale for the selection of these variables follows.

Maternal Contingency

The contingency or lack of contingency with which caregivers respond to infant signals has been of considerable interest to both attachment researchers and those interested in the general issue of emotion socialization.

Relevance to attachment theory.—From the point of view of attachment theory, caregiver sensitivity to infant signals is the sine qua non for the establishment of an emotionally secure attachment; in contrast, insecure attachments are said to accrue from selective ignoring of signals (Bretherton, in press). Accordingly, most ethologically guided approaches to studying the caregiver's role in fostering or impeding the development of attachment have focused on this particular dimension of caregiver behavior. (For an elaboration of this issue, see the previous chapter.)

Relevance to differential emotions theory.—Differential emotions theory also places great emphasis on the social-communicative value of expressive behaviors, especially with respect to the issue of emotion socialization. Affective signals are, by their nature, salient and compelling elicitors of responses between interactants. Affective exchanges between caregivers and infants provide infants with one of the earliest occasions for the learning of display rules, that is, the local cultural ideals of expressive behavior as well as individual-familial expressive patterns (Malatesta & Haviland, 1982).

A number of studies (Brazelton, Koslowski, & Main, 1974; Kaye, 1979; Malatesta & Haviland, 1982) have documented that young infants are exposed to modeling and instrumental learning conditions around different types of emotions very early in life during face-to-face play with their mothers and that mothers engage in attempts to moderate the emotional expressions of their infants. It has been demonstrated that mothers react in quite specific ways to their infants' various expressions of emotion (Frodi, Lamb, Leavitt, & Donovan, 1978; Malatesta & Haviland, 1982), and there is some evidence that these differential responses affect subsequent expressive development. For example, Malatesta et al. (1986) found that high rates of maternal modeling of joy and interest were associated with increases in infant joy and interest expressions between 2½ and 7½ months of age.

Beyond early infancy, there are few fine-grained, systematic, descriptive studies of children's spontaneous expressive behavior, especially in the context of interaction with social agents. Notable exceptions are Demos's (1986) naturalistic study of toddlers and the work conducted under seminaturalistic conditions at the Laboratory of Developmental Psychology, National Institute of Mental Health (e.g., Denham, 1985; Kochanska, 1987; Zahn-Waxler, Cummings, McKnew, & Radke-Yarrow, 1984). Collectively, these studies indicate that there are pronounced individual differences in the way in which mothers respond to certain types of children's emotion expressions and that these patterns may exert influence on subsequent child development. Kochanska (1987), for example, looked at developmental changes in the responses of (unipolar) depressed and nondepressed mothers to the anger expressions of 2–3-year-olds. She found that, in general, mothers became less tolerant, less affectionate, and less concerned when faced with their children's anger expressions over time. Depressed mothers responded differently than nondepressed mothers as a function of their children's gender—well mothers were more tolerant and supportive when confronted with their sons' anger, whereas depressed mothers showed more support and tolerance for the anger of daughters. In another study, this time with 2-year-old children of bipolar parents, Zahn-Waxler et al. (1984) found that children of depressed parents evinced poorer social interaction and emotion regulation than children from nondepressed families. In yet another investigation, this time involving seminaturalistic observation of the expressive behaviors of normal 2½-year-olds and their mothers, Denham (1985), using a contingency analysis, found that mothers responded to their children's emotional signals in a nonrandom fashion; in addition, multiple regression analyses showed that concurrent measures of children's and mothers' behaviors were related in important ways. For example, maternal emotional responses, current functioning, and/or prevailing emotional dispositions predicted children's various emotions and their socioemotional competence. Finally, a study by Demos (1986) focused on the expressive development and socialization practices of two mother/child pairs during the first 2 years of life. This detailed longitudinal study identifies what appear to be developmental sequelae of particular emotion socialization practices of the two mothers. In particular, Demos found that a child's ability to modulate and manage negative affective states was related to whether the mother helped foster self-regulating behaviors during early infancy.

These studies highlight the importance of interactive paradigms and the analysis of patterns of contingency between infant affective signals and caregiver responses in understanding emotion socialization and the development of individual differences in expressive styles. It also indicates how little we actually know about the process of emotion socialization over time. More studies, especially longitudinal ones, are clearly needed to validate and extend the patterns that seem to be emerging.

Because of the assumed formative role of maternal responsivity to infant signals for both the development of attachment and the socialization of emotion expression, we determined that it would be important to index and examine how early patterns of maternal responding might affect subsequent infant emotional development. Within the attachment literature, maternal sensitivity to infant signals has been studied by observing mothers and infants during routine caregiving interactions and by having judges make global assessments via rating scales. Occasionally, there is an effort to examine particular patterns of contingency, for example, the timing of maternal response to infant cries (Bell & Ainsworth, 1972). As seems warranted from a theoretical perspective, in the present study we evaluate affective exchanges at a more specific level of analysis. In attachment theory as originally formulated by Bowlby, sensitive caregiving is defined by the "appropriateness" of the intervention, that is, the signal-specific nature of the response. Within differential emotions theory as well, much emphasis is placed on the specificity of affective signals in terms of their social-communicative, phenomenological, and motivational value. Accordingly, in the present investigation we focus on mothers' affective (vs. general) responses to infant signals and examine both the degree of contingency and the type of contingent response vis-à-vis type of infant signal as predictors of attachment and expressive behavior in 2-year-olds. The types of contingent responses are those implied by differential emotions theory. These are discussed below.

Infant Temperament

A mother's tendency to respond to her infant in a sensitive or insensitive manner and the type of emotion socialization in which she engages are not, of course, unrelated to infant characteristics. It is obviously easier to be sensitive, accessible, cooperative, and accepting with infants who are easy to manage than it is with those who are difficult. The work of Grossmann et al. (1985) and Miyake et al. (1985) has demonstrated the way in which such infant characteristics as ability to orient and ability to tolerate frustration affect the nature of the interactions that mothers have with their babies.

There is now fairly substantial evidence that there are early, constitutionally rooted behavioral biases with respect to emotional dispositions (Bates, 1987). Evidence of innate differences in the predisposition to show certain patterns of emotional expression is suggested by individual differences that are detected early in life and that show continuity over time. Significant continuities over several years and beginning in early infancy have been found for "behavioral inhibition" (Garcia-Coll, Kagan, & Reznick, 1984; Kagan, Reznick, Clarke, Snidman, & Garcia-Coll, 1984), a behavior pattern that appears to index shyness or anxiety. Izard, Hembree, Dougherty, and Spizzirri (1983) have shown that individual differences in anger and sadness expressions persist over the first 18 months. Other data, based on parental report rather than coding by trained observers, are essentially consistent with this picture (for a review, see Izard & Malatesta, 1987).

In the present study, we were particularly interested in how a dimension of temperamental "difficultness" (Bates, 1987) might affect the development of attachment and the course of emotion socialization. To guarantee a significant number of infants disposed to temperamental difficultness early on, we drew on a population of infants who are known to be at risk for this condition, preterm babies. Prematurity is classically accompanied by developmental delay, difficult temperament, and interactive deficits (Field, 1987).

Preterm infants, moreover, have been found to differ from full terms in many ways thought to have an effect on the mother's attempts to interact with her child. For example, premature babies tend to be more irritable than their full-term counterparts. They show a lag in social smiling, are less ready to withstand the stimulation that occurs in playful face-to-face interaction, and show more gaze aversion. They also sleep a greater proportion of the time and are less alert and responsive when awake. Their motor organization is poorer, and their states of arousal are less well modulated. In sum, in the premature infant the caregiver is faced with a less adept social partner, one at risk for subsequent interactive difficulty. In fact, research indicates that the dyadic relationship of preterms both starts out and remains more disadvantaged than that of term infants. Parents of preterm infants make less body contact with them, spend less time interacting with them in face-to-face play, smile at and touch them less, and appear to be more emotionally withdrawn from their children even at 2 years of age (Barnard & Bee, 1982; Field, 1987; Goldberg, Brachfeld, & DiVitto, 1980). Consequently, it is assumed that preterm infants are exposed to a different pattern of emotion socialization and show a different course of socioemotional development than their full-term counterparts.

Research on emotional differences between full-term and preterm infants has only just begun. Recent studies of the relation between birth status and attachment have disclosed no anomalies in the distribution of the major categories of attachment types among preterm infants (e.g., Frodi, 1983; Gaensbauer & Harmon, 1982), and one study of the expressive behaviors of preterms based on assessments during the Strange Situation found that birth-status differences in expressive behavior did not obtain at the age of 1 year (Frodi & Thompson, 1985). The investigators concluded that there may be a rebound in socioemotional development among preterm infants during the second half of the first year of life. However, their measures of expressive behavior were dimensional rather than discrete, and they did not consider birth-status differences in interaction with other variables thought to moderate expressive patterns, as we do in the present study.

Gender

No single individual-difference variable is more frequently associated with group differences in the social-developmental literature than gender. With respect to socioemotional development, although differences in the distribution of attachment types by gender are typically absent, gender differences in expressive behavior have been demonstrated as early as infancy (for reviews, see Haviland & Malatesta, 1981; and Manstead, in press). Some investigators (e.g., Lewis, 1988) are presently engaged in attempting to identify how parents influence the different expressive behaviors of boys and girls, but little detailed data are presently available.

Summary and Prospect

The present study was designed to expand the existing data base on expressive behavior in early development and to elucidate the factors that influence its course. The investigation departs from previous studies in that it combines several important approaches within the same design. First, the design is longitudinal and involves four waves of data collection with a moderately sized population of infants. Partial results of the first three waves of data appeared in an earlier report (Malatesta et al., 1986); in the current report, we present data on the second year of life, provide more specifics concerning the earlier phases of expressive development (first three waves), and show how early patterns of interaction and expressive displays are related to later expressive behavior. Second, the design includes a sample of normal (i.e., nonrisk) infants as well as a sample of temperamentally difficult, at-risk, preterm infants. Third, the work provides one of the most extensively documented records to date of discrete emotional behaviors and their development over one of the most significant developmental epochs— the first 2 years of life. Fourth, the analyses seek to link constitutional differences, as well as early differences in the pattern of interaction with social agents, with subsequent expressive behavior and development.

Finally, the methods attempt to bridge the approach of attachment theorists to descriptions of emotional development, with a discrete emotion approach and the use of microanalytic coding strategies. It is only recently that developmentalists have begun to examine the relation between attachment status and more specific emotional parameters, and only a handful of studies have employed discrete emotion, microanalytic coding of emotional responses (e.g., Shiller, Izard, & Hembree, 1986). None to date have examined the predictive power of early discrete emotion patterns in mothers and infants as they relate to attachment, probably because of the time and labor involved in undertaking such detailed longitudinal work. The present study is unique in that it makes available such data. Further, our data allow us to begin to look at how one variable may not have the same effect on all individuals. For this reason, we look at interaction effects as part of our model.

METHODOLOGICAL AND DATA-ANALYTIC CONSIDERATIONS: OVERVIEW AND RATIONALE

The emphasis on both normative trends and individual differences in the development of attachment and expressive behavior led to a series of decisions that determined the design of the study. Here we provide the background and rationale of our choice of paradigm and of strategies for coding and analysis.

Paradigm Considerations

Our theoretical framework, with its emphasis on the relational context of emotional and expressive development over time, clearly called for an assessment of behavior during ongoing dyadic interaction, the elicitation of emotional behaviors, a longitudinal design, and the use of task-equivalent, age-appropriate measures at each wave of data collection.

To this end, we structured a series of play, separation, and reunion sessions at each of four ages: 2½, 5, 7½, and 22 months. The play sessions gave us an opportunity to observe a range of positive emotional behaviors and the separations and reunions a range of negative ones, thus permitting us to sample from the full array of affective reactions. All sessions were videorecorded for subsequent coding and analysis.

Coding Considerations

We were primarily interested in coding infants' and mothers' emotional expressions and signals of ethological interest—that is, attachment-related behaviors. Toward this end, we applied two well-validated coding systems: the Maximally Discriminative Facial Movement Coding System (MAX; Izard, 1979) for coding expressive behaviors and the Ainsworth attachment classification system, which evaluates the quality of attachment. Ainsworth's system is by now well known; details on the method of coding and classifying behavior can be found in Ainsworth (1972) and Ainsworth et al. (1978). Since the MAX system is less widely known, we take up a more extended discussion of its features.

The MAX system is one of the best-validated and most widely used facial emotion coding systems available. It is a theoretically based, anatomically linked facial movement coding system designed to identify fundamental emotions by coding movement changes in three regions of the face. The codes themselves are used in conjunction with formulas that are provided in a manual that comes with the videotape used in training. The formulas distinguish eight fundamental emotions—interest, joy, surprise, sadness, anger, disgust, contempt, and fear—and the motive state of physical distress or pain.

The MAX system demonstrates good content validity (for documentation, see Izard, 1979) and satisfies construct validity by social consensus studies (e.g., Izard, Huebner, Risser, McGinnes, & Dougherty, 1980). It also shows good criterion-related validity in studies involving assessments of predicted facial behaviors following emotion incentive conditions. For example, the fear expression has been reliably identified in young infants in response to extreme novelty (Schwartz & Izard, 1985), anger facial expressions in response to frustration of goals (Stenberg et al., 1983), pain expressions in response to DPT inoculations (Izard et al., 1983), interest expressions in response to the presentation of novel stimuli and as correlated with visual fixation time (Langsdorf, Izard, Rayias, & Hembree, 1983), and sadness and anger expressions in response to separation from the caregiver (Shiller et al., 1986).

In the present study, we coded the standard template emotions identified by Izard's system (i.e., the basic, unmodified expressions that one is likely to see in early infancy). In addition, we also wanted to consider signals that may be developmentally advanced modifications of the templates. The emotion socialization literature leads us to expect that one of the first voluntary modifications of expressive behavior will involve the dampening or minimization of negative affect expressions. Our previous work on adult facial expressions (Malatesta & Izard, 1984) was useful in alerting us to the likely configuration that such muted expressions might assume.

From preliminary inspection of our tapes, it became obvious that some of the 2-year-olds were engaging in facial behaviors that resembled dampened affect in adults, namely, biting the lower lip, pressing the two lips together, and using a slightly lowered brow during distress (rather than the sharply lower brow of anger or the sharply oblique brows of sadness). The slightly lowered brow can be represented by Izard's code 24. Biting the lower lip and pressing the two lips together are not, however, represented by codes in the MAX system. We therefore assigned codes of our own to these expressions (88 and 67) and coded all instances of their occurrence in each of the four waves of the study. One further behavior was of particular interest for theoretical reasons—eye contact between the partners. We coded infant gaze behavior directed at the mother because of its importance as an attachment behavior; correspondingly, we coded the amount of recip-

27

rocated gazing engaged in by the mother as a measure of her attentiveness and responsivity.

Another tactical decision involved choosing a frequency as opposed to a duration measure for quantifying facial expressive activity. In using the MAX system, one records the onset and offset of all facial muscle movement changes that are related to emotional expressions. One then has the option of subsequently entering from the recorded data frequencies of behaviors (i.e., each new "onset" counted as a frequency of one) or total durations of particular behaviors. Because "onsets" (i.e., changes in behavior) in the context of interpersonal communication are particularly salient and informationally rich, and because they are more reliably coded than offsets (which are needed for calculating durations), we decided to use facial expression onset frequencies rather than total duration of types of expressions as our dependent measures.

The measures outlined above allowed us to examine the types and frequencies of emotional expressions that infants and mothers display toward one another during playful and stressful encounters. For theoretical reasons, we were especially interested in a particular aspect of maternal expressive behavior, namely, mother's sensitivity (contingency or responsiveness) with respect to infant affective signals. Although maternal sensitivity is usually based on global ratings of the mother's overall responsiveness, we felt it particularly important to assess the contingency of her affective signals vis-à-vis those of her infant—it is known that infants are exquisitely sensitive to the affective expressions of others, and their own behavior appears to be modified by exposure to others' emotional expressions (Haviland & Lelwica, 1987; Malatesta, in press).

Maternal contingency was coded when a mother changed her facial expression within 1 sec of an expression change of her infant (i.e., a 1-sec lag). This 1-sec contingency window was chosen because it falls within the most optimal range of contingency learning. Infant and maternal expressive behaviors were originally coded separately and entered on joint coding sheets. After both partners were fully coded, instances of maternal contingency were noted. Because the intercoder reliabilities for separate scorings of infant and maternal behaviors were based on within-second accuracies, a final pass was made through the videorecords with both partners visible to ensure that in each case maternal behaviors followed rather than preceded or co-occurred with infant expressive behaviors.

Data-Analytic Considerations

The analyses were dictated by the developmental questions we were interested in answering (see the following section). However, given that the study involves several independent variables (gender, birth status, maternal contingency) and several dependent measures (emotion expression codes, other expressive signals) as well as the assessment of attachment—which can be treated as an independent or a dependent variable—we were presented with various analytic alternatives. Three major tactical decisions that were made prior to analysis require some explanation. The first had to do with which aspects of maternal contingency to evaluate, the second with how to analyze contingency patterns, and the third with whether to employ univariate or multivariate analyses of variance.

Analysis of maternal contingency.—As indicated earlier, attachment theorists stress that maternal sensitivity to infant signals is a critical variable in the infant's affective development and that it plays an important role in determining the quality of attachment. In addition, Izard's differential emotions theory and Tomkins's affect theory have also emphasized parental responsiveness as an important variable in individual expressive development. Therefore, we were interested not only in describing changes in the child's emotional profile over time but also in examining these changes in the light of differential parental responsiveness to affective signals.

Maternal contingency to infant affective signals was coded as described above. We noted both the overall level of contingency (i.e., the proportion of infant affective expressions to which the mother responded contingently) and the level of responsiveness with respect to certain types of infant affective signals (i.e., affect-specific contingencies) that are of special theoretical import.

Although the concept of maternal contingency as a general behavioral characteristic is frequently cited in the literature and is often equated with sensitivity, there have been few attempts to quantify different levels of contingency and assess their long-range effect on infant behavior (Belsky, Rovine, & Taylor, 1984; Malatesta & Wilson, 1988). Ainsworth (Ainsworth et al., 1978) has alluded to the possibility that a high rate of contingency (carried by an overwhelming physicality) might lead to a nonoptimal outcome for attachment. Consequently, we were interested in comparing the developmental profiles of children who had been exposed to varying levels of maternal facial contingency in early development. In this analysis, we looked only at the level of the mother's contingency, disregarding for the moment the quality and appropriateness of her signals. We hypothesized that high contingency would indeed be experienced as overstimulating and would override the effect of other factors, such as qualitative aspects. That is, even if maternal responses were in some sense "appropriate" (concern to sad faces, smiling to happy faces), the sheer amount of stimulating activity might exceed the infant's arousal tolerance.

While the attachment literature has been concerned with caregiver responsiveness to all infant attachment signals, it has been especially concerned with responsiveness to signals of distress (e.g., Bell & Ainsworth,

1972). We consequently decided it would be particularly instructive to examine our data for maternal responsiveness to distress emotions during the reunion episodes of our study. Since fear expressions are rarely seen in infants and rarely coded with facial affect coding systems (Campos, Barrett, Lamb, Goldsmith, & Stenberg, 1983), this meant paying particular attention to sadness and anger expressions.

We evaluated the contribution of both overall and specific kinds of contingency to subsequent infant affective development by resorting to ANOVA and simple Pearson r's. An alternative approach would have involved subjecting the expressive data of mothers and infants to sequential lag analysis. Our rationale for choosing the first alternative over the second necessitates a discussion of the strengths, weaknesses, and ambiguities surrounding sequential lag analysis.

Correlational techniques versus sequential lag analysis.—One way to evaluate contingencies between infant and maternal behaviors is to apply sequential lag analysis to the second-by-second changes in their expressive behavior. Although this technique is relatively new and still controversial (Bakeman & Dorval, in press; Moran & Symons, 1978; Sackett, 1987), it has the potential to provide affect-specific information about the shaping of emotion expression. In the final analysis, we decided that the nature of our data contraindicated the use of sequential lag procedures. First, these kinds of procedures are best suited to describing contingencies when the events that constitute a stream of behaviors are very frequent; beyond early infancy, emotional expressions are not high-frequency behaviors. Second, the most recent discussions of lag analysis recommend the removal of autocorrelation (Moran & Symons, 1987; Sackett, 1987), a practice we think may not be advisable for studies involving emotion expression in dyadic interaction.

As most researchers involved in the study of discrete emotional behaviors know, although emotional expressions (changes or "onsets") are salient communications and informationally rich, their occurrence is relatively infrequent. This presents a problem for lag analysis because, as Sackett (1979, p. 627) indicates, a minimum of 30 occurrences of the criterion behavior is required for valid application. The problem of infrequency of studied behaviors that one encounters in emotion research, moreover, cannot be easily remedied by coding longer segments of tape, for two pragmatic reasons. First, in longitudinal research, in which one hopes to see subjects repeatedly over time, it is neither wise nor humane to challenge them with too stressful or lengthy a procedure in order to obtain records more replete with expressive behavior. Second, the coding of facial expressive behavior is a labor-intensive task; a 1-min videotape can take 2 hours or longer to code (Izard, 1979). One potential solution is to sum over subjects so as to increase the reliability of the measure (provided the data for individual subjects are normally distributed so that outliers do not unduly distort the effects); however, this does not solve the second problem currently being discussed in the literature—that of autocorrelation.

A number of authors (e.g., Moran & Symons, 1987; Sackett, 1987) recommend correction for autocorrelation in sequential lag analysis, under the assumption that it represents a confound in estimating contingency effects. This is a statistical control (similar to that of covariance analysis) in which one assumes that the confound is independent of the variable of interest. Computing autocorrelations is also dependent on estimating base rates of the behavior; in the case of many dyadic analyses, especially those involving a particular focus of emotional behaviors, there are difficulties and risks attendant on this procedure.

The empirical problem here is that, without an independent measure of the base rate for the emotions we are studying, there is a risk of partialing out the effect of interest along with the autocorrelation. This is analogous to the misuse of ANCOVA when the covariate is not independent of the other predictor variables; one increases Type II error because the covariate is confounded with the other predictors. This is precisely the risk with the current data. Emotional behaviors are characteristically social behaviors that occur in the context of dyadic interaction. How does one get independent estimates of the base rates of such dyadically driven behaviors outside the dyad? In partialing out the autocorrelation of the child's expressive behavior, would we be removing the base rate of the child's behavior or the behavioral rate that is due to the dyadic effect in which we are interested?

In light of these considerations (also see Bakeman & Dorval, in press), we chose more conventional analytic techniques. As already noted, infrequency of occurrence poses a particular problem with emotion expression data. One solution is to block or sum across subjects or occasions; this increases the reliability of measures and avoids the infrequency problem as well as the doubts of autocorrelation adjustment. Because our data are longitudinal, examining the effect of maternal contingency on infant behavior is still possible: rather than predicting behavior from mother to child or estimating the autocorrelation for either individual within data-collection waves, we can predict behavior longitudinally. Data collected in waves 1–3 are independent of wave 4 data by virtue of being obtained at separate points in time. Thus, we can assess the stability of emotions by using subjects' earlier data to predict their emotion expression at a later wave and use an aggregate score of maternal contingency summed over the first three waves to predict infant expressive behaviors at wave 4.

Correlation and ANOVA give us the power inherent in parametric techniques without requiring that all the behaviors be frequent. Although these strategies are not without limitations and require that certain assumptions be met, they were viewed as the methods of choice for this particular data base.

ANOVA versus MANOVA.—Although it has become fairly common practice of late to prefer MANOVA to ANOVA when there are several dependent measures or to use it prior to univariate analyses, there are also good theoretical grounds for eschewing MANOVA in favor of multiple ANOVAs. Our main theoretical model, differential emotions theory, specifies distinct phenomenological, motivational, and signal properties of the discrete affects; as previously indicated, factor-analytic, concurrent, and criterion-related validation studies support this assumption of uniqueness. Consistent with this theory, our hypotheses do not specify covariation among the emotions used as dependent measures, thereby making multiple ANOVAs more appropriate than MANOVA.

A final comment about the statistical procedures chosen for this study is in order. Most of our procedures assume linear models; this is not to deny the complexity of the phenomena we are studying. Linear models provide a clear and simplifying place to begin an approach to complex problems. As our knowledge of the development of emotion and the complexity of mother-child interactions improves, more complex models may be warranted.

DEVELOPMENTAL QUESTIONS AND GOALS OF THE STUDY

Four major questions were posed.

1. *What are the features of expressive behavior during the second year of life?* Because data on emotional expression beyond early infancy are very limited, we were most interested in gathering detailed information on spontaneously generated expressions of 2-year-olds. We wished not only to assess general patterns of behavior (i.e., the relative distribution of different kinds of expressive behaviors) but also to index how these patterns might be altered as a function of the three individual difference variables of gender, risk status, and mothers' early contingency level. We also sought to examine how two dimensions of affective behavior—that of attachment and that of emotional expressivity—were related. These two concepts are theoretically relevant to one another but have rarely been examined together.

2. *What evidence is there for continuity or discontinuity in expressive style between early infancy and toddlerhood?* At issue are the stability of individual children's patterns across a range of discrete emotions and signals and the degree of continuity of maternal expressive behavior.

3. *What is the relation between affect at 2 years (expressive behavior and security of attachment) and particular qualities of affective interchange in early infancy?* Our aim was to explore the possibility that specific emotional qualities or patterns of early social interactions might predict the quality of attachment and/or certain styles of emotion expression at a later age.

4. *What kinds of models of expressive development might be proposed that take into consideration the contribution of children's dispositional tendencies as well as maternal behavioral style?* Using our data to construct tentative models of expressive development, we wanted to specify how child and maternal variables, singly and in interaction with one another, contribute to the development of children's expressive behavior.

III. METHOD

SUBJECTS

Mothers and infants were recruited for participation in a study of "personality development in premature and full-term infants." The mothers were not informed that we were particularly interested in emotional expressions or their development. Subjects were recruited by appeals to pediatricians, support groups for mothers of premature infants, childbirth preparation classes, and posted announcements. Both preterm and full-term infants were sought. Prematurity was defined by convention as a gestation of fewer than 37 weeks and/or a weight of under 2,500 grams at birth. Mothers and children were seen on four separate occasions, when the children were 2½, 5, 7½, and 22 months of age.

Subject Characteristics

The subjects we report on here consisted of 58 mother-child pairs. They were part of an original sample of 72 dyads on which we had complete data for the first three waves; 14 of these pairs either moved and could not be reached or declined to participate in the fourth phase of the study. Background data on the sample subjects as well as on those who dropped out of the study are presented in Table 1. The dropouts did not differ from those who remained on any demographic variable (not significant by t test and chi square). However, as described later, they did differ in one aspect of their expressive behavior, more dropouts showing a decline in smiling over time.

The sample subjects' ages (in days) at each of the four visits to the laboratory are shown in Table 2. Preterm infants were seen at ages corrected for gestational status. With this correction, there were no age differences (by t test) for birth status or sex at any of the assessment waves.

TABLE 1

BACKGROUND DEMOGRAPHICS ON WAVE 4 SAMPLE AND DROPOUT SUBJECTS

	WAVE 4 SAMPLE			DROPOUTS		
	Preterm[a]	Term[b]	Total[c]	Preterm[d]	Term[e]	Total[f]
Mean family SES[g]	57.78	56.18	56.67	58.14	58.85	58.50
	(6.35)	(9.73)	(8.67)	(12.63)	(3.98)	(9.00)
Mean maternal age at child's birth	31.75	33.90	33.27	32.57	33.43	33.00
	(4.82)	(3.89)	(4.24)	(3.41)	(5.03)	(4.15)
Mean level of maternal education[g]	6.17	6.53	6.41	6.71	6.71	6.71
	(.71)	(.75)	(.75)	(.76)	(.49)	(.61)

NOTE.—Standard deviations are given in parentheses.
[a] N = 18 (12 boys, 6 girls).   [e] N = 7 (4 boys, 3 girls).
[b] N = 40 (20 boys, 20 girls).   [f] N = 14 (9 boys, 5 girls).
[c] N = 58 (32 boys, 26 girls).   [g] Hollingshead Scale (Hollingshead, 1975).
[d] N = 7 (5 boys, 2 girls).

PROCEDURE

Overview

The four waves of data were collected on behavior elicited during mother/child play sessions as well as during reunion following brief separation. The first three experimental sessions (at 2½, 5, and 7½ months) involved a 7-min face-to-face play session followed by a separation of 5 min or less and a 1-min reunion. As a task-equivalent, age-appropriate analogue at age 2 years, we chose a modified Strange Situation procedure (Ainsworth & Wittig, 1969) because it permitted collection of samples of both positive and negative expressive behavior (as in the earlier waves), with the additional advantage of yielding attachment classifications.

TABLE 2

INFANT'S AGE (in Days) AT EACH ASSESSMENT WAVE

	PRETERMS[a]		TERMS		FULL SAMPLE	
	M	SD	M	SD	M	SD
Wave 1 (2½ months)	70.22	11.88	72.68	14.02	71.91	13.34
Wave 2 (5 months)	138.06	18.29	138.98	14.00	138.69	15.30
Wave 3 (7½ months)	205.11	25.83	209.58	20.75	208.19	22.32
Wave 4 (22 months)	657.72	94.01	657.13	117.50	657.31	109.92

NOTE.—Full sample (N = 58) at each wave.
[a] Corrected for gestational age.

The First Three Sessions

Experimental sessions took place in a 5 × 5-m room. A comfortable straight-backed chair was provided for the mother; an infant seat secured to a table (for 2½- and 5-month-olds) or a high chair (for 7½-month-olds) was placed directly opposite the mother at about a .5-m distance. The video-recording equipment consisted of two JVC color videocameras whose output went to a Sony SLO-383 record-and-playback unit via a special effects generator set for a split-screen image and digital time display.

Each appointment at the laboratory was scheduled around a time when the mother expected her infant to be rested and alert. On the first visit, the goals and procedures were reviewed and a consent form signed; mothers were informed that there would be a play session, a brief separation, and a reunion. When ready, the pair were seated, and the mother was asked to arrange her chair at a comfortable distance from the infant. She was told to feel free to talk to, touch, sing to, and otherwise play with her infant as she would at home. No toys were provided. Mothers were asked to distract or gently dissuade their infants from mouthing their hands or clothing during the taping so that the infant's face would not be obscured. Cameras were located 1.5 m from the mothers' and infants' faces so as to provide full-face, high-resolution tapes for later coding of facial expressions. Although some mothers at first appeared self-conscious before the cameras, it was evident that they rapidly habituated as they became engrossed in play with their infants; nevertheless, to circumvent any artificiality in the opening moments of taping, only the middle portion of the tapes was subsequently coded. A semiopaque curtain hanging from ceiling to floor separated the testing area from the rest of the equipment, which was monitored by an experimenter during the session.

Taping began when the infant was securely in place and attending to the mother. Mothers and infants were taped in face-to-face play for 7 min, after which the mother was signaled to leave the room; the experimenter remained in the room and out of sight of the infant. The mother was signaled to return to her infant either at the end of 5 min or after 30 successive sec of fret crying. After the mother rejoined her infant, taping resumed for an additional minute, during which the mother was not to pick up her infant but could minister to or play with her in any other way.

The Fourth Session

At 2 years, infants were seen for the Ainsworth Strange Situation procedure (Ainsworth & Wittig, 1969). The procedure was modified slightly to make it more comparable to the earlier sessions; this was accomplished by lengthening the initial mother/child play episode from 3 to 9 min. Thus, just as at the previous three sessions, at the fourth session there was a prolonged play period, followed by a briefer separation/reunion sequence; however, the sheer amount of time in play and reunion that was subsequently coded was greater for this assessment. This expanded window of time on mother/child play and reunion behavior was deemed appropriate for the 2-year visit since piloting had indicated that expressive behavior is in general less frequent then than during early infancy and we wanted to obtain sufficient data to permit use of parametric statistics.

Videorecording for wave 4 took place in the original experimental room; this time, however, the room was outfitted with a smaller $3\frac{1}{2} \times 3\frac{1}{2}$-m Plexiglas "corral" designed to keep subjects from moving out of range of the camera. Equipment again consisted of two JVC color videocameras with zoom lenses. The two cameras were trained on the mother and the infant separately; their output was fed to a special effects generator set for a split-screen image and digital time display. A third camera with a wide-angle lens provided a panoramic view of the interaction. This output was recorded separately from the split-screen close-up of the mother's and child's faces. The larger contextual view it provided was useful in scoring attachment classification later on. All videorecording was done from behind a partition fitted with a Plexiglas window and black drape.

Mothers were informed that the purpose of this part of the study was to observe children's responses to strangers and that the session would be videotaped. They were told that the first part of the procedure was designed to provide an opportunity for the child to become familiarized with the laboratory and toys (building blocks and two hand puppets). The mother and child interacted with one another while seated at a child-sized table. After 9 min had elapsed, mothers were instructed to move from the table to a nearby chair and begin reading a magazine. After 1 min, the remaining Ainsworth episodes (in which a stranger enters and leaves, the mother leaves and returns, the infant is left alone and with a stranger, and the mother returns once again) followed; each lasted approximately 3 min and followed the procedure originally established by Ainsworth and her colleagues. Mothers were told that they could end the session at any time if their child became unduly distressed; some children did, and thus a number of separation episodes were terminated early.

Coding of Videotapes

The First Three Sessions

The middle 5 min of the mother-infant play session and the 1 min of reunion were coded on a second-by-second basis for instances of facial expression changes using Izard's (1979) MAX emotion coding system. The procedure involves playing the videotape and noting facial expression changes as they occur in real time and then slowing or stopping the tape to record specific facial muscle movement codes. Both onset and offset of the expression changes are noted. Later, the codes are converted to emotional expressions via formulas provided in the MAX manual. As indicated earlier, this system distinguishes eight fundamental emotions—interest, joy, surprise, sadness, anger, disgust, contempt, and fear—and the motive state of physical distress or pain. Three other facial expressions—knit brow, compressed lips, and biting the lower lip—as well as gazing behavior were also noted and recorded because of their theoretical relevance to attachment theory and emotion socialization theory (see Chap. I); their description follows.

Knit brow.—The knit brow expression, which can be indexed by Izard's code 24, involves slightly lowered, drawn-together brows. The expression has been associated with states of mild tension (Darwin, 1872) and of cognitive activity or concentration (Oster, 1978). In infants, Stern, Beebe, Jaffe, and Bennett (1977) found that, during face-to-face interaction, eye narrowing and brow lowering were common signals to reduce or break eye contact. In adults, the knit brow expression has been identified as a "nonspecific" signal of distress, displayed under conditions of, variously, fear, sadness, and anger (Malatesta & Izard, 1984). It is our hypothesis that this expression occurs naturally during early infancy in the context of transition to more intense negative affect but that later in development it is used intentionally to signal imminent distress or as a control maneuver to down-regulate negative affect.

Compressed lips.—A second signal, which we have designated as "code 67" in coding protocols and refer to here as "compressed lips" (abbreviated in the tables as "pressed lips"), consists of lips that are pressed tightly together. In adults, this expression is found in the context of suppressed emotion, especially suppressed anger (Jonas, 1986). We hypothesize that children learn to use this expression in a similar fashion, namely, as a means of dampening or minimizing negative affect.

Lip biting.—A third signal, which we have designated as "code 88" in coding protocols, involves biting the lower lip. Informal observation suggests that this gesture indexes anxiety and suppressed fear in adults. We hypothesize that it may serve to dampen or control fear in children as well. As such, we would expect to see evidence of this signal during anxiety-provoking occasions such as separations.

Gazing behavior.—Because of its significance as an attachment behavior in infants and as a component of responsivity in mothers, gazing was a variable of special interest in this study. Thus, gaze direction (on or off partner's face) was coded as well.

After coders had trained on Izard's system and achieved the requisite

80% reliability with training-tape material on each category of expression, they then trained for reliability on samples of the experimental tapes. Intercoder reliability was calculated by counting movement-code agreements in each 1-sec unit. The formula consisted of dividing the number of agreements on movement changes for a particular section of coded material by the number of agreements plus disagreements; agreement on nonoccurrences was not included in the calculations so as to avoid spuriously inflating the reliabilities. Cumulative records on number of agreements and disagreements by category of affect code permitted calculation of category reliabilities as well. Intercoder reliabilities assessed before and at random during the coding of data tapes ranged from .80 to .98 for both expressions and gaze behavior.

Mothers and children were coded independently of one another and with the audio channel off. MAX coders were blind to the hypotheses of the study and to attachment classifications. At times, some coders could discern birth status, as they could sex, but there is no reason to believe that this influenced their coding in any way—robust intercoder reliabilities were sustained throughout. Gaze behavior was coded independently of facial expressions.

The Fourth Session

Facial coding.—The segments selected for facial emotion coding were those analogous to the first three sessions; this amounted to the approximately 9 min of mother/infant play interaction prior to the introduction of the stranger and the approximately 3 min of each of the two reunion episodes. These segments were coded in the same fashion as for the first three sessions with coders blind to hypotheses.

Assessment of maternal contingency.—After facial expressions of both mothers and infants had been coded, they were entered onto a joint coding sheet, and patterns of contingency between mother and child were noted. Operationally, a contingent response by the mother was coded when a maternal expression change occurred within 1 sec following an infant expression change. Each maternal response following each new infant onset of expression change increased the frequency of maternal contingent responses by one. The resulting sums were then nominalized into three groups—low, moderate, and high levels of contingency—and this three-level categorization formed one of the independent variables in our analyses.

Assessment of attachment.—Attachment classifications were determined following procedures described by Ainsworth et al. (1978) and on the basis of training and use of a training tape (provided by D. Cicchetti). As in the case of other studies, judgment of attachment security relied heavily on reunion behaviors. Subjects were assigned to the standard groups and subgroups, but only the most well-validated grouping factor, securely attached (B group) and insecurely attached (A and C groups), was used as an independent variable in subsequent analyses. Two trained judges blind to the hypotheses of the study coded the tapes; they were also blind to the mother's contingency level and, in most cases, birth status. Attachment classifications were made by judges who did not participate in MAX coding the wave 4 data. Intercoder reliability for major classifications and subgroups was .89; discrepancies were resolved in conference.

Of the 58 children, 20 (34.5%) were classified as A, three (5.2%) were classified as C1, and the remaining 43 (60.4%) were distributed across the four B subtypes. This distribution compares favorably with the one originally described by Ainsworth (1977; Ainsworth et al., 1978) and found in other samples (Van Ijzendoorn & Kroonenberg, 1987). For statistical analyses, the subtypes were collapsed to form an insecure group (A and C subtypes combined) and a secure group (B subtypes).

Some children failed to complete one or both of the reunion episodes because of extreme distress. Ten completed reunion 1 but not reunion 2, and two failed to complete either; 46 completed both. The data were examined to determine if the failure to complete reunion episodes was related to any of the main independent variables of interest. The birth status, gender,

TABLE 3

ATTACHMENT CLASSIFICATION, GENDER, BIRTH STATUS, AND MATERNAL CONTINGENCY
CATEGORY OF CHILDREN WHO COMPLETED AND WHO DID NOT COMPLETE
REUNION 1 AND/OR 2 OF THE STRANGE SITUATION

	COMPLETE		INCOMPLETE		TOTAL	
	N	%[a]	N	%[a]	N	%[b]
Attachment classification:						
Secure	26	74.3	9	25.7	35	60.3
Insecure	20	87.0	3	13.0	23	39.7
Total	46	79.3	12	20.7	58	100.0
Gender:						
Females	21	80.8	5	19.2	26	44.8
Males	25	78.1	7	21.9	32	55.2
Birth status:						
Preterm	15	83.3	3	16.7	18	31.0
Full term	31	77.5	9	22.5	40	69.0
Maternal contingency:						
High	15	78.9	4	21.1	19	32.8
Moderate	17	89.5	2	10.5	19	32.8
Low	14	70.0	6	30.0	20	34.5

[a] Percentage of row total.
[b] Percentage of column total.

maternal contingency level, and secure versus insecure attachment status of those who completed and those who missed one or more reunions are shown in Table 3.

Nonparametric tests (Fisher's exact and chi square) showed no significant differences. Although this does not demonstrate randomness, the distributions do not suggest that subjects completed or failed to complete in a systematic way that would confound other analyses; hence, completers and noncompleters were treated similarly in all subsequent analyses.

The next three chapters present the results of the study and are organized in terms of three foci: normative trends and dimensions of individual difference in the expressive behavior of 2-year-olds; continuity in expressive behavior over the four waves of data collection and prediction of wave 4 data from earlier factors; and models of prediction for particular outcomes.

IV. NORMATIVE TRENDS AND DIMENSIONS OF INDIVIDUAL DIFFERENCE IN THE EXPRESSIVE BEHAVIOR OF 2-YEAR-OLDS

As noted in Chapter I, there is a remarkable paucity of data on the expressive repertoires of 2-year-olds; we also know very little about what types of emotional expressions mothers typically display to children of this age. Thus, one of the principal goals of this investigation was to generate basic descriptive data on the expressive behaviors of 2-year-olds and their mothers. The data were collected under both stressful and nonstressful conditions so as to provide as representative a sample of everyday behavior as possible.

In the following, we first examine the general profile of expressive behavior of children and mothers as sampled during three episodes of the Ainsworth Strange Situation. We then consider the contribution of four individual difference variables that have been hypothesized to influence, or be related to, socioemotional development in significant ways, namely, gender, temperamental difficultness (operationalized by preterm vs. full-term birth status), quality of attachment, and the level of maternal facial contingency during early infancy. In addition to expressive behavior, we also examine differences in eye contact since gazing behavior is said to be a component of attachment and maternal responsiveness.

PREPARATION AND FORMATTING OF THE DATA

Findings reported in the text and in the tables are summarized by individual episode, that is, by play, reunion 1, or reunion 2, and by dependent measure. It should be noted that, unless indicated otherwise, all dependent measures have been proportionalized in order to deal with the somewhat variable length of sessions across subjects.

For the facial data, ratios were obtained by dividing the frequency of each expressive behavior in an episode (i.e., number of each type of expression "onset") by the subject's time spent in that episode. Thus, 20 interest expressions shown by a child during a play period of 540 sec results in a quotient of 4%, and 10 interest expressions shown in 500 sec yields a quotient of 2%. Because our expression frequencies are based on onsets rather than durations, these ratios should not be construed as indicating that 4% versus 2% of time was spent showing interest; instead, the values represent the frequency of onsets (i.e., frequency of signals) proportionalized for segment length. Because it is stylistically awkward to repeat "transformed" or "proportionalized" each time we refer to the data, we use the shorthand notation of "frequencies" with the understanding that this refers to transformed, not raw, frequencies.

Gaze behavior was indexed by duration for the child and by frequency for the mother. The duration measure was obtained under the hypothesis that time spent gazing at the mother might index how secure or insecure the child felt in the relationship, with longer durations associated with more insecurity; it was proportionalized for segment length (i.e., the total amount of time spent looking at the mother—whether or not she was engaged in reciprocal behavior—divided by number of seconds in the segment). In the case of the mother, the most significant aspect of her "responsiveness" was considered to be the ability to judge when to look toward her child; we therefore assessed the frequency of her gaze reciprocity rather than the sheer amount of time spent looking at the child. This too was proportionalized for segment length (i.e., the sum of frequencies of mother's reciprocal gazes divided by total number of seconds in the segment).

OVERALL PROFILE OF EXPRESSIVE BEHAVIOR

The profiles of mothers' and children's expressive behavior during play, reunion 1, and reunion 2 episodes are displayed in Table 4. (For data for waves 1–3, see App. Table A1; to facilitate comparisons, $N = 46$ in both tables.) A ranking of the various expressions reveals that both play and reunion sessions are characterized by predominantly positive affect in both mothers and children. Among the negative affects displayed by children during the reunion sessions, knit brow prevails in the first reunion but is superseded by sadness by the second separation/reunion. We next turn to an examination of how expressive patterns may vary as a function of certain moderator variables.

TABLE 4

PATTERNS OF EXPRESSIVE BEHAVIOR OF MOTHERS AND THEIR 22-MONTH-OLD CHILDREN DURING PLAY, REUNION 1, AND REUNION 2

	PLAY			REUNION 1			REUNION 2		
	Emotion	M	SD	Emotion	M	SD	Emotion	M	SD
Mothers:									
Rank:									
1	Joy	5.90	2.34	Joy	2.82	1.92	Joy	3.30	2.45
2	Interest	1.65	1.71	Interest	1.39	1.32	Interest	1.28	1.34
3	Surprise	.33	.51	Knit brow	.26	.74	Knit brow	.24	.58
4	Knit brow	.23	.43	Pressed lips	.20	.41	Pressed lips	.17	.51
5	Pressed lips	.21	.35	Surprise	.12	.30	Surprise	.07	.30
6	Sadness	.12	.25	Sadness	.10	.28	Sadness	.05	.16
7	Anger	.13	.92	Anger	.06	.27	Anger	.01	.08
Children:									
Rank:									
1	Joy	5.42	2.48	Interest	3.05	2.28	Interest	2.98	2.78
2	Interest	4.07	2.95	Joy	1.73	1.29	Joy	2.38	2.20
3	Knit brow	1.05	1.37	Knit brow	1.15	1.28	Knit brow	.80	1.18
4	Surprise	.73	.92	Sadness	.62	1.32	Sadness	.66	1.06
5	Sadness	.54	1.16	Anger	.26	.87	Surprise	.33	.83
6	Pressed lips	.47	.65	Surprise	.18	.38	Anger	.27	.57
7	Anger	.20	.48	Pressed lips	.17	.41	Pressed lips	.23	.52

NOTE.—All emotions are expressed as percentages of seconds in episode.

GAZING AND EXPRESSIVE BEHAVIORS OF 2-YEAR-OLDS AND THEIR MOTHERS AS A FUNCTION OF GENDER, BIRTH STATUS, ATTACHMENT CLASSIFICATION STATUS, AND MATERNAL CONTINGENCY

General Design

The design used was a 2 (sex) $\times$ 2 (birth status: preterm, full term) $\times$ 2 (secure, insecure) $\times$ 3 (maternal contingency levels summed over waves 1–3: high, moderate, low) analysis-of-variance design. With respect to contingency levels, the low group's mean score was 36.7 (SD $=$ 5.13), the middle group's 55.26 (SD $=$ 5.30), and the high group's 82.11 (SD $=$ 12.93). The cutoffs were created to make the groups approximately equal in size and resulted in $N = 20$ for the low group, $N = 19$ for the middle group, and $N = 19$ for the high group.

The dependent measures were (1) discrete emotional expressions that appeared with sufficient frequency for parametric analysis, namely, joy, interest, surprise, anger, and sadness; (2) three aggregate (dimensional) measures of emotion (for comparability with the previous attachment literature, which has tended to favor dimensional measures), namely, total expressivity, total positive emotion, and total negative emotion; (3) two eye-contact behaviors, namely, duration of child gazing at the mother and frequency of reciprocated gazes by mother; and (4) two facial signals, namely, knit brow and compressed lips (lip biting was observed in some children but did not occur frequently enough to permit analysis).

As indicated earlier, all dependent measures were proportionalized for segment length. Although many researchers automatically transform percentages (usually by means of arc sin), we did not take this route, for two reasons. First, examination of normal probability plots of residuals indicated that most variables met the standard assumptions of linearity necessary for the valid application of parametric statistics without further transformations. Second, although severe transformations of one form or another have become common (e.g., log, arc sin), it is our position that such transformations frequently distort the data in unknown ways and render them uninterpretable. Indeed, Winer (1971) clearly warns that even monotonic transformations may create or destroy effects and that interactions are particularly sensitive to power transformations. We thus preferred to take the conservative approach of staying as close to our data as possible. In the case of variables that did not meet reasonable criteria for normality, "significant" effects were simply not interpreted. Although we lose some of the data in this way, we also have greater confidence that the findings we do report reflect the important assumptions of normal residuals.

In the ensuing analyses, only main effects and two-way interactions are considered. Small within-cell sample sizes for higher-order interactions, as well as lack of hypotheses pertaining to interactions involving more than two factors, preclude higher-order analyses. (Appendix Table A2 provides the sample sizes for all two-factor interactions and main effects for play, reunion 1, and reunion 2 episodes.) In all analyses, the alpha level was set at .05, except where indicated otherwise. Post hoc tests were Fisher's least significant difference tests.

Infant Gaze and Expressive Behaviors

Separate ANOVAs for the dependent measures of gaze behavior and facial expressions were conducted. For the facial expressions, we first conducted ANOVAs on the overall level of expressive behavior or "total expressivity" (i.e., summed over all expression categories); we then split the data into "positive expressions" (interest, joy, surprise) and "negative expressions" (sadness, anger, knit brow, and compressed lips). Knit brow and compressed lips were considered negative expressions for this analysis because of the pattern of intercorrelations. In the case of knit brow, this expression correlates within wave 4 with the sad expression, $r = .40$, $p < .003$, and with the anger expression, $r = .43$, $p < .001$. Compressed lips tends to correlate with anger, $r = .22$, $p < .14$. In addition to the aggregate variables of total expressivity, positive expressions, and negative expressions, we ran separate ANOVAs on each of the discrete expressions.

Results of the various ANOVA tests, summarized by dependent measure, are found in Table 5 for mothers and Table 6 for children. (Appendix Tables A3–A6 provide the means and standard deviations for all main effects and all significant two-way interactions.)

As seen in Tables 5 and 6, a large number of significant main effects and interactions obtained. These effects are summarized by dependent measure in the tables; here, we summarize the results from the standpoint of how the major factors of interest—birth status, gender, attachment classification, and maternal contingency level—affected the kind of emotion expression displayed during the play session and in each reunion session. In the service of conserving space, individual tests and their results, already given in the tables, are not repeated here; however, the effects mentioned in the text are given superscripts that match superscripts for the effects of interest in Tables 5 and 6.

Behavior in the Play Session

Mothers.—As outlined in the tables, mothers showed more expressivity[a] and positive affect[b] to girls than to boys, the greatest amount being shown to daughters who were securely attached[c]. Mothers also appeared to allow

TABLE 5

SUMMARY OF ANOVA TESTS ON MOTHER'S GAZING BEHAVIOR
AND FACIAL EXPRESSIONS

Dependent Variable	Effect	F	df	p <	Direction of Effect
Play session:					
[e] Reciprocal gazing	Contingency	3.64	2,43	.04	LC, MC > HC
[a] Total expressivity	Sex	5.21	1,43	.03	F > M
[b] Total positive emotion	Sex	4.29	1,43	.05	F > M
[d] Total negative emotion	Class	5.23	1,43	.03	S > I
[c] Joy	Sex × class	4.02	1,43	.05	F(S) > M(S), M(I)
Reunion 1:					
[i] Total expressivity	Class	5.07	1,39	.03	S > I
[m] Total expressivity	Contingency	4.38	2,39	.02	HC > MC, LC
[k] Total expressivity	Class × birth	4.48	1,39	.04	P(S) > T(S); P(I) = T(I)
[j] Total positive emotion	Class	4.64	1,39	.04	S > I
[o] Total positive emotion	Contingency	5.06	2,39	.01	HC, LC > MC
[l] Total positive emotion	Class × birth	5.45	1,39	.03	P(S) > T(S); P(I) = T(I)
[n] Joy	Contingency	4.09	2,39	.03	HC > MC
[p] Joy	Class × birth	8.05	1,39	.01	P(S) > T(S); P(I) = T(I)
Reunion 2:					
[w] Reciprocal gazing	Birth status	7.65	1,33	.01	T > P
[r] Total expressivity	Birth status	6.57	1,33	.02	T > P
[s] Total positive emotion	Birth status	7.45	1,33	.01	T > P
[v] Total positive emotion	Contingency	3.55	2,33	.04	HC > MC
[t] Interest	Birth status	5.29	1,33	.03	T > P
[u] Joy	Birth status	5.28	1,33	.03	T > P

NOTE.—Superscripts in stub column correspond to those in the text. F = female, M = male; LC, MC, and HC = low, moderate, high contingency, respectively; I = insecure, S = secure; M(LC) = male of a low-contingency mother, etc.

themselves a wider range of affect with securely attached children; during play, they showed more negative affect to their securely attached children than they did to their insecurely attached children[d]. As far as birth status is concerned, mothers showed no evidence of differential treatment of preterm and full-term children during play; however, their earlier contingency level predicted the level of their child's gazing, with more gazing at mothers who had been low to moderate in contingency[e].

TABLE 6

SUMMARY OF ANOVA TESTS ON CHILDREN'S GAZING BEHAVIOR AND FACIAL EXPRESSIONS

Dependent Variable	Effect	F	df	p <	Direction of Effect
Play session:					
[f] Total gazing	Sex × contingency	5.57	2,43	.01	F(LC, MC) > F(HC)
[g] Interest	Sex × contingency	4.01	2,43	.03	M(MC) > M(LC); F(L&M) > F(HC)
[h] Pressed lips	Sex × class	6.00	1,43	.02	M(I) > M(S)
Reunion 1:					
[q] Interest	Birth status	4.77	1,39	.04	T > P
Reunion 2:					
[ii] Total gazing	Class	3.77	1,33	.05	S > I
[y] Total positive emotion	Birth status	6.43	1,33	.02	T > P
[gg] Total positive emotion	Contingency	4.35	2,33	.02	LC > HC, MC
[hh] Total positive emotion	Birth × contingency	5.02	2,33	.02	P(LC) > P(HC); T(LC) = T(MC) = T(HC)
[kk] Total positive emotion	Class × birth	9.58	1,33	.01	P(I) = P(S); T(I) > T(S)
[z] Interest	Birth status	6.66	1,33	.02	T > P
[ll] Interest	Class × birth	7.79	1,33	.01	T(I) > T(S), P(I), P(S)
[ff] Interest	Sex × contingency	5.63	1,33	.01	M(LC) = M(MC) > M(HC); F(MC) > F(LC) = F(HC)
[aa] Joy	Birth × contingency	7.04	2,33	.02	P(LC, MC) = T(LC, MC); T(HC) > P(HC)
[bb] Total negative emotion	Sex × birth	5.00	1,33	.03	F(T) = M(T), F(P) > M(P), F(T)
[ee] Anger	Sex	5.03	1,33	.04	F > M
[nn] Knit brow	Birth status	4.59	1,33	.05	T > P
[cc] Sadness	Sex × birth	7.63	1,33	.01	F(P) > M(T), F(T); F(P) > M(P)
[dd] Sadness	Sex × contingency	4.67	2,33	.02	F(LC) > All groups
[mm] Pressed lips	Sex × class	6.00	1,43	.02	M(I) > M(S); F(I) = F(S)
[x] Total expressivity	Birth status	5.05	1,33	.03	T > P
[jj] Total expressivity	Class × birth	7.57	1,33	.01	P(I) = P(S); T(I) > T(S)
[mm] Total expressivity	Sex × contingency	6.38	2,33	.01	M(LC) = M(MC) = M(HC); F(LC, HC) > F(MC)

NOTE.—Superscripts correspond to those in the text. F = female, M = male; LC, MC, HC = low, moderate, and high contingency, respectively; I = insecure, S = secure; M(LC) = male of a low-contingency mother, etc.

Children.—Recall that the mother's contingency score, a measure of her behavior during early infancy (waves 1–3), was based on the proportion of infant expression changes to which the mother responded with an expression change of her own. Boys appear to respond more favorably to higher levels of contingency in infancy than girls since level of gazing in boys at wave 4 was positively related to wave 1–3 contingency, whereas the highest level of gazing for girls occurred with low to moderate levels of contingency[f]. Also, males who had low-contingency mothers in infancy showed fewer interest expressions to their mothers and fewer knit brow expressions than full terms. Preterm females showed the highest negative affect (in terms of total negative affect[bb] and sadness[cc]) of all birth status/sex groups.

Girls showed more anger than boys when their mothers returned[ee]. In addition, gender frequently interacted with maternal contingency level. For example, boys' interest and total expressivity[mm] was highest at low and moderate levels of maternal contingency, and girls' was highest with high or low contingency[dd]. Girls of low-contingency mothers showed more sadness than the other gender/contingency groups[dd]. The latter finding is atypical of the more general pattern for low contingency to be associated with positive affective outcomes as described earlier in this section as well as in Chapter V below; since this breaks with the overall pattern, we assume that this result may be a chance finding.

Children of low-contingency mothers showed the most positive affect. In fact, there was an inverse relation between positive affect and maternal contingency in preterms[hh].

Securely attached children spent more time looking toward their mothers[ii] than insecure ones did, but the insecure children were more expressive[jj], at least among full terms, showing greater levels of positive affect[kk] and interest as well as the compressed lips expression[ll]. Among full terms, insecurely attached children showed less distress, broadly conceived; they were more positive, and this was mainly a function of their interest expressions.

DISCUSSION

During the second year of life, we begin to see what appear to be signs of instrumental control of affect signals. Three expressions that seem to function in the service of self-regulation (i.e., dampening negative affect) were seen in the wave 4 data: the compressed lips expression, the knit brow, and lip biting. Although the frequency of lip biting was not great enough to make statistical analysis meaningful, it is worth noting that this expression was never observed in early infancy. Another expression, that involving compressed lips, which is seen quite commonly in adults and appears to represent a muted form of anger (Darwin, 1872; Jonas, 1986; Malatesta & Izard, 1984), was also totally absent during the first few months of life (Malatesta & Haviland, 1982). It was observed, though infrequently, in some 7½-month-olds in the present longitudinal study; by 22 months, it was more fully established in the repertoire.

The third "nonspecific" negative affect signal, knit brow, was even more frequent than the compressed lips expression. However, in contrast to the earlier waves, in which knit brow occurred predominantly as a predistress face typically followed by crying, at 2 years the expression was less closely associated with crying. We suspect that during the second year children begin to use the knit brow in the same way as older children and adults. Adults often show the knit brow expression when recounting different kinds of negative affective experience. It has been speculated that the use of this nonspecific, low-level negative affect expression during interpersonal interaction is one of the means by which individuals signal their negative affect states to others without risking the "recruitment" of more negative affect either in the self or in the partner (Malatesta & Izard, 1984; Tomkins, 1962).

To return to the overall profile of expressive behavior in 2-year-olds, it is worth noting that interactions between mothers and children at this age are characterized primarily as positive, even during stressful situations. Although most children were distressed by the separations, they were able to recover relatively rapidly when the mother returned, and the reunion sessions were therefore dominated mainly by interest and joy and only secondarily by sadness, knit brow, and anger. However, these general trends mask a good deal of individual variation discerned through the ANOVA analyses.

Factors Contributing to Differences in Expressive Patterns

Four individual difference variables, alone or in combination, were found to influence the type and prevalence of different kinds of affect expression during both stressful and nonstressful encounters.

Contingency

In general, it appears that maternal facial contingency rates that are low to moderate in infancy have more favorable sequelae in children's expressive development, especially in the case of preterm infants. What might these rates index? There is some evidence that mothers with low to moderate levels of facial contingency may be more sensitive. In wave 4, these were the mothers who reciprocated more of their children's eye contact. Although high-contingency mothers showed more positive affect (both interest and joy) during the second reunion than did moderately contingent mothers, they did not do so during play; the elevated positive affect display during circumstances that are typically fraught with tension (i.e., the second reunion) suggests that it may reflect nervous smiling and nonauthentic joy.

One gender × contingency interaction deserves special attention. During play, boys who had high-contingency mothers in infancy showed more interest and gazing than did boys of low-contingency mothers, whereas the reverse pattern obtained for girls. However, following the stress of separation (reunion 2), sons of high-contingency mothers showed less interest than the other contingency groups did, and both boys and girls of low-contingency mothers showed the most positive affect. The differential effects of early levels of maternal contingency on the reunion behaviors of boys and girls may in part be a function of differential ability to modulate feeling state. Whereas male infants seem to prefer and to receive more gross motor stimulation and rough-and-tumble play than girls, there is evidence that boys have more difficulty controlling their affective arousal, at least early on (Malatesta & Haviland, 1982). It may be that boys, especially those of mothers who tend to be overstimulating, regulate their distress at separation by avoiding more stimulating contact with her through gaze aversion and other avoidance tactics. In fact, we found that boys with high-contingency mothers not only showed reduced levels of interest at reunion but also gazed at her less than did girls, though the effect did not quite reach statistical significance. (Note that these effects are not caused by differential maternal contingency rates toward males and females during the wave 4 play and reunion sessions—the ANOVA for contingency × sex was not significant.) In addition, although mothers responded somewhat differently to males and females during the play session (being more expressive and positive to girls), they responded similarly to their sons and daughters under conditions of child distress. Thus, differences in children's reunion behaviors do not appear to be attributable merely to mothers' differential behavior during reunions; they appear rather to have resulted from contingency rates experienced during early infancy.

Gender

As indicated above, mothers of 2-year-olds show greater expressivity to girls than to boys. A parallel finding was reported for younger children; Malatesta and Haviland (1982) found that mothers of 3–6-month-old infants smiled more at their daughters. The gender differences we observed in the present study—girls' greater exposure to a range of emotions and to more social smiling—may be part of a continuing program of gender-differentiated tuition in the use of affective expressions. If so, it might help explain why females smile more (Bugental, Love, & Gianetto, 1971; Man-

stead, in press), are seen as more sociable (Haviland & Malatesta, 1981; Maccoby & Jacklin, 1974), and are more expert than males at decoding the emotional expressions of others at all ages (Hall, 1978).

Boys and girls were found to display similar levels of anger during play; however, girls displayed more anger during the second reunion. A parallel gender difference with respect to anger was observed when the children were tested in a similar paradigm in early infancy (Malatesta et al., 1986) and in another study that used a separation paradigm with a different group of children (Malatesta, 1981). There has been some evidence, and much speculation, that mothers may encourage girls to remain physically and emotionally closer to them than boys (Chodorow, 1978); if this is so, then girls may tolerate separations from their mothers less readily than boys.

Attachment

Mothers appeared to allow themselves a wider range of affect with securely attached children (more expressivity and positive emotion shown to them during play, more knit brow during reunion). The greater degree of positive expressivity displayed during play may reflect the more positive nature of their relationship. In turn, during reunion, securely attached children were found to spend more time looking toward their mothers than did insecurely attached ones. However, it was insecure children, at least among full terms, who showed greater levels of positive affect, mainly consisting of enhanced interest expressions. Also, insecurely attached boys showed the highest level of compressed lips in both play and reunion sessions.

These latter findings are most interesting in the light of earlier comments in the attachment literature to the effect that insecure infants (typically classified as A) appear to be exercising restraint or control over their emotions during reunion episodes (Cassidy & Kobak, in press; Grossmann, 1981); in addition, although these children tend to avoid their mothers during reunion, they display what researchers have called covert or indirect hostility when observed at home (Main, Kaplan, & Cassidy, 1985). The picture, then, is one of children who are angry, vigilant, and emotionally controlled. Although the earlier reports are based on general impressions rather than discrete emotion coding, they seem consistent with the present findings. The heightened interest expressions during reunion, combined with the more frequent occurrence of compressed lips (which indexes suppressed anger in adults) in both play and reunion, appear to support the picture of a vigilant youngster who is trying to keep her anger under control. (These effects, incidentally, hold up even when the three C children are deleted from the insecure group and an ANOVA is conducted on A's versus B's.)

Birth Status

Preterm infants and their mothers (vs. full-term infant/mother dyads) have been found to display different patterns of emotional exchange during interaction in the opening months of life (Malatesta et al., 1986). The current data indicate that prematurity continues to exert a substantial effect on children's affective development, even into the second year. Although no differences as a function of birth status are observed in either children or mothers during the play session, differences begin to emerge in reunion 1 and become substantial by reunion 2. During reunion 1, full-term children communicated more interest than did preterms. We suspect that this may reflect a greater degree of mutuality between full-term children and their mothers and a better ability to reestablish positive communicative contact following a distressful episode. For their part, mothers showed the greatest amount of overall expressivity (which was mainly positive affect and specifically joy) to preterm securely attached infants. We suspect that mothers may go to special lengths to comfort preterm children who are securely attached because they view them as both needier and more rewarding than either full terms or preterm avoidantly attached infants. Preterm insecure children may be just as needy, but avoidant behavior may make them less rewarding to care for. At the second reunion, mothers showed more expressivity, especially positive emotion (i.e., interest, joy), to full-term children. In addition, mothers of full terms gave their children more reciprocated eye contact than did mothers of preterms. The reason perhaps is to be found in the children's data: full terms, especially those with low-contingency mothers, were more expressive, were more positive, and showed more interest and joy than preterms. Thus, the full-term children were apparently able to regain positive affectivity following the distress of separation more readily than preterms. Full terms did not display any more or any less anger, sadness, or compressed lips than did the preterms, but they did display more knit brow, which, as we have already discussed, appears to serve as a low-intensity signal of distress. Thus, relative to preterms, full-term children are able to communicate their distress without either becoming overly distressed or engaging in suppression (compressed lips); moreover, they show evidence of being able to recover their positive affect states fairly rapidly.

Preterm children with high-contingency mothers showed the least joy of all groups, and preterm females showed the highest negative affect (in terms of total negative affect and sadness) of all birth status/sex groups. The ability to communicate distress (especially the come-and-take-care-of-me kind of affect that is sadness; see Stettner & Loigman, 1983) would seem to operate adaptively for preterm children and may be especially reinforced in female children. By communicating sad distress, children motivate others to care for them. As Beckwith (1985) has noted, distressed preterms seem to have more difficulty in recovering from distress on their own.

Preterm children appear to be more negatively affected by a high level of maternal contingency. A number of authors have suggested that preterm infants have more difficulty modulating their levels of affective arousal and that they are more readily overstimulated (Beckwith, 1985; Field, 1987). If so, it is easy to see how high rates of maternal contingency/stimulation, which appears to be generally deleterious, could affect the preterm child even more adversely.

V. CONTINUITY AND CHANGE OVER FOUR WAVES: PATTERNS AND PREDICTIONS

In this chapter, we examine two sets of data that speak to the issue of continuity and change in expressive behavior over time. We first present correlational data on patterns of expressive behavior within mothers and infants as well as descriptions of mother/child concordance in expressive behavior over the four waves of assessment. We then examine particular patterns of intraindividual change in emotional expressivity during early infancy and their ability to predict subsequent quality of attachment and expressive behavior at age 2 years.

CONTINUITY OF EXPRESSIVE BEHAVIOR

To determine the degree of continuity of individual differences in expressive behavior from wave to wave, Pearson product-moment correlations were calculated for discrete expressive behaviors between each two successive waves; the results for mothers are displayed in Table 7 and those for children in Table 8. (Scores were based on expressive behaviors summed over play and both reunion sessions and proportionalized for segment length; data were summed over sessions in order to increase frequencies and hence provide more stable measures; see Epstein, 1980.) As can be seen from Table 7, mothers show a moderate to high degree of continuity in their expressive behaviors from the first to the second and from the second to the third waves. However, between the third and the fourth waves, only joy and knit brow (and total negative emotion, which appears to derive its strength mainly from the knit brow correlation) show significant continuity.

The correlations for children (Table 8) indicate considerable interwave continuity for a variety of expressive behaviors, although the strength of the correlations are not as great as those for mothers. The most stable period lies between the second and the third waves (5 and 7½ months of age). In

TABLE 7

CONSISTENCY OF MOTHER'S EXPRESSIVE BEHAVIOR FROM WAVE TO WAVE
(Pearson Correlation Coefficients)

	WAVES		
	1 × 2 (2½ × 5 Months)	2 × 3 (5 × 7½ Months)	3 × 4 (7½ × 22 Months)
Expression:			
Total positive	.34**	.54***	.10
Interest	.31*	.33**	−.07
Joy	.37**	.47***	.32*
Surprise	.36**	.59***	.02
Total negative	.39**	.66***	.49***
Sadness	.38**	.36**	.01
Anger	.13	.31*	−.03
Knit brow	.42***	.64***	.54***
Pressed lips	.11	.17	.12

NOTE.—N = 40–58, depending on wave and expression variable.
* $p < .05$. ** $p < .01$. *** $p < .001$.

addition, there seems to be both early and continuing stability of negative emotional expressions in infants.

The degree of concordance between mothers' and children's behavior at each of the four waves of measurement is shown in Table 9. The main concordance is for positive emotion, especially joy and surprise. As for negative affect, there is concordance in the use of knit brow during earliest infancy, in sadness and anger at 5 months, and in compressed lips at 7½ months; this last increases markedly at 22 months.

TABLE 8

CONSISTENCY OF CHILDREN'S EXPRESSIVE BEHAVIOR FROM WAVE TO WAVE

	WAVES		
	1 × 2 (2½ × 5 Months)	2 × 3 (5 × 7½ Months)	3 × 4 (7½ × 22 Months)
Expression:			
Total positive	−.04	.37**	.06
Interest	−.05	.30*	.01
Joy	.05	.35**	.14
Surprise	.32*	.50***	.05
Total negative	.28*	.22	.33*
Sadness	.28*	.34**	.37**
Anger	.39**	.42***	.32*
Knit brow	.16	.26*	.28*
Pressed lips	a	.16	.40**

NOTE.—N = 40–58, depending on wave and expression variable.
[a] No pressed lips observed in wave 1.
* $p < .05$. ** $p < .01$. *** $p < .001$.

TABLE 9

Correlation Coefficients Denoting Mother/Child Concordance in Expressive
Behavior over the Four Waves of Measurement

	Wave 1 (2½ Months)	Wave 2 (5 Months)	Wave 3 (7½ Months)	Wave 4 (22 Months)
Expression:				
Total positive	.28*	.38***	.54***	.41***
Interest	.12	.40***	.20	−.04
Joy	.18	.31*	.38***	.13
Surprise	.37***	.30*	.47***	.44***
Total negative	.12	.40***	.20	−.04
Sadness	−.03	.31*	.05	.10
Anger	.19	.27*	.20	.24
Knit brow	.28*	.08	.13	−.06
Pressed lips	a	−.11	.33*	.51***

Note.—N = 40–58, depending on wave and expression variable.
a No pressed lips observed in wave 1.
* $p < .05$.
*** $p < .001$.

The fact that mothers and infants show a good deal of concordance in their expressive behaviors—especially with respect to the compressed lips expression, which enters the child's repertoire relatively late in development and appears to index voluntary control of emotion—suggests that children's expressive patterns are at least in part determined by their emotional interactions with their mothers. This notion seems to be supported by the results of the previous ANOVA tests, which indicated that maternal contingency level (as assessed in early infancy) was related to particular patterns of expressive behavior in children at 2 years.

PATTERNS OF INTRAINDIVIDUAL CHANGE IN CHILDREN'S EMOTION EXPRESSIVITY OVER WAVES 1–3 AND THE PREDICTION OF ATTACHMENT AND EXPRESSIVE BEHAVIOR AT WAVE 4

Because we were interested in determining whether changes in infants' expressive patterns might index emergent difficulties in the mother/child relationship, we related individual shifts in emotion expression frequencies seen over the three successive waves to attachment security at age 2 years. The main interest was in comparing those infants who stayed stable to those who changed substantially; the more variable children were expected to be at greatest risk for developing an insecure attachment.

We also examined whether variability in maternal emotion expression during early infancy predicted attachment status at 2 years. There is some evidence that unstable environments are associated with an increase in the number of insecure attachments (Bretherton, 1985, 1987); we reasoned that unstable environments produce instability of maternal affect and that it is the latter factor that influences the development of insecure attachments.

We selected "variable" infants and mothers on the basis of first an ordinal and then an interval scale of measurement. In the former approach, we separated subjects into quartiles within each wave and defined as variable those infants who changed between waves by at least 1 quartile. Our aim was to isolate infants who showed substantial lability; continuous measures are more cumbersome for this purpose and tend to be arbitrary. We also wanted a measure that would be unaffected by outliers. At the interval level, we defined changes for each emotion by each subject's standard deviation across the waves; this yielded a continuous measure of variability of emotion expression within subjects. We used both measurements because we could not know a priori which level was best suited to our data; as it turned out, each provided different kinds of information.

Assessment of Change: Ordinal Level of Measurement

For each facial expression variable (interest, joy, surprise, sadness, anger, knit brow, and positive and negative emotion), subjects were rank ordered by frequency and then divided into quartiles; those who showed substantial change over the three waves—designated increasers or decreasers—became the focus of analysis. Increasers were defined as those whose interquartile rank on any one of the expressive behaviors increased by one or more ranks from the first or second wave to the third; decreasers were defined by the converse. A subject's status as an increaser or a decreaser could change depending on the emotion examined; rankings and analyses were strictly within emotion categories.

Children.—Change in infant joy (increase or decrease of one to three ranks) yielded significant results (see Table 10): the majority of securely attached children (62%) had displayed a pattern of increased smiling over

TABLE 10

ATTACHMENT CLASSIFICATION OF CHILDREN WHO INCREASED AND DECREASED
IN FREQUENCY OF SMILING IN WAVE 1–3 OBSERVATIONS

	SECURE		INSECURE		TOTAL	
	N	%	N	%	N	%
Smile increasers	18	62	5	28	23	49
Smile decreasers	11	38	13	72	24	51
Total	29	62	18	38	47	100

NOTE.—Increase and decrease are defined as a shift of at least 1 quartile in within-age frequency distribution.

the three sessions, whereas the majority (72%) of insecurely attached children had shown a pattern of decrease (Fisher's exact test, $p = .02$). It is possible that this association may be more pronounced in the population at large since a disproportionate number of our dropouts—nine out of a total of 14—showed a decline in smiling (of the remainder, two were increasers, and three stayed stable). Fisher's exact test applied to change in smiling (increase vs. decrease) × dropout status (in vs. out) was significant ($p = .03$), indicating that sample attrition was nonrandom in this respect.

We also looked at a more extreme subgroup—12 infants who showed a change of two to three ranks in smiling between waves 2 and 3. Six of the seven increasers (86%) were later classed as securely attached, and all five decreasers were classed as insecurely attached; this difference is significant at the .008 level by Fisher's exact test.

Mothers.—To determine how the mother's behavior might have affected change in the child's expressive pattern, the same ranks analysis was repeated on their data. Shifts in maternal rates of smiling over the three sessions did not predict children's attachment classification, nor did any other single expression variable. However, maternal contingency rate (as measured at wave 3) was related to attachment classification. Data for the full sample are presented in Table 11. Only 31% of the children of mothers ranked in the upper quartile of contingency scores in wave 3 were classified as securely attached, whereas children of moderate- to low-contingency mothers (lower three quartiles) were securely attached in 67% of the cases (by Fisher's exact test, $p < .02$).

In the subgroup of 12 infants who showed a radical change in their smiling pattern (described above), all but one of the seven increasers had mothers who were low to moderate in contingency, whereas all five decreasers had high-contingency mothers ($p = .008$ by Fisher's exact test). (Note that "high-contingency" mothers in this analysis are in the upper quarter of

TABLE 11

ATTACHMENT CLASSIFICATION OF CHILDREN WHOSE MOTHERS WERE CHARACTERIZED HIGH VERSUS MODERATE TO LOW CONTINGENCY IN WAVE 3 OBSERVATIONS

| | CHILD ATTACHMENT | | | | | |
| | Secure | | Insecure | | Total | |
	N	%	N	%	N	%
Mother contingency:						
High	4	31	9	69	13	22
Moderate to low	30	67	15	33	45	78
Total	34	59	24	41	58	100

NOTE.—High = upper quartile; moderate to low = lower three quartiles of the distribution in within-age frequency distribution.

the distribution, whereas in the ANOVA analysis presented earlier they were in the upper third.)

The significant relation between expressive patterns for joy and subsequent attachment classification appears to stem largely from the inclusion of preterm infants in the sample. We conducted Fisher's tests on increase versus decrease in smile rates by classification matrices separately for the two birth-status groups. The same trend appeared in both groups; however, with the reduced sample sizes, the effect reached statistical significance only in the preterms ($p = .045$). Of those preterms classified later as securely attached, 78% ($N = 7$) showed the pattern of enhanced smiling over sessions, and 22% ($N = 2$) showed a decline; of those classified as insecurely attached, all ($N = 3$) had shown declining smile patterns.

Assessment of Change: Interval Level of Measurement

As noted earlier, we used each subject's standard deviation (for each expression variable, summed over play and reunion sessions) over the first three waves as the interval measure of variability. Point biserial correlations for mothers and for children were computed between classification status and both the individual expression variables and their aggregates. A significant relation obtained between the secure/insecure classification and the standard deviation of the mothers' aggregate of negative emotion, $r = -.30$, $p < .03$. The negative correlation indicates that mothers of insecure infants had been on the average more variable in the expression of negative emotion across the first three waves than mothers of secure subjects had been. A Mann-Whitney U test, which has less restrictive assumptions concerning the underlying distributions, was also significant ($p < .01$).

RELATION BETWEEN QUALITATIVE ASPECTS OF EARLY MATERNAL CONTINGENCY AND SUBSEQUENT CHILD CLASSIFICATION STATUS AND EXPRESSIVE BEHAVIOR

In an earlier analysis, we looked at the relation between the level of maternal contingency in infancy and subsequent child development. In light of the theoretical importance of signal specificity in the literature on both attachment and emotion socialization, we now look beyond such levels to a more qualitative analysis by examining the child's expressive behavior at wave 4 as a function of types of maternal contingent responses to types of infant affect during the first several months of life.

Pearson product-moment correlations were run between specific maternal affective responses to specific infant affects (summed over waves 1–3) and types of children's affective responses during wave 4 reunion (summed over the two reunions). We also examined the relation between nonresponse to specific affects, termed "ignoring," and expressive outcomes; a mother's ignoring score consisted of the proportion of the child's affective responses to which no immediate contingent response was given.

We chose correlational statistics because we had no a priori notions of how maternal contingency would be related to the affective responses of children and hence assumed a simple linear model. (Examination of scatter plots also did not indicate the need of more complex assumptions.) To ensure that relations suggested by the contingency correlations were not artifactual, we examined the frequency distributions and scatter plots so as to spot departures from normality and linearity; "significant" correlations that did not meet the necessary statistical assumptions were judged spurious (e.g., where one variable in a pair was highly skewed or where the presence of outliers falsely inflated the strength of the correlation). The correlations that survived critical scrutiny are shown in Table 12. In brief, in wave 4 reunions, the compressed lips expression (which is viewed as associated with emotion suppression) was predicted positively by maternal surprise responses to infant anger and negatively by both mother's interest to infant interest and the total amount of contingency to infant interest expressions. Joy was negatively predicted by mothers' interest expressions to sadness faces, by her joy expressions to pain, and by her tendency to ignore sadness and pain. Child interest during reunions was negatively predicted by her interest expressions to anger and joy expressions to pain. Sadness was predicted negatively by interest to knit brow expressions, joy to interest expressions, and more overall contingency to interest during early infancy; it was positively predicted by ignoring of infant pain and sadness. Finally, knit brow was positively predicted by surprise expressions to infant pain, and anger was positively predicted by surprise to sadness and by ignoring of infant pain.

DISCUSSION

Continuity and Change in Expressive Behavior over the First 2 Years of Life

Wave-to-wave correlations indicated that children tend to show continuity in their emotional expressive patterns across a range of discrete emotions and signals. The correlations, however, tend to be low—this is as would be expected. The theoretical literature has stressed that, although the basic programs for the primary emotions are part of a common mammalian heritage and appear to be "hardwired" into the nervous system, expressive patterns are subject to the cumulative effects of enculturation and learning (Ekman, 1982; Izard, 1971, 1977; Tomkins, 1962, 1963).

TABLE 12

SIGNIFICANT CORRELATIONS BETWEEN EMOTION-SPECIFIC EXPRESSIVE PATTERNS
IN 2-YEAR-OLDS AT REUNION AND THEIR MOTHERS' CONTINGENT AND
IGNORING RESPONSES IN WAVES 1–3 ($N = 47$)

Child Expressions	Maternal Behavior in Waves 1–3	r	p
Pressed lips	Maternal interest to infant interest	−.31	.04
	Maternal surprise to infant anger	.45	.001
	Total contingency to infant interest	−.35	.02
Joy	Maternal interest to infant sadness	−.36	.01
	Maternal joy to infant pain	−.39	.01
	Ignoring of infant pain	−.31	.03
	Ignoring of infant sadness	−.28	.05
Interest	Maternal interest to infant anger	−.39	.01
	Maternal joy to infant pain	−.37	.01
Sadness	Maternal interest to infant knit brow	−.34	.03
	Maternal joy to infant interest	−.29	.05
	Total contingency to infant interest	−.33	.02
	Ignoring of infant pain	.35	.02
	Ignoring of infant sadness	.29	.05
Knit brow	Maternal surprise to infant pain	.29	.05
Anger	Maternal surprise to infant sadness	.42	.01

The wave-to-wave correlations (of frequencies of each expression) were stronger for mothers than for children, probably reflecting the greater degree of consolidation in expressive patterns that takes place by adulthood. Mothers showed a moderate to high degree of continuity from the first to the second session and from the second to the third. Between the third and fourth sessions, however, only two individual expressions and the aggregate of negative emotion showed statistically significant effects. Infant correlations from waves 3–4 were also weaker than those from waves 2–3. We surmise that the greater stability found in the earlier as opposed to the later waves can be attributed in part to the shorter interval of time between the earlier waves as well as to the greater degree of context change between the last two waves. Even so, four expressive behaviors of infants and two of mothers did demonstrate considerable cross-temporal and cross-situational continuity, even with our relatively limited sampling of behavior. In children, it is interesting to note that, whereas all four negative affect expressions showed significant continuity from 7½ to 22 months, none of the positive expressions did, suggesting that negative affect expression patterns may become more readily consolidated. Continuity for the negative affects was also greater between the two earlier waves, suggesting that there may be innate dispositional tendencies around negative affects. Children's affective behavior, however, is also changeable; the strength of even the significant correlations tends to be lower than that of those obtained for mothers.

Within waves, mothers and children show a moderately high concordance of individual emotion expression patterns. This mutuality or synchrony in affective behavior has been observed in other studies as well. Malatesta and Haviland (1982) found high mother-infant correlations for various emotion expressions as sampled from face-to-face interactions between mothers and their 3–6-month-old infants. In another study, Wolder (1988) found a high degree of synchrony in both rate and type (positive/negative) of affect expression between mothers and their 4–6-year-old children while they interacted during storytelling and a joint instrumental task. More important, Wolder's study demonstrated that, at least within this age range, children engage in more affect matching than their parents do. In the present study, we also see evidence that children may be modeling themselves on their parents' expressive patterns. One of the highest levels of concordance at wave 4 is for compressed lips, an expression that is absent from the child's repertoire until the second half of the first year and is not seen with much frequency until age 2 years. The expression appears to index not a primary emotion that enters the repertoire at a late date but rather an attempt to control negative affect. That children show concordance with the mother in its use after it enters their repertoire, that it seems to require voluntary control, and that the strength of the concordance correlation increases over time suggest that this is one expressive pattern that may be acquired by means of observation of parental expressive behavior.

In summary, we found substantial mother/child affect concordances over the first 2 years of life and a modest degree of intraindividual cross-temporal and cross-situational continuity in affective expression. The data indicate that maternal expressive behavior is more consistent across time than is that of children and that it may be somewhat dispositionally stable. Even so, there is enough variability and lack of continuity, especially in children and especially when moving from one context to another, to support Tomkins's (1962, 1963) assertion that the affect system is both flexible and susceptible to structuralization within the personality.

How Do Patterns of Early Emotional Interchange Affect Expressive Behavior and Security of Attachment at Age 2 Years?

Predicting attachment.—Some children changed in their expressive profile over the opening months of life. Those who showed a decline over the three successive waves in their apparent level of enjoyment during face-to-face interaction with their mothers (i.e., less smiling) and who were subsequently more likely to be rated as insecurely attached had mothers characterized by extremely high early contingency rates. It seems likely that infants experience such high facial contingency as overstimulating and aversive, and aversive experiences may provoke the defensive maneuver of avoidance (a key feature of children classified as A). However, since our measurements did not begin until 2½ months of age, we do not know where the aversive cycle for these mothers and children may actually originate. It is certainly conceivable that mothers may resort to high levels of contingency if their infants do not appear active or responsive enough, and it is important to take this possibility into consideration in future research.

That early decrease in infant smiling should predict security of attachment a year later is perhaps not surprising given the central role accorded the smiling response by Spitz (1965), who termed it the first psychic organizer. What is somewhat more surprising is that prediction can be made by sampling merely either 6 min of interaction on three different occasions, if the focus is the infant, or 6 min on one occasion (at 7½ months), if the focus is on the mother. To be sure, prediction rates were modest (72% of the insecurely attached children could be predicted by changes in the smiling pattern and 69% by the mother's data), but, as we noted, it appears that the effect was attenuated by selective attrition; prediction was increased to 100% when analysis was restricted to children who showed the most pronounced decrease in smiling. The relation between decrease in smiling and attachment was clearest in preterm children; thus, it appears that preterm infants, even those without medical complications, are more vulnerable to the effects of overstimulation than their full-term counterparts are.

The other maternal expressive variable that predicted attachment classification was variability (across sessions) in negative affect display, with more variable mothers being likely to have insecurely attached children. We hypothesize that the lower level of predictability of maternal negative affect may generate anxiety in the child and consequent avoidance of the mother. As Gunnar (1980) has shown, there is a relation between the experience of control/predictability and fearfulness, with predictability associated with reduction in fear. Negative affect displayed by mothers is clearly distressing to infants (Cohn & Tronick, 1983; Haviland & Lelwica, 1987); it is likely that, when its occurrence is also unpredictable, it is doubly aversive.

Predicting expressive behavior.—Several effects of level of maternal contingency on emotional expressivity at 2 years have already been noted (see Chap. IV above). In our more qualitative analyses, we additionally examined the child's expressive behavior in wave 4 reunions as a function of types of maternal contingent responses to types of infant affect. Positive emotion (joy, interest) was negatively predicted by patterns of maternal contingency during infancy involving what one can generally regard as insensitive behavior such as smiling during infant pain and ignoring infant sadness and pain. Similarly, negative emotion was positively predicted by ignoring of infant pain and sadness in early infancy and negatively predicted by maternal interest. The compressed lips expression, which appears to index attempts to suppress negative emotion, was positively predicted by maternal surprise to infant anger (surprise expressions typically took the "mock surprise" form) and negatively by maternal interest.

VI. MODELS OF PREDICTION FOR PARTICULAR OUTCOMES

In this chapter, we exploit the results of the various foregoing analyses to draft tentative models of differential expressive development, using multiple regression techniques to assess the relative contribution of individual difference variables in predicting certain key expressive and relational outcomes at age 2 years. Factors established as relevant by the previous analyses—gender, birth status, level of maternal contingency, and type of maternal contingency—were entered into regression equations to evaluate their differential contribution in the prediction of expressive patterns during reunion.

We focus on reunion behavior for both theoretical and empirical reasons. First, feelings, conceived of as internal states, are regarded as motivations or dispositions to act; emotional behaviors are viewed as adaptations to the environment. The demand for environmental adaptation is especially great during challenging situations such as separations from caregivers; thus, reunions can be predicted to be highly charged. Second, individual differences in expressive styles are most likely to be seen under conditions of stress. In fact, Malatesta and Wilson (1988) have proposed that individual differences in expressive behaviors (i.e., in emotion-specific patterns) during Strange Situation reunions reflect affective organizations that are part of personality. Finally, we wanted to predict behavior over the first 2 years of life; infancy is a particularly unstable time behaviorally since growth and differentiation are especially rapid. Accumulating data from studies of both human and nonhuman primate development indicate that prediction of behavior, and especially emotional behavior, is heightened under conditions that tax the individual's adaptive capacity (Suomi, 1985; Zahn-Waxler et al., 1984).

Shiller et al. (1986) applied a discrete emotions analysis to children's behavior during the separation episodes of the Ainsworth Strange Situation procedure and found that, whereas the typical response was anger, some children were distinguished by an unusual amount of sadness. Anticipating

65

that similar individual differences would exist as well in the reunion phase, we sought to predict anger and sadness in reunions from a composite of our early individual difference variables. Because these analyses were partially post hoc, conservative criteria were used in deciding which variables to enter into the model, and the number of models tested was restricted. The order of entry of variables was informed by a priori hypotheses as well as by post hoc components.

We assumed that birth status and gender would be important components in any model of expressive development and reasoned that, by virtue of being "givens" at birth and carrying with them dispositional aspects, these variables are logically prior to maternal contingency patterns. (One could argue from a systems perspective that neither infant nor maternal variables are "prior" since behaviors of both partners are interactive; however, we also make the assumption that maternal behavior is more flexible than that of a newborn child, and in that sense child variables may be seen as having more initial primacy.) Noting also that the main effects and interactions of these two variables were frequently significant in the preceding ANOVAs, birth status and gender were always included in the various models to be discussed as well as entered first.

The remaining components of the regression equations were determined by the following considerations. Our theoretical model assumed that mothers play an important role in the socialization of emotion (e.g., by modeling, contingency), but it did not specify which kinds of maternal behavior would be important in this process. Results of correlational analyses suggested some important linkages between maternal contingency patterns and expressive behavior outcomes. The maternal variables selected for inclusion in the models were chosen from among those that showed significant relations with anger and sadness in these previous analyses, namely, maternal contingency level and specific contingency patterns (see Table 12). Finally, the child's level of anger or sadness during the first three waves was also included in the model since it is conceivable that the socialization that intervenes between the early ages and wave 4 may be less significant than the initial base rates of these emotions.

PREDICTING CHILD SADNESS AT REUNION DURING WAVE 4

The predictor variables entered into these regressions were gender, birth status (and its interaction with gender), and the following measures from waves 1–3: the child's sadness expressions, the mother's total contingency score (squared to take into account the quadratic shape of interaction with the nominal version of this variable in ANOVAs), the mother's contingent interest to child knit brow, the mother's ignoring of sadness, the mother's ignoring of child pain, the mother's joy contingencies to child interest, and the mother's total contingency to child interest.

We began with a stepwise regression, eliminating variables that did not individually contribute an F statistic corresponding to an alpha of 5%—a conservative criterion was used in view of the partially post hoc nature of the model. The resultant stepwise regression eliminated all but two variables from the model: maternal ignoring of child sadness and maternal contingent interest to child knit brow.

At this point, we shifted to a hierarchical regression based on a priori hypotheses combined with the information from the stepwise regression. For the reasons noted above, gender and birth status were entered first. Neither gender nor the two-factor interaction contributed enough variance to the hierarchical model to be retained, leaving only birth status as a dispositional predictor. The child's early expression of sadness was entered next owing to the likelihood that this variable also shared some basic rootedness in temperament. Maternal ignoring of sadness and maternal interest to child knit brow were tried in several orders; the former was found to explain the same variance in the dependent variable as the child's early sadness expressions. We retained the latter variable in favor of the former because of our presumption that it might be at least partially temperamentally based. Maternal interest to the child's expression of knit brow entered the equation last.

The resultant model is shown in Table 13. At this last stage of model building, we relaxed the conservative criterion that each predictor be significant on its own and looked instead for a model that included our a priori considerations first, then adding what had appeared important in the stepwise regression. Setting these conditions, the overall model is significant, but the test for birth status does not reach the 5% level. (We elected this particular approach because of the demonstrable nonorthogonality of our predictors. As is well known, that which enters the regression equation first may predict the same variance as a variable entered later. This was likely to occur here given the inherent confounding of maternal behaviors and infant temperamental dispositions; a mother's behavioral style is not independent of her child's dispositions.)

In the present model, both maternal contingent interest to knit brow and child's early sadness had coefficients that were significantly different from zero. Inspection of the standardized coefficients suggests that no single predictor emerges above the others as being the most important; rather, all are contributory. The sign of the coefficient for the mother's contingency to knit brow is also of interest. Mothers who showed greater contingent interest to infant knit brow from waves 1–3 tended to have children who expressed less sadness at wave 4. We take this as evidence that mothers who responded with interest to the low-level distress expressions of their infants may have

TABLE 13

MULTIPLE REGRESSION MODELS PREDICTING CHILD SADNESS AND CHILD ANGER DURING REUNION IN THE STRANGE SITUATION AT AGE 22 MONTHS

PREDICTORS OF:	COEFFICIENT				MODEL			
	Raw	SD	T	p	df	F	p	R^2
Sadness:								
Birth status	547.22	.17	1.22	.23				
Wave 1–3 child sadness	.29	.28	2.04	.05				
Wave 1–3 mother interest to child knit brow	−151.83	−.31	−2.22	.03				
Constant	839.44	.00	1.68	.10	3,43	3.41	.01	.44
Anger:								
Gender	−1,223.7	−.63	−2.49	.02				
Birth status	−852.01	−.41	−1.89	.07				
Gender × birth status	1,258.67	.62	2.21	.03				
Wave 1–3 child anger	−.23	−.30	−2.05	.05				
Wave 1–3 mother surprise to child sadness	317.37	.43	3.19	.01				
Constant	1,643.09	.00	3.45	.01	5,41	3.37	.01	.54

NOTE.—Wave 1–3 variables are summed over observation waves 1–3.

contributed to their children's subsequent ability to withstand separation with only mildly sad distress.

PREDICTING CHILD ANGER AT REUNION DURING WAVE 4

Regression followed a procedure similar to the one described above. We began building our model with stepwise regression using the following predictors: gender, birth status, and waves 1–3 variables of the total sum of maternal contingency, the sum of the child's anger expressions, the sum of maternal ignoring of child pain, and the mother's contingent expression of surprise to child sadness. Using the conservative 5% criterion, three predictors were left in the equation: the child's expression of anger, total maternal contingency, and the mother's surprise contingencies to child sadness.

Hierarchical regressions followed in which gender, birth status, and the gender × birth status interaction were entered first and the child's expression of sadness second. We experimented with the order of entry and the possible removal of the child's expression of sadness, total contingency, and the mother's contingent surprise to the child's expression of sadness. The final model contained the a priori predictors of the child's expression of sadness and maternal contingent surprise to sadness; total contingency did not add enough variance when compared to that contributed by contingency to sadness and was thus dropped from the final model. This model is also shown in Table 13. Again, no single predictor emerged as being notably more important than the others. Inspection of the coefficient signs shows the importance of gender, birth status, and their interaction in the prediction of anger at wave 4. In rank order, the expression of anger is greatest for the female preterms, the male and then the female full terms, and the male preterms. Note that the negative coefficient for the child's early expression of anger does not indicate that subjects who expressed greater anger at the previous three waves expressed more anger at wave 4; the interaction of gender and birth status confounds direct interpretation of this coefficient. This confound also applies to the coefficient for maternal surprise to the child's expression of sadness. It appears that maternal contingency behaviors vary in their effect on the development of the expression of anger depending on the child's gender and birth history.

DISCUSSION

The foregoing regression analyses confirmed the importance of gender, birth status, and maternal contingency patterns in differential expressive development. By constructing our models, we attempted to assess the relative contribution of these factors to the development of children's emotional styles, specifically in the degree of anger and sadness displayed to mothers following separation. Overall, the regression models pointed to the combined importance of infant dispositional tendencies and maternal contingency patterns. Despite the fact that dispositional variables were entered first in the equations, maternal behavioral style variables still emerged as contributing new variance.

We were able to account for about 20% of the variance in children's anger at reunion and about 30% of the variance in their sadness. These results might seem disappointing; obviously, we would like to be able to predict more of the variance. However, considering that most research on personality and individual difference typically explains only about 10% of the variance (Mischel, 1968), we are heartened by models that explain two to three times as much. Nevertheless, one still needs to consider how the results might be enhanced and the model improved.

It is possible that the models themselves are neither wrong nor incomplete but that the R^2's are attenuated for methodological reasons. Epstein (1980) has argued that "personality coefficients" are typically low because researchers tend to sample behavior on only one occasion, demonstrating in his own research that prediction of individual differences can be enhanced substantially when behavior is sampled repeatedly and aggregated over time or occasions. In the present study, three samples of infant and maternal behavior were used to predict age-2 reunion behaviors, and it is perhaps this that accounts for our ability to predict as much variance as we did. To the extent that our problem is still a matter of too little sampling, our results would be enhanced if we were to assess emotional behavior more frequently and on more occasions. We also suspect that the models can be improved with the addition of other variables.

Two variables would seem especially recommended. As far as we can tell, our models contain all infant dispositional variables that are considered theoretically relevant—gender, birth status, and temperament (i.e., wave 1–3 child anger and sadness expressions). However, in terms of the influence of social agents, it may have been a serious error to restrict our sampling to mothers alone. We have as yet no way of knowing how influential a role fathers play in the emotion socialization of their children, but we suspect that it is considerable. In addition, a substantial portion of the mothers had returned to work during the infant's first year and had hired others to care for their children. One must wonder about the role that these other caregivers play in affecting the expressive development of young children, especially since many spend considerable time with them in a variety of emotionally charged circumstances. Future research on emotion socialization would be well advised to take into account the contribution of fathers and outside caregivers.

VII. SUMMARY AND CONCLUDING DISCUSSION

We summarize here some of the main findings concerning the course of affective development and the sources of individual difference that were detailed in the previous six chapters. We then engage in a more general discussion of the results as well as more free-ranging and speculative consideration of how the data inform our understanding of the processes of emotion socialization and personality development. In this respect, we agree with Grossmann (1988) that longitudinal data sets should be used not only in hypothesis testing but also, opportunistically, in hypothesis generation.

SUMMARY

In the present investigation, we charted the course of socioemotional development over the first 2 years of life and also confirmed the importance of several individual difference variables in differential expressive development.

Our data suggest that mothers' expressive behavior has a material effect on the course of infant affective development. Although we cannot rule out the possibility that maternal contingency patterns may be in part reactive to infant predispositions, both the theoretical literature and the pattern of our results assign an important role to maternal affective responses in altering the trajectory of children's expressive development. Both the general level of maternal contingency and the specific nature of the mother's affective responses were found to predict subsequent developmental patterns. Low to moderate levels appeared more salutary for a number of child expressive variables than high levels did, especially in the case of preterm infants. Displays of interest to early infant affect predicted positive affect, whereas tendencies to ignore sadness and pain (but not anger) were associated with more sadness and anger following separation at age 2 years.

Birth status affected children's emotional behaviors well into the second year of life. This finding conflicts with Frodi and Thompson (1985), who

71

found no significant differences in the emotional behaviors of 1-year-old preterms when compared to full-term infants and proposed a rebound phenomenon in the socioemotional development of preterms during the second half of the first year of life. However, these investigators did not use a discrete emotions microanalytic coding system, and we suspect that it is the greater sensitivity of this system that allowed detection of the subtle but important differences that we discerned. Birth status affected emotional behaviors under conditions of relatively little stress as well as under conditions of moderate stress, although individual differences were more manifest under the latter conditions in both preterm and term children. It is important to note that our preterm group consisted of children who had been only mildly premature, who came from relatively advantaged socioeconomic conditions, and who were born without medical complications. The effects described in the present report are likely to be even more pronounced in preterm children who are sicker, more premature, or come from less advantaged backgrounds.

Mothers responded somewhat differently to sons and daughters, in a manner that seems conducive to promoting the kinds of sex-differentiated affective patterns that have been reported in the literature. Boys and girls already showed evidence of dimorphism in emotional behavior, and gender differences obtained in both the play and the reunion sessions, especially the latter. How much these differences can be attributed to differential socialization histories and how much to innate factors is difficult to determine. Socialization may come to play a greater role as children mature; in the present study, gender differences were more noticeable in the second year than in the opening months of life (Malatesta et al., 1986).

Attachment classifications differentiated children's expressive behavior along a broad negative/positive dimension. During nonstressful interactions, securely attached children attended to their mothers more; this greater interpersonal attentiveness might help explain why such children perform more optimally under a host of conditions that involve interacting with another (Main, Kaplan, & Cassidy, 1985). During stressful situations—when it is more adaptive to communicate one's distress—insecurely attached children, paradoxically, displayed more positive affect (mainly interest) and showed the compressed lips expression more frequently; we interpret these findings as revealing a pattern of emotion suppression and vigilance.

Finally, although some interesting relations were found, expressive behavior as coded on a discrete emotions basis proved not to be reducible to attachment constructs, or vice versa, and our understanding of infant emotional development was enhanced by what should be properly regarded as two complementary approaches. Bowlby (1969) had indicated that attachment is concerned with feelings (i.e., internal states) about security; with the present study, we have come a bit closer to establishing what feelings may, or may not, be overtly revealed in secure and insecure children.

GENERAL DISCUSSION

This investigation was guided by two models of human development—that of attachment theory and that of differential emotions theory. Common to both of these is the emphasis on an organizational approach to socioemotional development; behavioral organization in general is viewed as being subserved by behavioral systems and oriented toward adaptation to environmental demands and conditions. In this concluding section, we consider our findings from within the larger framework of organization and adaptation, as we return to some of the issues that were first raised in Chapter I, namely, the relation between feeling and behavior, the role of maternal contingency in the socialization of emotion and in the formation of attachment, and the utility of employing both attachment and discrete emotions approaches in the study of personality development.

Feeling and Behavior

As noted earlier, a great deal of controversy still prevails with respect to two questions. Do infants have feeling states, and do expressive behaviors index such states reliably in early development? Attachment theory and differential emotions theory represent quite different paradigmatic worlds, yet both are in accord here. Both theories accept the notion of infant feelings either explicitly or implicitly and view infant expressive behaviors as indexing feeling states, even though the evidence for this is assessed in quite different ways within the two approaches.

We construe our data as supporting the stance taken by the two theories. Within the literature on emotions, three kinds of data are generally accepted as confirming that an observed emotional expression indexes a corresponding emotional state: convergent, predictive, and "contextual" evidence. All these sources of confirmation are to be found within the present data set; we refrain from detailing all the relevant examples and offer just a few instances of each case.

Convergent validation.—The fact that similar conclusions are generated by different theoretical approaches and diagnostics strengthens the assumptions of both theories. Within the attachment literature, the key diagnostic for assessing emotional organization is the child's behavior toward the parent following separation. Rather than focusing on discrete behaviors, assessment is made by taking into consideration the full complex of behavior and its organization over time. If a child feels threatened by separation and has no competing conflicts with respect to her attachment goals, emotional behavior should consist of greeting the caregiver on her return and approaching her for comfort, followed by relatively rapid recovery and return to play. If, however, anxiety over attachment co-occurs with the elicitation of anxiety over separation, conflict is experienced. The child may seem remote at the caregiver's return or filled with rage, may hesitate on approach or turn away, or, conversely, may cling unduly long and have trouble returning to play. Such differential patterns of organized behavior are used to infer secure or insecure feelings; note that it is the whole pattern of behavior that is important in interpreting the child's feelings. In contrast, a differential emotions approach to understanding the child's emotional organization centers on discrete emotion expressions—the nature of the expressions themselves, their context, and their patterning.

Our discrete emotions analysis of reunion behaviors cross-validated attachment researchers' assumptions that the avoidant behavior of children classified A is a mix of anger and fear. We found that such children were distinguished by their heightened interest expressions and tendency to engage in compressed lips; although very subtle, this pattern of discrete emotion expression was detectable by the coding system and was interpreted as evidence of heightened vigilance and suppressed anger.

Predictive validity.—Two types of predictive validity—proximal and distal—can be distinguished. Proximal predictive validity obtains when a behavior that is thought to index a particular state is reliably followed by a reasonably expectable consequence. Within differential emotions theory, discrete expressions are said to index differential feeling states; thus, smiling connotes joy, anger expressions connote frustration, sadness expressions connote distress, and so on. If a child is smiling while she plays with her mother, we expect her to continue doing so since she is presumably experiencing joy. Affective states are also held to be motivational, with each state providing a different motivation. If a child displays an anger expression during a frustrating experience, we expect that she will attempt to overcome the obstacle that is obstructing her way. When the first child continues to play and the second child bangs on the obstructing door, we propose that our assumptions of state have been validated.

Although we saw many examples of this kind, our analyses were not set up to demonstrate such proximal relations. Instead, most of our evidence of predictive validity is of the distal sort; that is, it involved predicting future behaviors from present ones over a period of development. Our finding of changes in level of infant smiling during the first half year constitutes one such example. If smiling indexes a state of joy or pleasure in the infant (as assumed by differential emotions theory), we expect a decline in smiling during face-to-face interaction with the caregiver to be ominous for the developing attachment relationship. A number of infants characterized by such a decline were identified in the present data set, and the prediction that they would have difficulty in their attachment relationship was sustained— smile decreasers were significantly more likely to develop as insecurely attached than were children who showed a pattern of increased smiling. We also expected that infants who were exposed to extremely high rates of contingency would experience this condition as overstimulating and aversive and consequently learn to avoid the caregiver. Supporting this expectation, children exposed to particularly high rates of facial contingency were indeed likely to develop an insecure (avoidant) attachment pattern.

Contextual validation.—Context validity is established in this instance by assessment of whether caregivers treat emotional expressions as biologically meaningful signals and whether their interventions produce the expected emotional reactions. There is every evidence that this was the case in the present study. As seen in ongoing interactions, caregivers' responses to infant signals of distress (sadness, knit brow) were typically accompanied by attempts to alleviate the conditions. In longitudinal assessment, children of caregivers who either ignored or responded as though they had misinterpreted their infants' distress signals reacted more acutely during the reunion sessions at age 2 years.

In summary, whether viewed from the perspective of attachment theory or from that of differential emotions theory, there appear to be reasonable grounds for inferring that infants' expressive behavior is coherently integrated with their feeling states.

There is some consensus in the literature that beyond early infancy expressive behavior (or the lack of it, in the case of affect minimization or neutralization) may be a less reliable index of state, at least on certain occasions. In the present data set, we observed three expressions (i.e., knit brow, compressed lips, and biting the lips) that appeared to be related to the suppression or dampening of negative affective state; these were most clearly evident in the wave 4 observations. We believe that the ability to self-regulate—subdue or modulate distress—is a developmentally advanced capability. In both the present data and in a longitudinal study by Grossmann, Grossmann, and Ernst (in preparation), it was clear that younger children recover less quickly from distress than do older ones.

In addition to this normative developmental trend toward more skilled regulation of state, individual differences are also observed. Some children fail to communicate the distress they experience under stressful situations (Grossmann et al., in preparation); these children appear to be overregulated and to minimize their affective expression to an excessive degree. Others, such as hyperactive children—who are known to be affectively labile and impulsive—are apparently underregulated. Deviations from the normative level of affect regulation seem to be constitutionally based in the case of some children and a consequence of idiosyncratic emotion socialization by caregivers in others. It is to this latter issue that we now turn.

The Role of Maternal Contingency in the Socialization of Emotion and Formation of the Attachment Bond

The attachment literature has stressed that caregiver sensitivity to infant signals is an important determinant of the quality of children's attachment; such sensitivity or responsivity typically has been assessed as a general component of the caregiver's interactional style.

In the present study, we focused on a particular feature of the caregiver's interactive style and investigated the importance of a particular kind of sensitivity, namely, maternal facial contingency to infant emotional expressions. Assuming that facial expressions are reliable and valid indices of infant states, we predicted that the mother's specific affective responses to her child's specific emotional signals—as an affectively charged form of dialogic interaction—would have a material effect on the development of both emotion expression and attachment. The early interactive exchanges of caregivers and infants are more than merely a form of nonverbal communication; they are affective imperatives that elicit mutual accommodation. This is illustrated by the work of Haviland and Lelwica (1987), who found that 10-week-old infants exposed to simulations of maternal anger, sadness, and happiness responded in an organized manner that revealed the differential effect of the particular affective properties of the mothers' communications.

Both the sheer level of maternal contingent facial responding and the more qualitative, affect-specific nature of her dialogic response early in infancy appeared to affect subsequent socioemotional development. As to the former, infants who had experienced extremely high rates of contingency were more likely to be insecurely (avoidantly) attached at 2 years. (For similar findings, see Belsky et al., 1984; and Isabella, Belsky, & von Eye, in press.) Why should this relation obtain, and what might an infant exposed to high rates of contingency experience at the affective level?

We know from previous laboratory research that infants exposed to intense looming objects act fearful and show avoidant responses (Malatesta, 1985) and that, when exposed to frightening toys, having control over stimulus exposure reduces fear whereas lack of such control amplifies it (Gunnar, 1980). It thus seems likely that extremely high rates of maternal contingency in close face-to-face play—a situation that is both highly salient and virtually inescapable—is experienced by the infant as unpleasant and aversive. It is also reasonable to hypothesize that such experiences produce a disengagement from the caregiver that functions as a means of self-protection from the disturbing effects of anxiety. Tomkins (1962) described fear as an emotion that is particularly "physiologically toxic" and noted that young infants have only the most primitive means of protecting themselves against such toxicity. This, in his view, explains the relatively late emergence of fear in the child's affective repertoire and reliance on escape and avoidance strategies. Tomkins's formulations appear supported by both proximal and distal evidence contained within the present study—that is, by the decrease in smiling during interaction in the early infancy sessions and by the avoidant responses during reunions at 2 years.

Although the developmental consequences appear nonoptimal, we think it important to view the infant's reaction to high contingency as a form of adaptive accommodation. We do not know as yet what consequences may follow from fear that is not regulated or avoided. If Tomkins is right, there may actually be some early built-in protective measures that guard the child against prolonged exposure to its own affect. The experience of fear may be gated out very early, while it is still in mild form, before it has a chance to produce toxic effects. If so, this would help explain why instances of facial fear expressions, especially the full template version, are rarely seen in children (Campos et al., 1983) and why the existence of fear and anxiety can be gauged only either inferentially or by the subtlest of facial cues. As a methodological note, we suggest that future investigators of discrete emotions who aim to capture instances of fear or anxiety score this affect on the basis of enhanced vigilance, bodily signs such as freezing or a reduction in activity level, and, in the case of older children, lip biting and possibly vocal expressions of fear. With respect to this last, note Thompson, Leger, Walker, and Garbin's (1988) recent demonstration that infant cries can encode a variety of affective and need states that can be differentially interpreted by adult listeners.

Children whose distress signals were either ignored or responded to in a generally insensitive manner by the mother in early infancy showed more anger and distress during the 22-month reunion episodes. We can perhaps refer to these early affectively compromised dialogues as instances of what the philosopher Martin Buber (1973) referred to as *Vergegnung* or "mismeeting." That such early mismeetings should be related to later difficulties in managing separations and reunions is not surprising in the light of Tomkins's (1962, 1963) theoretical model of affect socialization. Tomkins suggested that the classic principles of learning theory might not apply in the expected way, in that, rather than leading to extinction of the behavior, ignoring negative affect could lead to its monopolization in the repertoire. It is through assisting the child in the sympathetic experience and reduction of negative affect and by showing integrity with respect to their own feelings, behaviors, and ideology that parents can best avoid such an outcome.

Our data lend support to Tomkins's formulations. Overstimulation by the mother (i.e., extremely high contingency) during face-to-face play seems to qualify as an insensitive behavior, as does ignoring young infants' pain and sadness expressions and displaying mock surprise to their anger. Furthermore, mothers who had the highest levels of contingency also showed fewest reciprocating gazes with their children at age 2 years and more positive affect (both more interest and more joy) during the second reunion— but not during play—than moderately contingent mothers. The elevated positive affect display during postseparation reunion suggests a masking of other, more negative feelings, a phenomenon directly relevant to Tomkins's thesis that a parent's integrity of feeling, behavior, and ideology is an important aspect of successful socialization of children's negative affect.

Having touched on the issue of affective organizations, we turn now to a discussion of personality development.

On the Use of Attachment and Discrete Emotions Approaches in the Study of Personality Development

Earlier, we emphasized the similarities between the theories of attachment and discrete emotions; we now discuss their differences and evaluate their potential to provide alternative yet mutually informative sources of insight into personality development.

First, it is helpful to recall that, as it relates to early development, attachment theory is concerned basically with one core aspect of feeling—that of security or insecurity. Individual differences in personality types are similarly organized within the framework of differing qualities of felt security. As already indicated, this approach has been impressively useful in describing meaningful differences in behavioral organization and in predicting adaptive and maladaptive behaviors later in development. However, the range of personality types that can be reliably described in terms of differential predictive validity—typically two (secure/insecure), sometimes three (A, B, and C)—falls somewhat short of early expectations that each of the original eight attachment subtypes would show predictive validity (Campos et al., 1983; Lamb, Thompson, Gardner, Charnov, & Estes, 1984; Malatesta, in press). Success with the predictive validity of the latest major grouping factor—D—is also mixed (see, e.g., Bretherton et al., in press; Cassidy, in press; and Kaplan, 1984). Moreover, predictions based on attachment typologies are most relevant to assessments of behavioral competence in interpersonal contexts and of working models of interpersonal relationships.

Beyond these important distinctions, we must ask whether grouping children by some factor other than the quality of their attachment to the caregiver might have a broader, longer, and more specific predictive reach with respect to individual differences in personality functioning. Ideally, such a grouping factor should permit making more precise predictions about children's future expressive behavior, their perceptual biases, how they might interpret ambiguous social events, their reactions to stressors, their ability to introspect about feelings, and so on. The attachment literature, especially the most recent work on internal working models (Bretherton, 1987, in press), is increasingly moving in the direction of specifying differential functioning in these domains of behavior, although the most robust differentiation of personality types remains mainly that between secure and insecure attachment types (A and C groups combined) or between avoidantly attached (A type alone) and securely attached children (all B subtypes combined).

It is our hypothesis that differential prediction tends not to proceed beyond the important but limited distinctions between maladaptive and adaptive and between emotionally mature and immature behaviors (Malatesta, in press) because the attachment distinction indexes two ends of a broad, dimensional axis of hedonic tone, that is, negative versus positive affect. In general, insecurely attached children are more emotionally negative than securely attached children, as was borne out in the present investigation. (For similar data and views, see Thompson & Lamb, 1984.) Another factor is that sizes of most attachment studies are relatively small and C and D types are not very well represented in nonclinical samples, thus rendering validation of subgroups problematic. We believe that, applied to a large enough sample, a discrete emotions analysis might furnish evidence of differential and affect-specific characteristics of the various attachment classification subgroupings. In fact, in a recent paper (Malatesta & Wilson, 1988), we reviewed evidence suggesting that A2 babies are particularly fearful, C2s particularly sad, and C1s particularly angry. Had we had enough children of each particular type in the present investigation, we would have attempted to confirm the existence of such patterns with our discrete emotions analysis. (There were only three C children and too few in each A subtype to permit balancing for gender, birth status, and contingency.)

This is not to indicate that attachment subtypes should be reducible to discrete emotion profiles. In retrospect and from the vantage point of having compared videorecords of various children, it appears that, although discrete emotional organizations may overlap with attachment groupings, the two are not synonymous—nor, for theoretical reasons, would one expect them to be. What struck us most in these viewings, however, was the coherence and reliability of individual patterns of affect expression. For instance, some children appeared to be organized around the emotion of anger in that they had a very low threshold for frustration and were set off by the slightest provocation. Others showed a fear organization, as exemplified by a pronounced tendency to freeze under conditions of stress. Some tended to weep sadly and passively, while others seemed extremely shy. Still others showed a fear/anger organization, and so on. We believe that selecting groups of children who show such differentiated organizations and assessing how this grouping factor fares in terms of longitudinal prediction may be particularly productive in future research. In fact, the potential of this approach is already apparent in the work of Kagan and his colleagues (Garcia-Coll et al., 1984; Kagan et al., 1984) with respect to their longitudinal investigations of "behaviorally inhibited" (fearful/shy) children.

From a theoretical perspective, a one-to-one mapping of discrete emotion organizations onto attachment subtypes would not be expected. First, although the attachment construct implies affect as an essential motivational substrate for attachment-related behaviors, the attachment system, postulated to be an evolved, adapted behavioral system, is devoted to guaranteeing general survival rather than meeting specific kinds of adaptational demands. Second, as a goal-directed system, it is essentially and monolithically oriented toward maintaining homeostasis, that is, a balance between security (attachment) needs and exploratory needs. Securely attached children achieve such a balance, while insecurely attached children attempt to satisfy their attachment needs in a context of conflict, and this impedes exercise of the exploratory instincts that promote personal growth. To illustrate, the early goal of the attachment system is the maintenance of physical proximity to the caregiver, especially under conditions of threat. However, if proximity itself is experienced as aversive (because, e.g., the caregiver is too overstimulating or rejecting), the need to obtain physical proximity and the need to avoid its aversive concomitants place the child in a bind that jeopardizes the achievement of a proper balance between attachment and exploratory needs.

In contrast, the affective system—by which we mean the entire range of fundamental emotions, each distinguished by unique phenomenological, motivational, and behavioral properties—is another organ of individual adaptation that has both a broader and a more differentiated mission. With respect to the motivational element, Tomkins (1962) referred to the affective system as *the* primary motivational system in humans, one whose general property is that of amplifying the drive system. In fact, in what he believed to be one of his most important insights into the function of the affect system and its relation to drive, Tomkins maintained that drive is a "paper tiger" that derives its appearance of urgency and compellingness only from its co-assembly with the affect system.

Particularly germane to the present discussion is the fact that, as an informational signal to the self and others, each fundamental emotion is associated with different functional properties as well as with a specific, goal-relevant set of behaviors (Malatesta, in press; Malatesta & Wilson, 1988). For example, the emotion of fear, which is elicited under conditions of perceived danger, functions within the self-system to identify threat and to promote flight or attack; its function in the interpersonal system is as a signal of submission that may be instrumental in warding off attack. In the case of shyness, the elicitor is the perception that the self is the focus of intense scrutiny. Its function within the self-system is to produce behavior that protects the self against further violations of privacy; within the interpersonal system it functions to inform others of the signaler's need for privacy. Yet another emotion, anger, is elicited by frustration of goals. Its function within the self-system is to mobilize the self so as to effect removal of barriers or sources of frustration; interpersonally, however, it serves as a warning of impending attack or aggression. Similar specifications are made with respect to all the other fundamental emotions identified by discrete emotions theory.

In examining the functional properties of the primary emotions (Malatesta & Wilson, 1988), one of the striking aspects of the system is the diversity of goal-relevant behaviors that it contains and the flexibility that follows from access to differing modes of coping. The emotion system can adapt to a variety of threats and incentives and does so in a nonmonolithic way; different emotions are elicited under different circumstances, and the affective responses are specific to specific adaptive demands.

The emotion system is operative during the formation of the attachment bond as well as in its expression. But it is not limited in either manifestation or usefulness to the attachment relationship or its representations (Bretherton, 1987). Emotions are elicited in a variety of situations, and, although these commonly involve interactions and relationships with other people, they are not exclusive to interactional contexts. Anger may be elicited equally well when a door sticks, or when the car does not start in the morning, or if the temperature and humidity get too high.

Despite the inherent flexibility and generality of the affect system, it is also subject to structuralization within the personality (Tomkins, 1963). Almost all major affect theories (including that of Tomkins, which was described in some detail in Chap. I) maintain that affective organizations play a central role in differentiating among personalities, and several writers have implied that affective organizations may operate in a trait-like way to bias a range of psychological functions. This intuitively appealing idea, as well as a proposed developmental model of how such affective organizations/biases may be established initially and of the mechanisms by which they become consolidated over time, is discussed elsewhere (Malatesta, in press; Malatesta & Wilson, 1988). The only point we will make here is that these biases are seen as forged within the same relational context in which attachment is formed; as such, it cannot but be the case that some overlap will prevail between attachment and discrete emotions analyses of emotional development. Nevertheless, we suggest that functionalist analyses of children's discrete emotions afford a valuable tool in research on socioemotional development, one that has the potential to contribute information beyond that afforded by the attachment approach. Such analyses can help determine just how great the overlap between the heuristics of differential emotions theory and those of attachment really is; concomitantly, the use of procedural paradigms beyond that of the Strange Situation for exploring individual differences in personality will provide additional information on the specificity that each heuristic has to offer.

TABLE A1

PATTERNS OF EXPRESSIVE BEHAVIOR OF MOTHERS AND THEIR INFANTS
DURING PLAY AND REUNION

		AGE 2½ MONTHS				
	Play			Reunion		
	Emotion	*M*	SD	Emotion	*M*	SD
Mothers:						
Rank:						
1	Joy	8.50	3.01	Joy	8.04	4.70
2	Interest	5.31	2.77	Interest	5.40	4.62
3	Surprise	1.27	2.97	Surprise	1.31	3.23
4	Sadness	.84	1.53	Sadness	1.01	2.37
5	Knit brow	.64	.77	Anger	.98	2.35
6	Anger	.52	.83	Knit brow	.65	1.19
7	Pressed lips	.00	.00	Pressed lips	.00	.00
Children:						
Rank:						
1	Knit brow	4.12	2.90	Knit brow	4.16	3.99
2	Joy	3.57	2.93	Joy	3.51	4.02
3	Interest	2.60	2.57	Anger	3.45	4.50
4	Anger	2.09	2.85	Sadness	2.97	4.53
5	Sadness	1.69	2.08	Interest	1.78	2.45
6	Surprise	.51	.75	Surprise	.33	.67
7	Pressed lips	.00	.00	Pressed lips	.00	.00
		AGE 5 MONTHS				
Mothers:						
Rank:						
1	Joy	8.43	3.17	Joy	7.39	4.38
2	Interest	4.22	2.54	Interest	3.88	3.58
3	Surprise	1.21	1.78	Surprise	.94	1.95
4	Knit brow	.48	.86	Knit brow	.65	1.47
5	Sadness	.30	.63	Sadness	.47	1.20
6	Pressed lips	.30	.43	Anger	.29	.57
7	Anger	.26	.57	Pressed lips	.26	.43

	AGE 5 MONTHS					
	Play			Reunion		
	Emotion	*M*	SD	Emotion	*M*	SD
Children:						
Rank:						
1	Joy	3.93	3.42	Knit brow	3.26	3.08
2	Knit brow	2.94	2.74	Joy	3.08	3.39
3	Interest	2.92	2.06	Interest	2.86	3.06
4	Sadness	1.26	1.66	Sadness	2.43	3.31
5	Anger	1.11	1.68	Anger	1.92	2.74
6	Surprise	.89	1.62	Surprise	.61	1.38
7	Pressed lips	.02	.08	Pressed lips	.00	.00
	AGE 7½ MONTHS					
Mothers:						
Rank:						
1	Joy	8.73	2.77	Joy	7.54	4.92
2	Interest	4.66	2.70	Interest	4.31	4.00
3	Surprise	.98	1.10	Surprise	1.59	2.65
4	Knit brow	.51	.82	Knit brow	.80	1.68
5	Sadness	.34	.63	Anger	.40	.94
6	Pressed lips	.25	.42	Sadness	.36	1.11
7	Anger	.21	.39	Pressed lips	.22	.76
Children:						
Rank:						
1	Joy	5.88	3.03	Knit brow	3.52	3.52
2	Interest	5.01	2.92	Joy	3.48	3.33
3	Knit brow	2.99	2.51	Anger	3.04	3.54
4	Sadness	1.65	2.01	Interest	2.75	3.69
5	Anger	.85	1.05	Sadness	2.68	3.47
6	Surprise	.71	1.03	Surprise	.83	2.81
7	Pressed lips	.24	.45	Pressed lips	.00	.00

NOTE.—All emotions are expressed as percentages of seconds in episode.

TABLE A2

SAMPLE SIZES FOR TWO-FACTOR INTERACTIONS (within Cell) AND MAIN EFFECTS (Marginals) FOR PLAY, REUNION 1, AND REUNION 2

A. PLAY ANOVAs

ATTACHMENT × GENDER

	Female	Male	Total
Insecure	13	10	23
Secure	13	22	35
Total	26	32	58

CONTINGENCY LEVEL × GENDER

	Female	Male	Total
Low	8	12	20
Moderate	6	13	19
High	12	7	19
Total	26	32	58

BIRTH STATUS × GENDER

	Female	Male	Total
Preterm	6	12	18
Full term	20	20	40
Total	26	32	58

CONTINGENCY LEVEL × BIRTH STATUS

	Preterm	Full Term	Total
Low	5	15	20
Moderate	6	13	19
High	7	12	19
Total	18	40	58

BIRTH STATUS × ATTACHMENT

	Insecure	Secure	Total
Preterm	6	12	18
Full term	17	23	40
Total	23	35	58

CONTINGENCY LEVEL × ATTACHMENT

	Insecure	Secure	Total
Low	9	11	20
Moderate	4	15	19
High	10	9	19
Total	23	35	58

TABLE A2 (*Continued*)

B. REUNION 1 ANOVAs

ATTACHMENT × GENDER

	Female	Male	Total
Insecure	12	10	22
Secure	12	20	32
Total	24	30	54

BIRTH STATUS × GENDER

	Female	Male	Total
Preterm	6	12	18
Full term	18	18	36
Total	24	30	54

BIRTH STATUS × ATTACHMENT

	Insecure	Secure	Total
Preterm	6	12	18
Full term	16	20	36
Total	22	32	54

CONTINGENCY LEVEL × GENDER

	Female	Male	Total
Low	7	11	18
Moderate	6	12	18
High	11	7	18
Total	24	30	54

CONTINGENCY LEVEL × BIRTH STATUS

	Preterm	Full Term	Total
Low	5	13	18
Moderate	6	12	18
High	7	11	18
Total	18	36	54

CONTINGENCY LEVEL × ATTACHMENT

	Insecure	Secure	Total
Low	9	9	18
Moderate	4	14	18
High	9	9	18
Total	22	32	54

C. REUNION 2 ANOVAs

ATTACHMENT × GENDER

	Female	Male	Total
Insecure	11	9	20
Secure	10	18	28
Total	21	27	48

CONTINGENCY LEVEL × GENDER

	Female	Male	Total
Low	6	9	15
Moderate	6	12	18
High	9	6	15
Total	21	27	48

BIRTH STATUS × GENDER

	Female	Male	Total
Preterm	5	10	15
Full term	16	17	33
Total	21	27	48

CONTINGENCY LEVEL × BIRTH STATUS

	Preterm	Full Term	Total
Low	4	11	15
Moderate	6	12	18
High	5	10	15
Total	15	33	48

BIRTH STATUS × ATTACHMENT

	Insecure	Secure	Total
Preterm	6	9	15
Full term	14	19	33
Total	20	28	48

CONTINGENCY LEVEL × ATTACHMENT

	Insecure	Secure	Total
Low	8	7	15
Moderate	4	14	18
High	8	7	15
Total	20	28	48

TABLE A3

MEANS AND STANDARD DEVIATIONS OF MATERNAL EXPRESSION VARIABLES SHOWN IN PLAY, REUNION 1, AND REUNION 2 DURING WAVE 4 OBSERVATIONS (Infant Age 22 Months)

	GENDER		BIRTH STATUS		ATTACHMENT		MATERNAL CONTINGENCY LEVEL		
	Male	Female	Preterm	Term	Insecure	Secure	Low	Moderate	High
Total reciprocated gazing:									
Play	3.4 (2.0)	4.4 (2.9)	3.7 (3.2)	4.0 (2.1)	3.9 (2.8)	3.9 (2.2)	4.5 (2.7)	4.1 (2.2)	3.3 (2.1)
Reunion 1	3.4 (2.3)	3.9 (2.2)	3.8 (1.8)	3.8 (2.5)	3.9 (2.1)	3.5 (2.4)	3.1 (2.3)	3.3 (2.3)	4.1 (2.2)
Reunion 2	3.4 (2.6)	3.9 (2.3)	2.2 (1.8)	4.2 (2.5)	3.3 (2.4)	3.8 (2.6)	3.5 (2.5)	3.5 (2.3)	3.7 (2.5)
Total positive emotion:									
Play	7.1 (3.1)	8.8 (2.8)	7.6 (3.1)	8.0 (3.1)	7.5 (2.7)	8.2 (3.3)	7.4 (3.3)	8.1 (2.7)	8.2 (3.1)
Reunion 1	4.6 (3.3)	4.8 (2.3)	5.5 (3.9)	4.3 (2.2)	4.5 (2.4)	4.8 (3.2)	5.1 (3.5)	3.2 (2.0)	5.7 (2.4)
Reunion 2	4.3 (3.4)	5.1 (2.9)	2.9 (2.9)	5.4 (3.0)	4.8 (2.9)	4.5 (3.4)	5.3 (3.7)	3.5 (2.7)	5.5 (2.7)
Interest:									
Play	1.5 (1.6)	2.0 (1.9)	1.7 (2.0)	1.7 (1.7)	1.8 (1.9)	1.7 (1.7)	1.7 (1.8)	1.8 (1.9)	1.8 (1.7)
Reunion 1	1.5 (1.7)	1.8 (1.4)	2.0 (1.8)	1.4 (1.4)	1.4 (1.2)	1.8 (1.8)	1.8 (1.9)	1.2 (1.5)	1.8 (1.2)
Reunion 2	1.1 (1.5)	1.3 (1.0)	.6 (.8)	1.6 (1.4)	1.5 (1.5)	1.2 (1.2)	1.5 (1.6)	.9 (1.1)	1.5 (1.3)
Joy:									
Play	5.4 (2.5)	6.4 (2.4)	5.6 (2.5)	5.9 (2.5)	5.4 (1.6)	6.1 (3.0)	5.3 (2.3)	6.0 (2.6)	6.2 (2.7)
Reunion 1	3.0 (2.3)	3.0 (1.9)	3.3 (1.7)	2.8 (2.7)	3.0 (1.8)	2.9 (1.8)	3.2 (2.5)	2.0 (1.6)	3.7 (1.8)

	4.0 (1.8)	2.6 (2.3)	3.5 (3.0)	3.4 (2.5)	3.2 (2.3)	3.8 (2.4)	2.2 (2.2)	3.8 (2.0)	2.9 (2.7)
Reunion 2	4.0 (1.8)	2.6 (2.3)	3.5 (3.0)	3.4 (2.5)	3.2 (2.3)	3.8 (2.4)	2.2 (2.2)	3.8 (2.0)	2.9 (2.7)
Surprise:									
Play	.2 (.3)	.3 (.4)	.4 (.7)	.4 (.6)	.3 (.4)	.4 (.6)	.3 (.3)	.3 (.6)	.2 (.4)
Reunion 1	.2 (.2)	.0 (.2)	.1 (.4)	.1 (.3)	.1 (.3)	.1 (.3)	.2 (.3)	.0 (.1)	.1 (.4)
Reunion 2	.0 (.0)	.0 (.1)	.3 (.5)	.2 (.4)	.1 (.2)	.0 (.2)	.1 (.5)	.0 (.1)	.2 (.4)
Total negative emotion:									
Play	.8 (.7)	.7 (.8)	.5 (.6)	.8 (.8)	.4 (.5)	.6 (.6)	.7 (.9)	.8 (.7)	.5 (.7)
Reunion 1	.8 (1.1)	.7 (1.1)	.5 (.5)	.7 (1.1)	.5 (.7)	.6 (.8)	.7 (1.1)	.7 (1.0)	.5 (.9)
Reunion 2	.4 (.9)	.6 (.8)	.4 (1.0)	.6 (.8)	.4 (1.0)	.5 (1.0)	.4 (.6)	.4 (.9)	.5 (1.0)
Sadness:									
Play	.1 (.3)	.1 (.2)	.1 (.2)	.1 (.2)	.1 (.3)	.1 (.3)	.1 (.2)	.1 (.3)	.1 (.2)
Reunion 1	.1 (.3)	.1 (.3)	.1 (.2)	.1 (.3)	.1 (.2)	.1 (.3)	.0 (.1)	.1 (.3)	.1 (.2)
Reunion 2	.0 (.0)	.1 (.2)	.0 (.2)	.1 (.2)	.0 (.2)	.1 (.2)	.0 (.1)	.1 (.0)	.1 (.2)
Anger:									
Play	.0 (.0)	.0 (.2)	.0 (.1)	.0 (.1)	.0 (.0)	.0 (.1)	.0 (.1)	.0 (.1)	.0 (.1)
Reunion 1	.0 (.0)	.0 (.1)	.1 (.4)	.0 (.1)	.1 (.4)	.0 (.2)	.1 (.3)	.1 (.4)	.0 (.1)
Reunion 2	.0 (.0)	.0 (.1)	.0 (.0)	.1 (.1)	.0 (.0)	.0 (.1)	.0 (.0)	.0 (.0)	.0 (.1)
Knit brow:									
Play	.3 (.5)	.2 (.4)	.1 (.3)	.3 (.5)	.1 (.2)	.2 (.3)	.3 (.5)	.2 (.4)	.2 (.4)
Reunion 1	.4 (.1)	.2 (.8)	.1 (.3)	.4 (.9)	.1 (.3)	.2 (.7)	.4 (.8)	.3 (.8)	.3 (.7)

TABLE A3 (Continued)

	Gender		Birth Status		Attachment		Maternal Contingency Level		
	Male	Female	Preterm	Term	Insecure	Secure	Low	Moderate	High
Knit brow:									
Reunion 2	.3	.2	.2	.2	.1	.3	.2	.3	.2
	(.6)	(.6)	(.5)	(.6)	(.3)	(.7)	(.4)	(.6)	(.7)
Pressed lips:									
Play	.2	.4	.3	.2	.2	.3	.2	.3	.3
	(.3)	(.5)	(.5)	(.4)	(.4)	(.5)	(.4)	(.4)	(.5)
Reunion 1	.1	.3	.2	.2	.2	.2	.1	.2	.3
	(.3)	(.5)	(.3)	(.4)	(.5)	(.3)	(.2)	(.4)	(.5)
Reunion 2	.2	.2	.1	.3	.2	.2	.2	.2	.2
	(.5)	(.6)	(.3)	(.6)	(.6)	(.4)	(.6)	(.4)	(.6)
Total expressivity:									
Play	7.6	9.6	8.3	8.6	7.9	8.9	7.9	8.7	9.0
	(3.2)	(3.0)	(3.4)	(3.2)	(2.8)	(3.4)	(3.6)	(2.8)	(3.2)
Reunion 1	5.1	5.5	6.2	4.8	4.9	5.5	5.6	3.8	6.4
	(3.6)	(2.5)	(4.1)	(2.5)	(2.7)	(3.5)	(3.6)	(2.8)	(2.5)
Reunion 2	4.8	5.6	3.3	5.9	5.2	5.0	5.8	3.9	5.9
	(2.7)	(3.1)	(2.9)	(3.4)	(2.4)	(3.6)	(4.1)	(3.1)	(2.9)

NOTE.—Values represent frequencies of behaviors that have been converted to percentages to take into account variable length of episodes, that is, number of expression frequencies per total number of seconds in episode. Standard deviations are shown in parentheses.

90

TABLE A4

MEANS AND STANDARD DEVIATIONS OF INFANT EXPRESSION VARIABLES SHOWN IN PLAY, REUNION 1, AND REUNION 2 DURING WAVE 4 OBSERVATIONS (Age 22 Months)

	GENDER		BIRTH STATUS		ATTACHMENT		MATERNAL CONTINGENCY LEVEL		
	Male	Female	Preterm	Term	Insecure	Secure	Low	Moderate	High
Total gazing at mother:									
Play	7.9	11.2	9.6	9.3	10.3	8.8	10.2	11.4	8.2
	(4.1)	(8.6)	(8.2)	(5.9)	(7.9)	(5.7)	(7.1)	(8.2)	(3.8)
Reunion 1	9.4	11.1	12.2	9.2	11.1	9.5	9.5	9.9	10.7
	(6.1)	(8.1)	(8.1)	(6.3)	(7.1)	(6.9)	(7.3)	(6.9)	(6.8)
Reunion 2	8.5	11.6	7.5	10.9	7.0	11.9	9.9	9.7	9.8
	(9.2)	(7.9)	(6.3)	(9.6)	(5.9)	(10.0)	(8.4)	(9.2)	(9.2)
Total positive emotion:									
Play	10.1	9.5	9.3	10.1	10.5	9.4	9.5	11.1	8.9
	(4.4)	(4.1)	(4.8)	(4.0)	(4.7)	(3.9)	(4.7)	(3.8)	(4.0)
Reunion 1	7.0	6.7	5.6	7.5	6.7	7.0	5.8	8.3	6.6
	(4.4)	(4.1)	(3.6)	(4.4)	(4.3)	(4.3)	(4.6)	(4.7)	(3.0)
Reunion 2	7.1	7.6	5.0	8.0	9.1	6.0	8.7	6.1	7.2
	(4.9)	(5.0)	(5.0)	(4.6)	(4.9)	(4.5)	(5.2)	(4.3)	(5.3)
Interest:									
Play	4.2	3.2	3.8	3.7	4.0	3.6	3.6	4.8	2.9
	(2.7)	(2.9)	(2.7)	(2.9)	(3.7)	(2.1)	(2.9)	(2.7)	(2.7)
Reunion 1	4.7	4.1	3.5	4.9	4.4	4.4	3.7	5.1	4.4
	(3.1)	(3.0)	(2.0)	(3.4)	(3.5)	(2.8)	(3.0)	(3.5)	(2.7)
Reunion 2	3.9	4.0	2.8	4.5	5.2	3.0	4.8	3.4	3.7
	(3.3)	(3.3)	(2.8)	(3.3)	(3.4)	(2.9)	(2.9)	(3.3)	(3.5)
Joy:									
Play	5.1	5.6	4.8	5.6	5.7	5.1	5.1	5.6	5.3
	(2.5)	(2.1)	(3.1)	(1.9)	(2.2)	(2.4)	(2.4)	(2.2)	(2.4)
Reunion 1	2.1	2.5	1.8	2.5	2.0	2.4	2.0	2.9	1.9
	(1.8)	(1.6)	(1.7)	(1.7)	(1.5)	(1.8)	(1.8)	(1.8)	(1.3)

TABLE A4 (Continued)

	GENDER		BIRTH STATUS		ATTACHMENT		MATERNAL CONTINGENCY LEVEL		
	Male	Female	Preterm	Term	Insecure	Secure	Low	Moderate	High
Joy:									
Reunion 2	2.7 (2.2)	3.3 (2.6)	2.0 (2.6)	3.5 (2.1)	3.4 (2.4)	2.6 (2.3)	3.1 (2.8)	2.6 (1.9)	3.1 (2.5)
Surprise:									
Play	.8 (1.2)	.7 (.6)	.7 (.9)	.8 (1.0)	.8 (.9)	.7 (.9)	.8 (1.0)	.7 (.9)	.7 (.8)
Reunion 1	.2 (.3)	.1 (.4)	.2 (.5)	.1 (.2)	.3 (.4)	.2 (.2)	.1 (.3)	.3 (.4)	.3 (.3)
Reunion 2	.5 (.7)	.2 (.5)	.2 (.6)	.0 (.0)	.5 (.7)	.4 (.6)	.8 (.5)	.1 (.3)	.4 (.5)
Total negative emotion:									
Play	1.7 (1.2)	2.8 (2.7)	2.0 (1.6)	2.2 (2.3)	2.8 (2.1)	1.7 (1.9)	2.3 (2.4)	1.6 (1.4)	2.6 (2.2)
Reunion 1	4.1 (4.1)	4.6 (3.8)	3.5 (3.4)	4.7 (4.2)	3.8 (3.0)	4.7 (4.5)	5.0 (4.8)	3.4 (2.8)	4.7 (3.9)
Reunion 2	3.1 (3.3)	4.2 (3.1)	3.0 (3.7)	3.9 (3.0)	3.3 (2.5)	3.8 (3.7)	3.5 (3.2)	3.9 (3.9)	3.4 (2.4)
Sadness:									
Play	.4 (.7)	.7 (1.5)	.3 (.5)	.6 (1.3)	.4 (.6)	.6 (1.4)	.9 (1.8)	.2 (.4)	.4 (.5)
Reunion 1	1.5 (2.0)	1.0 (1.8)	.8 (1.1)	1.6 (2.2)	1.0 (1.3)	1.5 (2.3)	2.1 (2.8)	1.1 (1.4)	.7 (.8)
Reunion 2	1.1 (2.0)	1.4 (1.9)	1.1 (2.0)	1.3 (1.9)	.8 (1.2)	1.6 (2.2)	1.6 (2.0)	1.3 (2.4)	.8 (1.1)

Anger:									
Play	.1 (.2)	.3 (.6)	.3 (.7)	.1 (.3)	.2 (.3)	.1 (.5)	.1 (.3)	.3 (.7)	.1 (.2)
Reunion 1	.6 (1.4)	.8 (1.3)	.7 (1.3)	.7 (1.3)	.4 (.7)	.9 (1.6)	.4 (.5)	.5 (.9)	1.1 (2.0)
Reunion 2	.7 (1.4)	1.1 (1.3)	1.0 (1.7)	.8 (1.2)	.9 (1.4)	.9 (1.4)	.6 (1.1)	1.0 (1.6)	1.0 (1.4)
Knit brow:									
Play	.7 (.8)	1.3 (1.7)	.8 (1.0)	1.1 (1.4)	1.6 (1.7)	.6 (.7)	.8 (.9)	.8 (.9)	1.4 (1.9)
Reunion 1	1.6 (2.1)	2.7 (2.1)	1.7 (2.0)	2.3 (2.2)	2.1 (2.2)	2.1 (2.1)	2.2 (2.4)	1.5 (1.4)	2.6 (2.4)
Reunion 2	.9 (1.2)	1.4 (1.5)	.4 (.4)	1.5 (1.5)	1.4 (1.5)	.9 (1.2)	1.0 (1.1)	1.1 (1.7)	1.2 (1.3)
Pressed lips:									
Play	.4 (.7)	.5 (.9)	.6 (1.1)	.4 (.6)	.6 (.8)	.4 (.8)	.5 (.7)	.2 (.4)	.7 (1.0)
Reunion 1	.3 (.6)	.2 (.5)	.3 (.6)	.2 (.5)	.3 (.6)	.2 (.5)	.3 (.5)	.1 (.3)	.3 (.8)
Reunion 2	.3 (.6)	.3 (.5)	.4 (.6)	.2 (.6)	.3 (.7)	.3 (.5)	.3 (.7)	.4 (.6)	.3 (.3)
Total expressivity:									
Play	11.7 (4.5)	12.2 (5.4)	11.3 (5.6)	12.3 (4.6)	13.3 (5.4)	11.1 (4.4)	11.8 (5.9)	11.6 (4.3)	11.5 (4.7)
Reunion 1	11.1 (5.4)	11.4 (5.6)	9.0 (4.6)	12.2 (5.6)	10.5 (5.8)	11.5 (5.2)	10.7 (6.5)	11.6 (4.9)	11.2 (5.1)
Reunion 2	10.2 (5.4)	11.7 (4.7)	8.0 (5.0)	12.2 (4.7)	12.3 (4.9)	9.8 (5.1)	12.2 (5.0)	10.0 (4.7)	10.6 (5.7)

NOTE.—Values represent frequencies of behaviors that have been converted to percentages to take into account variable length of episodes, that is, number of expression frequencies per total number of seconds in episode. Standard deviations are in parentheses.

TABLE A5

MEANS AND STANDARD DEVIATIONS FOR SIGNIFICANT ANOVA INTERACTION
EFFECTS: MOTHERS' DATA

Dependent Variable	Effect	Gender	Attachment	M	SD
Play session:					
Joy	Gender ×	Female	Insecure	5.60	1.80
	attachment	Female	Secure	7.30	2.80
		Male	Insecure	5.20	1.80
		Male	Secure	5.50	2.90
		Birth			
Reunion 1:		**Status**			
Total expressivity	Attachment ×	Preterm	Insecure	4.40	3.50
	birth status	Preterm	Secure	7.00	4.30
		Term	Insecure	5.20	2.40
		Term	Secure	4.60	2.50
Total positive emotion ..	Attachment ×	Preterm	Insecure	4.00	3.30
	birth status	Preterm	Secure	6.30	4.00
		Term	Insecure	4.60	2.10
		Term	Secure	4.00	2.20
Joy	Attachment ×	Preterm	Insecure	2.20	1.80
	birth status	Preterm	Secure	3.90	2.90
		Term	Insecure	3.40	1.80
		Term	Secure	2.40	1.70

TABLE A6

MEANS AND STANDARD DEVIATIONS FOR SIGNIFICANT INTERACTION EFFECTS:
CHILDREN'S DATA

Dependent Variable	Gender	Contingency	M	SD
Play session:				
Total reciprocated gazing ..	Male	Low	6.9	2.30
	Male	Moderate	8.4	3.10
	Male	High	9.1	4.10
	Female	Low	14.8	3.20
	Female	Moderate	16.6	4.10
	Female	High	6.2	2.10
Interest	Male	Low	5.2	2.30
	Male	Moderate	3.0	2.20
	Male	High	4.25	3.70
	Female	Low	4.4	3.70
	Female	Moderate	4.0	3.60
	Female	High	2.1	1.50
		Attachment		
Pressed lips	Male	Insecure	.90	.90
	Male	Secure	.20	.40
	Female	Insecure	.40	.60
	Female	Secure	.60	.90

TABLE A6 (*Continued*)

Dependent Variable	Birth Status	Attachment	*M*	SD
Reunion 2:				
Total expressivity	Preterm	Insecure	8.7	4.90
	Preterm	Secure	7.5	5.20
	Term	Insecure	13.9	4.00
	Term	Secure	10.9	4.80
Total positive emotion	Preterm	Insecure	4.9	5.40
	Preterm	Secure	5.1	5.10
	Term	Insecure	10.8	3.70
	Term	Secure	6.5	4.40
Interest	Preterm	Insecure	2.90	2.70
	Preterm	Secure	2.70	3.00
	Term	Insecure	6.20	3.20
	Term	Secure	3.20	2.80
	Gender	**Contingency**		
Total expressivity	Male	Low	10.5	5.30
	Male	Moderate	10.8	5.00
	Male	High	8.3	6.70
	Female	Low	14.8	3.20
	Female	Moderate	8.3	4.00
	Female	High	12.1	4.70
Interest	Male	Low	4.2	3.30
	Male	Moderate	4.3	3.30
	Male	High	2.4	3.40
	Female	Low	5.6	2.20
	Female	Moderate	1.6	2.60
	Female	High	4.4	3.60
	Birth Status			
Joy	Preterm	Low	3.4	1.20
	Preterm	Moderate	1.1	1.00
	Preterm	High	.40	.50
Total positive emotion	Preterm	Low	8.9	7.13
	Preterm	Moderate	5.4	3.70
	Preterm	High	1.4	1.10
	Term	Low	8.9	4.70
	Term	Moderate	6.5	4.60
	Term	High	10.0	3.80

REFERENCES

Ainsworth, M. D. S. (1967). *Infancy in Uganda: Infant care and the growth of love.* Baltimore: Johns Hopkins University Press.

Ainsworth, M. D. S. (1972). Attachment and dependency: A comparison. In J. Gewirtz (Ed.), *Attachment and dependency* (pp. 97–137). Washington, DC: Winston.

Ainsworth, M. D. S. (1977). Attachment theory and its utility in cross-cultural research. In P. H. Leiderman, S. R. Tulkin, & A. Rosenfeld (Eds.), *Culture and infancy: Variations in the human experience* (pp. 49–67). New York: Academic.

Ainsworth, M. D. S., Bell, S. M., & Stayton, D. J. (1971). Individual differences in the Strange Situation behavior of one-year olds. In H. R. Schaffer (Ed.), *The origins of human social relations* (pp. 17–57). New York: Academic.

Ainsworth, M. D. S., Blehar, M. C., Waters, E., & Wall, S. (1978). *Patterns of attachment: A psychological study of the Strange Situation.* Hillsdale, NJ: Erlbaum.

Ainsworth, M. D. S., & Wittig, B. A. (1969). Attachment and exploratory behavior of one-year-olds in a strange situation. In B. M. Foss (Ed.), *Determinants of infant behavior* (Vol. 4, pp. 111–136). London: Methuen.

Arend, R., Gove, F., & Sroufe, L. A. (1979). Continuity of individual adaptation from infancy to kindergarten: A predictive study of ego-resiliency and curiosity in preschoolers. *Child Development, 50,* 950–959.

Bakeman, R., & Dorval, B. (in press). The distinction between sampling independence and empirical independence in sequential analysis. *Behavioral Assessment.*

Barnard, K. E., & Bee, H. L. (1982, April). *Developmental changes in maternal interactions with term and preterm infants.* Paper presented at the International Conference on Infant Studies, Austin, TX.

Bates, J. (1987). Temperament in infancy. In J. D. Osofsky (Ed.), *Handbook of infant development* (2d ed., pp. 1101–1149). New York: Wiley.

Beckwith, L. (1985, April). *Patterns of attachment in preterm infants.* Paper presented at the biennial meeting of the Society for Research in Child Development, Toronto.

Bell, S. M., & Ainsworth, M. D. S. (1972). Infant crying and maternal responsiveness. *Child Development, 43,* 1171–1190.

Belsky, J., Rovine, M., & Taylor, D. G. (1984). The Pennsylvania Infant and Family Development Project: 3. The origins of individual differences in infant-mother attachment: Maternal and infant contributions. *Child Development, 55,* 718–728.

Bowlby, J. (1969). *Attachment and loss: Vol. 1. Attachment.* New York: Basic.

Bowlby, J. (1973). *Attachment and loss: Vol. 2. Separation.* New York: Basic.

Bowlby, J. (1980). *Attachment and loss: Vol. 3. Loss, sadness and depression.* New York: Basic.

Brazelton, T. B., Koslowski, B., & Main, M. (1974). The origins of reciprocity: The early mother-infant interaction. In M. Lewis & L. A. Rosenblum (Eds.), *The effect of the infant on its caregiver* (pp. 49–77). New York: Wiley.

Bretherton, I. (1985). Attachment theory: Retrospect and prospect. In I. Bretherton & E. Waters (Eds.), *Growing points of attachment theory and research* (pp. 3–35). *Monographs of the Society for Research in Child Development*, **50**(1–2, Serial No. 209).

Bretherton, I. (1987). New perspectives on attachment relations: Security, communication, and internal working models. In J. Osofsky (Ed.), *Handbook of infant development* (2d ed., pp. 1061–1100). New York: Wiley.

Bretherton, I. (in press). Communication and internal working models: Their role in the development of attachment relationships. In R. A. Thompson (Ed.), R. A. Dienstbier (Series Ed.), *Socioemotional development* (Nebraska Symposium on Motivation, Vol. **36**). Lincoln: University of Nebraska Press.

Bretherton, I., Ridgeway, D., & Cassidy, J. (in press). The role of internal working models in the attachment relationship: Can it be studied in three-year-olds? In M. Greenberg, D. Cicchetti, & E. M. Cummings (Eds.), *Attachment in the pre-school years: Theory, research, and intervention.* Chicago: University of Chicago Press.

Bretherton, I., & Waters, E. (Eds.). (1985). Growing points of attachment theory and research. *Monographs of the Society for Research in Child Development*, **50**(1–2, Serial No. 209).

Bridges, K. M. B. (1931). *The social and emotional development of the pre-school child.* London: Kegan Paul, Trench, Trubner.

Bridges, K. M. B. (1932). Emotional development in early infancy. *Child Development*, **3**, 324–341.

Buber, M. (1973). *Meetings.* LaSalle, IL: Open Court.

Buehler, C. (1933). Social development. In L. Carmichael (Ed.), *Handbook of child psychology* (pp. 374–416). New York: Wiley.

Buehler, K. (1929). *Die Krise der Psychology.* Jena: Gustav Fiscer.

Bugental, D. E., Love, L. R., & Gianetto, R. M. (1971). Perfidious feminine faces. *Journal of Personality and Social Psychology*, **17**, 314–318.

Cairns, R. (1983). The emergence of developmental psychology. In W. Kessen (Ed.), P. H. Mussen (Series Ed.), *Handbook of child psychology: Vol. 1. History, theory, and methods* (pp. 41–102). New York: Wiley.

Campos, J. J., & Barrett, K. C. (1984). Toward a new understanding of emotions and their development. In C. E. Izard, J. Kagan, & R. B. Zajonc (Eds.), *Emotions, cognition, and behavior* (pp. 229–263). New York: Cambridge University Press.

Campos, J. J., Barrett, K. C., Lamb, M. E., Goldsmith, H. H., & Stenberg, C. (1983). Socioemotional development. In M. M. Haith (Ed.), P. H. Mussen (Series Ed.), *Handbook of child psychology: Vol. 2. Infancy and developmental psychobiology* (pp. 783–916). New York: Wiley.

Camras, L. A. (1988, April). Darwin revisited: An infant's first emotional facial expressions. In H. Oster (Chair), *Emotional expressions in infants: New perspectives on an old controversy.* Symposium conducted at the International Conference on Infant Studies, Washington, DC.

Cannon, W. B. (1927). The James-Lange theory of emotions: A critical examination and an alternative theory. *American Journal of Psychology*, **39**, 106–124.

Carmichael, L. (1971). The onset and early development of behavior. In P. H. Mussen (Ed.), *Carmichael's manual of child psychology* (pp. 447–563). New York: Wiley.

Cassidy, J. (in press). Theoretical and methodological considerations in the study of attachment and the self in young children. In M. Greenberg, D. Cicchetti, & E. M. Cummings (Eds.), *Attachment in the pre-school years: Theory, research, and intervention.* Chicago: University of Chicago Press.

Cassidy, J., & Kobak, R. (in press). Avoidance and its relation to other defensive processes. In J. Belsky & T. Nezworski (Eds.), *Clinical implications of attachment.* Hillsdale, NJ: Erlbaum.

Chodorow, N. (1978). *The reproduction of mothering: Psychoanalysis and the sociology of gender.* Berkeley: University of California Press.

Cohn, J. F., & Tronick, E. Z. (1983). Three-month-old infants' reaction to simulated maternal depression. *Child Development,* **54,** 185–193.

Cole, P. M. (1983, April). *Preschoolers' emotional display rules: Grin and bear it?* Paper presented at the biennial meeting of the Society for Research in Child Development, Detroit.

Cole, P. M. (1985). Display rules and the socialization of affective displays. In G. Zivin (Ed.), *The development of expressive behavior: Biology-environment interactions* (pp. 269–290). New York: Academic.

Darwin, C. R. (1872). *The expression of emotions in man and animals.* London: John Murray.

Demos, V. (1982a). Facial expressions of infants and toddlers. In T. Field & A. Fogel (Eds.), *Emotion and early interaction* (pp. 127–160). Hillsdale, NJ: Erlbaum.

Demos, V. (1982b). The role of affect in early childhood: An exploratory study. In E. Z. Tronick (Ed.), *Social interchange in infancy: Affect, cognition, and communication* (pp. 20–39). Baltimore: University Park Press.

Demos, V. (1986). Crying in early infancy: An illustration of the motivational function of affect. In T. B. Brazelton & M. Yogman (Eds.), *Affect and early infancy* (pp. 39–73). New York: Ablex.

Denham, S. A. (1985, April). *Maternal emotional responsiveness and its relation to toddlers' social-emotional competence and expression of emotion.* Paper presented at the biennial meeting of the Society for Research in Child Development, Beverly Hills, California.

Ekman, P. (1982). *Emotion in the human face* (2d ed.). Cambridge: Cambridge University Press.

Ekman, P. (1984). Expression and the nature of emotion. In K. Scherer & P. Ekman (Eds.), *Approaches to emotion* (pp. 329–343). Hillsdale, NJ: Erlbaum.

Ekman, P., & Friesen, W. V. (1975). *Unmasking the face: A guide to recognizing emotions from facial clues.* Englewood Cliffs, NJ: Prentice-Hall.

Emde, R. (1980a). Toward a psychoanalytic theory of affect: 1. The organizational model and its propositions. In S. I. Greenspan & G. H. Pollack (Eds.), *The course of life* (Vol. **1,** pp. 63–82). Bethesda, MD: National Institute of Mental Health Printing Office.

Emde, R. (1980b). Toward a psychoanalytic theory of affect: 2. Emerging models of emotional development in infancy. In S. I. Greenspan & G. H. Pollack (Eds.), *The course of life* (Vol. **1,** pp. 85–112). Bethesda, MD: National Institute of Mental Health Printing Office.

Emde, R. N., Gaensbauer, T. J., & Harmon, R. J. (1976). Emotional expression in infancy: A biobehavioral study. *Psychological Issues,* **10,** 1–193.

Emde, R. N., Kligman, D. H., Reich, J. H., & Wade, T. (1978). Emotional expression in infancy: 1. Initial studies of social signaling and an emergent model. In M. Lewis & L. Rosenblum (Eds.), *The development of affect* (pp. 125–148). New York: Plenum.

Epstein, S. (1980). The stability of behavior: 2. Implications of psychological research. *American Psychologist,* **35,** 790–806.

Field, T. (1987). Affective and interactive disturbances in infants. In J. Osofsky (Ed.), *Handbook of infant development* (2d ed., pp. 972–1005). New York: Wiley.

Frodi, A. (1983). Attachment behavior and sociability with strangers in premature and full-term infants. *Infant Mental Health Journal,* **4,** 13–22.

Frodi, A. M., Lamb, M. E., Leavitt, L. A., & Donovan, W. L. (1978). Fathers' and mothers' responses to infant smiles and cries. *Infant Behavior and Development,* **1,** 187–198.

Frodi, A., & Thompson, R. (1985). Infants' affective responses in the Strange Situation: Effects of prematurity and of quality of attachment. *Child Development,* **56,** 1280–1290.

Gaensbauer, T. J., & Harmon, R. J. (1982). Attachment behavior in abused/neglected and premature infants. In R. N. Emde & R. J. Harmon (Eds.), *The development of attachment and affiliative systems* (pp. 263–289). New York: Plenum.

Gaensbauer, T. J., Harmon, R. J., Culp, A. M., Schultz, L. A., van Doornick, W. J., & Dawson, P. (1985). Relationships between attachment behavior in the laboratory and the caretaking environment. *Infant Behavior and Development,* **8,** 355–369.

Garcia-Coll, C., Kagan, J., & Reznick, J. S. (1984). Behavioral inhibition in young children. *Child Development,* **55,** 1005–1019.

Goldberg, S., Brachfeld, S., & DiVitto, B. (1980). Feeding, fussing, and play: Parent-infant interaction in the first year as a function of prematurity and perinatal medical problems. In T. M. Field (Ed.), *High-risk infants and children* (pp. 133–153). New York: Academic.

Grossmann, K., Grossmann, K. E., Spangler, G., Suess, G., & Unzner, L. (1985). Maternal sensitivity and newborns' orientation responses as related to quality of attachment in Northern Germany. In I. Bretherton & E. Waters (Eds.), *Growing points of attachment theory and research* (pp. 233–256). *Monographs of the Society for Research in Child Development,* **50**(1–2, Serial No. 209).

Grossmann, K. E. (1981, April). Infant and social environment interaction: Epistemological considerations behind the ethological approach. In W. R. Charlesworth (Chair), *Back to nature, changing paradigms, and child ethology ten years later.* Symposium conducted at the biennial meeting of the Society for Research in Child Development, Boston.

Grossmann, K. E. (1988). Longitudinal and systemic approaches in the study of biological high-risk and low-risk groups. In M. Rutter (Ed.), *The power of longitudinal data: Studies of risk and protection factors for psychological disorders* (pp. 38–156). London: Cambridge University Press.

Grossmann, K. E., Grossmann, K., & Ernst, R. (in preparation). *Emotional communication in securely and avoidantly attached infant-parent dyads.* University of Regensburg, Lehrstuhl fuer Psychologie.

Grossmann, K. E., Grossmann, K., & Schwan, A. (1986). Capturing the wider view of attachment: A reanalysis of Ainsworth's Strange Situation. In C. E. Izard & P. B. Read (Eds.), *Measuring emotions in infants and children* (Vol. **2,** pp. 124–171). New York: Cambridge University Press.

Gunnar, M. (1980). Control, warning signals and distress in infancy. *Developmental Psychology,* **16,** 281–289.

Hall, J. A. (1978). Gender effects in decoding nonverbal cues. *Psychological Bulletin,* **85,** 845–857.

Haviland, J. M., & Lelwica, M. (1987). The induced affect response: 10-week-old infants' responses to three emotion expressions. *Developmental Psychology,* **23,** 17–104.

Haviland, J. M., & Malatesta, C. Z. (1981). The development of sex differences in nonverbal signals: Fallacies, facts, and fantasies. In C. Mayo & N. Henley (Eds.), *Gender and non-verbal behavior* (pp. 183–208). New York: Springer.

Hollingshead, A. B. (1975). *Four-factor index of social status.* New Haven, CT: Yale University Press.

Isabella, R. A., Belsky, J., & von Eye, A. (in press). The origins of infant-mother attachment: An examination of interactional synchrony during the infant's first year. *Developmental Psychology.*

Izard, C. E. (1971). *The face of emotion.* New York: Appleton-Century-Crofts.

Izard, C. E. (1977). *Human emotions.* New York: Plenum.

Izard, C. E. (1979). *The maximally discriminative facial movement coding system (MAX)*. Newark: University of Delaware, Instructional Resources Center.

Izard, C. E. (1984). Emotion-cognition relationships and human development. In C. E. Izard, J. Kagan, & R. B. Zajonc (Eds.), *Emotions, cognition, and behavior* (pp. 38–72). New York: Cambridge University Press.

Izard, C. E., Hembree, E. A., Dougherty, L. M., & Spizzirri, C. L. (1983). Changes in facial expressions of 2 to 19 month old infants following acute pain. *Developmental Psychology, 19,* 418–426.

Izard, C. E., Hembree, E. A., & Huebner, R. R. (1987). Infants' emotion expressions to acute pain: Developmental change and stability in individual differences. *Developmental Psychology, 23,* 105–113.

Izard, C. E., Huebner, R., Risser, D., McGinnes, G., & Dougherty, L. (1980). The young infant's ability to produce discrete emotion expressions. *Developmental Psychology, 16,* 132–140.

Izard, C. E., & Malatesta, C. Z. (1987). Perspectives on emotional development: 1. Differential emotions theory of early emotional development. In J. D. Osofsky (Ed.), *Handbook of infant development* (2d ed., pp. 494–554). New York: Wiley.

James, W. (1884). What is emotion? *Mind, 4,* 188–204.

Jonas, R. (1986). *A component analysis of the emotionality of type A behavior pattern.* Unpublished doctoral dissertation, New School for Social Research, New York.

Kagan, J. (1978). *The growth of the child.* New York: Norton.

Kagan, J. (1984). The idea of emotion in human development. In C. E. Izard, J. Kagan, & R. Zajonc (Eds.), *Emotions, cognition, and behavior* (pp. 38–72). New York: Cambridge University Press.

Kagan, J., Reznick, J. S., Clarke, C., Snidman, N., & Garcia-Coll, C. (1984). Behavioral inhibition to the unfamiliar. *Child Development, 55,* 2212–2225.

Kaplan, N. (1984). *Internal representations of separation experience in 6-year-olds: Related to actual experiences of reparation.* Unpublished master's thesis, University of California, Berkeley.

Kaye, K. (1979). Thickening thin data: The maternal role in developing communication and language. In M. Bullowa (Ed.), *Before speech* (pp. 191–206). Cambridge: Cambridge University Press.

Kochanska, G. (1987, April). *Socialization of young children's anger by well and depressed mothers.* Paper presented at the biennial meeting of the Society for Research in Child Development, Baltimore.

Lamb, M. E., Thompson, R. A., Gardner, W. P., Charnov, E. L., & Estes, D. (1984). Security of infantile attachment as assessed in the "Strange Situation": Its study and biological interpretation. *Behavioral and Brain Sciences, 7,* 127–171.

Langsdorf, P., Izard, C., Rayias, M., & Hembree, E. (1983). Interest expression, visual fixation, and heart rate changes in 2- to 8-month-old infants. *Developmental Psychology, 19,* 375–386.

Lewis, M. (1988, April). The socialization of emotions. In S. Friedman & J. Campos (Chairs), *National Institutes of Child Health and Development Workshop on the Socialization of Emotion,* Bethesda, MD.

Lewis, M., & Brooks, J. (1978). Self-knowledge and emotional development. In M. Lewis & L. A. Rosenblum (Eds.), *The development of affect* (pp. 205–226). New York: Plenum.

Lewis, M., & Michalson, L. (1983). *Children's emotions and moods.* New York: Plenum.

Maccoby, E. E., & Jacklin, C. N. (1974). *The psychology of sex differences.* Stanford, CA: Stanford University Press.

Main, M. (1973). *Play, exploration and competence as related to child-adult attachment.* Unpublished doctoral dissertation, Johns Hopkins University, Baltimore.

Main, M., Kaplan, N., & Cassidy, J. (1985). Security in infancy, childhood, and adulthood: A move to the level of representation. In I. Bretherton & E. Waters (Eds.), *Growing points of attachment theory and research* (pp. 66–104). *Monographs of the Society for Research in Child Development,* **50**(1–2, Serial No. 209).

Main, M., Tomasini, L., & Tolan, W. (1979). Differences among mothers of infants judged to differ in security. *Developmental Psychology,* **15,** 472–473.

Malatesta, C. Z. (1981, April). *Separation stress and the differential signalling behaviors of male and female infants.* Paper presented at the meeting of the Eastern Psychological Association, New York.

Malatesta, C. Z. (1985). Developmental course of emotion expression in the human infant. In G. Zivin (Ed.), *The development of expressive behavior: Biology-environment interactions* (pp. 183–219). New York: Academic.

Malatesta, C. Z. (in press). The role of emotions in the development and organization of personality. In R. A. Thompson (Ed.), R. A. Dienstbier (Series Ed.), *Socioemotional development* (Nebraska Symposium on Motivation, Vol. **36**). Lincoln: University of Nebraska Press.

Malatesta, C. Z., Grigoryev, P., Lamb, C., Albin, M., & Culver, C. (1986). Emotion socialization and expressive development in preterm and full term infants. *Child Development,* **57,** 316–330.

Malatesta, C. Z., & Haviland, J. M. (1982). Learning display rules: The socialization of emotion expression in infancy. *Child Development,* **53,** 991–1003.

Malatesta, C. Z., & Izard, C. E. (1984). The facial expression of emotion: Young, middle-aged, and older adult expressions. In C. Z. Malatesta & C. E. Izard (Eds.), *Emotion in adult development* (pp. 253–273). Beverly Hills, CA: Sage.

Malatesta, C. Z., & Wilson, A. (1988). Emotion/cognition interaction in personality development: A discrete emotions, functionalist analysis. *British Journal of Social Psychology,* **27,** 91–112.

Manstead, A. S. R. (in press). Gender differences in emotion. In M. A. Gale & M. W. Eysenck (Eds.), *Handbook of individual differences: Biological perspectives.* Chichester: Wiley.

Matas, L., Arend, R., & Sroufe, L. A. (1978). Continuity of adaptation in the second year: The relationship between quality of attachment and later competence. *Child Development,* **49,** 547–556.

Mischel, W. (1968). *Personality and assessment.* New York: Wiley.

Miyake, K., Chen, S.-J., & Campos, J. J. (1985). Infant temperament, mother's mode of interaction, and attachment in Japan: An interim report. In I. Bretherton & E. Waters (Eds.), *Growing points of attachment theory and research* (pp. 276–297). *Monographs of the Society for Research in Child Development,* **50**(1–2, Serial No. 209).

Moran, G., & Symons, D. (1987, April). *Using sequential analyses to quantify maternal responsiveness in early mother-infant interactions.* Paper presented at the biennial meeting of the Society for Research in Child Development, Baltimore.

Oster, H. (1978). Facial expression and affect development. In M. Lewis & L. A. Rosenblum (Eds.), *The development of affect* (pp. 43–76). New York: Plenum.

Oster, H. (1984, April). *Signal value of smiling and brow knitting in infants.* Paper presented at the International Conference on Infant Studies, New York.

Plutchik, R. (1980). *Emotion: A psychoevolutionary synthesis.* New York: Harper & Row.

Saarni, C. (1979). Children's understanding of display rules for expressive behavior. *Developmental Psychology,* **15,** 424–429.

Sackett, G. P. (1979). The lag sequential analysis of contingency and cyclicity in behavioral interaction research. In J. Osofsky (Ed.), *Handbook of infant development* (1st ed., pp. 623–649). New York: Wiley.

Sackett, G. P. (1987). Analysis of sequential social interaction data: Some issues, recent developments, and a causal inference model. In J. Osofsky (Ed.), *Handbook of infant development* (2d ed., pp. 855–878). New York: Wiley.

Schwartz, G., & Izard, C. E. (1985). *Emotion expressions of seven- and fourteen-month-old infants to three-dimensional masks.* Unpublished manuscript, Medical College of Pennsylvania, Department of Psychiatry, Philadelphia.

Senn, M. J. E. (1975). Insights on the child movement in the United States. *Monographs of the Society for Research in Child Development, 40*(3–4, Serial No. 161).

Shiller, V. M., Izard, C. E., & Hembree, E. A. (1986). Patterns of emotion expression during separation in Strange-Situation procedure. *Developmental Psychology, 22,* 378–382.

Spitz, R. (1965). *The first year of life.* New York: International Universities Press.

Sroufe, L. A. (1979). Socioemotional development. In J. D. Osofsky (Ed.), *Handbook of infant development* (1st ed., pp. 462–516). New York: Wiley.

Stenberg, C., Campos, J., & Emde, R. (1983). The facial expression of anger in seven-month-old infants. *Child Development, 54,* 178–184.

Stern, D. N., Beebe, B., Jaffe, J., & Bennett, S. (1977). The infant's stimulus world during social interaction. In H. R. Schaffer (Ed.), *Studies on mother-child interaction* (pp. 44–69). London: Academic.

Stettner, L. J., & Loigman, G. (1983, April). *Emotion cues in baby faces as elicitors of functional reaction choices.* Paper presented at the biennial meeting of the Society for Research in Child Development, Detroit.

Suomi, S. (1985, July). *Contribution of studies on animal behavior to human developmental psychology.* Paper presented at the biennial meeting of the International Society for the Study of Behavioral Development, Tours.

Thompson, R. A., & Lamb, M. E. (1984). Assessing qualitative dimensions of emotional responsiveness in infants: Separation reactions in the Strange Situation. *Infant Behavior and Development, 7,* 423–445.

Thompson, R., Leger, D. W., Walker, J. A., & Garbin, C. P. (April, 1988). Infant cries as graded or discrete socioemotional signals. In H. Oster (Chair), *Emotional expression in infants: New perspectives on an old controversy.* Symposium conducted at the International Conference on Infant Studies, Washington, DC.

Tomkins, S. S. (1962). *Affect, imagery, consciousness: Vol. 1. The positive affects.* New York: Springer.

Tomkins, S. S. (1963). *Affect, imagery, consciousness: Vol. 2. The negative affects.* New York: Springer.

Van Izjendoorn, M. H., & Kroonenberg, Pieter M. (1987, April). *Cross-cultural patterns of attachment: A meta-analysis of the Strange Situation.* Paper presented at the biennial meeting of the Society for Research in Child Development, Baltimore.

Van Leishout, C. F. M. (1975). Young children's reactions to barriers placed by their mothers. *Child Development, 46,* 879–886.

Watson, J. B. (1919). *Psychology from the standpoint of a behaviorist.* Philadelphia: Lippincott.

Watson, J. B., & Morgan, J. J. (1917). Emotional reactions and psychological experimentation. *American Journal of Psychology, 28,* 161–174.

Watson, J. S. (1972). Reactions to response contingent stimulation in early infancy. *Merrill-Palmer Quarterly, 18,* 219–227.

Wilson, A., Passik, M. A., & Faude, J. P. (in press). Self-regulation and its failures. In J. Masling (Ed.), *Empirical studies in psychoanalytic theory.* Hillsdale, NJ: Erlbaum.

Winer, B. J. (1971). *Statistical principles in experimental design.* New York: McGraw-Hill.

Wolder, M. (1988). *Emotional exchange patterns between depressed mothers and their four- to six-*

year-old children. Unpublished doctoral dissertation, New School for Social Research, New York.

Zahn-Waxler, C., Cummings, E. M., McKnew, D. H., & Radke-Yarrow, M. (1984). Altruism, aggression and social interactions in young children with a manic depressive parent. *Child Development, 55,* 112–122.

Zivin, G. (1982). Watching the sands shift: Conceptualizing development of nonverbal mastery. In R. S. Feldman (Ed.), *Development of nonverbal behavior in children.* New York: Springer.

ACKNOWLEDGMENTS

This research was supported by a National Institute of Mental Health National Research Service Award (1F32MH08773-01) to the first author and a grant from the Foundation for Child Development (Young Scholars in Social and Affective Development Program). We thank all the mothers and children who so generously gave of their time (again and again) to participate in this study and the following students who assisted at various stages of data collection and analysis: Cathie Lamb, Patricia Grigoryev, Melanie Albin, Sharon Leak, and Michael Obuchowski. We also thank the two reviewers for their valuable critiques. Address all correspondence to Carol Z. Malatesta, Department of Psychology, Long Island University, 1 University Plaza, Brooklyn, NY 11201.

ON THE PSYCHOBIOLOGY OF EMOTIONS AND THEIR DEVELOPMENT

ALAN FOGEL AND MARK REIMERS

A developmental psychobiology of human emotions should encompass the neurophysiological bases of the emotions, their linkages to expressive behavior, the ontogenetic sequences through which emotions typically develop, and the influences of early experiences on individual differences in emotion and its expression. Malatesta, Culver, Tesman, and Shepard highlight all these important issues in their *Monograph* on the development of emotion expression during the first 2 years of life. In the following, we comment on the explicit and implicit theoretical assumptions made by the authors when interpreting their data with respect to the issues of developmental psychobiology outlined above.

The work reported in this *Monograph* is nothing short of a remarkable achievement. It is the first longitudinal study of normative trends in the development of discrete emotion expressions during the early years of life. It is comparable to the normative studies on motor, language, and cognitive development done more than 50 years ago. This near half-century lag confirms the authors' indictment of the field's commitment to emotion as a viable and important area of developmental research. Although there is little evidence that the study of the development of the emotions per se (i.e., apart from attachment and temperament research) is growing, this *Monograph* will serve to encourage those in the field of emotion research that the ontogenetic territory now has at least a few guideposts to assist future explorers.

Partial support for the preparation of this Commentary was provided by a National Institute of Health grant (HD21036) to Alan Fogel.

The opening section of this work is a masterful historical review of the theoretical and methodological traditions in the study of emotional development and could stand alone as a tutorial for students and scholars not acquainted with this area. The relations between emotions, on the one hand, and constructs such as attachment and temperament, on the other, are clearly articulated and should leave no doubt about the value of analyzing the contribution of the emotions to these and other organized behavior systems.

The authors demonstrate admirable expertise in the methodology of coding complex facial expressive patterns and keeping those codes in their appropriate sequential context during dyadic interaction. The authors' discussions of the statistical processing of data derived, not from independent instruments, but from sequential behavioral observations are among the most insightful treatments yet written on this subject. See, for example, the rationale for *not* doing the traditional combined MANOVA analysis in favor of treating each of the behavioral measures with separate ANOVAs.

How Are Emotion Expressions Linked to Emotion Experiences?

Given, then, a unique data set of high quality and a longitudinal correlational design, what can be said about these findings from the perspective of the developmental psychobiological issues raised in our opening paragraph? The first two of these issues—taken together—relate to Malatesta et al.'s hypothesis that infant facial expressions are an accurate reflection of the infant's emotional experiences. Because the data on newborns show facial expressions to be discretely organized response systems, the issue, according to the authors, is whether the discrete emotion expressions correspond to discrete emotion experiences. Discrete emotion theory is clear in this regard, postulating that neural firings and feedback from sensations generated by the neuromotor aspects of the facial movements conspire to create a unique emotional experience (Izard & Malatesta, 1987).

In the present *Monograph*, Malatesta et al. argue that their data support this view via "convergent, predictive, and 'contextual' evidence" (p. 73). Facial emotion expressions appear to correlate in expected ways with contemporaneous attachment classifications (i.e., avoidant children show more discrete anger and fear), declines in smiling during the first year were predictive of poor attachments later, and caregivers' inappropriate responses to the emotions thought to underlie the expressions led to deviant behavior later.

Because of the combination of efferent and afferent processes, each discrete facial expression is thought to correspond to a different internal experience. Even though the experiences associated with a smile may be different for infants than they are for adults, the authors envision a "pre-wired and preadapted" (p. 19) linkage in infants between expression and experience. The authors rightly contend that social learning alone, of the sort imagined by Lewis and Michalson (1983), for example, could not account for the results presented in this *Monograph*. Yet they are aware that social learning processes become increasingly important during the first 2 years as children learn to blend emotions, to disguise their feelings, or to use socially sanctioned expressions regardless of internal state.

If we assume that emotion and expression are prewired to begin with, and if we also observe that these linkages become altered via socialization processes, we are left with the theoretical task of explaining how experience imposes itself on those wirings. One way to solve the theoretical problem is to assume not only that the linkage is prewired but that its potential for modification is also prewired: "The neuromuscular component of the emotions system shows features of both innateness and modifiability. The innate features are directed by genetic programs that have built-in allowances for learning or developmental modifiability" (Izard & Malatesta, 1987, p. 505). The emotion-experience linkages are thought to be encoded in the limbic system and in the amygdala, hypothalamus, and ventral midbrain regions, while the modifiability is believed to be due to the maturation of the cortex and pyramidal motor system (Izard & Malatesta, 1987).

This localization of invariant "native" behavior in the limbic system and "acquired" behavior in modifications of the neocortex is presented without support. Might not the limbic system itself, composed of neurons not unlike those of the neocortex, undergo modification that is manifest in the observed differences in emotion experience between infancy and maturity? Malatesta et al. assume that emotional expression is modified developmentally only by voluntary inhibitory masking of some set of underlying and invariant expressions.

This conception of invariant emotional essences raises considerable obstacles for building a theory of development. For example, if emotions are taken to be the fundamental source of motivation, how is the voluntary inhibition of emotion expression to be explained? Voluntary inhibition itself seems to require a motivation that presumably would have to arise outside the fundamental set of discrete emotions. This theoretical contradiction arises under the assumption of a developmentally invariant set of emotions in the limbic system prewired to a discrete set of facial expressions.

If emotions are not prewired to facial expressions, what are the alternative theoretical explanations for the evidence cited by Malatesta et al.? Clearly experiential learning, although necessary, is not sufficient since neonatal facial expressions have some congruity with concurrent experiences, for example, the classic connection of disgust expressions to unpleasant tastes and smells (Steiner, 1979). An alternative constructivist perspective is provided by Barrett and Campos (1987). They claim that emotion experiences are linked not only to specific facial movements but to a "family" of related events, including vocalizations, physiological arousal, action tendencies, goals, and cognitions. In their view, there are "intrinsic but not invariant" (p. 557) links between the experience and the expression. Thus, even though some linkages between an emotion and its facial and vocalic expression are "prewired," these linkages need not always be activated, and other forms of expression can be learned and substituted.

The advantage of this approach is that it postulates a more fluid linkage between emotion and expression; in other words, if certain preferred pathways are not available to the infant—because of the current configuration of goals, arousal, and context—infants will find alternative pathways to expression. There are data to support this view, although they are sparse. Infants express emotions with their whole bodies, either in gross or in subtle movements of the legs, trunk, arms, and fingers. Thus, distress may be expressed by crying (Wolff, 1969), turning away of the head or the upper body (Stern, 1981), kicking (Thelen, 1979), or bringing the hands to the mouth (Fogel, 1985). A host of other action tendencies symptomatic of distress have been recorded anecdotally in case studies, such as lowering of the eyes, clenching the hands, and disorganized limb movement (Brazelton, Koslowski, & Main, 1974; Fogel, 1985; Papousek & Papousek, 1977; Trevarthen, 1977). Although Malatesta et al. recognize and code two nonemotional facial motor actions, they seem unwilling to recognize a large variety of alternative expressive pathways that may or may not be accompanied by facial expressions.

Both Barrett and Campos (1987) and Izard and Malatesta (1987) view emotions as transient experiences that may be manifested in one or several rather stereotyped ways. Both views would deny that the same experience may be expressed with different facial expressions. Surprisingly, some recent evidence seems to suggest that this may happen. Camras (1988) reports that her infant daughter often used facial expressions usually associated with distress, sadness, and anger interchangeably on different occasions in similar situations. The data in the current *Monograph* also seem to support a similar interpretation. Many of the findings showing significant relations with emotion categories were with frequencies of "total negative" and "total positive" rather than with specific discrete emotion categories. One wonders why such collapsed categories were even used in a study subscribing to a discrete emotion perspective. Could it be that these broad-based categories reflect an underlying equivalence between discrete emotions related by general hedonic tone? Thus, while the facial musculature is capable of producing discretely different organized patterns of action, the internal states may not be so clearly parsed.

There is convergent evidence on several fronts for such a viewpoint. On the one hand, there is an established tradition of attribution theory within social psychology suggesting that a variety of indices of emotional experience and even of such seemingly clear-cut experiences as pain and hunger can be manipulated to some extent by cognitive priming (Schacter, 1971). More recently within neuroscience, Skarda and Freeman (1987) have shown that electrophysiologically discrete states of the olfactory bulb are not reliably produced simply by chemically distinct smells. Rather, distinct forms of EEG are produced by the interaction of a number of components of the olfactory system, in a way that is not driven or determined simply by the incoming smell. Should we expect the more recently evolved and complex limbic system to act in a more stereotyped manner than the ancient olfactory system? Such is the notion of discrete emotional states, produced time after time as the same pattern of activity within the limbic system, a position implicit in differential emotions theory.

How can organisms select pathways for expression that are neither entirely prewired nor entirely determined by goal and function? If we abandon prewiring, how can we explain even the fact that anger, sadness, and distress expressions tend to occur more often than chance in contexts that are "negative" in hedonic tone or that similar negative situations produce kicking and hand-to-mouth behavior? The alternative to prewiring is to assume not that organized motor patterns are controlled from the top down by inputs from the central nervous system but that patterns emerge at the periphery of the body as muscles—able only to flex and extend—interact with each other via linkages across bones and joints and in the context of biomechanical forces (Thelen, Kelso, & Fogel, 1987).

Although Malatesta et al. allude to feedback from the facial muscles as part of emotional experience, they do not develop the idea in any detail. The question to address is what accounts for the observed discrete facial expressions? Is the organizer behind the scenes, deep within the brain, or up front, within the face itself? It is tempting to account for regularities in the observable world by positing a template in a realm inaccessible to current investigation. If we imagine that the actions of individual facial muscles are translated from processes that occur deep within the brain (such as the limbic system), then information present in the face reflects details of brain state. The occurrence of relatively few clearly differentiated facial expressions, out of a large number of possible facial expressions, is then very suggestive of the same number of well-differentiated brain states. The face would then truly be a "window into the soul."

We suggest, however, that the details of the organization of emotive facial expressions occur through local interactions among facial features and between facial muscles and cranial nerve nuclei, in the presence of relatively nonspecific information from the deeper brain. For example, consider what would happen to the infant's face if all the muscles were simultaneously stimulated to tense but no sensory feedback loops were engaged to set the level of tension. Then the strong lower jaw muscles would pull the mouth open, the orbicularis muscles around the mouth and the eyes would contract these features, but the face itself would not be rigid. The characteristic distress expression could arise, thus, not from detailed individual coding of various muscle actions but through the interaction of various muscle groups when all are receiving the same level of tonic stimulation. We suggest that the process of forming and maintaining all the characteristic emotive expressions in infancy may be similarly explained. The crucial evidence would be electromyograph (EMG) recordings of neonatal muscles in the process of forming these expressions. We would expect that through motor learning the older infant's muscles would assume more characteristically distinct EMG signatures after considerable practice with expression.

Our point is that we may not be able to read from the detailed expressions of the young infant's face back further than a general quality of muscle tone. The information about the brain available from muscle tone is not so detailed. Whether there is only one limbic system state that produces this kind of tensing or whether there are a number of such states, each as clearly distinct from each other as from other states, is knowledge not available to us from the face alone.

This view of emotion expressions as self-organizing dynamic systems—in which muscles participate in the production of organized action and are not mere recipients of instructions (Thelen et al., 1987)—does not assume preformed, functional, or final causes for developmental changes (Fogel, 1985; Fogel & Thelen, 1987). Rather, developmental changes arise when any of the participating components of the emotional system are changed. Thus, as muscles develop, new coordinations are possible. In addition, other components may enter into the system and alter the pathways and sequences of expression through other interactions with the environment such as parental socialization.

What Is the Effect of Experience on Emotional Development?

We turn now to the third and fourth psychobiological issues raised in our opening paragraph. How do the emotions develop, and what are the experiences that engender individual differences in emotion experience and expression? Malatesta et al. suggest that the ontogenetic sequence in which new emotions arise and differentiate is part of a "basic maturational trajectory" (p. 1). They assume that "the child develops certain self-regulatory processes as a function of maturation (e.g., through cortical inhibitory controls) and socialization experiences" (p. 7). Individual differences arise in part because of "innate differences in the predisposition to show certain patterns of emotional expression" (p. 23), including "behavioral inhibition" and temperament, and also because of different socialization experiences.

How does one interpret high correlations between ages for the same expressions? Why would individuals who show a great deal of distress at one age continue to show high levels of distress at a later age? Do such correlations indicate innate dispositional tendencies? In Malatesta et al.'s data, all the negative expressions for the infants showed a high degree of stability across most ages (waves), but the positive expressions were not stable. According to the authors, this suggests that there may be "innate dispositional tendencies" for negative affects, but not for positive ones, and that negative affect expressions may become more "readily consolidated" (p. 62). This latter term is not defined, but in the context it seems to refer to innate disposition.

On the other hand, wave-to-wave correlations were considerably higher for the mothers than for the children, "probably reflecting the greater degree of consolidation in expressive patterns that takes place by adulthood" (p. 62). In this latter context, consolidation suggests that stability is the result of experiences that take place over life-span development.

What do the authors mean to suggest here? Do high wave-to-wave correlations reflect innate dispositions that persist in the face of environmental variability? Or do these correlations represent the cumulative results of learning and experience? Surely, Malatesta et al. do not intend us to embrace either horn of this old dilemma, yet such dichotomies are naturally forced on us by the commitment to invariant emotional essences that underlies differential emotions theory.

The fact is that stability correlations tell us nothing about the source of individual differences. Stability can arise because behavior remains intrinsically stable or because a stable environment scaffolds a stable performance. Just because infant stability correlations occur earlier in life than stability correlations for adults does not mean that the former correlations reflect innate dispositions and the latter the cumulative effects of experience.

In lieu of experimental manipulations of the sort done to study developmental process in other species, human developmentalists must often be content with between-individual variance and cross-time stability. The problem is not in the use of such methods but in how we interpret them. While the theoretical orientation of Malatesta et al. revolves around the expression and modification of brain-behavior linkages *within* the individual, their correlational data can yield information only about the statistical structure of *between*-individual groupings. As Nunnally (1982) points out, "In studying individual differences, one does not really investigate persons but rather the statistical spaces between them . . . but somehow in the process, the individual and people as a group can become lost" (p. 146).

Just because we can predict an outcome does not mean that we understand its origins. Before Copernicus, astronomers had mapped regularities of planetary motion and were able to predict the seasons, the moon's phases, and eclipses. They interpreted these regularities in terms of supernatural forces, laws of pure form, and a moral commitment to a geocentric universe. Constructs that prove adequate for a particular predictive task are not thereby validated as general explanatory principles. We would like to engage Malatesta et al. in a questioning of the philosophical commitments inherent in the constructs of differential emotions theory, in the hope of finding such more general principles.

References

Barrett, K. C., & Campos, J. J. (1987). Perspectives on emotional development: 2. A functionalist approach to emotions. In J. D. Osofsky (Ed.), *Handbook of infant development* (2d ed., pp. 555–578). New York: Wiley.

Brazelton, T. B., Koslowski, B., & Main, M. (1974). The origins of reciprocity. In M. Lewis & L. Rosenblum (Eds.), *The effect of the infant on its caregiver.* New York: Wiley.

Camras, L. A. (1988, April). Darwin revisited: An infant's first emotional facial expressions. In H. Oster (Chair), *Emotional expressions in infants: New perspectives on an old controversy.* International Conference on Infant Studies, Washington, DC.

Fogel, A. (1985). Coordinative structures in the development of expressive behavior in early infancy. In G. Zivin (Ed.), *The development of expressive behavior: Biology-environment interactions* (pp. 249–267). New York: Academic.

Fogel, A., & Thelen, E. (1987). Development of early expressive and communicative action: Reinterpreting the evidence from a dynamic systems perspective. *Developmental Psychology,* **23,** 747–761.

Izard, C. E., & Malatesta, C. Z. (1987). Perspectives on emotional development: 1. Differential emotions theory of early emotional development. In J. D. Osofsky (Ed.), *Handbook of infant development* (2d ed., pp. 494–554). New York: Wiley.

Lewis, M., & Michalson, L. (1983). *Children's emotions and moods.* New York: Plenum.

Nunnally, J. C. (1982). The study of human change: Measurement, research strategies, and methods of analysis. In B. Wolman (Ed.), *Handbook of developmental psychology* (pp. 133–148). Englewood Cliffs, NJ: Prentice-Hall.

Papousek, H., & Papousek, M. (1977). Mothering and the cognitive headstart: Psychobiological considerations. In H. R. Schaffer (Ed.), *Studies of mother-infant interaction* (pp. 63–88). London: Academic.

Schacter, S. (1971). *Emotion, obesity, and crime.* New York: Academic.

Skarda, C., & Freeman, W. (1987). How brains make chaos in order to make sense of the world. *Behavior and Brain Sciences,* **10,** 161–195.

Steiner, J. E. (1979). Human facial expressions in response to taste and smell stimulation. In H. Reese & L. P. Lipsitt (Eds.), *Advances in child development and behavior* (Vol. **13,** pp. 257–293). New York: Academic.

Stern, D. N. (1981). The development of biologically determined signals of readiness to communicate, which are language "resistant." In R. Stark (Ed.), *Language behavior in infancy and early childhood* (pp. 45–62). New York: Elsevier.

Thelen, E. (1979). Rhythmical stereotypes in normal human infants. *Animal Behavior,* **27,** 699–715.

Thelen, E., Kelso, J. A. S., & Fogel, A. (1987). Self-organizing systems and infant motor development. *Developmental Review, 7,* 39–65.

Trevarthen, C. (1977). Descriptive analysis of infant communicative behavior. In H. R. Schaffer (Ed.), *Studies of mother-infant interaction* (pp. 227–270). London: Academic.

Wolff, P. H. (1969). The natural history of crying and other vocalizations in early infancy. In M. Foss (Ed.), *Determinants of infant behavior* (Vol. **4,** pp. 81–109). London: Methuen.

SOME BASIC CONSIDERATIONS IN THE FIELD OF EXPRESSIVE BEHAVIOR DEVELOPMENT

GAIL ZIVIN

Malatesta and her colleagues have produced a remarkable longitudinal study of mother-child expressive interactions that provides a first rough outline of expressive/emotional development from age 2½ months through age 24 months for term and preterm infants of different attachment classifications. Making clever and sensible cuts in a potentially overwhelming data set, Malatesta et al. have presented a clear picture of important outcome patterns that, as they point out, is mostly consistent with predictions derived from attachment theory, differential emotions theory, and what is known about preterm infants' interactive tendencies.

It is crucial to Malatesta et al.'s study that 2½-month-olds have emotional states shown through facial expressions. Differential emotions theory, in which this work is grounded, supports this assumption by positing that physiology, expression, and subjective experience are organized into discrete emotions at birth. This assumption is one of central dispute in the current field of expressive/emotional development. Fortunately, there is a new scholarly review including empirical evidence for and against it (Camras, Malatesta, & Izard, in press). The review shows sufficiently equal support both for and against this position that good sense requires the provisional acceptance of Malatesta et al.'s assumption and serious examination of their study.

I greatly appreciate the comments that Willis F. Overton and Laurence J. Stettner contributed to the Commentary's preparation. A more extensive version of this Commentary, introducing the basic definitions, issues, and classic references of expressive development, is available on request.

A further proposition that is also fundamental to their study, and crucial but controversial in the field, is that infants' facial expressions can be reliably discerned by mothers and coded by observers. In my Commentary, I outline a variety of suppositions that this proposition entails, consider how Malatesta et al. are affected by the problems posed by each, and then propose a hypothesis to reconcile contradictory data on infant expression perception. The issues to be discussed can be grouped under two general assertions: that the codes used in this study are adequate to capture infant emotions and that mothers and infants can reliably discern each others' emotional face signals.

Adequate Codes

To be informative, Malatesta et al.'s observed infant expressions must approximate their assumed emotion meanings and must be adequately captured by the coding system in use. At least three notions are at issue here: that relations between observable actions and internal emotion conditions can be validated with current technology; that the particular coding system they use has been shown to index such internal conditions; and that no additional information, such as context, is needed to judge the meaning of facial expressions.

Asserting the importance of code validation is not to deny that expert intuitive judgments often yield exquisite insights (see Field & Fogel, 1982; and Tronick, 1982); moreover, such intuitions reflect the integration of many dimensions of information, which tend to be fragmented by instruments with specified criteria. The problem lies in finding standards by which to recognize accurate intuitions. Casual guesses may be avoided by keeping observations on the level of descriptions of apparent social function (Charlesworth, 1982; Zivin, 1977b) or interactional structure (Kendon, 1982) or by setting up naturalistic or quasi-naturalistic experiments requiring differential behavioral outcomes of the expressive behavior (Camras, 1977; Klinnert, 1984; Zivin, 1977a). However, these less intuitive approaches may fail to convey the human meaning of complex patterns.

Validation's technical limits.—Straightforward convergent validation of codes requires correlation of codes with independent measurement of internal emotional conditions. Confidence in such measurement is restricted by strong disagreements on the definition of those internal conditions (e.g., whether they necessarily involve distinctive physiological states) as well as by limitations of emotion assessment methods. Thus, *self-report* of emotion is problematic for adults and out of the question for infants; *judgment* techniques attribute emotion by judging nonverbal behavior and hence are circular for validating observational codes; *clinical rating scales* may reflect traits rather than state durations; initial findings of *physiological patterns* for emotion (heart rate, temperature, EMG, EEG) show rather gross distinctions, often only between groups of emotions (e.g., Ekman, Levenson, & Friesen, 1983); and *inductions* (emotion elicitation situations), used as indicators of emotion presence, reduce to whichever of these four emotion-measuring techniques had been used in piloting. Thus, straightforward convergent validity strategies are questionable, and the best we can do is accumulate diverse studies that offer indirect predictive validity (Landy, 1986, offers guidelines for this).

Validity of MAX emotion codes for infants.—Young infants pose special coding problems: they have fleeting expressions, and their faces differ from adults' because of baby fat, different proportions, and lack of wrinkles and teeth. The MAX system (Izard, 1980) was developed on and taught with adult faces, but it has been widely applied to and validated on infant faces. Although the recent modification of MAX (called Affex) is taught with infant exemplars and a new Baby FACS (based on the widely used adult Facial Action Coding System; Ekman & Friesen, 1978) modifies criteria for infants (Oster & Rosenstein, 1988), these refinements occurred while Malatesta et al. were already collecting their data. All this opens the question of whether MAX was adequate to code their infants.

Although there is no direct way to assess this issue, high intercoder reliabilities can be taken to indicate adequate codes (assuming that inadequate criteria would prevent coders' agreement and that no systematic biases are present). Several authors do report high intercoder reliabilities (76%–98% on emotion categories: Izard & Dougherty, 1982; Izard, Hembree, & Huebner, 1987; Malatesta et al., this volume; and 88%–91% on muscle action categories: Haviland & Lelwica, 1987), suggesting that MAX can indeed be adequately applied to infants. Further indirect support follows from several studies that have been able to apply MAX or Affex to infants as young as age 2½ months, variously finding faces of interest, anger, sadness, joy, and fleeting fear and disgust (Haviland & Lelwica, 1987; Izard, 1980; Izard et al., 1987). It should be noted that Oster and Nagel (1988) have recently questioned the comprehensiveness and consensuality of the emotion discriminations made by MAX on infant faces, but whether these criticisms should affect confidence in MAX use is not yet known.

Validity of the meaning of partial patterns.—The intuitively appealing interpretations of the partial patterns coded by Malatesta et al. must be viewed as only provisional. Relying on the facial feedback hypothesis, the authors assume that knit brow for mild transitional distress, compressed lips for suppressed anger, and lip biting for suppressed fear are examples of developmentally advanced, minimizing expressions that reflect the infant's attempts to regulate emotional intensity. Although the age distributions of these patterns are believable, concurrence on these interpretations is still lacking: a number of references are cited for a variety of knit brow interpretations, none for lip biting, and one in adults for compressed lips. Malatesta et al.'s hypotheses suggest an additional function for the general developmental trend to expressive miniaturization and deserve further testing.

The authors' interpretation of infants' gaze direction differs depending on context: it is seen as positive in most situations but as wariness in insecurely attached boys on reunion. Although this disjunction may be accurate, Malatesta et al.'s post hoc interpretations—while plausible—fall short of citing the needed general criterion for attributing different meanings to behaviorally identical gazes. This and the knit brow interpretations are among the very few instances of the authors' sheer hunches that remain unsupported by additional data.

Sufficiency of facial information in the absence of context.—Malatesta et al. are well aware that facial emotion expressions alone cannot guarantee the presence of associated emotions, and they discount for their results three sources of unreliability: they hypothesize that infants' expression minimizations prepare for *display rule* use; they indicate emotion *blends* as more important in later development; and, by holding to the facial feedback hypothesis, they need not consider the problem that *low-intensity* expressions may contract muscles but be too mild to be seen by trained coders, as suggested by a recent EMG study (Cacioppo, Martzke, Petty, & Tassinary, 1988). They do not, however, consider the possible need to use *contextual information* to modify simple interpretations of facial patterns.

They cannot be severely faulted for this omission; with some notable exceptions—primarily in interaction studies—interpretation of expressive actions without attention to context predominates in psychology. This focus fits traditional approaches to laboratory control; it is methodologically convenient; and it fits received, if often erroneous, understandings of Darwin and of classical ethology that are taken as authoritative in the study of emotional expressions. I devote the remainder of this section to clarifying the assumptions that underlie these misunderstandings.

Contextual information and developments in ethology.—Ethology and the field of animal communication have shifted away from and then back to the importance of context in decoding animal and human nonverbal behavior, creating confusing impressions of the role of context in an "ethological approach" to expressive behavior. Darwin's argument in *The Expression of the Emotions in Man and Animals* became the basis for ethological (and other) study of expressive behavior. Because that book emphasized the innate link between internal states and behaviors that express them, and because it described behavior forms apart from context, Darwin can be read to imply what he surely would not have endorsed: that behavior form alone, without context, always provides sufficient expressive information.

The early ethologists (1910–1930) were dedicated naturalists who used all observable information to decipher the functions of the actions they observed. As their work coalesced into the field of ethology, the concepts of evolutionarily selected, stimulus-bound, and response-bound innate communication behaviors emerged and are still useful today. The most prominent of these are *ritualization*, the process of naturally selecting increasingly noticeable forms of a potential signal behavior; *display*, a ritualized behavior that functions as a signal; *sign* or *key stimulus*, any stimulus for which responsiveness has been naturally selected; *social releaser*, a stimulus (usually the display behavior of a conspecific) that elicits a specific social response; and *fixed action pattern*, a rather rigid behavior pattern that is inherited in outline or whole (later recognition of subtle variability changed this concept to *modal action pattern*). Human facial expressions of fundamental emotions can be viewed in these terms as modal action patterns that have been ritualized by natural selection to produce visible displays that act as social releasers for potential emotional responses. Notice how, by emphasizing innate stimulus-response patterns, these concepts can suggest that context is irrelevant.

Two further factors kept descriptions of animal signals away from context and tied to (inferred) state into the early 1960s. One was that much ethological interest centered on behaviors attached to obvious motivational states, such as mating and feeding, and hence did not require contextual information. The other was the effect of the new semiotics of animal and human nonverbal behavior, strongly influenced by anthropological linguistics. It asserted that nonverbal signals always are evoked by the individual's internal state and are thus spontaneous, involuntary, and veridical indices of state (not, except trivially, of context). These features, which are still used to characterize immature, spontaneous human nonverbal communication, link the received Darwinian idea of state-tied expressive behaviors directly to the study of human emotional facial expressions. As long as all spontaneous human expressions were thought to refer to and be products of unique state, contextual information would not be important to an observer's interpretation of them.

However, contemporary ethologists questioned the simplicity of these characterizations, particularly the tie of a signal to one state and the implied irrelevance of contextual information. Although signals were cataloged in the field, state was no longer inferred, and "meaning" became limited to behavioral predictions of the signaler's or receiver's next behavior. Apes were found to be voluntarily deceptive (e.g., de Waal, 1986), and monkeys were found to refer to classes of objects such as predator type (e.g., Seyfarth, Cheney, & Marler, 1980). Invertebrates were seen to convey additional self-identifying information in display messages and to use context to clarify display message information (Smith, 1977). Detailed interaction analyses showed that signals occur when animals are in conflict between states, making those signals yield probabilistic, negotiated information about a signaler's next act (Hinde, 1985), and that contextual and other experiential factors, not just state, strongly influence the presence and intensity of signals (see Mason, 1985).

Despite these variations, the older display-state model (or a less centralized display model such as Fogel's in this volume) is at least partially accepted by almost all researchers of human facial expression. Immature, unsocialized, and involuntary facial expressions may indeed fit a display-plus-biological-condition model, and distinctive physiology accompanying facial expressions (Ekman et al., 1983; Fox & Davidson, 1988; Izard, Cohen, & Simons, 1988) and their perception (Zivin, Doghramji, Carroll, & Breuninger, 1988) may argue for it.

Clearly, what we need at this point is a mixed model, showing rather precisely how inherited displays, internal biological conditions, and responses to them are open to and modified by experience. No one doubts the reality and importance of this transformation—whose social learning component is often called emotion socialization—and several recent works have outlined broad features of the mixture (e.g., Lewis & Saarni, 1985; Zivin, 1985). However, besides studies of the acquisition of display rules and of blends (and a few searches, including Malatesta et al.'s, for infantile precursors to socialized emotion), there have been few specific suggestions of how the mixture arises and proceeds.

Assumptions That Mother and Infant Read Each Others' Expressions

I examine here three questions to which Malatesta et al. must presume specific answers. Do mothers perceive the same emotions in their infants as the codes assign? Do babies as young as 2½ months perceive maternal emotions through mothers' expressions? How might infants experience the maternal behaviors counted by Malatesta et al. as maternal contingency?

Mothers' perception of infants' facial expressions.—Mothers have long attributed fundamental emotions, particularly happiness, interest, and anger, to their young infants, and Izard has repeatedly shown that adults' consensual attributions of such emotions to infants conform with MAX codes (e.g., Izard, 1980). It is consequently highly likely that the mothers in Malatesta et al.'s study perceived the same fundamental emotions as those that were coded.

Infants' perception of mothers' facial expressions.—The many partial interlocking answers to the question, When do infants perceive facial expressions? have been detailed in excellent reviews by Dolgin (Dolgin & Azmitia, 1985) and Nelson (1985, 1987). One of the disputed issues is paramount here. Must an infant scan all relevant expression features and integrate them into a gestalt (that could be generalized across many persons who make the expression) in order to perceive emotion expression meaning, or is discrimination of only some of the features sufficient? If the former, then much evidence coincides to show that infants do not begin to have most of these capacities (including integrated scanning, the concept of facedness, differential response to feature vs. gestalt, and generalization) until about 5–7 months of age. If the latter, then several controlled studies support the notion that infants perceive (something of) facial expressions soon after birth (see, e.g., Meltzoff & Moore, 1977).

Several considerations argue against accepting the more stringent conditions as prerequisites for any perception of facial information; these include the coherence of Malatesta et al.'s continuous data across waves, the research reports that neonates respond nonarbitrarily to facial expressions, and the uncontrolled clinical observation that young infants respond appropriately to expressions in natural interactions.

I suggest here how young infants may have partial, but real, perception of mother's facial expressions (fitting the less stringent criteria and one data set) and how they go on to gestalts (fitting the more stringent criteria and another data set). It seems clear that the mechanisms and percepts of facedness differ before and after 5–7 months of age, moving from focus on discrete, ungeneralizable, nonconceptualized features to perception of integrated gestalts backed by a category of facedness (Nelson, 1985, p. 121). It also seems clear that infants are perceiving and reacting to something specific in facial expression information long before the more complex mode arises. Following the notion that preprogrammed processing of important social information needed before more mature systems are in effect could be adaptive in human infants, I propose that the infant shifts from taking information from features to perceiving gestalts, with perception of each type being informative and effective at each developmental level. I suggest that preprogrammed facial expression features act as key stimuli releasing facial attention (Eibl-Eibesfeldt, 1975, pp. 75–103) and guiding early attention and differential reactions to facial configurations. What is new with my notion is that the local key stimulus system would be in effect only or predominantly until it is surpassed by (or absorbed into) the more developmentally advanced mode of perception and that this system shift reconciles the contradictory data of different perception modes. (My hypothesis assumes that the preprogrammed salient features do not require extended attention. Thus, data on young infants' scanning—e.g., Haith, Bergman, & Moore, 1977—that show relatively infrequent sampling of internal features with concentration on the face outline and that have been used to argue against young infants' "reading" internal face features do not contradict this hypothesis.) The idea that preprogrammed capacities are functional early in life until they are enriched or transformed is one of the primary tenets of ethology that has been generally accepted in developmental psychology through the influence of attachment theory. What is suggested here is a similar early preprogrammed assistance for expression perception that is superseded when facial gestalt capacities have been developed.

Meaning of expressions and features.—As regards the meanings that facial configurations acquire in the early months, all researchers in the field must rely on their own intuitions since the infant perception paradigms (paired comparisons and habituation studies) reveal only that a difference has been perceived. With this as the state of the field, Malatesta et al.'s interpretations of their 2½-month-olds' perceptions seem as well founded as more skeptical interpretations would be.

Meaning of maternal contingency.—Maternal changes of facial expression within 1 sec of infant's change were initially counted by Malatesta et al. in an attempt to measure maternal sensitivity. However, correlations of high and even medium frequencies of this count with children's negative emotion led them to interpret such levels as being aversive and experienced similarly to "looming" or intrusiveness. The consistent findings of negative emotional correlates are provocative, and the looming interpretation is an interesting metaphor, but I question its validity.

My reservations arise from consideration of real-world characteristics of mother-infant interactions: these are only briefly stationary and face to face (mainly during feeding, diaper changing, and some play), and, during such times, mothers speak, make noises, sing, and act silly; the bulk of interactions occurs at varying distances and not face to face. It simply seems unlikely that the cumulative effect of mothers' contingently changing facial expressions during any of these interchanges would, in itself, have the measurable relations indicated by the correlations.

A "qualitative analysis" that would look for vulnerable children's aversion behaviors within, or immediately following, a series of frequent maternal contingencies might support the looming interpretation and allay this objection. In the absence of such additional support, it seems more likely that high maternal contingency—and, for vulnerable mother-child pairs, medium contingency—indexes some more generally prevalent maternal variable. It may be that high-contingency mothers do not back off when their infants show negative reactions. Other possible candidates are overall high maternal reactivity, which could result from many personality and temperament types and/or hypervigilance to the child's emotions; either could lead a mother to be generally overstimulating or intrusive. Malatesta et al.'s attributions of self-defensive, avoidant, and hostile behavior to children of highly contingent mothers would still fit if the maternal contingency measure indexed a broader maternal characteristic. This measure does appear to sample an important maternal interaction variable, and exploration of its relation to broader characteristics could further our information on structural harmony in mother-infant pairs and its contribution to the development of relationships and personality.

Summary.—Malatesta et al.'s assumption that mothers and infants read each others' facial expressions to mean the same emotions as coded by MAX emerges as being approximately as well founded as alternative positions. Out of the several points through which I examined their assumptions, only two very minor ones (whether gaze and minimal expressions are validly interpreted and whether infants experience their high- and medium-contingency mothers as "looming") seemed seriously unfounded. These points are of small overall importance and are in principle easily remedied: the first requires further empirical study and some provision of general criteria for changing interpretations of the same expressive form, and the second simply needs reinterpretation as a sample of more pervasively intrusive or frenetic behavior. Based on these considerations, there is no question that Malatesta et al. present plausible working suppositions and that we can suspend these distracting reservations as we study their work for its rich and original information.

References

Cacioppo, J. T., Martzke, J. S., Petty, R. E., & Tassinary, L. G. (1988). Specific forms of facial EMG response index emotion during an interview. *Journal of Personality and Social Psychology,* **54**(4), 592–604.

Camras, L. A. (1977). Facial expressions used by children in a conflict situation. *Child Development,* **48**, 1431–1435.

Camras, L. A., Malatesta, C. Z., & Izard, C. E. (in press). The development of facial expressions in infancy. In R. Feldman & B. Rime (Eds.), *Fundamentals of nonverbal behavior.* Cambridge: Cambridge University Press.

Charlesworth, W. R. (1982). An ethological approach to research on facial expressions. In C. E. Izard (Ed.), *Measuring emotions in infants and children* (pp. 317–334). New York: Cambridge University Press.

de Waal, F. (1986). Deception on the natural communication of chimpanzees. In R. W. Mitchell & N. S. Thompson (Eds.), *Deception: Perspectives on human and nonhuman deceit* (pp. 221–244). Albany: State University of New York Press.

Dolgin, K. G., & Azmitia, M. (1985). The development of the ability to interpret emotional signals—what is and is not known. In G. Zivin (Ed.), *The development of expressive behavior: Biology-environment interactions* (pp. 319–346). New York: Academic.

Eibl-Eibesfeldt, I. (1975). *Ethology: The biology of behavior.* New York: Holt, Rinehart & Winston.

Ekman, P., & Friesen, W. V. (1978). *Facial action coding system.* Palo Alto, Calif.: Consulting Psychologists Press.

Ekman, P., Levenson, R. W., & Friesen, W. V. (1983). Autonomic nervous system activity distinguishes among emotions. *Science,* **221**, 1208–1210.

Field, T., & Fogel, A. (Eds.). (1982). *Emotion and early interaction.* Hillsdale, NJ: Erlbaum.

Fox, N. A., & Davidson, R. J. (1988). Patterns of brain electrical activity during facial signs of emotion in 10-month-old infants. *Developmental Psychology, 24,* 230–236.

Haith, M. M., Bergman, T., & Moore, M. J. (1977). Eye contact and face scanning in early infancy. *Science, 198,* 853–855.

Haviland, J. M., & Lelwica, M. (1987). The induced effect response: 10-week-old infants' responses to three emotion expressions. *Developmental Psychology, 23,* 97–104.

Hinde, R. A. (1985). Expression and negotiation. In G. Zivin (Ed.), *The development of expressive behavior: Biology-environment interactions* (pp. 103–116). New York: Academic.

Izard, C. E. (1980). *The maximally discriminative facial movement coding system (MAX).* Newark, Del.: Instructional Resources Center, University of Delaware.

Izard, C. E., Cohen, B., & Simons, R. F. (1988). *Covariations of young infants' facial expressions and patterns of autonomic nervous system activity.* Manuscript submitted for publication.

Izard, C. E., & Dougherty, L. M. (1982). Two complementary systems for measuring facial expressions in infants and children. In C. E. Izard (Ed.), *Measuring emotions in infants and children* (pp. 97–126). New York: Cambridge University Press.

Izard, C. E., Hembree, E. A., & Huebner, R. R. (1987). Infants' emotion expressions to acute pain. *Developmental Psychology, 23,* 105–113.

Kendon, A. (1982). The organization of behavior in face-to-face interaction: Observations on the development of a methodology. In K. R. Scherer & P. Ekman (Eds.), *Handbook of methods in nonverbal behavior research* (pp. 440–505). Cambridge: Cambridge University Press.

Klinnert, M. D. (1984). The regulation of infant behavior by maternal facial expression. *Infant Behavior and Development, 7,* 447–465.

Landy, F. (1986). Stamp collecting vs. science. *American Psychologist, 41*(11), 1183–1192.

Lewis, M., & Saarni, C. (1985). *The socialization of emotions.* New York: Plenum.

Mason, W. A. (1985). Experiential influences on the development of expressive behaviors in rhesus monkeys. In G. Zivin (Ed.), *The development of expressive behavior: Biology-environment interactions* (pp. 117–152). New York: Academic.

Meltzoff, A. N., & Moore, M. K. (1977). Imitation of facial and manual gestures by human neonates. *Science, 198,* 75–78.

Nelson, C. A. (1985). The perception and recognition of facial expression in infancy. In T. M. Field & N. A. Fox (Eds.), *Social perception in infants* (pp. 101–126). Norwood, NJ: Ablex.

Nelson, C. A. (1987). The recognition of facial expressions in the first two years of life: Mechanisms of development. *Child Development, 58,* 889–909.

Oster, H., & Nagel, L. (1988). The differentiation of negative affect by infants [Conference abstract]. *Infant Behavior and Development, 11,* 465.

Oster, H., & Rosenstein, D. (1988). *Baby FACS: Measuring facial movements in infants and young children.* Unpublished manuscript. (Available from H. Oster, Derner Institute, Adelphi University, Box 701, Garden City, NY 11530)

Seyfarth, R. M., Cheney, D. L., & Marler, P. (1980). Monkey responses to three different alarm calls: Evidence for predator classification and semantic communication. *Science, 210,* 801–803.

Smith, W. J. (1977). *The behavior of communicating.* Cambridge, MA: Harvard University Press.

Tronick, E. Z. (Ed.). (1982). *Social interchange in infancy: Affect, cognition and communication.* Baltimore: University Park Press.

Zivin, G. (1977a). On becoming subtle: Age and social rank changes in the use of a facial gesture. *Child Development, 48,* 1314–1321.

Zivin, G. (1977b). Preschool children's facial gestures predict conflict outcome. *Social Science Information, 16,* 715–730.

Zivin, G. (Ed.). (1985). *The development of expressive behavior: Biology-environment interactions.* New York: Academic.

Zivin, G., Doghramji, K., Carroll, J., & Breuninger, W. (1988). Physiological patterning in observers: A pilot study providing evidence for emotion-specific observer patterns that parallel reported performer patterns. Paper presented at Jefferson Medical College, Philadelphia, January.

ENGAGING THE COMMENTARIES:
WHEN IS AN INFANT AFFECTIVE EXPRESSION AN EMOTION?

CAROL Z. MALATESTA, CLAYTON CULVER,
JOHANNA RICH TESMAN, AND BETH SHEPARD

We welcome the opportunity to respond to the thoughtful and stimulating Commentaries by Fogel and Reimers and by Zivin. It should be clear to the reader who considers our study and the two Commentaries that the field of emotions research is not of one mind—or, perhaps more appropriately, of a singular feeling about a number of critical methodological and theoretical issues. When given a forum for discussion, these kinds of differences of opinion or perspective often take the form and tone of *Methodenstreit*. Seldom does one have the opportunity to address such a debate-ridden field in as mutually tolerant and respectful a climate as the one created by Fogel, Reimers, and Zivin.

We respond to Zivin's Commentary first, noting that it is an abridged version of an earlier draft. The present response refers to both the published article and the longer version. Zivin's thorough exposition of the historical changes in ethological conceptualizations of behavior makes a contribution in its own right as well as creating a context for the further enunciation of our theory.

Differential emotions theory, like attachment theory—as originally presented by Bowlby—is grounded in both ethological and general systems theory assumptions. However, these assumptions have been largely implicit in earlier formulations. Zivin does us the service of bringing the ethological assumptions into relief; moreover, she deftly explicates variants among

We thank B. Dorval, C. Izard, and J. Panksepp for their comments on an earlier version of this Reply.

these and convincingly reconciles apparently contradictory data concerning infant perceptual abilities (with respect to whether infants can apprehend changes in the facial expressions of their mothers)—a premise on which our interpretation of the data is based.

A portion of Zivin's Commentary concerns itself with an examination of whether there are good grounds for the assumption that infant facial expressions reflect internal emotional states. She notes that we deal adequately with three sources of unreliability that would undermine the results and interpretations: display rules, blends, and low-intensity expressions. However, she argues that we do not consider seriously enough the "contextual" challenge to the interpretation of facial expressions—that is, we do not address nor have we examined context closely enough to determine if facial expressions relate to eliciting conditions in a way that would substantiate assumptions of face/state linkages. Let us examine this issue further.

On Context and the Use of Context to Examine Feeling State/Expressive Behavior Concordances

While Zivin urges infant affect studies to use context as one convergent basis for inferring emotional state (as per current trends in the field of animal and human ethology), Fogel and Reimers claim that context may be uncorrelated with differential facial expressions and states—that is, that context does not help clarify infant emotion—and cite Camras's (1988) data on the infant Justine as evidence. The discrepancy between Zivin's and Fogel and Reimers's views on context indicates that the issue of the relations among context, state, and behavior requires further discussion and amplification.

First, let us review the procedures of the present study to determine whether the assertion that we have failed to take context adequately into account in fact applies. This is important because the procedures that we followed were dictated by our views on context and our attempt to reconcile the clash of opinion on the utility of using context in such a fashion. We briefly sketch how the context issue was addressed and then examine the rationale behind our decision. Finally, we elaborate on the whole problem of the relations among context, expressive behavior, and internal state from a developmental perspective.

How the Present Study Took Context into Account

Although it might at first appear otherwise, the present study did in fact take context into account—as a vehicle for exploring the density of display of a *range* of emotional expressions (and for locating individual differences therein). Context was manipulated so as to induce more than one emotion, as indicated by our deliberate use of play, separation, and reunion sequences. It is clear that the experimental manipulation was successful in this regard. The play session elicited several emotions and signals predominantly within the positive domain, whereas the reunion episode—as expected—was found to contain various positive and negative emotion expressions, confirming the intent of the contextual manipulation.

Although we took context into account in the above sense, it is equally true that we did not look for the kind of context/emotion specificity that others (e.g., Camras, 1988) have tried to identify—such as the relation between an immediately prior maternal behavior or other contextual event and the likelihood of a specific emotional response. This approach, of course, is a matter of choice and is contingent on the research agenda as well as on certain underlying assumptions about event/behavior relations in the domain of emotions and expressive behavior. It is the underlying assumptions that we would like to address in some detail because they involve the larger question of whether infants have differentiated feelings and how we can go about gauging them. Although Zivin would have us look more closely at context to judge the validity of assumptions underlying the facial coding scheme we used, data from both the present study and that of Camras (1988) challenge the notion that looking at specific context/behavior linkages in young infants is the best or most legitimate means of validating behavior/state concordances.

To restate the problem, the assumption of behavior/state linkage is the assumption that a particular expressive behavior indexes a particular feeling state (a stance that has been taken by differential emotions theory) and is referred to by Camras as the "innate tie" hypothesis. According to contemporary ethological thinking, expressive behaviors should also relate to context. Among species that are capable of deceptive behavior, mature individuals can manipulate their expressive behaviors to achieve certain goals; as such, their expressive behavior may or may not match underlying state at any given moment, and thus a contextual analysis may reveal the real underlying motivational state. One is less concerned about the threat of deception with young infants because, as our review has shown, they do not appear to be capable of deliberate dissembling—though, as Zivin notes, this assumption is rarely explicitly examined. Theoretically, one should be able to test this notion by checking to see whether the occurrence of a particular emotional pattern is preceded by a stimulus that is logically linked with that emotion. Sometimes the additional assumption is made that there should be a more or less one-to-one correspondence between certain elicitors (contexts) and certain responses. These kinds of notions imply "specificity." However, the assumption that different contexts should elicit different kinds of emotional expression in a context-specific/emotion-specific way is closer to older ethological models than to contemporary formulations (see Zivin's unabridged Commentary). One of the reasons that we did not look for this kind of specificity inheres in the theoretical assumptions of differential emotions theory; moreover, this assumption appears to be supported by Camras's data as well as by other studies that have looked at the relation between context and behavior.

A number of researchers have relied on context-manipulation studies to validate the assumption of state/behavior linkages, and the results suggest that the method is valid within certain limits. For example, DPT inoculations have been used to validate the coding of pain expressions, frustration paradigms to validate anger expressions, and placement on the deep side of the visual cliff to validate fear. What goes unmentioned, however, is the fact that, in each of these studies as well as in a dozen others, infants have not been found to emit just one type of emotion in response to an eliciting situation, even in situations in which the state/behavior relation appears to be very close. In each case, a number of expressions are elicited, but the researcher typically relies on the *predominant* expression as a means of validating the relation. This means that infant affective expression shows sufficient categorical specificity to place some faith in the notion of a differentiated and preprogrammed emotional response system. However, it also challenges the notion that the emotion system may be understood as a functionally fixed system with a reliable input/output organization (as per earlier ethological formulations).

The latter point requires additional comment because Fogel and Reimers appear to understand differential emotions theory as asserting that the emotion system operates in such a fashion. These authors draw on the results of Camras (1988) as an example of research that challenges the notion of stimulus/response specificity. Camras's study involved video and diary recordings of the early expressive development of her daughter, Justine, during routine caregiving. Her data indicate that "similar" contexts elicited a range (though a restricted one) of different emotion expressions on different occasions. Camras also found that certain emotion expressions occurred in a range of contexts. These data seem to refute the idea of specificity (i.e., one context or stimulus elicits one emotion). Correspondingly, they seem to imply either random behavior or flexibility. A random interpretation is contradicted by well-controlled studies with large data bases that demonstrate a relation between certain eliciting conditions and prototypical or predominant (though not fixed) behavior responses, as already reviewed.

Differential emotions theory has stressed that the emotion system is characterized by generality (Tomkins, 1962) and flexibility (Izard & Malatesta, 1987). Yet it is often misinterpreted as implying stereotyped behavioral patterns driven by a fixed input-output apparatus. The misperception that differential emotions theory requires stimulus/response specificity may derive from two sources: (1) our use of the term "prewiring" to denote the innate properties of the system and (2) the emphasis the theory places on the assumption that each of the primary emotions has distinct phenomenological, motivational, and signal properties. We take the opportunity to expand on these notions further.

On the Use of the Term ''Prewiring''

Fogel and Reimers interpret our use of these terms as connoting a type of fixity. However, we use these terms to denote an evolutionarily based, functional preadaptation of patterns of expressive behavior. The universality of emotion expression prototypes and their reliable association with generic feeling states—as established by cross-cultural research and the observed phylogenetic continuity between the expressive patterns of human and nonhuman primates—would seem to support the notion that expressive patterns are phylogenetic adaptations and that certain expressive propensities are innate. This is not to say that expressive patterns and the linkages between internal state and expressive behavior are immutable. In fact, differential emotions theory specifically deals with transformations that occur within the emotion system—as assisted developmentally by the growth and elaboration of language and representational thinking—in its formulations concerning emotion socialization.

What Is Fixed, and What Is Flexible?

The basic premise of the theory is that, before the onset of enculturation and learning, there is an innate connection between feeling states and behavior. However, it is a sine qua non of social development that raw expressive behavior needs to be modulated in the context of developing interpersonal relationships—masking, simulation, exaggeration, miniaturization are all tools at the service of accomplishing such social goals. For example, when the contempt expression is first observed in children, it appears in what parents would consider an embarrassingly crude form. In our videotapes of 12-year-olds interacting with peers (Malatesta & Dorval, in preparation), contempt is typically expressed with a full complement of expressive gestures—head tossed back, upper lip curled, retraction of head and body—all of which is often accompanied by a snort or laugh of derision. By adulthood, one rarely sees such unmodulated expression of contempt during face-to-face communication. Instead, the contempt expression may take the form of tilted head and slighty raised brows (the "William F. Buckley face") or mild supercilious tone of voice (Dorval & Malatesta, in preparation). Expressions can even be miniaturized to such an extent that they are all but unobservable, or other maneuvers can take the place of expressing contempt directly, such as removing oneself from the scene. In instances in which the target of contempt is so contemptible as to be "beneath contempt," the contempt expression may be absent entirely; one refrains from even interacting with the odious individual so as to avoid contact and contamination. In Timon's words, "Thou art not even clean enough to spit upon." One could describe these different expressions and nonexpressions as differential responses to similar inputs; thus, in this case, context (stimulus) does not predict response. Nevertheless, across the modes of expression for the particular emotion, we discern one common appraisal (superiority) and one functional property—the tendency to avoid contact with the inferior object of scorn. Thus, different forms of contempt expression, even its suppression, constitute a common family in the emotional/motivational states associated with them, and collectively these are different from those found with other primary emotions. As far as eliciting conditions go, although the stimulus for an expression (say, the stimulus for the smile) may change during early infancy (auditory and tactile stimuli early in development with visual stimuli becoming more important later on), the response (smile) elicited appears to index a similar underlying state—that is, pleasure —since repetitions of such stimuli produce more smiling (up until a point of saturation). Moreover, auditory and tactile stimuli are not exchanged for visual stimuli as *the* prototypic elicitor of the smile; instead, visual stimuli are added to the set of natural elicitors. Thus, we have a situation that does not necessarily involve qualitatively different changes in "coordinative structures" so much as it does an expansion in the forms that can elicit the same functional category of emotion. Still later in development, the connection between an expressive behavior is not so much broken as modified, as in the case of mixed emotions; moreover, spontaneous displays may be overridden for other preemptive motives. A spontaneous smile is still likely to index joy, but it may also combine with other elements—say, contempt—in the case of the smile of derision. Or it may be deployed as a mask to hide feelings of anger or fear—in which case, elements of expressive behavior are summoned by will but assembled in a classic pattern (e.g., a recognizable smile rather than a new form of behavior).

On the "Distinctiveness" of Types of Emotions

The emphasis of differential emotions theory on the "distinctiveness" of different emotions may also create the impression that emotions are fixed response categories. However, as indicated elsewhere (Izard & Malatesta,

1987), emotions are best conceived as instinct-like behaviors (patterned and organized but flexible) rather than reflex-like behaviors, a distinction that has been emphasized in contemporary ethological theory. As such, there should be a range of elicitors that can provoke a particular response (although one expects that the range of elicitors will form some kind of identifiable "family" of provocations). Moreover, because emotions are flexible response patterns and not reflexes, and because any particular adaptational demand may be met by alternative emotional strategies, it is also the case that we cannot expect a one-to-one correspondence between a particular eliciting event and a particular emotional response—instead there may be multiple emotional reactions. Bereavement, for example, typically produces not one emotion but several—grief, anxiety, and anger, to name a few of the more salient experiences. The fact that Camras's Justine emitted three different kinds of expression during a crying bout following a "single" event is problematic only for a theory of emotions that assumes that infants, unlike adults, can have only one emotional response to a given situation. Such a view is sensible if one asserts that emotions are products of thought processes and endorses a kind of adult chauvinism that denies infants various cognitive capacities because of their immature status. Although it is our position that emotion and cognition are separate systems and that emotional responses can occur in the absence of appropriate cognitions (as in free-floating anxiety), we recognize that emotions and cognitions often, if not nearly always, intereact. We also suggest that infants may be capable of more sophisticated appraisals than they have previously been given credit for. Stern's (1986) sensitive analyses of the synchronization between infant behaviors and those of their caregivers illustrate that infants are capable of sophisticated responding that seems tailored to their emotional "appreciation" of the content of communication. Even more to the point, Lewis and his colleagues (Lewis, Sullivan, & Michalson, 1984; Sullivan & Lewis, 1988, in press) have demonstrated that, during conditioned learning and extinction training, young infants display a range of emotions, including interest, joy, surprise, sadness, anger, and fear, all within short order, and that the different emotions are meaningfully related to stages in the learning process—and, it is assumed, to the infants' cognitive appraisals. Thus, the notion that rapid changes in infant expressive behaviors constitute random facial grimaces unrelated to state does not seem warranted.

Facial Behavior as a Privileged Form of Emotion Expression? Yes and No

Let us address two other points raised by Fogel and Reimers that bear clarification. These authors hold the impression that differential emotions theory equates emotions with facial expressions (rather than viewing the

131

latter as a component of the expressive system) and indicates that there is only one preferred pathway to expression. We would like to correct this impression. First, the theory recognizes that the face is not the sole vehicle for expressive behavior; instead, it states that patterned feedback from affective vocalizations and from muscular and kinesthetic movements in the rest of the body also plays a role in emotional behavior (Izard, 1977; Izard & Malatesta, 1987; Malatesta, 1981) and even that emotion in the young infant is originally a "whole body" phenomenon (Malatesta, 1981). It is easy, however, to see how Fogel and Reimers might have come to construe the theory in the way that they have. Despite the fact that the theory notes the importance of these other expressive behaviors in experience and communication of emotion, much contemporary research, including the present study, has focused on the face, a circumstance that can be attributed to the groundbreaking success of the cross-cultural facial recognition studies of the late 1960s and early 1970s as well as to the recent availability of sophisticated facial coding systems. Moreover, the degree of specificity and differentiation in other channels of emotion expression has yet to be systematically documented. In one preliminary study (Malatesta, Davis, & Culver, 1984), we found that vocal expressions of emotion were less differentiated than facial expressions, at least between 3 and 6 months of age. The apparently lower level of specificity of other communication channels in early development suggests that these systems may be more modifiable and also that they may be instrumental in affecting modification in the facial affective program. For example, an infant may tense the fist during states of distress but learn, through accident or a preadapted propensity, that putting the fist or fingers in the mouth soothes the pain directly through distraction and through the comfort of sucking. This maneuver may also affect modification of the emotion expression system in another, indirect way. Tomkins (1962) has suggested that affect has a self-recruiting and self-sustaining property. For example, hearing the sound of one's own voice crying may make one feel even sadder and thus intensify the crying. In the case of the infant who puts hand to mouth and begins sucking, the distress signals from the patterned shape of the distress mouth and distress voice are temporarily disrupted, thus breaking the cycle of recruited distress. The interruption of distress, we may assume, is rewarding in its own right, as is the satisfaction derived from sucking, and this may enhance the likelihood that the thumb-in-mouth activity will occur again when the child is in distress. In such a fashion, one aspect of the affect system becomes incorporated in modifying another. Such dynamic system properties are not alien to the formulations of differential emotions theory but rather consistent with it. We admit, however, that this aspect of the theory is rarely spelled out, and we are pleased that Fogel and Reimers have given us an opportunity to expand on it.

Can Emotions Be Inhibited through Emotional Means?

The above example clarifies the role of the face and its interaction with other somatic aspects of the emotion system. It also provides an illustration of the way in which the emotion system may inhibit itself—which relates to Fogel and Reimers's query, How can an emotion inhibit itself? The commentators believe that one would have to go outside the set of discrete emotions to provide inhibition. However, the notion of one emotion inhibiting another or of one part of the emotion system influencing another is not as paradoxical as it might first appear; instead, it is consistent with the theory. One way that one part of the emotion system can inhibit another has already been described; another example follows.

Differential emotions theory is formulated in such a way as to accommodate the facts of everyday emotional life. Emotions rarely occur in isolation; rather, they tend to occur in combinations or patterns. Different qualities of emotion allow one to be simultaneously of two or more minds. However, this collegiality of emotions also permits competition. Discrete emotions are of different qualities, and these qualities generate different motivational goals. Thus, emotions may covary in time, but they do not have to covary in goals; the goals may themselves be in competition with one another, which may result in any number of resolutions.

Let us take an example of a situation in which two emotions obtain. A particular event occurs, and anger is elicited; the resulting anger activates behavioral propensities toward aggression. This pattern of expressive display may be adaptive in certain contexts but maladaptive in others. The emotion system requires both a means of communicating intentional aggression as well as a means of inhibiting the display if that is required by a particular situation. For this purpose, a more general emotion, such as interest, is functionally relevant. Among its several functions, interest instigates programs that plan long-term adaptation and mastery over the environment. One maintains interest in manipulating and controlling one's environment. This is as true for a baby manipulating a mobile over a crib as it is for a worker who maintains a job by not expressing anger at an immediate supervisor. In the latter instance, anger and interest compete; if the motivation to save one's job is stronger than the need to ventilate temporary frustration, the motivations inherent in interest can subjugate the powerful motive of aggression. The point of this example is that individuals are thrown into a wide variety of situations that instigate complex goals; in the case of thwarted ambitions, an individual requires both a powerful motivator toward aggression and a powerful motivator to modulate that aggression. Whether the threat is a fabled saber-toothed tiger or an irascible boss, adaptation requires both a means of aggression and a means of planning the inhibition of that aggression. As such, different emotions are recruited for different ends.

Central versus Peripheralist Explanations of Expressive Development

Fogel and Reimers contrast differential emotions theory with the dynamic systems perspective of Fogel and Thelen (1987), emphasizing the dynamic modulating influence of peripheral muscles. Since differential emotions theory includes many dynamic systems properties—most notably, concepts of feedback and modulation—the theories are not at great odds on this point. However, while we agree that peripheral influence occurs, it does not seem reasonable to look for a peripheralist explanation as the primary means of explicating the complexity of facial expressions and their development over time. In the first place, although every expression is surely constrained by muscular characteristics, the patterned triggering of contractions and relaxations has to be a function of the central nervous system. Second, certain patterned consistencies would also argue against a peripheralist explanation. Negative facial expressions occur in negative situations. Children are not pleased by frustration as a general rule. Some will express anger, others may be fearful, but it would be an odd child indeed who would be delighted by frustration. The peripheralist heuristic would also be hard pressed to explain data indicating that electrical stimulation in areas of the limbic region of the brain results in fearful or aggressive responses, including facial change, or that humans and animals tend to respond to emotional stimuli as though these stimuli were releasers for the motor patterns described in the ethological literature.

There is one other related point that we would like to clarify. In earlier formulations, differential emotions theory made a distinction between subcortical centers, where emotion programs were thought to be stored, and higher cortical inhibitory centers. In rough outline, this distinction still seems tenable; however, we eschew the notion of strict localization of function and especially the idea that there is one "center" for each of the discrete emotions. Instead, it would appear from recent neurophysiological and neuroanatomical research that emotion functions are organized in neural command circuits (Panksepp, 1982, 1986; Panksepp, Siviy, & Normansell, 1984). As such, organized patterns of emotional behavior are seen as related to neural activation in command circuits that have connections with pathways and nuclei at higher and lower levels; this conceptualization also recognizes that efferent feedback from sensory and motor modalities has the capacity to alter activity in these circuits and even that "biasing" of the circuits may occur (i.e., that some circuits may become more readily activated than others—an idea consistent with our notion of emotion biases in personality). Panksepp's theory of neural command circuits subserving the primary emotions is based on a substantial body of new neurophysiological research. Thus, at this point in time it seems safe to say that, although the brain may not be very well lit, it is no longer a black box.

The above notwithstanding, we are in clear accord with Fogel and Reimers's notion that the emotion system is a complex, dynamic one and that it may be found to behave in both linear and nonlinear ways. Moreover, we believe that the concept of "emotional biases" as outlined in our discussion shows some of the properties of what dynamic systems physicists have described as "attractors" (Miles, 1984). In dynamic systems, attractors act like magnets, gathering the current of everyday life phenomena to their centers. It is our hope that this concept will prove to be important in helping resolve a number of developmental enigmas.

References

Camras, A. A. (1988, April). Darwin revisited: An infant's first emotional facial expressions. In H. Oster (Chair), *Emotional expressions in infants: New perspectives on an old controversy.* Symposium conducted at the International Conference on Infant Studies, Washington, DC.

Dorval, B., & Malatesta, C. Z. (in preparation). Ethnography of the family: Affect and speech event organization. Long Island University, Psychology Department.

Fogel, A., & Thelen, E. (1987) Development of early expressive and communicative action: Reinterpreting the evidence from a dynamic systems perspective. *Developmental Psychology,* **23,** 747–761.

Izard, C. E. (1977). *Human emotions.* New York: Plenum.

Izard, C. E., & Malatesta, C. Z. (1987). Perspectives on emotional development: 1. Differential emotions theory of early emotional development. In J. D. Osofsky (Ed.), *Handbook of infant development* (2d ed., pp. 494–554). New York: Wiley.

Lewis, M., Sullivan, M. W., & Michalson, L. (1984). The cognitive emotional fugue. In J. Kagan, C. E. Izard, & R. B. Zajonc (Eds.), *Emotion, cognition and behavior* (pp. 264–288). London: Cambridge University Press.

Malatesta, C. Z. (1981). Infant emotion and the vocal affect lexicon. *Motivation and Emotion,* **5,** 1–23.

Malatesta, C. Z., Davis, J., & Culver, C. (1984, April). *Emotion in the infant voice.* Paper presented at the International Conference on Infant Studies, New York.

Malatesta, C. Z., & Dorval, B. (in preparation). Shame and contempt in family systems. Long Island University, Psychology Department.

Miles, J. (1984). Strange attractors in fluid dynamics. *Advances in Applied Mechanics,* **24,** 189–214.

Panksepp, J. (1982). Toward a general psychobiological theory of emotions. *Behavior and Brain Sciences,* **5,** 407–468.

Panksepp, J. (1986). The anatomy of emotions. In R. Plutchik & H. Kellerman (Eds.), *Emotion: Theory, research, and experience* (Vol. **3,** pp. 91–124). New York: Academic.

Panksepp, J., Siviy, S., & Normansell, L. (1984). The psychobiology of play: Theoretical and methodological perspectives. *Neuroscience and Biobehavioral Reviews,* **8,** 465–492.

Stern, D. (1986). *The interpersonal world of the infant.* New York: Basic.

Sullivan, M. W., & Lewis, M. (1988). Facial expressions during learning in 1-year-old infants. *Infant Behavior and Development,* **11,** 369–374.

Sullivan, M. W., & Lewis, M. (in press). Emotion and cognition in infancy: Facial expressions during contingency learning. *International Journal of Behavioral Development.*

Tomkins, S. (1962). *Affect, imagery, and consciousness* (Vol. 1). New York: Springer.

CONTRIBUTORS

Carol Z. Malatesta (Ph.D. 1980, Rutgers University) is associate professor of psychology at Long Island University. She is a charter member of the International Society of Research on Emotions and associate editor of *Cognition and Emotion* and the *International Review of Studies on Emotion*. Her theoretical and research interests are centered on the growth and differentiation of emotion expression and personality over the life span. Her publications include "Differential Emotions Theory of Early Emotional Development" (with Carroll E. Izard), in the *Handbook of Infant Development*, ed. J. D. Osofsky, 2d ed. (New York: Wiley, 1987), and "The Role of Emotions in the Development and Organization of Personality," in *Socioemotional Development*, ed. R. A. Thompson, Nebraska Symposium on Motivation, vol. 36 (Lincoln: University of Nebraska Press, 1989). She is also the editor (with Carroll E. Izard) of *Emotion in Adult Development* (Beverly Hills, CA: Sage, 1984).

Clayton Culver is a doctoral candidate in clinical psychology at the New School for Social Research. His research interests are the development of emotions, the phenomenology of emotions, schizophrenic cognition, and mental imagery. His publications include "Change and Continuity in the Affective Themes of Adult Women" (with Carol Z. Malatesta), in *Emotion in Adult Development*, ed. C. Z. Malatesta and C. E. Izard (Beverly Hills, CA: Sage, 1984), and "Patterns of Recall in Schizophrenics and Normal Subjects" (with S. Kunen and S. Zinkgraf), *Journal of Nervous and Mental Disease* 174 (1986): 620–623.

Johanna Rich Tesman is a doctoral candidate in developmental psychology at the New School for Social Research. She is currently completing her dissertation, which is concerned with the effect of mothers' mixed emotional messages on infant development.

Beth Shepard is a doctoral candidate in psychology at the New School for Social Research. She is currently completing her dissertation, which deals with the intergenerational transmission of shame in personality organizations. She is the author (with C. Malatesta) of "Socioemotional Development in Children with Craniofacial Anomalies," in *Developmental Perspectives on Craniofacial Problems,* ed. R. Eder (New York: Springer, in press).

Alan Fogel (Ph.D. 1976, University of Chicago) is professor of psychology at the University of Utah. Related work includes "Development of Early Expressive and Communicative Action: Reinterpreting the Evidence from a Dynamic Systems Perspective" (with Esther Thelen), *Developmental Psychology* 23 (1987): 747–761. He is also the editor (with Tiffany Field) of *Emotion and Early Interaction* (Hillsdale, NJ: Erlbaum, 1982). His research interests include emotional and communicative development in infancy in relation to social and cultural contexts and the application of dynamic systems principles to the ontogeny of social action.

Mark Reimers (Ph.D. 1986, University of British Columbia) is a postdoctoral fellow in psychology at the University of Utah. His training was in mathematics, and he is interested in the description and modeling of developmental processes.

Gail Zivin (Ph.D. 1972, Harvard University) is professor of psychiatry and human behavior at Jefferson Medical College. She is the author of "Processes of Expressive Behavior Development," *Merrill-Palmer Quarterly* 32 (1986): 103–114, and "Innate Communication Behaviors," in *For a Semiotics of Emotion,* ed. W. A. Koch (Bochum: Bochum Publications in Evolutionary Cultural Semiotics, 1988). She is also the editor of *The Development of Expressive Behavior: Biology-Environment Interactions* (New York: Academic, 1985). Her research interests are in specifying interactions between experience and genetically preprogrammed capacities of expressive communication and perception.

STATEMENT OF EDITORIAL POLICY

The *Monographs* series is intended as an outlet for major reports of developmental research that generate authoritative new findings and use these to foster a fresh and/or better-integrated perspective on some conceptually significant issue or controversy. Submissions from programmatic research projects are particularly welcome; these may consist of individually or group-authored reports of findings from some single large-scale investigation or of a sequence of experiments centering on some particular question. Multiauthored sets of independent studies that center on the same underlying question can also be appropriate; a critical requirement in such instances is that the various authors address common issues and that the contribution arising from the set as a whole be both unique and substantial. In essence, irrespective of how it may be framed, any work that contributes significant data and/or extends developmental thinking will be taken under editorial consideration.

Submissions should contain a minimum of 80 manuscript pages (including tables and references); the upper limit of 150–175 pages is much more flexible (please submit four copies; a copy of every submission and associated correspondence is deposited eventually in the archives of the SRCD). Neither membership in the Society for Research in Child Development nor affiliation with the academic discipline of psychology are relevant; the significance of the work in extending developmental theory and in contributing new empirical information is by far the most crucial consideration. Because the aim of the series is not only to advance knowledge on specialized topics but also to enhance cross-fertilization among disciplines or subfields, it is important that the links between the specific issues under study and larger questions relating to developmental processes emerge as clearly to the general reader as to specialists on the given topic.

Potential authors who may be unsure whether the manuscript they are planning would make an appropriate submission are invited to draft an outline of what they propose and send it to the Editor for assessment. This mechanism, as well as a more detailed description of all editorial policies, evaluation processes, and format requirements, is given in the "Guidelines for the Preparation of *Monographs* Submissions," which can be obtained by writing to Wanda C. Bronson, Institute of Human Development, 1203 Tolman Hall, University of California, Berkeley, CA 94720.